THE CENTURION'S SPEAR

STEVEN MAINES

ACKNOWLEDGEMENTS

I wish to thank the following people for their
encouragement, support, contributions
and love.

Ann Maines. Barry Maines.

Michele Genovese-Maines.

My sounding board and Muse,

Lita Fice.

This book is dedicated to my children:

Liam Maines
Genavee Maines
Mattea Fiona Maines
Elizabeth Maines

I love you all more than you'll ever know.

VOLUME I

LONGINUS

LONGINUS

Hours and hours had passed. People had come and gone all day, weeping and wailing and gnashing their teeth with despair at the sight of their Savior and his two companions spread out and dangling upon their wooden beams. The sky had become grotesquely dark and ominous at one point, instilling a palpable fear among the mourners and the curious who had gathered. I, too, felt a twinge of irrational foreboding at first, but quickly dismissed my dread as ridiculous. I was simply witnessing an unusual weather-storm for this time of year. That this man was being crucified at the same time was mere coincidence. And, I believed that. Until, that is, the Earth shook.

It only lasted for a moment, the shaking. But, it left no doubt in my mind that it was directly correlated to this dying man on the cross.

In that moment, I looked up at him. Though the sky behind his body was dark with clouds, there was a beautiful, unearthly glow emanating from around his slumped head. He muttered something then. Something like, they know not what they do. Though somewhere deep within me, I knew this man to truly be a Holy man, connected to a power—perhaps, to The Power above us all—my heart was still the hardened stone of a soldier of Rome, dispassionate and immune to all but death and orders. My orders here included staying with the doomed One until he was dead.

Some versions of my duties, or what took place next, proclaim that I was a hero; that my next act actually saved the Christ's skull from being crushed. It was the custom at that time in this particular region that one who was hanged from the cross would remain there until dusk only. No prisoner was to be left on the cross overnight. If he had not died by dusk, his skull would be crushed by a soldier standing guard, thus

4

insuring death. It was brutal, yes. But nothing I haven't seen in many a battle. Besides, by that time, there was no feeling left on the part of the condemned, as he long since would have passed into unconsciousness. But instead of having his skull crushed, this man that hanged before me had another fate. Here is what really happened.

His eyes closed, his chin on his chest, the Christ appeared to be in the state of eternal sleep, his spirit departed. The only way to be certain that he had passed on was to reach up with my spear and prod. This I did, to the gasps of horror of the remainder of those present, which included his mother and another woman to whom she clung. What did I care? I had my orders. I pierced his side, between his ribs. A sickening moan came from his mouth as blood and body fluids seeped down the length of the protruding blade and shaft from his ribs. Some of it even spattered on my face and into my eyes. Contrary to what some believe, however, my poor eyesight was not suddenly and miraculously restored to normal at the touch of the Christ's blood and body fluids. In subsequent years, however, my eyesight became nearly perfect the older I got, instead of degenerating with age, as is usually the case.

Before I could withdraw my instrument, I felt a vibration come from the body on the cross. It came down my spear and into my own body. It paralyzed me. The air around me instantly filled with a static tingle, like a localized lightening charge. I felt as though I were floating. A man's voice then whispered to me, saying, "What have you done, my child? What have you done?"

An Otherworldly fear overtook my mind and with all my strength, I cursed and yanked on the spear, finally pulling it free of the body. I spun around to see who had said the words to me. But no one was close enough to have whispered and be heard, save for the two women, and, as I said, it was a man's voice.

Confused, I looked back up at the man on the cross.

His now vacant, dead eyes stared at me from a corpse no longer occupied by the spirit. Or, so was my assumption, until I had heard what had happened three days later. But for the moment, I gave the orders for him to be removed from his death-perch. His loving, weeping mother and a few others moved forward to take him away.

I stood there for a few moments, staring at his mother and then staring at him. The voice once more whispered in my head, and I found myself saying out loud, "What have I done? By the Gods, what have I done?" I felt a tear roll down my cheek, though inwardly, I felt no emotions. But, again, somewhere inside of my being, I knew who this Man truly was; an emissary from God or the Gods. Nevertheless, I convinced myself that I had followed and executed the orders given to me with my usual exemplary proficiency. Commendations would be forthcoming, I was sure. However, my conscience and spirit would show me something else.

That night I was able to keep sleep at bay for a long while. I knew that if I gave into slumber, I would have to face my conscience, my fears and truths of the day's events, and this, of course, I could not allow. So I spent the night in the arms of the local whores. When one would tire, I would find another to play with. This went on throughout the night. I spent nearly half-a-year's wages that evening. I was possessed, so to speak, by the gods of sex. I could not be satiated. I had the virility of ten bulls. I would no sooner spend my seed in one woman, when I would rise and swell again. On more than one level, I hoped the night would never end.

But it did finally end. As dawn approached I drifted off into a strange slumber in the arms of the two women sharing my bed. Unwillingly, as my eyelids began to close, I found myself glancing in the direction of the corner of the room. There, propped up against the wall, was my spear. Though I had thoroughly cleaned his blood from the blade—actually, I had cleaned the blade three times, the last one especially being quite unnecessary—the blade now gleamed crimson with blood once again. Impossible!! It must be the light within the room! But nay, it was clearly blood that dripped down the blade, seeping along the shaft as well. I tried to disentangle myself from the limbs that lewdly entwined my body, but found that I was paralyzed, as I had been momentarily on the field of crosses the previous day. My eyes, though I endeavored to keep them open, closed of their own accord.

Images thrust themselves at me in my mind's eye. Horrifying images of death and destruction, of torture and foulness beyond human comprehension; of wars and rumors of wars being fought on the planes of the heavens, as well as of earth; of Evil reigning in the minds and hearts of men the evils that he can and will inflict on his fellow man. The visions showed the fall of my beloved Empire and the rise of another; then the fall of that one and the rise and fall of another, then another, and so on. They showed the swift boats going to new lands and the killing and torture of humans unknown. They showed men flying in great machines that rained down fire and death. They showed flying objects that carried no man, but delivered swift and massive destruction and fates worse than death. They showed bodies alive but burning, screaming for their very souls. Could this all be true?

This and more I saw in the sleep of that dawn. Then the voice, the whispered voice from the field came to me. "Fear naught," it said. Even so, terror infused my being. I tried to speak, but found that I could not. I continued to see the horrific images play out in front of my mind, as the voice continued: "This and more shall you see, for I tell you now that you have been chosen. You will not leave here until this world is consumed. Until this world has run its course, shall you wander and learn and teach. You will long to leave, for death, on many an occasion, but true death will never come, because it cannot. Ah, you think this to be punishment, but it is not, not at all. There is nothing for which to be punished. It is your desire."

At the ceasing of the words, the words which came from I knew not where, nor from whom—though, much later, I would come to realize it came from the depths of my own being, the eternal, ever-present Oneness of all within—I realized that my fear was of this world. That was all.

At the ceasing of the words, the images increased in speed and ferocity until all I could see was the earth from the vantage point of the stars. She was now a very old and very dead planet. I was not completely aware at the time of what I was looking at, but knew, nonetheless, that it meant the utter annihilation of all existence as I then understood it.

In the trance state—the dream state—I screamed. With my entire being, did I scream. A silent one at first, but it grew, and it grew.

I heard the scream far off in the distance and tried to move away from it. But instead, of moving away from it, it simply grew closer. As it did, I realized that it was my own voice; my own scream emanating from my own body. A bright light exploded in front of me, and I found myself in the bed, swimming in a pool of my own fetid sweat. The two women were trembling at the foot of the bed, staring at me as if I were the foulest of Demons. I sat up, breathing hard and looked at the spear, the blood now dried as if it had been there forever.

I looked back at the women and, in unison, they jumped back as if I were going to pounce and devour them in one-felled swoop.

"What do you stare at?" I bellowed.

"I...we...you became violent, thr...thrashing at us as if the devil was in you," squeaked one.

"Truly," moused the other.

I rubbed my head, trying to make sense of the vision or dream I had just had, as well as what these women were saying.

"Leave me," I finally mumbled.

Slowly, the women backed away toward the door. Just before they passed through it, though, one of them, Irena, a beautiful, green-eyed, dark-haired, Roman-Hebrew woman whom I had known since first being stationed at this hole of an outpost, stopped and boldly brought up a fact. This was her...house, so to speak, after all.

"Longinus, there is one other matter..." she hinted.

Ah, Irena. She was ever the business woman. Her eyes always conveyed a strength and confidence that were accentuated by the high cheekbone structure of her lovely face. If I was meeting her for the first time, I would assume she was noble born. But, I knew better. I nodded to the clump that was my clothes and armor near the spear. "There is coin in the bag on my tunic. Take what you will."

She did as she was bade. But then, curiously, as she stood from retrieving the money, she stared at the spear as if transfixed by enchantment. She had not been on the field of crosses on the previous day. She could not have known how I had used the instrument, nor had she been a follower of this so-called Anointed One. Yet, there she stood, under the spell of the spear. She reached out to touch it.

I exploded, leaping out of the bed. "No!" I screamed, violently grabbing her arm and throwing her across the room back onto the bed with the strength of three men.

She bounced off of the skins of the bed, smashing her head against the wall.

"Do not touch it," I snarled at her, caring not whether she had died from the impact. She had not. She lay clutching the back of her head and whimpering, blood oozing between her fingers.

Irena then looked up at me weepily, yet angrily. I suddenly felt like the ass that I was. I tried to mouth an apology, but nothing came out. Irena's green eyes flashed a mixture of disbelief, fear, and above all, defiance. Irena. I so loved her boldness. With as much dignity as she could muster, she collected herself, stood, and walked toward the door. Taking the other still trembling woman, girl, really, by the elbow, they both left me alone with my apparent dementia.

~||~

I sat in the deafening silence of the room for over an hour, staring at the spear against the wall. Aside from, or because of, the apparent permanent blood stain on it, it now looked like any other spear of a Legionnaire. But I knew otherwise.

I finally came to my senses and began to put on my clothing, my uniform, my duty regalia. I did so as though in a fog, as if my body was detached from my very essence; as if I were watching someone else donning his uniform. It doesn't matter, I kept telling myself. What's done is done. The soldier in me was clearly trying to reassert himself.

But it did matter. Nothing would ever be the same again. Ever. I reverently approached the spear, half fearing it might come to life. But ultimately, that's not what I began feeling from it. I paused, sensing its... what was it? Divine energy? It seemed to glow. I finally shook my head, nonsense, plucked it from its resting place, and departed the stuffy room.

The sun beat down harshly as I stepped outside. Curse this region! Perhaps if I asked the General for transfer to the homeland, I thought. The gods knew I deserved it. Yes, a transfer would not be too much to ask.

A crowd had gathered at the far end of the street. They seemed to be watching something, or someone. I couldn't really hear anything. Two of my platoons were there as well, milling about, apparently not too concerned with whatever was causing the crowd to gather. Still.

A Legionnaire trotted by, oblivious to me, clearly quite intent on joining his comrades down at the end of the street.

"You there!" I yelled at him.

The young man stopped and looked at me. Recognition

appeared on his face, and his eyes grew large. He trotted up to me, saluting fist to chest much too hard and crisply, clearly trying to impress his Centurion with the polished moves. Green, this one is, was all I thought. My thoughts, however, quickly returned to the reason why I had stopped him. I nodded toward the crowd. "What goes on down there?" I asked.

"The people...," his voice cracked.

Inwardly, I had to smile. This lad couldn't have been more than fifteen summers. He cleared his throat, and tried to deepen his voice with age and authority.

"The people," he began again, "are listening to someone speak, Centurion. I believe it is one of those who followed the Jew-King that was hanged yesterday." This last part, the lad spat with sardonic contempt.

"Hold your tongue, boy, or I'll have it on a platter!" I bellowed angrily, though I must confess that I wasn't sure why I was angry. "You know nothing of this man."

The boy-soldier before me began to tremble, fearing my wrath and clearly confused as to what possible transgression he could have committed.

"Dismissed!" I barked.

Again, his crisp, forced salute. He almost fell over his own feet in his flight away from me. I watched him run toward the crowd; and then I turned toward the tavern next to the place where I had spent the night of debauchery, now intent on finding food.

But something stopped me. I slowly turned and found myself looking back down the street at the crowd once again. The next thing I knew, my feet were moving, seemingly of their own accord, guiding me forward toward the crowd.

A string of thoughts and voices went through my mind. Why am I going there? What do I care what one of His followers has to say? Well...what if this person speaks against Rome? No. He never did, did he? I heard tell that he even said, 'render unto Caesar, that which belongs to Caesar,' so why would a follower of his say otherwise? Besides, his own people condemned him to death.

My inner dialogue, or argument, went on like this as I walked toward the crowd. "Silence!" I finally declared out loud, apparently none too quietly, for two women stared at me from a nearby doorway as if I were mad.

No matter.

The voices stopped. I decided to go check on the situation anyway. It was my duty, after all, to investigate any impromptu gathering. I am a Roman officer here, I reminded myself.

The lad whom I'd stopped a moment before saw me coming and alerted his comrades, all of them snapping to attention as I approached. I simply gave them a curt nod and maneuvered my way into the crowd to get a better look at the cause of it.

A man, a Jew by the look of his unkempt beard and robe, stood on a table in the center of the crowd. He was talking to a couple of other men in a normal, though slightly raised, conversational tone, a combination of awe and reverence laced into his speech. The crowd here was pressed tight, straining to hear what this person had to say.

The dirty, sweating bodies around me began to become oppressive. But it didn't seem to matter, as I found myself drawn into this moment, to hear what this man was saying. Though I could only pick up snippets, he was clearly talking about the man hanged the previous day—his, Teacher, he was saying.

"But he told us! I'm speaking the truth!" he insisted.

"Impossible!" said another. "No one rises from the dead!"

"Did he not command Lazarus to come out of his tomb?" countered the first man.

"So it is claimed, but, I was not there to see it."

"I was. And I tell you, that happened. So shall this. On the third day," declared the man on the table.

My heart began to thump. "On the third day?" I found myself saying out loud.

The crowd turned to me in unison, fear suddenly spreading on the face of the two men who had been conversing. Clearly, they had mistaken my reason for saying the words.

"No, no," I said. "I sincerely wish to know. For myself. Not for any other reason. Not for State reasons, certainly. Please."

The two men looked from one to the other. They were Hebrew. The first, the one on the table, stepped gingerly down to the ground, all traces of fear evaporating from his craggy face. He was older than the second by far.

He then stepped forward and looked me squarely in the eyes, peering into my soul, I felt. Apparently satisfied that my inquiry was of a true and sincere nature, he spoke. "So said my Lord."

He continued to look at me, assessing me. I suddenly felt vulnerable. I could have arrested this man for the way he dared to look a Roman in the eye, for the way he was inspecting me at the moment. But I simply stood there. He then looked at my spear and his eyes grew wide.

"You!" he said. "You are the Centurion who pierced my Lord's side."

A murmur rose from the crowd. I stood my ground. Where are my men, I found myself thinking. But I needn't have been concerned. The man reached for the blade of my spear. I jerked it back out of his reach.

"Please," he said. I looked closer at him. Covering the lower part of his craggy, aged face, he had a scraggly grey beard. He wore an old and tattered robe—though of which tribe I could not tell—its hood covering most of the top of his head, though I could see wisps of thin grey hair hanging limply near his temples. His eyes were kind and full of depth. Still, he was just an old man. That's all he was. He was harmless.

I felt myself compelled to put the blade of the spear within his reach. He touched it tenderly with his hand, caressing it almost lovingly. A tear rolled down his cheek and he put his lips to the metal, kissing it respectfully. I felt a moist drop descend my cheek as well. I was moved beyond words, though I knew not why.

"Thank you," he said, looking into my eyes. Slowly, he turned and walked into the crowd, the people moving with him. Soon, I found myself standing in open space, the crowd having dispersed.

"Sir?" a voice said. I looked up to the source of the voice. It was my young legionnaire, along with his fellow soldiers. "Are you well? You've been standing here for a while now," he said hesitantly.

I blinked as if waking from a dream. "Quite well, soldier," I said smiling. I looked from his face to those of the others. Boys, all of them. They could not have been more than sixteen summers. "Come," I said. "Let's find food." We began to move off, and I took one look back at where I had stood with the crowd and the man who had kissed the blade of my spear.

I looked at the weapon myself, cradled in my hand, feeling the power it held. Something was moving me, beginning to shape my destiny. I could feel it, but denied it in that moment. Sometimes, the Universe will move us whether we acknowledge it or not. Destiny will not be denied.

That night, true sleep was a foreign thing, kept at bay by the deep thoughts, voices and images within my mind. I saw many things in my tumultuous dreams. Again, as before, they were things that were violent and seemed to be off in the future. But there were also things that were pertinent to the present, to me. One voice in particular, came through.

It was familiar. It was his, the One from the Cross.

"Longinus," he said to my dreaming mind. "Longinus, I will see you again. You will see that I live. In heart, mind and body, I live. All will see that they, too, will live forever—that they have always lived, always will."

I knew not then what he was saying. I now know, however. It is a wondrous thing. Why do we not give in to these Truths? We spend millennia and then some, hearing these things, but not listening—not listening to the Spirit within which houses all Truth, houses our very Truest Self.

I awoke in a sweat and more fatigued than when I retired the previous evening. I looked at my surroundings. I was in the same room as on the night of His death; the same room of debauchery; now two nights ago. For an instant I was confused.

In my fogged mind, I thought it was the night of His death. I thought that perhaps it had all been a dream: the death, the night of debauchery, all of it. But then I saw my spear leaning against the wall in the corner, dried blood still caked on parts of the blade, in spite of the many times I'd already scrubbed it, and I knew it was no dream. I didn't remember coming to the same room on the previous night, but obviously, I had. Too bad it wasn't all a dream.

Something was rattling around in my brain. Was it something about today? Yes. That was it. But what? There was indeed something about this day that was to set it apart. But in that moment, for my life, I could not remember.

I lay there for some time, soaking in the newness of the day. Or rather, absorbing the newness of my Self, for that is actually how I felt. Inexplicably. After a time, I slowly got up and splashed water on my face from the basin that had been left for me. Then I donned my uniform and breastplate. Taking the spear in hand, I headed out in search of food.

"Ah, Longinus," came the sweet, familiar voice. Something in it this time, however, gave me pause. I turned to see Irena's eyes piercing me with feathered contempt. What could she be angry about? Was it my outburst from the other night? Perhaps. But it wasn't like her to hold a grudge. Still, she was vexed by something. "I demand payment," she blurted out.

"For what? I already paid for my room, gave you something for the night. I told you to take what you wanted from my coins, which you did," I said.

"The girl!"

I was confused. "Irena, I was with no one last night, so I

don't owe you..."

"...She left. You had us both two nights ago—all night long. And in the morning, you scared demons out of the girl, myself as well, for that matter. But I know you. I took it as just another of your moods." She paused briefly, calming herself before continuing. "We've known each other a long time. I won't pretend that there's ...something... between us as man and woman, because there's not. It's business. Which means, I don't mind sharing you. But I draw the line when you cause my business to suffer with your temper or anything else."

I did not understand at all what she was talking about. Bewilderment must have splashed across my face.

"She's gone, Longinus! Because of you! She wouldn't take anyone last night, and this morning, she left, saying she couldn't forget the madman."

"Maybe she was speaking of another soldier. After all, if it weren't for the Roman army, you'd probably have scant few customers, my dear," I said in desperation.

"No!" was her emphatic reply. "It was you she spoke of. 'The madman with the spear,' she said."

I forced a smile. "Are you sure she meant my Legion issued spear and not my man-spear?" My feeble attempt at humor only served to incur Irena's wrath all the more.

"No, damn you! You know she meant this spear!" She reached for the weapon at my side. Something inside me snapped. Reflexively, I yanked the weapon out of her reach, and violently threw up my other arm to block her from getting to it.

But the force of my block was much more than I had intended, and, for that matter, much greater than I thought I was capable of. With a gush of air from her chest, Irena flew back some ten feet, sprawling and flopping on her back like a child's straw doll. For a moment she lay motionless and I shuddered. By the gods, I thought, what have I done?

Since the time I had been assigned here, Irena had become much more than just a bed-companion. She had become a friend. No, even more than a friend. In that moment,

I suddenly realized that I cared for her on a much deeper level.

My heart leapt into my throat as she lay before me. "Irena!" I yelled, leaping to her side and kneeling before her. Why had my reaction to protect the spear been so strong? And what of my physical strength in that moment? Where had that come from? I was becoming unstrung; like a damaged archer's bow, I was quickly becoming useless.

"It is you, is it not, Longinus?"

Her voice brought me back to myself, and my nearly overwhelming concern for her. "Yes, I'm here. I'm so sorry."

"No, I mean, it is you they speak of," she said, gaining her strength with each word. Her demeanor had completely changed; no longer angry, as if her anger had been used to cover something else. A fear, perhaps? She sat up and fixed her beautiful eyes on mine. "It is you who pierced the side of the Jew-King, I know it now; the way you protect that spear. Does it hold magic now? Some say that it must."

I was speechless. What was she saying? To whom had she spoken? A few moments of silence filled the space between us. Irena smiled, a teardrop rimming her eyes. "I'm...I'm," she stammered. "I'm sorry I yelled at you about the girl. I don't think she was cut out to be as the likes of me anyway."

My heart swelled. "The 'likes' of you? You're, well, I'm proud to be your friend. You're a smart woman, Irena, and more."

It was then that I felt myself opening up to yet another new sensation. It was the inexplicable feeling that I'd known Irena for a very, very long time, long before I was even born. But how could that be? Yet, something deep within my Being recognized that same something deep within hers. I felt myself drifting in a fog, an ethereal mist. What was wrong with me? I had had thoughts like this before: a deeper recognition of someone, but dismissed them, relegating the thoughts to imagination.

Yet somehow, this was different. Somehow, I knew this feeling to be correct. I knew that I was grasping a deeper

Truth, a deeper Mystery.

"Oh, Longinus," Irena said, once again pulling my attention back to her. "I am your friend?" she asked tenderly.

"And more," I replied. I gazed at her again, my full awareness coming back to the present; to myself, Longinus, Centurion to Caesar. "Who has told you that it was I who pierced the side of the man on the cross?"

"Two men. And a woman."

"Who were they?"

"I don't know who the men were, but the woman, her name was Mary. She used to work in a house a short distance from here. Then she started to follow the man you crucified."

"Why?" I asked.

"She said his words cleansed her, freed her," replied Irena.

I thought about this for a moment. Then another thought took its place, one with more urgency. "When did you speak to them last?" I asked.

She pondered the question for a moment. "Two hours ago. They were elated over..." Her voice trailed off as a look of understanding and awe crossed her brow.

"Over what?!" I insisted. But a feeling crept over me, an awareness of the answer that had been there all along.

"Over the 'fact,' as they put it, that this crucified 'Jew-King', Jesu, I think they called him, had arisen from the dead early this morning."

Of course. That was it. That's what today was about. "And they saw this feat?"

"Mary did. And then one of the men, later."

"And you believe them?" I asked, somewhat incredulous.

She hesitated. I could tell that she wasn't sure whether she was speaking to Longinus, her friend, or Longinus the Centurion.

"I...no," she said, but her face betrayed her, as it had a moment before.

Deep within my own being, I knew the truth even then.

But Centurion Longinus was in command. I had to check into this. By now, rumor, myth or truth, this would be spreading throughout the city. Things could get out of hand very quickly. Was this the real reason that I wanted to delve into this? No. But in that moment, it was the reason I allowed my mind to believe. The spear in my hand seemed to pulsate in that moment, almost as if it were divining, pointing the way to go.

I ran for the door and was out in the street before I knew it. My heart was pounding. A sensation, an urging, was compelling me to go north. It was coming from the spear. Just as I was about to step in that direction, someone was next to me.

"I'm going with you," Irena said, her jaw set in that stoic and defiant way that I'd come to love.

All I could do was smile. "Of course, you are," I said. We set off down the street. We'd gone about a hundred yards when I noticed something odd; the street—indeed, the whole area—was empty. No one was about. Irena and I exchanged a wordless, questioning glance.

One of the men, one who had been at the gathering on the previous day, the old man who had so reverently kissed the spear, suddenly and mysteriously stepped out from behind a tree on the edge of a path, one leading northward off the street. The hood of his tattered robe or cloak was up over his head, but I could still see most of his face and knew it to be the same man. But, he was different, somehow, from that moment of yesterday. I stared in amazement, for his face glowed with a light; a light of the Gods; a light of the divine. His eyes, though filled with depth yesterday, now showed even more profoundness. In those eyes seemed to be the knowledge of creation and the awareness of having seen first-hand the Great Mysteries. Our eyes locked only briefly. I had to avert my own eyes, so deep was his gaze.

"Centurion," he said. "I have seen it, Centurion. I have seen him. I have witnessed the Resurrection."

I knew what he said, but feared it. "What say you, man?" I replied.

"The burial chamber lies empty," said the old man.

Again, Irena and I exchanged a look. "Do you speak of the one they call Joshua, or 'Jesu'?," she asked the man before us.

"Yes, I do."

"Take us there," I commanded, the Centurion in me taking control.

The man was about to protest because of my tone, I could tell. But then his demeanor shifted, and he suddenly smiled instead. "Follow me," he said. He turned and headed up a path. Irena and I did as he bade.

~ ||| ~

Several things kept pushing into my mind as we walked to the burial site, the tomb. Most of these things were of a superficial nature, such as thoughts that amounted to justifying why I was making this trek to the burial chamber, not much more than a cave really, of a man who had died on a Roman cross. One of thousands who had perished that way, and certainly not the first I had helped to speed on the way to meeting his gods, or his God, in this case.

I glanced at the spear in my hand. It still seemed to be pointing the way, pulling me along. Nonsense! I yelled silently. Yet, along the path I went, Irena at my side, the raggedy old wise-man before us. I'm going to see this cave, this tomb, for security reasons, I rationalized to myself. If the body were to be missing, then it could present a reason for the locals to become agitated. Even now, there were those calling this one Joshua, as he was called in his Hebrew language, or Jesu in the Greek, or Jesus in my Latin tongue (I never had been one for the pretentious Greek that the Patrician classes of Rome were so fond of espousing)—even now, there were those calling this Jesus a Savior. But it was not a savior from Rome that he was to be.

I should have checked in with the garrison by now. My men will be wondering about me, I thought. Still, I walked on. We came to a clearing. The smell of sage and dust hovered in the air. Somewhere in the distance, a sheep bleated frantically, urgently. Where's her shepherd? I wondered. Before us, between two sets of ancient cedar trees, was the mouth of a tomb. It was not very impressive, yet it was more than just a cave.

The opening itself was not as high as an average man, and only slightly wider. On the outside entry frame, extending some fifteen feet up the top of the tomb-cave, and off the right and left sides, were carved ornate Kabalic symbols. Set to one side, resting in its carved-out rolling track, was what could only be the Sealing Stone. It was large: approximately my finger-tip to elbow thick, twice the height of a man, and the same width.

The Sealing Stone was not round. Not really. It resembled a severely damaged stone wheel; a huge, broken and largely chipped stone wheel. Thus, it was more square than it was round. It was apparent that it had always been square, and at some point, someone had tried to make it round, unsuccessfully. It would have taken at least four strong men to even budge it, let alone to put it in place to seal the tomb and then remove it again.

As we approached the cave or tomb, the old man spoke. "I assure you, Centurion, the stone was in place, the tomb had been closed," said the old man.

I then looked at him, studied him. That feeling I had a while before with Irena—that overwhelming sense of familiarity, of recognition—now hit me with this man.

From over his shoulder, I suddenly noticed two other men. Had they been here when we arrived at the tomb? If so, I had not seen them. Each of them looked on with expressions of fright and awe. They were Legionnaires, but not in my charge. Regardless, I was a commander, a senior officer to them, and thus, was about to question their presence.

But the spear began to vibrate in my hand. I almost dropped it. For an instant, it felt alive. I found that I didn't have the need to question this, however, but was instead compelled to go in the direction that the spear seemed to be insisting I go, into the mouth of the tomb. Slowly I walked forward, Irena right on my heels. She too had seen the spear's demand.

Cold and dank was the tomb. Musk and death were its smell. The coppery smell of old blood lingered as well. And there was something else... Nay, two other things: A tingling charge was in the air, as if the lightning bolt of a god had been thrown through the tomb's air. With it was the unmistakable smell of something burned. Was it an offering that someone had made and left? No, not likely. It smelled more like slightly burnt cloth than anything else, not the incense or wood figure one would burn in an offering such as this.

The burnt smells were faint, wafting on the stale air of this place as an afterthought. If something had burned here, it had only been singed.

"Come, see," said our guide, the old man. I hadn't even noticed that he had walked past me and was standing in the center of the tomb, or more accurately, the center of the burial chamber near a large, rectangular slab. Obviously, this was where His body had been placed. But, all that remained there now was a large cloth, a shroud. I approached the slab, and hence the shroud. It almost seemed to glow of its own accord.

I reached out to touch the cloth. Irena's breath caught in her throat. I stopped in mid-reach and looked at the old man. He smiled and nodded his...encouragement, approval—I knew not which—compelling me to pick it up and see. I did, slowly lifting it up for inspection.

"His shroud," I said reverently, to no one in particular. I suddenly dropped the thing, afraid. Why was I doing this? What did I care about this man? As if to answer, I felt the spear vibrate again. Was I imagining it? It did not matter. The message the spear was sending me was clear.

I placed the spear on the slab so that both my hands were free. Gently, I lifted the shroud once again for a better look. Now, my breath caught in my throat, for on the cloth, an image appeared. A face. Though its eyes were closed, the face watched me, its face staring at me, its features connoting a peaceful bliss. I looked even closer, and as I did, the strange odor of singed cloth grew stronger. It was coming from this cloth! How could that be? I held it higher, examining more of the cloth. As I looked further, I saw that the image of an entire body had been...imprinted, singed (however one wished to describe it), onto the shroud.

"That is Holy cloth, touched by God, as an Anointed One was raised from death," said the old man.

I could not deny the feeling that I held something beyond my comprehension, the same type of emotion that the spear had affected upon me for three days past. I was completely overwhelmed; overwhelmed by a number of things that I simply could not fathom. They coalesced into that state of being most prevalent in humans when faced with that which they do not understand: fear. When fear spoke to me, I simply hardened the heart, walling out the threat of the unknown, so that I stayed in control. Invariably, this took the form of my Centurion mantel shining forth. It was always such a nice guise to hide in. Such was the case in that instance. I dropped the shroud and turned to the old man.

"Where is He?" I demanded. The old man's face became taut as he heard the shift in my voice, command bordering on menace.

"But, He is risen," he said.

"Impossible," I stated flatly.

"Longinus," Irena said, "what are you doing?"

"Stay out of this. Go back to the house."

"But—"

"Go!" I barked. I then spun on the two Legionnaires standing dumbfounded at the entrance to the tomb. "What do you know of this?" They looked at each other as if I'd spoken Greek, or some other language their feeble minds were too illiterate to grasp. "Well?"

"I, we, don't know, Centurion," stammered the boldest of the two, a short, dark-haired, middle-aged soldier of about thirty-six summers, with a nasty scar on his left cheek. The other, a light-haired boy of perhaps seventeen, was trembling. This one had something to say.

"You. Out with it!" I demanded.

"I am Legionnaire Gaius. I...we were assigned here by Centurion Cascie, sir, to watch the tomb so no one would steal the body. Mine was the second watch, sir," said the boy. My gaze wandered to the scarred one.

24

"I am Legionnaire Romi, Commander," he said, saluting me crisply. It is true. I had first watch. When..." he hesitated, looking at his comrade, not wanting to implicate him in anything.

"The tomb was sealed and all was well when I relieved Legionnaire Romi, Centurion," said Gaius, saving his friend from having to continue on. "No one was around. The night was cold and quiet, and after a time...after a time..."

My eyes narrowed, piercing the boy's. His shame-filled gaze dropped from mine.

"It was my fault, sir," spouted Romi. "I should've taken the second watch."

"No," interrupted Gaius. Summoning his courage, he pulled his gaze back up to me. "After a while, I fell asleep. When I awoke, the sealing stone was moved and the corpse was gone." He stopped, waiting for me to respond. I did not.

The truth was that I did not know how to react. As a soldier, this man's severe dereliction of duty had to be punished, even if with his own life and those of some of his company. But I knew that something else had happened in the night; something infinitely bigger than a mere soldier falling asleep.

No, I thought. Someone must've stolen the body. I did not want to believe in the alternative. I looked at the ground. Too many feet had trodden over the earth here to yield any evidence of a theft. And the only potential eye-witness had been asleep. But if the body had been stolen, could the thieves have made the image on the cloth? And if they did make it, how'd they do it? Obviously, they'd have made it to bolster their claim that He'd risen, but...

I couldn't think anymore. I was confused. But, I certainly could not let these men see that.

"There was no one around when I awoke," continued the lad, "so I ran to summon help. When Romi and I returned, a woman was near the opening of the tomb."

"What woman?" I asked.

"Don't know, sir."

"You didn't get her name?" I asked, incredulous. The two soldiers exchanged another fearful look. Another transgression. "No wonder you're still just a Legionnaire, soldier," I spat at the middle-aged one.

"Yes, sir," was all he said.

I took a breath to hold my temper in check. "Proceed. The woman..."

"Yes, sir. Well, the young lad here asked her what she was doing. At first, she said nothing. She looked as though her mind were gone, far away, like. When she finally did speak, all she'd kept sayin' was that she'd seen him, that He's alive, and that He'd spoke to her."

"I...figure she meant the dead Jew in this cave, sir," said Romi, clearly thinking that I had not grasped the meaning.

I came close to hitting the man.

"But, she never talked right to us," put in Gaius. "More to the air, to the spirits," he said, dreamily, as if he were also talking to the spirits.

"Then she left," offered Romi.

"To, 'spread the news,' she said," added Gaius.

"And neither of you stopped her," I reprimanded. Their faces fell in shame again. "You, Legionnaire Gaius, fell asleep on guard duty. Neither one of you detained a witness, let alone even got her name? What is wrong with you? Especially you, Legionnaire Romi. This is obviously not your first tour of duty!" My anger was beginning to get the better of me.

"But...but that's just it, sir," stammered Gaius. "We both know that we should have done those things, but—"

"But what, soldier?" I exclaimed, almost yelling.

"We weren't really thinking straight. It was as if something was in the air here..." Romi trailed off, his brow crinkling, eyes looking down. He seemed to realize how stupid that must sound.

I became silent, thinking. My anger was getting back under control, and it was because what Legionnaire Romi had just said somehow made sense to me. The two soldiers, however, took my silence as a malicious sign. The younger one began shaking, one of his hobnailed sandals actually clattering on the ground.

"You should be flogged, flayed and executed," I said, then fell silent again for a moment, allowing those images to sink in.

I thought Legionnaire Gaius was going to piss his Carass, or at the very least, burst into tears. Romi, on the other hand, was blank faced, stoically rigid. A lifer, this one, I thought. He's seen many a battle; a true soldier.

"However," I continued aloud, "you are not in my Command. You will have to explain yourselves to Centurion Cascie, and probably to Horse Commander Luctus. I pity you. Right now..."

"Longinus," whispered the voice, interrupting my speech.

I whirled around to see Irena still standing there, near the slab. But, I knew, the whisper had not come from her. Nor had it come from the old man, also still standing near the slab.

Suddenly, a knowing smile splashed onto the old one's face. "You hear him, do you not, Centurion? He calls to you."

Shocked by his words, as well as by the voice in my head, I stood there gaping at him.

"I...I do not know what you speak of," I replied lamely. I forced myself to gain back my composure and spun back on the two Legionnaires, intent on reasserting my authority.

"And, you two," I said with inflated gruffness. "Report immediately to your commanding officer and inform him of the events here."

"Yes, Centurion," they said in unison, shocked that I wasn't going to turn them in personally. They both slammed their closed fists to their chests in salute, then spun on their heels, leaving as quickly as they could.

"And send back three others to guard this place," I called after them.

"Yes, Centurion!" Romi yelled as their footfalls receded in the distance.

The inside of the tomb was now utterly silent. Outside,

a bird sang a joyful tune, and the distant sheep's mournful bleating drifted to my ears once again. Still have not found your shepherd, little one? I thought. Or, was that the voice addressing me again? I began to back out of the tomb.

"Longinus," said Irena.

I stopped and stared at her. There was something different about her entire countenance. My eyes saw it, but my spirit and mind perceived it more. She seemed somehow transformed, and a light emanated from her. She reminded me of the Ones in the stories the Hebrews tell; stories I've heard told around even a Roman soldier's campfire. This region infected us all. What was it they were called? Ah, yes: Angels —a race of Divine beings that helped humans on behalf of the Hebrew God.

We did not really have anything like them in the Roman pantheon of gods and demigods, although, one could argue that local deities filled that role -- and, I was certainly not Hebrew. Still, Irena stood there glowing. Was it a trick of my mind? It must have been. Or, perhaps it was a spell.

Ach! I yelled at myself in my head. I had never adhered to such nonsense. I would not journey down that path now.

I glanced at the old man. He had the same glow emanating from him as Irena. An odd thought impinged itself in my brain; I suddenly realized that I did not yet know his name.

"Peace, my friend," he said. "We have all been touched by the Divine this day."

I looked back to Irena, who now appeared normal, though the old one still glowed. He now held the Shroud rolled up and cradled in his arms, with the gentle touch of a doting mother holding her newborn. I was about to say something when my gaze caught sight of the spear still lying on the slab where I had left it. I picked it up and left the tomb, leaving the others looking silently after me.

I did not know why I left so abruptly, other than to say that something was happening to me; something was stirring to life within. And, it was terrifying.

~IV~

After leaving the tomb that day, I went straight into town. Legionnaires had been sent in to make sure the people stayed more or less in line. Word had spread quickly of the Master Teacher's rising from the dead, or alleged rising. By late afternoon, early evening, all of his followers—his disciples, they called themselves—were found, gathered in one place. Soldiers I encountered on my way through town were only too eager to tell me where the disciples were.

    I arrived at the courtyard of this place just in time to see a lieutenant thwacking the one I took to be the owner of the house, the one called Paul, with a standard issue short-club, while the rest of the flock looked on helplessly, including a woman I recognized as one of the locals. I was later told that she, too, had become one of the Teacher's disciples, a questionably close one. Five legionnaires also looked on, nearly salivating with sadistic pleasure at the misplaced and trivial display of Roman power.

    "Lieutenant!" I yelled. His arm froze in mid-strike. He turned to see who dared interrupt his fun. Upon seeing that it was a superior officer, he lowered his arm and assumed a look of guilt. But I saw right through that look.

    Insincerity cascaded forth from this one. His eyes showed not true guilt, but a cruelness and defiance masked by a veil of good. Hardness and cruelty is all he would understand. So be it. I did not gain Centurion rank by being a pleasant fellow. Before I could speak, however, he spouted off.

    "Centurion Longinus," he began arrogantly, summarily losing the facade of guilt.

    I did not know this lieutenant. Obviously, though, he knew me. And, judging by his posture, his arrogance, was probably from a prominent Roman family. But I cared little about that.

"I was merely attempting to...to—" he tried to continue.

"To what, you shit-hole? Were you told to beat him?" I bellowed. My gaze landed on Paul. His lower lip was ripped and bleeding profusely. His nose was smashed on the bridge, and bleeding from that wound and the nostrils. A dark, painful-looking mound was already forming under his left eye. Yet, it was none of those ugly things that stood out about him to me in that moment. It was, instead, the stupid, childlike smile which adorned his face; a smile that seemed to glow and grow in radiance the more I looked at it; to pull me in to a whole other world; nay, a whole other Universe.

But my heart and head had to stay rooted here, in what was happening at this moment. I had to control this entire situation. "I should let this officer hit you once more just to knock that smile off of your face," I caught myself saying to the man, Paul.

"It would not matter," Paul replied through his broken lips. "Nothing can hurt me on this glorious day."

"Your spilt blood bespeaks otherwise," I said.

"'I am in this world, but not of this world'. My Master said that, and on this day, it was shown true to me. You may hurt this corporeal form, but it is not who or what I truly am," said Paul.

"What you are, is a madman," quipped one of the legionnaires, thus inciting a round of laughter from the other soldiers.

"Silence!" I commanded, with the wrath of the gods. "You will stand at attention, all of you." I narrowed my eyes at the lieutenant as I spouted the order. They obeyed.

With them all lined up at crisp attention, I grabbed the short-club from the young officer and hit him upside the helm. His head snapped to one side and his helmet shot off, clattering noisily to the floor.

Slowly, dramatically, almost menacingly, the lieutenant brought his head, and thus his face, back to attention, boring his eyes into mine. Death and malice flashed in those eyes—for half-a-heartbeat only, but they had been there, nonetheless. This one was not only cruel, but dangerous.

To his credit, though, he said nothing. The other legionnaires were stunned and shocked by my violent outburst. The air seemed to be sucked out of the courtyard as they made a collective, shocked intake of breath.

I turned then, and addressed all the soldiers as their clearly superior officer. "Your insubordination and lack of discipline disgusts me! You speak out of turn. And you, lieutenant," I said, rounding on him again, my spittle spraying his face, causing him to blink involuntarily. "I should drop you where you stand."

The legionnaires seemed even more shocked at this. But, it wasn't shock. There was something else beginning to creep into their faces, their countenance. I could see it in her eyes; they were thinking, Why would a Centurion care if we were beating Jews, especially if they might be hiding something, in this case, possibly a body, a possible rallying point for those civilians wanting to revolt?

"Do not be angry with them, Centurion," Paul said, intruding upon my thoughts. "They were only doing their duty as they saw it."

I stared into this man's pale-brown eyes. That light was there; the same light that was in the old-man's eyes, the one in the tomb. "Leave us, all of you," I said to the men while still staring into Paul's eyes.

Legionnaires and Paul's flock alike began to file toward the front gate. "No, no. Not you," I said, motioning to the civilians. "Just the soldiers." I turned to the lieutenant. "You wait for me on the road," I commanded, none too gruffly. They marched away. Paul and the others who were left stared at me, waiting.

Paul's eyes, still alight, glanced down at my spear. His face beamed all the more. "That is the instrument, is it not?" he asked.

"Yes."

"May I?" he asked, reaching gently, slowly for the weapon.

I said nothing, but allowed him to touch the shaft, then the blade. He caressed it as if it held the Master himself. My soldier-self wanted to yank the thing away from him. But, I knew he was no threat. I felt a certain inexplicable bond with this man through the instrument.

Finally, he pulled away and looked deep into my eyes. I felt his soul touching mine. "You will go beyond your bounds, my friend. You will leave all this behind," he said indicating my uniform, "to seek and speak the Truth. This will occur soon. Very soon. Of course, it is up to you. You could choose to turn your back on it all. The choice is yours."

I stood speechless. I knew naught of what he spoke. The path before me was dark, save for the knowledge that I was Centurion Longinus, Centurion Gaius Cassius Longinus of the Imperial Roman Legions. Yet, within my being, I was unfolding into much more. I could feel it.

I finally gathered myself back together. "See..." I stammered. I cleared my throat and began again. "See that you stay out of sight for the day."

Paul simply inclined his battered head in response, giving away nothing.

Good enough. I turned on my heels and left the courtyard.

~V~

I had left Paul's home that day, ignored the lieutenant and his soldiers waiting for me on the road, and all but staggered to the Legion base.

In truth, the Legion base was barely an army encampment, save for some stone and concrete dwellings: barracks, that the men had managed to erect since my arrival. That particular day had turned out to be unusually hot and dry. It seemed the gods had sucked all the moisture out of the air.

I rarely came to the base at mid-day. I was usually out in the field, as we called it, with only a handful of my soldiers at a time, while the rest stayed behind to attend their assigned duties, so my men were surprised to see me wandering back in alone. At least, that's what I took to be the reason, at fist, for the look on their faces. But then, I came to realize what that look truly was: deep uncertainty.

Word had quickly spread throughout the area, including throughout Rome's Legion of the land, that this Jew had supposedly risen on the third day after his death, as He Himself had foretold.

Many of these men were indeed superstitious to a fault, as well as uneducated, and so undoubtedly believed the tripe of a risen body. This, I thought, was their reason for the look of trepidation.

But, that was not the only thing that had them uncertain. Word had indeed traveled fast, for they had already heard that a guard, a fellow Legionnaire, had fallen asleep on duty, an offense serious enough in its intensity to invoke the rule of Decimation, the rule of one-in-ten. The rule had not been implemented in some time, to my knowledge, but that did not mean it would not be in the future. In fact, somehow, that was the rumor that was floating about: that the rule of decimation was going to be implemented for this offense, which was also why the men were on edge.

Simply put, the rule of decimation states that if a soldier—a Legionnaire—committed a grievous error or offense, a gross dereliction of duty, then all one-hundred men in his century, and or his fellow centuries, were lined up by officers. One soldier was selected at random, and executed on the spot. Then, every tenth man in either direction from the first, was also selected, and executed on the spot. Usually, after watching in horrified, bowel-loosening terror, the offending Legionnaire was also slaughtered. The remaining Legionnaires would never forget the lesson: Obey, or be the cause of death to your comrades and yourself, and the befalling of shame on your family's honor.

Rome ruled by many methods. Not the least among them was fear, in various forms. That was especially true within the ranks of the military.

As if it were not enough, the men were agitated for yet another reason. By now, they all also knew that mine was the spear that had pierced His side. Thus, these soldiers embraced the gods of fear on more than one count.

In my mind, at that moment, however, I dismissed them all, intent only on going to my quarters. I did not know what I was thinking. Or perhaps I would not admit to myself then what I was thinking, but now I must reveal the truth of my mind. I wanted to escape to the familiar: the military, my command, my home.

A soldier's life; it is blessed among all professions for its regimentality. Although, I will admit now that in my case, established structure was the coward's refuge.

As the days, then weeks, passed, I went beyond my usual gruff self, and became an abusive tyrant to those around me, particularly, to the men beneath me in my command. Those closest to me, when in my presence, began to walk as if on burning coals, and if possible, did not subject themselves to my person at all.

Even Irena, my sweet Irena, was loath to venture near me. She tried on several occasions. I found myself enraged by her mere existence. I insulted her profanely each time. She was still effected and affected by that day in His tomb, and simply wanted to enrich her understanding of the experience by talking with the one who had shared it with her, the one she cared about, and the one to whom she was now bound in a most profound and unusual way. In the time since the experience, however, I was of a mind to destroy its reality, or at the very least, push it into the oblivion of the irrational.

"What you think happened, you stupid whore, is the farthest from the truth," I had said at our last meeting. "There are logical explanations for everything that happened that day."

Something in our perceptions of each other shifted in that moment.

Irena was never one to back away from an argument with me. She would turn her back on others in the same context, not caring about them or what they thought or said enough to engage them, but not me—never with me. Yet, now she did. A long silence ensued before she spoke.

"Maybe the girl from that night was right, Longinus. Perhaps demons do possess you," she said.

She was not serious, of course. Was she? She had said it with a smile upon her face. But, it was the smile of pity, of indifference; the kind one might give to another whom they feel is beneath them, or is simply ignorant. I knew in that moment that I had lost her. I realized once again what I had truly shared with Irena. Not just at the cave—the tomb, of course—but what we had shared since my arrival in this desolate place which the gods had forsaken.

We had shared our bodies, for one. On so many, many nights, we satisfied the primal, animal urgings of our bodies. It wasn't mutual at first. It was a business transaction. But, it blossomed into much more. Soon, our spirits and minds began to intertwine as well, profoundly. We would become enveloped as one in spirit, merging together in mind as our sweating, writhing bodies melded together in the climactic ecstasy that was the reflection of the divine, explosive creation of the Universe. Am I exaggerating? Not at all. For that is how I came to view our coupling. In that final moment of climax, I was the Highest of Gods, creator of all. I realize this now.

I acknowledge now, too, that I had never experienced anything like it with another human being. Ever. I knew she felt it, too, though we never spoke of it. I could see it in her eyes, feel it in her embrace. From there, we became very close on all levels. She was a confidant, a partner, a friend.

Appearances, however, were important in my line of work or duty. As a Roman officer, I could not be seen to have a relationship, let alone a serious one, with a woman of her profession and nationality, even if she was part Roman. So, I continued to pay her. At one point, she began to refuse to accept it, even becoming angry when I insisted. But, insist I did, almost becoming belligerent about it. I know I hurt her then. For, I said things I did not mean in order to force her to accept my money. I know this diminished me in her eyes, and caused her to question what was really between us. Yet, our passion for each other only grew. And, yes, I would call it love. Even in argument.

If someone were to see us or hear us arguing, on occasion, they would have sworn that we hated each other. However, the opposite of love is not hate. Love and hate are two sides of the same coin. The opposite of love is indifference.

Such is what I felt from her in that last moment, when she had said that perhaps the girl had been right about demons possessing me. And, it saddened me.

She left me then. I was told that she left the city entirely shortly thereafter. I know not where she went. North, was all that I was told, upon inquiring. I convinced myself that it did not matter at all. I was a Centurion, and thus above such things. How absurd. Nevertheless, it is what I told myself.

I was in the command tent when I received a visitor. It

was someone familiar.

A young legionnaire swept into the tent with the self-importance only reserved for the young and naive. "Centurion Longinus," he said with his formal salute.

"Yes," I replied, pretending to ignore him, not looking up from the report I was studying.

Quite apparent was the lad's disappointment in my seeming lack of interest in him, for his voice fell in volume and assertiveness substantially. "There is a man here to see you, Centurion. An old man," he said.

Though my eyes stayed on the report, the writing became a blur. My hand, for some reason, drifted to the spear leaning against the table at my side. I rarely left it more than two feet from my body now. I had no explanation for this, other than that it had become more important to me than my own arm. I was connected to it in a way I could not explain nor understand. Or, perhaps I simply feared to.

"His name is Jacobi. The old man has been waiting since dawn to see you. We thought he was a little...off, so we kept him away until now. He's persistent in saying that he...a...," the lad stammered.

I looked at him then. "He what?" I asked. But I already knew.

"He says he met you before at the...a..."

"Tomb. And, once before that," I finished for him.

Perplexity ran across my legionnaire's face. "Yes," he said. "But the old man said that he never said his name."

"'Tis true," I admitted. "But I know it now." I thought for a moment, not sure whether I wanted to hear anything that the old man had to say. Curiosity got the better of me, though. "Show him in."

"Yes, Centurion." With that and a salute, the lad disappeared and returned a moment later with Jacobi.

The older man's face still had the glow which had descended upon him that day in the tomb. But now, as I looked at him, something within me quickened, as if, for the first time in a decade, I was seeing a dear old friend. His semi-toothless smile beamed when our eyes met, as if to confirm my thoughts.

"Ah, Centurion Longinus. Thank you for seeing me," he said reverently.

"I apologize for not seeing you before now. I was just informed of your presence," I found myself saying. But why? I was a Roman Centurion, and made no apologies for lack or delay of audience with a Jew civilian! Still, as before, for some reason, something compelled me to administer to this one with respect.

"How goes it with you, Centurion Longinus?" he continued. I found the question odd, yet oddly comforting, as if I could unburden myself of anything to him.

"Quite well." I lied.

His eyes left mine for a moment and landed on the spear, then came back to me. My fingers, resting on the spear, now closed, gripping it in a gesture of protection, or more accurately, of coveting. "Jacobi," I said amiably, "an interesting name. Why have you come to see me?"

Again, his eyes drifted to the spear, then back. "Does It speak to you still?"

I brought the spear closer to my body. "Speak to me?" I asked, playing the fool. He simply smiled.

"Come, Centurion. I know The Voice has spoken to you through it. Does it still?"

I pondered for a moment as to how or why I should answer that. Indeed, as I have pointed out, odd voices in and out of my dreams, and one in particular, had plagued me since that day Jesu was hanged and I stabbed His chest. But, as of a while ago, I simply chose to push them aside, ignore them, and they had stopped. Though it had been only a little more than a month, I had convinced myself that the voices—the voice— was gone, and, indeed, had only been a phantom of my mind. Yet, now with Jacobi in front of me again...

Still, I denied it. I did not want to hear It again. "My dear Jacobi, I fear I know naught of what you speak."

He looked at me then with piercing eyes, as if looking

into my very essence. "Have you no shame?" he asked. "You deny the greatest gift that could be bestowed upon anyone?"

My anger began to rise. "Take care, old one," I breathed. "Do not forget your place here."

"Do I forget it?" he declared sarcastically. "What difference? You deny your True place," he countered.

His statement was confusing. Yet, there was a part within me where it made perfect sense.

He sighed then, as if letting go of a hope. "I came because I feared this, but had to see for myself. You have turned your back on the gift of Your Self. Alas, it is a shame, but it is also your choice. Yet, know this: It will always be there for you when you are ready."

I looked at the spear. For one of the few times in my life, I was speechless. Yet, part of me wanted to rail at this little old man for his presumption. Part of me grappled with a truth which I knew he was trying to teach me. Before I could find my tongue, however, he was gone. I looked up from my spear and he had vanished.

I ran around the table to where he had been standing, then to the tent flap. Peering out to the area beyond my tent, there he was, walking away. Jacobi was now approximately two-hundred yards from my tent. By the gods, how could he have walked so far so quickly?! Or could I have been staring at the spear that long?

"Sir?" came my guard's voice. I looked at him with what must have been astonishment. "Are you all right, sir?"

"Yes. Yes, of course. Carry on," I said and ducked back into the tent.

I sat down again behind my make-shift desk, piled with reports and maps, when one I seemed to have overlooked caught my eye. I picked it up: A leather-rolled missive with the seal of the Emperor's Guard, the Praetorians. "Guard!" I yelled.

The lad came rushing in as if a demon's teeth were chomping into his ass.

"Yes, Centurion?"

"When did this arrive?" I snapped at him, waving the

leather roll.

"I...do not—"

"When, damn it?"

"This afternoon, I presume, sir."

"You presume? Why was I not told? Can you not see the seal? It is from Rome herself!"

"Yes, sir, but it was not accompanied by a royal courier, sir," he said. "It must have come through with other reports. I did not know it was here until just now. Sir."

The boy was right. This should have been accompanied by a high ranking minion of the Emperor's Guard, a glorified courier. "Are you sure, Legionnaire?

Are you sure this was not accompanied by anyone?" I asked, with the edge of a razor, challenging him to defy me.

He straightened and lost all fear, exuding the confidence of one who spoke the truth. "Yes, Centurion. I am positive. I have been here since dawn and personally inspected those reports that came in this morning. That message was not there, so it must have arrived after the noon meal without royal escort. I would have seen otherwise."

"Yet, you did not find out if any reports came in after the noon meal, else you would have notified me of this, the only one with the royal seal," I pointed out.

The lad's confidence evaporated, his chin dropping to his chest.

"I do not know the seal of the Emperor's Praetorians. This...this is my first post, sir. I—"

"What? Every soldier knows the Praetorian Seal...," I started. But my heart suddenly went out to the boy. Ignorance. That's all this was. Indeed, I had committed a similar sin in my first year of duty. My slip had cost the life of my Centurion's servant. I had allowed a missive to slip through, containing a powerful poison. Upon opening it, my Centurion's servant spilled some of the foul substance on his skin. Blisters formed on his hands almost immediately. It ate through to the bone and a grizzly death ensued.

Surprisingly, my Centurion had not punished me beyond

a month of latrine duty. I never understood that, until now. This lad's transgression of not notifying me of this leather-bound message, was nowhere near my sin.

"Son," I began, "your lack of attentiveness could cost you someone's life, even your own."

His brow crinkled. Clearly, he did not grasp my meaning. "See that you go through the deliveries and arrivals everyday, anytime and every time they come. Understood?

"Yes, Centurion."

"Dismissed." He saluted so hard that I thought his clenched fist might go through his chest-plate. And, he nearly tripped over himself in his hasty retreat.

A smile tickled my lips. Had I ever been that young, that eager, that...green? I must have been.

My eyes dropped to the leather scroll still cradled in my hand. Trepidation crept into my mind. Why had there been no escort accompanying this? Of course, perhaps there had been an escort with the missive, but he had traveled in common civvies instead of the Praetorian uniform. And, perhaps further, he simply got tired of waiting. It was most unusual if that were the case. Then again, the Praetorians could be an arrogant lot.

The escort to this thing, or lack thereof, suddenly became irrelevant as my curiosity to its contents finally got the best of me. There was only one way to find out what it contained. I slipped my finger under the wax seal and pried it from the leather. Expensive parchment greeted my eyes as I unrolled the communication. I read the words, not quite comprehending what I was seeing.

"Come now. The message cannot be that glum."

I was startled by the voice. I looked up to see before me once again the old bright face of Jacobi. Speechless was I again.

"Well, when do we leave?" he continued.

"Leave?" I stammered.

"Is that not what it says? You are being recalled to Rome, are you not? And, I shall be your servant on the journey," he stated flatly, conveying the obvious.

"How could you know that? The message was sealed. It is death to view a royal communication meant for another!" I said. "And, and, I thought you'd left!" I was babbling. Why could this one unnerve me so?

He simply stood there smiling. "As you pointed out, it was sealed. I could not have seen it as you think because I did not open it."

A silence ensued. I was, once again, speechless.

"Well?" he finally said. "Do I speak the truth?"

"Are you a magician?" I asked lamely.

He laughed. In fact, he rolled with laughter. It was actually quite refreshing, that laugh. It immediately put me at ease. I found myself smiling, smiling as much at this little man as I was laughing at myself for my inane question.

"No," said Jacobi at last. "Unless, of course, you consider running into a young, drunk courier, who was blabbing how he was of the Praetorian ranks, though he was dressed plainly, and asking him why a Praetorian was here, an act of a great Magician!" he laughed again, showing a wonderful, toothless grin, full of life and warmth. I could not help but be drawn in by it. He also had graciously explained what had happened to the Royal Courier.

~VI~

The heat was oppressive, burning the lungs as it entered, deflating the soul as it left. Overall, I was glad to be leaving this barren place. The gods baked this land and its people, scrambling the brains and creating a ripe environment for one to lose one's mind; actually, for the many to lose their collective balance.

For example, more than a few people were beginning to view me as some kind of demi-god. My spear and my contact with the Anointed One, as many were now calling him, had caused this. Ignorant fools. Jacobi was among them. He certainly held me in this reverent light, but, only to a point. He was continually harping on me that my human part, my Roman part, kept getting in the way of the True Gift and Realization which I had been given.

At first, I would simply bellow at him to leave me alone; that he was an old fool. But his deflection of my words and attitude was done with the gentle demeanor of a wise old sage and father-figure. And, with persistence.

Once, I yelled at him with such wrath and violence that I was sure he would piss his robes and lose his bowels. Any of my soldiers would have, and then fled for their lives. But not Jacobi. Dear Jacobi. He simply smiled his toothless grin; that Otherworldly glowing Presence emanating from his whole being. I had tried to drive him away. I failed. I could have had him forcibly removed from my post forever. But I did not. I could not. He was here for me. He was a guide of sorts. I do not know how I knew this. I just did.

Thus, I accepted him into my circle as my "servant." Some of my men snickered at this, behind my back, of course. It was not uncommon for an officer to take a young man-servant into his tent to be part of his staff. Some preferred the sexual pleasures of a young man, as well as those of a woman, or even instead of. Perfectly fine. But not me. I had always preferred the company of women. My men knew this, which made their jokes about the older Jacobi becoming my man-servant all the more humorous. Again, these hilarities were never told to me or in front of me, but I heard them, nonetheless. And, it mattered not.

Even at the time I was leaving this place, I had still received no official word as to why I was being recalled to Rome. My superior officer would only say that in the official missive he received, the reason stated was reassignment. As to where and why, he would not say, if indeed he even knew. My missive said nothing save for recalling me to Rome. The General, my superior officer, was also obviously quite perturbed with the whole thing. There was more going on here than I was being told. For instance, why was I not being allowed to take my men with me, if, in fact, this was simply a reassignment? One hundred of the finest lads I have ever had the honor of commanding were they. Although, it was true that since the great Julius Caesar, or rather, just thereafter, an officer was not allowed to take all his men when transferring— too much loyalty can be a dangerous thing. But, I was only a Centurion in command of a hundred; not a General in command of a Legion of thousands. Besides, when previously I'd been reassigned, my men had always come with me. Why not now? I was told to pick a platoon and support crew only. Why?

No matter. I was a soldier of Rome. I obeyed orders. I told my men I would see them again, and then chose two Decurion officers, seven legionnaires, and four servants to man supplies and domestics. My replacement had arrived the next day, so off we went—me, my nine men, plus four, and supplies. And, of course, Jacobi.

The first two days of the journey were utterly uneventful; hot and boring. We were to stop in a small village on the third day to replenish our food and water, and rest our mounts. Two more days and we'd reach the coast and passage back to Rome herself. Approximately half a mile from the village, my two scouts returned to report that the place seemed empty. Though they had not actually ventured into the village itself, there appeared to be no one about at all. This was somewhat odd, but not that unusual. The sight of Roman soldiers often instilled fear in the locals. Fear enough to stay inside or, out-and-out hide. Still, someone should be around.

"You did not see anyone?" I asked, for clarification.

"Not a soul, sir," the scout replied.

"Any holiday that we know of?"

"Sir?"

"Any observance, holy or otherwise, that would draw the people elsewhere or keep them indoors?" I restated.

"Ah, well, I don't know, Centurion," the scout replied sheepishly.

Then, as one, our gaze turned to Jacobi for an answer. This area was still Jewish, after all. "I do not know the local customs of these parts, but I assure you that in the general sense of the Law of Moses, this is a day of normal enterprise," he said as he casually leaned on his walking staff.

"Can you never speak plainly?!" I retorted.

"This is a normal work day," Jacobi said simply. "But..." he said, eyes narrowing.

"Well, what is it?" asked the scout.

"I... I'm not sure," answered Jacobi. There was a silence. The raspy caw of a vulture sounded in the distance.

"It's the heat, is what it is. It's cooking your brain, old man!" quipped a legionnaire, and the rest laughed.
"All right, enough," I said. "Proceed with caution," I told the scout. "Lead us in."

Indeed, no one was about as we went in. Small plumes of smoke were hovering just above the ground in various places around the village. One of the servants suddenly made a grotesque guttural noise and vomited. In an instant, we realized what had made the poor fellow wretch. It was not smoke hovering above the ground, but dust; the dust surged up from the wings and jostling of dozens of scavenger birds as they vied for their place at a gruesome feast. The heat-filled light breeze suddenly shifted and brought the stench of the slaughtered villagers into our nostrils. My scout had been correct; not a soul was here, not any longer. But their hacked and disemboweled corpses were.

The bodies were in groups. The mutilation was an abomination; a child's arm hacked off and protruding from a woman's vagina; a severed penis and scrotum stuffed into an elderly man's mouth; the hilt of a sword standing out of the anus of both men and women, the blade still up inside the victim; heads and torsos on pikes. There were other atrocities that went beyond the imagination. It was obvious that these horrors were performed on the people while they were still alive. The final look on their faces was beyond unspeakable pain and terror, frozen there forever. That servant was not the only one to lose his breakfast at this point. Even two of my hand-picked, battle-hardened legionnaires did, as well. I could not blame them. The wrath of the gods coursed through my veins in that moment. I knew not these people, cared naught for them. Yet, something inside me wanted to avenge them, if only on the basis of human dignity. There was another reason, too, going through my mind—not quite as lofty; this was a slap in the face to Rome. "You see?" it bespoke. "Rome is nothing! She cannot even protect her subject people!" I looked at Jacobi and was quite surprised to see his reaction. He was calm, almost serene. Though he surveyed the scene with eyes wide open and obviously smelled the rotting stench, he was unaffected, at least in the way the rest of us were. For some reason, I was angered to see him thus.

"Jacobi!" I yelled. "What in the name of the Gods? Are you dead yourself? These are your people, destroyed. Yet, you stand there as if... as if..." I could not finish.

"'As if' what, Longinus? These are not my people alone. All are one People, within the One. Their eternal spark or spirit is not here any longer, but it is not gone. This," he said gesturing to all the death, "is tragic perhaps. Yet, it is what it is; an experience in the Mind of God. There is no judgment."

I was astounded.

"That is not to say," he continued, "that those who are guilty will not meet justice; 'those that live by the sword, shall perish thereby,' it has been said. Again, no judgment. It is simply the way of it, reaping what one sows, the Law of the One."

"Of course, you old shit!" squawked Decurion Demitri, clearly tired of Jacobi's rants. "I choose to live a soldier's life. There is no more honorable way to die than by the sword!"

In spite of everything right then, I had to smile. Demitri was the son of a dear friend of mine. He was part of the equestrian class. He was educated. And, he had been my ranking Decurion for some time. He could have left the army the previous year, but chose to stay with me. At times, he over stepped his bounds. But, usually, he was both amusing and insightful.

"As you say," Jacobi said with a bow.

Demitri made a move to strike the old man. Jacobi moved not a muscle.

"Hold, Decurion!" I commanded. "Stand down. We have more important matters here."

"Centurion!" said a legionnaire. "All the water supplies are contaminated. There are corpses down the wells.

"Understood. We'll ration what we have," I said. "Gather any arrows and weapons left behind. I want to know who did this. Dispatch two men to search for any survivors." The soldier opened his mouth to speak. "I know," I cut him off. "It's futile. Do it anyway. Have the rest of the men pile the corpses in the center of the village. Burn them."

The soldier saluted fist to chest and left to fulfill his unpleasant task. There was then a preternatural silence, as if all the air in the immediate vicinity had been sucked away, taking all sound with it. The spear began to vibrate in its harness on my saddle. Jacobi and Demitri both saw it as well.

"They're still here," said Jacobi.

Across the center of the village, one of my men dropped, an arrow protruding from his back. "Form up!" I commanded, my mount dancing nervously beneath me.

A score, plus ten filth-encrusted bandits, poured out of the humble dwellings, screaming with blood-lust. "Shit on Rome!" yelled one. "Kill them all!" yelled others, all waving swords and weapons.

"To the outskirts," I directed my men. I was proud of them at that moment. We were outnumbered three to one. Yet, there was not a hairsbreadth of fear between them. One man had gone down. He would be avenged. There was nothing else to be done. Of the remaining eight, six were legionnaires on foot. Demitri and my other Decurion quickly remounted and moved rapidly, the way we had come. The other servants had remained outside the village with the supplies. Only Jacobi had ventured in with me. He, too, was on foot. But, unlike my well trained young legionnaires, Jacobi could not run in formation to a protected site. He could not even move his sack of bones faster than a brisk walking pace. He was standing next to my horse's flank. Without so much as a "by-your-leave," I bent down and grabbed the scrawny old man below the armpit. I kneed my horse hard in the sides, urging him to a sprint from a standstill. Using Jacobi's own weight and the horse's momentum, I simply swung the old man up behind me on the mount as we galloped off.

"STOP, Longinus!" yelled Jacobi.

"I'll not leave you to these barbarians, Old One!"

"So you would sooner break my old bones this way? I've had a long life. I've seen the One incarnate, and now I see It within myself. I fear not the next life. Now put me down!" demanded Jacobi.

"You'll not venture to that next life just yet, my friend. You belong with me!" I yelled over the pounding hooves and screaming bandits.

My men and I met up where we had left the other servants and the supplies. The servants had already been slaughtered. Seven more bandits awaited us at the bodies. They were easily taken down. Demitri and my two mounted lieutenants sliced their heads off where they stood. I felt bad about the servants. Ordinarily, I would have assigned guards to them and the supplies but I had not the man power. Besides, all the servants I had picked had battle-practice experience. I had used them for skirmish practice when I was short of troops. They were loyal and knew how to fight. But they had been outnumbered and not properly armed.

The remaining murderous scum were running out from the village. They came at us in a rag-tag group, no organized attack formation whatsoever. This would be easy. With a light nudge from me, Jacobi slid gently to the ground. My men and I regrouped, forming a small wedge; a miniature version of a tried and true battle formation that would slice through and divide an enemy horde. The screaming, murderous filth was now running full tilt right at our v-shaped wedge. Our horsemen were at the front of the wedge with myself at the point. I pulled my spear from its harness and lofted it, ready to signal our own charge.

"Hold, Longinus," said the Voice; that same voice, from my dreams. Now, though, it seemed to be coming from the spear—from the blood stain on the spear's blade.

Fear gripped my heart. "You again!" I heard myself whisper. I quickly pushed the fear away and replaced it with anger. "Hold?" And what, allow ourselves to be slaughtered?!"

"Sir?" said Demitri from behind me. Apparently, I had answered the Voice a little too loudly.

"Nothing, Decurion," I said.

"Longinus," continued the Voice in my head, "that will not be the way of it."

I watched the oncoming scum. Against my better judgment, I held; did not move a muscle. Though I could not see my men because I was at the point of our little wedge, I sensed their agitation; could almost hear their thoughts. "What in Hades does he wait for?"

"Sir?" Demitri's voice.

"Hold your ground, Decurion," I said.

The horde, if you call them that - thirty or so

disgusting, smelly, disorganized, marauders and murderers, a mob, really—were still running at us full speed, still screaming at full throat. But then it began to happen. When they were about forty yards from our position, their voices began to falter, their sword arms began to drop. Some of them began to fall back. By the time they were within fifteen yards of us, the "mob" had dwindled to about ten. The rest had stopped at various points on their charge and were now bent over, hands on knees, panting for their lives. The final ten had also stopped, fatigued. They could not maintain a full sprint to engage us. They had expected to pounce on us in the village. They were not the well-conditioned legionnaires of Rome. Drawing them outside the village at their frenzied pace had fatigued them completely. It was time to destroy them.

"You will not kill them," said the voice.

"Like hell, I won't!" I said through clenched teeth. "Advance!" I yelled. As one, my men and I sprang forward.

"You will not kill them," repeated the voice. I tried to turn a deaf ear. I glanced back at Jacobi. His eyes were closed. I know that he had heard the voice, too. No matter. Our wedge sliced through what was left of the mob and dispersed; no need to keep our formation. Individual fighting broke out. In outright defiance of the voice—I would not obey a phantom!—I made a violent stab down with my spear from horseback at the first enemy I came to. It should have run him through, skewered him where he stood. Instead, to my horror, the spear snapped. The lance shaft broke at the place where it joined the blade, the blade itself falling harmlessly to the ground. The enemy was as stunned as I. He stood there. Frozen. I reigned in and drew my sword. My mount's momentum had taken us a few yards beyond the man I had thought to spear. I turned and spurred my horse to a gallop back at him. Before I could reach him, however, one of his comrades stepped into my path, stabbing his short sword at my horse's legs, but missing. I cleaved the lad in two with my sword, swinging down and slicing through his shoulder, collar bone and ribs. Almost in the same motion, I smashed his face in with my stud-soled boots to dislodge my weapon from his body. I galloped on to the first enemy. To my amazement, he had picked up the spear blade. For some inexplicable reason, I was angered by this beyond comprehension. How dare this pig even think of touching it! I thought. Even more amazing was the awe with which he now looked upon it.

I reached him and reigned in, stopping my mount within arm's reach of him. I swear that in that moment, as he looked into my eyes, he knew who I was and what he held. I raised my arm, and severed his head from his body. It dropped off his shoulders and thudded to the ground, its eyes still blinking at me with comprehension. For five heartbeats, his body remained standing, blood spurting in a rhythmic fountain from the neck stump. Then, the truly astounding thing happened: The hands, still holding the spear blade, raised in the air toward me, clearly offering the blade back to me. As soon as I took the blade, the body's legs crumpled in death.

A silence filled the air. Fighting had ceased. I slowly became aware of many eyes being upon me. Everyone had witnessed what had happened. The enemy began withdrawing. The man I had beheaded had apparently been their leader. They had also taken in how I had killed him and his offering up of the blade, the significance of which was not lost on them. A superstitious lot, was my first thought.

"You did not heed the voice," said Jacobi from behind me. I turned to see the old man standing there, stern disappointment splashed across his face. At his side, he held the shaft of my spear. I had dropped it when it broke, unaware, to free my sword hand.

I was confused and angry. Why was Jacobi reprimanding me, and how dare he presume? I was also afraid. Why was he hearing the voice, too, yet no one else heard it? To dispel this confusion and fear, I did what I always do; I hid behind my mantel of being a Roman Officer. "Who are you to question me? This man led the killing here," I said. Then I remembered something else said earlier. "Why do you care, old man? You said earlier that, what was it? 'Their eternal spark is not gone...an experience in the mind of God...no judgment...and yet you stand there in judgment of me? Take care, Jacobi!"

"It is your intent here, your lack of heed to the Higher voice within you that is at issue, not this one," he said, indicating the headless form before me. "He chose his path as we all do."

"I tire of your riddles, old man. I don't know why I keep you around," I said.

"Yes you do. I am one of your inner voices," he retorted with a toothless grin.

I could not tell whether he was serious.

"Sir!" yelled Demitri. "They get away!" All eyes swept to the retreating, more like slinking away, outlaws.

"Take them," I began. I locked eyes with Jacobi. "Alive, if possible."

"But Centurion, there are too many and they are unworthy," continued Decurion Demitri. "They cannot be allowed to escape. It would be simpler to kill them with arrows and—"

"Enough! You will not question me thusly! You will follow my orders or end up like this piece of shit," I said, commandingly, pointing to the decapitated corpse. "I don't care whose son you are. Is that clear, Decurion?" My anger, though misplaced, silenced him utterly.

"Yes...yes, sir," he stammered

~VII~

We headed for the coast, arriving two days later. I had repaired the spear, reattaching blade to shaft as best I could given the tools at hand. It wasn't pretty, but it would hold solid. Of the murderous raiders that had been left alive, we captured fifteen. The rest fled, eluding us as they ran back into the maze of rock formations in the hills that surrounded the village.

Eluded is perhaps the wrong word. Eluded implies pursuit. I was not about to order my men to pursue them all the way. We had neither the manpower, nor the time for that. So, I settled for capturing a handful as an example. As I had implicitly promised Jacobi, we took them alive. Foolish, that was. Once I turned them over to the Roman regiment at the port to which we were headed, they would all be crucified. It's not as if any of them were of note, from a wealthy family of the occupied territory who could be ransomed back to their people. They were nothing, worthless. Capturing them alive had, in some ways, been crueler then killing them outright. Then again, perhaps one or two of them would make it to the arena to fight for his life and maybe even live, for another day or so. Still, I was of the mind that that would not happen. They would be crucified.

I pointed this out to Jacobi. "'Twas stupid to take these men, Jacobi. You know that. They are going to be executed anyway, in a much more prolonged and brutal fashion than they would have received by our hands."

"Then why did you spare them?"

I felt the flush of anger color my face. "What say you?!" I growled through clenched teeth. "You bid to spare them! That..." I lowered my voice to a conspiratorial whisper. "...That voice, too. You heard it. I know you did."

"No, I did not, Longinus," he said.

"But?" I began, confused. I was sure by the look on his face, at the time, that he had.

"I knew it was there, however. I knew that you were hearing it," he continued. "In that moment, Longinus, it was a lesson for you to learn. It was not about saving those men. Their fate had already been sealed by the choices they had made and believed in. In that moment, it was for you to acknowledge your own conscience, your highest Self through compassion, to step outside of your Roman persona and—"

"Stop!" I pleaded. "Why must everything with you be in the form of a riddle?"

"'Tis not a riddle if one understands its point."

"Ach!! I surrender."

* * *

The port city of Najaffi—as it was now called, at least, perhaps, until the next solstice; it had changed names so many times over the past two decades, that it was somewhat difficult to keep an account of what it might be called at any given time—was as beautiful to the eye as it had been when I first arrived in this region of the Empire. For the most part, however, its beauty ended there.

As we approached the city, we were first met with the smell of the salty sea, the ocean. I always warmed to the smell of the ocean. It bespoke travel, adventure, going home. But this time, there was no opportunity to revel in the feelings that scent conjured. For, no sooner had the ocean smell wafted to us, when it was rudely usurped by the offensive stench of the city itself: stale urine and excrement, thousands of unwashed human bodies, not to mention unprocessed and rotting trash and refuse. As it had been the last time I had come through Najaffi, its waste disposal system was still apparently non-existent. It baffled me as to why the city leaders, who changed almost as frequently as the name of the place itself, did not develop some way of dealing with this problem, or, indeed why the Roman Prefect, the military head of this realm, did not simply implement his own solution. Then again, very few cultures other than that of the Roman people had as an acute sensibility to personal cleanliness and hygiene, which, of course, extended to their surrounding living environment. And, as to the Prefect stepping in, well, when occupying a region, a province, a people, we did try our best to respect their customs and ways of living, even if they were disgusting to us. Such was my train of thought as we approached the city.

That train of thought was all but forgotten, however, when the next wave of smells happened to hit us. Food! Cooking meats and vegetables; that wonderful smell made our mouths water and our taste buds lust for gratification. I had not realized how hungry I was until that moment.

We arrived at the outskirts of the city. I ordered Demitri to stay outside and make a temporary camp with the prisoners. I would send out supplies and food as soon as possible. I was not about to march the filth through a crowded thoroughfare. I took my other mounted Decurion and Jacobi to seek out the local Roman authority. If my information was accurate, then the Prefect, the man in charge here, was still Maximus Centilius, a somewhat brutal lower General turned Prefect for Rome, who thought nothing of flogging and flailing prisoners for entertainment; even those whose crimes were petty: the stealing of bread, for example.

The main thoroughfare into the city was flanked by several Roman Guards as was appropriate. We dismounted and I approached the soldier nearest us. He was obviously a Gaul, a Celt, as evidenced by his mane of red hair and mustache. No Roman-born soldier would be allowed to keep that mustache and that length of hair, though it was tied back to flow out the back of his helm. Certain allowances were beginning to make their way into Rome's military mind with regard to the recruitment of foreign fighters. The Celts from Gaul were among the fiercest fighters in the world, though tough to discipline. A handful of them were starting to make their way into Roman life, including, and especially, the army.

"You there. Where might I find your Prefect, Centilius?"
I asked.

The Celt studied me as if I were a fly on shit. Though
recognition of my uniform and rank finally dawned on him, he
was still clearly unimpressed. His silence dragged on to the
point of utter rudeness, not to mention insubordination. My
patience by this time was non-existent. Though he was almost
a head taller than I, we both stood on uneven ground. By
stepping toward him, I actually came eye-to-eye with the
brute, as I was on slightly higher ground. As I did this, I could
smell his rancid, stale-ale breath, no doubt the result of the
previous night's inebriation. My nose was practically on his.

"Take care, soldier. I am Centurion Longinus and I am
here to see your Prefect, who is an old acquaintance of mine.
You will take me to him now, or I will rip your balls off where
you stand and feed them to the hungry prisoners I've dragged
here. Is that clear, my ignorant Celtic friend?" There is a point
at the beginning of any confrontation where it will explode or
snuff. I could see in his eyes that in any other time and place,
he would have done the former, attempting to, and probably
succeeding in, tearing my head from my body. But,
fortunately, his Roman training was paying off; he maintained
his discipline. The Celt stepped back from me and eyed my
dirty uniform again, then looked over my shoulder at my
companions. "My Decurion and servant," I offered.

"Follow me," he said, and turned on his heels without
the customary—actually required—salute to a senior officer.
So much for discipline.

I started to follow, when I heard the voice. "Do not
leave it," It said. I didn't flinch at hearing it. Perhaps I was
getting used to the unbidden inner commands. Jacobi was
staring right at me. The old fool knew I had heard something.
The "it," of course, was the spear. I stepped toward my horse
and retrieved it. My Decurion raised an eyebrow, but said
nothing. I motioned to my companions to move out. The three
of us followed the Celt, leaving our horses with one of the
other city guards, a decidedly more Roman-looking soldier.

The Celt led us through the crowded plaza of the city. There were all numbers of merchants, vendors and sellers of everything imaginable, and some quite unimaginable: fine linens and jewelry, cooking wears, meats and other food, spices, soothsayers—everything that one would normally expect to find in a port city. But, then there was the bizarre things; magic potions made from the dung of priests, animals being sold not as food, but as sexual surrogates, and naked humans being led by twine tied to their genitals, being marketed specifically as sexual playthings. I ignored most of what I saw. I turned to see my battle-hardened, yet worldly-naive Decurion's face writhing in disgust. Jacobi, however, was smiling his toothless grin at one and all. My first thought was that the old fart had gone off his nut and didn't realize what some of these people were peddling. But then I looked into his eyes. And, there It was: that other-worldly glaze; the depth that I'd seen many times. He was looking at all these people as equals, distaining none of them. I turned back to look at our Celtic guard as he continued leading us to the Prefect. Clearly, he had been observing me and my little party as we progressed.

His face was difficult to read. There was a mixture of contempt and respect. He turned away as we walked on. Though it mattered not what this one thought, I was curious.

"Speak your mind, soldier," I said.

"Very well. Your officer is puss-food," he said, prompting my Decurion, whose family name was Flavius, to begin to unsheathe his gladius at the insult. A subtle shake of my head and the blade was re-sheathed, much to Flavius' disappointment.

"He is one of the finest soldiers I've fought with," I countered. The Celt simply grunted, but said nothing else. "Well? What else?" He stopped and turned to look at Jacobi who was now quite a few paces behind us. I stopped next to him. Flavius walked on. The Celt and I simply observed the old man for a moment. The Celt's contempt had obviously been for Flavius. The respect was for Jacobi.

"That one. Where I hail from, we would say the he has the look of The Old Ones," the Celt stated with reverence.

"He is old," I said, confused.

The big Celt looked at me as if I were a stupid child. "Not 'old' in the man-sense, sir, but as in one of The Old Ones —he God-Men that created all—that my people are descended from."

Now I understood. So, it was not just me who saw this light in Jacobi. I suddenly felt a bit of a kindred spirit with the Celt. I felt that this might be someone, even as obviously barbaric as he was, who might understand some of the things I'd experienced over the past few months. But, the feeling was short-lived. My reason kicked in. He was an ignorant Celt, after all. He was a subordinate, not to mention that I did not know him; not even his name. "As I said, he's simply my servant," I impotently stated.

The red-haired man smiled and said, "Are you sure who is the servant, and who is the master?" He laughed and we walked on.

I had exaggerated a bit to the Celt when I said I was an old acquaintance of Centilius'. In truth, it was an out-and-out lie. I'd never met the man before. I knew him by name and reputation only. His reputation of cruelty was not exaggerated. We heard the squealing pleas for mercy as we approached the huge wooden doors. The door-guard obviously recognized the Celt. But, to my surprise, he did not give me, Decurion Flavius, or Jacobi a second look; he opened the doors right away, as if we had been expected. An uneasy feeling began to wrap itself around me. Before I could give any thought to it, however, my uneasiness gave way to nausea. As we entered the great hall behind the doors, we were greeted by the sight of a man stretched on some kind of wooden device. He was lying on his back, the contraption at an angle so that the man was leaned back, but not quite lying flat. His arms were outstretched on wooded planks, his head tied back to a post from which extended the two planks holding his arms. No, his head was not tied back. The post had an indentation which cradled the back of his head. His head was being held there by his ears; his ears had been nailed to the post with two very large nails—spikes, really—to help keep his head back. If he lifted his head too much, his ears would rip off his head. His hands were also nailed to the planks. The source of his screaming pain, however, quickly became apparent: His scrotum had been nailed to a separate piece of wood and was being twisted in the hands of another man in a black robe.

A short distance away, across the plush black marble floor, reclined several well-dressed men, their togas rimmed with gold. They were eating what appeared to be a very sumptuous lunch. A couple of the men were obviously as disgusted by the sight of the man being tortured during their meal as I was. I am all for disciplining someone, flogging, even. But I have never been one to torture, especially in the context of what is clearly nothing but entertainment. Yet, I stomached it; made no indication that I was bothered by it. The Prefect, after all, who was apparently the man in the middle of the rest —as he seemed to be the one enjoying the display the most— far outranked me. Besides I needed him. I looked to my Decurion and subtly shook my head; not a word, my thoughts were to him.

Slowly, the spear's tip began to glow softly. I looked from the spear to Jacobi. The old man had stopped in his tracks, eyes closed as if in some kind of trance. The tortured man began to become still, his screams turned to simpering moans. Finally, he was silent, as if asleep. My spear returned to normal, Jacobi opened his eyes and came to stand beside me. The Celt smiled and looked at Jacobi with revered awe. He then looked at me, eyebrow raised, silently telling me that Jacobi was indeed one of the Old Ones.

Prefect Centilius, however, was not so reverent. "What is this?" he bellowed, looking from the racked prisoner to myself, then to Jacobi. A most awkward silence ensued, during which Jacobi made his way to my side. The Prefect's gaze was intense, almost demonic. But, Jacobi merely yawned.

Prefect Centilius was a short, stocky, petty little man, with the brains to match his stature. It was widely rumored that in addition to his cruel nature, he had a taste for young boys. The latter is ultimately what had forced him out of the military; he allegedly had raped a senator's thirteen year old son. The only reason he didn't lose his life, so I'd heard, was that there had been no direct evidence; no witnesses, just the boy's sketchy accusation—his word—against the then second-rate General. Glancing around at the young man-servants doling out the food and wine, I had no doubt that the General's lust for the youthful male was true. Looking at his ugly, almost demonic, expression at that moment, I felt certain that the charge of rape also had been true. I suddenly hated and distrusted this fecal excuse of a man, this putrid example of a Roman.

Fortunately, our Celtic friend spoke up, breaking my thoughts and the silence. "Noble Prefect. Please forgive the intrusion, but this is Centurion Longinus. He has been escorted to your presence as requested," he said, rather too formally and with a sarcastic edge.

Escorted to his presence as per request? I was stunned. Perhaps we had been spotted on the road, but to know my name and for someone to be commanded to be escorted to the Prefect immediately was something else. The uneasy feeling in my gut tripled. "What is the meaning of this?" I demanded. "I am simply on my way to Rome as ordered."

There, behind a partition, near the couches where the diners were reclining, appeared a Praetorian Guard, then another, then another, and yet one more.

"It appears that you have something the Emperor desires," giggled the Prefect.

"Shut-up, Centilius!" barked the lead Praetorian, a General by rank. That, too, was quite odd. Why was such a high-ranking officer in the Emperor's Guard here? And what could I have that they, or the Emperor, wanted—if indeed the whore-spawn Prefect was correct? Then it became clear. All of

60

their eyes simultaneously drifted to the spear in my hand. I should have known. It was strange that no one questioned me about it coming in to a Prefect's court hall. True, I was an officer of Rome, and thus, a side arm gladius was permitted on my person. But, bringing in a weapon such as a spear was simply not permitted. It had not even dawned on me that I still carried it until that moment.

"You let quite a few of the murderers from that small village get away," continued the Praetorian. "That was a mistake."

How could he have known? Spies? Some of the escapees made their way here, told their stories, perhaps? But what of it? "I had not the man power to capture them all," I said, defensively.

"You could have, should have, killed them. 'Twas your duty. But we saw what we needed to see, on more than one level."

I was outraged. "You've had spies watching me?"

"Of course. And then some. You and your weapon performed most admirably. It even speaks to you, does it not?"

There was much more going on here than just espionage. Though he outranked me, I had gone beyond caring about the consequences. "Explain yourself!" I commanded.

"Why, Centurion, you forget your place."

"I don't care who you are anymore. Something is happening here, and I want to know what it is."

"Very well. Your village raiders were hired thugs; a chance for us to see the spear in action. It's becoming the stuff of legend, you know," confessed the Praetorian.

I was utterly confused. My rational mind could not get itself around the notion that my own beloved Rome would stoop to such a feat simply to watch a meaningless piece of wood "in action." I had seen many atrocities during various campaigns, most of them displayed by the cruelty that human nature can turn to when allowed. Yet, most had been products of a confused circumstance of the moment, or of desperation.

But this... "I don't know what you're talking about," I replied. "The spear did nothing."

"The man you struck with it, his headless corpse handed it back to you."

I said nothing.

"And, it glows while in your grasp, then it speaks to you, does it not?" he reiterated.

Glows. Yes, it has, but usually not before I hear the voice. It shakes, or vibrates, and even then, sometimes the voice is simply there, in my head. How could he know even a twisted version of these things. Perhaps...enough. This had gone on long enough. I held the spear aloft, over my head, but in a non-threatening manner. "This is nothing but wood, metal and—"

"And magic," interrupted a burgundy-robed wisp of a man. Obviously, he was one of the court soothsayers or Apollo Temple priests.

"You're a fool if you truly believe that," I said.

"But it soothed and silenced the prisoner," he said, indicating the motionless wretch on the rack. Had that too been planned?

"I, the spear had nothing to do with that," I said, holding the spear by my side and turning to Jacobi. Why was he not saying anything? It certainly was not for fear of offending a superior. That had never stopped him before.

Before I could say anything to Jacobi, the Praetorian mistook my glance at the old man and stepped forward to get a better look at Jacobi. "Yes. This one, too. This one silenced the prisoner, but in conjunction with the spear's tip glowing. He will come with us too."

"Too?" was all I could stammer.

"Yes. The spear, you and this old man. You see, Centurion, rumors have been infiltrating the palace in Rome. And, as I said, the priests convinced our emperor that the spear must have powers beyond this world, and therefore, his highness should be in possession of it, being that he is a living god and the most powerful man on earth. The thought was to have you simply bring it to Rome on a recall mission. But then, our sources," he continued, as he made the subtlest of head nods to Flavius, "indicated that you'd die rather than part with it. So, we organized the assault on the village to test it, and you."

I turned and glared at Decurion Flavius, hatred spilling from every one of my pores. The spear began to shake in my hand violently. The movement was not lost on the Praetorian, nor on anyone else in the room.

"There! See there! It responds to you. You know now that Flavius was our man and that angers you. The sense of betrayal, and so forth. We came here to take the weapon from you. But I think now that you must come."

~VIII~

I was now completely ignoring the purple robed figure, seething in my anger at Flavius. Betrayed, yes. Though I hadn't known this one all that long, it was long enough to believe that I could trust him. "How much did they pay you, Flavius? You have disgraced yourself and your family forever."

"Quite the contrary, Longinus," answered the Praetorian. "He has done his patriotic duty, as I expect you to."

I said nothing.

"Come, come, Longinus," the Praetorian said at last.

"No," I said, burning my disgust into the bastard's eyes.

"Do not look at me like that, Centurion. It is not I who demands this, but the Caesar himself.

"He has no idea what this is," I said, holding up the spear.

"Exactly why you must come with us—to show us."

For a moment, I faltered. Could I go to Rome and presume to show them...show them what? I had not the faintest idea myself what this...thing was all about. I had been denying it all along. And, it was only just in that moment that I fully acknowledged to myself that there was something here; something larger than myself happening to me, through me, and the spear was a part of that, but certainly not the thing itself. In truth, it was only a very small part of the overall story that was beginning to take shape within my mind's eye, my soul. The fools in Rome would never understand this. "If it's such a small part, then simply give it to us," they would say. Never!

"My patience is done," said the Praetorian, interrupting my thoughts. With the snap of his fingers, all became chaos.

Purple-robed figures descended on us from all sides. I spun, and the spear caught two of them with barely a touch, yet both crumpled to the floor as if scalded by hot oil. Spinning again, I caught another Praetorian's sword with the blade of my spear. It did not parry his weapon, but sliced through it as though it were lard. Stunned, he stepped back, afraid, that dumb look of the superstitious splashed across his face.

"Take him!" the General Praetorian commanded, pointing to Jacobi.

I could not get to him fast enough. The four remaining Praetorians pounced on him like lions on a rabbit. But, they were in for a huge surprise. The butt of Jacobi's walking staff stabbed into the balls of the first Praetorian to reach him, the head of it under the jaw of the second, drawing the first up off his feet in excruciating pain, shattering the teeth and jaw of the second.

Two other Praetorians wrapped themselves around Jacobi, though, smothering him with their bulk. The spear left my hand before I even realized that I had hurled it. It slammed into the side of the Praetorian on Jacobi's front, sending the guard screaming to the ground in a crumpled heap of fury and burning pain. The stench of searing flesh filled the air. He yanked the spear from his side and a wisp of smoke trailed from the wound.

For an instant, no one moved; frozen, stunned by what we had just witnessed. In that moment, I covered most of the floor between me and the spear, now resting at Jacobi's feet. I stopped short, though. The last Praetorian now had Jacobi in a choke-hold from behind, jewel-encrusted knife at his throat. In contrast to his burst of heroic fighting a moment ago, Jacobi was now quite relaxed and, so it seemed, almost limp in the guard's arms, with that odd smile upon his face. Then my eyes met the Praetorian's. I saw fear there. Hesitation, indecision. He would not slice the old man's throat. Not because he was afraid to, but because he saw the prize on the floor: The spear, the Lance, the supposed Magical Staff of the gods, the blade of which carried the blood of the Powerful Prophet.

I could see the dilemma play out in his eyes; to grab the spear, he must release Jacobi and face me—hence, the fear in his eyes. Is this Centurion a powerful prophet of some kind as well? he would be thinking. It is he who wields the spear, after all. The fool was giving his own power away to me with such thoughts, because it paralyzed him. He could not decide.

Then I would. I had to.

The Praetorian General was still there, and no doubt, more Palace Guards would enter at any moment.

"Guards!" squealed the snake-of-a-Prefect. Indeed, I would not have long to wait at all before his reinforcements came.

I saw movement out of the corner of my eye. The Praetorian General had started to move toward the spear. And then it happened: The act, the deed, that would forever change my career, my path, my very life. Although, one could argue that my path, my life, had already been forever changed back on a lonely hill many months before, where three souls had hanged on lonely crosses.

His sword drawn, the General lunged toward me and the spear. I could not draw my gladius quickly enough. The General's sword was almost upon me. Suddenly, there was a flash of metal from another sword, and the General's sword arm was lopped off in a spray of blood, arm flopping to the floor, his sword clattering some eight feet away. The General fell to his knees as the death thrust came into his side. My Celtic friend now stood next to the fallen Praetorian General, bloodied sword in hand, his mustache tugging upward at the corners, framing his grinning mouth.

A hand and dagger suddenly appeared from behind the Celt, moving toward the center of his back, unseen by the big man. My instinct took over, unfortunately. That is when, without conscious thought on my part, my short-sword gladius left my hand. I had become adept at throwing this weapon many years before. There was quite an art to it, or, at least, to doing it well. The trick was to flick the arm, so to speak, from the elbow down—not from the wrist, as so many assume—at precisely the right moment, so that the blade, which is lighter in weight than the hilt, will fly lead and land true in the target. Within a fraction of an instant, it was done. Within a quarter of a heartbeat, I had become an enemy of the state, an enemy of Rome. The hilt of my gladius protruded from the chest of the Prefect.

The Celt had seen my eyes, my body language, assessed my intent, or what he thought to be my intent, in a split second, and ducked as I knew he would, thus exposing the Prefect behind him. The big man looked at me, amazed. "I thought," he began with the awe of one whose life had just been spared, "I thought that you were aiming for me."

The Prefect now lay on the floor, gasping for breath, gurgling air escaping from the bloody hole in his chest.

"No," was all I could manage to say. I had instinctively come to the aid of a comrade-in-arms, a man who had just defended my life against one who was not supposed to be an enemy. But the man I had defended was a Celt! Not even a true Roman. Obviously, though, that didn't matter. In the inferno of battle, your comrades are those you fight with as one, each an extension of the other. Personal origin, individuality itself, was rendered meaningless in that instant.

And yet...and yet...By the Gods, what had I done? This Prefect—Maximus Centilius—was a piss-ant. All of Rome knew that. But, he was still, or rather, had been, a Prefect of Rome, appointed by Rome to govern here. My life in the Roman military machine was over; the only life I had ever really known. Certainly, the only one I had ever loved.

"Centurion!" It was the Celt, shattering my self-loathing. I simply looked at him, dazed with disbelief. "Where is your officer?"

He was right. Flavius was gone. No doubt he had slithered off when the commotion started. Aside from the Celt and myself, the only ones left alive in the large room were the dancing girls-prostitutes, and the men—so-called dignitaries—

cowering behind the reclining cushions. And, of course, Jacobi, who was still being held by a Praetorian.

I managed to come out of my daze, and saw that the Praetorian was still in a bit of daze himself. Indecision is the worst of enemies. It is paralyzing, allowing the depth of fear to swell up within one's being, bubbling to the surface in heretofore unimagined ways. I could see it in his eyes. The problem was, he still held his arm around Jacobi, knife at the old man's throat.

Then, to my amazement, Jacobi calmly lifted his free hand to the sharp blade under his chin, and gently pushed it away. The Praetorian complied as if he were in a dream, slowly backing away, eyes betraying a glazed, trance-like stare, probably in disbelief over all that had just happened. Reverently, Jacobi, leaning on his staff, bent down and picked up the spear, handing it to me as he stood once again. I accepted it back with the same respect and reverence with which it had been retrieved and offered.

"It is not yours, Longinus," began the old man, "but It has been entrusted to you for a goodly amount of time. It is nothing in and of Itself; wood, metal. But, It has His blood, and will aid those who Know and are on the Path. You are not only on this Path, but are a leader on it. You may not accept this yet, but your higher-self—that part of you that is Truly Eternal, and that is him—says it is so. And so it is."

For the first time since I'd known the old man, I was consciously aware that he was making sense. Sort of.

But there was no time to dwell on it. The large doors crashed open and a half-century of legionaries and local palace guards poured in, led by Flavius and a Tribune.

"Centurion Longinus, in the name of the Emperor, you will cease hostilities and surrender your weapons and person!" ordered the Tribune.

"This way!" yelled the Celt, before I had a moment to think. I grabbed Jacobi by the wrist and half-dragged him as we began to run to the back of the large room. I let go of him long enough to yank my gladius out of the now dead Prefect, never breaking my stride or pace as I did so. I now had no free hands with which to pull Jacobi along. Yet, to my surprise, when I looked to Jacobi, he was right there with me, keeping up with the Celt and myself, step for step. For the second time that day, I was amazed at his youthful bursts of energy.

We had been heading toward a rear door that led to a balcony. At least, it appeared to lead to a balcony as I glanced out its adjacent window. Suddenly, a platoon of soldiers barged through the door and into the room. We stopped in our tracks. I looked to the Celt. He was unsure. Obviously, he did not know the palace as well as I thought. No matter. They were coming for us; for me, in particular. I had been branded an enemy of Rome—though those in power now had scarcely ever exhibited the ideals of Rome, twisted and perverted power-mongers that they were, and therefore, in my eyes, were not true representatives of what Rome is, or was. That was the only idea that made me feel that I was in the right. And, as such, I had to turn and fight, then and there, and die the only honorable death left to me. But then I heard Jacobi's words echoing in my head, "...It has been entrusted to you for a goodly amount of time."

"My lady," came Jacobi's live voice. Yet I paid no heed, thinking that it was still the one in my head. Until, that is, I heard the other voice in reply; a decidedly feminine one. And, familiar. Lovingly familiar.

"Yes! It's me, Longinus!" it said in a loud, urgent whisper. She was standing in the shadows, dressed in the bright colored silk and satin of a palace mistress. I could barely see her face. But I knew her. Irena. My Irena. My heart leapt. "This way, quickly!" She disappeared down a dark narrow hallway off to our left.

"Seems you have a friend," observed the Celt. Jacobi simply smiled. We ran into the dark hallway without hesitation.

Light spilled from four open doorways, two on either side of the hallway, approximately fifty paces or yards down the otherwise dark corridor. We stopped momentarily, not wanting to cross the doorways. Shadows played frantically in the light. More soldiers massing, I assumed. Though I knew not what lay beyond these doorways—the outside, more rooms— one thing was certain: we were not entering them. Irena, still in shadow, was already well beyond them.

"Hurry!" she called.

We were at a full run in an instant, passing through the light as quickly as possible. Still, I stole a glance through the first doorway on my right as we darted past. What I glimpsed confirmed what I had suspected; soldiers. They were scrambling up the stone steps leading up to the balcony off the main room we had just come from. Apparently, this doorway also had a side-landing for the steps, before they continued on the balcony. But it had been just a glance and I had seen no more.

The corridor remained dark, but my eyes had adjusted and told me that the way was becoming narrow. Something else, too: our flight was becoming easier. We were heading down, the path becoming a steep downward gradient with every step.

We reached a circle, a point where the corridor we were in emptied into a room or anteroom, and halted. Off of this anteroom were three other corridors—one directly ahead, which seemed to be a continuation of the one we had just come from, one to our right, one to our left. Irena paused just long enough to make sure we were all together, then headed off to the corridor on our left.

"This way," she said.

"Wait!" I said, grabbing her arm and stopping her for an moment. "Irena," I breathed, almost panting, partly from our pounding flight and partly from my disbelief at seeing her, the not so buried feelings for her still pining within me. My eyes washed over her, taking in every bit of her. "It really is you! But how? What are you...?"

"There's no time, Longinus. Please, this way," she pleaded.

"Where are you taking us, woman?" the Celt demanded gruffly, before Irena could move.

Having been insulted by his tone—when she was trying to help us, after all—and in her typical defiant way, she shook off my grasp and stepped fearlessly up to the Celt, the top of her head barely reaching his ribs, and locked eyes with him. "This passageway," she pointed, indicating the corridor to our left, "leads to a cave that's partly under water. It's an underground dock. The underground canal to which it's attached leads to the harbor. There is a boat mastered by a countryman of yours named Ventrix. He's a trader and is set to leave for Gaul on the evening tide. He will take you."

"Why? Why would he do that?" I asked. "We've just killed a Prefect and the Emperor's guards."

Irena spun back to me, fire in her eyes. "It's because of that! He hates Rome. Yes, Rome has made him a rich trader. But he hates what Rome has done to your people." She said this last bit to the Celt, then turned back to me. "More than he likes being a successful trader. Besides, he's...a friend. He'll do it because I ask him to."

My heart began to race, my emotions wavered, and a hundred different questions came to mind. But there was no time. The spear began to glow. We could hear faint voices and see the distant flicker of torches from back down the corridor from which we had just come. They would be upon us soon.

"Quickly now! No more questions!" commanded Irena as she ran down the new corridor.

As we all entered the narrow stone passageway in single file, Irena suddenly stopped and jumped up, attempting to grab a dangling leather strap that protruded from the ceiling. She jumped once, twice, thrice, and missed. The strap was just out of her reach.

"Allow me," offered the giant Celt. Casually, he reached up, wrapped his large hand around the leather and looked to Irena.

"Pull hard!" she ordered.

He did.

The crash of iron made us all jump. Then there was another, and another and another. An iron gate now blocked the entrance to the corridor we were in; another blocked the corridor across the ante room, and still another blocked the one next to it, and finally, an iron gate blocked the opening of the passageway we had originally come down.

"But," I lamely began.

"The royal family had built these for their escape, but never got the chance to use them," she called over her shoulder as she continued on the run, and we followed. "There's a separate pulley system to open them all up again."

"Who else knows about the passages?" asked the Celt.

"The Prefect and a few of the palace staff."

"And you?" I had to ask.

Before she could answer, we were upon a set of steep stone stairs leading what seemed to be straight down.

"Watch your footing. These steps crumble easily."

Down and down we went. It seemed an eternity as we descended into the bowels of the palace. It certainly smelled like bowels. The air became musty, moist, rotting—rank. It smelled of wet death. Yet, we pushed on.

I began to hear the sound of trickling water. It became louder and was suddenly accompanied by a larger, subtle rumbling sound—the ocean. Our staircase turned right, then left and we were standing on the edge of water, with a seven man boat in front of us, tied to a short wooden dock. The area was lit by the daylight coming in at the small mouth of the cave off to our left. It was about 80 yards away, but allowed enough sunlight in to reflect off of the water and the sparkling shards of crystals in the cave.

"It is beautiful," intoned Jacobi, who had remained silent up until now. I had assumed he had been conserving his energy. But perhaps he simply had had nothing to say. He was fearless, it seemed, even now; placing his energy not in complaining of our plight, but instead, using it to praise the beauty of our immediate surroundings. "Is not our creator wondrous?" he asked, to no one in particular.

"Yes, Rabbi. The Creator truly is. But now you must go. Into the boat with you," Irena said, as she gently helped the old man into the craft. The Celt climbed in and helped settle him. I handed the spear to Jacobi, and put my gladius in its scabbard.

"I must get back before it's too late" said Irena.

"What?" I said, still standing on the dock. "You must come! You can't go back!"

"I have no intention of going back. There's another way that leads out and off the palace grounds."

I didn't move.

"Please, Longinus. There's...there's someone. Someone I need to go to."

I was crushed. I felt my face flush with anger and embarrassment. "But," I stammered.

"There's no time to explain. But I will. I will find you. There's another ship taking your same route in a few days. If all goes as planned, I will be on it."

"And if it doesn't?" I asked.

She was silent.

"How are we to know which is Ven...Vent..."

"Ventrix. Master Ventrix. He flies the Boar. Here," she said removing an onyx and diamond necklace. And what Cretan gave this to you? I thought, but said nothing. She placed it in my hands and folded my hands in hers. "Give this to Ventrix. He will know it's from me and it will more then pay for your passage."

There was an awkward pause. We looked into each other's eyes, deeply. It was still there; that old spark, the ethereal connections that had been there since time began. "Irena," I started. "When you left..."

"I know, Longinus. I know. Much has happened since then. I have much to tell you and I will. But you must go now. Please."

She released me and guided me into the boat as she had with Jacobi. I complied. It was all I could do. The Celt had untied the little boat and we slowly began to drift toward the cave opening. A short oar was thrust into my hand. I looked at it, then back to where Irena had been standing. She was gone.

"Come, Roman," the Celt said gently. "Let's go find the Boar ship."

~IX~

The ship rocked gently as it cut through the small waves on its way to the gods knew where. Actually, I did know—more or less—where we were headed. But it might as well have been the end of the world. I had been informed that we were going to a specific "outland" region of Gaul, a place where Romans had come years earlier, conquered, and then essentially, moved on. Our captain, for want of a better title—these people did not really have organized military or naval rankings as did we Romans; Owner and Master of the ship would be more accurate—declared that we would go to this region for goods which he could only procure there: exotic wines, herbs, certain leather goods, for example. But he was not very convincing. Obviously, at least to me, he was attempting to display his authority. I believed that the real reason for our specific destination was that my Celtic friend had convinced him to take us there. Whatever the reason for our destination, I was not a man at peace.

I sat huddled in the prow, my back against the rail, legs tucked up under me, chin upon my knees; a ball of sunken humanity. The sun had set an hour earlier, and darkness enshrouded me except for the occasional light from a sliver of a waxing moon somewhat obscured by clouds. How in Hades did I get to this point? Only a matter of days before, I had been a proud Centurion of Rome. And then it was all gone. So, this was despair. There was no other word for what I felt in that moment. But I would not let it consume me. I swore it. And yet...and yet...

Finding the vessel with the flying boar had been easy enough. The Celt knew exactly where in the harbor to look, as all ships landing from Gaul were quartered in a specific region of the docks. There had been several ships moored that hailed from various parts of Gaul, but the banner/flag with the boar insignia had been the largest of them all. In fact, some of the ships or vessels had no identifying flag or insignia at all; an illegality in a Roman port. But the boar flew on the largest flag, on the largest ship.

Her captain, a man named Ventrix, had been dubious at first when I addressed him. But when the Celt spoke to him in their guttural tongue, and then instructed me to hand him the necklace, Ventrix immediately warmed to us, inviting us onto his boat without further delay. Our eyes locked as I passed him and boarded his vessel, and I saw no hostility there.

"Yah, Irena," he suddenly said, with an indefinable smile. I was not sure what he meant. Was it meant for us—he and I—as if we shared some lecherous bond through the favors of Irena? Or, did he simply mean to say, "Irena. She is quite a woman, is she not?," as in a simple statement of respect. I chose to believe the latter. Otherwise, I would have killed the man right then and there, and I had killed enough for one day. Besides, he was our only chance of getting out of this place alive.

Master Ventrix ushered us into the hold immediately. Or, rather, he tried to. Something possessed Jacobi just then, and he took it upon himself to walk to the prow of the boat, which faced the open sea, stood on the forward gunwale and began blessing the boat and all aboard in a none-too-quiet voice. His Hebrew tongue grated on many of those on deck and even a few close by on the docks. More than one person made the hand gesture, the sign against the evil eye.

"Jacobi!" I barked for him to stop, more out of fear for his safety from fellow Romans on shore, than out of embarrassment. He made no sign that he had even heard me. I looked to the Celt with a silent command. He simply sighed and stepped up to Jacobi.

"Forgive me, old one," he said, and gently picked up the old man, who, oblivious, kept speaking his blessing as he was carried into the hold.

There was cargo already locked down and ready for

transport back to Gaul. Ventrix said something to my Celtic friend and they had a brief conversation, after which the ship's master looked at me with a new respect, even bowing at one point. He then disappeared across the hold.

"What was that?" I asked.

"I will tell you later. We must hide now. The Romans will be all over every ship looking for us," answered the Celt.

"I know that, but where are we supposed to hide? There's a lot of cargo here. And what space there is left, is too open," I said as I looked around. Indeed, there was a lot of cargo, but the hold was not completely full.

"I believe the captain wants us to follow him," came Jacobi's voice from underneath the Celt's arm. We had both forgotten about the old man, still gently slung through the big man's arm.

"I am sorry!" said the Celt, flushing redder than his beard as he placed Jacobi on his feet.

"Bless you, my son. I enjoyed the ride, though I was not quite finished on deck," Jacoby scolded gently.

"Yes, well," stammered the Celt.

Just then, we heard Ventrix call us. We made our way through the labyrinth of crates and boxes and bundles of goods to the far wall of the hold. The ship's master stood by the wall, beaming with pride. He had pushed aside a huge crate to expose a section of wall; a wall, on the other side of which, I thought was the ocean. What was he so proud of? And then he showed us.

He placed a chubby, grimy finger on a wooden knot in one of the planks and pushed. A section of the wall slid open, but instead of revealing the ocean, it exposed a very slim passageway with very narrow steps leading down. His face exploded into a huge grin, then into an opened-mouth laugh at our astonishment. Ventrix motioned for us to follow as he led us down the steps, all eight of them, and into a cramped little room beneath the hold. Obviously, he dealt in human cargo as well, probably smuggling escaped slaves back into Gaul. Is this what Irena had been planning for herself? Is that how she had known about Ventrix and his ship? She had been a free woman when I had known her in Jerusalem; a business woman—albeit, the owner of a brothel. But here...

Ventrix and the Celt began talking to one another again, interrupting my thoughts. When they finished, the big Celt turned to me and Jacobi. "We are to stay in here no matter what we hear going on up above. He will come for us when we are safely away."

"You mean we are to be locked in here," I stated flatly.

"He must seal us in for a time, yes. But he will come for us when all is clear."

No, I thought. I should end this now; go up and onto the docks. Fight them and end it. Honor dictated...

"He will," asserted the Celt, obviously misreading the expression on my face. "I trust him. He will come for us when the time is right. We are distant cousins, it turns out," he added, as if that meant Ventrix was the definition of trustworthiness.

I looked at Jacobi, who simply nodded toward the spear in my hand, reminding me of my new charge. "Fine," I said. "We wait."

The Celt turned and said something to Ventrix. They then quickly embraced and the Ship's Master was gone, up the steps, sealing us in behind him.

Three-and-a-half days, we spent in that room. We ate old bread and dried meat and drank water. The Celt pulled them from a box in a cabinet, obviously having been told of their presence by his cousin. There was even a piss-pot.

A few hours after our sort-of imprisonment, if you will, we heard thumps and raised voices outside. The Romans had come. But, the thumps and voices were gone soon enough. And then we and the ship waited, and waited and waited. We lost track of time. Two days later, we were eventually told, the ship left the harbor. The three of us felt the ship's movement at the time and expected to be released within the hour. We were not. I hoped it was to make sure that no ship followed us.

It was. I was assured by Ventrix.

"Centurion Longinus," the Celt broke into my thoughts. His face was silhouetted against the dark sky, the waxing, small crescent moon behind and above his head. "We are free," he declared.

"Are we?" I asked rhetorically. I began to formulate other questions in my mind. But before I could put these questions into words, my thoughts changed again, and I suddenly realized something for the first time. "What is your name?" I asked. "I've no idea what it is."

Although his face was mainly in darkness, his white teeth shined with his smile. "Thought you'd n'er ask, you bein' a high Roman and all," he said in mock submissiveness, bowing his head once.

Obviously, in his mind, because of my fall from Roman favor, we were now more or less equals. Unlike Roman society, where one was almost always born to position, the Celts could move "up" or "down" in their culture's structure. Some of the Kings or Chiefs of the various tribes were even chosen by the people, changing every so often to ensure balance. Oh, true enough that many stayed King by force throughout Celtic history, but even that was usually relatively short-lived. No wonder we thought of them as inferior; what society could survive by electing their own Kings? Not all are equal. And, their women; I had heard that their women could even lead men into battle. Madness! The only branch of their society that seemed to always be above everyone else was the Druidic priesthood.

Yet, Rome was once a Republic, her leaders, senators, elected by her citizens—albeit, the Patrician class—and then sometimes, two overall Councils, Leaders or rulers, elected by the Senate. I could hardly fathom allowing a commoner, an uneducated peasant, to be allowed to vote for a leader. Yet, I was from that humble class, I reminded myself. Within Roman society, there was only one way to better one's allotted place in life: the military. And, I had done so. I had through intelligent deeds and uncommon soldiery and valor, risen from common foot-soldier through the legionnaire ranks, at least as high as Centurion. But now it was all gone. There would never be another way to redeem myself in the eyes of Rome. I envied this Celt and his free ways.

"Dosameenor," he said. "My name is Dosameenor. 'The Seer,' it means."

I gave him a quizzical look.

"When I was young," he continued, "I glimpsed certain future things on occasion. I was going to enter the sacred brotherhood, even took preliminary studies for a year."

"A Druid. You were to become a Druid?" I asked, surprised.

"You know of them?" asked Dosameenor, with none-too-little pride.

"Yes, I have heard. I have heard your Druids burn folks alive for your gods; enemies, displeasers..."

"We did. But, most were given the sacred potion of the mistletoe made by the Druids. It dulled their senses from much pain, enabling the spirit to soar free in the flames."

"Oh, well of course! That makes it all perfectly fine then!" I retorted sarcastically. "Barbaric."

"All things not of Rome are barbaric to you people. But it matters not. That ritual practice ended a long time ago. Banned, actually. 'Tis no longer performed."

"Hmph," I grunted, not quite believing him.

"'Tis not. It was a complex ritual having to do with releasing the spirit, the soul, as a Roman would say." He paused, reflecting, I presumed, on what he had just said. Then he went on, "Not important anyway. The Brotherhood is much more than one ritual," he said in a far-off tone. "They hold secrets—secrets that are ancient. Secrets of the workings of all things."

"Hmm," I grunted again, doubtfully. "You speak as if your Druids are still around. They were disbanded, even outlawed when Gaius Julius Caesar swept through Gaul and beyond."

"Perhaps. But they thrive still, as you shall well see," he

replied.

I simply stared at the silhouette before me, the eyes sparkling, the teeth glinting in the moonlight. There was something about this man, this Celt named Dosameenor, The Seer. There was a depth there beyond what the eyes could see. The spear quivered ever so slightly as if to confirm my feeling. I glanced to my left and saw a figure sitting, not far off, leaning against the railing as I was, but asleep. Or, perhaps he was in a meditation. The figure was Jacobi.

I looked back to my Celtic friend, and was about to ask him if he still "saw" future things on occasion. I thought better of it, however—though I wasn't quite sure why—and simply said, "Yes, we shall, Dosameenor. We shall see." He smiled again and left me.

Daylight finally dawned and I sat where I had through the night. At sea, one has only his own thoughts for company, in spite of the occasional interruptions by other souls traveling on board. My thoughts were becoming darker by the league; my self-loathing more profound by the breath. I had destroyed everything in my life; all I had known; all I had achieved. Gone.

"Let go, my friend," came Jacobi's soft voice. He sat next to me, apparently having moved closer during the night. Dosameenor was nowhere to be seen. "Trouble not over what is done, what is passed," he finished.

"Easy for you to say, Jacobi," I replied. The spear, the lance, lying across my lap, grew slightly heated for a moment, as if to accentuate what Jacobi had just said. I peered at the thing. I still was not convinced that its quiverings and heatings and doings were simply not the product of my imagination. But I could not deny the now permanent dark red stain on the blade. I had cleaned the fresh blood off when we were in our tiny hovel-hideout in the bowel of the ship as a way of passing the time; cleaned it easily of the traces of killings in the palace. But his blood remained, as it always had, regardless of how many times I cleaned it. My life was changed completely and forever, inexplicably wound and bound to a power, a mystery beyond my comprehension.

We traveled for several days. After the third rotation of the sun, I stopped counting. The further we sailed from the port city, the more despondent I became. I was lifted only briefly. Not because of the clear skies and smooth waters, both of which were our constant companions, but because, for a time, I believed that we had sailed only miles from Rome. The area felt of home, the air smelled of it too. Indeed, when I asked Ventrix, he confirmed my belief.

"You made for seas," he said in his broken Latin, meaning, I assumed, that I should have been in the Roman navy instead of the army. Perhaps. My senses on the water told me we were close to my home—well, somewhat close to my home—and my stomach had been stable, unlike even a couple of the more "seasoned" ocean farers on board. Although, I suppose I should not make too much of my stable stomach. As I said, we had traveled through fairly mild conditions. No matter. I belonged on Terra Firma, in the army, leading men to glory on the battle field! But, alas.

We had passed about six miles off the coast near Rome because of the ocean currents, Ventrix said, which were aiding us on our journey to Gaul. His boat had sails, but his Celtic crew was not the most adept at using them. Most of the men were rowers, but they could not row all the way to Gaul, Ventrix said.

"Why not?" I inquired of the ship's master. "They can be pushed, forced to," I said, assuming the rowers to be slaves, as they were aboard Roman Triremes.

His face crinkled at my ignorance. "Deese men are free men. Some serve me for debt. Dat iss all," he explained.

"You mean, they're indentured," I offered. His brow crinkled again, but this time in confusion at the new word. "Indentured," I began. "One who becomes a slave to someone to pay a debt to that person," I explained.

"Dey not be slaves!" he insisted.

"No, no. At least, not forever. Only until they pay the debt." Ventrix's face showed near malice. It was useless.

"Never mind. Yes, they are freemen, free Celts," I acquiesced.

I had taken to sleeping and spending much time in what had been our locked room. It offered the isolation I desired. I did, though, make brief visits on deck to take fresh air and to see where we were. On these occasions, I usually would observe Jacobi holding court with two or more crew mates, discussing philosophy, religion, God. God. His One God. The God of all things, including, or rather especially, man. What a strange concept. I had heard this only once before; from this Jesu—The One God, The One "Father" concept.

Most of the time when I saw Jacobi speaking, Dosameenor was also there listening, absorbing. Invariably, Jacobi would see me, and with a slight head nod, or the raise of an eyebrow, beckon me to join them. Always, I would decline, gently shaking my head "no," and move on. Until one day...

I awoke at dawn on what was to be the final day of our journey at sea. There was a tentative knock on the door.

"Enter," I said groggily.

The door slowly creaked open, and a boy stepped in, bearing a tray with an offering of fresh bread, cheese and wine.

"Master says we land at dusk," said the boy, unsolicited, in perfect Latin.

"You are Roman?" I asked, astonished. I had not seen the lad at all, let alone heard him speak, on this trip. He was about fourteen summers with short brown hair that curled about his forehead. His eyes were blue, his frame was thin; too thin.

"Roman, yes. Well, Spanish," he answered.

"Your Latin is flawless," I said.

"My father was of the Horse-class, my mother was a mistress to my father—a whore. She died when I was very young and my father took me in. He had had only daughters with his wife," he explained, matter-of-factly. "My father declared me his son. Thus, I began my studies, Latin, Greek, among others. I even now speak several dialects of the Celtic language."

"I see," I said contemplatively. "Unusual. Bastards are rarely acknowledged publicly."

"Yes, but as I said, he had no other sons. And, once acknowledged publicly by the father, then a bastard is a true son of Rome. Was this not so of Caesarian, Julius Caesar's bastard with Egypt's queen?" he questioned pointedly.

I laughed out loud. "Indeed! And you are quite educated. And bold. But we know what happened to young Caesarian, don't we?"

The lad was silent, assessing whether my last statement was a veiled threat or a simple statement of fact. I changed the subject. "So, how came you to be Ventrix's slave?"

The young lad bristled with indignation. "I am no one's slave! Master Ventrix saved my father's life—twice." He lowered his gaze and plunged ahead. "My father's—my family's —money was almost gone. My father drank and gambled and dumped his seed in anything female," he said, clearly ashamed of his father. "Master Ventrix and my father became friends after the first time he rescued my father. He offered to help pay father's debts."

"In exchange for you."

"And my older half-sister. She's in Gaul."

"I see," was all I could manage.

"That was two years ago, and I have served Master Ventrix well. I mainly served in his quarters and the galley," he finished.

"Which explains why I've not seen you until now," I said.

"Yes, sir. That and the fact that you have remained down here during much of our trip."

I cocked an eyebrow at the lad's impertinence, but let it go. I tore off a piece of the fresh bread and placed it in my mouth. It seemed to melt there. For some reason, in that moment, nothing had ever tasted so good. "Why..." I started, then swallowed the bread, "...are you telling me all this?"

"When we land, I am free to go. I am ill aboard the ship more often than not and therefore, inefficient. Master Ventrix loves my sister. He truly does and she asked him to release me. He has, as of the end of this trip," he explained.

"Again, lad, why are you telling me all this?" I asked.

"I wish to accompany you when we leave this vessel," he declared, as if it were the most obvious thing in the world.

The look of utter surprise on my face must have been quite comical. The boy simply smiled and hurriedly said, before I could speak, "You will need a translator, you will need a guide, you will need someone to prepare your meals, you will need someone to carry your belongings." His eyes drifted to the lance on this last point.

Possessively, I placed a hand on it for a couple of moments. But it was unnecessary. I sensed that there was nothing malicious about the boy; nothing hidden or dark. He was a servant and a seeker. His eyes glazed over as he continued to stare at the Lance. He had that same awed, reverent expression on his face as Jacobi had when he had first seen the spear.

"What is your name, lad?" I asked.

"Paulonius. Paulonius Renius," he replied, finally taking his eyes off the weapon.

"I thank you for your offer, but I travel light and I already have a translator and guide in Dosameenor," I patiently explained.

"The Celt you travel with is a good man, according to Master Ventrix. But he intends to find his family and be with them for a time," the lad imperiously informed me.

"Then I will move on."

"To where?" asked Paulonius.

"You're impertinent, boy. Take care," I said between somewhat pursed lips. Obviously, he knew everything.

His tone abruptly changed, realizing that he'd overstepped himself. "I'm sorry, sir. I did not mean to offend.

It's just..." he trailed off, eyes downcast in a gesture of respect. "The rabbi says that you are an instrument of God. That you are to help spread the word of an anointed One, the Word of...of God's true nature, and—"

"Rabbi?" I interrupted. "What rabbi? You mean Jacobi? Most of the time Pauli... Paulo..."

"Paulonius."

"Most of the time, boy, Jacobi rants like a lunatic!" I nearly shouted.

A long silence ensued.

Finally, Paulonius began to back out of the small room.

"Wait," I said. I paused in thought before I continued. "I did not know you listened to his...sermons on deck."

"No, sir. Well, a couple. He has frequently visited Master Ventrix, even taken meals with him on occasion," explained Paulonius. The Master and the Rabbi both wanted you to come too, but...but it was seen that you preferred, um, solitude," said Paulonius, timidly.

"Hmm. And who 'saw' that?" As if I did not know.

"The Rabbi, Centurion," replied Paulonius.

"The question was rhetorical! And, he's not a rabbi! He's...he's Jacobi!"

"He is a knowledgeable Teacher. The One God, the One Source of All, clearly speaks through him. A Master Teacher in his tongue is called a Rabbi," stated the lad quietly, firmly, factually.

"Well, I'll see about that," I said, and nudged past Paulonius to head up to deck.

Jacobi was in his element. I saw him at the stern as I arrived up on deck, Paulonius at my heels.

"How? I hear nothing," said a quizzical-faced, grizzled shipmate in broken Latin. He was sitting on the deck with a handful of others, Dosameenor among them, at the old man's feet. Jacobi himself was seated on a crate, facing the little group. His aged-pruned hands were wrapped around the neck of his walking staff, the tip of which was firmly on the deck; a

King's scepter to a King and his court. Well, not exactly a King was Jacobi, but he did look like he was holding court.

"It is not a hearing with the physical senses, good man," answered Jacobi. "To say that, 'all are called, but few are chosen,' is to say that one simply feels, knows, that God calls him. It is this inner feeling, this inner urging, this inner knowing that is God's voice. To acknowledge this feeling or knowing is to 'hear' the call."

"But," began another man seated in the group, "I never had that thing; a feelin' or knowin', like you talkin' 'bout."

"Yeah," another put in.

"But you are here, my good fellows, listening to what I'm saying, to what the God says," explained Jacobi. "Something moved you to be in this moment with our little group. That something is the One God in you, the Voice, calling you, moving you. Do you understand?"

They both nodded duly understanding, but not fully grasping.

"How can all be called? Many, maybe. But look around. Not everybody everywhere, not possible," said yet another man, an old man. This shipmate had to be even older than Jacobi. His thin, withered features betrayed a hard life. Yet, his eyes were still stark-green, bright, youthful, intelligent. Several of the others nodded their agreement with his sentiment.

Jacobi became silent for a moment, his body still, his eyes closed. He was deep in thought, or waiting for that Knowing voice from within. His stillness dragged on, and his listeners began to wonder if he was not actually asleep. They looked to one another, not quite able to make sense of the awkward silence.

"All," Jacobi suddenly said, eyes popping open, startling everyone and gaining their full attention once again. "All is possible with the One, and the One is all there is! Master Jesu knew this. And, therefore, all of us, every one, without exception, is from and of the One God, and thus, the One is in all of us. Now, not all choose to 'hear' the call, or rather, at their deepest levels, choose not to recognize it," Jacobi finished, to blank looks of confusion.

"You see?" Paulonius whispered from behind me. "He is a great rabbi."

I looked at the boy with a cocked eyebrow, sardonically conveying my disbelief that he had actually understood what Jacobi had said.

Jacobi observed the faces in front of him. "Ah..." he finally said to their blank stares. "I see that I get ahead of myself." His gaze swept the rear deck and landed on the boy and myself. "Hello, Centurion Longinus," he greeted me.

I was no longer worthy of the title or rank of Centurion and cringed inside as he said it. "Jacobi," I stated simply.

"And my boy, Paulonius. Are you both to join us?" asked Jacobi, clearly delighted at the prospect.

"No," I said flatly, before the light of excitement in Paulonius' eyes could reach his mouth. "I need to speak with you and Dosameenor."

"Ah, well then," he said, and then turned back to his listeners. "Shall we continue this another time?"

"But we land tonight," protested the bright-eyed, wrinkled old man.

"Yes, we land tonight," echoed another of the listeners.

"We will find a way, my friends," declared Jacobi. "We will find a way either on board or on land." With that, Jacobi stood and the others followed suit, dispersing to their various posts or duties. All, except of course, Dosameenor.

I approached my two companions with Paulonius again at my heels. I wheeled around on the lad with more intensity than I meant to. "Are you now my shadow, boy?!" I barked. "I would speak to my friends alone."

Paulonius looked as if I had slapped him. He flushed red with embarrassment at the public rejection. With downcast eyes he mumbled, "Yes, sir," before skulking off toward the bow. He glanced back once, an expectant look on his face. He opened his mouth to speak, no doubt wanting to remind me of his request. But then, wisely, he thought better of it, closed his mouth, turned and was gone.

Dosameenor, Jacobi and I were left alone. I waited until I was sure no one would overhear.

"I need to know your intentions," I said, addressing both men.

"Our intentions?" asked Dosameenor, as if buying time to phrase his answer.

"Yes. When we land, what will you do?" I then looked to Jacobi. "I am asking you both."

Dosameenor looked away, seeing something far off in his mind. Jacobi simply looked confused.

"Why, I go where you go, of course. I serve God within and you without," Jacobi answered. "Why would you even ask?"

"One might say you serve two masters," I said somewhat facetiously.

"We all serve the One. And I serve you to remind you of that fact," said Jacobi.

"You're a clever one," I said with a chuckle. I quickly turned serious again, though, and looked to my Celtic friend. "And you, Dosameenor?" I asked. He had become very quiet.

Finally, he looked me in the eyes, his brow somewhat crinkled. "Who do I serve?"

"No," I said. "What will you do when we land?" I repeated. "I thought you were going to be with me, guide me, help me in this land of yours, until I determine what I am to do."

"And so I shall. But ..." he hesitated, stiffening almost to attention, as if what he was about to confess would earn him a reprimand from his superior officer.

"Speak your mind, my friend," I said reassuringly. "I certainly won't judge you."

"I have," Dosameenor continued, "been away from my family, my wives, my children, for three years. Soon after I was 'recruited,'" he nearly spat the last word, "conscripted, into the legions, my clan...left the regions which had been our ancestral home for centuries." His eyes narrowed, anger brimming to the surface. "Actually, we were forced out, to put it mildly," he said, his tone laced with bitterness. He took a moment to release the anger before he continued, breathing steadily, as a legionnaire is trained to do in any tense situation. "I have had no word on their whereabouts for quite some time," he continued. "I have been wanting to go and find them."

"Why have you not done so before now? Surely you've had opportunity."

He thought for a moment before going ahead. "Legionnaires watch each other. Sometimes, inform superiors about each other. Especially those of us not Roman born, we in particular are scrutinized. Deserters are hunted and killed. I had to be sure I could make it all the way back. You were the catalyst and all the conditions were right," explained the big Celt.

"Hmm," was all I could manage. In truth, I felt for the man.

"Please come with me. My people will welcome you."

"Your people will hate me! I epitomize Rome. I represent those who drove your people out of your homeland, raping and killing and enslaving in the process," I said. There was no point putting a sweet glaze on it. We both knew how the Roman Military machine worked.

He frowned. It was a hard, sad look. "No," he said at last, his frown leaving, confidence in his people replacing it. "When they know the truth, they will embrace you," Dosemeenor assured me.

"Which truth, Dosameenor? That I've been a soldier of Rome all my life, or that I am a fugitive of Rome?"

"Yes!" he said, laughing.

We were still at the stern and I looked out to sea, to where we had already passed, back toward Rome. In every way, I was going farther and farther away from her. "Your people," I finally said, "are noble. You have proven that. But then I think I always knew it. Still, not all of your folk will embrace me. Some never will."

"Perhaps," he said, after a moment of thought. They are of no consequence, though."

I said nothing to that. My thoughts drifted to something else. "We are bound to run into Roman patrols," I finally said.

"Maybe," Jacobi put in, "and you will know what to do then."

"I suppose I will," I admitted. I looked the old man in the eyes. "You are not my servant, Jacobi. You never really were."

"Oh, but I am!" Jacobi declared. "I serve those who truly serve the One. And that you do, or will quite soon," he insisted.

There was nothing I could say to that. I had tried before to deny those types of statements from him. It was futile.

He could see my thoughts. "Think of me as a guide for your soul. For now," he offered with a toothless grin.

"A teacher?" I asked, smiling back.

"Of sorts," he said.

"Then, so it is...Rabbi." With that, I turned to Dosameenor. I placed a hand on his shoulder and nodded. We would stick together. For now. I had a sudden urge to go back down to the room; to hold the lance. I left my friends then to do just that.

We first heard the drums a few miles out, when it was still daylight. It was daylight no more. Trudging through the wilderness at night was disturbing enough. But, to have the rhythmic, primal percussion piercing the darkness as well, was to have the demons of Hades gnawing at your bowels. Dosameenor, on the other hand, was elated.

"We are close to home!" he said.

His home, or rather, his people. Not mine. I still questioned why I had come. But there I was. Where there was, however, I was not certain.

We had landed and disembarked from the ship during a busy evening at the port. The Celtic celebration of Samhein—the fall celebration of the harvest and fertility, among other things—was in preparation by the locals. We found a stable in which to spend the night. It smelled. Horribly. The fodder was rotted, but at least it was dry. A light rain had begun to fall earlier and was continuing still. Every other lodging option was already taken. Even camp space outside the port city was non-existent unless one went quite a ways out. Many folks were coming and going for the celebration, which was four days off.

Dosameenor did not spend that night with us, at least not most of it. He left us to secure supplies for our journey on foot and verify, as much as he could, the information he had on the whereabouts of his clan, his family. It took almost all of the coinage we had between us, which was not much. Yet, apparently, it had been worth it. For, upon his return, late into the night, he not only had secured ample supplies, but was himself light of being and happy as a child whose wish had just been granted; his information had been correct.

We left the following dawn. Our group was eight: Dosameenor, leading the way, Paulonius—against my better judgment—Jacobi and myself, and four men from the ship who were also heading to their families, part of a neighboring clan to Dosameenor's. One half-lame, half-blind old mare, which cost us the last of our coins, carried most of our supplies.

"We could all carry the supplies on our backs. Why did you waste our silver on this thing?" I demanded, upon seeing the decrepit pack-beast the night before.

"What difference does it make?" asked the Celt. "She'll do for the journey and save our backs. We don't really need the coin where we're going."

"And after? I am not staying in this land forever," I retorted.

"Then we will trust that a way will be revealed at that time. Live in the moment, Longinus. Tomorrow will take care of itself," replied Dosameenor.

"You've been listening to Jacobi too much. You sound just like him," I said, irritated.

"Perhaps. But maybe it's just my way of thinking, too. A Celtic way."

I said nothing for a moment. We were getting off the point. I said, "Well, the money was partly mine. You should have asked before buying that mare."

"Ah," interjected Jacobi, who, as always, stood close by, almost invisible until he spoke. "That's it then, is it not? You are used to being consulted on matters, Centurion Longinus, yes? But here, you know as well as I, you must defer to Dosameenor. Besides, truthfully speaking, you are no longer a Roman officer, so do not expect everyone to act as if you still are."

"What?" I said, almost yelling in anger. The old man had struck the most tender of spots.

"What I mean, is that you are no longer an honorable one in Rome's eyes," Jacobi continued. "But that is not to say they are right, Longinus, or that you are not a most capable leader. You simply are no longer an officer of Rome. You must trust in those around you now. Equals, one and all. Your time to lead will come again very soon, though probably not in the way you are expecting."

As usual, he spoke in riddles. I was silent. Perhaps that was the best tact to take; be silent and let it go. I retreated back to the corner of the stable where I had been sleeping, lay down and blanketed myself in the comfort of self-pity, the reassuring presence of the lance by my side. All that had happened, and whatever was to come, was inextricably linked with this instrument.

As I said, we left the following dawn, walking by day, camping by night. Four days had past. The land was beautiful and rugged. I had never seen so much dense greenery; untamed and intimidating, yet exhilarating and inspiring. The giant oak, or the "Sacred Oaks," as I quickly learned was the proper and respectful way to speak of these majestic trees, were much more than just trees to the Celts. They were beings, housing the divine, in service to humans. A lot of Celtic society's belief system revolved around the sacred oaks and the rituals the Druid caste performed around the trees on behalf of the people.

The weather had been mild: fairly warm days, cool nights. There was no rain as on the night we landed in the port, but there was a perpetual dampness in the air, which, I supposed, helped to account for the lush greenness throughout most of the region. It was wonderful! Nothing like the hot, arid, dust-plate I had been serving in.

On the fourth morning, we had set off again. This time, however, we did not stop when the sun disk went down, but pushed on, because we had begun to hear the drums.

Jacobi heard them first. At an age when most men are at least half-blind and half-deaf, Jacobi's senses were seemingly more acute than one a third his age.

"How is that possible?" I asked him.

"It is not that my ears are better. It is that I use them more. It is not that I hear better. It is that I truly listen."

"Yes, yes!" squawked the young voice behind us. "I understand."

Jacobi and I both stopped and looked back to see

Paulonius trailing us closely on the narrow forest path. I should have known. He had barely left the old man's side since we left the boat.

"Paulonius," I reprimanded, "you shouldn't eavesdrop on others' conversations. 'Tis a good way to lose an ear."

"Yet," Jacobi said, "he exemplifies my point. How will he learn if he does not truly listen, regardless of where the instruction comes from or when?"

I looked at Paulonius. "All right, then. What did he mean, boy?"

"Rabbi Jacobi meant that his hearing is no better than anyone else's, simply that he better turns his attention and full awareness to that which he is listening to, thereby completely drawing it in and discerning it," the lad said.

Jacobi threw back his head and released a guttural, cackling laugh. The noise sounded like a chicken being strangled; a happy strangled chicken, but still a chicken. "That, my boy, is precisely right," Jacobi said, tears of mirth streaming down his cheeks.

"By the gods, I give up!" I said, rolling my eyes in resignation to the absurd. I turned and resumed my trundling walk, Jacobi and Paulonius in tow. I caught up to Dosameenor, who was leading the way on the path. "Do you mean to push on through the night?" I asked him. The shadows were long and it was getting gloomy on the forest path.

"If necessary," he said with an amiable smile. "You hear the drums? We are not far off. Besides, I do not believe it will take us through the night to get there."

But then, his smile faded. He suddenly stopped on the path, all of our little party doing the same. Dosameenor's initial excitement was now tempered by something else: concern. He was listening. Truly listening. Something in the sound of the drums had caught his attention. He took a few more paces on the trail and stopped again, peering over the ridge into a valley. We had been marching on a path through a tree-filled area, up on a ridge. The path or trail had begun a slow descent about a mile back.

I caught up to Dosameenor again and followed his gaze over the ridge and into the valley, both of which had been off to our right. My gaze landed on our apparent destination. The valley was lit up by fires; huge controlled bonfires. The ridge opposite our position was also lit up. "The Samhein fires you spoke of. We <u>are</u> close," I said. But there were two fires in the center of the valley that were larger than any others. It was almost dark and they stood out like two moons on earth.

The lines in Dosameenor's face became deeper, etched with concern, almost fear.

"Not just celebration fires," observed Jacobi.

"Then what are they?" I asked, confused.

"We must make haste," spat Dosameenor as he broke into a legionnaire's trot down the path. We all followed suit.

"Answer me!" I demanded as we ran down the trail, which was now partially lit by the glow of fires. I looked down at the fires, my breathing in rhythm with my jogging steps. "The fires in the center; they're too large to be celebration fires," I observed. "Are your people under attack?"

"No. No attack. They are all celebration fires—of Samhein, yes. But those two are more. Celebrations of victory in battle," he replied, pausing briefly for his own breath to fall back into rhythm. "Only they," he continued "could make flames as big."

"You mean...you mean victory over Romans?" My stomach lurched at the thought. It made sense. We had not seen one Roman patrol since leaving the port. We had noticed two patrols within the port city itself—only two—which now struck me as odd. It did not at the time because I was too preoccupied with avoiding them, which had been easy. That ease meant there were very few patrols within the port, probably only the two we saw. When I thought about it, I remembered that the patrols had seemed oddly agitated, almost fearful. You could see it in their eyes, the stiffness of their bodies. They were alone, but trying not to show it. But, as I said, at the time, I must have taken note of these things, though they hadn't sunk in 'til now.

I had changed my clothing to avoid the patrol's attention. Even now as we trotted through the forest, I looked down at my Celtic garb: leather breeches, drab gray woolen tunic, green cape pinned back over my shoulder with a copper broach. The shoes, however, were my Roman-issued laced, hob-nailed sandal boots. They were too comfortable not to wear. I had packed the rest of the Centurion uniform, which was now being carried by Paulonius. My gladius, however, was at my side, and the spear, of course, was in my hand.

I shivered just then. I suddenly felt an overwhelming, oppressive weight from within tugging at my bowels. Then the realization hit. Oh, Mithras, god of the warrior, god of the soldier, no! I held my tongue, did not voice my fear, willing it to leave my mind. But for naught.

We finally came off the forest path, down off the ridge and into a clearing. We began to run, to sprint, following Dosameenor to the largest of the central fires. And there I had my nightmare confirmed.

~XI~

We were on the valley floor. Knee-high grass now replaced the huge trees that had been our constant companions; flowers dotted the whole area, a variety of colors twinkling in the light of the fires and the crescent moon.

We ran, urgency feeding our steps. The din of the drums was nearly deafening. Their tempo was frenetic, building to a climax that we could yet discern. But then, another sound took over; agonized, feral shrieks and screams. Animals. The sound could only be coming from animals in searing, unearthly pain. In the next moment, yet another sense took over—smell. A grotesque stench filled our nostrils. Burning flesh.

Dosameenor stopped in his tracks, staring. The rest of us did the same and I, too, stared at the most unholy sight I had ever beheld: The Wickerman: a big, wooden cage in the shape of a man, with arms and legs and chest and head filled with prisoners.

There were three Wickermen. The two outer ones, about twenty-five feet high, were aflame. These were the two larger flames or fires we had seen from the ridge. The center one, the biggest of the three at around forty-feet high, was not yet lit. But it was full of the doomed: those awaiting the same fate as the occupants of the other two Wickermen. The screams were not from animals. They were from men. They were from the men trapped in the burning Wickerman.

And they were Romans. Romans being burned alive and screaming in agony as the skin boiled off their bones.

We were so frozen with the shock of what we were witnessing, that it took a moment to realize the drums had stopped.

I was the first to come out of my stupor, throwing Dosameenor a look of disgust and revulsion. So much for this ritual being banned. A group of shaggy-looking Celts were coming towards us, weapons out, yelling some primal battle cry, ready to destroy the newcomers who dared to intrude upon their sacred rituals. Their fierce battle-cry was rendered rather impotent, however; all but drowned out by the shrieks of the fire victims.

"Dosameenor!" I yelled in alert, ready to command evasive, defensive maneuvers. I stopped short of that, though, remembering who my cohorts were, and where I was. Old habits do not die. "Dosameenor!" I yelled again.

He looked at me, then at the oncoming warriors, locking eyes with the apparent leader. Again, I assessed the odds and hence battle tactics. As I said, old habits do not die. Or, perhaps I should say, loved habits do not die. We were eight against thirty, with dozens, no, probably hundreds, more warriors and defenders behind them if needed.

But apparently, they would not be necessary.

The leader and his band halted not ten feet in front of Dosameenor. I thought it was to address the intruders. But it was not, for they said nothing. A soft glow from the fires and waxing moon cast an eerie light on both Dosameenor's face and that of the warrior leader. It was then quite apparent why they had stopped. Their leader's face; his nose, his forehead, his eyes, even his mane of hair was almost identical to Dosameenor's.

"Dosameenor," smiled the warrior. "My brother! Is that truly you?" he said in Celt. I had obviously picked up the language since boarding the Flying Boar in Najaffi; at least, in the hearing of it. I could understand most of what was being said.

"Aye, Renaulus. 'Tis I," replied Dosameenor.

The one thing the brothers did not share was their smile. While Dosameenor's was pleasant, his brother's was rot: missing teeth and dark, broken ones adorned Renaulus' mouth. He gave a belching laugh and stepped forward to embrace his brother.

Dosameenor's response was chilly at best, returning his

brother's embrace only to the degree that custom apparently dictated so as not to offend.

Just then, a tremendous crash of wood and debris was heard, startling us all, as one of the burning Wickermen collapsed into the pit where its foundation lay. Burning bodies and limbs flailed as the structure fell in upon itself. Once again, the drums beat on and the screams from the other still burning Wickerman continued to fill the night. Then suddenly, the second one collapsed as well. It did so in a hail of embers and death-throw shrieks. It sobered us back to the horrendous event taking place before us. It was all I could do to keep myself rooted, waiting to see how Dosameenor's unscheduled reunion would play out.

Finally, Renaulus spoke. "I regret that your homecoming is in the middle of this madness," he said sincerely.

Dosameenor exuded genuine warmth then, seeing that his brother was apparently not a part of the human sacrifice before us. "Why is this happening?" he asked.

"They are Roman?" I interjected in broken Celt. I was sick from the thought and would not be silent, even if it meant giving away my Romaness by my clear mangling of the Celtic language.

Renaulus' demeanor changed. He was once again the guarded warrior, ready to pounce on the enemy. He stared hatefully into my eyes, my soul, but spoke to his brother. "Who is this?" he demanded of Dosameenor as if I were a worthless pile of horse shit.

"Peace, brother," replied Dosameenor. "He is my friend. His name is Longinus, Centurion, or former Centurion of Rome. He is no longer favored with Rome."

"Why?" asked Renaulus suspiciously.

"Later. Just know that he is my honored guest. He will be treated accordingly," answered Dosameenor forcefully.

Renaulus paused. He clearly did not like the answer, but accepted it as custom dictated.

I took advantage of his momentary silence. "Why are you burning Romans?" I blurted out as I involuntarily stepped toward him. His men, three of them, immediately stepped to his flanks to protect him. At the same time, Dosameenor extended an arm to my chest to halt my progress.

The shrieks of terror and anger from those in the center Wickerman, the only one left, rose to a deafening volume, as they knew they were next to be put to the flame. I looked even closer at them to be doubly sure. They were Romans. Even the naked ones had the short cropped hair and relatively clean-shaven faces of the legionnaire, but most still wore their wool army issued tunics. These were light-blue or gray when new. They were still their original colors—so it seemed in the available light—but battered. The garments were torn and stained with the blood and mud of battle, and with the shame and guilt of utter defeat. "Who are they?" I demanded.

"'Who are they,' you ask?" repeated Renaulus as if I were a stupid child. "As you see, Centurion," he continued sarcastically, "they are legionnaires of Rome."

"No! Which legion?" I shouted in bitterness, wanting nothing more than to strangle this hairy, ignorant fool where he stood. On my arm, I suddenly felt the calming touch of Jacobi's hand. At the same time as Jacobi's touch, came that inner voice again; His voice. "All is well," He whispered in my head. It had been awhile since last the Voice, He, had spoken to me. "All is well," He said again. "Their spirit, their soul, is freed this night. It matters not how."

"Stop!" I hissed between clenched teeth. Only Jacobi heard me. Only Jacobi knew that I was hearing something in my mind. I could tell by his touch.

"Your spirits are Free. They have always been and always will be Free. You imprison your spirits, your souls, yourselves, by your thoughts, your beliefs, your actions. Almost all must be freed eventually because you believe so. When you come to truly understand, to remember your Truth, you will no longer need even death," the Voice whispered.

I was speechless. The absurdity and madness of the evening had been punctuated by the voice in my head. I looked at Jacobi. The old man simply smiled calmly.

"I do not know," Renaulus declared, breaking the spell I had been under.

In that moment, I chose to ignore the voice in my mind. At least for now. So, I pulled my attention to Renaulus, gently taking my arm away from Jacobi's touch.

"I don't know what legions they're from, Centurion," continued Renaulus, condescension dripping from his words. "The battle went on for three nights."

"How could you see?" Paulonius chimed in.

Renaulus scowled at the insolent lad, truly confused by the boy's ignorant question.

"I'm sure my brother means that the battles were fought in the light of day. We Celts measure time by nights, not days. I would think you'd know that by now, boy," Dosameenor answered for his stupefied brother.

Renaulus, ignoring the boy entirely, said to me, "These were the legionnaires left after our victory." He spoke almost as if it were nothing. "Their leaders, their officers, were allowed to fall upon their swords. Then we took their heads and—"

"You did what?" I exclaimed, appalled.

"We took their heads for only a while. They were placed with their bodies in the cages, the Wickermen, as you call them," spat Renaulus contemptuously, as if he had no cause to explain this to an inferior such as me.

"The head is the seat of the soul. Possess your enemy's head and you have his soul," Dosameenor said offhandedly. "I'll explain more at another time."

Enough. I had had enough. "There's one of those things left not yet aflame. There's still time to stop this," I said, trying to sound firm, not wanting to reveal my own terror.

"No," Renaulus said flatly, arrogantly, regrettably.

"It is the Druids' doing. Their word is Law," Dosameenor explained. "But why, this is beyond me."

"An evil one has seized control," said Renaulus, bitterly.

"For now."

Dosameenor suddenly had a glazed look in his eyes. But it quickly turned to one of hostility. "Draco," he stated, disgustedly.

"The only Druid in recent memory to revive all of the old rites of sacrifice. You remember him, eh brother?"

"Yes. But how? How is it that he is in control? When I left, he was still only an apprentice on the council. How could he have risen so quickly? I haven't been away that long." Dosameenor said.

"How'd you know it was him I meant, then?"

"A feeling. You forget, Renaulus, I was one of them for a time." Dosameenor then paused reflectively. "Actually, who else would it be?" he asked rhetorically. "Draco tortured animals when he was young, when we were all young, remember? He said he was driving out demons! Of all the stupid ..." he said, caught up in that moment in the past. "Then the time that he insisted a boy caught stealing pelts in winter—for his mother, no less—should be burned alive for the crime. Thank Dana the elders didn't listen then."

"Aye. I remember that," replied Renaulus.

"Please!" I interrupted. "We must stop this," I said, as the spear vibrated again. "We must stop them from lighting the third Wickerman! No matter who's responsible."

"No, Roman," said Renaulus, "As my brother said, 'Tis the Druid's doing. One does not defy the Druids." But, Renaulus' tone was edged with sarcasm. He, too, hated what was happening this night, but certainly could not admit that to the likes of me.

"Are the Elders agreed, or is Draco alone in this? asked Dosameenor.

Renaulus' eyes narrowed, "What do you think, my brother?" he queried. "Draco seized the head of the Druid body, it is true. And, most of the Elder Council of Druids, so I've heard, are against him—at least in private. But they fear him. And he does have supporters. I know you were a Druid once, Dosameenor, but that was a long time ago. There is much under-handing and back-knifing amongst them in these times."

Dosameenor thought for a moment. I was almost jumping out of my skin. Much more talk and I would stop the last Wickerman from burning, myself. Or die trying. The latter, of course, being the more probable outcome. Then Dosameenor's face changed. "What of Detrom?" he asked, slightly smiling, clearly reliving a fond memory in his mind.

"Your teacher, yes?" said Jacobi.

Dosameenor smiled. The old man's perception was amazing. "Yes," he said. "My Druid Mentor, Teacher, Rabbi, if you will."

"Gone. Driven off by Draco," Renaulus said grimly.

Dosameenor's face lost all ease, ripping him back into the present moment. Anger filled his being. "Then, by Dana, I will put a stop to this and find out the meaning of all of Draco's doings."

"Could be suicide, brother," Renaulus smiled, gritty maliciousness showing through. Obviously, Renaulus hated this Draco as much as Dosameenor. "Forget what I said, Roman," Renaulus said to me, then turned back to his brother, "I'm with you Dosameenor. To the end." Both men embraced, then turned as one and sprinted toward the center of the crowded festivities, toward the large Wickerman.

We all followed, Paulonius aiding Jacobi. I ran faster than all. I may have been a fallen Roman officer in the eyes of Rome, but I was still a Roman. And, those were my people stuck in the cage.

Yet, we were too late. As we sprinted toward the midst of the barbarity, the third Wickerman burst into flames.

"No!!" I howled like an angry, wounded beast. It was useless. I could hardly hear my own voice. The screams from within the Wickerman were horrifically loud, as were the still pounding drums. Adding to the cacophony was the noise of the Celts around it. Madness reigned this night.

There was a throng about the wooden structure.

Closest to it were many white-robed, hooded figures. They formed a loose circle around the Wickerman and were chanting. The chant itself was a rhythmic and morose, yet, lilting melody. The robed, hooded figures—whom I took to be Druids—were repeating the chant over and over again, holding their arms spread wide toward the Wickerman as they chanted, as if to embrace the souls agonizing within. (Indeed, I was later to find out that they were doing something quite like that. They believed they were mentally and spiritually aiding the souls of the doomed to cross over to the Otherworld into complete freedom through the purity of the flames.) The rest of the throng seemed to be regular Celts; ordinary folks. There were hundreds of them: men, women and children. They were all there bearing witness to the sacrifice, the archaic rite, the macabre spectacle.

None of them, however, were celebrating Samhein, as I understood it. Most were simply staring blankly, numbly, at the Wickerman. Until, that is, the stench of burning flesh again reached their nostrils. At that point, most had a look of utter disgust splashed across their face. Many turned away, or covered their face in a vain attempt to hide from the horror. Some could not take it at all and vomited at their own feet. Mothers pulled their children into the folds of their clothes, attempting to shield them from the terrible deaths before them. But, alas. This was also in vain; they could not be hidden from the sounds and smells of grizzly death this night.

Yet, as shocked and disgusted as most of the people were, none of them left. No one turned and walked away. No one backed out of the crowd and ran home. No one. It was as if they were all anchored there by some unseen force, or rather, perhaps, by some unseen threat.

Our group came to an abrupt halt at the outer edge of the crowd. We then pushed our way through to the inner circle, to the Druids. Once there, Dosameenor's brother pulled out a hollowed beast's horn, placed his lips on the small end, tilted his head back and blew.

The sound of the horn blasted through the valley,

drowning out even the drums and screams of the victims. Those closest to it slammed their hands over their ears lest their insides burst and bleed. When the single note blast trailed off, all became silent. Even the screams in the burning Wickerman had become whimpers, though that was probably more because of death and the final throws there-of than because of any herald. Most of the Druids, too, had ceased their chanting, and some had even thrown off their hoods to gaze at the intruders. Others, however, continued their vocalizations, oblivious, obviously deep in a trance.

One, the tallest of them, and the only one wearing a light blue robe, turned slowly to face us. Looking into his face, though, was like trying to look into the mouth of a cave. For, his hood was more of a cowl: long and tubular in the front, thereby completely obscuring the wearer's face, and thus, invoking in the viewer a sense of awe mixed with fear—as if some demigod from the Otherworld stood before them, not simply a man.

"Who dares disturb this sacred rite?" boomed the deep voice from within the cowl.

All at once, the spear began to vibrate in my hand.

"Who?" he demanded again, anger and hatred and darkness seething from his being.

"Dosameer dares, Draco!" answered my Celtic friend with the power and authority of a god.

The spear continued to vibrate in my hand, though subtly, as if growling. Or, more accurately, as if warming up for a release of power. I pulled it closer to my side, hoping no one would see it.

The blue-robed figure before us pulled back his cowl, revealing the head and face beneath. Draco.

He had long black hair that reached down to the center of his back. It was slicked flat and back with lard. His eyes were an unearthly ice-blue, which contrasted intensely with the pasty-white skin. He was not ugly, but rather had a comeliness that struck from the Otherworld, as the spawn of a demon may be glamoured (glamoured being a magically induced spell or veil), with beauty.

There was something else.

I thought at first they were dirt smudges and shadows playing upon his features. But then he stepped closer and into the light. They were not dirt and shadows, but tattoos and scars. Obviously, the tattoos had been tapped into the skin purposely, but to my surprise, the scars appeared to be self-inflicted, as well; they both—scars and tattoos—wove together in intricate circular knot-patterns on his face.

I admit that in that moment, looking into those eyes—that face—I knew a jolt of fear. But then I felt the spear in my hand, still quivering and thought of him, the One on the cross, and heard the Voice in my mind saying, "Fear not, for I am ever a part of you. Fear not, for I am ever your-Self." As usual, I did not completely understand the statement, the riddle. But, this time, rather than thinking about it with my head, I let it seep into my being—deeply. The result was profound; I was instantly soothed at the deepest level of my soul. I lost all fear —of anything—because I had a sudden realization of my own eternalness, not of the flesh, but...

"Dosameenor," Draco hissed between clenched teeth, thus interrupting my split-second of contemplative, spiritual awareness and snapping me back into the moment. Draco was surprised to see Dosameenor, but hid it well.

"What is this?" bellowed Dosameenor. "These rites were banned generations ago."

"They have been revived, and you of all people know that it is death to disrupt them," replied Draco, threateningly.

Several of the Druids threw off their hoods and withdrew swords from beneath their robes. From shadows close by, we heard the unmistakable smooth-sliding sound of blades being removed from scabbards and belts.

"Since when do Druids carry weapons during rituals?" demanded Dosameenor,

"Prisoners may escape," Draco replied casually, dismissively, deceptively. He then smiled maliciously. "Also, because your coming was foretold, though we did not really expect you so soon. I did not think you would be in agreement with us on our...revival." He said this last bit with an arm gesture to the Wickermen, or what was left of them.

Dosameenor, his brother, and his men drew into a tighter group, forcing the rest of us into it, as well. My soldier instinct fought this; we were too close together to function in a fight. But it didn't really matter. We were hopelessly outnumbered.

Suddenly, the spear began to vibrate violently in my hand, the tip—its blade—to glow. Those closest to me quickly moved away, clearly afraid of what they were seeing the lance do. I spun to Jacobi, silently questioning him, imploring him to advise me. He smiled and nodded toward the spear. I understood. Let It guide you, he was silently saying. I had no choice. But how? Was I simply supposed to ask It for guidance? I closed my eyes for a moment to think. And then it hit me: Do not think. Do not think at all. Let go.

So, mentally, I did just that; I let go of any and all thoughts, of any and all feeling; of any and all attachment to a given outcome to this madness and turned my entire being over to the spear or to that which was working through the spear: to him, the Voice, the Power within.

I felt a complete change in my perception of the moment. I was detached, but present; an observer and a participant. I realized in that instance that I was infinitely more than the present situation, yet at the same time, an integral part of it.

I opened my eyes and was compelled to step forward, raising the glowing, quivering lance as I went. All could see It, the Lance. Fear and awe came into their eyes. They parted for me as I walked toward Draco and the remaining Wickerman. The latter, amazingly, was still standing, but raging ever more intensely with angry flames.

I was being guided, for I knew not what I was going to do. I was not in control of my actions; yet I was in complete control, for I allowed it all to unfold: An Infinite Power, an Infinite Intelligence was working through me, as me, because It was me. I do not mean to paint this a mystery. It is not. When one has the experience I speak of, he or she knows It for what It is: the Infinite Mind—or God, or call It what you will—working through him, as him, period.

Draco stood stalk-still, eyes glinting in the firelight and moonlight. There was a hint of fear in those eyes as he watched me approach. None of his followers moved to flank him. I stopped five feet in front of the dark Druid. His eyes suddenly darted to the lance's tip, the blade now pulsating with an intense bright glow. Somewhere in the back of my finite, human mind, I dismissed the glow as reflective light from both moon and fire.

But then it happened. The Lance's tip, the spear's blade, continued its pulsating glow as the entire field and valley grew dim by nearly half as the moon was suddenly shrouded by dark clouds. I quickly realized that I had been thinking of something, imagining it in my mind's eye for quite a few moments. Rain. Rain is what I desired to end the mad fires of this night. But how, I had asked myself, could that happen on an apparently clear night with a bright crescent moon? I had doubted.

But right then, it was as if the conditions surrounding me were responding to my intensely doubtless desire to end the torture. Rain! I commanded in my mind.

The Lance, as if to amplify my thought, glowed brighter. "Rain!" It was my own voice this time, yelling, commanding the desire into reality. I felt detached, in a trance. I simply allowed what was happening to flow through me, to channel through.

Now, some have said that what occurred next was perhaps coincidence. I know otherwise.

I turned my face skyward and the deluge began.

The first drops hit Draco on the head. He turned his face skyward as well. He began to mutter something: a spell, an incantation, perhaps, or a counter-spell. Whatever he was saying, though, was useless. Sheets of water from the heavens fell. The mass of people began to murmur in awe and confusion. The noise was drowned out briefly by the sudden loud hissing of the fires being extinguished. The hissing died away and the crowd's noises became louder, near panicked as darkness completely engulfed us.

The fires were out. Smoke enshrouded the last standing skeleton of a Wickerman, but the rain rapidly cleared it as if it had never been there.

Then, it stopped. The rain suddenly stopped as if someone had closed a valve. The spear tip no longer glowed. The people became silent, awed once again. The only sounds were the pathetic moans coming from within the last Wickerman. Some of the sacrifices still lived.

Soft light began to blanket the valley. We all looked upward and saw the clouds peeling back from the moon. The sight inspired more murmurs from the throng. Then, all eyes fell upon me.

Some of the people made a gesture with their hands and arm—the sign against evil. Most, however, looked at me reverently; a few even dropped to their knees worshipfully. More than one began to whisper a name—"Grosgon". "Grosgon," Dosameenor later told me, was their clan's name for the Elemental God. I was he, incarnate, they believed. Others called me "Merlanco"—their word for a master magician, a master wizard; one who through years of study and many blessings by the gods is able to command the elements. Still in a trance-state, I looked at Draco then—who was rigid with fury—and back to the Celtic tribe around me.

Jacobi stepped up to me smiling. "You have taken a large step tonight, Longinus," he said.

I came back to my senses just then. I was in a state of peace I had never known. Yet, my normal Roman self began to quickly reassert its position in my mind. I found I had many questions about what had just happened. And, as usual, I wasn't entirely sure of what Jacobi was talking about. A step to what? I thought.

But before I could ask him, I saw movement out of the corner of my eye. From the edge of the tree line, from the edge of the darkness, they came. A new murmur arose from the people as everyone saw the figures approach like spirits from the night mist.

~XII~

The murmur rose from the crowd, panic laced within. The figures appeared like spirits. They seemed to materialize out of the mists as they came rushing from the edge of darkness.

"Antewonc!" The Ancient Ones!—the people whispered fearfully. Ghosts, they thought. I could almost agree with them. Even my heart pounded with apprehension as the strange apparitions approached. But it quickly became apparent that they were neither spirits, nor ghosts, nor strange apparitions of the night, but flesh and bone and blood.

Dosameenor was the first to recognize one of them. "Detrom?" he said in breathless disbelief.

Detrom was the one leading the group from the darkness. He wore a heather-colored robe, torn, tattered and stained from living in the wild. In his right hand was a tall, intricately carved walking staff. Something on the top of it gave off a greenish, pulsating glow, though I could not tell exactly what it was.

His aged face peered out from a shawl of dark blue, equally as torn and worn as his robe. There were dirt smudges and wrinkles of time on that face. But beneath those was a look of intensity and determination of one who could not be denied. His dark brown eyes were portals to the Otherworld, allowing one to glimpse the Infinite, as well as the mundane. There was a depth of Kindness in those eyes, as well. Intriguing, was this one; one of infinite strength and courage, yet also of eternal patience and goodness. And Knowledge. In those eyes and in that face was pantheistic Knowledge; the Knowledge of the gods; the Knowledge of the Universe—True Knowledge. There was something else there, too: familiarity. I suddenly had the overwhelming sense that I knew this man. Or rather, had known him in some way, some form, in a distant past. That was impossible, of course. At least, that's what I professed to myself then.

He was immediately flanked by several others who were similarly clothed. Holy ones. Druids, they were. But many in the group were clearly warriors. Some of them wore short battle tunics. Some, nothing at all, but the colored wode smeared and painted on their skin. They had weapons brandished, their bodies rigid and flexed, ready to fight. Detrom and the others halted near us. As with Dosameenor, the people began to recognize loved ones and kin within Detrom's ranks.

"Ronas!" someone called to a face near Detrom.

"Tramon!" a woman squealed to someone else as she ran forward, falling into the man's arms. Happiness swirled around us as spontaneous reunions took place. Dosameenor embraced his mentor, the former High Druid Detrom.

But the reunions were over quickly. A multitude of questions abounded. I listened and observed, and was able to piece together that most of the returning folk, nearly a century in all, had been driven off by Draco and his followers under threat of death. Others from the community had run off to join Detrom, despising Draco and his new regime. Later, still others had urgently left the tribe to find Detrom, and alert him and the outcasts, about Draco's plans for the Wickerman fires. It was hoped that this news would spur Detrom and his group to retaliate against Draco and stop the abominable ritual sacrifice. Yet, even with skilled trackers, it had taken many, many days to find Detrom. Draco had chased them far and away, 'tis true. However, Detrom, being the powerful High Druid he was, had caused himself and his group to magically disappear for a time. Or, at least it seemed that way. They reappeared when Detrom had a vision of the impending sacrifice and literally bumped into those searching for them while on the way to stop the evil proceedings. But alas, the vision had come too late for those being fed to the flames.

The questions and talk died down and all turned to confront the instigator of the night's madness. Draco was pensive, to say the least. He had the demeanor of a snake, cornered and coiled, ready to strike at a threat. The number of his followers had dwindled, substantially. During the brief, spontaneous reunions and the delightful ensuing chaos of such things, most of Draco's people had put down their weapons or shed their robes and drifted back into the populous, absorbing into the throng when it became obvious which way the wind had blown. Others had slunk back beyond the burnt Wickerman.

Confronting a Druid is no easy thing. The Celtic people revered their Druids; indeed, their whole Druid class, and stood in utter respect, awe and even fear of their knowledge and power. No one wished a dark hex cast upon himself by any Druid, let alone a mad, dark one. Yet there is strength and courage in numbers; there is power and movement with like thought. A palpable change in the atmosphere took place. Anger charged the air. Almost as one, the people advanced a step toward Draco. He backed away three paces, angling toward the edge of the clearing, toward the edge of darkness. Fear was in his eyes. But he cloaked it with empty arrogance, draping Druidic power, or more accurately, Druidic status, over his being, preying on the people's fear of that status. He attempted to glamour his person with power; attempted to create the illusion that he was larger than life, powerful as a god. Indeed, for an instant, a dark glow of deep magenta pulsed around his body, expanding to twice the size of his form.

"Cease and obey me or be cursed! All of you!" he hissed.

For a brief instant, all were still. I knew not if others saw the evil glow about him. Perhaps not. It was clear, however, that for a moment those present warred within their mind as to whether or not Draco's statement rang true. But their single-mindedness—their anger—led them to see through the dark Druid. Draco's 'power' was naught but a shallow understanding of true workings of the Universe and hence, any strength derived from that understanding was depthless, a perversion of Truth. As such, it was only as powerful as people believed it to be, allowed it to be.

"Kill him!" someone shouted.

"Burn him!" demanded another.

Draco backed away, impotent against this onslaught of hostility. The mob took another step toward the dark one. Any farther and a murderous riot would add to the night's insanity.

"Stop!" boomed Detrom's voice as he stepped between the people and Draco. Detrom was glamoured with power, too. But, unlike Draco's paltry aura, all could see Detrom's Otherworldly glow. The look of awe on their faces told of that. Detrom's Power was True. He seemed larger than any mortal; truly, a god among men. Then, his aura decreased in size somewhat. He appeared a man once more. "There has been enough killing this night, enough death," he said with heart-penetrating sincerity.

Silence reigned for a moment. The fact was, Detrom did not have to glamour himself with power. His people revered him, even adored him. That was clear.

"But...but," someone tentatively began, "he deceived us all." The man, a medium-sized, balding Celt in his middle years, gestured toward the carnage in the wreckage of Wickerman. "These were not rites to be brought forth again. These were not Romans deserving of this burning death!"

"'Tis true!" shouted someone else. "They were withdrawing, going elsewhere in their Empire. 'Twas Draco who spelled us with his dark magic to hunt the Romans down, High Druid Detrom. You know this to be so. He drove you off before we went to battle with these Romans," he said, again gesturing angrily toward the charred corpses. The man paused then. His head bent forward and a shock of thick, curly, red-blonde hair fell across the left side of his face, only partly obscuring his eyes as he began to weep. "I lost my son, my only son, that day in the fighting. And for what? 'Twas not an honorable battle." He paused again until he gained control of himself. Then, in true Celt fashion, he looked straight into

Detrom's eyes, straight into his soul, speaking to the gods through the once and future High Druid, and said with controlled rage, "'Tis my right. I want revenge."

"Yes!" cried a voice in the crowd.

"Vengeance for Draco's deceptions and evil!" yelled another.

Others quickly joined in the call for Draco's blood.

Detrom let them rant on for a moment; let them vent their frustration and anger. But, only for a moment. "Peace!" he finally said once again, in that booming voice of the gods.

"Peace," he said again.

A silence filled the air. The anger abated momentarily as all heeded Detrom. He had garnered their attention. But it lingered not long. It was broken by the dawning realization that moans and groans of pain and agony came from the half-dead.

"Oh, Dana!" exclaimed a woman. She stood staring into one of the burned Wickerman, or what remained of it; looking at the charred carnage. "A few still live!"

Tortured and guttural sounds emanated from black, smoldering forms. Yes, some still lived; if it could be called living. The agonized noises had been drifting around us for several minutes, along with the crackling of the dying fires. We had all been too preoccupied with Draco to hear them—until now.

We turned our attention to the victims of Draco's twisted plans, the Dark One himself forgotten for the moment.

A tribesman, a warrior by the look of him, began to gently pull apart the frame of a Wickerman. He yelped with pain and quickly yanked his hand away, causing that section of the now fragile wooden cage to crumble into sizzling embers. The wood in the Wickerman's frame was black and wet and only barely smoking. Deceiving that was. Beneath the damp, blackened outer layer, the wood still burned at the core. Fire can be a warm and gentle lover; a servant sent from the gods. Or, it can be an evil, deceptive monster, bent on torturous destruction. Someone tended to the man's scorched hand

116

while others, following his initial attempt, but with a bit more caution, made their way through the first two dilapidating cages to the remnants of burnt and twitching Romans. My people. My stomach churned yet again.

"Please!" someone yelled in crisp Latin.

The last Wickerman's flames had also been put out by the rains. But, having been lit the very last, only moments before the mysterious deluge from above began, for the most part, it still held strong. Most of its occupants were either lying on the cage's floor, or dangling limply from where on the cage they had been tied; unconscious, but hardly burned. Hardly burned, perhaps, yet most were still dead, nonetheless. If the flames do not engulf the victim, then the smoke will usually destroy him from within, filling his lungs with poisonous breath. There were only two men standing on their feet, their lower appendages precariously perched on a rung of the frame, ankles tied to the frame itself. Their hands clung white knuckled on higher wooden bars. Except for the second fellow: one of his arms was hooked round a bar at a strange angle.

"Please," said the first one again. His blue eyes were piercing, his tunic barely singed.

"Help us," croaked the other, a pair of blood-shot eyes looking at me wildly, beseeching me from a dark, sooty face.

They were both speaking to me directly, begging for liberation. The second one did indeed have something wrong with his left arm; it was bent at a backward angle at the elbow. It wasn't a fresh break -- no swelling where it was bent abnormally. And, its bend to the wrong angle was slight. But its appearance just accentuated the gruesomeness of the evening.

"Sir," said the first man. "Centurion Longinus," he addressed in a tone of familiarity.

Did I know this man? I took a closer look at him, stepping up to the cage. He was a legionnaire, but not a young one. His tunic though filthy, was clearly a Roman soldier's, as was his crooked-armed friend's. And yes, he did seem familiar. But then again, I have commanded so many. After a time, their faces all blend together. Plus, it was hard to tell with this one; his face was dirty and swollen in places from battle. Or abuse. Still...

"How do you know me?" I asked without suspicion, and not without compassion.

"From..." his voice cracked and broke. He swallowed hard, his throat obviously damaged and painful from the fire's heat and smoke. He gingerly swallowed more and tried again to speak, attempting to sound as crisp as a moment before when first he'd captured my attention. "From the cave," he rasped, not sounding at all crisp. "The Prophet's tomb, the day he had risen. We," he continued, indicating his bent-arm comrade, "had been guarding the tomb and...and..." The man's voice gave way again.

"Yes," interjected Jacobi. The old man apparently had been shadowing me the whole time. "Yes," he repeated. "You were so instrumental that day and the night preceding. Bless you. Both of you. Longinus," he said turning to me, "free them from their cage."

I felt my left eyebrow cock up out of indignation. Jacobi was ordering me about? "I was about to, Master Jacobi," I snapped at him. I immediately felt embarrassed at having done so.

Jacobi simply smiled and gave me a slight nod.

I looked again at the soldier who had spoken. "What is your name?" I asked. "Romi, sir. Romi Romanus. This is Gauis Henatpas," he replied, indicating his friend.

I stepped closer still to the cage, this time searching for a weak spot in the wood.

"We are in your debt from that night, sir. We...fell asleep...somehow -- though I assure you, it'd never happened before, as I think I -- well anyway, we fell asleep at the tomb, but were never reprimanded because of you, though it was common knowledge what had happened there. He had risen, they said... a woman was there and saw him, and us asleep...I think. You said nothing, but even our superiors didn't want to scold us..." Romi went on, now on the verge of babbling with fatigue, trauma, injury.

I did remember him now, and his friend, though they were hazy in my memory; there had been a more important event that day. Although, I was quickly realizing, as Jacobi had pointed out, these two were also a part of that event in one form or another. I still was not totally convinced that the Prophet had indeed risen that day. Well, actually, I simply hadn't thought much about it since then. Fear, I suppose. "And you'll owe me twice-over after tonight," I said, more to snap me back to the present than allow myself to stay in thoughts about the past.

I and several others began to break open the cage near the legionnaires. We had to use large stones to smash through. The Wickerman was a sturdy prison.

Hard, urgent whispers clumped from behind me. I turned to see the big Celt engaged in heated, but low-toned, conversation with a few fellow tribesmen. "What is it?" I called to him.

He broke from the others and approached. "Draco has vanished. We must pursue him," he replied.

"No," said Detrom.

"But," began Dosameenor.

"He is gone, Dosameenor," Detrom continued. "You will not find him now."

"But he must be punished!" cried Renaulus, now standing next to his brother.

"And so he shall," Jacobi said calmly, "In his own way, in his own time."

"Indeed," agreed Detrom smiling sagely at Jacobi. "Indeed!"

Dosameenor grunted, clearly not happy, but let it go.

"Come," I said. "Plenty of time to get that piece of shite. Right now, I need your help."

He paused, looked over the cage in front of us, then at the remnants of the other two and nodded. He turned and yelled orders in Celt. The mass of people formed into several loose groups around the Wickerman. The rescue and recovery effort thus began in earnest.

~XIII~

And so it was that twenty-two men—twenty-two Romans—
were pulled from the ashes and timber that night. Of the
twenty-two, thirteen succumbed to burns or smoke inhalation
by the next morning, crossing the river of the dead to the next
world. A blessing that was. One of them in particular was so
badly charred that he was more skeleton than flesh. How he
had remained among the living for even the night was beyond
any of us. His strong spirit finally knew it was time to move on,
though, when morning came. Five more were balancing
between this life and the next come mid-afternoon, with no
one expecting them to make nightfall.

We did what we could for them. Detrom and his Druid
physicians had a salve for burns concocted from plant extracts
and oak sap and crushed mistletoe. It was laced with herbs
that gave the salve a vaporous quality, thus allowing those
with severely afflicted lungs to inhale temporary relief. These
same herbs also gave the salve a numbing agent. When rubbed
on the burned area of skin, the victim often felt a temporary
relief from the pain. But, ultimately, it did not matter what we
did. These five would not make it for long.

The remaining four, however, were another matter.
Amazingly, for the most part, they were unscathed. This
included Romi and Gauis.

We had not yet moved from the site of the Wickerman.
I insisted on cremation of the Roman remains -- an honor
usually reserved for officers and nobles and heroes. But in this
case, they were all heroes to me, thus cremation was totally
appropriate.

We could also not move the more severely injured until
they left us or healed a bit, the latter being very unlikely.

I was resting my eyes, my mind, my soul, my heart, in a make-shift sheepskin lean-to shelter that Dosameenor had erected. He and some men had erected several, three of which had been used for survivors. This one was now empty. Jacobi was off helping Detrom. I was alone. The stench of the burned and dead still filled the air. I tried not to dwell on that or my own circumstances. What now?

The shelter's flap whipped open, spilling light from the late afternoon sun into the space. A figure was silhouetted at the opening. "Yes?" I said.

"Sorry, sir," said Romi as he stepped into the dimly lit shelter. Mr. Jacobi wished you to know that three more have ... have died," he managed to croak out, as much from emotion as from a ravaged throat. "Just within the past hour." Romi was cleaned up, but his face was still bruised and that scar -- yes, I definitely now remembered this one from the cave.

"Not at all unexpected. And the other two?"

"One is dead to this world, but still breathes. Barely. The other, well, uh, the other has awakened and asked for death, for someone to send him on his way," said Romi sadly.

"And no one has yet obliged him," I stated.

"No, sir. You are now my senior officer. I'll do it if you order, but..."

"Make no mistake, soldier," I interrupted. "I am not your officer or anyone else's. In fact, Rome hunts me."

"Yes, sir."

"Mind you, boy. Stop addressing me as your superior."

Romi paused then, and simply looked at me, unflinchingly. There was no fear in his eyes. "I meant that as an agreement with your statement. I know Rome hunts you," he said. He then nodded at the spear, which leaned blade-up against a wall of the shelter. "You, It, is what brought several of us here, searching for you."

"Ah, yes. You and your crooked arm friend thought to cash me in. Me and this thing I carry. I see how it is," I snapped.

"No, no," he bristled at the misunderstanding. "You do not see how it is, sir. We came to find you, to join with you, to help you. You are helping to create a new world, and we wish to be a part of it."

"What are you talking about?" I asked, stupefied.

He looked at me as if I were daft. "That day at the tomb, He rose from death. Your spear has his blood on it. It, he, speaks to you, guides you..."

"You know naught of what you speak," I interrupted, anger momentarily seeping into my being.

Romi ignored that, pressing on. "And last night, out there," he said, pointing to the killing field where the Wickerman had stood the night before. "You called rain from a nearly clear night's sky with the spear's aid, I believe."

I said nothing.

"Something is happening," he continued, "the likes of which has not been seen before. It's bigger than me or you alone, bigger than Rome. Yes, even that. I am no traitor to pursue this in spite of Rome. But I have heard a call. So has Gauis."

Again, I said nothing. By the gods, I thought, I should just throw the spear away. But it would not help; it would make no difference. The change surrounding me was actually from within. Something infinite, profound—even magical—had opened deep within my being and there was no closing it. And, yes, the spear was guiding me in all of it, or something divine was working through It. I could feel the power that coursed through It. Rome did not pursue me. She wanted the lance and Its power.

I suddenly became aware of a head poking through the shelter's front flap just behind Romi. It was quite still. The eavesdropper had probably been there awhile, listening. I needed only one guess at who it was, since I knew Jacobi simply would have burst in, and no one else would have dared listen in on my private conversations.

"Gauis, I presume?" I said. "You might as well come in, too." He entered slowly, cautiously. "Come on, man. I won't bite you."

He obeyed, stepping in fully. He stood five-feet in front of me. He was only slightly older than when I met him at the tomb—perhaps eighteen summers now. But his demeanor had aged considerably. He had obviously been through a lot since last I saw him. And, indeed, his left arm was slightly bent in the wrong direction at the elbow. It looked to be from an old injury. How could he be a legionnaire? Even if the wound was from battle, he would not be allowed to remain a soldier as a cripple. His arm made me look at him more closely. He was not Roman born. He had darkish skin, but light brown hair and grayish eyes. Then I remembered his family name. Hentapas. Definitely not Roman. I noticed that he wore something around his neck. It was an Ankh, the key of life, an Egyptian symbol that dated back thousands of years. It was an elongated crucifix or cross, somewhat like those Rome used to hang prisoners. But instead of a vertical top bar, there was an oblong vertical loop, almost like a head. Rome's cross meant death. This cross meant life and resurrection into the afterlife. This boy, Gauis, was Egyptian. I had not seen it on the previous night; it had been dark and he had been covered with ash and soot – not to mention all the other distractions of the evening. But now it was obvious; his skin color, noble lined face, grey eyes and name. "Egyptian," I said aloud.

"Yes. Gauis Hentapas is Egyptian," answered Romi.

"What happened to your arm? I do not believe that you had a crippled arm at the cave, the tomb." I said.

"No, sir," Hentapas began, his voice also still scratchy. I am from a noble Egyptian family near Aswan. When I arrived back there on leave, one month after the day at the tomb, the military governor there ordered me to his presence. It was almost as if he'd ordered my leave from duty and waited for me." He said this last part shuddering, the revelation still fresh. "He tortured me for information about you and the day at the tomb, I think to make an advance for himself, or maybe to get the...that," he said pointing to the spear. He paused then and stared at it.

"Go on," I prompted.

"Yes: He did this to me," he continued, holding up his bent arm. "It was on the first night, and then he threw me in an isolation cell for two weeks when I could not give him any useful information. It healed wrongly because it was never reset properly." He paused then, looking at the arm. A proud, defiant look came into his eyes after a moment. "But I can do anything a normal legionnaire can do. I have hidden the defect from my superiors. It's simple," he insisted.

"I'm sure," I said. "Aswan, Egypt. That would be Prefect Murius. Molonus Murius. A Spaniard. He is a pig, a sadistic fuck-hole by reputation. I'm sorry he did this to you," I told him. I was indeed changing. In my past, I never would have apologized for the actions of a superior officer to a legionnaire, especially to the face of the legionnaire in question. "Why didn't you report it?" I found myself saying. I knew it was a stupid question before it was even out. No one would ever take the word of a legionnaire over that of a Prefect. "Never mind," I amended.

"Sir," said Romi, ignoring my demand not to address me so. "The survivor wishes an honorable death," he said, bringing us back to the reason he was here.

"Yes. We will see," I replied, rising and picking up the lance.

"I wish to clarify...I want to..." the Egyptian began.

"Spit it out, Hentapas," I said, without patience.

"Romi misspoke last night. I was the one who fell asleep at the tomb, not Romi. Remember?" confessed Hentapas.

I softened. Something about this lad was touching, calming.

"It does not matter now, my young friend. As Jacobi said, you were instrumental in the happenings that night. All was as it was supposed to be. Now, let's go aid our fellow legionnaire." I clapped the young man on the shoulder and led us out of the concealment of the shelter.

The day was beautiful, despite the horror of the

previous night. It was bright and crisp, affirming the promise that life moves on, always changes, quite often to newer and better things.

Romi, Hentapas, the Egyptian and I made our way across the field to another hastily erected shelter. (Although Hentapas was also known as Gaius—a common Roman family name which he no doubt adopted when he became a Roman citizen—I now preferred to call him by his birth name, though I didn't quite understand why, at the time—it simply felt more honorable somehow.) The field itself was mainly clear now. Scorched earth was all that remained where the Wickermen had been. Off in the distance, some three hundred yards away, smoke still rose from the pyre we had lit to cremate the dead. I had refused to honor the deed by cremating their remains in the same spot where they had been tortured by flame. We had lit the funeral pyre earlier in the day. Bones took long for fire to consume.

Not many of the tribes people remained. Most of them had finished with their helping tasks and returned to their respective clan villages a mile or two away.

We entered the shelter, which was open-walled on two sides, and consisted of several animal skins sewn together for the other walls and roof. The whole thing was held up by the strong oak branches of an adjacent tree.

I have seen horrible things in battle. But what I saw before me now shocked me to a new stomach-churning height: a living corpse. Over most of his entire body, his skeleton showed through the thinnest of blackened-pink tissue. There was barely any skin or muscle on his head. There was no face; only a blackened skull and shreds of flesh clinging to it here and there. But his eyes! His eyes were more than intact. They were huge in their lidless, hollowed-out sockets, but they were bright and clear and could see. Yet, it was more than that. They were bright with their light-brown coloring, yes, but they were bright with something else as well. I was hard-pressed to figure out what it was -- love, happiness, peace, all of them? He stared off, seeing something. But it was not something on the outside; it was something within and beyond this world.

The pallet the man was lying on held him approximately six inches off the ground. Cowled Druids stood silently, near it with Jacobi and Detrom at the foot on either side. They both of them were silent as well; solemn, but not at all downcast. In fact, I began to feel a lightness in the atmosphere of the shelter, and my shock at the man's appearance suddenly abated. The form on the pallet slowly shifted his gaze to me, then to the spear, as if to say, "I'm ready for you." But, I stood impotent with indecision.

"Longinus", came Jacobi's soothing voice. "Open yourself. Let it wash over you and you will know what to do."

I looked into the eyes of the man who lay before me, and breathed deeply. I focused on my breathing for a moment, then shifted my attention to the spear, silently asking for guidance from It, from the power that coursed through It. After several breaths, I knew what I was supposed to do; I was to ease this man's spirit through its transition. I was not there as an officer who had been requested to perform an honor killing. I was there to aid his soul with its journey, as a guide of sorts, to the next world. The spear, the lance, began to vibrate ever so slightly; its blade aglow. I knelt next to the pallet and touched the lance's tip to the man's charred forehead. His eyes shined with joy.

He should not have been able to speak. But he could and he did. "I...I see a palace. A glass—no, a crystal, palace!" he rasped. "And...and..."

"Shhh," I gently hushed. I closed my eyes and continued to focus on my breathing; inhale deeply, hold for a beat, exhale thoroughly, repeat. I was in the flow and rhythm of my breath when I suddenly felt a floating sensation. In the next moment, I was there; in front of the palace. I controlled my awe at what was happening, what I was seeing, by simply allowing it to happen without censor, without judgment. The palace did indeed seem to be made of crystal. The bright light that hit the structure from a brilliantly blue sky was bent and split into an infinite variety of beautiful colors within its walls and within its endless number of rooms. Mere glass, at least in the world of men, could not do this: reflect and refract the light of the heavens into an infinite variety of colors, thus reflecting the infiniteness of creation itself.

In the palace, in all the rooms that I could see and sense, there were people; many, many, many people. They were all looking at me, including, and especially, one in particular. He was standing quite close, not far in front of me. It was him; Jesu, the one whom I had pierced while on the cross. Instinctively, I looked at my hands. I held a shadow of the lance, but not the thing Itself. I did not panic, but knew this to be the way of it in this realm. There were several others who stood close to Jesu, shoulder to shoulder. They, including Master Jesu, seemed to be their own clan -- not separate or above any of the other people in the palace, but somehow special. Though I did not recognize any of those surrounding Jesu, I knew in my heart that when these individuals had been alive in the world, they had all been anointed ones in their own cultures. Curiously, too, at least as they appeared to me, they all had similar facial features to Jesu -- or he to them -- even the heavier, far-eastern Asian looking sage who was standing just to Jesu's right.

Someone stepped from behind me and stood next to me on my left. I turned my head and looked him in the eyes. It was the man from the pallet. He was whole. Not burned. I had not known this man in life and certainly could not tell what his features had been like, given his charred condition back on the pallet. But I knew it to be him. I knew those eyes.

"Thank you," he said to me in a whisper. He then faced the anointed ones and the crystal palace, and walked forward.

I started to follow, taking a tentative step forward, as well. But Jesu held up a hand and stopped me. "No, Longinus," he said in a familiar voice. "This way is not for you."

I paused. Of course this way was not for me. At least for now, it was not. There were so many things I wanted to ask. But one question stood out above all. "What am I to do?" I asked.

"You already know. You are here, helping one in need to cross, are you not? You breathed and opened and asked, and the way was made known to you. That is all you ever need do to know an answer."

"The spear guided me and..."

"No. You guided you. The lance is simply a tool, a point of focus just as your breath is."

"And you. You guided me."

"I am your-Self. All that I am is within you," he said.

"I don't understand," I replied.

"I believe you do in your heart, in your soul. There is a part of you, Longinus, that you know is eternal. It is your true, infinite self, that part of you that can never be separate from the source of all things. And it has been awakened within you and is ever expanding. You are here because on some level, you know this, you feel this, you are listening to this. Continue to listen and to trust and you will be guided every step of your path," he concluded.

His words, his thoughts, infused my entire being. They cleansed my mind, my body, my soul. I found myself crumpling at his feet in emotional and spiritual awe and humility. I touched the ground with my face. I stayed that way for what seemed a long while. When I finally looked up, I was back in the shelter, on the floor. I stood and looked once again into the eyes of the man on the pallet. Those eyes now stared blankly into space. The charred shell remained. The soul had made the transition.

A soft white light surrounded me and the man's body, Jacobi and Detrom. The other Druids were also attuned to the holiness of the moment. With eyes closed, they chanted softly in prayer. Hentapas too was chanting rhythmically, softly in Egyptian. Their prayers and chants had helped me, had sustained me and aided our burnt patient on the journey to the Otherworld. The light, the aura, which surrounded us gently began to fade. The chanting of the Druids and Hentapas quietly faded, as well, and ceased. They all stared at me.

"I...saw..." I began.

"We know," Jacobi smiled.

Detrom smiled as well and simply nodded.

How they could know where I had been and to whom I had spoken, I knew not. But it mattered not. They had sensed, or somehow seen, what had transpired and were in reverent awe. Though not nearly as much as I.

~XIV~

It had rained during the previous night. Vapor appeared before my eyes as I took in and then released my first conscious breath of the day. Cold it was this morning. My lodge, my quarters, in the village was small, but sturdy; a mud-brick hut with a thatched roof. It was large enough for a sleeping pallet made of rushes, a stool, and a small fire-pit which was in the center. The structure was round, the roof conical with a hole in the top-center for the fire-pit smoke to escape. It had belonged to Detrom's second, the High Druid Mallard. He had been among the first killed during Draco's insurrection. Word had spread of my "participation" in the burned legionnaire's "Journey of Spirit," as the people were calling it. I was now truly being hailed as some kind of Roman healer and magician, equal to a powerful Druid. Appropriate, the people thought (indeed, even insisted), for me to have the Malard's dwelling.

I could smell freshly cooked oatcakes and hot mead. That and cheese had been left for me every morning at the stooped doorway entrance to the lodge since I had come to the village nearly three weeks ago, two days after the night of the Wickermen. I had kept to myself since arriving in the village. Much of that time had been spent in quiet reflection; reflection upon the experience with the burned soldier, my own soul's journey to the crystal palace (What was the crystal palace?); the experience of the rains that seemingly came at my will to dowse the flames of the Wickermen, and all of the experiences profound and otherwise, that I'd had since that day on the hill of crosses. And Irena. I even thought of Irena. What had become of her? But mainly, I thought about the spear, the words that had come to me, the guidance in times of need, and the attunement I was feeling with all creation because of It.

Jacobi said I was in meditation and prayer. He and Detrom would visit me once a day, to check on me. They both seemed immensely pleased with my desire for solitude, the opposite of how I thought they would feel. But then again, I was probably putting that opposite attitude on them myself. In my past, I would have interpreted someone's desire for solitude simply as laziness, a rouse to shirk a duty. Not anymore. At least, not in this context.

Perhaps Jacobi was right; I was in a sort of period of meditation and prayer. I simply thought about my experiences in the recent past and asked the Gods, the God, the Universe, for guidance. No concrete answers came, but intuitive feelings abounded as to what was to come. Of course, my reasoning mind asked for more details. But they would not come from the intellect. Patience and trust of my intuitive faculties had to be allowed to grow. Just this last thought alone made me realize for certain that I was truly a changed man. A passion had bloomed within me; a passion to know the truth behind all that had happened -- which seemed to inevitably include knowing the truth of my own nature and the powerful source within.

I threw back the stag-skin blanket and rolled off the pallet. Groggily, I staggered to the entrance to retrieve my meal. I pulled back the entrance's flap to reveal the platter of cheese, oatcakes and mead, and the three pair of feet just next to it. I looked up and there stood Jacobi, Detrom and surprisingly, Hentapas, who stood next to them shoulder-to-shoulder as an equal. They had plans of a sort; that much was obvious. "You are early today," I said somewhat annoyed.

"Forgive the intrusion, Longinus," said Jacobi, his usually light demeanor slightly heavier.

"Longinus," began Detrom, "tonight marks Luna Prima. It is the rise of the awakened mother. It is an extremely powerful time. It is the perfect time for one to be initiated, formally, into The Mysteries. You have been chosen by the Gods and God. Your abilities are raw, but they will grow. The ritual we will perform will help you immensely."

I stood there stunned. "What? You want me to be part of your Pagan rite?" I said a little too harshly. Yet, images of the last ritual of theirs I had witnessed still lingered.

"That's unfair of you," replied Jacobi, reading my thoughts as usual.

"Yes. I apologize, Detrom. You are no Draco. I know that," I said.

"No, I am not," said Detrom. "But make no mistake; Draco and I wield the same infinite power – as we all do. We just use it for different purposes.

"This rite, the Luna Prima. What is it?"

"That it has to do with the full cast moon on its first night, I'm sure you've already surmised. As to its exact meaning and ritual aspect, well, you will see," was all Detrom would say.

"Hmm," I grunted. "And you, Hentapas? Are you here with these two or do you disturb me this early as well, but for another reason?"

"I am with Master Jacobi and Arch Druid Detrom, sir," he stated in a manner that did indeed indicate equality with the other two.

I was not sure what to make of this and it must have shown on my face.

"As it turns out," offered Detrom, "Hentapas was raised in Thebes, Egypt, at Karnack Temple. He was a priest of the old religion there; a strong priest, powerful, despite his young age. He will be joining us tonight, assisting in the rite, which is not unlike those he's performed in his homeland. He has demonstrated much power, and much knowledge of the sacred arts."

A part of me was a bit stunned by this, although the larger part of me was not surprised at all. There had been something about the lad... Still, the old religion of Egypt?

"I left the temple to become a legionnaire only because I had been conscribed to," said Hentapas.

"I thought," I began, "that all the temples of Egypt had long since been abandoned and left for ruin, or at the very least, rededicated to Roman gods. And your land's old religions, aren't they long dead, too?"

"Appearances. Do not always trust appearances, sir," answered Hentapas. "The old ways thrive, though not in the open, nor exactly as they once were. But they are there, nonetheless."

"Hmm. I never really...I never gave it much thought," I confessed.

"Someone will come near midnight to escort you, Longinus," Jacobi said, somewhat abruptly.

"Jacobi," I said, "are you assisting in this too? Is it not an unclean thing for you?"

"I am an observer. And no, I don't believe it to be the unclean, undivine thing you may think it is. I have seen that all power, as Detrom pointed out a moment ago, is from the same place and source. It is simply seen in different ways and in different things by different peoples. It is all of God," he concluded.

"Until tonight, then," stated Detrom. "Forgive the intrusion this morning and forgive us for rushing off, but there is much to do."

I said nothing. It was time for me to move to the next part of my life. Rome was nearly dead inside of me. She would always be a part of me, but that part was shrinking. I looked at all three of them, one by one. "As you wish," I said, and slipped back inside with the food to break my fast.

I went for a walk after my morning meal. The village itself was a simple place. Twenty-five or so, small, circular wood and mud structures—huts, really—sat on either side of a narrow main thoroughfare. All this was surrounded by small oak trees and pine trees. I had been out and about several times since my arrival in the village, but I still received glances of curiosity mixed with reverence as I strolled along. The spear received as many of these looks as I did. I took It with me everywhere. As the people looked my way, I would simply smile and walk on.

I left the village and walked a short way down a path which wound through a stand of trees and ended at a lake. The lake was a fairly small body of water, only about a-hundred yards in diameter, and fed by an abundant fresh water stream. On its tiny beach, I removed my tunic, folded it and placed it on top of the spear, which I had already put under a nearby bush, along with my hob-nailed sandals. I turned and plunged into the cold water. Oh, how I missed the hot Roman baths. Hot baths were the gods' gift to civilized man. I could have asked the locals to heat some water for me in one of their large cisterns, but the lake was much simpler. Besides, a part of me did not like the thought of the Celts laughing at the tough Roman's prissiness, his delicate sensitivity to cold water. But, as it turned out, it only took a few minutes to get used to the lake's temperature. I scrubbed and cleaned myself, then simply enjoyed a relaxing, gentle swim, all the while contemplating the coming night's ritual.

Half an hour went by. Or, maybe it was an hour. I lost track of time. I was floating on my back, basking in the peaceful surroundings: the serenity of the lake, the brilliance of the clear blue sky. And then, I became aware that I was not alone. I saw movement out of the corner of my eye. I turned and clumsily stood in the somewhat shallow water, leaving barely my head above the surface. A distance away, a naked female form entered the lake with a splash. Did she not realize I was there? I could not believe that she did. Why would she jump into the water naked, knowing a strange man was there? But, then again, these Celts were a very open people.

Still, courtesy dictated that I make my presence known to the woman, and the sooner, the better. But I did not. I was enthralled with the sight of her and did not want to break the spell. Seeing her long brown hair, full breasts, round buttocks and small, but shapely feminine form, made me realize just how long it had been since I had laid with a woman. Once again, Irena came into my mind. I missed Irena. I missed our love making, certainly. But I also missed her, the person. Yet, the truth was that probably, I would never see her again. That thought made me sad. But I had known that I'd probably not see her again for some time. I was resigning myself to the fact. Life moves on. And there I was, in the present moment, with a nude woman swimming about. I was quite aroused by her and her nakedness as she glided through the water. My immediate desire was to stay silent and simply enjoy the sight of her. Yet, I knew I could not do that. I had to let her know that she was not alone.

The lake's shore was only about seventy feet from my position. The woman was now much closer, leisurely swimming right toward me. I cleared my throat aloud. It was a feeble and cowardly attempt at declaring my presence, and did not work. I had not made the sound at all loud enough, especially since I'd made it at a moment when her head was submerged. Her upper body sprang above the surface for an instant before going under again. I opened my mouth to speak, but was too slow. I stood there, my toes barely touching the lake's bottom, open-mouthed, as her snow-white buttocks broke the surface briefly, as well, before disappearing as she dove under the water. She continued her underwater sojourn, swimming right at me. Gently, I swam a few feet to my right to avoid her. But she veered to her left in the same instant. I tried to reverse my course, but it was too late. I bumped right into her -- or she into me. She broke the surface in a gasp, her face contorted with what appeared to be mock surprise and anger. She stood there, seemingly on higher ground than I, or on an underwater rock or something, for she stood almost a third of the way out of the water. There in the water, I could not tell exactly how tall she was, but I refused to believe that she was taller than I, let alone by almost a third! Yet, there she stood, her bottom two-thirds in the water, top third above. Her breasts floated, or appeared to, her dark, wet hair clung seductively to her shoulders.

"I'm sorry," I said stupidly, not sure whether I was apologizing for bumping into her or for staring at her bobbing breasts. She still looked angry, but there was something not quite sincere about the look. However, I did not know this woman. Perhaps this was her look of genuine anger.

She studied me with bewitching hazel eyes and then said quizzically, "You are not as tall as I thought."

"I...what?" I stammered, caught completely off guard.

"And you are older too. I am twenty-eight summers. You are obviously much, much older."

"I am not!" I blurted out defensively, feeling like an awkward schoolboy. "Well, I am older than twenty-eight summers for certain—by eleven, in fact—but..." I stopped myself in mid-sentence as a thought occurred to me. I found my own bearings again and looked to where I had put my clothes and more importantly, the spear. The area was undisturbed. I looked back at the woman, studying her for a moment. Her eyes were actually more green than hazel. A small nose and mouth adorned her face. Her lips were full and curled up at the ends on both sides, giving the impression that she had a perpetual smile. She was beautiful. But that was irrelevant. "Are you spying on me? What is your name," I demanded.

"Camaroon," she replied, with a bit of playful haughtiness. "And no, I am not spying. I simply wanted to see you up close."

"So, you waited 'til I was naked in a lake?" I asked. "You're an odd one."

"Not really."

"Does your husband know where you are?" I asked, with an air of superiority. At twenty-eight summers, she would be, should be, married.

"Husband or no, I do as I please," she answered.

"Really!" I said with mock arrogance. "He must be very understanding," I said sarcastically.

"He? I never said I was married to one man. Nor even to a man," she said mischievously. "In fact, I never said I was married at all."

"Camaroon!" came a child's yell from shore. A girl of about ten, dressed in a long white hemp gown, stood waving at us, or rather, at Camaroon. "You are needed!" the girl said, not urgently, but leaving no doubt that the woman before me was about to get back to shore.

"I am coming," Camaroon replied.

"Your daughter?" I asked playfully. She gave me that quizzical look again. "Well, you never said you weren't married either."

"Silly Roman. You needn't be married to have a child. But no, she is not my daughter. She is what you Romans might call a Vestal."

A Vestal Virgin? I asked myself. Vestal Virgins were young virgin girls who were keepers of the eternal flame in the temples of Rome, and priestesses in waiting and training. They were very highly regarded. Before I could ask anything, though, Camaroon spun in the water and swam back to shore.

"Wait," I said. She stopped for a moment and looked back at me. "Just like that, you're off? You swim out here to view me, then leave?" Again, I felt like an awkward schoolboy.

"You heard the lass. I'm needed. Goodbye for now, Centurion Longinus." She swam the rest of the way to shore, got out of the water and dressed. With a wave to me, she and the girl headed off hand in hand.

"I'm no longer a Centurion!" I called to her, receding back for no particular reason. No response. She and the girl disappeared into the stand of trees, headed back to the vicinity of the village.

~XV~

The full moon was bright and clear, nearly at its zenith. After returning from the lake, I spent the rest of the day and evening in solitude. But this solitude felt different. Something compelled me to mentally prepare for that night's activity, not just to reflect upon it, as I had been doing in the lake, but to open my mind and soul and spirit to it. I knew not from where the compelling came; whether from my own instinct or a higher power or a higher voice guiding me. But then, much of the time, in essence, instinct and a higher power's guidance are one in the same thing.

The flames in my shelter's fire pit were flickering, dwindling, dying. No point in feeding them. The spear stood near the entrance, waiting as I was. I couldn't tell completely in the dim light, but it looked as if the tip, the blade, was glowing slightly.

"Centurion Longinus," came the voice from outside. How I wished they would stop using my former rank. "We bid you join us." The voice was feminine. I stepped to the lodge's entrance and pulled back the flap, hooking it from above so it would stay open. Ten robed figures stood just outside. Six of them were in white robes. All of them were hooded with large cowls; all of them had their faces obscured. The leader, however, the one closest to me, the one who had called me out, pulled back the cowl of her white robe just enough for me to see part of a face splashed with moonlight. I could also see one bright green eye peering at me from beneath the cowl's edge.

It was Camaroon from the lake; I was sure of it. And, she was indeed a tall woman. We were eye to eye, at least. She may have even been slightly taller. I chuckled to myself; it was now apparent that she had indeed been standing on something in the water earlier in the day. "You are..." I began.

"We are the guardians and keepers of the Mysteries," she interrupted. "We have no names but Guardian or Keeper. You will address those of us in white as such. Those in blue, you will address as Guide. But you will only address any of us if asked to do so. Do you understand?"

I hesitated briefly. I had questions to ask her. But, obviously, that would not be acceptable. I gave in to the moment. "I do, Guardian," I replied.

"Good. For now, you will be known only as the Seeker or the Neophyte. Come with us now to be initiated into the ranks of the Mysteries. Do you accept this invitation, Neophyte?" she asked.

"Yes, Guardian."

"Excellent." With a nod of her head, two blue-robed Guides stepped forward and stopped in front of me. One of them ceremoniously held out a small white sack made of linen and a neutral colored robe. "You will wear this robe and the sack, the ritual hood, over your head, for you are not yet worthy to behold the path to the place of enlightenment," Guardian Camaroon continued. I started to protest, but thought better of it. "It is also so that you may learn trust—trust in your guides and Guardians, in no matter what form they appear. Do you object to this?"

I picked up the spear, holding it at parade rest. I could see that my white-hooded Guardian was about to say something. Obviously, no one was allowed to bring a weapon to ritual ceremonies, except for the High Priest or the one performing a sacrifice, if indeed there was one. However, for every rule, there are exceptions. This was no ordinary lance, and she knew it. "I do not object," I said, and stepped over the threshold of my dwelling and between the two blue-robes.

My Guardian looked at the spear's tip, which was indeed aglow. "So be it," she said.

The linen bag or hood was placed over my head, blinding me to the night. I felt hands on either side of me gently grasp my arms and guide me. I walked and knew that we were all walking in unison. And so, with the rank precision of a small military unit, we silently and reverently marched out of the village.

The ground beneath my feet was smooth and packed. No doubt it was a well-worn path. I was a bit nervous. It seemed as though we had walked for some time, but it had probably not been more than a few minutes. I assumed we were going to the sacred grove of oak trees. It was the Holiest place in the area, where many a ritual had been performed over the centuries. Supposedly, it was quite close to the village. Yet, it was a risk. By now, once again, Roman patrols and military would be coming into the area. Dangerous it was, then, to hold a ritual in a grove of trees, regardless of how sacred they were. Caesar had shown this when he burned down the sacred groves of oak to the east and north of us a few decades before. It had been the largest and most sacred grove of all; a place where all the continent's Druids and those from beyond as well, would flock once a year. It was there no more. Although, amazingly enough, I had heard that it had already begun to grow again.

We came to a halt and I stood in blind silence. Faintly, I could hear extremely muffled voices chanting in slow, rhythmic unison. Why were they so muffled? I wondered. It wasn't because of distance, for they did not sound far off. Nor was it because of dense tree growth. That would have merely filtered the sound. The chanting voices sounded as if they were coming from beneath thickly packed wet blankets. Then it dawned on me.

The guides released me. The hood which had blinded me, was removed. I was not in a grove of trees. I stood at the threshold, the entrance to a passageway that led into a hillside. The stone frame of the threshold was intricately carved with many Celtic symbols. The bright moonlight lit the hill well. I studied it for a moment. There was something not quite right about the hill; something not quite natural. And then I realized what it was. It was a hill made by the hand of men and women. A King's Burial Mound. Roman historians had written about these mounds. They were intricate structures built by the people for their dead king or leader, not unlike the great pyramids of Egypt, except for the fact that these structures were then covered with earth, rather than built upon. The end result was that from the outside they looked like a formation of the earth itself, a hill. But inside, they were the resting place for a king and much, much more. They had even been constructed to display astronomical events on specific days, or nights, of the year. That they were used for rituals, however, I was not aware. But, nor was I surprised.

"Neophyte," said Guardian Camaroon, whose face was once again completely obscured. "You stand at the threshold of the Temple Mound. Within is sacred and holy ground, and this is a sacred and holy night. Do you still wish to proceed?" she asked. I opened my mouth to respond, but she quickly held up a hand to silence me before I could speak. "Know before you answer," she said ominously, "that if you choose to proceed, there is no turning back." She let this hang in the air for a moment. "What say you, Neophyte?"

I was not quite sure what would happen if I changed my mind once inside the Mound, but it mattered not. "With heart and soul, I wish to proceed," I replied.

"So be it," she said. She turned and entered the Mound, followed by three of the other Guardians, Keepers or white-robes, then two Guides, myself, the other two Guides, and finally the last two Guardians. The spear tip glowed, and my heart beat quickened, but not from fear; from ecstatic anticipation of the divine. For the intensity and the importance of the moment was becoming more palpable with every step I took.

From there on, the night was a blur. Upon entering the Temple Mound, I began to slip into a trance-like state of being. I thought at first that perhaps someone had slipped a mind-altering substance to my food. I had not eaten anything since that morning—which in and of itself shows that no one had slipped me anything. It would have taken effect long before midnight. Or, perhaps it was the smoke from all the torches lighting the inside of the mound. But that was unlikely, as well. My lungs felt no discomfort, whatsoever. My mind, my soul, were simply surrendering to what was happening. A strange sensation was that. I was unaccustomed to giving in or surrendering in any circumstances. But this was much bigger than just me.

I remember winding through a maze of tunnels to the heart of the mound. Soon, though, I found myself in the center of the structure, deep inside the earth. I was surrounded by all manner of hooded figures, whose faces and identities were hidden by cowls. There was some kind of large stone altar in the center of the room we now occupied. Someone, it sounded like Detrom, began speaking in an ancient Celtic tongue. I understood not a word of it. I stood before the altar for quite a few minutes, listening to the voice drone on in the ancient language. Though I could not understand what was being said, there was something calming and soothing about the words, the voice. It was an incantation invoking the divine presence of the Universe, I decided: a calling forth of the blessings of the gods; of the One God. The trance I felt myself drifting into now became profound. I experienced that floating sensation again; the same one I felt when I was in front of the burned legionnaire. Strangely, I welcomed it. It was beginning to feel familiar; almost like I was about to go home. I don't mean the kind of home that we all might abide in here on earth. I mean the Home of all; a remerging with my soul's Source, the way a drop of water falling from the sky into the ocean is remerging with its source.

Two hands gently touched my sleeves. A slight tugging ensued. I sensed all this, more then actually felt it. And then it happened: I was outside my body, floating above all who were there, looking down on the proceedings as if I were an observer. Panic began to seep into my mind.

"Fear not," the voice said. His voice. Jesu was next to me. We were not floating, exactly. But we weren't standing, either. We simply were there, above the heads of all the others, who were now shrouded in a thin, mysterious type of fog. "The world they are in now appears as it does because you see it through a veil," He said.

"Are we in the Otherworld?" I asked.

"No. All are in the Mind Of The One. There is no separation, only gradations of form and phases of existence. But all swirl in and through each other."

We watched the rite continue, as the two robed figures pulled on my sleeves and helped me to disrobe. My earthly form stood before the congregation, still holding the spear, but naked. My awareness, my consciousness, though in astral form felt a twinge of embarrassment. I looked down at my ethereal body hovering there with Jesu. It was robed. "For a minute there..." I started.

"You are only clothed in the form of Longinus now because it is familiar to you, to your human self. But, of course, there are no forms to your True Nature. You simply are. Consciousness. An Individualized point in Mind—as mind," said Jesu.

My earth self handed the spear off to someone, Camaroon, I believe, who, in turn, handed it to the Head Druid standing before the Altar, Detrom. I was surprised at my actions, but knew all was unfolding as it should. My naked form was then led to the altar, and aided in climbing onto it and lying down.

The chanting continued. It now sounded more like a dirge, but was not mournful. It was full of depth, aiding me on this leg of the journey. I felt my astral form beginning to fade. I looked back at my earthly body lying on the stone altar, and noticed something for the first time: a white cord extending from the navel area of my body on the stone to the navel area of my soul-body. I was about to ask Jesu about it, when I noticed something else even more intriguing. Someone else was disrobing. It was Camaroon. She proceeded to step up to the altar. The scene continued to fade.

"It is time to go, Longinus," said Jesu. "Come. I have much to show you."

The interior of the Temple mound faded entirely. In its place, appeared the Crystal Palace.

~XVI~

My head ached. My legs felt tangled, as if I were wrapped in a cocoon. A brief flash of panic ensued, but was quickly quelled as I opened my eyes to see the familiar surroundings of my own lodge. I started to disentangle myself from the skins on the pallet, but bumped into a form lying next to me: Camaroon. Her naked body was next to my equally nude self.

"Hello, Longinus," she said. "How do you feel?"

I was somewhat at a loss. "I...feel fine. Head hurts a bit," I said. "Why...uh..."

"Why am I here? To watch over you and keep you warm."

My brow crinkled in question.

"You were not entirely yourself after the ceremony," she continued. "You were shivering and chanting and conversing with... Jesu, I believe?"

Bits and fragments came into my mind. Jesu. "I don't remember much of the actual ritual," I said. "But, yes, Jesu came to me." I thought more about it and decided that was not quite the way of it. "Actually, I went to him." More of the whole night was coming back, and excitement grew within me at the memory. "Yes! I felt myself lift out of my body and float upwards. I could see all of you from above, performing the rite, and we, Jesu and I, went away, to the Crystal Palace, the same one that was there when I aided the legionnaire to the other side, and..."

"Longinus," Camaroon interrupted, "it is best to keep the actual events or happenings of your vision, or your journey, private. They were meant for you and you alone. What you learned from it may be shared with a chosen few, but the fine points of the experience are yours alone."

I understood what she meant, but was a bit

disappointed. I felt a strange connection with this woman. I was excited about the experiences and wanted to share them with her. I fell silent for a moment. I threw the skins off both of us and truly took in her naked form. "Did we?" I began. There was that school boy feeling again.

"No," she smiled. "You had trouble coming out of your trance. Your body was cold to the touch. I came into your bed to keep you warm. As you can see," she said, indicating the healthy fire in the fire pit.

'Tis true, I thought. I would have let the fire die out in the night. Plus, it was indeed stiflingly hot in the lodge. Another thought occurred to me; another memory from the previous evening. "When I was watching from...above," I began tentatively, "I saw my...self, my physical self, being disrobed and laid upon the stone slab or altar."

"Yes."

"Then I remember seeing you disrobe and...well, I don't know exactly, but it seemed that you were led to the altar too. What happened?"

"You don't remember?" she asked, in a tone of mock disappointment."

"I'm afraid not."

"Well, let's just say that the two halves of the Universe were joined to completion."

"Hmm. Sounds fairly pagan to me," I said, only half-joking.

"Those that look down upon our rites look from a place of ignorance and their own unfettered lust. They have no understanding of the balance of the Universe and the need to keep that balance in check. Besides, what was accomplished on the altar last night was only one aspect of the night's ritual. There were many other facets to it." She paused then, and I thought about it all. "You really do not remember much of it, do you?" she continued.

"No. I do not. At least, not the ritual part of it. It seems I was in a trance from the time we walked into the Mound."

"Well, that's not unheard of, but it's very unusual. You are powerful, Centurion Longinus, or, should I say, Master Longinus."

"Master? What does that mean?"

"It means that you gave quite a demonstration of your ability last night. You and the spear, that is. Twice you drifted into prophesy. Twice you healed individuals in the rites who were infirmed. One of them was the Egyptian, Hentapas. You straightened his arm perfectly without pain. It was as if it had never been crooked."

"What are you talking about?"

Before she could respond, though, there was a rustling sound from outside. Someone began to mumble. We both strained to hear the conversation, and suddenly realized what it was. Whoever was outside was mumbling to himself, rehearsing a prepared speech for me. I looked at Camaroon, and she at me, and we both burst into laughter. 'Twas time to let the person off the point of the sword, so to speak. "Who is there?" I called out.

"I, um, it is me, Centurion Longinus."

The voice was definitely familiar. "Who is 'me'"? I asked.

"Paulonius, sir."

Paulonius! I had not seen nor heard from the lad since the night after the Wickermen. Jacobi had sent the lad away on an errand when I took my recluse upon arriving in the village. The errand, I believe, was to scout the surrounding countryside with some warriors, for Roman patrols.

"I have your meal, sir," he continued.

My thoughts were still on what Camaroon had just told me, but I quickly realized how hungry I was. And, it would be good to speak with Paulonius. So I pushed the previous night's events out of my mind for the moment. Camaroon and I would talk more later. "Excellent!" I said, as I jumped up and threw on a robe. I motioned for Camaroon to do the same. "Come in, lad."

He entered the lodge with a tray of delectable foods—

oat cakes and mead, cheese and smoked fish, dried venison
and herbs. He placed it on the table near the fire pit. I stepped
up to him and embraced the boy. "It is good to see you," I
said.

"And you," he replied, keeping his eyes lowered as
Camaroon finished placing the robe about her.

"Please join us. Help us break our fast," I said.

"Oh, I do not wish to intrude."

"Nonsense," said Camaroon.

"Indeed, I insist," I added. "We've much catching up to
do."

"I would be honored, sir," he said timidly.

And so, we sat together and feasted on the morning
meal.

From then on, I spent a lot of time in a haze of study
and duty: study with the Druid sect; duty to the people of the
community. It seemed that my status had indeed changed to
that of a "Master," at least in the eyes of the villagers. Many
came to me with various ailments and, much to my surprise at
first, and after much prompting by Camaroon, I found that I
could help them. Or, more accurately, I found that some kind
of healing energy, ability, was coming through me and the
spear.

I reached a point where I could nearly always call upon
the trance state that I had found myself in on the night of the
ritual. I would then concentrate on the individual in question,
seeing in my mind's eye that this person was whole and
perfect on a spiritual/physical level, regardless of the present
appearance of his or her physical state of being. It simply was
a knowing, left over from the enlightenment I had received on
the night of the ritual: There is only One Mind, One Source, and
all, everything, is from this One Source. Spirit, the Gods, The
One, God, whatever name it is called by, is knowing and
experiencing Itself through that which it creates; the good and
the bad. Good and bad are mainly just human points of view.
Everything simply Is in the Mind Of the One, because

everything Is the Mind of the One. Therefore, there can be no separation from something of which we are all intrinsically a part.

It is this perception of separateness on a very deep level of the individual's human mind that causes the disease or unhealthy conditions.

Hmm. I thought I sound a lot like Jacobi. Well, I finally understood a lot of what the old man had been saying.

The spear was the focal point through which the healing power seemed to come. And, admittedly, much of the healing that took place was due to the strong belief on the part of the person involved. In fact, their belief in the healing was at least as important as anything I could do. That was the first step in healing oneself. Change the core beliefs at those deeper levels of the human mind and one would indeed go very far in the healing. But aiding in the belief that they could be healed was the spear. I doubted that many of them would have come to me for help if I were without it. No matter.

Camaroon was instrumental in my studies. She mentored me in the use of herbs and other medicinal aids in the realm of nature. I was also under the tutelage of the High Druid Detrom, as well as Jacobi. Though Jacobi was not a Druid, he was given the unofficial title of Merlin, for he had become somewhat of a Grand Master of the natural laws of the universe. He had been busy with his own studies and had developed a particular ability that was quite astonishing.

One day, as Camaroon and I were sitting under an oak, plying at the great tree's roots and slicing up the mistletoe we had gathered earlier, Jacobi, Paulonius, Romi and Hentapas—whose once crooked arm was now perfectly normal—approached us.

The younger lads were grinning from ear to ear. Romi was stoic as always, but there was a twinkle in his eyes. Jacobi's face was adorned with his usual friendly, toothless grin.

"Show him, Merlin Jacobi!" exclaimed an excited Paulonius. "You have never seen the likes!" he said to me.

"Boys, this is simply a tool. It is not a plaything," Jacobi

150

reprimanded, more, I thought, for show than for any other reason.

"Please," Romi said, maintaining his stoicism, yet lighting the area with a flash of excitement from his eyes.

"Very well," said Jacobi.

"That was an easy battle," I observed. "What are you to show me, Merlin Jacobi?"

"Watch," he said.

He lifted a hand toward a large ceramic bowl next to my leg. It was nearly empty, not yet filled with the root stuff we had been extracting. The old man's face contorted with concentration. I looked at the bowl. "What are you—" I began.

"Shhh!" Hentapas, Romi and Paulonius responded in unison.

The look on Jacobi's face became calmer, detached. Suddenly, a tingling sensation filled the space around us. Camaroon's hair, which had been hanging loosely over her shoulders, began to lift into the air. And, the bowl next to me began to shake, rattling on the hard-packed ground. And then it shattered, fragmenting into a hundred pieces. I quickly covered my face to protect it from the flying shards of clay, as we all did, but only for a brief moment. Within an instant, the tingling sensation in the air was gone, and Camaroon's hair was resting on her shoulder as if nothing had happened. All was back to normal, except, of course, for the shattered bowl.

For a moment, all were silent.

"What...what have you done?" I asked in disbelief.

"The bowl is easily replaced, Longinus," said Paulonius.

"I don't give a goat's ass about the bowl. I mean, what have you learned, Jacobi? Doesn't this seem...I don't know...violent? Even dark?" I asked the old one.

"Longinus, my boy," the old man began, "what have I told you? What has Detrom told you? Hmm? It is not the power itself that is dark. It is the use to which it is put. It is in the heart of those that wield the power as to whether it be dark or light. What I just demonstrated is the use of a law of the Universe—a mental, spiritual law that responds to my mind when my mind is aligned with it properly, because it is Mind Itself, and must respond by its own law. Is an arrow, or a spear, light or dark when it finds its target? Can it be blamed for an evil wound or death? No, Longinus. The arrow and spear are subject to certain laws of nature set in motion by the one who wields them, and the arrow or spear cannot help but abide by those laws once set in motion. It is the same with the power I just demonstrated, but on a much larger, universal scale. You know this to be so."

"All right, all right," I said, throwing up my hands in mock surrender. "I understand the point. And, yes, you and Detrom have certainly said that before! I get it!"

Camaroon laughed at my discomfort, and the others joined her. Obviously, some things were never going to change between Jacobi and me. Thank the gods, or God, for that.

After a moment, one by one, we all became silent, soberly pondering the significance of what we had just witnessed. Truly, all things are possible with the One when the workings are understood properly.

"You are an amazing talent, a powerful Merlin indeed, Jacobi," said Camaroon, the first to speak again.

"No, I am just attuned to the laws of the Universal Mind. We all have The Merlin inside of us, all of us."

Much time passed. I reached a point where I tapered back on the healing work and became more of a Monachus, a sort of Monk, or Ascetic, than anything else. I loved nothing more than to spend days on end studying and meditating, sometimes with the others, but most of the time alone. I felt most connected with the All in the state of meditation, for it was in such a state that I was truly at one with my eternal nature. The feeling or experience itself is difficult to describe; to put into words. The spoken or written word is by its very nature finite and, therefore, limiting, and how is one to use a finite medium to describe something that touches on the infinite? While in the meditative state, I was truly myself; at one with creation; seeing my human self as just a small dot on the map of expression; a blink of God's eye, even as the Eye Itself.

But as profound as that sounds, I was also still Longinus the man, and Camaroon had become my wife. At least, that was what everyone was saying. We had shared my lodge ever since the initiation ritual. And, of course, we shared the bed, as well. We devoured each other's bodies nightly. Our parts were as made for each other. Exploding inside of her brought me a momentary oneness with the Source of All akin to that which I felt during deep meditations. Sexual climax can be fragmentary enlightenment.

I was still Longinus, the soldier, as well. Paulonius had briefed me that morning over the meal, and continued to do so. Many Roman patrols were in the land. Many of the other villages had been hit. Some of the lads from our village rallied to their aid, and had never been heard from again. Our village was safe for a number of reasons. Rome still hunted me and the spear, so a plan of deception had been implemented to lead them off in different directions. We were also located in a valley that was dense with oaks, forested from prying eyes. Finally, Detrom and the other powerful Druids had placed an immense Glamour of protection and obscurity over the valley, concealing us and rendering us invisible to those who meant us harm.

I had been part of the ritual to invoke the Glamour. Was it working? We had been left alone, after all, for well over a year now. Actually, it had been much longer, two years or more. I had lost track of time, for awhile. Ever since the night of the Glam ritual, a mysterious fog or mist hung over the valley, veiling us from the rest of the world and, it seemed, from time itself, for a year felt as only a month. But I think I might have been the only one who felt this way about the time passing; a carryover from my Roman sensibilities and training, perhaps. The Celts didn't seem to notice or care. But then again, they wouldn't; they've always had their own sense, definition, of time.

It was indeed a strange thing, this mist. In addition to

invoking a feeling of time-lapse, the mist was also thin enough during the day to let sunshine through normally, and thick enough at night to prevent our cooking fires from being seen from afar, as reported to us by our scouts that were sent out nightly.

Then, one day, a group of strangers arrived—peaceful travelers who were fleeing Rome.

They came into the village in the early afternoon, escorted by two of our perimeter guards. As I stepped out of the lodge, I saw that Camaroon was talking with one of the new strangers, a woman, who appeared to be cradling a child in her arms. Hentapas was standing with Romi and a group of our people. The local folks were curious and excited about the newcomers.

"They made it through the mists," a villager whispered.

"Obviously, they mean us no harm then!" observed another.

The former legionaries, however, were white as ghosts. They stared at the newly-arrived entourage.

"What is the matter with you two?" I asked. "Have you not seen travelers before?"

"It's her," Romi said, as if I'd not said a word.

"Who?" I demanded.

"It is her. The woman holding the child," answered Hentapas, as if I should know her.

I looked at the travelers. They all looked weary, about fifteen in number; more men than women, and mostly on foot. Many of them were in the shade of one of the big oaks, so it was difficult to see all their faces. The woman whom Romi and Hentapas were talking about, though, stood in the light. She was the one speaking with Camaroon. Through the dirty face and travel ravaged clothing, I could still tell that she was attractive, probably twenty-nine to thirty-three summers. The child, asleep in her arms, appeared to be a girl of about three.

"All right," I said. "I see her. Now tell me who she is."

"She... is the woman from the tomb that day. His Tomb," Romi stated tonelessly.

154

"What woman?"

Hentapas turned to me slowly and looked directly into my eyes. There was intensity in his gaze, a kind that I had never seen before. It conveyed the seriousness of what he was about to say.

"She is the woman who was first to find the tomb opened when Romi and I had fallen asleep, sir. The one who said she had seen Jesu risen from the dead," he stammered.

I stared at the woman and my heart began to pound. I thought at first the pounding was due to what the lad had just told me. But it was not; at least not entirely, for I began to sense something else—something else altogether. I could feel it in the air; it rode on the mists.

Then I saw her.

Another woman stepped out from the shadows and stood next to the one holding the child, and Camaroon, and I knew my life was once again changed.

~XVII~

Dosameenor, who had escorted the outlanders into the village, ordered his troops, which amounted to several platoons of men and women warriors, to gather food for the newly arrived contingent of travelers. It took me a moment to get over the shock of seeing Irena standing with Camaroon and the other woman, before I realized that Jacobi was speaking to me. He was standing next to me. I had not heard nor seen his approach.

"Did you hear me, Longinus?" Jacobi asked. "Of course, you didn't. How could you? You are clearly in a state of disbelief, are you not? Yes, it is her, Longinus. And the other is Mary of Magdalene."

"She, Mary, was the one at..." began Romi.

"I know," Jacobi interrupted. He looked closer at Mary, and then especially closely at the child in her arms. The child; the little one sparked something in the old man. That light, that brilliant other-worldly glow that I'd seen on Jacobi before, began to project from his entire being, but this time, it had an intensity to it that I'd never seen before. "Is that...could it be?" he asked with reverent awe, more to himself than to anyone else.

And, just like that, he was off, shuffling toward the group.

"He may be somewhat of a Merlin now," observed Romi, "but he is still odd."

"He knows things that you and I may never understand," said Hentapas sagely.

"Hmph," was Romi's skeptical response.

I watched as Jacobi approached the group of travelers slowly. Irena took notice of him and released a squeal of delight. Tears filled her eyes as she embraced the old man, nearly crushing the life out of his seemingly frail body in her excitement.

They conversed then. I was not close enough to hear them speak, but I watched intently and could see words tumble from their mouths. The words, combined with an animated flurry of hand gestures, told each in a moment, the basic journey of life for the other, as it had unfolded over the past years since last they'd seen one another. Jacobi kept looking at Mary and the child, clearly wanting to speak with the woman. Finally, Irena placed her hand lovingly on Jacobi's cheek, drawing his full attention back to her. I saw her mouth the words, where is he?

Jacobi turned to me, smiled from ear to ear, and pointed.

I thought my heart would leap out of my chest.

Tentatively, on wobbling legs of anticipation, I stepped forward to meet my past, my destiny.

She wiped the tears from her eyes as she walked toward me. We approached each other slowly at first, as if in a fragile dream whose world would dissolve with a sigh. But the reality was that she was here; I was here. Our steps picked up as we got closer to each other, until we were covering the ground in a flying run. We slammed into each others' body with the force of a long-exile-ended. Our arms wrapped tightly around one-another, as if we wished to never again be separated. After a moment, I pulled back, cupping her dirty, but still lovely face in my hands.

"Where have you been? I thought you were going to follow us. You never came. I thought I'd never see you again. Why didn't you come?" The words just shot out of me. I couldn't help myself. I had not realized until that moment how much this woman had meant to me.

She simply smiled. A solitary tear rolled delicately and meanderingly down her cheek, leaving a streak of contentment on her face. "Oh, Longinus," she said. "I have sorely missed you, too."

We stood there and stared at each other for a moment. I looked over her shoulder and could see that most of the villagers had come out and were now watching Irena and me. Irena's fellow travelers were also gazing at the odd reunion here in the middle of a glamour-affected valley. Then there were the others who were watching us with even more curiosity; Jacobi stood with them. Mary looked at me, with what thoughts, I could not say. Her child, too, gazed at me, but with eyes as old as time itself. And, Camaroon—there was something forlorn in her face as she stared at me; a resignation, perhaps.

Jacobi shuffled his way toward us, motioning Mary to follow him. Camaroon hung back for a moment, but quickly caught up.

"All right, then!" boomed Dosameenor's commanding voice to the rest of the villagers. "Come on now. Let's get busy and make our guests feel at home!" The other villagers quickly obeyed and scurried about their work.

Hentapas and Romi still stood close by. They wanted to stay—I could feel it—but they both began to step back, believing that it was not their place to be present for this meeting. "Remain here!" I ordered. "We are all a part of this."

Hentapas nodded, clearly pleased.

The little group arrived and halted before Irena, myself and the other two men. An awkward silence filled the space around us. Or, perhaps it was only I who felt the awkwardness. For a brief instant, I focused on other things; I heard birds singing, the chatter of the villagers around us and my own breath going in and out. I stared at the woman, Mary. Yes, thirty-three summers at the most, wavy brown hair with shades of auburn. Dark, dark brown eyes accented with long dark lashes; a beautiful woman. But she was much more than just a woman. Her countenance seemed to radiate a depth and a wisdom that transcended all the knowledge of the Universe. It reminded me of the power I had felt from Detrom the first time I saw him. This, however, felt even more powerful. So much so, that a sudden feeling of complete unworthiness at being in her presence swept over me. I almost felt compelled to drop to my knees in awe. I stopped myself from dropping, though, and stood my ground in front of her, but with eyes lowered.

Other thoughts then began to gnaw at me. In spite of all the training and enlightenment I had received over the past couple of years or so, I was still very, very much human. I felt guilt, tremendous guilt, over what I had done to Jesu, her Master and Teacher...and...and...

I looked at the child and suddenly realized who the father was, or had been. The babe, the girl-child, stared at me with his, Jesu's, eternal eyes.

"Longinus," said Jacobi, interrupting my thoughts, "none of it matters. It all took place as it was supposed to, as Master Jesu wanted it to," he explained, reading most of my thoughts as always. "Detach yourself, as you have been taught, and look at it all from the true perspective of your Higher, Eternal Self. You will see that what I say is true."

I closed my eyes briefly, willing Jacobi's words into my mind, attempting to shove out all other thoughts. I opened them at the sound of her voice.

"Centurion Longinus," Mary's sweet voice intoned, as but a whisper. She smiled a radiant smile of forgiveness and Love, the Love of God.

"I...am just Longinus now, please," was all I could manage to say.

She inclined her head in acknowledgement, stepped up to me and touched my face with her free hand. A feeling of divine warmth and comfort coursed through my entire being. "Let it go now, my friend," she soothed. "I know that he speaks to you, for he speaks to me, as well. You think that it's through the spear, but it is not. But you know that, too, don't you?" She laughed, a sweet, tinkling sound. "I think we all have crutches that we must let go of." She stepped back then.

I had the inane thought that perhaps she would like to see the spear, which I now kept, some of the time, at least, well hidden in the lodge. A stupid thought, that. Why would she care to see that thing? It had been a thought born of my own insecurities; a juvenile need on my part for her to accept me and forgive me, or for me to forgive myself. But all I had to do was to open my heart and mind and spirit, and hear what she was saying to know that there was nothing to forgive.

Irena spoke then. "Mary is the reason I could not come to you when I said would, or rather, my vow to help Mary was the reason," she explained. "When you left on the boat that day from Najaffi, Mary was due to give birth at any time. Sara here," Irena said, gently tousling the child's hair, "was longer in coming than we thought she would be and there were complications with Mary afterwards."

"I was in a fever for a very, very long time, Longinus," Mary said. She smiled, recalling the memory. "While I was in the fever, I spent all that time with Jesu, you see, learning so that I could teach and carry on his work, too, when I was well again. Oh, I had been his disciple when he walked among us, but the teachings he taught me while I was with him on the Other Side for a time were even more infinite in their scope." She studied me for a moment. "But I think you know what I speak of, Longinus, or you soon will." Adjusting the child in her arms, Mary held Sara so that I could see her face more clearly. "Can you say hello, Sara?"

The child said nothing, but stared at me until a smile to light up the world splashed across her little face. The smile quickly grew until it burst forth into peels of glorious giggles of happiness, which, in turn, rapidly infected us all. We burst into laughter of our own.

"Camaroon?" sounded a young female voice. It was Rintinau, the young girl who had come to the lake, calling for Camaroon. She was no longer a little girl, but blossoming into a young woman. She had been Camaroon's shadow and student for some time now, "Guardian of the Temple Mound Flame" and "Apprentice Priestess of the Mist", she was called.

"Grand Master Detrom asks for your council," Rintinau said.

"Yes, of course," Camaroon replied.

We looked at each other then, Camaroon and I. She had not been laughing with the rest of us. Her face was smiling but I saw emptiness there.

"Excuse me," she said, and walked off with Rintinau.

~XVIII~

The rest of the day was spent helping our guests to clean up, settle in and generally shake off the road. As it turned out, the group was not going to be here for all that long; they were headed to a community up in the northern region: a community of Jews. Mary would be safest there, according to Irena and Thomas, the leader and Rabbi of the group. Mary was being hunted by Rome for a couple of different reasons, the most obvious of which she had been carrying in her arms. I was quite disappointed, for Irena was going with them. I tried to talk to her about it at the feasting that evening, but could not. Every time I tried to corner her, it seemed that someone else needed her attention, thus thwarting my effort to speak to her. No matter for now. They would probably not be leaving for many days. Surely, I could change her mind by then.

The cooking fires remained stoked, and the feasting and celebration around them went on into the night. It was mostly our people of the village who carried it on. Not all of the group of newcomers were Jewish, however, and those who weren't stayed out celebrating and regaling the village folk with their tales of travel. But most were Jewish, as it turned out, and had their own strict guidelines on food and drink. Most of them retired when their appetites had been at least partly satiated.

Irena had merely smiled at me when the time came for her to take leave of the celebration. Mary wanted to go, as well, so Irena escorted the woman and her child to their lodgings. I sought out Jacobi then, but could not find him near the cooking fires. Nor could I find Dosameenor, nor Hentapas, nor Romi, nor Detrom, nor even Camaroon. So, I left the cooking fires and their celebratory congregants and headed back to my own lodge.

Pulling back the flap and entering my living space answered one question, at least: where Camaroon had gone. She was not lying on the sleeping pallet, though. She had not retired. Quite the contrary. She was piling her belongings in a stack near the entrance. Obviously, she was leaving.

"What is this?" I inquired.

She stopped what she was doing and stared at me as if drinking me in for the last time. She smiled then. "What does it look like?" There was no anger in her voice, no sarcasm, no hostility of any kind. She was leaving, and that was that.

"You are going somewhere, without even discussing it or a courtesy goodbye or explanation?" I asked, feeling both angry and guilty. I found that a part of me actually wanted this: a confrontation with her—perhaps, even for her to leave me all together.

Camaroon put down the fire tools she was packing away and came face-to-face with me, looking me straight in the eyes, soul-to-soul. She gently touched my cheek then, stroking it lightly. "My Longinus," she began. "Yet, mine no more. Nor ever really, were you, I suppose. Do you remember the night of your ritual, how, the next morning, I told you that you had made prophecies?"

The question caught me off guard. "What does that have to do with anything?" She waited patiently while I thought about it. "All right, yes. I recall that you said I had babbled a couple of prophetic phrases or something or other, but I couldn't remember anything about them and you certainly wouldn't tell me no matter how many times I asked, nor would anyone else who was there."

"That's right and do you remember why I wouldn't tell you what you said that night?"

I could feel my face blushing. She had always retained that ability to make me feel like a school boy. "Something about that they were meant for me and that I'd remember eventually. Well, guess by the gods what? I still haven't remembered them. So, I imagine they weren't altogether such important prophesies after all, eh?" I was becoming flustered, though I was not sure why.

"They were meant—" she began.

"I know," I interrupted. "They were meant for me. They came through me, so were for me to interpret, and so on."

"No," she stated so abruptly that I was utterly silenced. "They were meant for you because they were about you."

The air was still. A piece of wood cracked and popped on the fire in the pit, spitting an ember onto the surrounding dirt floor. I simply stared at it, as it harmlessly cooled and died. "What do you mean? I thought I had said things that concerned everyone."

"Oh, you said a couple of things that pertained to the Romans destroying our culture and so forth. But the main things you said concerned yourself and the future." Camaroon looked away then. She sat on the edge of the sleeping pallet and caressed the cover, the place where we had relished each other's bodies night after night. "I kept hoping that it was a false-prophesy. I even began to believe so," she continued, "until they arrived: Irena and the others," she finished, a tear glistening in one eye.

I went to her then and knelt in front of her. I placed a hand on her chin and lifted it, thus looking again into her eyes. "I am sorry. I do not want to cause any pain. But I don't understand what you say. Please. Please explain it to me. What did I say that night? What does it have to do with you, with her?"

She gazed back at me, surprise subtly drifting across her face. "You truly do not remember any of it, do you?"

I gently shook my head.

"Very well, then." She took a breath, released it with a sigh, and plunged in. "You...said that your bloodline, 'a descendent of Longinus', is going to found a new nation, one based on truth and justice—one where the weaker are defended and treated well. This is to be in a place, on an island, where the last of the Celts live, some three-hundred years hence. The other thing you stated was that your spirit will incarnate during that time and in that place as the greatest of all wizards, the Merlin of Merlins. So powerful will you be, that the title 'Merlin' will lose all meaning, for it will be your name: a name that you will pass on to a son who will crown a true High King of that land. You said you will do this—incarnate as this being—to aid in the birth of this new country and her King, her King being the descendent of Centurion Gauis Cassius Longinus," she finished.

The crackling of the fire was all I heard for a moment. I remembered nothing of these prophesies. But they rang true, completely true, resonating with every fiber of my being. I could hardly speak.

"Reincarnate as a Master Merlin?" was all I managed to say.

"Not just a Master Merlin, THE Greatest Merlin, and father to the final Merlin," she added.

I didn't know what she was talking about, so I focused on the generality. "I know the Druids convey the belief in reincarnation, but I've never really thought about it."

"Why do you think our warriors are so fearless? It's one of the reasons anyway. They know they will be born again, into this life, to continue their schooling, to advance to a point spiritually where they will choose not to come back here. Even your Jesu alluded to it," she said.

"I don't know about that," I said. I thought about it for a moment. "I don't remember anything about that in our...I should ask Jacobi."

She smiled sagely. "I believe Jacobi would say that with an Infinite God, all things are possible, and must be—by the definition of what it is to be infinite—truly possible. But you are placing attention on only one part of the prophecies."

"Yes, my descendent. I don't understand that part."

"Oh, Longinus, stop it!" she blurted out in frustration. "You are not daft! Figure it out. You will have a child that carries on your bloodline."

"I know what it implies," I said, staring deeply into her eyes.

"Do you?" She cupped my face with her hands and stared right back into my eyes. "Yes, it means that you will have a child. But not with me, if that's what you're thinking, and you know that in your heart."

It is in part what I was thinking. I thought that perhaps she was pregnant, but she had just dashed that idea. Several years we had been together and she had never become pregnant with my child. The subject was never brought up. I never questioned why. I know now that it was never brought up, by me, at least, because I had other priorities embedded deep in my mind. Since she never talked about having children together, I, consciously or not, or for whatever reason, did not want to, either.

"I cannot, Longinus, not any longer," she continued, the tear now rolling down her face. "I had a child many summers ago, a girl child. The birthing was very difficult for me and left my insides ravaged. I am barren."

I did not know what to say. You can never know someone fully, no matter how intimate you become; no matter how long you are with that person.

An awkward laugh escaped her lips. "You never knew? Why do you think I never became pregnant with you?"

"I...assumed you knew of a special way of controlling it. You are a powerful herbalist and Druidess," I said.

"Is that all you assumed?"

I paused in silence for a moment. "I don't know what else to say, Camaroon. But I never thought that you were barren." A gulf of awkwardness yawned between us. "What of your child?" I finally asked.

"What of her? You've seen her a thousand times, spoken to her almost as many."

My brow crinkled in confusion.

"'Tis Rintinau, Longinus."

My mouth must have dropped agape, for she laughed again.

"You never suspected?" she asked astonished.

"Why should I? That first day at the lake with you, I

asked you directly if she was your daughter. You said 'no,'" I answered, feeling utterly foolish. I thought about both of them. On some level, I suppose I knew. "Why did you lie? Why did you never tell me?"

"As I believe I told you then, she is what you call a Vestal. 'A Vestal Virgin,' as a Roman would call her. She was chosen at birth by the Druids. Once a girl-child enters into the service of The Light, The Temple, she is no longer the child of a man and a woman, but a divine child-being of the Goddess. From that point on, we neither speak nor think of her in terms of 'our child'. That is the way of it." explained Camaroon. "So, I told you the truth."

"I see," I said. "And her father. Her human father?" I asked, trying to smile.

"He was killed in the battles preceding your arrival. We were never close. In fact, Rintinau was begotten in a ritual designed solely for the purpose of bringing into being a new 'Vestal' servant to the Great Goddess."

"How...that is, why the two of you?" I couldn't help asking.

"We had both been servants to the Goddess in the Temple. Rintun, that was his name, was a powerful Druid, but equally, a powerful warrior. A rare combination. There were several other factors, too—our ancestral paths and so on," she finished, rising from the sleeping pallet. She stared back at the pallet for a moment, letting go, I could feel, of her distant past, and shifting her thoughts to us once again. "So you see, Longinus, it is not with me you will beget a child to continue your bloodline. And it is obvious the time has come for me to move forward so that you may move forward." With that, she turned and resumed gathering her things.

I still knelt at the pallet. I came partially to my feet, turned and sat down on the pallet where Camaroon had been a moment before. "Where will you go?" I asked.

"To Rintun's family's lodge," she said matter-of-factly.

"I thought you said you and he were never close?"

"We were not. But his sisters and I were. Besides, Celts

take care of their own. You don't have to be blood to be sheltered for a time or taken in as family. We foster out our children all the time, for instance, allowing them to be raised by another member of the community, and not just in the sense of service to the Goddess as with Rintinau, but ordinary folks do it. They foster their children with some other member of the village. Almost all of our children are raised by the whole community. You've seen that. I could stay with Rintun's sisters forever, but I'll build my own dwelling soon enough." Obviously she'd thought this through.

"I see," I replied. She continued to gather things and I continued to watch in silence. In silence, that is, until I began to hear a slight, quiet rattling, as if something close by were vibrating against a piece of wood. I knew what it was. I went to a spot against the wall near the pallet, pulled back the long vertical panel of wood I'd carved out, and saw that the spear was indeed vibrating slightly, its tip aglow. I took it out of its hiding place and headed for the entrance, knowing full well that it was indeed time for me to move on into the future.

I stopped before leaving and faced Camaroon one last time. "I wish you well. I wish you prosperity in all things. I wish you long life and happiness. Thank you for all that you've given me: your mind, your knowledge, your love. I will always remember you. Please remember me, too," I finished.

"I will, Longinus. How could I ever forget you," she said smiling.

We kissed then; a final, passionate embrace; a remembrance of that which once was, but would be no more.

I left my lodge then. When I came back three hours later, all traces of her were gone. I never saw her again.

~XIX~

I spent the next few weeks in contemplation, and service to the village. The travelers had made themselves at home, joining in, for the most part, with the community's daily activities. The day finally came, though, when Thomas announced that the group would be leaving the next morning.

Irena and I had hardly spoken to each other during the whole time she had been here. We had exchanged pleasantries and courtesies, pretensions more accurately, but that was all.

Instead of going to the lodge of her ex-sister-by-marriage, Camaroon had left the village entirely. She had told no one of her plans, not even Rintinau. As a result of that and the gossipers of the community, some of the folks in the village cast a disapproving eye at me, and more subtly, so as not to offend our guests outright, at Irena. I believed this was why Irena had kept her distance from me; she was merely being diplomatic, not wanting to give offense overtly to any of the villagers.

But the time for her leave-taking had come. She made it clear that she was going to fulfill her promise and see Mary and Sara all the way to their destination. I had made a decision as well: I was going with them.

The evening meal was being held in the Great Hall, as it had come to be known. It was a fairly large round wooden structure, complete with a beamed roof. The Hall had been used for feasts and celebrations, as well as village meetings, for as long as most folks could remember. The villagers had not used it for a long, long time, however; for it had been the sight of bloody executions by Draco at the time of his short-lived rise to power. Many had wanted it burned to the ground, but Detrom convinced all to let it stand. With a ritual for cleansing and a rite aiding the remaining tormented spirits of those who had been killed there, the Hall was purified, and once again became a lively place for the people. What better way to counteract death in a place than to celebrate life there.

The meal turned into a feast to celebrate the group that would be leaving. Most of the villagers were in attendance. I, too, made my way there.

The sun had long set by the time I went to the Hall. The night was calm, cool and bright with a rising full moon, but the Hall inside was noisy, hot and slightly dim with smoke. The cooking fires were in the center of the large room, and smoke was doing its best to escape out the small hole in the center of the roof, but for the moment, more of the cloudy substance appeared to be staying in the Hall than not. The celebrants didn't seem to mind, though, for they were boisterously oblivious to it.

In Rome, for meals such as this, it was customary for everyone to be seated on cushions on the ground in front of several low tables piled with food and drink. Such was the way in the Great Hall. Jacobi and Irena sat with Mary and the child, Sara, Detrom and Thomas sat with Dosameenor and Dosameenor's brother Renaulus, and several of the Hebrew guards the group had traveled with. The guards were not armed; no one was allowed weapons in the Hall—not even Dosameenor and Renaulus—but they still wore their military-type tunics denoting their station in the group.

The Hebrew guards eyed me curiously, with a twinge of anticipation as I approached the table. They glanced periodically at my side. Clearly, they were hoping to see the spear. I probably could have brought it; the spear would be the only weapon exempt from the rule concerning arms in the Hall, but I had not. It was back at the lodge in its paneled hiding spot. The guards took note that they probably would not see the famed lance that evening and went back to their meal, albeit, obviously disappointed.

"Longinus, my good man," Detrom said, as I stopped in front of the table. "You've come out to join us. Please, sit." He moved over slightly on his cushion to make room.

"Yes, my friend!" exclaimed a slightly inebriated Dosameenor.

I was about to decline. I simply wanted to announce my intent to travel with the group. I thought better of it, however. "Thank you," I said and sat between Detrom and Jacobi, the old man smiling at me in that knowing way of his, probably reading my mind, my intentions.

A goblet of mead was placed in front of me, then a platter of meat and cheese. I drank the mead and nibbled on the cheese, somewhat lost in my own thoughts.

"You have something to tell us, do you not?" asked Jacobi.

I looked at him and smiled. "Indeed," I began, and turned my attention to Thomas, The Learned, as many of his people called him. This was my first face-to-face meeting with the man. I had only seen him from a distance these past weeks. A handsome face, he had. An ample shock of red-brown hair mixed with grey waved from atop his head, and a bright red beard, somewhat trimmed, adorned his cheeks and neck. Topping off his facial hair was a not-so-red mustache. It was dark brown, also with streaks of grey. His eyes were a piercing watery brown. They had that same type of depth as did Jacobi's eyes and Detrom's and Mary's, though the latter's were definitely in a class alone. "I intend to accompany your group on the morrow," I stated flatly.

The table fell silent. The sounds of the feasting impinged themselves on us with deafening loudness. The faces of those in my company seemed to be frozen, though why or with what I could not tell. No one really expected me to stay here forever. Perhaps it was because of the way I said it; as a matter-of-fact, no negotiation on the subject. I saw Dosameenor and Renaulus exchange a glance.

Thomas, though, was the first to recover. "Delightful!" he exclaimed. "Yes, indeed, you would be most welcome. Is that not so, ladies?" he inquired, directing his attention to Mary and Irena.

Mary smiled. "Why, certainly. How wonderful."

Irena smiled, too. She looked deeply into my eyes, deep into my soul; the deepest since our reunion on the day of her arrival.

And I looked deeply into her soul, as well. There was something there that she was attempting to conceal. Was it joy? Yes, I believe it was.

"But you have made a home here, Longinus," Mary continued. "The people will surely want you to stay. Are you sure that journeying with us is what you wish that you do it for the reasons of your spirit?"

What she was really asking was whether or not I was doing it for reasons of the flesh, for Irena. My heart, certainly, and my body, perhaps, belonged with Irena, 'twas true. Yet, it was my higher soul that was telling me that I must go with them. Whatever awaited, whatever my ultimate destiny, it was much bigger than just Irena and I. I had given much thought to what Camaroon had told me the night she left; what she had said about my Prophecies. I had even tried to ask Detrom about them; about exactly what I said the night of my Initiation. He would not speak of it, echoing part of what Camaroon had said: that it was for me and me alone.

My thoughts had drifted on the topic for a few days, but in the end, I let it go. If I were going to have a child eventually, that would carry my blood to far away lands and change the world, then the event of my coming together with this child's mother would play out in its own time and with whom it was supposed to. The only conclusion I had come to in the past weeks was that it was time to leave the village, and it was appropriate to do so with Irena's group.

"Yes," I finally said. "I've thought much and meditated much. It is time to go. Besides, I was once a Centurion. You could use an extra man at arms.

"Ah, but I thought you were more Druid now, a priestly man, a man of peace," commented Thomas.

"Aye, 'tis true, he is that" interjected Renaulus, slurring his words slightly. "But once a warrior, always a warrior.

Besides, a man of peace is only at peace when all agree to be at peace. But one must always be on guard. Is that not so my friend?" he inquired, addressing the question to me.

"Well," I began, but stopped. I had come to respect Dosameenor's brother. I even had feelings of fondness for him. But he was a simple man. He was a warrior and thought like a warrior and only a warrior. "'Tis true that one must always practice awareness, Renaulus," I answered vaguely, which only seemed to confuse the man. I glanced quickly at Dosameenor and saw him hide a smile at his brother's puzzled expression.

I then turned my attention back to Thomas. "I am many things, as are we all, and I practice many things. Yes, I practice healing, meditation, the elevation of my soul to salvation and enlightenment. And, I also still practice the art of war. It is a necessary evil," I finished. I had indeed kept up my skills with sword and spear, drilling with Dosameenor and his brother and their men on a semi-regular basis. My body was not, however, in the type of military shape that it had been in the past. No matter.

"I understand," replied Thomas. "We all have many layers, and I, too, practice salvation even in turbulent and violent situations."

"What does that mean—salvation?" Renaulus interrupted. "Salvation from what? I'm no sinner like you people believe."

"That is not what we believe, my friend," Thomas said gently.

"But you are Jews, are you not?" Renaulus asked harshly, yet with sincerity, not contempt. Anyone just joining us would have thought that Renaulus was becoming belligerent with Thomas. But he wasn't. Renaulus' way was simply gruff, even when he was not angry. It could be frightening at first until one got to know this bear of a man.

"Most of us in the group are Hebrew, yes, but many of us practice what is becoming known as a 'Philosophy of Knowing' or a 'Gnostic Philosophy,' as it is called in Greek," explained Thomas. "Part of the philosophy is the belief that the only definition of sin is that it is a missing of the mark, so to speak. That to not heed to one's higher soul is the only sin; that there is nothing intrinsically wrong with drawing all one's attention to things of this world, it just means that one will stay in this physical realm longer. That in and of itself is the punishment, if you really must label something as a punishment," finished Thomas.

"But I love it here! I love women! I love battle! I love food and drink!" countered Renaulus, hoisting his goblet of mead, slopping some of its contents onto the table.

"So you do," put in Detrom. We all laughed. "Our friend is merely saying that that is fine and good and garners no such thing as punishment in and of itself. But the greater joy and higher purpose of your soul is to realize its divine nature and turn to it to lift you to your highest possibilities. I believe your Jesu conveyed this belief," continued Detrom, glancing at Thomas.

Thomas nodded sagely.

"And that can only happen," Detrom went on, speaking again to Renaulus, "through your own awareness and learning and contemplation, not by any set of rules which are imposed from without by someone else."

"Precisely," added Thomas.

Poor Renaulus fell silent. A new and much more profound expression of confusion furrowed his brow.

Dosameenor clapped him on the shoulder. "Fear not, my brother. These things will come to you in time. If not in this life, in the next one, then, or the one after that, or the one after that!" he laughed. He then looked at me in all seriousness. "I go with you, Longinus."

I did not know what to say. I thought for sure that he would want to stay with his people. I looked to Mary and Thomas almost expecting a negative response. But they were simply smiling, awaiting my reply to my friend. I then looked at Jacobi.

"Yes, Longinus. I go with you, too. I am, by the One God, still your servant." He smiled affectionately.

"You are no such thing. You may do as you please and you know it," I replied.

"And I please to go with you. Besides, someone has to watch out for you. And, as always, that duty falls to me," he said jestingly in the manner of a frustrated parent, inciting another round of laughter.

"So be it," I said, looking from him to Dosameenor.

"Good," replied Thomas.

Mary began to rise. "Please excuse us, but Sara and I must retire. It is good to have you with us, Longinus," she said.

Irena also rose to leave. "I will say good night, as well."

"We will see you all at the dawn," said Mary to those of us remaining at the table.

"To the dawn," toasted Dosameenor. We all raised our goblets as the women nodded in acknowledgement and retreated from the hall.

~XX~

The morning came quickly. I was up with the Druids performing a rite to welcome the returning sun, the "Disc Of Life," as they called it, or "Amon Ra," as Hentapas called it, and to secure blessings for safe travels. The morning ritual was performed outside of the mists enshrouding the village, on the eastern high ridge of the valley. This was only one of a handful of times I had participated in the dawn rite. I don't really know why I had not joined in more often. Perhaps I simply was not an early riser, although, my military career would argue otherwise.

Looking down toward the valley floor and the village, the protective mists enshrouding the community seemed thinner this day than they usually did. A feeling of foreboding passed through my being at the thought, though I could not put my finger on what caused it. Detrom and the others would surely keep the mists strong after I had gone. Reports now came back with every scout sent out; the Romans were everywhere.

For the journey, I wore my Centurion cuirass, but I wore it underneath the robes and cape of a Celtic elder. I abandoned my Roman sandals, something I was loath to do, and donned traditional Celtic warrior footwear: sturdy leather boots. They bit into my feet, but would do for the time being.

To further cover my Romanness, I even allowed my beard to come in a little. I had been doing that for several weeks, since Irena and the others had arrived. I suppose that a part of me knew I'd be going with them when they left, even before I actually realized it, and thus started to conceal my identity as Centurion Longinus. I kept it quite trimmed, however. I refused to give up all semblances of being civilized.

Detrom and some others had given me a horse, a large

and magnificent beast by the name of Macha, the Celtic Goddess of War. The horse was indeed powerful and full of life and rage, traits usually reserved for steeds of war, yes, but steeds of war were also usually male. She warmed to my touch from the first, though. A good match we were.

Mounted on Macha, I came to the center of the village after breaking my fast with some of my fellow travelers. There were many people there, and much activity had been underway; seeing to last minute provisions by the men and so forth. Irena, Mary and Sara, however, were nowhere to be seen.

Jacobi was mounted on a horse of his own, an ancient mare about half the size of Macha. "It appears your mount has seen the light of a few summers," I couldn't help but tease.

"Yes, yes, she has indeed. But let not the wrinkles of time fool you, or the fool you will become!" he quipped. "She has many summers and miles left in her."

"No doubt, no doubt," I said, standing corrected. "Have you seen Irena?"

"She was here mere moments ago. That is her chariot and provisions there," he said, pointing to the large four-wheeled wagon-type vehicle some twenty-feet away. It had the appearance of a large, extended chariot and was drawn by two strong horses who waited patiently, already harnessed to the wagon. The vehicle was laden with provisions and covered. The covering was over a frame that rose a few feet into the air to conceal contents and to comfortably, more or less, seat passengers. It almost reminded me of some wagons I had seen Roman royalty transported in across vast distances, except without all the pretentious accoutrements and silk trappings, and refinements in drapery.

Just then, I saw the child, Sara, crawl out from the covered portion onto the back of the wagon. "Please stay with me, Sara," came Mary's calm, tinkling voice as she, too, appeared at the back to retrieve the errant child. Sara simply giggled at the game as her mother wrapped her arms about the babe and pulled Sara to her body.

"It would appear that Sara is anxious to go," I observed to Mary.

"Good morning, Longinus. Yes, I believe most of us are," she replied. She glanced down at my horse's side. There, in its sheathing, was the spear. The blade itself was well hidden. Only the shaft protruded out of its nest. Nonetheless, she knew what it was. Her eyes lingered only for the briefest of instances before returning to me. "And you, are you anxious to be away?"

"It's time, yes."

"You've much history here. And, you've learned much and progressed much to know the Truth, have you not?" she asked, as she looked into my eyes.

Sara was staring intently at me as well, as if she too awaited my response; as if she, too, would weigh my answer.

Foolish, Longinus, I thought. No one was waiting to judge me, but me. "Yes, to all. But, as I said, it is time for me to move on."

"Indeed it is," said a familiar voice. I looked down to see Detrom standing beside Macha, patting her flanks with affection. Behind Detrom, sitting atop their mounts were Dosameenor, Romi and Hentapas. Paulonius, too, was with them, but on foot, holding a small shaggy horse of the hills, by its long mane. Most Celts did not ride with stirrups or reigns, and only rarely with saddles, preferring instead to ride bareback and using the animal's mane as the main control and command device. Paulonius had taken to this form of riding. There was another animal behind Paulonius' little horse that looked just like the first one. The latter was loaded up with supplies. I simply took note of the lad, his horses and the others, then turned my attention back to the High Druid.

"Detrom. I'm so glad to see you," I said as I dismounted. Truth was, I was glad to see all of them. Though Detrom was staying, I was not sure until that moment if the others—Romi, Hentapas and Paulonius—were actually going to come with me. I had given them all leave to stay if they wished it. More than one of them had become involved with the local women over the course of our stay here. Paulonius, in particular, had become attached to a fetching lass with the most beautiful emerald eyes and flowing auburn hair I had ever seen.

That same fetching lass suddenly appeared, stepping out from the other side of Paulonius' horse. She was in full travel attire. Obviously, she was coming, too. I looked from the lass to Paulonius, who was turning all shades of red, and seemed completely at a loss for words. Ah, the idealistic impulsiveness of youth! Would that we all retain that quality as time marched on. But then again, perhaps that would not be such a good idea.

"He was too afraid to speak to you last night," said the lass.

Sixteen summers, I judged her to be, and brash, but in a cute and charming way. Hopefully, that would not turn to a sour way as she aged. "I see," I replied, in a non committal tone.

"So, I will speak in his stead," she said with nervous determination.

I put my hands up in mock surrender. "Wait," I said. "There is no need to speak of anything. You already have made your decision to accompany us as evidenced by your clothing. There are no restrictions as far as I'm concerned, as to who comes with us. Thomas voiced the same. So, there is nothing to say. Paulonius has leave to do as he wishes. If that is to bring you along, then so be it. The rest is up to your people."

"Yes, sir," she said looking surprised. She obviously had been expecting to meet with resistance.

"But," I continued, "you will serve the needs of the group. What can you offer?"

"I make and repair weapons: arrows, bows, lances," she said, looking at my spear shaft on Macha as she stated this last information. She glanced back at a pair of proud people, a man and woman, standing just beyond our group. "My mother and father taught me," she said, indicating the two. "They have been the village's armorers for many, many summers."

"We hope not to need those services."

"Even so, we may. But, I can also cook and..."

"All right," I said, laughing. "We are glad to have you, as I know Paulonius is."

"Thank you, sir," she said.

"Just one more thing. Your name?" I asked.

Paulonius opened his mouth to speak, but was beaten to it by the lass.

"My name is Genevieves, The Seventh," she replied.

"Carry on, Genevieves, The Seventh. You too, Paulonius," I said, and smiled. They both darted away with their beasts of burden before I could change my mind.

I looked at Detrom and we both laughed.

Jacobi sided up to us then.

"Ah, I am going to miss you, my friends," Detrom said, looking from Jacobi to me.

"And we you, High Druid Detrom," replied Jacobi.

"Yes, indeed," I said.

"Yes. I will, however, look in on you from time to time in the waters of the lake, Master Longinus, and in the light of the sacred flame. In that way, I will still be with you. Open your heart to me. Open your mind and spirit to me, always, both of you, and I will commune with you on the planes of the Otherworld, and impart any information to you that I can, whether of the mundane or of tantamount import," Detrom finished.

"So be it," I replied.

"So it is," said Jacobi.

"And, one more parting gift for you both," Detrom said, handing Jacobi and me each a beautiful and intricately carved gold broach. On the circular portion was the image of the mighty oak tree surrounded by the swirling knot-work which represented the eternal journey of spirit. In the center of the tree was a delicately carved image that looked like a snake, a serpent, which symbolized the Highest Wisdom, as well as the office of the High Druid. Even the pin that went through the middle of the broach to fasten it to one's cloak was intricately carved with the knot-swirls.

"Detrom..." I began, astounded by the gift, even more so than the gift of Macha.

Jacobi had dismounted and was embracing the High Druid. "Thank you, my friend, but I also sense that there is a practicality to this as well," said the old one.

"Indeed," smiled Detrom. "I know not what you will find, how many of us, the Druids, there are truly left throughout Gallia. But we are here and always will be. These will show that you come from and represent the office of the Highest Druidic authority in the land, should you need to show it. But beware, for it may also be your undoing should the wrong eyes land upon it."

"Thank you," I said.

"Yes. Thank you. And your warning is duly noted," said Jacobi, gingerly remounting his mare.

Thomas and Irena and Dosameenor finally arrived then, arms loaded with the last of the supplies.

I caught Irena's eye and smiled.

She smiled back, a loving glint in her eye.

So began our trek out of the village and out of the valley of the mists.

~XXl~

Our first three days of travel were relatively uneventful. The worst thing that happened was that one of the mares pulling Mary's chariot-wagon broke an ankle and had to be killed. The poor beast simply took a bad step, lodging a fore hoof in a forest rodent's large hole. She panicked and began to buck wildly in her harness, kicking the wooden panel behind her: the panel in front of the driver's platform. It splintered the panel and knocked the driver to the floorboards, unhurt, thankfully.

But the mare was not so lucky. The force from her hind leg kicks against the panel completely shifted her whole body weight to her front legs and beyond, toppling her over onto her muzzle. Of course, the stuck fore leg could not budge, and with the beast's momentum hurtling forward, it snapped at the ankle.

Howling sheiks of pain tore from the animal, causing all of us within earshot to grimace in sympathy. I had witnessed the whole incident and instantly gave the order to slash the mare's throat. I hated to do that, but allowing it to suffer was crueler.

It was strange; watching one of Thomas' guards carry out my order; I caught myself looking away. Was I squeamish just then? No, mournful is more accurate. I had come to fully appreciate life in all its forms. This horse had been a faithful servant. She had worked unconditionally, yet met with a tragic end.

Some would say that I was attaching too much value to the beast. It was, after all, simply an animal; a dumb beast of burden. But I had come to believe that all of life was sacred. All of life was sacred, and all of life carried on after this existence in some form. Detrom and Jacobi believed that we come back here again and again to learn and learn, until our souls have learned enough and move on. I was still not sure if I held with them in that thought. But if it were so, would this animal also come back here again? Did that mean it, too, had a soul? On that point, as well, I still debated with myself. I did believe that something of the animal's spirit carried on, though, so better to release it from its suffering here and now.

I do not think that I would wax so philosophical over killing a man again, however. I had killed many in the past under the guise of duty and, I confess, simply out of the blood-lust of battle frenzy, even enjoying the act at the time. I was different now, 'twas true. As I said, I now valued all life; saw the God-Spirit in all men and women. We are all brothers and sisters in The Great Light, as the Druids call it.

But men make choices. Quite often, they are choices that consciously and purposely bring harmful consequences upon others. They must be met with equally harmful, even savage, repercussions. But I did not believe that I would seek out battle and death, any longer, as a matter of stately duty or war, or for some other idealistic reasons.

I would, however, brutally defend myself and those close to me, and in that context, I would have no inhibitions whatsoever in killing a man. In spite of my Druidic studies of natural laws and spiritual principles and Godly Truths, I was still a soldier on many levels. I did not believe, as many did, and more were coming to believe, that a path of spiritual study and practice, and a soldier's life were incompatible. How could they be if everything came from the One?

We left the mare for the forest beasts and carrion animals to feast upon. Life's circle. We thought briefly about cutting up the carcass and taking it with us, but decided against it. We had not the time or inclination to prepare the meat properly for travel: to dry it and salt it for preservation, not to mention storing it. Besides, no one really wanted to eat horse meat when we had plenty of venison, goat meat and beef on hand.

Toward the end of the third day, a short while before

we stopped to make camp, I was hailed from behind by a familiar voice. "Longinus," she said, approaching me on foot.

I halted, and spun my mount around, not because of any urgency in Irena's voice, but because I was at last, apparently, going to get the chance to speak with her. I confess to resentment in minute proportions directed toward Mary for her coveting of Irena's time and services. Of course, it was all by Irena's choice. She did nothing against her will and took orders from no one.

I dismounted and stood stiffly at Macha's side, nervously stroking her flank as Irena came to stand before me. Although, Camaroon had had the ability to make me feel like a school boy on occasion, that paled as compared to what I was feeling now: sweaty palms and an eagle's wings flapping in my stomach. Even the spear in its sheathing was vibrating slightly, not as a sign of danger, but simply in empathy with my state of being at Irena's appearance. Macha, too, sensed my nervousness, for she craned her neck and looked back at me as if to say, "silly man."

Control yourself, Longinus, I thought.

Irena stood silently before me.

"Hello," I finally managed.

"Hello," she replied, her own nervousness evident in her voice.

Awkward silence filled the space around us for a moment. I took that time to simply drink in her beauty. I had almost forgotten how lovely she was. Oh, I had seen her at the village, of course, but it was only now that I allowed myself to take her in without inhibition, without censure of myself.

"I..." we both said simultaneously.

The shell had been cracked. We laughed together with the ease of two souls a long time attached, all the awkwardness fallen away. I reached out and touched her hand, caressing it gently. I then pulled her close, embracing her, while looking into her eyes, as she looked into mine. After a moment, we both became aware of other eyes; some of the others in our traveling train were watching us, smiles on their faces as they hiked along.

"Come," I said as I took Irena by the hand and stepped away from the horse. Macha would stay in place, nibbling on the green grass at her hooves. I led Irena into a nearby stand of trees. We stepped behind an oak, out of view.

Pent-up passion spewed forth from our beings; our bodies intertwined as if we could mold ourselves into one person. Our mouths found their counterpart; our tongues also intertwining in a dance of love, lust, longing and spirit. Just kissing her made me feel a oneness with creation that I had never known. I think it had always been that way with her. I was simply just now realizing it.

I wanted her, right then and there; body, mind and spirit. A soft moan escaped her lips as my hand drifted down and over her breasts to her hips, searching, in part, for the opening to her mantle.

She pulled away slightly, but I continued the search with my hand, as well as kissing her neck. "Longinus," she whispered out of breath.

I stopped and looked at her.

"We must wait 'til tonight at least, when we're at camp. I'm sorry I've waited so long to come to you," she said, "but we can wait a little longer. I... I actually wanted to find you just now to ask your help in securing another horse for Mary's wagon."

I looked at her, dumbfounded. She could not be serious.

We both suddenly burst into laughter.

"Well," Irena continued when our laughter subsided, "that's what I told myself and Mary. Mary just smiled and nodded. She knew." Irena paused then, and looked at me lovingly. "Oh, Longinus," she said. "My Longinus, my Gaius."

"Yes, my love. I am yours. But you've never used my family name, so don't start now," I admonished teasingly. "And you're right. We will wait 'til tonight. But no longer!" I added, only half joking.

I took her hand once more and we walked out of the

stand of oaks back to Macha. The others had moved off up the road.

I mounted Macha and held my hand out to Irena. "Come," I said. "Ride with me."

Hesitation splashed across her face. I knew that it was not Macha she feared, but what others might think upon seeing us together. Ultimately, though, it mattered not what anyone else thought and she knew it. Besides, most of those who traveled with us knew that Irena and I had a history, so why would they be surprised to see us together? She took my hand and leapt up as I pulled and swung her onto Macha's back behind me. We trotted up the road to catch the others.

Irena's arms were wrapped around my waist and after a moment, she playfully tickled my ribs. "Mary's wagon really does need another horse, you know," she said.

We caught up to the others in no time. Once again, smiles greeted us as we rode through the group to catch Mary's vehicle. The group overall had a couple of supply wagons, but Mary's was easy to spot. In addition to the fine draperies covering it, one solitary mare now labored to pull the laden chariot-wagon. Mary and Thomas both walked beside the vehicle, in an attempt to help ease the animal's burden. The effort only produced a minimal relief for the beast.

I was still unsure of what exactly was being carried in Mary's wagon; supplies for Mary, Sara, Thomas and a few others, certainly. But it was too large for just supplies. Something else was in there, too. I gathered, from overhearing bits of conversations, that it was a fairly sizable item, significant in a personal, mystical sense. Neither Mary nor Thomas would reveal precisely what it was, and I don't believe Irena knew any more than I did. It was a genuine curiosity, but I left it at that and respected their wish for privacy on the matter.

We arrived at the chariot-wagon and I halted Macha briefly, so that Irena could slide off and rejoin Mary and Thomas as the entire company kept moving.

"Well, well," Thomas began playfully.

He was prevented from continuing the thought, however, by a none-too-light elbow jab to the ribs. Mary retracted her elbow quickly and gave Thomas a look which said, That's enough out of you! She turned to Irena and said, "Sara sleeps. You needn't have come back so soon, you know."

Irena paused for a moment, not quite sure how to respond to that. "Thank you," she finally said with slight embarrassment. "If that's the case," she said turning to me, "perhaps we could find that other horse now."

"Uh...oh, yes," I stammered, caught off guard. "Let's go find Paulonius. I think he and—Genevieves, isn't it? I think they would spare one of their animals for a time."

"Splendid!" exclaimed Mary.

I turned and addressed Thomas. "We should make camp soon," I said, glad to change subjects. 'Twas true, though. The sun was dropping quickly. The road we had followed thus far was surrounded by green grasses and meadows interspersed with stands and groves of pines and oaks. But aside from the small stand of oaks that Irena and I had ducked into briefly, we had not seen many clumps of trees this day. 'Tis better to make camp hidden among trees than exposed in an open meadow. But either way, we needed to stop soon.

"Agreed," replied Thomas, his tone all business this time. "The scouts have just reported a large grove about two miles up the road. We'll stop there. We should reach Alesia by midday on the morrow."

"So be it," I said. Turning to Irena, I held out my hand for her to once again vault onto Macha's back; then we trotted off in search of Paulonius and Genevieves.

"Has Thomas or Mary revealed to you why we must first go to Alesia?" I asked after a moment.

"No," she answered. "But it's something to do with what they carry. That much I'm sure of."

The community that Mary and Thomas wanted to eventually reach was well west of the village we had left, just outside of Jubionyus. The community, which apparently did not have a name as of yet, was comprised of Hebrew outcasts, as well as others, who had formed a growing sect called Gnostics; the same sect, at least in thought, that Thomas, himself, belonged to. Yet, for shrouded reasons, we were first heading north to Alesia—the famed location in which Vercingretorix (the first and last unifier of Gaul) surrendered to the great Caesar—then traveling west, southwest to Jubionyus.

An hour and a half later, and with the mighty sun disk just sinking over the horizon, we came to the grove of trees and made camp. I helped many put their shelters together. I had shown them how to put together a quick, temporary one in the manner of a legionnaire, but some were a bit slow to grasp it. I then set up my own, making it clean and spacious in the hopes that Irena would indeed be able to join me later.

We had found Paulonius quickly enough before making camp. He was quite amiable to giving up one of his horses for Mary's use when I asked him to. I think there was a part of him that was still grateful to me for allowing Genevieves to join us. Then again, seeing the way they interacted now, I was not sure that he should be grateful; she was quite the bossy one.

Irena had taken the beast back to Mary. I had not seen her since. Paulonius had come by my shelter to see if I needed anything, which I did not, and a while later, Jacobi brought me food: oatcakes and venison. He stayed while I ate and we chatted. I brought out the spear at one point during our conversation, as we were talking of the healings and seemingly magical energies that came through this weapon, this instrument. As if it knew we were speaking of it, its blade began to glow, pulsating ever so slightly.

But that was incorrect, for I began to sense that there was another reason it vibrated. An ominous wave of foreboding washed over me. It was momentary, brief, and then it was gone at the same instant the blade stopped glowing.

Jacobi, too, had seen the blade glow and observed my reaction. "Longinus, what did you see?" he queried. "What did you feel?"

"I...I know not," I replied, still trying to decipher what I had sensed.

"Be still. Breathe deeply. Let the feelings, the images, whatever, come through unfiltered, uncensored," Jacobi said, guiding me to that higher place within.

I did as the old man bade. I stilled my mind, breathed in and released and then saw it in my mind's eye: fire, violence death, all in the near future, and two figures that I took to be nemeses, though I could not tell whether they were foes of ours or someone else's. Such is the nature of visions; clarity is illusive at best. I conveyed what I'd seen to Jacobi.

"We must be vigilant," he said.

"We are always vigilant. Besides, I did not sense that the victims were of our group," I replied.

"Regardless, we must be especially watchful. I will speak to Thomas." Jacobi stood up gradually, his old bones slowing of late, and walked out.

I sat in silence for a moment. Then, I thought about seeking out Irena, but decided against it. If she were busy with Mary and Sara, then I would be intruding. So, I sat on my sleeping pallet with the spear, the lance, across my lap, closed my eyes and began to meditate on the vision I'd just had, as well as my own place in the vision and everything else.

I was drifting in an ethereal realm of the mind. The Mind in which all creation is one. During this meditation, no new information on the vision I had came through. Nothing. So, I instead focused on achieving a deeper connection with my Inner Self. In the process, many Divine Masters, so to speak, Jesu among them, appeared to me, spoke with me, imparting knowledge to me, to my soul.

Perhaps it was all just my imagination, these visions of Divine Masters and the conversations with them; a way of escaping. Sometimes, I had trouble believing in all of the mysterious and mystical experiences I had since the night of the Wickermen. I had not doubted them while I was still in the village and near Detrom and the Druids. But now that I was away from them all, back in the real world, all of those experiences just seemed a bit...unreal. I had even voiced my feelings to Jacobi. But he had just laughed and called my doubting natural and good.

"'Tis only natural. Questioning things is always good. But you know in your soul what the truth of it is," he had said.

Another figure came into my mind during this meditation: Irena. She was suddenly floating with me in this realm of Mind. It was her spirit, her soul.

This did not feel as though it was a conjuring of my imagination. Her soul was there with me in that moment; I knew it, I felt it. Our minds, our beings suddenly merged as one; two souls, one mind. The sensation was overwhelming. I welled up with emotion, with happiness, with, with...

My eyes flew open. I was back in my shelter, sitting on the pallet with the lance still lying across my lap. Five feet in front of me, sitting on a stool, was Irena in the flesh. I had no awareness of her coming in. Her eyes were closed, so I simply watched her for a moment.

Her eyes came open. A smile slowly grew on her face; a smile to melt a snow-capped peak.

"That was simply..." I stammered.

"...Wondrous," she finished.

"Yes. You were with me in my meditation, on the..." I wasn't sure how to say it; how to put into words where it was we had been; what had happened.

"I was." She paused for a moment. "I...came in, to your shelter, I mean, a while ago," she continued. I was going to call to you from outside, but something told me not to; to just come in and join you."

"I'm glad you listened to that 'something,'" I replied.

We stared at each other then, each silently reliving that moment of disembodied oneness. As we did this, a connection began to reveal itself; a tugging sensation began in my chest. I physically reached out to Irena and drew her to me. We lay on the sleeping pallet, she atop me, chest to chest. The tugging sensation grew. It was as if a rope, a line of energy, connected our hearts and the sacred energy center there; the most powerful of the seven in the body as taught by the Druids.

She moaned slightly. "Do you feel that, Longinus?" she asked nearly breathless.

"Yes," I replied, equally breathless.

Our chests were touching. In addition to the tugging, I could feel her heartbeat. It was my heartbeat. Our pulse was exactly the same. As in the meditation, suddenly, there was no Irena. There was no Longinus. We were one being.

Soon, our oneness of spirit broadened to include oneness of body. We loved; our bodies joined together in one explosion after another. Then we talked. She told me everything that had happened to her since last we saw each one another, and I shared all of my experiences with her. Then, we made love again, and again, 'til almost dawn.

Shortly before the sun rose, we finally collapsed from exhaustion, falling into each other's arms. Our eyes grew heavy, but sleep would not come. For, it was then that we heard the first screams of terror.

~XXII~

Irena and I bolted awake and out of my shelter as soon as we heard the first scream, our night of passion all but forgotten for the moment.

The camp was in chaos. Animals were running in panic, their owners doing their best to control them. But the chaos was not caused directly by any outside source; we were not being overrun by an enemy. The chaos apparently had been caused by the panic of the animals, mainly horses, and the screams of terror had come from two women who had been trampled in the process.

One had a partially crushed leg; the other, surprisingly, only a single cracked rib. Dosameenor had the men already about, gathering the animals back together and aiding in the restoring of calm. Thomas was in the midst of it all as well, lending whatever help he could. Jacobi was tending to the wounded women near a fire pit—who apparently had been trampled while piling wood for the morning cooking fires—and waved me over. Irena and I ran to where he was and I knelt next to him.

"These woman need your healing touch, Longinus," said Jacobi.

I hesitated. In my desire to get out of the shelter, I had forgotten the spear, something I had not often done. I was about to voice the fact that I needed to get the lance when Irena suddenly held it out to me.

"Thought you might want this," she said slyly. She had come out of the tent-shelter right behind me, right on my heels, yet had the presence of mind to grab the spear on the way out. Seeing her there holding the spear, I was instantly catapulted back to the time when I had nearly knocked her out when she attempted to touch the thing. Guilt flashed briefly though my mind over that. But that was then, and now it was more than appropriate that she held it.

"Thank you," I managed. I took it from her and turned to Jacobi. "I can't heal a smashed bone, Jacobi." The woman's leg was nearly flattened at the shin of her left leg. A mass of blood, skin, tissue and splintered bone.

"Of course you can't, because you believe that you can't. And you don't need that to heal," he said, pointing to the lance. "Never mind. Come. Help me get them both back into their tent. We will set the bones or whatever needs to be done. You will ease their pain with your skill."

"How are you going to set that mess?" I asked, indicating the leg.

Jacobi clucked like a disappointed old hen. "Master Longinus, you really have begun to doubt things, haven't you?"

The question was rhetorical, so I didn't answer him. Instead, I gently picked up the woman, balancing her against the spear, as Irena helped the other injured woman, and took her into the nearby shelter-tent, where I placed her on a sleeping pallet.

We had just set the women down when a voice hailed me from outside. "Longinus," called Dosameenor.

I stepped back out of the tent and came face-to-face with the big Celt. "Yes, my friend."

"Don't be long. We must be under way soon," he said with a warrior's intensity. Something was happening.

"What is it?" I asked, and then realized it for myself. The smell of smoke permeated my nostrils: fire. I could see the smoke just through the trees; too much of it to be from any cooking fire. In fact, the women who were injured had not even had the chance to start our cooking fires. This was coming from somewhere well outside the grove of trees we were camped in; probably from over the next hill.

Dosameenor saw the realization dawning on my face. "Yes. The horses sensed the fires before we did and panicked. Those fires are not from anything natural. A village or town burning, if you ask me. Romans," he spat with disgust. Almost in the same instant he had said it, he became aware of the insult. "Agh, Longinus, I'm sorry. I did not mean you. And, I know I was once a legionnaire. It's just..."

I smiled and put a hand up in friendship to silence him. "Please, I take no offense. You know that."

"Very well," replied the big Celt. "As I said, we must leave soon."

"We will. Jacobi and I will help the wounded while you ready the camp to leave."

"Done," he said, and walked off to do just that.

We took care of the women's wounds. Jacobi was simply amazing. Truly a Merlin, as it were, for he seemed to have learned a great deal in the art of healing from the Druids; much more than I. He nearly reshaped the crushed part of the one woman's leg with the ease of a magician. The other one, with naught but a cracked rib, was simple enough to bind. For my part, I had simply used a calming spell or prayer—however one prefers to think of it—on the women by holding the spear's blade tip over the first woman's leg and muttering the incantation of healing and calming that Camaroon had taught me.

The incantation itself was nothing but words aimed at putting me in the right state of mind to allow certain healing energies to come through. They did. The spear tip began to glow and a warmth of energy went through my body, down the spear and into the leg. The woman winced at first, having barely maintained consciousness to begin with, but soon relaxed with her eyes closed, the pain subsiding, which allowed Jacobi to do his work. All that remained was to secure adequately comfortable transport for them, for which Mary volunteered her wagon.

The whole company, several dozen of us, were on the move again within an hour. Scouts reported back to Thomas, Dosameenor, and myself that it was indeed a village on the road to Alesia that Romans had sacked and burned. It appeared to have happened at some point deep in the night. We had not detected any smoke until dawn because the winds had been blowing in the opposite direction. I had no doubt that whatever legion was responsible for destroying the village, they were still in the area and knew of our presence. They probably were watching our every move.

Why they had not approached us was the mystery. We were a fairly sizable contingent of men, women and guards; not an army, granted, but any Roman patrol coming upon us would have stopped us, at the very least. Why then had they not done so?

Another mystery to me was why Thomas insisted that we stay on the road to Alesia. Both Dosameenor and I counseled him to go around the village and off the main road if he still wanted to take us to Alesia. But he would have none of it.

"Staying on the main road shows that we're not hiding anything," he argued.

He did have a point, but it was not a point that I shared; stealth was more of the ally that I wanted in situations like this, not trusting a potential enemy to believe my innocent intentions. But in the end, we stayed on the main road.

Irena was with Mary in her wagon helping with Sara and the two injured women. I would not see her much the rest of that day. We passed the burned village about an hour after leaving our encampment of the previous night. Many in our group turned their faces away, covering their noses and mouths to keep them from gagging at what they saw.

Perhaps it was my jadedness as soldier, but the sight was not nearly as bad as what I had been expecting. True, there were a few charred corpses on the ground, but for the most part, the village was empty. No doubt, most of the inhabitants had either been driven off or taken as slaves.

Still, my heart and soul went out to those who were slaughtered here, and whose lives had been forever altered by Romans. I was ashamed, perhaps for the first time in my life, that I was Roman-born.

Suddenly, a sound permeated the air. It was a high-pitched, rhythmic whirring sound. I thought at first it was the wind. But there was no wind. I realized that the sound was coming from within the village. I scanned the village remains for the source of the sound. There, about fifty yards in toward what looked like the center of the place, or what had been the center, was a toddler wailing with all its might.

It—she, by the looks of it—was standing next to an unburned adult female corpse. Dosameenor had been quiet, maintaining a discipline in passing by the village. But at the child's cry, he lost control of that discipline. He turned his mount toward the sound and bolted into the shell of a village.

"Dosameenor!" I called. But it was no use. The people in this village had been Celts, and Dosameenor was taking their destruction personally.

Hentapas and Romi came up next to me on their mounts. Macha was skittish under me because of the smoke and stench of death and the sudden approach of Romi and Hentapas, but stood her ground, maintaining her own discipline.

"What should we do, sir?" asked Romi.

"We shall stop and bury the dead," interjected Thomas from behind me.

I turned to see Mary and Thomas riding at the front of the chariot wagon, and pulling up to a stop next to me.

"I thought you wanted to move through this place," I said.

"I was wrong," he said, deferring to Mary.

"We cannot leave these people this way," she said, clearly having been the one to convince Thomas to have a change of heart.

But I did not agree for a couple of reasons. "I'm not sure we have the time. Also, these are Celts. They have several different customs of disposition of the dead depending on the region. You should consult Dosameenor. Furthermore, whoever did this is still in the area." I paused while she thought about that. "Besides, didn't Jesu say 'let the dead bury the dead?'" I added.

"Not the same context, Longinus," Mary said, in a near scolding tone.

"Perhaps, but you get my point."

"I do and I will ask Dosameenor, nonetheless," she replied.

We all looked in the direction of Dosameenor. He was kneeling in front of the little one. She seemed to grow calm at his presence. A moment later, she held out her arms to be hugged, and he scooped her up as if she were a feathered pillow. The little girl clutched his beard as he leaped onto his horse. The child would surely squall from fright at any moment I thought. I was wrong. Instead, she giggled, her troubles forgotten for the moment.

Mary had a smile on her face. Even in the midst of death, life can seem to magically assert itself.

Dosameenor rode straight up to us. "The other men searched the place. I fear only this one lived," he stated flatly.

"We will find a place for her," said Mary.

"No, I will care for her," Dosameenor asserted powerfully.

We were all shocked by the statement. How in the world was this man going to care for a girl of about two summers? Why would he want to?

"But..." Mary started. She stopped when she saw the look in Dosameenor's eyes. It wasn't hostility, just finality; there was no arguing the point. It would have been absurd to try. When the big Celt made up his mind about something and stated that something was a certain way, then that was it. No room for negotiation.

"So be it," Mary said. "We must bury the dead left here," she continued on, changing subjects.

"No," Dosameenor said in that tone of finality again.

"Burn them?" asked Hentapas. "Will that not alert the Romans?"

"Are we sure it was Romans?" asked Thomas.

"Who else?" answered Dosameenor. "Your own patrols

have seen them.

"Yes, Hentapas. They would probably be alerted, if they aren't already watching us. I still say we leave the dead to bury the dead," I said, looking from Dosameenor to Jacobi, the latter just joining us, his old mare hobbling up to our group very slowly, even under the old man's slight weight. I made a mental note then and there to secure a new beast for Jacobi. The poor thing he was on now looked as though it would collapse at any moment.

"Agreed," said Dosameenor.

Again, we were all left speechless at his decision. I expected Jacobi to agree with me; he had said as much in the past in similar situations. But I did not expect it from the big Celt.

"If you still wish to make it to Alesia with your precious cargo -- whatever it is—without interruption," Dosameenor continued to Thomas and Mary a little gruffly, "then we leave this place now and do not stop."

So, I thought dryly, I was not the only one who was curious about the contents of Mary's wagon.

Mary bowed her head.

Thomas stared at the big man. "So be it," he finally said.

Thomas' calculations had been off. We did not make Alesia by midday. Nor by dark fall. We made camp in a small stand of pines under a near full moon. My senses were peaked. The spear tip was even at a constant but slight glow. We were being watched. I could feel it.

I sat at the campfire. No shelters tonight. We needed to be mobile fast. All would sleep in the open, near the central fire. Even the horses pulling the wagons would remain harnessed. Hentapas, Romi, and several of Thomas' guards were at the perimeter of the camp. Dosameenor was with me, awake at the fire, the babe asleep in his arms.

"What do you call her?" I asked in a hushed tone so as not to wake the others.

"Mattea," he replied fondly.

"Mattea," I repeated. "What does it mean?"

"'Beloved,'" answered Dosameenor.

To my surprise, the big Celt was near tears. I said nothing. If he wanted to tell his tale, he would.

"I..." he began. "When we got back to my village, after the dust settled from the night of the Wickermen, I found my wife and family, or what was left of them. My wife had been raped by one of Draco's worthless followers. She had born him a bastard boy that my wife had drowned when the lad had been born.

"When Draco's man found out what she'd done, he took my only daughter, raped her and drowned her," he paused, his face crinkling with renewed agony, as if it had just happened, muffled sobs shuddering into his beard. "She was only three summers," he said when he was in full control again. "Her name had been Matteoua. It means 'Beloved of my soul.'" He paused a long while then before continuing. "You see, this little one," he said brightly, looking at Mattea, "looks a great deal like her. Same hair, same eyes..."

Yet again on this day, I was fully surprised by the man before me. I had known nothing about this. Nothing. I looked at Mattea then. She could easily pass as Dosameenor's daughter. But she wasn't. "You," I started delicately, "you know that it's not Matteoua, right?"

"Of course, you stupid Roman," laughed Dosameenor. But then he turned serious. "It is her spirit, though," he said as a matter of fact. "Her soul, you know."

I must have looked confused.

"Mattea is two summers," Dosameenor went on. "She barely walks or speaks. Matteoua was killed at three, over three summers ago."

I thought for a moment. I would not argue against the man's belief, though I could not fathom it.

"You want proof, don't you?" he challenged.

I could not deny it.

"This little one called me 'Frap-Frap,'" he said.

I shook my head, not understanding.

"So did Matteoua."

"Your first daughter called you that, too? What does it mean?" I asked, trying desperately to get my tired mind to accept what he was saying.

"That's just it. Nothing. It means nothing. It's a nonsensical pet word—a pet name Matteoua had made up. At the village today when Mattea looked right at me and said it..." he trailed off.

I could see why he would believe this little girl was the reincarnation of Matteoua. Indeed, I could almost believe it, too. I wanted to. Very well. For him, I would accept it; the little one in his lap was his daughter. Period.

We sat in silence for a few moments. I was about to ask him about the rest of his family.

He was reading my thoughts, as he spoke of it before I could ask. "My wife went mad. Demons took over her mind. She ran off into the hills two days after I had arrived home. My oldest boy had already run off to another tribe. My youngest son blamed me for it all. I had not been there to protect them, you see," he said.

"Dosameenor, you can't believe that," I offered lamely.

"I don't," he said, not very convincingly.

"Why am I just now hearing of this?" I asked. Truly, I could not understand how he had kept it quiet.

"You must understand that in our culture, if one turns his back on something, then that is all. It is never spoken of again. To do so would bring shame on your family and clan, and possible exile. Besides," he smiled, "you were...busy when we first arrived. You had exiled yourself to the quarters you'd been given, remember? This was something I dealt with and tried to put out of my mind forever. Until today."

"You are one of the bravest men I've ever known," I declared. "I'm proud to be your friend."

"And I, you," he said.

"Even though I'm Roman?" I quipped.

"Even so. Besides, you're more Druid, which is

decidedly not Roman."

Silence again fell between us.

After a few minutes, I began to drift. My eyes closed. I did not sleep, but my mind calmed and I saw things within the mind's eye—the same things, the same vision, that I had had in Jacobi's presence. Only now, I was in the middle of the visionary mayhem; a future event that I would be a part of?

Suddenly, the spear, which had been resting next to me, began to vibrate, snapping me out of my semi-trance state. After less than a minute, it stopped as suddenly as it had started. Dosameenor had also seen it.

Silence again. We both sat for a moment, trying to deduce the spear's meaning.

Then, off in the near distance, at the perimeter of the encampment, we heard a dull thump, a grunt and a thud.

They were unmistakable sounds to the trained ear; an arrow finding its mark in a man's chest, the grunt of the victim upon the arrow's impact, and the landing of the body on the ground. Our perimeter had been breached.

Dosameenor and I wasted no time. We jumped up and shouted for all to awaken at the same moment Romi was yelling from halfway between the perimeter and my location near the fire.

"To arms! To—" he called.

He was close enough that I could see the whites of his eyes and the enemy just behind him.

His call was cut short when a gladius blade pierced him from behind, the point protruding grotesquely through his front ribs. Shocked, but not frozen, Romi turned and sliced the neck of his assailant: a pimply-faced legionnaire, who crumpled to the ground like a whimpering dog, his life's blood saturating the ground. Romi turned back to me, saluted fist to chest, then fell to the ground, dead.

There was no time to think about him. Chaos was overtaking us again, this time perpetrated by a definite enemy. Legionnaires poured into the stand of trees, rapidly approaching the campfire.

But our chaos was short-lived, for everyone in our company was armed, including the women, producing weapons from within their bedding as they came awake. I was shouting orders, but it was not necessary; they all began defending themselves, fighting as a cohesive unit. It was amazing to behold. I looked to Dosameenor, who simply smiled proudly.

"You were busy before we left," I said to him.

"Indeed I was," he said, laughing. He ran with Mattea to Mary's wagon a short distance away, handing his daughter to Irena.

I caught her eye briefly before she popped back in with the child. She looked at me. Be careful, her eyes said.

Something was off. There were not as many Romans as I had thought. The group did not comprise a Century, barely a platoon. I saw no officers. All of the legionnaires were in single combat here and there. They also seemed to be fighting for an objective other than killing everyone. Many of the legionnaires were fighting to incapacitate their opponent, but not delivering a death blow. Instead, they would shake off the one they were fighting and move toward one objective: Mary's wagon.

"Rally to me!" I shouted as I ran to the vehicle.

Then I saw their leader atop a black stallion. Draco.

What in Hades was happening here? Why were Roman soldiers following a Dark Lord of The Druids?

The answer to those questions could wait. Right now, we were under attack. For the most part, our people were gallantly holding their own, but that wasn't going to last long. The Romans were a few less in number than we, but much greater in skill, despite Dosameenor's training of those in our group.

"Form up to me!" I commanded, as I arrived at the wagon.

The men in the group, Thomas' guards and others, did just that, as did Dosameenor and his men. The women bounded to the wagon as well.

The Romans ceased their fighting when our people

disengaged, but began to encircle us. I looked about, trying to find the rest of the guards who had been manning the perimeter. I only saw Hentapas, kneeling next to Romi's body.

He looked up. We made eye contact and I motioned my head for him to join us. He was loath to leave his comrade's body, but knew the greater good of the moment demanded it, and ran over to me.

"Thank the gods you made it," I said.

He said nothing but his face was a mask of angry grimness.

Next, I saw Paulonius and Geneveives coming from behind the wagon, the latter just finishing a last violent hack with her short sword into an attacking legionnaire. They came toward our group.

We were all near the fire and Mary's wagon, with the enemy closing around us. Irena, Thomas, and Mary descended from the chariot wagon. The two wounded women's heads poked from the curtains. I could only assume that the babes, Sara and Mattea, were tucked safely inside.

But was that safe? As I said from the start, the invaders seemed to be after the wagon. More than one of them had been cut down in their path to it.

Jacobi? Where was Jacobi? Dread began to creep over me. I looked around frantically. He was nowhere to be seen.

~XXIII~

"Halt!" came a booming voice. It was a glamoured voice, infused with more power, false power, than was actually there. And it came from the Dark Druid atop his horse.

"Draco," hissed Dosameenor under his breath, vengeance and murderous intent seeping from every pore.

I placed a hand on his arm, silencing him.

Then my own blood boiled as I looked up and saw that the Dark One had something lying across his lap, a human form draped across his legs: Jacobi, unconscious, or worse. He looked dead, his skin was pasty-white. I covered the fact that all I wanted to do was rush to the old man's aid. To do that at that particular moment would have ensured the death of us all. So, I endeavored to remain calm and in control. At least, in appearance.

"I should have killed you the night of the Wickerman," spat Dosameenor.

"But you did not, did you? And here we are," gloated Draco.

I glared at him and at the lifeless Jacobi.

Draco looked down at the old man. "Fear not, Longinus. He merely...sleeps. For now."

"Release him!" I demanded.

"No. We must talk first. Then perhaps I'll think about it," Draco said, toying with me.

"Why are you with Roman soldiers?" I demanded.

"That is none of your concern," retorted the Dark One.

"Now, now, Arch Druid Draco," said another voice. "He should know that Rome and you have reached...an agreement, shall we say?"

The owner of the voice came forward into the light on a brown bay and stopped next to Draco. He was dressed as a

Roman Tribune.

"Detrom is Arch Druid—not that piece of shite!" said Dosameenor.

"Who are you?" I asked the apparent Tribune.

"You don't remember me, do you? Pity. I remember you," he said, in a mock hurt tone.

I looked at him carefully. Yes. There was something familiar about him, but I did not voice that.

"I'll help you remember then. You reprimanded me, chastised me in front of my men," the Tribune said, anger exuding from his being. "'Twas a long time ago, but I never forgot. Or forgave. Remember?"

I did not remember any of what he was saying.

"No? It was at a man's house by the name of Paul, a follower of that pathetic false Messiah, Jesu. Do you remember yet? I was giving the man a well-deserved beating for speaking against Rome, and you, the mighty Centurion Longinus, interrupted me and belittled me in front of my men!" he shouted, nearly losing his control.

This one's whole demeanor was off; not normal. Demons had him, or he was simply insane. Either condition was unpredictably dangerous.

"Of course, I was just a young lieutenant then. Green, was I then, or I would have killed you for that insult. I was from a prominent Roman family, after all, and you, you were from...what, a whore's ass?"

I had been born into the plebian class. That much was true. But both my parents had been honorable citizens. My father, a legionnaire, had been killed in a street-brawl outside of an Egyptian beer house in Thebes, while trying to drag a drunk comrade away from a fight with some locals. It was a pointless death. But it happened before I was born, so I never knew the man. My mother had been a well-paid servant in a senator's household, as her mother before her. She certainly had not been a prostitute. She died shortly after I first became a legionnaire. One day, her heart simply stopped.

Obviously, this Tribune was trying to inflame my anger.

He was failing. But I did remember him now, and the incident he was talking about. However, I would never give him the pleasure of knowing that. "No. I do not remember you. Apparently, you were not worthy of remembering."

That struck a nerve, I could tell. He fumed at it, but to his credit, maintained control.

I glanced at Jacobi. His motionless form still showed no sign of life.

"Get to it, Draco," the Tribune said to the Dark Lord. "The General will not wait long for these things. But leave that one to me," he said, pointing to me.

Draco turned to Mary first. "You and your brat will come with me. The contents of your wagon will go with the Tribune, as will your spear, Longinus."

He lied. I could see it in his eyes, sense it in my soul. He had no intention of giving my lance to Rome. Nor the contents of Mary's chariot wagon, either.

"Draco lies," I said to the Tribune. "If you think I wronged you in the past, then you must understand that it was in the context of my duty. But believe me now. This one lies to you. He may have led you to the items Rome seeks, but he will not part with them and you're a fool to think otherwise."

"Shut up, Longinus," said the Tribune, drawing his gladius, "or I will drop you here and now. I'll not do permanent damage to you, though. Did you know that there's a bounty on your head? You're an enemy of the State—deserter, among other things. Much gold awaits the one who captures you. I stand to become even richer." He then turned to Draco and made the biggest mistake of his life, and the last. "Seize the wagon, seize the spear!" he yelled to his men as he struck the sword tip out at Draco's throat.

But the Dark One was much faster; Otherworldly fast. He was also Otherworldly strong. In the blink of an eye, he grabbed the Tribune's sword wrist and snapped it like a twig, even before the sword really got close to his neck.

In the next instant, Draco's free hand had clamped

onto the Tribune's face, crushing the facial bones like a dried-up egg shell.

The legionnaires were oblivious to the Tribune's plight. They had their orders and were already beginning to slash in earnest at everyone in their way.

Draco pushed the dying Tribune, now screaming in muffled agony, from his mount to the cold ground.

Then Jacobi slipped to the ground. I rushed over to him, scooping his fragile frame into one arm, and at the same time, hurtling the spear with the other.

It found its mark, landing with a loud thud into Draco's shoulder. He howled, not with pain, but delight. What had I done? I had all but given him the lance!

But then its imbedded blade began to smoke. The smell of burning flesh permeated the air. Draco's howls of delight now turned to cries of tormented pain as the lance and its power burned him from within. It was more than he could stand. He yanked out the weapon, letting it fall to the ground, smoking and glowing with heat at the blade tip. I snatched it up before Draco could recover himself, Jacobi still in my arms.

"Leave us!!" commanded Dosameenor to Thomas and myself, "I will deal with this, me and my men. Go! Take Mary and the wagon and go!"

I was about to protest, but did not. Instead, I turned to Thomas. "Go," I said as I loaded Jacobi into the chariot wagon under a side flap. I wanted nothing more than to examine the old man right then and there. If he were not dead, then I would heal him and bring him back to full consciousness. Yet, there was no time. We had to leave this place immediately, but the soldiers who came with Draco and the Tribune must not be allowed to follow.

"But—" he said.

"No, go."

"Longinus, you must come," Irena implored.

For the first time that I could remember, I saw genuine fear in her eyes; fear for me. "It's all right, my love. I will be right along."

"You better be!" she commanded.

Mary jumped into the back of the wagon as did Irena. Thomas took the driver's place and they were off, rolling quickly through fighting bodies and dead ones. A minor contingent of Thomas' guards went with them. But many brave ones stayed to fight alongside Dosameenor.

I wanted to, as well. But something was compelling me to go with the wagon. They would need my protection, true, but...

I ran to Macha, still tethered to a tree, dancing nervously at all the activity. "Shhh, girl."

I mounted Macha and took one last look at Dosameenor, who was in the throws of battle, and loving it. I turned in time to see Hentapas joining the fray. "No! Hentapas, come with me!" I barked.

"Romi must be avenged, sir!" he countered, tears of rage and anguish in his eyes.

Paulonius and his young lady had jumped upon one of their horses, Paulonius in the front. They were now next to Hentapas, clearly unsure of what they should do. "All three of you—I need you with me! Hentapas, you are not mine to command, but I tell you, I need you with me. Romi is gone, lad. Nothing you do here will change that. You both said you came to find me, to join me. Well then, come with me now! It's what he'd have wanted."

Hentapas thought about it for a brief moment. Then, with a shout of rage, he turned and threw his drawn sword at a nearby Legionnaire. It landed true, catching the man in the chest, splitting him open. The legionnaire was dead before he hit the ground.

Paulonius kicked his horse's ribs. He and Geneveives galloped past me, following the chariot wagon.

I held out my hand and Hentapas ran to me, leaping onto Macha's back behind me without my aid. I dug my heels into Macha's side and we were off to catch up to Mary's wagon.

We caught up to them quickly. They were moving as swiftly as possible, but even with two horses now pulling the wagon, it was quite a burden with two injured women, two children, Jacobi, Irena and Mary, supplies and the item, whatever it was, all inside.

Irena looked out from the back of the vehicle, poking her head through the drapery coverings. She simply nodded her head in acknowledgement that I was once again with her. There were only seven guards escorting the chariot wagon and about twelve civilians, all running on foot, who had been traveling with Mary and Thomas from the start, back in Palestine. The rest had stayed to fight Draco and the Romans.

There was no sign of pursuit. Still, I urged them on. "Keep moving! Do not stop 'til I give the order!"

We traveled the rest of the night, which wasn't very long. An hour and a half later, just after sunrise, we had to stop briefly, to rest the horses and the folks on foot. There was no other source of water, so we let the animals drink from our own water supplies.

Still, there was no sign of pursuit by Draco. I had no illusions that the spear had killed him. It would take much more than just that to send him to the Otherworld. Perhaps the legionnaires had turned on him when they saw that he had killed their Tribune?

Not likely. I don't believe that any of them had witnessed the Tribune's death, having been preoccupied with carrying out their orders of slaughter and theft. Besides, Draco could easily blame one of us, who were resisting them, for killing the Roman officer. Or, if a young legionnaire had witnessed the event, Draco could use his Dark power upon the mind of the impressionable legionnaire, steering him in a completely different direction. The point is, Draco was alive, no doubt, and would continue his Dark quest at all costs.

But, for the moment, we seemed to be relatively safe.

We were tucked into a hillside just inside a stand of trees. I did not like having our flank being drawn up against a mound of earth, no retreat for us on that side. But the animals, and especially the people, were too tired to continue on.

We had only been there a few minutes, everyone trying to catch their breath and satiate the need for water, when Irena came forward and threw herself into my arms. "Damn it, Longinus!" she declared. "You scared me. I thought you were going to stay and fight them."

"I wanted to, but I couldn't," I said, not quite knowing what I meant.

She obviously saw confusion in my face over the matter, for she looked at me quizzically. "You mean, you didn't come just for me?" she asked only half in jest.

"Of course, but there was something else. Something was telling me that I had to stay with the wagon and you, and..." I was starting to babble.

"Shh, Longinus. As much as I love you and want you with me, you must always follow that inner voice of yours. It guides you for the highest good," she replied. "Trust me when I say I understand."

Just then, Thomas stood on top of a tree stump where all could see him. He had a frantic look on his face, a fearful look. "We've been going east! We must go back northwest, to Alesia. We must get to Alesia!" he declared.

I would have none of it. I was not going to let him lead any longer. "Are you mad? The roads will be scoured by the Romans. A Tribune of theirs is dead, and one way or another, we will be blamed for that. We will never get close to Alesia. "And what you carry in that wagon is not remotely worth the risk."

"You have no idea what you say, Longinus," countered Thomas.

"Then show me! I demand it! Show me what it is and explain to me why it is so important that it go to Alesia!" I said, my anger boiling up inside at the man's impudence.

"You would not understand," was all he said.

"Thomas," said Mary, "for one who has been given an inner knowledge and enlightenment, you can still be a fearful doubter. This is Longinus. He possesses the other great treasure touched by him—the other great relic that has on it His sacred blood. Who else to better understand what we carry?"

Thomas was silent for a moment. He collected himself, and seemed once again to be in control. "Yes, you are right," he said to Mary. He then turned to me. "Forgive me, Longinus."

I simply bowed my head slightly in acknowledgment of his apology. "What is it that you have that could possibly be related to my spear, which is, I assume, what you're referring to?"

"Come, Longinus," Mary said.

Irena took me by the hand. Did she now know what it was? Together, we followed Mary and Thomas to the wagon. Mary lifted the back flap, hooking it open, and I climbed in, the rest remaining outside the back of the vehicle, but looking in, watching me.

The interior of the wagon was spacious, nearly enough for me to stand up in, even with the arched covering. Deceiving, that was, from the outside. Despite the ornate drapery that clung over the outer frame of the raised portion of the wagon, the inside was plain, a pallet to one side for lying on, a stool on one end, and, surprisingly, only two small boxes of supplies at the very rear. I had thought there to be much more in the way of supplies. Those folks who were occupying the inside had moved to the front. Jacobi was sitting up on the pallet, smiling, as was the woman with the injured leg, which now seemed to be miraculously better, almost completely healed. Not even a bandage on it.

The old man also looked invigorated. "Jacobi!" I said, surprised, but grateful, to see him looking so well. He said nothing, but looked at the item which took up most of the rest of the space in the wagon.

I looked down at the item in question. At first, I was not sure of what I was looking at. It simply looked like a few pieces of large, squared lengths of wood, darkly stained by time. But then I noticed that some of the darkest stains were not from age, per se, but from a liquid substance in a time past. There was something familiar about the shape of this thing. I stared at it for a moment. And then it hit me: it was a crucifix cut into several large pieces.

But it was no ordinary cross. By all the gods! By the God! My heart began to race, my breathing to quicken. I reached out to the thing and, closing my eyes, I touched it.

Blinding white light flashed before my inner sight. I was transported in spirit and mind to a hundred years in the future, two hundred years into the future, a thousand, and back again, in less than a moment. Then I found myself in a holy place, though I knew not where that was, with all manner of strange beings before me; some of the flesh; others of a form that I cannot begin to describe. Divine Masters, one and all I knew them to be.

"Longinus," came His voice. "You have come far."

He was standing before me. "Jesu," I breathed.

"The cross that your earthly form now touches, and the spear that you carry, are touchstones for all who believe in me. But I fear they may not understand the Truths of themselves and what I taught, and instead will rely on the power of these things to venerate the Man and not the lessons and knowledge. You must help them see the way, Longinus. You and the others," Jesu said.

"But how? I am wanted for worse by many. Anywhere I go, I will be captured or killed," I replied.

"You will do what you can in this life, but will not finish, 'tis true. You will continue in your next life upon returning here."

"You believe in rebirth to this place?" I asked, astonished.

"All things are possible with the Infinite Mind of the Universe. Never forget that. But it is up to the individual soul when, or even if, to return. Not all come back to the earthly form. But you will. You are the Teacher, The Merlin, for the ages. Go now and take these things away so that those who mean evil do not get them, and those who do not understand the Truth, fall to worship of me through them. Get them not to Alesia, but to the land of your next birth—to the island in the west," he finished.

The vision, the place I was in, began to fade.

"Wait!" I pleaded. "I know naught of where you speak!"

I suddenly found myself back in the wagon, slumped over the Rood, the wooden cross that Jesu had been crucified on.

Tears filled my eyes. My body felt weak, as if I'd had been on a hundred-mile forced march. The others were staring at me, waiting to hear what had happened; what I had seen.

"We...I...spoke to Jesu. He said I...we are to take the Rood not to Alesia, but to the Island in the west," I managed to say.

"What?" asked Thomas, his tone laced with disbelief. "That is rather a coincidence, isn't it? After you were just saying we shan't go to Alesia?"

"Do not doubt what Longinus says he saw or heard in the vision, Thomas," said Irena. "He speaks the truth and you know it."

Thomas fell silent.

"What island, Longinus?" asked Mary.

"I don't yet know. But I will find out," I said.

"What else? What else did the Master say?" queried Thomas.

I simply shook my head, still trying to grapple with the vision myself.

"That's enough for now," said Irena, fending the others off.

Sara giggled then, and Mattea followed with peels of laughter, reminding us of their presence, and Jacobi and the wounded women were smiling in a way that conveyed they knew what the wood was before us. Perhaps that is what accounted for Jacobi's rejuvenated condition and the woman's leg healing so fast and well. I trusted the other woman's ribs were just as healed.

"Come and rest for a few minutes, Longinus," Irena said, beckoning me to come out of the chariot wagon.

"Rest in here on the pallet," offered Mary.

"Thank you," I said, climbing over to it. I put my head down and slipped into a deep sleep.

The sleep was short-lived. I awoke two hours later to commotion outside in our makeshift camp. I thrust my head outside the wagon. Irena was a few feet away, talking to Jacobi. "What is it?" I asked them.

Irena ran over to the wagon; Jacobi hobbled. "Thomas sent two of the men back the way we came to see if Draco was following," she said.

"And?" I questioned impatiently.

"They are about an hour behind us," said the old man.

"They are numerous. One of the scouts said two Centuries strong at least," added Irena. "What are we to do?"

"We cannot outrun them," I said, trying to think of something. Anything. I looked up to the steep hillside next to us. "I knew we never should have stopped where we did. A death trap, it is," I railed under my breath.

"Or...a help in concealing us," Jacobi countered.

"What are you talking about?" I asked him, incredulous.

The old man simply spread his arms wide as if to say, Look around, my friend.

I looked about me, searching for his meaning. The morning had dawned cloudy, foggy, misty. And then I realized what he was trying to say. The fog, the mists, somewhat buttressed up against the hillside, could be amplified to conceal us. But could we do it? Could we veil ourselves in a glamoured mist the way Detrom had? Even if we could, would we be able to maintain it? Perhaps it would only be necessary for a short time, until we figured out our next move.

"Jacobi," I said with awe and respect, "can we do it?"

"Not if you have to ask! Of course we can! The mists are already here. We need only grasp their element, their essence, and create them anew!" he exclaimed with delight.

214

"Do it!" I commanded.

"Oh, not me. You," he said.

"Me?"

"From a clear sky, you brought down the rains the night of the Wickermen, and you think you'd have problems with this? This is child's play for you!" he said.

Thomas and Mary approached us then, and Jacobi and Irena explained what we intended to do, as I thought about how to go about it. Mary and Thomas went off to gather everyone together to be near the wagon, so we might all share in the calling of our only hope.

As if it knew our minds, the foggy mist began to become thicker in our general area, not lesser as it would seem it should normally be as the morning wore on. Within a few moments, each person in our dwindled party had gathered near the wagon awaiting further instructions. They understood in general that Draco and the Romans were coming, and that we were going to attempt to—no, not attempt to, but do— shroud ourselves in a mist. Some had fear in their eyes; not from the pursuing Romans, but from the thought of a conjuring, as one of them put it, that I was going to perform.

"'Tis demons' work," said a woman, an older woman with white hair and stark grey eyes. She was one of our group, but I had not heard her speak until now.

"No, it is not," Mary said, gently, going on to explain in abbreviated terms, that there are natural laws that govern the universe, and how these laws respond to everyone according to one's mind and thoughts. The higher the training in such things, the more adept one can be at controlling or using these natural laws.

The woman -- whose name was Leona, I was to later find out—looked doubtful. But she trusted Mary, so she agreed to at least be passive in the proceedings. Negative thoughts in the group during the ritual, for want of a better term, could adversely affect the outcome.

Hentapas offered to help in the proceedings and I

gratefully accepted. "Please sit," he said to all gathered. They did as he bade and sat on the ground. Hentapas remained standing near me.

I, too, remained standing, breathed deeply and pushed all doubt from my mind. "We will do this quickly, and well," I declared. "All of you close your eyes and breathe deeply and steadily," I continued, "holding in your mind only the following thoughts: The power of the Universe flows effortlessly through us, protecting us in the Veil Of Mists. We command this to be so! So be it!" I said.

"So be it!" echoed Hentapas, Jacobi and several others.

The others all had their eyes closed and breathed steadily, focusing on my words. But words are just empty shells without the thoughts and images behind them, and the thoughts and images come from the mind. Thus, the real work of making the mists mask us was done in the mind.

I had the lance in my hand and held it aloft with one hand, blade tip pointing to the Heavens. I closed my own eyes and created in my mind the image of the mists presently surrounding our physical forms becoming thicker, enshrouding us and the entire immediate area. But we needed more. I felt the spear begin to quiver in my hand, and then I felt myself, my mind, my spirit, exit my body.

I traveled to the smallest level imaginable within the mist itself. Down and down within it I went, until I felt as if I were the mist; its fundamental essence. I stayed there for what seemed liked a long time, all the while knowing that I, the mist, was infused with Divine power and protection, and that no one, no-thing, could penetrate it to see our group's sanctuary unless they meant us only good.

Then something AMAZING happened. Where I was with my mind, with my spirit, in and as essence of the mist, all the others suddenly were too, with Jacobi and Hentapas leading them. We all merged as one in the protective mist. The combined power of all of our spirits as one was almost overwhelming. We sustained this feeling for a while, etching solidly our desires for protection into the mists core.

Slowly, very slowly, the others faded from my awareness. I, too, began to withdraw from the mist, having completed the work needed.

I opened my eyes and was back in body, holding the spear tightly at my side. I looked around at the awe-struck faces. They were, no doubt, astonished by their experience. But equally, I think, they were astonished by the appearance of our immediate area, for many of them were looking around with wide eyes.

The area we were in was now fairly bright with the sun. As with Detrom's valley village, a slight layer of mist covered us like a ceiling—like a sheer, nearly transparent dome made of wispy threads of cloud. It was thin enough to allow ample sun in, but, I trusted, that as with Detrom's mist, no one could see in from above it; from on top of the hill.

Off in the distance, some one-hundred yards or so in all directions, through the surrounding trees, was a wall of mist extending up from the ground to meet the dome mist. The wall mist was thick as honey and marked the perimeter of the forested side of our sanctuary. From where we stood, to the wall mist, was bright and clear.

My eyes met Leona's. There was no fear there at all, only awe. Her eyes said, Perhaps this was not demons' work, after all. "Master Longinus," she said aloud, "I was there with you, with everyone, there in the mists. I felt the Goodness all around!"

"Quiet!" ordered Thomas suddenly. "Listen!"

We could hear them, off in the distance: horses trotting and men tramping at a forced march pace, which amounted to a half-run in unison, for miles and miles at a time. Panic started to rise in our midst; I could feel it. It was palpable. Murmurs began to filter among the people.

"No," I said. "Fear not."

I did not know whether my words would sit with them. But Jacobi backed me, saying in a hushed voice, "Yes! Do not concern yourself. They will pass us by."

All of them became silent once more, waiting patiently

to see what would transpire.

The noise grew louder. We could hear voices now, commands and responses. "You there! Tighten the flank! We should be upon them at any moment!" barked an officer to a subordinate.

"Trying to, sir! Can't see shite for this fog, Centurion!" came the answer.

It was strange: We could hear the commands and responses, and the scuffles of feet and hooves, and shouts of confusion. They all sounded as if they were right next to us, not more than a few feet away. But they were not. We could see no one; no origin whatsoever for the sounds. It was as though we had suddenly entered an unseen land parallel to the normal earthly world.

I heard the voice of Draco. "This is a mist of Glamour. Curse you, Longinus!" he shouted from outside the mists. "Curse all of you. I will find you. You will not escape me!"

Soon, however, the noises and voices receded; moved off to continue their futile search for us elsewhere.

"God of Abraham!" exclaimed the woman. "'Tis truly magic, what ye've done, Master Longinus."

"Merlin Longinus, or, just Merlin, I think. He's earned that title with this bit 'o 'magic,' don't ya think?" said the familiar voice.

I turned and saw a sight for weary eyes: Dosameenor and ten men who had stayed to fight Draco and the Romans. I stepped forward and embraced the man as my brother. "I thought...I didn't know what to think," I stammered.

"Aye, the fight was hard, but we held our own and then some. After an hour, they broke off and ran. We began to follow your trail. We'd just come to the outer portion of this small grove when the mists descended. I knew it was more than natural. More than the gods' work. I knew it was you!" exclaimed Dosameenor. "You are surpassing even the Arch Druid himself! I therefore declare you to be a Merlin, my friend!" He paused for a brief instant, then added, "I can declare that, you know."

Before I could say anything else to Dosameenor, Leona looked at him and threw him a question of her own. "But, you came through the fog, I mean the mists. The Romans could not. Why?" asked the woman, now utterly intrigued.

"Only those who mean us harm are repelled by the mists. Those who mean us no harm will pass through, which means we can pass in and out," I explained.

"But, how? How does it know?" she inquired.

"It has to do with the state of mind or kind of Thought with which we infused in it, and the state of mind of those who come upon it," I answered.

She looked at me, trying very hard to understand.

"Simply trust that It knows, my good woman," said Dosameenor.

She nodded and said, "It has its own spirit, then."

That sounded as reasonable as any other explanation. "As you say," I replied.

Dosameenor then turned to the group in general. "Is there no food with which to break our fast? I could eat a horse," he joked.

Macha, tethered a short distance away, seemed not only to have heard and understood the comment, but to have taken offense. She whinnied very loudly in protest.

"Sorry, girl!" said Dosameenor.

Several laughed, albeit nervously. Dosameenor's words, though, made everyone realize how hungry we all were. None of us had eaten since the previous day.

We quickly set about to remedy that.

~XXIV~

The first days spent in the misty sanctuary consisted of regaining our strength and, for the most part, planning our next move.

Dosameenor organized hunting parties while I organized the perimeter guards and their shift roster, though I was confident that a guard posting was unnecessary as long as I reinforced the protective mist regularly. The guards, however, made everyone else feel better.

We had decided to stay for only a few days, a week at most. Enough time, we thought, to allow those pursuing us to move on. At the end of that time, we would split up into small groups and trickle slowly out of the mists one group at a time over several nights.

The hunters had no problem going out and coming back through the vaporous clouds. The game was plentiful, and a source for water, a stream, was found a short distance away. Surprisingly, they encountered no search parties, no Roman patrols, no one at all. Many attributed this good fortune to the mists, as well as to my magic powers. I was not so sure. I was sure that the hunters would have seen someone.

We rested and ate, and ate and rested. Temporary shelters were put up around the area, and we came to feel a sense of security for a bit. Deceiving, was that, for we found ourselves lulled into a feeling of being at home.

As with the mists that Detrom and his Druids manifested, time seemed to stand still for those within these mists, or simply didn't exist at all. I was aware of that fact, as were Jacobi and Mary and Thomas, and I determined not to let it influence me or any one of us.

But some of the others in our party seemed oblivious to the lack of a time definition, even going so far as to sight that here in the mists, we might establish a whole new community free of religious persecution, free of the political oppression, free of any constraints or conventions at all. A nice thought, perhaps. But dangerous. No one really wanted to stay here forever.

For the moment, it did not matter. When the time was right, I would convince them that we should leave. If I had to, I would lift the mists altogether, and then we would have no choice but to go. But, I let the matter rest for now.

Irena and I put up our own shelter, a large tent of skins given to us by the two women who had been injured the morning we saw the smoke. They were grateful for the healing and the protection of the Rood and mists. Irena and I fell into a comfortable routine; we were up in the morning to break our fast with a morning meal, which usually consisted of bread, cheese, apple mead and sometimes venison, with the whole company and then attend to the needs of the people. Then we would share the evening meal with everyone in the communal center of the encampment, and afterwards, Jacobi and a few others would tell tales in the bardic tradition, shortly after which Irena and I would retire to our sleeping pallet for anything but sleep.

One morning, Irena could not get up from the pallet. After a bit of fussing, and at Irena's insistence, I left to attend to the camp. By the noon meal, she was still not off the pallet, so I asked Jacobi to look in on her.

When I returned later in the afternoon to check on her, I saw not only Jacobi, but Leona, as well, just exiting my tent. Why were they both there? Panic struck me suddenly. I ran up to them. "What's wrong?! Is she ill?"

Leona burst into laughter and Jacobi just smiled his toothless grin.

"Irena is quite fine. Perfect, in fact," offered the old man. "Leona, as it turns out, is a midwife. I asked for her expert opinion."

They were both silent for while, allowing me to absorb what they had just said.

Finally, the implications of what they were telling me sunk in. "By the gods!" I said. "You mean...I'm to be a father?"

"Yes," replied Leona in a sarcastic tone which meant, why is it men never grasp the obvious when it comes to these things?

"You're sure?" I asked.

"Yes," she stated in a hard, matter of fact tone. But her tone softened as she went on. "I have been a midwife for a very long time. On many occasions I know these things even before the mother-to-be does."

I was at once excited beyond belief and nervous beyond comprehension. "Can I see her?" I asked.

"Of course, Merlin Longinus," said Leona.

I started to head into the tent, but Jacobi placed a hand on my arm, halting me before I could enter. His whole countenance had shifted. "After you see to Irena, please come see me, Longinus," he said, in all seriousness.

"What's wrong, my friend? Why so grave?" I asked, fear for Irena again gripping my heart.

"No, no, nothing grave. Do not be alarmed. Just come and see me."

"I will," I said, clapping him on the shoulder. I then turned and entered the tent.

Irena still lay on the sleeping pallet. Though she looked a bit peaked, the mother-to-be of my child now wore a bright smile. "You beam," I said.

"'Tis because of you, you know," she replied sleepily.

"No, it is not. 'Tis because of what you carry," I pointed out.

"Which you implanted in me," she countered. "And thus it is because of you that I beam."

"You sound like a logician," I said teasingly. I walked over to the pallet and sat on the edge. Tenderly, I reached out and placed my hand on her belly. "It's a marvel," I said after a moment, with more than a little awe.

She saw the contemplativeness in my eyes; heard it in my tone. "Are you all right, Longinus?"

"Yes, of course. This changes everything, doesn't it?" I said. "Perhaps we should stay here, make this place our home."

"Permanently?" she asked with distaste.

"Well, I don't know."

"No, Longinus. You know we cannot. You have too much of a destiny. We," she said, placing her hand on mine, which was still on her belly, "have too much of a destiny. Your son is to carry our bloodlines to an island world, a new world, remember?"

I was shocked. How did she know of the prophecy I had uttered during my Druidic initiation? "How...how did...?" I let the thought dangle without completing the sentence.

She sat up on the bedding. "That is not important, my love. Really. The important thing here is that I believe our son will help to create a new people in a new land. I feel it in my heart, in my very soul. But it is not going to happen if we stay here."

I thought about what Irena had said. I thought about all that Camaroon had said on the last night that I saw her. It appeared that the prophecy was about to come true, or at least part of it: my bloodline was about to be carried on. "Well," I finally said, "you can't go anywhere for awhile. We'll take it a day at a time, at least until your sick feeling passes. Then again, we could travel when you do feel better, but we'll have to stop again before too long, for you to give birth. I will not let my child be born on the road. But where is that to happen? We're without a country right now. I could be arrested almost anywhere. Maybe—"

"Longinus," interrupted Irena, "you're starting to sound like a whiney old man!"

I smiled and fell silent, and lost myself in thought again for a moment. Something Irena had said finally hit me. "A son, you say?"

"Yes. I know it."

"So be it," I said, smiling. I stood up and took the spear from its secured place. "I must see Jacobi. I'll bring food back when I return."

I bent down and kissed her forehead as she slid back under the skin covers, closing her eyes. With a last stroke of her hair, I slipped out to find Jacobi.

I found Jacobi with Dosameenor, Thomas, Hentapas and Paulonius near the central cooking fire. Mary and Genevieves were there, too, but excused themselves to pay a visit to Irena as soon as I arrived. I was going to tell them that she was resting, but they looked too excited to be dissuaded from the visit.

"She is well, as I said. Is she not?" Jacobi asked.

"'Twas as you said," I replied, lightheartedly. The lightness of my mood shifted, though, when I felt the concern in the air. "What is it, my friends?"

"We have been here a very long time, Longinus," said Dosameenor.

"Couldn't be," I said, dismissively. "A few weeks perhaps, but—"

"Actually, it's been more than a few months," Jacobi interrupted.

I thought about it for a moment. It was inconceivable. "That can't be so. Irena and I, we just put up our shelter last week. We..." I stopped. No. That had actually been...how long ago? More than a week; perhaps, but not by much.

"Several of the hunters just got back. They'd not been out for at least a week, by their reckoning. They killed plenty 'o game last time, so no reason to venture out again for a bit, save for reconnaissance, which is what they did today," explained Dosameenor. "When last they were out, the air was a bit crisp. But this time, blankets of snow were everywhere, freezing conditions. Dead of winter it is out there right now." Impossible, I thought. It was still mild here in the mists. It had not been close to winter when we came in here.

"I knew there'd be a bit of a time distortion from the last misty place we'd been in," I said. "It did not seem all that bad back there, though—barely perceptible."

"Not so here," said Hentapas. "I've been calculating our stay here as it pertains to the outside world; I went out briefly myself to measure the amount of snowfall in the surrounding area. I've talked to two of our people who grew up about five miles from our present location.

"The amount of snow fall I measured on the ground is normal for the month of March, late March at that. Which means we've been here in this misty sanctuary for approximately ten moons," Hentapas finished.

I was astounded. "But, it can't have been more than four or five weeks," I said.

"Indeed, for us, that's about right," admitted Jacobi. "But when invoking the laws that govern the mists, we are also invoking other laws of the Universe that we don't yet comprehend."

This put a wrinkle into things that I'd not anticipated.

Jacobi saw my apprehension. "Longinus, ultimately it matters not. But we need to be aware and more vigilant about the time difference. That's all. I suggest that it is time for some of us to leave."

He was looking at me when he said that, but I was not ready to go yet. I would not leave without Irena, and there was no way that I would force her to travel just then.

"Not you," Jacobi said, reading my thoughts, as usual. He looked then to the Egyptian. "Hentapas has volunteered."

I looked at Hentapas. He had come a long way since the day I had first seen him at the tomb, in more ways than one. He'd been but a boy then. He was more than a man now. He was a mystic-warrior with no equal.

But, I could see something else in him now, too: purpose. I could see it in his eyes. "What else is there to it?" I asked. "It's not just about the leave-taking."

Hentapas looked at Thomas, who stepped forward. "We —Mary, Jacobi and myself—thought that perhaps it would be best to take the Rood out and away in pieces so as not to jeopardize losing it all to the Romans, or worse, to Draco, if some of us are eventually caught or stopped," he explained, clearly not happy about the decision. "I'm loath to do it that way, but hopefully, all the pieces can eventually find their way back to us in Jerusalem."

"That's where you're going?" I asked.

"Yes. Well, eventually. Hentapas will go first. Then we'll send more out later, with more of the Rood," said Thomas.

"I will try to send word back as to what is happening in the outside world as often as I can," added Hentapas.

We were all silent then. I was particularly reflective.

Thomas took my silence, at least in part, to mean something else. "Forgive us for not consulting you, Longinus, but this all just came up this morning, and you were, well, a little busy. Congratulations, by the way."

"Thank you, and I do not take any offense whatsoever by your 'not consulting me,' as you put it," I said. Then I turned to Hentapas, clasping him on the shoulder with my free hand. "When do you leave, my friend?"

"Within the hour, sir," he stated as a matter of fact.

"So be it," I said, embracing the lad.

And, true to his word, within the hour, Hentapas was packed, saddled and ready to go, with one-thirteenth of the Rood hidden in a bag tucked into a larger wrap all stuffed into a fairly large backpack. The number 13 was an ancient mystical number. We had thought of cutting the Rood into more pieces but, any more than thirteen would have been too many, so thirteen pieces was perfect, on more than one level.

Four others were to travel with Hentapas: two from Thomas' original group, who had come from Palestine, and two who had come with us from Dosameenor's home. Hentapas, as it turned out, wanted to go back to Egypt, and one of the Palestinians, a beautiful young woman with silky black hair and deep brown eyes, clearly wanted to go with him wherever he went. The two from Dosameenor's home were his own fighting men and volunteered to go with Hentapas. They had voiced an interest in seeing the land where Jesu had walked, dangerous as it might be.

"Protection of the gods, protection of the God, goes

with you, Hentapas," I said.

"The One Mind blesses your way, know that to be so, my lad," said Jacobi.

"Thank you. We will see each other again," Hentapas declared.

"Indeed, we will," I said, smiling. "Irena sends her regards, apologizes for not seeing you off in person."

"Please, sir, I wish only that the lady Irena be healthy and deliver you a fine, strong son, which I know she will," he said. "Goodbye one and all!"

With that, he and his small group, all on foot, turned and hiked out of our sanctuary, disappearing into the mists.

* * *

We, Irena and I, were going to go next; leave in a week or so with a thirteenth of the Rood. I thought she would get better, well enough to travel for awhile at least. But, it was not to be. She was to have a very difficult time of it throughout the whole of her pregnancy. Extreme fatigue and nausea plagued her constantly. I was concerned at first, but was assured by Leona, the midwife, and Mary, as well, that it was not uncommon for one to have a difficult time of it. "She's strong and no doubt will weather this just fine," Leona asserted.

I had my doubts, but left it at that.

It was many weeks before she could get out of bed, and even then, she could only go for very short walks before the need to lie down struck again. Obviously, we were not going to make it out of the camp any time soon.

But group by group, by twos, fours, and sixes, we watched the occupants of our little sanctuary dwindle, each group taking with it a part of the Rood and heading off in a different direction about two to three weeks apart. Two to three weeks apart by our figuring, anyway.

Paulonius and Genevieves left, Genevieves with child as well, as it turned out, but seemingly completely unaffected by her pregnancy. "You'll be a fine father," I told Paulonius. He was quite frightened by the prospect, as his father had been ill-suited to the role.

"Thank you," said Paulonius. "I'd like to stay here with you, but..." he trailed off.

"You must consider what is best for you, your lady and the little one to come," I pointed out. "Thank you for your service to me."

"Yes, sir, and you for the honor of it," he replied.

Dosameenor and Mattea also left for his home with two of his men. They would stay there for an indeterminate amount of time before then getting the portion of the Rood they would carry to its final destination.

The rest of his men, six more, were instructed to stay with me until I saw fit to give them leave to go, no matter how long that might be, and no matter what corner of the world I dragged them to. I told Dosameenor that it was greatly appreciated but not really necessary; however, he insisted. Truthfully, I was relieved at his insistence; very grateful for the added men at arms. Of the six, four seemed more or less ambivalent about the order. But it didn't sit very well with two of the men, who had wives and families back in Dosameenor's village. In the end, however, I won them over to the cause of hiding the Rood and Spear from Rome, and by the promise to release them of their duty to me sooner, rather than later, despite what Dosameenor might say.

The day of Dosameenor's leave-taking was difficult. We had been through a lot together and I had not realized how much I loved this big Celt. "My friend," I said with tears brimming my eyes.

He made a show of bringing his hand to his face and bowing his head as if to show respect. But we both knew that it was to conceal his emotions more than anything else. "I will miss you my brother," he said, as he embraced me in a squeezing bear hug. He then held me at arms' length and said, "I look forward to the time when we will hoist mead together again."

But as soon as the words were out of his mouth, my stomach lurched and fell, and I knew that it would not be so; I would never again see this man—in this life, anyway. I knew not how I knew, nor how each of our lives would play out. I only knew that our paths would not cross again.

"Yes, I look forward to that as well," I said feebly, trying to hide the additional emotion I was now feeling over this latest revelation.

I remained silent as he said goodbye to Thomas and Mary and Irena, who, having one of her better days, made it out of the tent to say farewell to the big Celt. "Thank you for being with him, for protecting him, for being his 'brother' in so many ways and for being my friend, too."

I had never in all my years seen anyone turn so many shades of red as did Dosameenor in that moment. "Th...thank you, me lady," he stammered, then added, "I only wish I could see your son born."

"Well," said Irena, "we'll just have to make a point of coming to you eventually so that you and Mattea may meet him."

He nodded. After a moment, he stepped away and turned to Jacobi. He looked at the old man and finally genuinely burst into tears. "You are revered in my eyes. You are a Druid of old, truly one of the Ancient Ones," he said once he gained control of himself again.

"'Tis you, Dosameenor, who have honored me by being my friend, listening to the ravings of an old man," Jacobi said.

"Even when I've been less than gentle with you?" the big Celt quipped, probably referring to the time he had carried Jacobi under his arm aboard the ship shortly after our first meeting.

"Even so!" laughed the old man.

Slowly, Dosameenor turned and looked at us all one more time, drinking in the sight of us. Something told me that he also felt deep inside that this would be the last time he would see any of us. Finally, he mounted his horse, a large pack behind the saddle, which I assumed to contain the Rood piece. He gave us all one last nod goodbye, turned with his traveling companions and trotted off into the mists.

I looked at Irena, belly now swelling with about eight moons of child. Had it been that long already? What was the outside world doing? Had it advanced in time by the same amount of time as first calculated by Hentapas, or had that changed? Perhaps time had slowed in comparison to us. Perhaps it had sped up. It was mind-numbing to contemplate.

We had heard nothing from any of those who had already left; no word from the outside world at all. A bit troubling was that, but not too much so. At least not yet.

Then, one day, something happened that shook me to the core. Jacobi took ill. Age was part of it to be sure, but something else afflicted him that we could not define; something within his lungs.

His breathing became extremely labored to the point that he, too, was confined to his sleeping pallet.

I was beside myself. Nothing I tried seemed to work in healing him. I enlisted Leona's help, as well as Mary's. Nothing worked.

For some time, he faded in and out of consciousness. I meditated, prayed and conjured healing energy over him night and day, seeing in my mind's eye that I merged with his spirit, his body; going to the deepest levels imaginable of his lungs to aid and cure his breathing. I used the spear in conjunction with these treatments. I used what remained of the Rood, hoping beyond hope that it would aid in healing as it had miraculously done in the past. Nothing. He was indeed dying. There was no other way to put it.

Finally, one day when I was sitting by his side, on his pallet, he inexplicably awakened into one of his more lucid moments, and managed to rasp out more than a few words. "Longinus, Longinus! I was dreaming just now," he began with a cough, but was excited, nonetheless.

I motioned for him to be still and not spend the energy on speech, but of course, he wouldn't hear of it.

"I dreamt that I was young, oh so young. Just a small

lad. Not as I had been in this life, but in a life anew. You and Irena were there, too." His brow became furled, trying to figure out what he had experienced in the dream. "Though I'm not sure as to..." he coughed violently. It took a moment before he could continue. "Though I'm not sure as to the capacity...I mean, why you were in it."

"Please, Jacobi. Rest. Save your strength. Speak no more," I pleaded.

"Save..." he coughed, "...my strength for what? It's time for me to leave, Longinus."

I felt this to be so, but to hear him say it stunned me terribly; it confirmed my worst fear.

"I need you to aid my journey."

"What do you mean?" I asked suspiciously.

He gave a retched, liquid-lunged laugh which turned into a fit of coughing. "No, no, lad!" he finally managed. "I need no help in bodily demise. I would like you to bury me here, in this misty sanctuary, and cast a spell, or a blessing, whatever you wish to call it, of rebirth for me upon the grave. There is magic here. Who knows what may happen, eh?"

I remained silent. Of course, I would honor his wish. For a moment, though, I had thought he was going to ask me to burn his remains in the Celtic manner to release his soul.

"I'd thought about that, you know," he said, reading my thoughts.

I smiled. Even in death, I could keep nothing from him.

"But, I'd rather be buried," he finished, with a cough.

I was silent for a moment, and then said, "Certainly, I'll honor your wishes." Profound sadness overcame me and I wept.

"Stop, my son," said Jacobi. "I will see you again and again for many lifetimes to come." He paused briefly in thought. Then a gleeful look of realization suddenly donned on his face. "And the very next life, I believe, will be much sooner than you think!"

I wasn't sure what to make of that, but did not question it. Instead, I fell quiet, reflecting again on the loss I was about to experience.

"Longinus," he said coughing. "Longinus, be not sad for me, or for yourself. You know I go simply to my Source, merging with God as One, as one can never do completely while in the body. 'Tis a thing to be celebrated, not mourned."

"You know you will be missed. Very deeply, Jacobi. You've," I had to stop briefly. Tears stung my eyes. Though I knew what he said about merging with the Source to be true, that did not take the absolute pain away from losing him in this life. And that loss deserved the honor and solemness of mourning, regardless of his words to the contrary. "You have been more a father and mentor to me. More than you'll ever know. So whether you like it or not, you will be mourned."

"So be it," he said after a moment. "But always keep in mind where I am truly. My Highest, Truest Self -- your Highest, Truest Self -- lives forever. You seem to lose sight of that fact quite often. Focus on that, always," he said, before breaking into another round of rattling coughs. "Always heed the voice within, always! Because, whether you think it's Jesu or your own inner Self matters not, for..." he struggled for breath, "...they are one in the same."

I simply nodded my head.

"One more thing," he whispered with labor. "Would you bring the spear to me? I should like to kiss His blood one more time."

I thought it a strange request. He had kissed the lance's blade the first time I met him, but I considered him to have grown, evolved, beyond that sort of thing now. Still, if that was his choice for his final moments, then I would indeed comply. "Yes."

I had brought the spear with me each time I visited these past days in the hopes that it would eventually aid in his healing. This day was no different. I held the lance horizontally over him, blade near his face.

The blade was dark with age, stained with years of trials and service; stained still, too, with Jesu's blood. It had never come off. I had stopped trying to remove it a long time ago.

A tear rolled down Jacobi's cheek as he looked at the Holy stain.

Instinctively, I moved the blade closer to his mouth so that he would not have to strain to reach it.

He lifted a frail hand and pulled the spear the last couple of inches, placing the flat of the blade, the stain Itself, on his lips with reverence.

I bowed my head respectfully and stayed that way until I felt the spear's weight shift in my hand, indicating that Jacobi had released it.

I then placed the spear on the pallet, laying it alongside my friend.

He closed his eyes and we both fell silent.

Thirty minutes later, Jacobi was gone.

I wrapped his body in some of the fine draperies that had hung over Mary's chariot wagon, torn and cut specifically for Jacobi's burial shroud. I dug the grave myself and tenderly laid him to rest. All those left in the encampment attended the funeral.

I spoke of my love for him and the teachings he had passed on to me. Then, I asked everyone to leave, and I laid the dirt back over him, planting a sapling on the spot. I then spoke the words of power that would aid him on his journey to and through the Otherworld, and then the words of power that would help him to pick the rebirth that suited him perfectly, though I knew he had somehow already picked that even before leaving here.

I went back to my shelter a hollow man. It would take a long time for me to let him go completely. In spite of my enlightenment, I was still human and would grieve for him. But I knew in my soul that the rites I had performed at the grave would aid him. Perhaps that sounds contradictory. But as I said, I was human, and as such, I could know that my friend was in a wonderful place, even help him to it, and still grieve for him profoundly.

I carried on as best I could. There were many things around the camp that needed my attention, not the least of which was taking care of Irena, whose time was near.

Mary was a constant figure in our lives, looking after Irena as much as I did. Though they never said it, I believed that she and Thomas stayed in camp to make sure the child was born healthy before leaving. I also felt that Mary wanted Thomas and herself to stay with Irena and me until we decided to leave.

But Thomas would not wait much beyond the birth. I had no doubt that they would go on without us. It was not prudent for us to leave right after the child was born. Given Irena's frail state during pregnancy, she would need time to recover. In addition to that, traveling with a newborn is ill-advised even during the best of times, so we would wait before we left the encampment, even if it meant that Irena and I would be the last to leave.

I awoke one morning when the mists around the encampment seemed particularly thick. Despite that, a musical, joyous chorus of bird songs could be heard coming from all directions. The air was light and smelled of...happiness. That seemed to be the best way to describe it. 'Twas true that birds could often be heard in the forest near us. On this particular day, however, they were louder and more musical that I'd ever heard.

I was searching for a reason for the profundity of bird songs, and the other things I felt in the air, when Irena stirred next to me.

She moaned slightly and rolled onto her back. I lay motionless next to her, on my back, as well, and with the covers off. I was about to say good morning when her hand suddenly clamped onto my bare stomach, nearly clawing out a handful of flesh.

Before I had the chance to yell in pain, she shrieked in agony.

"What? What is it?" I cried frantically.

"Aghhhhh!" was all she managed to say as she arched

her back in the throws of pain. She had let go of my stomach and now clutched my hand, nearly crushing the bones.

I did not feel any pain, though, as I was too intent on her. What the devil is happening to you? was all I could think.

Then, quite unexpectedly, I felt a warm liquid spreading on the sleeping pallet and knew what was happening.

"Get Leona and Mary," she hissed through clenched teeth.

"Yes, yes," I said, partly horrified and partly ecstatic with joy; my child was about to be born!

It took the whole of the day. She labored for over twelve hours. I was crazed for a while, but Mary came out for a breath of fresh air at midday, and assured me that a long labor was not unusual, particularly for a first birth. Irena seemed to be weathering it as well as could be expected.

I had been exiled to the outside, where I spent the better part of the day with Thomas and a couple of the other men, who found my nervousness most amusing.

Then, well into the thirteenth hour, as quickly as it had begun, it was over. The sudden squalling spilled out of our shelter, announcing the arrival.

Mary poked her head out of the tent flap. "Longinus, you have a strong son, just as Irena had predicted!" she said.

I laughed out loud and received a round of claps on the back. But I was not relieved yet. "And Irena?" I queried.

Mary's hesitation said much. "She will fair well in the days to come," she finally replied.

"And now?" I demanded.

"She's very weak, but she will get better. I'm sure of it," she said with sincerity.

I believed her, but I needed to see for myself. I entered the tent and crossed over to the sleeping pallet.

The whole of the place smelled of musk and copper – blood. Leona looked at me from the bedside, a scowl of ridicule splashing across her face. "Here now," she spat at me in hushed tones. "You shouldn't be in here."

Mary entered just then and stood next to me.

"Irena?" I said, ignoring the other women.

"Longinus," she said, in utter exhaustion. She was drenched in perspiration, her beautiful hair plastered to her head. And she had the bloodless coloring of a corpse. For a moment, my heart fell to the floor. "Do not worry. I am fine. Have you seen your son?" she asked, speaking in slow and slurred speech.

Slowly, I became aware of a cooing sound coming from a blanketed bundle on the pallet next to Irena. Leona, having dispensed with her initial wrath at my intrusion to the birthing chamber, picked up the bundle and brought it over to me.

I ever so gently took it from her and placed it in the crook of my left arm. Then, with my free hand, I pulled back the part covering his little head.

I was humbled by the little life before me. As with all newborns, his eyes were still closed, but he seemed to be smiling at me with a familiar, toothless grin. I stared at the babe for a few moments.

"We," Irena began, "we never decided on a name."

I thought for a moment, but the name was obvious. "Jacobi," I said.

"Yes," she said smiling. "Jacobi Arturius Longinus," she added.

"Arturius? Wasn't that your father's name?" I asked. She had never mentioned naming our child after her father.

"Yes. I loved him very much, you know." she said, reminiscing, almost deliriously, through the haze of fatigue. Her father had become a legionnaire, was conscripted as one to be more precise, when Irena had been a lass. He had gone off to Britain with a legion and was never heard from again.

"Jacobi Arturius it is," I agreed.

~XXV~

He was a healthy boy, Jacobi Arturius. He had thick, dark hair and lashes, and bright green eyes. A curious and infectious smile seemed to always play on his face, which instantly garnered gushing attention for him and his parents.

As I predicted, Thomas insisted on leaving shortly after Jacobi Arturius was born, three weeks to be exact. Mary did not wish to, but deferred to Thomas. They left with a portion of the Rood on a morning when the protective mists seemed to be especially thin.

"Be sure and shore up the barrier," said Thomas as we all stood next to the chariot wagon, which was loaded and ready for the journey. "I could help you do it right now if you wish."

I looked around at the mists. I thought about taking him up on the offer and performing the rite then and there. We had been able to hear passersby a few days before. That hadn't happened since the first day we called the misty barrier into being, when we heard Draco and the others on the outside. I did not think, though, that it would be difficult to reinforce the mists on my own. "Thank you, Thomas, but I think I can manage it. You two are ready?"

"Yes," Mary said with a touch of sadness. Sara, her thumb in her mouth, stood next to her mother. She was getting big, Sara. Perhaps one day, in a different land, she and Jacobi Arturius will be able to grow up together in peace and safety. I pray it will be so, I said silently.

"Well then," Thomas said, interrupting my thoughts. "We should be off."

He ushered Mary and Sara into the back of the wagon, and gave a couple of last minute orders to the people going with them; the rest of Thomas' guards and three women. That left Irena, me, Jacobi Arturius, Dosameenor's men, Leona and Jenus - the woman who had been injured in the ribs that day along with Leona. Leona and Jenus had both wanted to stay to help with Irena and Jacobi Arturius.

On the previous evening, we, all those who were left in the camp, met to discuss the present and future. The two women insisted on staying with us and Dosameenor's men. Everyone else felt that it was time to leave. We discussed plans and strategies well beyond that, too, one of which was that at a point two years hence, on the Ides of October, Irena and I and Jacobi Arturius would meet up with Thomas and hopefully Mary and Sara, to give them the Rood. The place we would meet would be Antiochia or Antioch. Irena had family there. It was where we decided to go when she was better and our baby boy was fit to travel. At last accounting, Rome was certainly an occupier there, but not in full force.

"Goodbye," said Thomas from the driver's platform, standing alongside the driver.

"Farewell!" called Mary from the wagon's back, tears brimming her eyes.

"Byeeee," squealed Sara with delight, beside her mother.

We stood and waved as the entourage disappeared into the mists.

Time created a void into which we seemed to fall. Or, more accurately, we simply lost track of time. Caring for an infant is an all-encompassing job in the best of times. Yes, we had the help of Leona and Jenus, but even so, Jacobi Arturius kept us extremely busy.

He grew rapidly and we had the time of our lives with him. But before we knew it, he was near his first natal day. Almost a full year had passed. Irena and I were astounded when we stopped to think about it.

Then we awoke one morning to something surprising and quite frightening. The mists were gone.

We had stopped posting a guard through the night a

long time ago. The mists had always been a solid presence since the time we first came to this place. Of course, it needed to be shored up on occasion with a ritual similar to the initial one used to create it, but that was simple enough. Yet, nothing had happened to indicate that the mists might vanish outright.

Leona was the first to find it so. She had risen early just before full dawn, as she always did, to prepare the breaking of the fast. We all rose quickly when we heard her cry out.

"What is it?" I called, as I bolted headlong out of the tent, the lance in one hand, my gladius in the other.

Then I saw it: Nothing but green and open forest surrounded us, except for the hill on one side. No mists. Birds were singing their morning tune and a slight breeze was soughing through the trees. But there was no other noise. One could see beyond the trees now, nearly out to the main road.

One by one, all came out of their shelters to greet the new day, and one by one, had expressions of surprise and fear on their faces.

Jenus was the first to regain her voice. "Merlin Longinus, what has happened?"

"I do not know," was all I could manage. I quickly regained my senses, though, and barked orders to the warrior guards who remained with us. "Go out to the road. Scout the area quickly, but thoroughly. Report back to me within the hour."

"Aye, sir," said the eldest, a grizzled old bear of a fighter, named Fracix, who had barely said three words since we all arrived here.

He and the others left at once. The women looked to me for more guidance. "Leona, prepare to break fast as you usually would. If someone was here and meant us harm, they would have already attacked," I reasoned.

Leona gave a curt nod, took the younger Jenus by the wrist and went about her business.

I heard coughing and turned to see Irena, looking a bit

pale, holding Jacobi Arturius in her arms, both still in their sleeping wraps and rubbing sleep from their eyes.

The coughing was coming from Irena. It had taken her quite some time to get back to resembling the normal, healthy woman I had always known. Even when she got back to that point, she still tired easily. Now she seemed to have something happening in her chest. "You're coughing. Are you all right?" I asked, trying not to sound overly concerned.

"I'm quite fine, my love. Just a bit of a chill, that is all," she replied.

"Sorry, but I'll take no chances with you," I said.

"Thank you, Longinus, but your doting isn't necessary. What happened to the mist?" she asked, tactfully changing the subject.

"I don't know," I said.

Longinus, said the voice in my head. Heed the signs.

"Yes," I said out loud.

"What, my love?" asked Irena, looking at me with a mixture of fear and awe. "You swooned."

"What?" I asked, and then noticed that I was sitting on the ground. "How—"

"You went into a trance mumbling something and then went to the ground," said Irena.

I said nothing, but tried to recall what she said I'd done. All I could remember was the voice in my head.

"Longinus? What is it you saw?" Irena prompted.

"Not what I saw—what I was told: 'Heed the signs,' is what I remember."

"'Heed the signs?'" she repeated.

"Yes. I believe that it means it is time for us to leave here," I stated flatly.

"Yes," Irena said after a moment. "Yes, I agree. It is past time for us to do so."

An hour later, with the morning meal nearly done, the scouts came back to report that no one was in the immediate area. Not a soul. We could easily venture out and probably not run into anyone until the morrow at least. That settled it then.

It was indeed time to leave our sanctuary. I felt it in my heart, in my soul. The vanishing mists and the fact that we were alone were the signs.

I thanked the men and dismissed them to eat, but urged them to be ready to leave when the sun was at her zenith. The day was warm and bright and we would have much time to travel. I then informed the rest of our party of the plan.

"Where are we to go?" asked Jenus.

"To Antioch," I replied.

"I have family there," Irena put in as she cleaned up the meal dishes. "You are all welcome to stay with us there."

A slight frown crossed Leona's face.

"Or we will make other arrangements for you to go wherever you wish," added Irena.

"No. It is not that," said Leona. "I really have nothing to go back to. I was just trying to figure out where Antioch is. I've never heard of it."

Jenus laughed. "You tain't never heard of any other place, either, have you?! You never been anywhere outside 'o home but here!"

"And you have?" the older woman countered.

"Not what I'm sayin'—"

"All right," I said, interrupting the little feud. It is quite some ways south, southeast of us right now."

"Is Romans there?" asked Jenus.

"Yes, but I don't think many," I replied.

Irena coughed several times then.

I waited patiently until she finished and cocked an eyebrow at her that said, Are you sure you're all right?

She simply gave me a look of annoyance.

I would take her at her word then. I turned my attention back to the others. "Please be ready to leave by noon. We will eat an afternoon meal on the road, so prepare something and pack it," I ordered.

"Yes, sir," said Leona and Jenus in unison and left us.

Irena, Jacobi Arturius and I also went to prepare for the

leave-taking.

We entered our tent. Irena yanked the sleeping skins off the pallet with her free hand and put the boy down on the bare pallet. She gave him the warrior-doll that Fracix had made for him, a toy that was not exactly a favorite of hers because of what it represented. But Jacobi Arturius loved the doll and it had been a very pleasant gesture from the old warrior. It was something that displayed his loyalty, albeit in an abstract way.

Jacobi Arturius babbled incoherently with excitement as he shook the doll. His mother kissed his head and tried to comb the lad's unruly dark locks to the left so they were out of his eyes.

"No," he frowned, as he pushed away his mother's hand.

I had never heard him speak beyond a baby's gibberish. "Well," I said in surprise. "That's wonderful!"

"Not really. 'No' is all he seems to want to say thus far," answered Irena.

"It's a start," I countered.

She coughed again. The bout only went on for a few seconds, but it did not sound good.

"Irena," I started.

"Longinus, don't," she said. "I tell you it is a slight chest cold, nothing more. It will pass in a matter of days. Right now, we must leave as you said. Come, we must ready ourselves."

I stood there, lost in thought. Despite the trance voice, and the signs, we could easily stay a while longer. True the mists were no more, but I could put them back or try. And even if they never came back, we seemed to be alone in this little forested valley.

Yet, I knew that the voice had been right; knew it deep within.

"So be it," I said. "You're right. Let's get ready."

Irena started to roll up the bedding.

An urge suddenly hit me. "Wait," I said, taking her by

the hand.

I pulled her close, kissing her on the mouth passionately, rubbing my hands through her hair. She returned my kiss with equal passion, opening her mouth invitingly.

After a moment, we simply held each other, her head resting against my shoulder. As it happened so many other times, I could feel her heartbeat through my chest, my own heartbeat matching hers in rhythm, our souls merging as one. We stayed that way for a few minutes, savoring the feeling of exquisite closeness.

Finally, she looked at me and crinkled her brow. "Longinus, are you trying to become ill?" she teased.

"I would have whatever ails you as long as we could be together," I replied. I truly loved this woman with all of my being.

We continued holding each other and I became aware of something: a fire was burning within me. I wanted her then and there.

And then I looked at Jacobi Arturius, staring at his silly mother and father with that grin of his. He was innocence personified, and I knew that my fire must cool for the time being.

I pulled away then, gently stroking Irena's lovely cheek with the back of my fingers.

I thought of something then; something that had crossed my mind several times of late. "Irena, my love. I have to ask you something."

She must have seen a shift in my countenance; seen a seriousness come into my eyes. "What is it?" she asked, a look of fear in her eyes.

"Nothing, nothing," I answered soothingly, reassuringly. "It's just...it's just that, if something befalls me, if something happens while we're on the road, I want you and Jacobi Arturius to take the spear and go with Mary and Thomas. Stay with them even if it means going somewhere far away."

"What are you saying? What have you seen?" she pleaded.

"No, nothing. I am just saying...I want you to be prepared just in case," I replied.

She didn't answer right away. "You assure me you have had no vision to prompt this...this request?" she finally asked suspiciously.

I laughed. "Yes, my love. I promise. 'Tis pure precaution."

"All right then. You have my word. We will go with Mary and Thomas even if it means going to the ends of the earth," she said.

"I thank you," I said, embracing her once again. For some reason, I felt relief at this; relief at having voiced my desire for this type of arrangement.

While it was true that I had not had a vision or dream, something in my being had compelled me to get Irena to make the promise. Whatever it was, it was not in the forefront of my consciousness, my mind—at least, not yet.

~XXVI~

We left one half hour after the sun had reached its zenith. One of Fracix's men questioned why we didn't just wait until the following morning.

"'Tis foolish. Won't get far this day. May as well wait 'til the morning. More time to supply up, too," he had said.

Ironically, this was also one of the men who had complained bitterly at being ordered by Dosameenor to stay. I would have thought him anxious to leave at any time. But I think in the end, he was just the complaining type.

His comments this time, however, earned the young man three sharp cuffs on the side of his head, administered by Fracix himself. "You show respect to Merlin Longinus and do as he says, you damned whelp, or I'll gut you and leave you here for carrion!" yelled Fracix for all to hear.

As with most bellowers, the young complainer was full of naught but air when confronted with firm authority.

The first few hours on the road were spent marveling at the sights and smells from the surrounding woods. The greenery was beautiful and lush; yews, pines, and oaks abounded. The smells were astonishing. For the first time in quite a while, we all realized that we had been missing a lot of smells altogether. The mists had dampened our surrounding environment at the encampment, laying a type of blanket on the trees, shrubs and ground. The result was that not much in the way of scents escaped our detection. We had simply become accustomed to it to the point that we didn't notice a lack of forest smells.

Now, out in the open once again, the scent of pine, mistletoe-laden oaks, and the musk of damp dirt—the skin of the earth—wafted to our nostrils. It was delightful.

Most everyone seemed to be in a jovial mood, probably

due to the fact that we were once again in the world of men and not hiding in a secluded, misty, hillside glen. We were all quite grateful for the protection of that enchanted place. But a gilded cage is still a cage, even if it's of one's own making. We should have left the misty glen a long time before. But then, from atop Macha, I looked into the small open wagon that Irena and Jacobi Arturius were riding in and I remembered the reason that I had refused to leave sooner.

Irena caught me looking at her, smiled seductively and winked, then coughed. I couldn't help but laugh. The cough rather shattered the alluring seduction of the moment she'd created. I sobered quickly and silently prayed that her cough was indeed just a chill of the chest and did not portend something more serious. Though Jacobi had been an old man even when I'd first met him, his final demise had been due to the lung disease. I could not help having that in my mind when I heard my love cough.

For the time being, however, I respected her wishes and paid no mind to her cough; at least outwardly.

The first day was short. We got our bearings and traveled south, by southeast, enjoying the environment as we went along. As Fracix and the scouts had reported before we left the encampment, we had not seen another soul that first day. We halted at sunset and made camp for the night.

I sent two of the men out to scout in the direction we were headed. Still, they saw no one. But they did see definite signs of people; the road we were on came to an intersection with three other roads, all of which headed in very different directions. There was no one at the intersection, but there was ample evidence to suggest that vendors had carts set up there on occasion, and heavily-laden wagons rolled through. There were many deep wheel grooves in the wet dirt of the roads to support their belief. The road we were on curved a bit at this intersection, but clearly continued in a southeasterly direction, which is what I required. My objective was to reach one of the ports along the border of Gaul and Italy, and secure passage on a boat for myself, Irena, Jacobi Arturius and the two women.

It was not likely that we would find a boat going directly to Antioch. In fact, that would probably be impossible. Antioch was many, many leagues from where we were now. To reach it by sea would be an arduous journey. But, the alternative was a combination of a very difficult journey over both land and sea. Besides, if we stuck to the ocean ways, there would be much less of a chance of being stopped by a Roman patrol.

Whichever port we reached, and once our passage was secured, I would then release Fracix and his men from their obligation of service to me. If one or more wanted to come with us, then they would be most welcome to do so. But, I'd not hold a man any longer than necessary. I thought about some kind of gift or reward for them. I even thought of giving Macha to Fracix. As much as I would have liked to, I was not going to take her all the way to Antioch. Upon rethinking it, though, it would not be fair to the other men to give Fracix such a fine gift when I could not match it for the others. Macha would also fetch a handsome price in the market; money was something we'd certainly need for the rest of the trip.

But securing the boat trip and saying farewell to our escorts was still a few days away at best. For now, it was enough to enjoy our first night out of the mists; our first night of freedom in many moons.

We sat on the ground around the cooking fire and I explained my plan for the rest of the trip. At one point, Jacobi Arturius crawled onto my lap, gurgling what sounded like "Da!" He settled quickly enough and seemed to quietly observe everyone and listen to everything that was being said, as if he were taking mental notes.

The spear lay by my side and began to give off a perpetual soft white glow which remained the entire time the lad was on my lap. The energy I sensed from the glow was that of protection; protection for the boy. Others around the fire periodically looked at it, some with a bit of awe on their faces;

others with unmasked curiosity. I finally pushed it under my leg as much as possible, out of sight, to minimize the distraction.

"...And once we've obtained passage," I said, continuing what I had been saying to Fracix and the men, "you and your men are free to go home."

The men murmured. Five of them were obviously overjoyed that their tour of duty with me would be coming to an end soon. A couple of them even began to boast in explicit detail of the sexual pleasures they would experience with their wives the moment they got back home.

This banter proved very entertaining to Leona and Jenus, who were sitting with us around the fire, and who, in turn, seemed to delight in this change in conversation. Celtic women were anything but prudish when it came to the subject of sex. To the Celts, sex was the most natural and wonderful thing that Dana, the Mother Goddess of all things, bestowed upon earth. It balanced the Universe.

Irena was not present, having excused herself after the meal to wash up, which I was glad for since young Jacobi Arturius was sitting on my lap and his father was almost as entertained by the conversation as the two women.

"All right, you animals," interjected Fracix. "Can't you see there's a little one here, too young to be hearin' such shite from the likes of you?"

One of the men looked at me, fear in his eyes. "Sorry, Merlin Longinus. We meant no offense. It's just...we're excited to be going home is all."

"No offense taken," I said quickly. "And, I'm sure the boy's a little too young to comprehend most of what we say on any given subject, let alone the topic you were just in."

"Thank you, sir," said the lad whom Fracix had cuffed earlier.

"No. Thank you. Thank you for your service and devotion. You do Dosameenor proud," I said. "Now, I suggest we all retire. I would like to leave at first light."

"Aye, sir," said three of the men in unison. Everyone got up to gather their bedding. Most were sleeping by the fire.

Irena and I were the only ones who put up a small shelter for the night. She had started to almost argue with me about it, but I insisted on putting it up both for her sake and Jacobi Arturius', and I was not going to take no for an answer.

I was about to walk to the shelter to be with my family when I saw Fracix unrolling his sleeping skins near the fire and I approached him.

"Yes, Merlin Longinus?" he said with respect.

"Please, Fracix, you needn't be so formal with me. Longinus will do," I said.

"How 'bout Merlin?" he offered.

"I'd prefer Longinus."

"As you wish," he said sincerely, but with some distance, and continued to unroll his bedding.

"Why did you not celebrate as your men did when I said you'd soon be released of your obligation?" I asked.

"No reason, really. Just not my way," he answered vaguely.

"Have you a family to return to?" I asked. But as soon as I asked it, I realized that perhaps I'd overstepped my bounds. "I'm sorry. It's none of my business."

"No," he replied. He stopped fussing with his bedding and faced me. "No. I've no family. I had a boy and a wife. And a dog. They were all killed by Draco."

I sank inside. Draco had destroyed so many lives. "I'm sorry. I'm so sorry."

"Thank you, Mer— I mean, Longinus, sir. It's just...well, I have nothing to return to."

"You are more than welcome to come with us, you know," I said. "In fact, I would like it very much, and I know Irena would, too."

"That's very kind," he said. He paused then, thinking about my offer.

"Besides, Leona's coming with us. I've seen the way she looks at you," I added, trying to make things a little lighter.

His lined faced creased a bit into a smile. "Leona aside,

I would like to accompany you to Antioch. From there, who knows."

I clapped him on the shoulder. "Excellent. Very good. I'll see you in the morning, then."

"Yes, sir."

"Again, please call me Longinus and not sir or Merlin. All right?" I asked.

"All right," he said, chuckling.

With that I bid him to rest well and retired to my shelter.

Irena and I were up before the new day was lighted. Jacobi Arturius slept on. He was wrapped in skins and laid underneath an oak while his mother and I took down the tent and prepared a small meal. By the time the sun's light was cresting the horizon, our little company was once again on the move.

We had traveled the better part of the morning. I was on Macha, riding at a gentle pace alongside the tiny wagon which carried Irena, Jacobi Arturius and the two women, when Fracix and one of the other men I'd sent with him to scout ahead came back at a trot, halting their mounts in front of me.

"What is it?" I asked apprehensively.

"Nothing to worry about, I think. There is a very small village, maybe a couple families, about three miles ahead," answered Fracix.

"Any Romans?"

"No, sir," he replied.

"All right. We'll pass through, maybe garner a few more supplies, some information," I said.

We pressed on, coming to the village a while later. Indeed, the village was tiny: three small mud buildings and a fourth structure made of grass and branches.

At the edge of the road, just on the outskirts of the village, a small, filth-encrusted child of about six summers, whose gender was indeterminable, yelled out at our arrival. The little one's eyes lit up as he or she turned and ran back to the structures, yelling something which seemed to be in a regional form of the Celtic dialect, which I could not understand.

I assumed it was an alarm of some kind. Yet, I halted in drawing a weapon. Something stayed my hand, my intuition saying that it was fine. I turned to Fracix, "What is the child saying?"

Fracix looked perplexed, apparently at what the child was saying. "She says, 'More are coming! More are coming!'"

That was indeed perplexing. What did she mean? Even more interesting, I thought, smiling to myself, was how Fracix could tell it was a girl. I gave voice to that thought, "You can tell it's a girl?"

"Of course," he said as if it were the most obvious thing in the world. "But, what does she mean by 'more are coming?'" he added, drawing his sword.

"No," I said. "That won't be necessary."

"But—"

"Trust me. I feel it," I said.

"As you wish," he said, sheathing his weapon.

We proceeded into the village. A small, hobbled old man came out to greet us, the rest of the clan waiting cautiously behind him.

"Greetings, friends," said the elder in a heavily accented dialect that sounded similar to Dosameenor's. I understood him, though. His voice had a high-pitched quality to it, and his breath and words whistled through his lips as he spoke. His tone and demeanor were quite friendly, yet not pretentiously so. There was no fear in him.

I dismounted and faced him, allowing him to clearly see that my weapons were not drawn. "Greetings," I said. "We are simply traveling through and wonder if we could barter for some supplies and perhaps some news."

"Supplies we can help with. News is rather short. We don't really go to the outside world. All we need is here, don't you know," he said smiling, and holding his hands out, gesturing to the plush greenness and beauty surrounding us.

Though I could understand the man's love for his home, I was very disappointed. I wanted to know what year it was, how long we had spent in the mists as compared to the real world of men, and did Tiberius Caesar still rule Rome?

"I must say you are the second visitor we've received in two days!" the elder added excitedly. "Perhaps our other guest can give you news."

My years as a Centurion pricked my skin. Who was this other visitor? But then the inner voice calmed me again and I knew that there was nothing to fear from this other visitor.

I was about to ask about the guest when a familiar voice hailed me from a short distance away. "Longinus, sir!"

I spun around to see Paulonius standing there. He looked weary from travel and thinner. But he was wonderful to behold. There was something else about him, too; there was a bearing about him now. It dawned on me that he was no longer the young lad whom I remembered. He was a man now. "Paulonius!" I exclaimed. I rushed up to him and embraced him as a brother. "'Tis good to see you!"

"Yes, and you," he said.

Irena called out from the wagon. "Paulonius!" she exclaimed joyfully, Jacobi Arturius giggling in her arms.

"Miss Irena!" he said. "And who is the strapping young one?"

"That is my son, Jacobi Arturius," I said proudly.

"A son. How wonderful," replied Paulonius, smiling like a proud uncle.

We stayed in the tiny village for the rest of the day, and that night, too. I did not intend it so, but after a midday meal, Paulonius took to filling us in on the events of the outside world, after which we found the day to be rapidly waning. I decided that it would serve no purpose to be on the road again for only a couple of hours. Besides, Irena's cough seemed to be particularly acute that day, and thus the rest would do her well.

Five years had passed while we had been in the misty sanctuary. Five years. Though that did not equal the pace originally put forth by Hentapas' calculations, it was, nonetheless, nearly impossible to comprehend; my thinking had us in the mists only two to three years at the most. No matter; the whys of that mystery could be left for someone else more adept at deciphering the mechanical workings of the Universe, perhaps to some philosopher/mystic/mathematician of the future.

Five years, though, was a long time. I had apparently become the stuff of legends. Me and the spear, that is. Rumors had started some years before that the spear and I had performed miracles of healing and divine magic that, somehow, allegedly proved the divinity of Jesu the Christ, the Son Of God, as many now called him. The spear and I, according to these stories, had been called to Heaven by God, Himself (which is why I had not been seen all these years) after I had been preaching the so-called word of God to the heathens and barbarians of Gaul and beyond. I had become, according to these misguided folks, the next messenger of God and Jesu.

It was apparent that there was a whole new religious movement growing. Christians, they were being called, for they purportedly followed the teachings of the Christ or Jesu. Unfortunately, from what Paulonius told me, it sounded more like most of them were worshipers of the man, Jesu, looking to him for salvation, for the Kingdom Of Heaven, rather than following His teachings of turning within oneself to seek God and the Kingdom.

Many of these so-called Christians were counting me among their numbers, based solely on the rumors and interpretations of certain events that they chose to call miracles of God, instead of understanding them for what they were: conscious workings with, and of, the natural Laws of the Universe. Adding to the perception that I was one of them was the fact that I had left the Roman military machine and indeed had turned my back on Rome altogether. In other words, I was still a fugitive of Rome which added more to my mystique for them.

But I was not one of them. I had experienced enough events and manipulations of the Universal laws that led me to know that a potential Christ existed within each one of us; that A Master Druid, a Merlin of the highest order, is within every one of us. There is no reason to look to the outside for anything of this nature save for a certain amount of guidance in unlocking these inner mysteries; these eternal secrets that are housed at the core of our beings.

Toward the end of the day, the village elder who had first greeted us—Rhetter, was his name—led me to a pile of supplies that his people had put together for us. There were dried meats, furs for warmth, skins filled with water; even a few filled with mead.

I was overwhelmed by his generosity. "I thank you from the bottom of my heart. But, I fear I cannot pay for such riches," I said.

"Pay?" he queried, obviously having no concept of the word.

"Trade, barter," I clarified. "We really have nothing to trade you for these riches."

"No trade," he insisted.

It seemed to me that especially with the meats, these were indeed riches for the villagers. I got the feeling that they were part of their winter stores. But in the end, it would have been much more of an insult to turn down the gifts. "Thank you," I said again.

"Please to take this, too," he said, handing me a ceramic jar about the size of a small goblet. "It is salve from our Shaman," he said. "Even a great healer such as you can use help sometimes, no?" he said in his whistling manner of speech.

"What is this for?" I asked.

"Your wife," Rhetter said. "For her lungs. Rub it on her chest and under her nose before she sleeps. The spirits in the salve work to help her breathe."

I opened the jar and sniffed the contents. Tears came to my eyes as a vapor, the spirits, from the salve wafted into my nostrils. The immediate effect was amazing; even I, who was not at all ill, could breath clearer than I could moments before. "Thank you!" I said excitedly. Perhaps this would indeed help Irena.

I asked Fracix and two of his men to help secure the supplies before retiring. The sun was sinking and we would leave early the next morning. I embraced Rhetter in another gesture of thanks and excused myself to go back to the central fire where Paulonius was waiting for me.

"They are generous people, are they not?" he observed of Rhetter and his people.

"They are indeed. They are indeed!" I replied. I paused briefly, wondering at the lad. "Are you coming with us?"

"Of course," he replied, clearly surprised by the question.

"I mean, are you coming with us all the way to Antioch, which is to be our final destination?" I clarified.

"I know it is and well, yes."

"You knew about Antioch?" I asked, intrigued.

"Yes. I found Mary in Jerusalem. She told me of your plans to meet in Antioch. I thought you'd stay on or at least near the main road when you left the mists, so I was confident I'd find you even if you'd already left that place," he said.

"Mary and Thomas are well, then?" I asked, not meaning to change subjects, but still interested in my other friends.

"Uh, Mary, yes. I suppose Thomas, too, but he was in Egypt. Mary was with a man named Joseph. He seemed kind enough. Quiet sort, though. He owned the tomb in which Jesu had been laid to rest, you know. Joseph of Arimathea, that's it," Paulonius said.

Interesting turn of events, I thought to myself.

"Anyway," Paulonius continued, clearly becoming excited at what he was about to tell me, "before starting on my journey to find you, I took the liberty of securing passage for us all from the Port city of Nicxa. It's just over the border into Italia from Gaul," Paulonius explained. "It's not a straight trip, mind you. There'll be several stops at ports of call along the way. But I think you'll be pleased with the accommodations, providing it all goes as planned."

I was quite surprised and pleased by the lad's initiative. "What...how—"

"You'll see," he said, putting up a hand to silence me, clearly quite pleased with himself.

I trusted Paulonius implicitly and looked forward to seeing what he had procured for us. Another thought occurred to me then. "What of Genevieves and your child?" I asked. "Last I saw you two, she was expecting."

"Twins, we had! Can you believe it?" he said. "Two girls. They're just like their mum. Bossy little things! It's all I can do to get words in on the edge!" he said, laughing with affection. "They, and my two brothers, will meet us in Antioch —if that's all right with you," he added tentatively.

"Of course it's all right! Congratulations!" I said, embracing him. "Irena will be thrilled."

"Thank you," he said timidly, shying from the acclaim.

"All right then," I said. Let's get some rest. I'll see you at first light.

"Yes, sir," he said, giving me a playful legionnaire salute.

The whole of the little village came out to see us off at first light. A couple of the children, one of whom was the filth-encrusted little girl who had first announced our coming, chased our traveling party with delight for nearly a quarter of a mile or so. She finally stopped when her mother called for her. The little one stood and waved to us until we had gone too far and could see her no more.

We headed south, following a trail that somewhat paralleled the main road we had been on.

Paulonius led the way. I was still very interested in how he had secured passage for us and on what kind of vessel, but he remained tightlipped about it until, as he put it, "all things were confirmed," just in case the captain of the vessel was unable to make it after all. "That's very unlikely, though," he added.

The day progressed uneventfully. Irena seemed much better from the use of the salve. She was hardly coughing at all. Still there, however, was the ever present rattling in her chest. I was truly beginning to fear that it actually was more than just a chill. It just seemed to linger. She remained strong, though, even if she tired easily. She had been gracious enough when I presented the salve to her the previous night, if not a bit dubious about it. But, in the end, she tried it and it gave her some relief almost instantly.

The surrounding area was, for the most part, quite lush and green. Patches of dried foliage and leaves were only here and there. There was a slight bite of cold to the air, but nothing intolerable. According to Paulonius, it was actually late fall. Winter would be upon us before long. But, he assured us, we would be at the port city of Nicxa well before the onset of winter; in just a matter of a couple of weeks or less.

Late in the afternoon, I sidled up to Paulonius. "We need to stop soon for the night. Fracix spotted a secluded glen about three miles from here that will do."

"Yes, good. I think we've made good progress for the day," he said.

"Indeed." A silence fell between us for a few moments; the horses' hooves and the chirping of birds were the only sounds to be heard. "So," I finally said, "what of Mary and this Joseph fellow? How did you meet up with them? And Thomas is in Egypt you say?" I asked.

"Well," began Paulonius, "Genevieves and I just kept traveling. Oh, we stopped for a bit when her birthing time came, but not for long, even with twins. We originally had planned to stop and make a home somewhere near her village, near Dosameenor's clan-hold. But I wanted to keep going. Something in me, as it turned out, just wanted to see where you had first met...him; you know...Jesu," he said a bit timidly.

"No reason to be shy about it, lad. None at all," I said.

"Anyway," he continued, "We ended up there and heard about a woman speaking in public, talking about the teachings of Jesu. We went to hear for ourselves and lo and behold, it was Mary. Joseph was with her then. Still not sure how they met. She was quite pleased to see me and asked after you and the lady and the little one, of course. She said Thomas was in Egypt establishing a community of his Gnostic types. They were going to join him at a later time. She even talked of going with him, Joseph, I mean, back into Gaul at some point in the not too distant future, maybe even to a large island in the west called Briton or Britain or something."

My heart suddenly thumped in my chest. I felt the world around me close into darkness. A vision came upon me: one of a brilliantly green land surrounded by the sea. It was a place that abounded in beauty: a place that had within it a large lake that contained a small island that was always shrouded in mystical mists. It was a place with giant stones standing in circles that were once places of worship, but now stood as ancient sentinels to a long-forgotten race of peoples whose descendants presently inhabited the marshes and nearby hills of the land, rather than the entire island.

I saw the land as from the air; as if I were a bird. As if I were a powerful Merlin who had taken on the form of my namesake and was flying over the land, and I knew unequivocally that my descendants, too, would thrive in this land. I even saw Irena there and Jacobi Arturius as a grown man and...

"Longinus," called the voice from far away. "Sir!" It was Paulonius' voice.

I came back to myself, still mounted atop Macha, but slumped over in the saddle. Our whole party had halted. The vision had been strong, so real. I ached all over, as if I had actually been flapping my arms, my wings, on the journey over the island in the vision. "Yes," I said.

"Longinus, are you all right?" This was Irena. She had apparently jumped from the wagon the moment she saw the trance state assert itself on me. She turned to Paulonius. "What did you say to him?"

"I was speaking of Mary and Joseph and Thomas and-"

"And the island of Britain," I said, interrupting Paulonius.

I knew the moment I said the words Island of Britain that it had been a vision of truth; my immediate descendants would indeed thrive in that place, would become native Britons. But I would never live to see the land. At least, not in this life. That thought saddened me, yet excited me, too, for it made the future clearer.

"Longinus?" Irena repeated.

"I'm fine, my love. I'm fine." I answered.

"You're sure?" asked Paulonius. "I did not mean to-"

"Stop right there, my friend. These things come upon me as they will," I said. "No need to worry. Now, let's proceed before we lose daylight altogether."

"Let's go then," Irena said, coughing slightly.

The company began to move down the trail once again.

~XXVII~

I was floating, floating above the Isle of Mists in the lake, the lake that was in the middle of the strange land, the large Isle of Britain, it was. Ruins of standing stones dotted the landscape of the small isle as well as its mother, the larger one.

The image changed. I was part of a large circle of white-robed figures. We were a smaller circle inside the circle of ruined stones. A ritual to welcome the full moon is what we were doing.

That image faded and was replaced by another one; another ritual, another night. Many robed figures were in a circle, just as before. This ritual was different, though, an important event: the conjuring of the unifier of Britain. A priest and priestess were naked, performing the essence of the rite atop the center stone altar. All were chanting, including the two on the center altar.

I was there -- not just in the vision, but in physical form as one of the participants. Longinus was not who I was here in this place. I was who I would be in that life. This was a distant future. I knew this to be so. The naked priest upon the altar was me.

That image faded, too, replaced this time by a horrific scene in the present, but still yet to come; the not so distant future of this life. Roman soldiers. They were crucifying someone, but I could not see who. The prisoner was being crucified upside down.

Smoke filled the image. I struggled to see more, but could not.

I began to shake. Or rather, someone began to shake me. "Longinus?" Irena said, coughing. "Wake up! Wake up!"

I left the realm of dreams and visions and returned fully

to the present moment, opening my eyes to see her beautiful face hovering above me, filled with concern.

"I'm here, my love," I said.

"You were dreaming. What did you see?" she asked.

"The Island realm," I answered, still in the fog of sleep and dreams.

"You were...chanting, too. In a foreign tongue," she added.

"Hmm," was all I could manage to say.

"Well come, then. We need to be up. Light is already breaking in the camp," she said.

Indeed, outside of our tent, I could see light and hear others already up and about.

Suddenly, something hit me in the ribs. I looked and saw a little foot pushing against my side. Jacobi Arturius lay between us, stretching to give rise to the new day.

I sat up then bent down and kissed the boy's cheeks then looked at Irena. "How do you feel today?" I asked.

"Well," she replied. "The salve is quite good."

"Take a deep breath," I said.

"What?"

"Please. Take a deep breath."

She sighed, a bit annoyed, but did as I asked. The rattling wasn't quite as prominent, but it was still there. Or, perhaps she has found a way to mask it, I thought, smiling to myself. That would be typical of her.

"Thank you. All right, then," I said letting go of the matter. I got off of the sleeping pallet and froze. Something...something...a wave of foreboding washed over my entire being.

Irena was watching me. "Longinus?"

I said nothing; could not even move. There was no vision, nothing other than a...feeling; as if a squashing weight had just been placed on me.

Do not worry, Longinus, said the voice in my head, His voice. All will be as it should.

"My love, you're frightening me," said Irena, now

standing before me, touching my arm.

Slowly, the feeling left me. I looked at her and smiled. "It's fine. I'm fine. Just an odd feeling, but it's gone," I said.

"What kind of odd feeling?" she pressed.

"Worry not. All will be as it should," I said, echoing the voice within.

She gave me that look of annoyance once again, but let the matter rest.

"Shall we join the others?" I asked

"Hah, nah, gah," giggled Jacobi Arturius as he played with his toes.

"You go ahead," Irena said. "I'll get the little prince presentable."

Something in her phrasing caught me off guard, creating in my mind an image of a future King in a future land that I, Longinus, was related to. "What did you say?" I asked.

"What?" she replied, not having heard my question over the lad's laughter.

The image in my mind was quick and fleeting. "Never mind," I said. "I'll go help the others get ready." I left the tent wondering about the meanings of the images and visions I'd had that morning.

The day proved to be as beautiful as the preceding one. Nicxa was not far, not as far as Paulonius had thought. It was perhaps only a week away at most, at least according to the two old women we met on the trail. They took to bickering between themselves when they could not agree on the exact distance. They were sisters as it turned out and the elder of the two said that it was six days hence; the younger, seven.

We thanked them for the information, though I'm sure they did not hear, for as we moved off, they were behind us in the middle of the trail, facing each other, hands on hips, each yelling to convince the other that she was right.

All we could do was bless them, laugh and go on.

Later in the day, I was riding alongside of Paulonius and Fracix. Fracix was commenting on where we should stop for the night.

But his voice began to fade in my mind. It quickly became as a distant ring in my ear. Something else was attracting my attention; something from a source outside the realm of the physical.

The feeling of foreboding crept into my being again, but this time, there was a specific reason for it; we were being watched. There was no one in the bushes, no one in or behind the trees, of that I was sure. It was not that kind of reconnoitering work.

This was the work of one who understood the laws governing remote viewing: a magician, a sorcerer, as the layman would say. In other words, someone was looking into dark waters or a flame to view us from a distance.

An interesting side effect of that type of magic, or so I had been told by Detrom at one point, was that more often than not, it took a part of the viewer with it; part of his or her energy. You often could feel the personality of the one performing the remote viewing.

In this case, I knew exactly who was watching us. "Draco," I whispered as I stopped Macha.

The others stopped with me.

"What did you say?" asked Fracix.

"Where is he?" asked Paulonius nervously, drawing his sword as he spun his mount in survey of the area.

"He is not here, Paulonius. Not in the flesh, anyway." I explained. "Yet he watches us all the same," I said, again trying to feel Draco's presence.

Neither of the men questioned my assertion. They simply took it as truth.

"Don't worry, even if he watches us from afar, he does not know our plans," I continued after a moment, as much to convince myself as to assure Fracix and Paulonius. I let the matter drop for now, focusing my attention back to our immediate needs. "Speak naught of this to the others. "We'll be on the boat soon enough and out of here altogether. Agreed?"

"Yes," said Paulonius.

Fracix, however, remained silent. For the first time, I sensed that there was something simmering in this one, a rage that was just below the surface, but mostly kept in check, except when I mentioned the name Draco.

"Fracix?" I said. "What say you?"

"Of course, I won't say anything," he replied.

"Is there anything you want to say to <u>me</u>?" I asked.

He hesitated, then said, "I will kill Draco if I can," he confessed.

This actually explained a lot. I had started to wonder why this man had really wanted to come with me. It's true that he had said he did not have anything or anyone to go back to, and I had taken him at his word. But now I could see that wasn't the only reason.

"You stayed with me believing that Draco would probably continue to chase me. That way, you'd eventually have a chance at him, is that it?" I asked, accusation dripping from my words.

"No, sir! I mean...that was not my intention in staying with you. Please, you must believe me," Fracix pleaded.

I said nothing for a moment, letting him ponder my silence. But then I softened. I liked Fracix, truly I did. "Perhaps you don't really know your mind. But then, who among us does?" I asked rhetorically.

"Yes, sir," he said, bowing his head in shame.

"It doesn't matter. I'm glad to have you here, regardless of the reason," I said, smiling. "And I've told you before, don't call me sir." With that, I nudged Macha back into motion and we headed down the trail once again.

That night, I slept peacefully and the following night, as well. In fact, the next few days were uneventful as we traveled down the trail. We ran into several people, locals of the surrounding area, as well as others traveling on the trail, but never got wind of any Roman patrols, even though either Fracix or one of the other men was constantly scouting the way ahead.

Even so, I could not shake the feeling of being

watched. Draco's presence I felt, but another's too—a Mage of some kind, one of Rome's pretentious Priests of Apollo or the like. They were working together to find me, the spear, and the Rood.

No matter. I did not sense they were anywhere near us. Surely, we would make the port and be away before they could catch us.

We started on our way on yet another bright, crisp, clear day. Fracix and one of his men went on ahead to scout, as was the usual routine. They had not been gone long when we smelled something in the air: the ocean. Excited murmurs ran through the group as it was now apparent that this phase of our journey would end soon. As if to confirm this, two gulls circled above us, chirruping to one another.

"I should ride on ahead, make sure the ship's there. We're earlier than I thought we'd be, you know," said Paulonius as he came up alongside me, his mount dancing beneath him. Macha snorted in annoyance at the other horse's exuberance.

"Well, if you think it's necessary," I said.

"I think it's a good idea. Hopefully, it's already there. If so, I can encourage the captain to ready sail. The sooner we leave this land, the better," he added.

"All right, then. Be off," I said.

He kneed his mount to a near gallop.

"Wait!" I called.

He stopped and spun around.

"How will we find you? Where shall we meet?"

"Of course, sorry! Ask for me at the Porpoise Inn. It's a few streets in from the docks. You'll come to it first before you see the boats," explained the lad.

"See you there, then," I said.

With that, Paulonius was gone.

A short while later, Fracix and his man came back. They had gone as far as the top of a grassy green hill on the outskirts of Nicxa, which overlooked the port city and the bay. Fracix was confident that we would make our destination by late afternoon. We did not stop for the midday meal, but ate on the trail.

As Fracix had predicted, when the sun was nearly touching the earth towards day's end, we crested and descended the grassy green hill and headed into the city by the water.

It was easy enough to find the Porpoise Inn: a large building made of brick and wood. It had the look of a well-made, Roman-engineered structure. The sign hanging in front had a huge dolphin or porpoise painted on it. We passed several Roman patrols scurrying here and there on the way to the inn.

I had dismounted upon entering the city and walked in with the rest of our party on foot. I pulled my cloak up around my head, but that was probably unnecessary, for not one person, legionnaire or otherwise, paid us any mind. Everyone we passed seemed oblivious to all else except for their own mission of the moment.

The city was crowded, smelling of humanity and the sea, but it was exhilarating. The closer we got to the inn, the more anxious I was to be away on the boat. The next step to that was asking after Paulonius at the inn. I told the others to wait outside the Porpoise Inn while Fracix and I went inside. I thought about bringing the spear in with me, but decided that fewer arms were better. So it remained secured in its place on Macha's side.

The inside of the Porpoise Inn was a contrast from its outward appearance. Outside, the structure looked strong, even dignified, promising an ample bill of fare and comfort within. But it seemed a questionable promise. The main room was dimly lit and smoky from cooking fires. Various sorted types—dirty, nearly rag-clothed sailors, filled the nooks and crannies of the place; denizens of the sea, aliens of the land. Women served those denizens with the vivaciousness akin to the professionals which they probably were. Surprisingly, there were also a couple of tables filled with legionnaires, drinking loudly and playing equally as hard with the serving wenches as the denizens were.

The Centurion in me wanted to walk over to their tables and box their ears, demanding to know who their superior officers were. Of course, I was not about to do that. Instead, Fracix and I stealthily made our way to the right of the room, to what appeared to be a counter for guests to inquire for accommodations.

The robust woman behind the counter grinned toothlessly as we approached. "How may I help you?" she asked in Latin, with surprising articulation. It caught me off guard. For the most part, I had been speaking in the Celtic tongue for a few years now. I simply assumed someone in her station would not know Latin very well, if at all.

"We seek a friend," I said.

"Don't we all," she replied coyly, batting her eyes at Fracix.

"Uh, yes, well this friend's name is Paulonius," I said.

"Here now, woman. The legionnaires at table four need another round. Go," said a tall man, wearing a mead and beer splattered apron. He swatted the woman's ample rump. She sighed, obviously disappointed, but left.

The man seemed of sixty-some-odd summers, but still had a commanding presence. "Whom do you seek?" he asked in northland Celt, Dosameenor's dialect.

"Who are you?" Fracix asked, a little too gruffly and unnecessarily. If the man answered, courtesy dictated that we identify ourselves, as well. If it came to that, obviously, I would have to lie.

"The owner and proprietor here, Jamsonis," the man said with a smile. "Don't be fooled by the raucousness here right now. Three ships just came in, you understand. I keep a good place with very clean and nicely appointed rooms, providing of course, you have the means."

We had little to trade and even less money. I would have to sell Macha. Indeed, all our horses would have to be sold before the voyage.

"We have the means. But before we discuss that, let's

see if there is even a need," I said. "We're looking for a lad named Paulonius."

Jamsonis' eyes lit up. "Ahh," he said. "Yes. He gave me instructions to have you wait here in a couple of our rooms. Your ship is readying herself for passage. You are to leave on the high tide at midmorning on the morrow," he said. "Your man Paulonius will meet you here later this evening."

"I see," I said, pleased, but rather surprised he knew so much.

"I know Paulonius. We grew up very near each other, you understand," Jamsonis offered.

"I did not know that," I said. "Listen, my friend, we cannot pay you for the rooms until tomorrow. We have fine animals but need to sell them before we leave."

"I can help with that. Are they horses, oxen?"

"Horses."

"Good animals?"

"Yes, especially one that I'm loath to part with," I said.

"I understand. I can get you the most denarii. I deal exclusively with the Roman Garrison here, you understand. I'll even be your middle man—show the beasts to the garrison commander myself," he said.

Something in his tone gave me indication that he knew I wanted anonymity. I was not sure how much Paulonius had told his childhood acquaintance, but something told me that he could be trusted. "That would be good," I said. "Perhaps first thing in the morning?"

"I don't know that the commander is available then. Perhaps tonight? Later, of course, after you've spoken to Paulonius," Jamsonis offered.

"Tonight? He would do business at night?" I asked.

"He prefers it, actually."

"Very well," I said.

"I'll show you the rooms myself," said Jamsonis.

I sent Fracix to fetch the others while I followed the proprietor.

We all fit into two fairly large rooms that connected

through a large door. The rooms were scrumptious, according to Leona, complete with easy access to the baths in the building next. After visiting the baths myself, I snuggled in for a nap with Irena and Jacobi Arturius. Leona and Jenus shared our room; everyone else was in the other. Two of the men were outside the doors at all times, keeping watch in shifts.

I was awakened around midnight by the sound of coughing; Irena was having a rough night.

"I'm sorry, my love," she said. "I fear I keep everyone awake."

"Don't worry," I soothed. "The salve no longer works?"

"Sometimes better than others," she answered.

I kissed her then, a simple, loving peck on the lips. Something wiggled against my side; Jacobi Arturius rolled over in his peaceful sleep, oblivious to the cares of the rest of the world.

"He's beautiful, is he not?" Irena asked in a rattling whisper.

"As beautiful as his mother," I replied.

"I was thinking more like his father," she said. She coughed again, though gently, quietly.

"That chill should have left you by now," I said.

She started to protest, but stopped when I threw up my hand.

"Before we leave tomorrow, we are going to seek out a doctor. I'm sure there's one around here," I asserted. I would not be silenced this time about the matter.

She opened her mouth to speak, but was halted by a knock at the door.

Leona answered it. "'Tis master Paulonius," she said.

"Come in," I said, getting up off the bed.

Paulonius entered with Jamsonis right behind. "Are you comfortable?" asked Paulonius.

"Quite," I replied. "Good to see you."

"And you," replied Paulonius. "All is ready. We leave top of the eleventh hour in the morning." He turned to the proprietor.

"And here is the money for your horses," Jamsonis said, stepping forward and holding out two bags of coins."

It appeared to be much more than I expected. "Thank you. This is...generous."

"My pleasure. The garrison commander fell in love with yours, you understand—your Macha. I saw it in his eyes. So, I held out for a good price, a very good price," he said with a chuckle.

I would miss Macha. I had said my goodbyes earlier when first I showed her and the others to Jamsonis. I only prayed that she went to a good home.

"Ah, I know that look, my friend," Jamsonis said, staring straight at me. "Fear not, the commander is a good man. Macha will be loved and pampered."

I believed him. "Thank you for that also." I shall have to tip this man well when we leave, I thought. Indeed, Fracix's men too. I now had enough coins for it.

"There is something else," I said, after a moment. "A doctor. For my wife's cough."

"Well, Chefren the physician travels with us tomorrow. He's on his way home," Paulonius put in. "He's renown in Greece and Egypt and much of Rome. Do you wish to see him now, my lady?" he asked of Irena.

"No, no. Do not disturb him at this hour. I will see him tomorrow," she answered, looking at me, playfully challenging me to protest.

"The morrow is fine," I said to Paulonius, but looking at Irena. "Tomorrow is fine."

Tomorrow came quickly. Now that the day was here, I was more anxious than ever to be away. Our things, such as they were, had been stowed aboard the vessel early, before dawn. I only carried a shoulder skin of water, a sleeping Jacobi Arturius and the spear, wrapped in a sheathing of cloth. Irena walked at my side, hand on my arm, the other women and men just behind us. We were all following an excited Paulonius down to the docks.

"You'll see. The ship is as strong as...well, you'll see. And the rooms you have aboard are very comfortable," said Paulonius.

I was not paying attention to the lad. The feeling of foreboding was back; of being watched. This time, however, it did not feel as though the viewers were all that far away.

I looked around. Roman soldiers were here and there in clumps. Some would look at us as we passed; others would simply glance, then look away, at other citizens making their way about. None of them seemed to be paying undue heed to our group.

"Did you hear me?" Paulonius inquired.

"Uh-huh," I said absently, still scanning the crowds for...what I was not sure.

Then I saw it; a darkly-cloaked figure some twenty or so yards away, darting in and out of the people, all the while keeping pace with us. He—I assumed it to be a man for the figure's size—disappeared behind a large vending cart. When he did not reappear on the other side of it, I handed Jacobi Arturius to Irena. "I'll catch up to you in a moment," I said.

"Where are you going?" she asked.

"I just need to check on something." With that, I hurried off.

I quickly walked over to the cart and stepped behind it. The cloaked figure was nowhere to be seen. It was as if he had vanished into thin air. My first thought was of Draco. Perhaps he was not as far away as I had felt him to be during the remote viewings I sensed that he was conducting. Or, perhaps the cloaked figure I'd just seen was his apparition; his projected self. I thought this latter point hardly probable. I spent another minute or two looking over the immediate area. He was not there. It was time to leave.

I quickly caught up to the others.

"What was that for?" Irena asked, concern etched on her brow.

"I thought I saw something, someone," I replied honestly.

"Shall I take a couple of the men and go back and look again?" Fracix offered, having run up to meet me at my return.

"No, no. 'Tis not necessary," I replied. "I don't believe there to be any danger." I smiled, changing the subject. "Besides," I continued. "I have released you and your men. You are free to go home!"

It was true. I had given them all coin. It was a small gesture of my appreciation for their service.

"You are not yet away on the boat," Fracix explained. "They are your men until that time."

"All right then, but all's well," I asserted, while at the same time looking back to where we had just come from, attempting to catch again a glimpse of the cloaked figure. Still, he was not there.

We arrived at the docks. I said thank you and farewell to Fracix's men. Fracix, himself, was still determined to accompany us to Antioch and I made it clear that he was welcome.

Several large vessels appeared ready for the sea; ready to depart at or near the same time as us. Roman patrols were walking the docks, but not harassing anyone; simply observing. Many smaller boats, fishing boats and the like, appeared to be readying themselves for a day on the water, as well.

"Come," said Paulonius, "do you not recognize her yet?"

I was not sure of what the lad was talking about. But then I saw it: the Boar banner flying on the mast of the ship we were about to board. Standing at the plank, a one-man welcoming party, her Captain; Ventrix.

"'Ello, my friends!" exclaimed Ventrix, when he caught sight of us.

"Hello," I said as we boarded. I embraced him as a brother. "Captain Ventrix! What a surprise. I am so pleased to see you!" And I truly was. He had been marvelous to me and Jacobi and Dosameenor, and to Irena as well, as it turned out. He had been nothing but a very caring, good friend to her back in Najaffi.

"My lady Irena," he said with a respectful bow when he saw her.

"Stop it, Ventrix. We've known each other too long for such formalities. How are you, my friend?" she said, kissing the old salty dog on each cheek.

"I am well. I am well," he said. "But come. It is time. We must be underway. Me first mate will show you to your rooms below, or actually, why don't ye do it, Paulonius, my boy?"

"I'd love to," Paulonius said. "Follow me."

"We will meet for midday meal in two hours, yes? Much to talk about!" said Ventrix

"Indeed. I look forward to it," I said, and followed Paulonius below deck.

The rooms were spacious, considering we were aboard ship. Irena and I and Jacobi Arturius shared one room. Leona, Jenus and Fracix shared another. Although, throughout the voyage, Fracix actually ended up sleeping most often on the deck with the ship's crew. Once we had settled in, there was a knock at the door. I opened it and there stood a dark-skinned short man clothed in a white silk tunic. His head was shaved as was his face, lending him to look more like an Egyptian priest than anything else. The bag he carried, however, was not that of a priest.

"I am Chefren, the Physician," he said with kind eyes. I understand your wife is not well?"

"Uh, yes. Please come in," I said, standing aside for him to enter. "Irena, this is Chefren," I told her.

"Thank you so much for coming. I hope it is not too much trouble?" Irena inquired.

"No, no not at all," said the physician. "Shall we begin?"

To start with, he listened to her breathing, using a conical device. The small end went in his ear; the larger end against Irena's upper chest, all the while having her take deep, rattling breaths. He then listened from her back.

After a couple of other procedures, he asked her to hack and cough purposely, to draw up mucus from deep within the lungs, instructing her to then spit the slimy substance into a small glass bowl. He visually examined the stuff, smelled it, too, and even dipped his fingers into it to feel its properties.

Next, he requested a urine sample. Irena squatted while we turned our backs, and piddled into a glass cup. She stood and offered the physician the sample. Chefren eyed the liquid carefully, smelled it, and even tasted it.

"Well, my lady, you do not have the lung disease; yet," Chefren concluded.

"What does that mean?" I asked, bristling at the vagueness of his statement.

"She has a high-grade chest chill, it's true, but the liquid within her lungs is pooling, not flushing itself out. I have seen cases where this has led or been the precursor of the lung disease," he answered.

"Will it happen to me?" Irena asked, alarmed.

"Not likely. I said it the way I did to frighten you."

I was confused and a little angry. What game was this doctor playing?

"Please, forgive my bluntness," he said, "but you have not been taking care of yourself, have you?" It was more a statement of fact from the man, than a question.

Irena looked at me sheepishly. I simply smiled. I liked this doctor's way, after all. Maybe she would listen to him.

"Well..." she began.

"No, she hasn't," I volunteered. "We've been traveling, 'tis true, but—"

"Longinus—" she began to protest.

"It's fine," said Chefren. "The past is done. It does not matter now. Here," he said, holding out a small pouch to Irena. "It's an herb to mix with tea. Use a pinch in the morning, one in the afternoon and one before bed. It will help you rest and rid you of the chill before it does become something more. Besides, you will need your rest now more than ever. In fact," he said looking off, now clearly speaking to himself, "that obviously, at least in part, explains why the chill's held onto you so long."

"I don't understand," I said.

"Why, my dear friends," the doctor said, sounding surprised. "You are going to have another child. Truly, you didn't know?"

I looked to Irena.

"My cycle is late, to be sure, but I thought it due to the illness," she explained, wonder and excitement tingeing her voice.

"No. You are with child," Chefren said again.

Silence filled the room for a moment. "Well!" I finally said, laughing.

I crossed the floor and hugged Irena, picking her up off the ground.

"Careful," the doctor chided playfully. "I will take my leave of you, now. We depart in moments and I always like to be on deck when we set off."

I turned to the man. "Thank you, doctor. Thank you so much."

"Yes, thank you," Irena said. "Longinus, why don't you go with him?"

"Uh, I suppose I could. Are you trying to get rid of me?" I teased.

"Yes. Let me make the room presentable," she replied.

"All right, then. After you, doctor," I said, motioning to the door.

Up on deck, Paulonius was helping Ventrix with his duties.

I stopped them both briefly and told them that I was going to be a father twice over. They both laughed aloud in happiness. "Excellent, my friend!" exclaimed Ventrix.

I let them go about their business as Chefren and I stood at the stern, watching the people on the docks as we pulled away.

A crowd milled about near the slip from which we had just launched. A shadowy figure weaved in and out of the people, coming to a halt near the water. It was the cloaked figure I had seen earlier.

He appeared to be staring right at me, but I could not tell for sure; the cloak's hood was covering his head. Slowly, he removed the hood and I stared straight into his eyes; the eyes of the Dark Druid Draco.

Sailing was smooth. We had several stops to make for cargo and passengers along the way. The first was a quick stop not too far from our initial point of departure on the island of Corsica. Ventrix had a shipment of spices and herbs to pick up. We made the pick-up and were away again before long. The stop had been completely uneventful.

I told Ventrix and Paulonius about my sighting of Draco. There was no accounting for his being there other than simply following us on the land and by way of remote viewing. He had appeared to be alone on the dock, but that was far from certain. It would also be easy enough to find out where the ship flying the Boar was destined and follow her. "Be not concerned, my friend. You are safe here, and we are not followed. I've had my men in the nest since we left," offered Ventrix as we sat at his table the next evening eating.

Even so, my mind was not eased.

"You have powerful magic now, yes? Or so I heard," he said, changing the subject.

I looked at Paulonius.

"You've been gone awhile. As you know, more than few have begun to mythologize you," Paulonius explained.

"Some say you speak to Jesu—you do God's work in His name and you preach his teachings," added Ventrix. "Is it true?"

I thought for a moment about how I should answer this. "I speak to Him, in a way. I believe He exists in all of us. As for doing God's work, I suppose you could say that too, in a way. I use the natural laws of the universe to achieve results that could not be achieved otherwise. If you believe this is God's work, then so be it," I said. "I do not preach Jesu's teachings. I don't even know most of His teachings. In fact, I don't teach or preach anything."

Ventrix looked confused, and disappointed, as well.

"Sorry. I don't wish to perpetuate a false belief," I said.

"It may not matter," Paulonius put in. "Folks are going to believe what they will, no matter what you say. And I'm sure Draco and his cronies are aiding in the spreading of rumors about you, too. Rome will think you could be a threat down the road. It'll make them want to catch you, all the more."

"Hah! That won't happen," Ventrix chimed in.

We fell silent for a while.

"How is lady Irena?" Ventrix asked.

"Fine, fine. Resting," I replied.

"Good. Good," said Ventrix. "We were good friends for a long time, you know. I mean, just friends, mind you, not—"

"I know, Ventrix," I said, laughing. "She's told me all."

We finished our meal talking of things of the world. By the time I retired, Irena and Jacobi Arturius were fast asleep.

~XXVIII~

Our final stop before continuing the last leg of the sea trip, which was also the longest, was at Sicilia. A Roman officer, a Prefect no less, came aboard with several legionnaires, commandeering passage to Antioch. It was unusual, but certainly not unheard of. Apparently, the only Roman military vessel in the area was dry-docked. Since the Boar was heading to Antioch anyway, the commandeering was inevitable. Unfortunately for Ventrix, it meant relinquishing his cabin to the Prefect. None of us aboard the ship were comfortable with the Roman military with us, but there was nothing to be done about it.

The legionnaires and their Commander kept to themselves; too much so, I thought. They seemed to be going out of their way to avoid contact with us, or perhaps were under specific instructions not to interact with us at all. That in and of itself would have been fine, except for the fact that on several occasions over the next few days of the journey, I saw more than one of them in a huddled whispered meeting. During this time, they would sneak peeks at me or Irena when she was out of our room, averting their gaze quickly if they thought I or someone else would catch them watching. It was very strange.

At first, I thought I might simply be imagining things, making something out of nothing. But the spear was beginning to say otherwise. It was constantly aglow. On the one occasion I took it up on deck, it began to shake violently. I immediately took it back to our room and wrapped it up tight.

Then one night, Paulonius approached me when I was at the bow. It was late. I normally would have been with Irena, but something compelled me to the deck. He was scared, I could see it in his eyes, feeling the distress seeping from his pores.

"What news?" I asked, keeping my voice even.

He looked around to make sure we were not being watched or listened to. "The Prefect summoned Master Ventrix to dine with him," he said in a whisper.

"Not unusual. Ventrix is the owner and captain of the vessel," I pointed out.

Paulonius ignored the point. "The conversation revolved around you. Or at least, the Prefect tried to make it so."

"Explain."

"He wanted to know who you are, who is traveling with you," said the lad.

"Again, that is within protocol, as well..." I began.

"He joked that perhaps you were the 'traitor Longinus,'" Paulonius blurted out, almost too loudly.

"Calm yourself," I said.

"I tell you, they came on board for you, these soldiers did," said Paulonius.

"You don't know that—"

"Then why, by the gods, would the Prefect make such a joke? Draco is looking for you. Rome is looking for you. They are all working together!" Paulonius said, exasperated.

"Stop it! You sound like a hysterical little girl," I reprimanded him.

He was right, though, and I knew it. I had sensed for some time that the net was closing around me. Two things warred within me: the soldier and the Druid—the man wanting to fight and the sage who knew that there was a much bigger vision unfolding here. All will be as it should, the voice had said. But what of Irena and my son and my unborn child? And what of the spear? I could not let Rome or Draco, especially, ever get to Irena and the spear.

"What did Ventrix tell him?" I asked.

"He said he didn't know you—that your passage was arranged by a contact in Gaul. That you are a merchant with family in Antioch," replied Paulonius.

"What name did he give for me?"

"He didn't. He pretended not to remember, claimed he never kept records of passengers because he hardly ever had them."

"What about Irena? What relationship did he give us?" I asked, anxiety lacing my voice.

"None. Said you were sharing the room for belongings but that the lady and her child slept there alone, you with the crew mates," said the lad.

"What if the Prefect asks the men?" I asked.

Paulonius smiled. "They know who you are—have heard about you and the spear, too. Every one of them was serving aboard when you were here before and remember you. They love you the way they loved the old man Jacobi and would do or say anything for you, or nothing at all if it meant protecting you.

I was shocked. "I had no idea."

"And that's the way it is supposed to be. It's what Ventrix instructed them to do; pretend like you're not here, draw no attention to you and yours whatsoever," he explained.

"And they can be trusted?" I asked.

"To the death. Remember, I know them, too."

The sound of the waves lapping against the prow filled my ears, the noise of the flapping sails their counterpoint.

I knew I must speak with Irena immediately. I had to tell her what was happening, or seemed to be happening. It would be necessary to separate for now for the safety of all, at least until we made landfall; at least until the Prefect and his men were gone. "Thank you, Paulonius. You would do best not to be seen with me anymore for a while. I'm going now. I must tell Irena."

"Please, Longinus, let me. Stay here. I'll come back in a few moments. I'll explain everything to her. Give them no reason to question lady Irena by perhaps seeing you go to her.

I thought about it for a moment. She was the love of my life. I could not, would not, send another to do this. "Thank you lad, but no. I will be quick, but I must do this. Wouldn't you in my place?"

I could see him thinking of Genevieves and the twins. "Yes, of course. But be swift."

I snuck below deck, casually but with stealth. I saw no one as I slipped into our room and sat on the bed. "Irena, my love," I said gently.

She awakened slowly. Irena was getting more and more beautiful every time I looked at her. "Come to bed, my love," she whispered sweetly.

It pained me. In that moment, I wanted nothing more than for us to be away, to have a spread of land, a home, a hearth. A place where I could watch my children grow, and I could grow old with my love. With sad discipline, I pushed the wonder-filled thought aside. "I cannot, my dearest. Are you awake enough to listen?" I asked with some urgency.

"What is it?" she questioned, alarm in her voice.

I explained to her all that Paulonius had told me. She did not like my idea of separating for the protection of her and Jacobi Arturius, but managed to come around to it after some convincing. "There's one more thing," I said. "You must keep the spear. It is wrapped and stowed behind a loose panel near the door," I said, nodding to our room's entrance. "Take it and keep it with you until we are safely off and away from the ship."

"You don't want it with you?" she asked.

"They will recognize it for what it is: a Roman issued Centurion's lance," I explained. "And by that, the Prefect will know who I am. Keep it with you."

"Of course. Oh Longinus," she said, fighting back tears.

"Stay strong, my love. This will all be over soon," I added, as much to convince myself as to reassure her.

We embraced. I stayed in her arms for awhile, savoring every second of her presence; every nuance of her smell. After a few moments, I kissed her passionately on the mouth, kissed my sleeping son on the head, and slipped out of the room.

Flying, I was, once again above the small misty isle in

the lake of the larger island of Britain.

Jesu was with me on this flight, whispering into my soul. "All is as it should be, Longinus. There is no beginning, there is no end. Only changes in form, only changes in levels of being, of awareness, of growth."

Next, I saw that I was performing a ritual in the form of some future smaller self: a priest of the Druidic sect on that same misty isle. Jesu was there, too, standing next to me assisting in the ritual. He was not a physical form, though, but a vaporous presence. He was there briefly, then faded from sight.

"Land ahead! Land ahead!" came the voice from afar. "Land ahead!"

The priest that was myself in this future life, this future realm looked up as if he heard the call.

"Land ahead!!" came the voice again. My future self and life faded from view.

I awoke. Neck aching. I had slept yet again on the hard wood of the deck, starboard side, near several of the shipmates. They were all awake and looking at the posted lookout perched on the mast. "Land ahead!" yelled the lookout again.

"We make land, Merlin," whispered the man next to me.

"Please don't call me that," I said.

"Sorry, sir. Me apologeeze, Master," said the grizzled old fool. "I remember you."

I concluded that the old man was a few candles short in the head. I had spent the previous night next to him, as well, yet he acted as if he had just seen me for the first time, or at least for the first time in a long time.

"Shut up!" said one of the other mates, clocking the first one in the head. This one was muscled and young. "Shut up. You know what you were told."

"Sorry," the old man said again.

I looked across the deck. Some thirty feet way, on the port side, two of the legionnaires were sitting on the deck staring straight at me. Had they heard the exchange? At least the old man had not called me Longinus.

"Means we land in a couple of hours, don't you know," said the old man, referring to the sailor calling out the land sighting.

"Hmm," I said looking out to the horizon.

I kept to myself for the next hour, to keep low and make sure that I was the last one off the ship. My plan was interrupted, though, when a legionnaire approached me as I was making my way to the cargo hold. "The Commander wishes a word," said the soldier.

I knew that tone well. It was an order, not a request for my presence. Thus, it was pointless to resist.

"Lead the way," I said, meeting his eyes.

I was taken to Ventrix's room, the captain's cabin, and ushered in. The Prefect was seated at an oak wood table perusing papers and maps. "Leave us," he commanded to the legionnaire. The soldier exited, leaving the Prefect and me alone in the room.

I stood there silently for five minutes. Ten minutes. Fifteen minutes. The Prefect never even glanced at me or acknowledged my presence in any way. The arrogance of the man was revolting.

Finally, I lost my patience. "Your man said you wished a word. Would you share that word before we make landfall?" I asked sardonically.

After yet another three minutes, he finally looked up and studied me for another minute or so. "No," he said flatly. He then smiled, malice dripping from his lips. He made a brushing motion with his hand, as if brushing dirt off the table —as if brushing me away. "You may go now," he said at the same time.

I felt myself growing angry. It was all I could do to keep myself contained. I backed out of the room slowly and returned to the deck, to the spot where I had been that morning.

"What did he want?" Paulonius asked from behind.

"To look me over. To see if it was Longinus who stood

before him," I answered.

Paulonius stood with me for the remainder of the trip. We docked in Antioch at midmorning. The lad, who insisted on staying with me all the way to our final destination, as he put it, and I, remained until all the others had disembarked.

We stood near the main sail mast and watched as one by one, the passengers left. Irena sneaked a look at me, at which point Jacobi Arturius saw me too. The boy yelled something unintelligible, but something that I knew to be, "Da!" Irena turned the boy's face away and quickly left the boat.

Lastly, after all but the ship's crew left, the soldiers went. The Prefect looked back at me, once again smiling malevolently, as he walked off.

I waited for about thirty minutes. The soldiers disappeared into the crowds on dock. Ventrix was still aboard seeing to the unloading of cargo. Our eyes met. I mouthed the words thank you, and Paulonius gave a nod to the captain, his former master. It angered me further that I could not give the man a proper thank you and goodbye. But things being what they were, it was clearly best to feign unfamiliarity.

Together, the lad and I left the ship. We made our way through the crowd, working ourselves to the center of town. This port city was not unlike any other; similar smells and many people. The difference here, however, was that there seemed to be a large contingent of Roman soldiers; many more so than any other place we'd been recently. Certainly more than I was expecting.

Still, we proceeded unhindered. After a few minutes of walking through the people, I spotted Irena, holding Jacobi Arturius, up ahead in the distance, perhaps fifty yards away, Leona and Jenus right next to her; Fracix and two dock workers carting our belongings behind them.

They seemed to be heading toward a couple: an older man and...Mary! I assumed that the man was Joseph, the Joseph of Arimethea of which Paulonius had spoken.

I was about to call out to them when I was grabbed

from behind. Strong hands seized my upper arms and spun me to face a platoon of Roman legionnaires led by the Prefect from aboard ship. Standing behind the platoon was the darkly cloaked figure, hood off, of Draco. How did he get here? Dark, negative use of the Laws, no doubt, were my first thoughts. Stupid, that. Of all the things to be concerned about in that moment...

"Centurion Longinus, traitor to Rome, preacher of the alleged Christ's doctrine against Rome, murderer of Roman Officers, Dark Sorcerer who seeks to destroy Rome...shall I go on?" yelled the Prefect as he stepped up to me eye-to-eye, spewing his words into my face and his spittle along with it. His mouth curved into that now familiar malicious grin.

This time I lost control. I hit him square in the face with my fist. I had always been told that I was unaware of my own strength. It must have been true, or else I had Otherworldly power coursing through my being in that moment, for the Prefect's nose was more than splattered; it was no more at all. In fact, the whole front of his face had caved in from my blow, as if I had hit him with a fist of iron, or an anvil. The Prefect went down in muffled screams of agony, dieing within seconds.

Immediately, the soldiers drew their weapons and advanced.

"Hold!" came the command from their rear, freezing the legionnaires in their tracks.

It had not come from Draco, but from the one who stood next to him. I had not seen him before. He was dressed as an officer; not just any officer, but a General, judging by the scarlet cloak he wore.

And then there were the others. There were two behind the General, who were dressed in the traveling togs of Roman officers. But their cloaks were the purple of the Praetorian Guard.

"Centurion Longinus," began the General in a deep, authoritative voice honed by decades of commanding others. "You've heard the charges put to you. And you may now add murder of a Prefect to it..." he said, glancing down at the officer I had just killed, "...as well as murder of a Tribune. Am I right, Master Draco?" he asked offhandedly, as he looked at Draco and back to me. "Will you not come peacefully, or do we have to kill you here and now?"

"I did not kill the other officer, the Tribune. Your man Draco, here, did. But, what difference if I come peacefully or not? You will kill me anyway," I replied.

"Now, now. No need for such pessimism. You don't know that," he said, softening his tone. He looked at Draco. "Is that true? Did you kill the Tribune in the forest, then blame this poor fellow?" he asked, with utter sarcasm. He turned his attention back to me. "Ah, well, Longinus. Never mind that. You and I simply need to...talk."

I had not drawn my short sword, but was in a fighting stance. I looked to my left and saw for the first time that Paulonius was being held by three legionnaires, one of whom had him in a choke-hold. I relaxed and looked to the General, nodding my head.

"Splendid. Move out," he said and the soldiers escorted Paulonius and me away. I peered over my shoulder trying desperately to catch sight of Irena. I could not see her, but I felt her watching me. I felt them all watching me.

~XXIX~

I came awake in a dank cell somewhere below the city, alone. Paulonius was not with me. My head throbbed. A lone barred hole at the top of the wall near the ceiling, about a foot in diameter, was my only source of air from the world. The hole was at ground level outside and let in only enough light, or darkness as the case might be, to tell me that it was deep night.

How many days I had been there, I did not remember. I had not eaten in days—that much I did remember. Water had been scarce, I believe. A little rain had seeped in through the hole, I think. That had helped. I had been whipped and beaten severely and often; that much I knew. Why? I wondered. Oh yes, the spear.

I had a wife, too. I called her my wife. She was the only woman I had ever loved; the only one I ever would love. We had started a life together. Irena.

I had a son too, Jacobi Arturius, and another babe on the way. Life was good. Except for this place. I was stuck in this place. I could end this myself easily enough.

Gradually, I came to my senses, letting go of the delirious thoughts. The General wanted the spear. The Prefect I had killed had been under orders to make sure that I was indeed Longinus, and to covertly escort me to Antioch, where Rome would exact her revenge on me and take the spear. Draco had bartered some kind of deal with them, no doubt to get the spear for himself eventually. I remembered during one of the interrogations that Draco had claimed to be the only one other than I who knew how to wield its powers. He lied.

I had told my interrogators over and over that I had tossed the spear. It was no longer with me; that it was in Gaul.

"You lie!" had been the response from one of the

interrogators. "You lived in a mist enshrouded village that you created through the lance's magic!"

"And the 'magic' stopped, which is why the mists left us and I left the spear," I had said.

Fools. I almost had them convinced.

I looked down at my wrapped hand, blood seeping through the bandages. Two of my fingers were now missing. A memento from the torturer, was that.

"Can you not grow another? You are the great Longinus. Perform a miracle for us, I command you!" my tormentors had teased.

In the end, they had received nothing from me; no information, no spear, no miracle. I suspected that even they were getting bored.

But had my powers, my abilities, abandoned me? Every time I had been thrown back into this cell, I had tried to conjure up a mist in which to escape in when next they came for me. I had also tried to control certain of the Otherworld elements to do my bidding; to aid me in masking an escape from this place. Nothing had worked. I could no longer even focus to go to that place within which Jacobi and Detrom and Jesu had taught me to access; that Higher place within that was my Truest Self. I had never felt so alone.

I was angry and numb. I cared for naught any longer.

Yet, that was not true. I cared about Irena, my son, my unborn child and all that I'd learned. And I cared that I would not be able to pass on the knowledge I had learned.

I wept. I slept. I dreamt.

Floating, I was, above myself in the dank cell. I looked down and saw my own huddled figure there on the floor, and realized I was not in my body. I was not dead, though. I could see the white cord attached to the body lying there and ascending up to the vaporous form that was me. It reminded me of the night of my initiation at Detrom's Temple mound.

"Strange, isn't it?" He said.

I turned my astral form and saw Jesu.

"We place so much attachment to the physical form,

yet at its earthly end, it is nothing," Jesu said.

"I am not dead yet," I said.

"You might as well be. You are too attached to the form of things. You have forgotten much. But that happens when we're in the physical," He said.

"We love things, people. They become a part of us," I countered.

"Yes, but that attachment is only in the context of the physical realm. You've lost sight that existence is forever in one form or another. If you choose it, your loved ones will always be with you and you with them, not just here on the earth plane," He said.

I said nothing; just looked with sadness at my physical form down below.

"Be at peace, my friend," said Jesu.

"I just didn't want them to get the spear," I said.

"I know. It is a powerful conduit. But they won't retrieve it. It is already gone from this place," He said.

I didn't question him as to what he meant.

"Let go now. Release all attachments—to this life, to that body, all of it, and simply Trust. Non-attachment is the essence of peace and happiness. Achieve this, and cross over with ease," He said as he faded.

I awoke huddled on the floor of the cell. Had I only dreamt the floating with Jesu? No. Its reality was palpable. I could feel it still.

Sunlight was streaming in through the little hole. Seabirds were calling to one another outside. A beautiful day, it seemed. It did not matter what happened to me. I was at peace.

They were coming; I could hear the footfalls. Guards marched in unison down the hall that led to my cell. There were four of them. They stopped in front of my barred door.

"Good morning, gentlemen," I said cheerfully, even energetically, though I struggled through the pain to get up. They looked at each other, not sure if I were mad or if I was displaying a miraculous recovery.

"Afternoon, more like," said one of them, a Centurion. "But not good for you, I'm afraid."

"More interrogations?" I asked.

"No. Done with that, we are," he said.

"Master Draco won't like to hear that," I said.

"Humph," said one of the others in contempt. "That one's gone, left this morning. Disagreed with the General, he did."

"Over what?" I asked, already knowing the answer.

"Enough outta you!" the Centurion said, slapping me in the face.

"Chain 'is legs, then bring 'im up and tie the wood to his arms and shoulders. You know the drill," the soldier said to his companions.

The sun was indeed bright. The day was hot. It was also beautiful. The colors on the trees and flowers were vibrant as I had never before seen or noticed. The smells were more luxurious than I remembered smells ever being. The twilling of the birds were all meant for me; for me to truly understand the beauty and diversity of the Creator and the Created.

The wood they tied across my shoulders—the cross piece to my crucifix—was heavy, blood-stained and splintered. I felt it dig into my skin as the ropes were tied to my wrists; felt my own blood begin to trickle down my back, my arms, and add to the wood's collection of stains.

"Move!" the Centurion called. We began a slow march to a hill some four hundred yards away. I knew it was our destination, for several other crucifixes dotted the landscape at the top of the hill. As we moved along, we passed a table in the shade of a tree at which several officers were seated, taking afternoon drinks. One of them was the General.

Though I was hunched over from my burden, I could still make eye contact with him. It was unavoidable.

"Halt!" he ordered.

We complied, the Centurion poking me in the ribs to

hold me upright. I all but fell over backwards, straining painfully and terribly to keep from doing so.

"Centurion Longinus," said the General, as he and the other officers got up and walked the short distance to us.

"Yes, sir," I replied.

"You seem chipper for a man about to be crucified," he stated.

"It matters not what you do to me," I said.

"You are not afraid to die?" he asked.

"No reason to fear. 'Twill not be the end," I said.

"Maybe his spear will magically appear and save him," said one of the other officers, inciting a round of laughter from the others.

Even the General laughed. "The spear matters not. Our idiotic priests claimed it to be powerful, as did that stupid sorcerer. What was his name?"

"Draco," said the other officer.

"Yes. Him. Ridiculous. A hunk of wood and metal. Absurd what fools will believe. I'm simply tired of you, Longinus. Time to make an example of you. Yet, you are not afraid, I truly see that."

"No. In fact, you honor me," I said.

"How's that?" asked the General. His demeanor had shifted to that of one who was now being insulted.

"You crucify me."

"Are you daft? How is that honoring you? I could see if we were to allow you to fall on a blade, but—"

"Because you crucify me the way we crucified him, Jesu," I said.

They all fell silent.

"You think this is a joke?" the General was enraged. "We shall remedy that. You, Centurion," he said turning to the officer that had been leading me, "you will crucify this one upside down, do you hear me?! Hang him upside down on the cross!!"

"Yes, sir!" replied the Centurion.

With that the General turned on his heels and went

back to his table in the shade, the other officers following in his wake.

The weight was crushing my lungs. I could no longer feel my feet or lower legs. Nor could I feel my hands. Where the nails were driven through my wrists, a stinging sensation was all there was. My head pounded fiercely. Blood was in my eyes. I don't know how long I had been there. It was night, I could tell. The immediate area was lit by torches. I craned my neck to view the crucifix next to mine. From my inverted position, all I could see were feet: Paulonius' feet.

He was hanged with me, next to me. He had been bloodied and missing all his front teeth when I had first arrived at the hill. He had already been attached to his cross and was lying on the ground before being hoisted to the upright position. His guards had abandoned him for the moment, drinking water and taking a break from their duties.

"I said not a word to them. Not a word," he whispered to me as I fell to my knees next to him.

"Thank you, my friend. For everything," I had replied.

He was dead now. I heard his last rasping breaths during my previous waking moments.

Something was moving in the torch light. A guard? Yes, a few yards away. A lone guard of the dead and dying.

But there was someone else. My eyesight was nearly gone because of the blood and pressure on my head. Someone was trying to get my attention. A figure crouched on the edge of the hill behind the guard. I did my best to focus my eyes.

The figure held a torch near her face. Irena. My love, my life. Was I dreaming? No, it was her.

I tried to call out, but I had no voice.

She made no noise, but tears streamed down her face. I craned my head again to try to see her right-side-up, but I could not move.

She was saying something, or mouthing something. I was in a daze; could not hold on much longer. What was she trying to say?

Then, I could see it, in my mind's eye, I knew what she was saying; could hear her in my heart: "I love you, Longinus."

"You are my heart, my soul, my love," I replied to her in my mind.

I left my body then for the last time. I would be Longinus no more.

~EPILOGUE~

It was 322 in "The year of our Lord," as the Christian monks would say. Their monastery was across the lake and up the hill. The lad did not have much contact with them.

He was growing up on the Island of Britain, in the realm of Avalon amongst the Druid priests and priestesses.

Ten summers he was, with long auburn hair and a thin frame. One beautiful day, he rummaged through the partial ruins of an abandoned underground sanctuary temple.

Going into this old place in and of itself was not unusual. The young lad loved coming to it. It was his sanctuary. He'd spend hours there digging, looking for precious relics from the past or just sitting in silent meditation, imagining that he was participating in some ancient rite.

On this day, however, he decided to venture deep into the very back portion of the temple, to its most inner sanctuary; a place he did not usually visit, and, in fact, had not visited in many a summer because it was so deep within that it was always shrouded in darkness. But something compelled him to go there. So, the lad took a torch on this day.

Shadows jumped to and fro as he entered the inner sanctuary. The smell of must and age filled his nostrils. When his green eyes adjusted to the darkness and torchlight, he noticed something under one of the toppled stones in the very back of the place. It looked to be wrapping of some kind. The boy placed the butt of the torch in the sconce hole of a nearby wall and attempted to move the stone trapping whatever it was that was beneath. He used all of his might. It was useless. Then he realized that what he took to be a stone was actually a large sarcophagus tipped on its side. Have I found a body? he wondered.

He decided that the portion of the stone on the

wrapping was the lid of this sarcophagus. Breaking it might be possible. The young lad picked up a nearby fragment of hewn rock and threw it hard at the lid. A loud cracking sound filled the room, as well as a cloud of powdered granite and dirt. There was nothing in the sarcophagus, but the item that had lain beneath the crumbled remains of the lid was now easily retrievable.

The boy pulled on the wrapping and dragged the thing free. It was long and thin, certainly not a body. Suddenly, he felt a tension grow within him as he touched the wrapping, trying to feel what was inside.

A treasure perhaps! he thought with excitement. He remembered a story, a legend really, of a man who visited this place three centuries earlier. He was from the Christian's Holy Land and had come with a woman and two children—boys, if the lad remembered correctly—and three treasures that purportedly had belonged to the very first Christian.

Could this be one of those treasures? Slowly, carefully, the lad unwrapped the thing.

A spear it was. An old Roman lance. He held it. It felt strangely...familiar.

He stood at mock attention, spear at his side pretending to be a Roman legionnaire. After a moment the boy looked closely at the thing. The shaft was still strong, but it was splintered in spots. The blade at the tip was bent slightly and the whole of the metal was stained with rust, and something else. The boy drew the blade close to his face and squinted his eyes to try and make out what, besides rust, was on the blade. It looks like blood! he thought.

Then a strange thing happened: the spear vibrated in his hands, and its tip began to glow softly. It was as if the thing was alive and simply waking up from a long nap.

He dropped it with a start. After a moment, the spear stopped the vibration, ceased its glowing.

The lad picked it up again. A fine weapon this is, he thought to himself. But I'm not a soldier.

The boy thought for a moment, then realized it would

be wonderful for another purpose.

He looked at the spear and said in a loud voice, "I declare you the wizard's staff!" His words echoed off the cavernous walls. He held the spear high for a moment, vertically, blade pointing up, then brought it down, tapping the shaft's butt end on the ground three times to make his declaration so.

"Hello!" called the female voice from outside. "Master Merlin, is that you? Are you in there?"

"Yes, priestess!" answered the boy.

"Come. Time for studies," the priestess called back.

The boy wrapped the spear back up and tucked it under his arm. He took his torch and treasure and headed out of the ancient temple.

VOLUME II

MYRRIDDIN

MYRRIDDIN

The moon was high and full. Its silver light bathed the valley and road with a brightness that seemed more akin to midday than to midnight. I saw the road clearly through a nearby cluster of shrubbery. My sight was so clear, in fact, that it was as if I were actually there.

The traveling party approached on the road from the east, just as my Druidic Master had predicted. There were three wagons drawn by two horses each. The wagons were surrounded by horsemen; Romans, to be precise. They were a contingent of soldiers, perhaps two Decades strong, their Decurions leading the way. Seeing an escort of Roman soldiers was an increasingly rare sight in this place and time, but certainly not unheard of. Rome still had Britain in her grasp, though that grasp was becoming looser by the day.

"Well, boy, what do you see?" asked High Druid Master Moscastan. He was young for a High Druid Master. No more than forty-five summers.

Moscastan was a striking figure: over six-feet tall, broad of shoulder and thick of muscle. He had an exotically handsome face with eyes as black as coal, and skin as brown as baked bread. He had been born in the land of the Jews, but Hebrew he was not. He was Persian by paternity. Moscastan had come back with his mother to her homeland, the isles of Britain, when he was but a child.

His mother being a Britton explained Moscastan's shock of red hair. She had been taken as a slave by Rome when she'd been but a lass and sold to a wealthy Persian noble for his harem. She had been freed by her owner, Moscastan's Persian father, upon his death, as set forth by his posthumous wishes. She then made her way back to Britain, child in tow. "I ask again, Master Merlin, what do you see?" he repeated.

Master Moscastan knew that I preferred one of the ancient Gaelic spellings and pronunciations of my name, as opposed to the common one propagated by the Romans. But he used the latter when he wished to chide me. Merlin. Merlin had always been a title, a level of achievement within the Druidic ranks, and, therefore, a special word, even a sacred one. But as with so many of our ways, the Romans—and the new peoples calling themselves Christians—had destroyed, or at the very least, bastardized them; the old Celtic and Druidic traditions. The title, or word, "Merlin," was one such example. The word Merlin had become almost more of a meaningless name now than anything else. But, there were many of us who knew that the old ways still existed, and hence their titles and words still held not only meaning, but power. Though I was given the name Merlin, I had too much respect for the title to use it as my name. Instead, I used Myrriddin, one of the more ancient and obscure spellings. This particular spelling also meant the learner, which I certainly was still, even at thirty summers and with my many years of study with the druids.

"I see three wagons and a Roman escort," I finally replied.

"Look within the wagons," commanded Moscastan.

"What?"

"Do it!" he ordered.

I peered through the shrubs again just as the wagons were passing in front of my view. I concentrated on the wagons, commanding my inner eye to see their contents. Indeed, after a moment, I could perceive the parts of Roman war machines beneath the wagon's canvas covering.

"Siege engines!" I shouted.

As I did so, one of the Decurions on the road reined in his mount and looked in my direction.

He could not have heard me, I thought. After all, I wasn't actually there.

But then the Decurion, the leader of one of the groups of Ten, nudged his mount toward me; toward what was my viewing position.

As the Roman officer did this, I jumped back with a start and bumped hard into Moscastan. My surroundings were no longer the moonlit valley and road and shrub, but Moscastan's sparse, dank, underground dwelling. Though its floor was dry, hard-packed earth, its walls always seemed to be damp; they were made of dark, soft clay. The whole dwelling only measured about ten-feet by ten-feet. It was dug out of the earth by Moscastan, himself, many years prior, and had a five-foot high, thirteen-foot long tunnel leading to the surface on a semi-gradual incline as the only way in or out. Three holes, a foot each in diameter, were scattered around the dwelling. They were ventilation ducts that led to the surface.

I stepped forward once again and cautiously peered back into the waters of the large scrying bowl through which I had been remotely viewing the moonlit valley and Roman-escorted wagons. The image I had been viewing and the scene I had been living was gone.

"I could swear an oath that one of the Roman officers saw me," I said, disappointment and embarrassment at having lost the images seeping into my voice.

"Not saw you, sensed you. Outbursts of emotion project your essence. Those whom you are viewing will sometimes sense your...presence, so to speak, if they are sensitive enough," Moscastan explained. "But you know this already, do you not?"

His half-smile was mocking, though not unkindly so. He was right. I knew that control of emotion in this instance—indeed, in most instances—was paramount to a successful viewing. More specifically, in the case of remote viewing, it was the control of one's thoughts that counted the most. An emotional outburst signaled the loss of this control, even if it was for only an instant.

"Yes, yes," I said. Though I wanted to try the remote viewing again, it was late and I was tired.

"The night is nearly gone, Myrriddin," said Moscastan in an echo of my thoughts. "We've seen what we needed to. The Romans come again."

"I admit I was surprised to see the siege engine parts in the wagons, but I'd hardly call twenty some-odd soldiers and three wagons another coming of Rome, even if they do carry war implements." I replied. "Perhaps they're leaving for good," I added, sardonically.

"Hmm," said Moscastan, noncommittally.

"Well, I should be off," I said, after a moment of silence. "Must be on the drilling field at dawn."

"Then you'd best be gone. The sun appears again in but four hours," replied the Master Druid.

"Peace be yours, Master," I said.

"And with you, lad."

With that, I headed up the tunnel and into the night air.

Luna went to slumber quickly, the sun birthing again much sooner than I had wanted it to. I had not yet developed the ability to gain a full night's replenishing sleep on a half-night's (or less) turbulent rest. Only a Druid Master like Moscastan was capable of such a feat. Though I had been a student of Master Moscastan's for many summers, twelve thus far, I was far from being a Deryddon—a full-fledged Druid; a full- fledged Magi or Magician. I had moments when I felt connected to this caste of Druid, the Magi, but not very often. There were actually three castes of Druids and I felt more a part of the other two than I did the Master Druid caste. The other two castes were known as the Bard, which was the historian or poet caste, and the Vates, which was the caste of the Prophet. It was especially this latter one that I felt most connected to because, more often than not, and more often than the average person, I would have prophetic visions during my sleep.

Yet, this was probably due not so much to my Druidic studies as it was to two other facts: The fact that I slept nightly on wattles from the Rowan tree, which were known to quite often produce visionary experiences in one who slept on them, and the fact that I also slept with my staff, which was formed from a Roman spear I found in the ruins of a nearby ancient Druid Temple when I was a lad. It was barely still recognizable as a spear. Its blade now cradled a Druid Egg, a rough, apple-sized crystal. The blade itself was straight and intact, not bent to cradle the crystal, though I had tried to bend it by heating the metal. No matter how hot it became, the blade would not bow. Nor would the hot flames cause any discoloration to the metal, or cause any of the corrosive stains that had been there for centuries to burn away. There was one cluster of stains on the blade that was definitely not corrosion. I was convinced that it was blood; it had the color and thickness of dried blood. But if it was blood, why could I not clean it off or burn it away?

On more than one occasion, the spear-staff had vibrated or become warm in my hands for no apparent reason, and seemed to convey something from the Otherworld. Exactly what that something was I still could not decipher, but I knew, felt, that it was something important and profound. I was not frightened by these occurrences.

When the blade wouldn't bend to cradle the crystal, I created a small, oval-shaped binding wicker cage made of oak and rowan sticks. It is called binding, for as one makes the cage, one speaks and thinks his desire and intent for it, thus binding it to those intents and desires. In this case, the intent was to protect and conceal the spear. I then secured it to the base of the blade, keeping the blade with it. Before securing it completely around the blade I placed within the cage, resting against the blade itself, the Druid Egg. This was not only to further aid in the protection and concealment of the spear's identity, but a Druid Egg, being a conduit of energy, also served to amplify the spear's power. Or so I chose to believe. I secured the cage and Druid Egg with leather thongs. The whole thing was impressive, a true Merlin's staff. Why didn't I just keep it as a spear? I was more of a wizard than a warrior, to be sure—though I enjoyed my youthful daily warrior training. But the spear, I knew beyond dreamy, idle wishing, was something special and was not to be paraded forth—at least, not as a spear.

Having the knowledge that the spear was something special, however, sometimes made me feel unworthy of it. Yet, as I said, occasionally when I touched it, it seemed to communicate with me, not in words, but with a small vibration or warmth. I almost felt that it was alive or even that something divine could come through it, though that had not yet happened. Other times, however, and in fact, most of the time, I knew that the spear, my staff, was meant for me and me alone. On the two occasions I had let friends handle it, they both had burned their hands quite severely when they touched the shaft. The warmth that I felt when touching it was more of a loving caress channeled from the Otherworld. It was a warmth that never exceeded the temperature of comfort. In addition to this, there was one other very important reason why I knew this spear was meant for me: it had always been mine. Not just in the life I now led as Myrriddin, but in a previous life as a Roman centurion, had this very spear belonged to me, this soul.

The combination of sleeping on the power-laced wattles and next to the spear would, on occasion, produce in my mind the vivid images and experiences of this man of the Empire from over three centuries prior. Yet, it was more than just the images and experiences of this centurion, whose name had been revealed to me as being Gaius Cassius Longinus that impinged themselves on my mind during my nocturnal sojourns. It was also the certain knowledge that I had been him in that very life; that my soul and his soul were one-in-the-same soul. Even more, was that according to Moscastan, I, Myrriddin, was related to Longinus, the man, by blood! This he had yet to explain to my satisfaction. But, he had assured me that it was so, and that he would explain it all to me in due time.

"It is enough for now that you have the spear, and that it speaks to you. Guard it well," he had said to me on the day

303

that I had revealed my treasure to him, and the fact that it communicated with me. Guard it well, I did. No one knew that my Merlin's staff, my Magi's wand, was the spear of Longinus, Roman centurion. I had disguised it well.

As the sun crested the hills to the east, I left my small round, thatched dwelling on the western outskirts of the village with staff in hand, and made my way to the cooking fires at the center of the village. There were a few people at the fires breaking their fast of the previous night. A bit odd, that was. Usually, there were many more on hand at that time for the morning meal.

"Ach, Master Merlin," came Leoni's familiar, deep, husky voice. I had assumed since my childhood that her deep voice was due to her hefty girth, and that its raspiness was from years spent in the smoke of the cooking fires. She had been with me since I was a tot. Her plump face and black hair had been the first images my eyes saw. My parents—having been told by the then High Druid Aberdinus that my coming had been foretold, that I was to be a great Druid—had given me up at birth for rearing by the community on the island of Avalon, the Isle Of Mystery, at the High Druid's insistence. Avalon, a small island in the middle of the Lake Essex, was where all prospective Derwyddons and Dryadesses, Druids and Druidesses, and all manner and levels thereto, were trained and housed. Many, such as myself, arrived not long after birth, if, that is, they had been chosen for it. And, one could only be accepted into the Mystery School on the island if chosen, as I had been.

Once the choosing had taken place, all ties to one's actual parents were severed for fifteen summers or so, at least. One did not actually begin formal Druidic studies until the age of eight. Before that, in addition to being allowed to just enjoy childhood, the little one was groomed for his or her future education in many ways; being taught to recognize the Spirit, the God, in all things, was one example. When I had first arrived on the island as a babe, Leoni had been a caretaker in the community's nursery. She had already achieved the status of a low-level priestess, but chose to go no further with her Druidic studies. "You must recognize your pattern," she had said to me once. "Know your meaning. Mine is to serve the younglings of this place and beyond." Leoni had been the one to call me from the ruins the day I had found the spear. I had taken it with me that day, removed it from its place of rest, concealed, wrapped in its rotting cloth. She had looked askance from me as I came out of the ruins of the Temple, silently asking, What is that you carry? But she never actually asked, never mentioned it. Now, even here, in our village off the island, she is with me still, not in the same way as when she was my caretaker, of course, but seeing her daily at the village's cooking fires reassured me that all was right with the world.

* * *

"Ach, forgive me, Master Myrriddin, I mean," Leoni corrected herself. "You did not join this morning's Sun birth rite."

"No," I replied. "I was with Master Moscastan until quite late last evening."

"And yet, Master Moscastan was there. Hmm," she said with mock bewilderment, bordering on reproach.

I said nothing. She could still disarm me as if I were naught but a very young lad.

She smiled broadly, a clean, dimpled smile. She still had most of her teeth. "Ah well," she said. "I'm just glad you're still at the study, even if it is a private tutelage with Master Moscastan. Concerned, we were, when you announced your leaving the Mystery School all those summers ago. We thought, 'Why? Why would the lad do this?' We all said, 'What with only half his years of study done...?'"

She continued rambling to herself as she resumed her duties at the cooking fire, poking the embers while reliving the events as she remembered them, all but forgetting my presence. I quickly took advantage of the moment, grabbing two oatcakes hot off the fire pan, a small wedge of cheese, and a cup of mead. "I'm off to the drill field, Leoni. Blessed day to you!" I called as I trotted away, all the while trying desperately to balance my mead, oatcakes, cheese and staff.

"And you, Myrriddin," Leoni called back to me. I hadn't thought she heard my goodbye. "You'd best be quick," she continued. "There're things swirling in the wind."

~ || ~

Whatever Leoni meant by her last statement, I hadn't a notion so I did not attempt to understand it. I made my way to the drill field, stuffing my face as I went.

My staff, mead and oatcakes were not the only things I carried. Tucked under my tunic in my leather belt strap was my sword. It was an old Roman gladius, refurbished, polished and honed to a deadly sharpness. I found it the day after I had found the spear in the Temple ruins. The gladius, however, I found in another set of ruins altogether. These ruins were near the village of the Ruthernus clan. They were not as dramatic as the Temple ruins where I'd found the spear, my staff; not by any means. That place had been a sacred stone Temple built by the Antewonc, the Ancient Ones, or more accurately, my ancestors. The exact function of the place in ancient times was now only known to the oldest of our Druids, although I suspected Moscastan held the knowledge, as well. Still, the place was considered hallowed ground. No doubt, I would have been severely reprimanded had the fact that I'd removed an artifact from the place become common knowledge. Yet, I knew my secret to be safe with the two besides myself who held the awareness of my possession.

I found the gladius, however, in a not so sacred place: a dilapidated Roman fort long since abandoned. I had also found a legionnaire's shield; three, actually, and two helms, also common legionnaire issue—the helms each had the tell-tale ring atop, not the cresting plum of an officer. I kept one of those along with the sword, but gave away the other items. I might as well have given away the helm, too. I never touched it after that day—no real Celtic warrior would ever use a helmet, after all.

Staff in hand, gladius tucked away under my tunic, I arrived at the drill field just as I finished stuffing food into my mouth. I thought I would be early. Yet, the field was already packed with many, young and old. Leoni had said to be quick; that there were things swirling on the wind. Indeed, I now understood at least part of what she had said; there was something on the wind, an air of tension wafting on the breeze. It appeared that most of the village was in attendance, as well as many from other villages around the area. No one was in drill formation. In fact, most everyone was cloistered about in groups, talking and whispering in anticipatory, if not anxious, tones.

As I approached the first group, I saw that it was made up of villagers and clan members, around my own age. They, too, were chattering excitedly like a flock of geese. Among them was my good friend Baldua. He was a mixture of the small, dark Hill People and Saxon: short, stocky and dark of skin, but yellow of hair and light of eyes. Though we were the exact same age, he was a good foot shorter than I. "Baldua," I said as I approached.

"Merline, mihi amice!" (Merlin, my friend!) he said in perfect Latin.

Though most in the region knew Latin, we mostly spoke in our native Gaelic. I loved my friend Baldua: we had always shared everything—from the same nurse-maid as infants, to the same lovers as grown lads—but he was a pretentious sort. For example, he preferred to speak mainly in Latin, convinced he was, or so he claimed, that it was the language of the future. For the sake of friendship, I let him get away with it while most others ridiculed him for it.

"Myrriddin, you sod," I said in Gaelic.

"As you wish," he replied in our native tongue, to my surprise.

"What is happening?" I asked.

"Horse Master Kindrixer says we must ready for battle. The Picts come from the north and Saxons from the northeast.

They are fighting together. Apparently, they have one leader," he said excitedly.

"They're one force?" I asked, dumbfounded. No such thing had ever happened before. The Romans had, for the most part, kept the region free of the raiding Picts and Scotts, as well as the Saxons. But lately, Rome seemed to have abandoned her charge, leaving us open and susceptible once again to these brutal raiders. I often wondered which was worse, the oppressive yoke of Rome, or the bloody and frequent skirmishes with our natural enemies and neighbors. One question that had been on my mind seemed to have been answered right then and there. The vision in the scrying bowl from the previous evening had shown Roman soldiers and their war machine on the move. They had been leaving us, I was now sure.

The rumble of pounding hooves sounded from behind. I turned to see a contingent of horsemen, among them, Horse Master Kindrixer—a half-Roman, half-British bear of a man. Tall, even in the saddle of his giant steed, he had dark hair and blue eyes. His face had the handsome features of a man in the classic Roman sense, as Leoni had crooned, whatever that meant. Her description must have been accurate for the reaction from women was the same everywhere the man went; a ridiculous swooning and faint glassing of the eyes, as if the female, upon laying eyes upon the man, had suddenly been rendered under a glam of love and lust. Even some of the males had the same reaction when they gazed at Kindrixer.

Aside from, or perhaps because of, his amorous affect on the lasses, and some of the lads, he was also a wonderful and charismatic leader. He had retired from the Roman military at the ripe age of thirty summers, having served his conscripted service of fifteen years. He had worked his way up to and through the ranks of the Roman military machine to the unprecedented level of Horse Master, a rank one was traditionally born into. Yet, as I've pointed out, much about the Empire and her might was changing almost daily.

Horse Master Kindrixer and his party halted now, his large brown bay neighing loudly at the hard yank on her bit from her Master. Kindrixer looked over the assembly, seemingly eyeing every one of us. "To the east!" he commanded in his deepest, authoritative voice. The urgency was unmistakable. "We leave now!" With that, he spun his mount and led the way off the drill field, followed by the rest of his mounted party.

The spear, my staff, began to vibrate quietly in my hand. Whether as a portent or not, I could not tell. It stopped as quickly as it had started. Then, almost as one, the throng that was assembled on the field moved to follow Kindrixer, not a one of us knowing our destination, let alone what awaited us at day's end.

My village must have been nearly empty, as with the surrounding villages. Everyone, it seemed, had answered the call to assemble with arms on the drill field outside our clan's village—the call that runners had apparently yelled throughout the villages after the morning's sun-birth rite. Obviously, the morning's ritual was not the only thing I'd missed.

"Form up!" someone shouted. The mass of people that followed Kindrixer attempted to do as ordered. There were more than a few clan members among us who had served in the legions of Rome. These men brought their experience and knowledge of Roman warfare and military back home with them. Some of them became leaders of our village's fighting army and even those of other villages. A given village's army, though, was probably a misnomer; my village's so-called army, for example. At first, we drilled in secret because of the Roman presence. But as more and more time went by, less and less of Rome was seen in the area. Gradually, our fighting group became bigger and a little better, drilling and training more in the open.

But two things became apparent quite soon. The first: though our group became bigger, no one really took the organized body of fighters seriously, especially the fighters themselves. It was thought to be too Roman. Celts fought as individuals within a group, not together as a unit. No matter how much we trained—no matter how much discipline was imposed on us by our actual battle experienced—Roman-trained brothers and fellow clan members, we were still Celts; group discipline was a foreign thing. Yet, that discipline is in part what had made Rome so great militarily. She could put thousands and thousands on a field of battle, and those thousands and thousands would fight as one; cohesive and deadly in the execution of its duty, efficient and precise in the carrying out of its objective. The forces of Rome had inspired awe and fear across the world. With that, however, she also left in her wake experience and knowledge of her techniques in the ways of war. Yet, those of us who tried to emulate the techniques for our own purposes often found ourselves ensnared by our own cultural habits and fighting techniques, or lack thereof. We were nothing like Rome. Thus, these exercises were more sport than anything else.

The second thing that became apparent was that although we used real weapons for our sparring—sharp swords, daggers and spears—most of us had never seen actual battle. Oh, there were certainly injuries from these practice battles, such as deep cuts from blades, broken teeth, bruised and bloodied bodies and body parts, but in the end, it was all just that; practice, not the real thing. Most of us had never seen any real fighting because for as long as I could remember, at least, we had always been a subjugated people; Rome had always been here. And, of course, we had never had an army of our own. But Rome's time among us was ending. So, threatened with raids and warring parties from other regions, other peoples, we tried to stand an army of our own.

Such was the case on this morning's march behind Horse Master Kindrixer. Our acting centurions formed us up into the tight rows of a legionnaire force. Though we numbered far less than any legion—a few hundred as opposed to a few thousand—we looked liked a formidable Roman force, minus the matching tunics and leather carassi of a real legion. And, for a while, we actually marched as one small army, comprised of many small Centuries, behind the Horse Master and his mounted men. As the morning wore on, however, the whole of our large group lost interest in being one force and walked as individuals once again; without formation, laughing and talking, and carrying on almost as children.

Toward the end of the morning, we stopped for a short rest. We had marched out of our valley, through a dense forest of small oaks and maples, and across a meadow plain of poppies and grass; then into another larger forest, this one comprised of ancient and sacred oaks and willows and dubbed by some the Dark Forest.

Though over time, this forest had become a place of mystery and even fear to many—indeed, more than one child had wandered in never to be heard from again—its name, Dark Forest, was originally derived from the fact that its trees were so tall and its canopy so dense that barely any sunlight slipped through to the forest floor. Still, many maintained that it was a place of spirits and hauntings. It was no wonder, then, that we made it through the Dark Forest in tight formations. Well, as tight as could be managed while dodging and darting around the mighty, sacred oaks. Finally, when we were nearly through to the other side of the forest, we stopped for a rest.

The respite was short-lived, however, and we were rudely summoned back to the task of marching. "Come now!" shouted Cramusin, a dark haired, short tyrant of a would-be centurion, whose only real skill, militarily or otherwise, was constantly annoying the general population of the clan—and everyone else with whom he came into contact—with his empty arrogance. "Form up. I order you!"

"Shut yer yap, Cramusin, or I'll kick ya like the mut ye be," replied an older clansman named Trastonus, who had served as a conscripted legionnaire for some twenty-five years.

"I am your centurion," cowed Cramusin in a whiny, nasally tone.

"Yer nothing, I say," answered Trastonus as he rose off his seat on a fallen tree. Trastonus, though around fifty-five summers in age, had the dried, leathery skin of one who had been exposed to the elements for a century of seasons. "We only follow you at times cuz Kindrixer, for his own odd reasons, likes ye, Cramusin. Make no mistake, lad."

Several of the others in our century—more a couple of dozen; our little group was no more a century than Cramusin a centurion—began to grumble their agreement with Trastonus. Trastonus and Cramusin had served together for one year under a brutal Roman commander. According to the older clansman, Cramusin was a coward, usually hiding behind a shield on the battle field. He excelled in the field ranks of the legionnaire and was granted certain privileges in rank and title because of particular favors he gave the Roman general, much to everyone's consternation. Those privileges seemed to have carried over to his service under Kindrixer.

"Be-s-sides, we've not be-een told wh-where we are going," stuttered a slight lass of about nineteen summers, by the name of Igraines. She was quite thin and pale, with emerald-colored eyes and chestnut shaded hair that hung in ringlets down to her underdeveloped breasts.

But her breasts and slight body were the only things underdeveloped about her. Beneath her chest beat the heart of an old soul and truly-tried champion. I had first met her on the Isle Of Mystery when she was very young, where she had come to study for what turned out to be a short time. Once back in the general population, and still a wee lass, she had taken much teasing and abuse over her stammering way of speech. She finally snapped two winters past when two lads, one sixteen, the other seventeen, had cornered her in the horse paddock to tease and torment the girl. Their fun turned violent, though, when some of Igraines's clothes were torn. It became clear that the young men were interested in more that a malicious game of mockery.

In short, Igraines smashed one of the lad's balls with the heel of her foot and cracked open the skull of the other with her bare fist, gouging out one of his eyes in the process. Once the lads had recovered from their injuries, they were banished from the clan and vanished from the village. No one ever dared mock Igraines again. She further proved her fighting prowess on the drill field. Her combat-sparring abilities were so impressive that most of the boys and many of the men voiced openly that they would not at all mind having her next to them in a fight.

While she was a good fighter, I was also of the mind that adding to the sentiment of wanting her next to them in a fight was the fact that Igraines was budding into a beautiful young woman, as well. I had heard as much on more than one occasion while the drink of mead went around an evening's cooking fire, after the women had gone, of course. Many of my fellow clansmen had commented on the girl's impending womanhood. And, I admit that I, too, was enamored with her. It was obvious that in a short time, she would be ripping out the hearts of men, young and old, in more ways than one.

I smiled. Yes, I was charmed by her. She may have had a stutter, but to me, her voice had the same sweetness of sound as the good fairy folks did, or, I imagined, as the angel folks. The latter I'd heard about through the new religion people—the Christians, as they called themselves. "Yes," I heard myself agreeing with the lass while staring into her lovely eyes. I then turned my gaze to Cramusin. "The point is made. Where are we going?"

~|||~

"East," said the brick-headed Cramusin, once again donning a false mantle of authority.

"That don't tell us nothin' we've not heard yet," countered Trastonus.

"Well, that's all you get," replied Cramusin, again cowering under the older man's gaze, yet holding in his tone; a haughtiness which was clearly meant to imply that he knew more about where we were going than the rest of us. But it rang false.

"Cuz that's a-a-all you know," observed Igraines, garnering a round of laughter from those within the hearing of it. She had simply voiced what the rest of us had been thinking.

Bested, Cramusin said not a word more. He turned and made his way back to join the larger group assembling in the nearby clearing.

"All right, then," Trastonus declared to the rest of us after a moment. "I s'pose we should join 'em, eh? We'll see soon enough where we go." We gathered with all the others in the clearing and continued the trek east.

However, approximately three miles into the next leg of our march, the question of our destination was suddenly and brutally rendered irrelevant.

We had come away from the so-called Dark Forest and traveled through a valley for nearly two miles. We then passed through another forested region, though this one was much more sparse than the Dark one, and then into yet another valley after nearly a mile of the sparser forest. Baldua and I walked side by side, had done so for miles, when he suddenly said, "Here now, what's it doing?!"

I followed his gaze to my staff. The Druid's egg atop was glowing red, as if a fire had been lit from within it, the

staff itself was beginning to get warm. Others around me
began to mumble to each other in fear at seeing the red
glowing orb, some even making the gesture to ward off evil.
But I knew it for what it was: a warning, but a warning too late.
Then all at once, its glowing stopped; its warmth ceased.

The sudden screams were guttural, primal and seemed
to come from everywhere at once. Hundreds upon hundreds of
them came pouring into the valley, swinging their weapons:
battle axes, swords, spiked balls on chains, even long pikes
with iron nails sticking out horizontally and curling upward at
the tip beneath the blade; one and all of them screaming a
blood-curdling cry of battle, and heading straight for us.

For an instant we froze; indeed, all time seemed to
freeze. Only the voice of Kindrixer snapped us out of our
reverie of disbelief. "Tight formations, now!" bellowed
Kindrixer. Most obeyed, drawing their weapons and bumping
into each other as we tried to form ten tight rows as we did
on the drill field.

Unfortunately, there were a few who panicked, young
and inexperienced in the ways of war—as I was myself, but
there was no panic in my bones this day—who dropped their
weapons and ran. But the handful that did this—lads between
ten and fifteen summers—ran straight into the enemies'
blades, for the Saxons and Picts were everywhere. Those that
ran were cut down instantly, mercilessly. In the future, their
deaths would be remembered for more than they were worth
that day. A Celt does not run from battle. But the runners
were the first to die in battle on that day, and they would be
remembered in song for it.

"Shields up, first rank down!" ordered Kindrixer from his
mount.

Many of us had no shield so we doubled up with those
who did. Little good it availed, however, for the enemy, whose
number seemed to swell with each passing moment, pinched
us from all sides like the claw of a giant raven. Yellow-haired
Saxons from the eastern shores; dark, squat Picts from the
northern regions, engulfed us. The noise was deafening;

hundreds and hundreds of men, and none-too-few women, yelling at the peak of their lungs; some in the crazed ecstasy of battle frenzy, some in the horrifying agony of unimaginable pain, as weapons found their marks on the bodies of my people. Added to the din was the clash of weapons, metal upon metal, sword to sword. What shields we had were either made of wood and split at the first violent stroke from the enemy, or were old Roman left-behinds and crumpled in the fight from mere age and corrosion.

Baldua and I were near crushed in the middle of the melee. The tight rows we Celts had started with had collapsed in on themselves, until we were nothing more than a tight onion ball. There were about seventy-six of us left layered in this ball, which the enemy was peeling back layer by bloody layer. Soon, there would be none of us left.

"What, by the Goddess, do we do?!" Baldua screamed above the din.

Dirt and dust kicked about by the crush and chaos of fighting filled my mouth, the stink of loosened bowels and fear filled my nostrils. I was being crushed and smashed from all sides. Looking down, I saw the face of Cramusin staring back at me, eyes wide open and vacant in death, his body broken underfoot. He had been trampled by his own people in the fighting.

I suddenly felt something violently shaking in my hand; it was the staff. I had not even had time to draw my sword. But I had held fast to the staff, always the staff. And then, I heard it. For the first time, I heard it! In my head, came the voice of my staff, the voice of the spear. "He returns," it whispered—I say it, for, indeed, it sounded like neither a man's nor a woman's voice, which spoke the words, "Leave here."

For a moment, within my own being, time stood still; all was silent. Though the battle and its din raged on, I heard it not. What, who, was this voice? I asked myself. Was it indeed the spear? A spirit? My own self? My imagination? Or all of those things? Images came to my mind, flashed inside my head: a crucifixion, a Roman soldier piercing the side of one being crucified with the very spear I held, my staff. He was an important person, the one being crucified. I felt it. And the Roman soldier, a centurion...

Pain was in my arm. Far off, I heard Baldua speaking in perfect Celt, his Latin abandoned for now, his hand roughly clenching my arm. "Myrriddin!" he screamed.

The noise of battle, the crush of bodies, returned to me, or I to it.

"What's wrong with you?" Baldua yelled. "You became rigid, like a stone. We must do something!"

I nodded. Looking at the spear, I willed it to guide us. It seemed to tug me, pulling me in one direction. Perhaps I was causing it to do this. But for the moment, it didn't matter; I followed the spear, my staff, and Baldua followed me. We squeezed our way through the mass of struggling bodies towards its perimeter, beyond which, on the side of the valley to which we were headed, I now remembered there being a stand of pungent smelling saplings nearby in which we might hide.

We had almost reached the edge of the fighting mass. I could see the stand of saplings, possible sanctuary within reach. And then I heard the voice—not the spear's voice this time, but a human voice thunderously projected from a man sitting atop the largest white horse I had ever seen. "Halt! Halt and heed!" the man bellowed.

I froze. For a horrifying instant, I actually thought he was yelling at me and Baldua. But as I turned and looked closer at the man, it became clear that he was yelling for everyone, all those fighting, to cease their combat.

The man raised a hand, palm opened, and called again, "Halt, I command it!" His voice boomed with such depth, volume and authority that one by one, all ceased their fight, disengaged the opponent and turned to face this imposing figure on the white horse.

He sat tall in the saddle: six-and-half feet tall when standing on his own feet, I guessed. Straight, glossy, black hair hung down to his chest. His deep-set eyes were a piercing light-gold and his nose was slightly hooked. All that, plus his slightly protruding rigid brow, gave him the look of a demon. I shivered for an instant with awe. And fear! This one projected evil; was evil. I could feel it emanating from his being as surely as I could feel my own breath.

He was clearly the leader of the Pict-Saxon horde, for all of them, to a man, looked to him now, stiff at attention. Strange, that, I thought. All my people—those left alive—stared at him, too. It was my people that the man now addressed.

"I...am Lord Creconius Mab," he declared.

My heart thudded, pounded. Though I was already sweating from the fight, even more began beading on my brow, my palms. A tingling of intense nervousness swept through my being. This man, this Lord Creconius, was an old and bitter enemy of mine. I felt it. I knew it. Though I, Myrriddin, had never laid eyes on him, Creconius and I had known each other before, many life-times before. As a Celt, I knew I had occupied a physical body before this one; in another life and in many a life. Being born again into a new body was a choice one's spirit made in the Otherworld. The Christian folk were trying to change that belief—called it pagan, they did. Some of our folk had abandoned the belief. But if ever there was confirmation on this side of the veil as to whether I had lived before, what I felt in that moment toward Creconius was it.

I studied him even closer. He wore dark riding breeches and a black cloak with matching black gloves. A gold torque studded with rubies adorned his neck. I looked at his face again. Yes, his face was nearly as my mind remembered it, though it was decidedly more feminine. It also glowed softly, as if a glam or spell surrounded it. But, there was no mistaking whom this face belonged to or whom he had been in a previous life. "Draco!" I whispered, not knowing exactly where the name came from, but knowing beyond doubt that was this dark lord's name in a previous time.

"What?" Baldua whispered urgently. "Come, we can still make it to those trees there. 'Tis where you were leading us, yes?"

I nodded and continued pushing my way through the people and slipped out past the last man to a boulder lying in front on a tree. We hid for a moment behind the boulder. I looked back at all the people, now transfixed by the figure on the white steed.

"C-c'mon," came the familiar stutter.

Baldua and I looked to our right, and there, next to us behind the boulder, crouched Igraines, breeches torn at the knees, grey tunic splattered with dirt and mud, as was her face, but still in one piece.

"This is m-my spot!" she declared.

"Puella fatua! (Stupid girl!)," said Baldua finding his Latin tongue. "You'll be found if you stay here," he said in our native tongue.

"Yes," I added, and began crawling on my belly to the trees. Baldua followed. I looked back at Igraines. She hesitated, looked back at Creconius, then followed Baldua and me into the trees.

Rocks dug into my stomach as I crawled, dragged myself, along. Looking behind me again, I saw that both Baldua and Igraines were close behind me. Looking beyond, them I saw Creconius on his mount. He was saying something about absolute surrender.

"Attack!" came the reply from someone in the crowd—Kindrixer, on foot, in the middle of those of my countrymen left alive.

I stopped.

Baldua nearly crawled over me, but stopped just short behind me. "Are you mad? Why'd you stop?"

"Kindrixer," was all I could manage to say. I was suddenly torn between continuing on to apparent safety and joining Kindrixer in fighting Creconius, the evil one I've known in one form or another for some time. Ancient, confusing animosity welled up within my being.

Someone was pulling on my shoulder, dragging me onward. "C'mon!" cried Baldua. It was he who dragged me toward the safety of deeper cover in the trees. It was now Igraines alone who was behind me. I was unaware of it at the time, but Baldua had maneuvered around and ahead of me during my hesitation. "There's no use in fighting. There are too many of them."

"F-for once I agr-ree with Baldua," whispered Igraines.

A huge battle cry went up then from all the Celts present. Though surrounded and outnumbered, the Celts, with Kindrixer leading the way, began an assault, breaking the tight ball they had been in and attacking the enemy. I felt shame. As I said, Celts do not run. Yet, that is precisely what I was doing. I looked at my two companions. Baldua had no compunction about saving our skins, or more accurately, his own. In spite of what she had said, however, Igraines did. I saw reflected in her eyes a similar shade of shame to my own: dishonor. I was about to disengage from my friend, Baldua, and abandon our flight to safety, in order to join the fight instead. But then the slaughter began.

~IV~

Kindrixer was the first to fall, his head nearly severed from behind by a wickedly wielded battle axe, his assailant unseen in the throng and confusion of battle. I was shocked. All of us who saw him fall were shocked. Kindrixer had been the only cohesive element keeping the Celts in any semblance of a fighting unit. When he fell, many were easily cut down as they froze, startled at the sight of their leader killed. Others ran, some heading straight toward us.

"That's it then," Baldua said with finality. Obviously, he had read in my eyes the intent to stay and fight. "Come! Now!" He took the lead, crawling further into the bush before anyone could get even close to us. I followed, as did Igraines, as if in a daze.

The urgency of our plight shifted into a more desperate form. We could easily be revealed if those coming toward us overran us. So the three of us got to our feet and ran for our lives.

Deeper and deeper into the stand of trees we went. The further we went, the thicker the forest became. Deceiving that was. From the outside—from the clearing we had been ambushed in—it simply appeared that the stand of trees was deep, but thin. But here we were, trudging through a wooded area that was becoming thicker, denser and darker by the moment. The sound of the battle was receding quickly. I was not sure whether that was because of the distance we were putting between us and the fighting or because it had become such a rout that it was almost finished. I tried not to think of that, but kept moving.

In addition to the darker, denser forest we were now in, something else suddenly became clear: we had been making a steady climb; an ascent up a hillside. And, it was becoming steeper by the step.

Baldua stopped, hands on knees, head hanging low, panting to catch his breath. Igraines and I stopped as well. It was a strange respite in a mad day. "Where are w-we going?" asked Igraines, after a few moments.

Baldua looked at me.

"Well, don't ask me," I said. But it was not me that Baldua was asking with his eyes. His gaze drifted down to the spear, all but forgotten in our rush to escape. It vibrated again, slightly, its tip moving toward...what, I could not tell. No matter. It seemed as good a direction to go as any at that point. "This way, I guess," I said, my voice laced with uncertainty. My companions looked at each other, apparently none too pleased with my reply. "C'mon," I said more forcefully. "At this point, we've naught to lose."

We continued our trek, up the hill and through the dense forest.

We walked for hours, trudging uphill, then down, then up again, all the while surrounded by huge oaks and pines standing as sentinels. We no longer heard the noise of battle. Instead, the sounds of birds twittering and breeze-blown trees soughing, filled the air with a beauty that only the mother goddess could produce. I felt at peace as I walked along. But it was a brief and fleeting thing; a temporary false sense of security on a violent and terrifying day. The fact was that we were escaping from certain death. And, even if we survived, we would probably become refugees in our own lands, for I had no doubt Creconius would raze our village once he had finished off our so-called army. Such were my thoughts as we continued on our forced march. But then I realized something that was of a more immediate urgency. We were lost.

I believed we were heading west, toward home, or what was left of it by now. But it was difficult to tell for two reasons: the forest was getting denser and the light was fading. The light was fading because of the thick forest top, yes, but also because the sun was setting. Still, the spear, my staff, led us on with its insistent vibration and definite pull in a particular direction. It was acting as if it were a divining rod leading us to water. Yet, where it was actually leading us I knew not. No matter. Since it was getting dark, I would see to it that we stopped soon to make camp and find food. Traveling through an unfamiliar forest at night would be foolish at best. And our dinner would have to consist of scavenged nuts and edible roots. I would not risk being spotted by an enemy because of a cooking fire. We would not hunt for meat this night. Igraines was the only one of us who had a water-skin. I could tell by its sloshing throughout the day that there was precious little of the liquid in it, but it would do for the night. She had already offered to share it earlier, but Baldua and I had declined at the time.

We reached a small clearing that had flat ground and was well protected. One side of it faced the hilled forest through which we had just marched; the other half faced rock outcroppings: large boulders that seemed to be at the base of a mountain. It was difficult to tell in the twilight how large it might be. We will find out in the morning light, I thought. "We should stop here," I said out loud.

"I agree," said Igraines, for once unstuttered.

I half expected Baldua to give a sardonic reply in Latin. But he said nothing. He simply plopped down on a rock, exhausted. This day had taken a toll on all of us.

"I s-saw f-ficob-berry bushes a quarter l-league back," Igraines said.

"Good. Just be careful," I said. "Anything else you can find, too – nuts, anything. No meat, though. No fires."

The look she gave me was incredulous. "Just because I stutter, does not mean I'm stupid," she said.

I looked away from her, blushing, I'm sure.

"Can I have some of that water now?" Baldua mumbled. "I'll only sip it, I promise."

Something was wrong. My friend was not just tired from our march. I looked at him closely. He was pale and he grimaced with every breath. Obviously, he was in pain, a lot of it. Then, for the first time, I noticed that he was intently clutching his right side. "Baldua?" I asked, concern grasping my throat.

He looked into my eyes, courage and sincere pleas dripping from his gaze. He lifted his tunic, with much difficulty at that movement, to reveal two grotesque lumps which had formed over the region of his right lower ribs. In addition to the lumps, there was a hideous discoloration; a dark purple had spread across the affected area. "I think they're broken, these two," he said, pointing to his two bottom ribs.

"You would n-not have been able to come this f-far if they were broken," Igraines declared as she knelt next to Baldua to examine the ribs. She gently traced the fingertips of her right hand back and forth over the lumpy, discolored region, finally letting them come to rest between the two lumps. Slowly, she began to push.

Baldua's face contorted in agony.

"W-well, say it hurts. Don't b-be an ass!" she said reprimanding him.

"All right! Stop, you wench. It hurts!"

"Fine. They're c-cracked. B-badly. But they're n-not broken," Igraines diagnosed.

"Why didn't you say something?" I asked angrily.

Baldua simply shook his head. "Quorsum istuc?" (To what purpose?) he countered. "We had to get out of there. I had taken someone's sword hilt in the side. Hurt like fire at the time. Didn't think it to be this bad, though."

"You n-need a moss and mistletoe poultice p-placed on it," Igraines said.

"Sure. I'll pull one out of my ass," Baldua replied.

"You are n-not doing anything," Igraines stated flatly, as a matter of fact. She was small in structure, but huge in stature, especially in moments such as this, when she was clearly in command.

"Is that all you need—moss and mistletoe?" I asked her.

Igraines nodded, then added, "But m-moss from the m-mighty oak's trunk only. Nowhere else."

"Very well," I said, and slipped out of the clearing in search of the medicinal items.

I walked for a while and found only saplings and pines. I should have gone back the way we had come, not further up the mountain. I remembered there being several ancient, sacred oaks about a half mile back from the clearing. But that was moot now. Presently, I was about three-quarters of a mile farther on from the clearing.

Finally, after nearly an hour of searching, I found two gigantic and clearly very ancient oaks. As I approached them, I found myself becoming reverent, as if I were approaching two sacred sentinels. The staff in my hand felt warm as if it, too, were solemn. The mighty oak has been a sacred entity and symbol to Celts for thousands of years. It was engrained in my mind and blood to respect and honor these trees. But for the first time, I was truly feeling a sacredness emanating from an oak—from both of them. Something tangible was occurring. The lower branches of both trees intertwined, though their trunks were some thirty-feet apart. The uppermost branches were not only intertwined, but in some places were grown together as one—not fused together, but grown as one, as if from one tree.

Then I touched the one closest to me. Emotion welled up within me; the staff began to chill in my hand. Sadness. I was astounded to feel sadness emanating from this mighty tree. I looked to the other tree and understood. I walked over to the second tree to touch it and had my thoughts confirmed; it was dying. Its bark was without moss, dry and brittle, its life and spirit nearly gone. These two trees had grown together, seen centuries of life together and intertwined in a marriage of oneness. And now, one of them was dying. Would the other be far behind?

After a moment, I snapped myself out of this reverie, remembering my purpose for being there. But I didn't just start searching the healthy oak's trunk for moss and the lower branches for mistletoe. Instead, I felt compelled to ask. I stepped back a few paces and looked at both trees, addressed both in a reverent manner.

"F-forgive my intrusion," I stammered, suddenly feeling as Igraines must have on occasion. "I am sorry for the state of your being, your partner's being, for both of you, and ask that the blessings of Dana be upon you," I found myself saying. On the Isle Of Mystery, I had chanted and sung to mighty and sacred oaks in a large circular group of other initiates, but never alone. I had been with Moscastan on several occasions when he had addressed prayers to the earth Goddess, Dana, through the oaks, but those too had been in groups. Yet, here I was, alone and beseeching these living things. On the one hand, it felt strange. But on the other, it felt completely natural. "I seek your help. I need moss from your body and the healing of your mistletoe for my injured friend. With your permission, of course." I paused. Silence. A slight breeze rustled the branches. The sound of a small forest creature scurrying through the undergrowth came and went. Again, silence. Fool, I thought. Did you expect them to speak?

Then it happened: The staff, the spear, began to vibrate; to point to the healthy tree. I walked back to it, around to the other side of it and there, on its far side was a thick, moist blanket of moss. A rustling in a branch just above the moss blanket drew my attention. A beautiful cluster of mistletoe hung there. "Thank you," I said out loud, and began to gather the items for my friend's poultice. By the time I had gathered all I needed, it was almost completely dark. No matter. I could still make out the pseudo trail I'd used to come to this point. I would simply follow it back.

I left the two wondrous oaks and made my way back toward the clearing and my friends. But after a few minutes, the way became more and more difficult with each and every step. Darkness descended like a cloak over my eyes. I kept forging ahead, carefully, knowing Baldua needed what I carried, yet cursing myself for taking so long as to allow darkness to become a barrier. I silently asked the staff to help guide me, but silence was its only response.

Finally, I broke into the clearing which was adequately lit by a half-moon in a cloudless sky. But my heart dropped! This was not the right clearing. The surrounding rock formations were different, and, of course, my friends were not to be seen. I almost yelled for them. Foolish that would have been. I stood in the clearing and looked all around. Now what? I thought. My staff began to vibrate, tugging me in the direction to my right. I looked that way and saw in the distance through the trees, a glow. This was not the glow of a camp fire. It was larger, eerie, and at a constant, steady pulse. It was like something from the Otherworld. In spite of my better judgment, I found myself walking toward it. What I would find there, I knew not. But what I would discover there would change my life forever.

~V~

I cautiously made my way through the undergrowth, quietly moving toward the glow. All the while, the staff vibrated harder in my hand. Usually, if the vibration were some sort of warning of danger, the staff would change its temperature, too. But there was no such temperature change this time; just the vibration which was more on the verge of becoming a shaking. In fact, if anything, I would say it was... excited— excited at the prospect of going to the source of the glow. I tried to dismiss that thought. It seemed ridiculous. But I could not dismiss it outright. It's what I was feeling, sensing from the staff, the spear.

I drew nearer the source of the glow, the pulsating light. It was emanating from a cave whose opening appeared small; perhaps four feet-high and five-feet wide. It was located on the side of a huge granite rock formation lodged in the mountainside. The light itself escaped from the cave's mouth in more of an undulating, intense rainbow, but washed out to appear bright white, especially from a distance. So bright it was that the little glen just outside the cave's opening was bright as day. There was no telling how deep into the mountainside the cave went. Because of the smallness of the cave's opening and the intensity of the light escaping from it, 'twas tempting to say that it was shallow. But I knew that both of those things were deceiving when it came to judging the cave's depth. My mind suddenly shifted back to my friends. Baldua! I thought. I must get these things back to Igraines so that she can help him. But how? I was lost before, in the wrong clearing when I saw this glow. How will I find my way back? The staff! I looked at the still-shaking lance in my hand. "I don't care about this place," I said aloud, speaking to the lance. "Find my friends!"

It continued its shaking, not altering it in the slightest. I turned to leave, still looking at the staff. After one step, it gave a last shudder and stopped, laying still in my hand. I stopped in my tracks and noticed that a cold was descending in the air and with it, a mist, thick and dense, enshrouding the immediate area completely. If someone had been standing fifty feet from me back up the path from where I had come, I had no doubt that they could not have seen me nor even the glow from the cave.

"What is this?" I asked out loud, suddenly feeling trapped and angry. But the sound of my voice was deadened by the mist. It was obvious that no one could hear me even if they were near and I yelled. Something was compelling me to the cave, to the pulsating light. I looked at the staff. "So this is the way of it?" I asked rhetorically.

Silence.

I turned back around and looked at the bright cave opening some forty feet away. "So be it," I said, and walked to the cave's mouth and entered.

I was momentarily blinded by the brightness as I ducked into the opening in the hillside. The light was intensely bright. Feeling my way along one side of a wall, I found I could stand upright. I stood there for a moment, shading my eyes with one hand as I stared at the ground, allowing my eyes to adjust. And listening. I just listened, trying to discern any sound but the silence that assaulted me. Then, out of the silence, very faintly, came the sounds of what could only be described as the very quiet tinkling of tiny glass bells. Yet, the sound was more pure than that, more crystalline. The smell of this place was unique, too. It smelled of fresh spring water and mint. The cleanest aroma I had ever experienced. Next, as my eyes adjusted, I truly noticed the ground that I'd been staring at. It sparkled. Even in the brightness of the space, it sparkled dazzlingly, as if a billion-and-one little stars were embedded at my feet. Slowly, I looked up, trying to peer through the brilliant light at the rest of my surroundings. My eyes adjusted further and the bright pulsating lights seemed to dim.

The cave's interior was vast, at least four times as large as any village's central lodge I had been in, which granted, in my whole life had only been two. The cave was large enough to hold several hundred people, perhaps a thousand. Its floor and walls were jagged rock-type formations and its ceiling was breathtakingly high. It seemed that this cavernous space touched the sky, or rather, was its own sky. Amazing! But what was even more astounding was the fact that the pulsating light seemed to be coming from millions and millions of crystals embedded, or rather growing from, the walls and stone formations everywhere in the cave. They were of every color. I then noticed that some, in fact most of the jagged rock formations I had seen a moment ago, were not comprised of plain rock with crystals growing out of them, but were themselves, in fact, huge crystal formations. I was awestruck.

"Twilight of the gods," a man's voice said.

I nearly dropped the staff and medicinal collection I carried. My heart pounding, I spun to my right to see the figure of what looked to be a very old man standing some fifty paces away at the opening to a passageway leading deeper into the mountain from within this main cavernous chamber. Though he was fifty or so paces away, his voice had sounded mere inches from my face.

"The domed shape of the cavern does magical things with sound," he explained, apparently reading my thoughts.

Looking up, I noticed that in addition to having some rock formations, the high ceiling to this place was indeed a curved dome shape. It was like being on the inside of a giant egg.

"Twilight of the gods," the old man repeated, resuming his initial line of speech, referring, I assumed, to the twinkling of all the crystals.

My heart still raced at the surprise of seeing someone else in there, let alone an old man. I took a breath to calm myself. The old man walked toward me. My first instinct was to duck out of the cave. But I held my ground for curiosity's sake, if for no other reason.

He appeared quite old: ninety summers at least, although that was probably not accurate. He was skin and bones. His skin was so wrinkled, it was as if it had been flayed from his bones, stretched and wadded, then placed back over his skeleton. His hair was white as snow with streaks of red. Surprisingly, he apparently still had all his teeth, all of which were also a snowy white. He smiled as he approached and that smile reflected the light in the room, as did the countenance of his whole being. He wore a cloak that looked fairly new. Black, it was, with little gold and silver stars all over it. You're a strange old man, I thought. He did not walk like an old man though. His gait was steady and sure. He stopped before me and I looked into his dark eyes.

"I've waited for you to find this place," he said.

"I don't..." I stammered. Then it hit me—the familiarity of his voice and eyes. "Moscastan?"

The old man's smile now beamed.

"You've known me by many a name," he said. "Presently, it has been Moscastan, yes."

I searched his eyes, his face. Beneath the aged surface, it was indeed my mentor. I was stunned beyond belief. "But how?"

He looked at me quizzically, even pityingly. "You have studied the Druid ways and the mysticism therein for many a year. Have you learned nothing, Master Myrriddin?" he asked.

I felt a flush of embarrassment. Of course, I had learned a great deal about the nature and workings of the world we live in and the greater universe as a whole: How to control various elements in the world around me by joining with them at the level of thought, for example. Higher Truths about the oneness of our world and the Otherworld are things that I learned, too. And, glamour—the ability to cast certain spells, if you will; to cloak oneself or his or her surroundings so that they appear as something different to others—is also something I learned. All of these things were simple applications of natural laws properly understood and utilized. But this! Was this how Moscastan actually appeared? Was his appearance as the younger Moscastan that I knew and loved naught but a glamour, or was this old man-persona before me the glamour?

"Ah, Myrriddin. Do not look so perplexed. Come," he said soothingly. It is time for you to venture deeper into this Crystal place." He gestured to the whole of the sparkling cavern. "And hence, deeper into your soul."

I looked at the mistletoe in my hand.

"Fear not. Baldua will be fine. Presently, he is on his way to feeling much better. Trust me," Moscastan said, reassuringly. "Leave all but the spear, your staff. The spear will aid you on the journey you are about to embark upon."

Reluctantly, I placed the medicinal items on the ground and clutched my staff, the spear. There was nothing to do but follow.

~VI~

We entered a low passageway through which Moscastan had
come into the large main chamber. He led the way back
through it and it seemed to go on for a long while—five-
hundred paces and more. We remained stooped the whole
way. The light had not diminished at all, nor had the pleasant
smell of spring water and mint. In fact, if anything, these
smells became more pronounced the deeper we went.

We were indeed traveling deeper and deeper into the
mountainside, going down at a slight angle, too, into the
bowels of the earth. I wanted to ask where exactly we were
going, but knew in my heart that trust was in order here. I
trusted Moscastan implicitly. I always had. Not only that, I
sensed that I was about to experience something beyond my
comprehension. But I was not apprehensive in the least;
Moscastan was with me; my spear was with me. That last
thought struck me as odd when I caught it, but I also knew
that old Moscastan was right when he had said the spear
would aid me on this journey.

Presently, my staff, the spear, began to feel warm in
my hand, soothingly warm. I felt that it was telling me we were
close to our destination.

Finally, Moscastan halted. He turned to face me, still
hunched over because of the low-ceilinged passageway, and
motioned for me to enter an opening in the wall that was now
between us and to my right. I had not noticed it until that very
moment.

It was a round, roughly-honed hole in the rock and
crystal wall that was only about three feet in diameter. The
bottom portion was approximately a foot off the floor of the
passageway. It appeared to have been made by the hand of
men, not naturally formed. I did as the old man bade and

stooped even lower as I entered the hole or entryway. Moscastan followed.

I entered another room, a fraction of the size of the main chamber I had been in earlier, but no less bright. The walls were ten-feet high and composed of solid crystal, reflecting a light that seemed to be generated from within. The room itself was oblong and only as big as a large sleeping chamber. In the middle was a solid, rectangular crystal slab that stood in the center of the space. It was just large enough for a fully grown man to lie on comfortably. The slab was a beautiful deep-blue in color. It looked like a solid block of the ocean set still in the middle of the room. I then noticed something that filled me with awe: the crystal slab had a glow at its center. It pulsated, the glow did, as if a heart of light beat within, as if it were alive.

"Please, Master Myrriddin," Moscastan said softly, reverently. "Lie on the Altar. Go within and attune with the Mind of All to know your Self, to know your purpose. It is time." He slowly retreated back out the small entryway and stood in front of it out in the passageway as if guarding it. What or who he could possibly have been guarding it from, I had no idea.

I looked at the Crystal Altar and felt my pulse quicken. I admit, however, that a part of me felt silly. How was this thing going to attune me with the Mind of All or tell me my purpose? Yet, another part of me already knew the answer to that: It wasn't the thing itself that would tell me about anything; it was simply a tool to help amplify my attunement with a higher nature within my being. I stepped up to it. Its flat top came up to my navel. I climbed on and lay on my back placing the spear at my left side close to my body. For a moment, I stared at the ceiling. It sparkled with crystals, each winking at me. I closed my eyes, breathed deeply, slowly and rhythmically, as I'd been taught to do on the Isle Of Mystery when calling on the Natural Powers of the Universe. Thus, I began to go deep within my own mind, to my very soul. As I did this, the spear began to vibrate in a pulse that matched the rhythm of my breath.

Soon, I was floating. I felt no substance to my self, to my body. That was because I was no longer in my body. I knew that for sure. A mist surrounded my mind's eye. I could see nothing. Floating, floating, and floating still. Finally, I felt a slight jolt, as if I were entering something. Slowly, the mist began to clear.

I heard a woman—no, more than one woman—sobbing softly. I looked over to its source and saw three women shrouded in dark robes, on their knees consoling one another as they kept glancing up in my direction. But it was not me they were looking at, or so I thought. They were looking at the person in whom my consciousness had entered. In effect, though, they were looking at me, for I had entered into the body, the time, the moment, of my former self; the Roman Centurion Gaius Cassius Longinus. How could this be? I thought. My Myrriddin self or soul was that of Longinus, this I already knew. So, how could the same soul occupy the same space in two different times at the same time?! But then I realized what I was experiencing. Though real in every sense of the word, it was a moment in what we call "time" as stored in the Universal Mind. As such, it was quite easy to experience something that has already happened, or re-experience it, if one attunes to it properly. Many lives I had lived on the planet we call earth. But for some reason, it was this one of Longinus that I needed to see now, relive now. But I wasn't the man himself, as I was then. Now, I was a witness, looking out from his eyes, but merely as Myrriddin, the observer, not the participant.

The women looked at me/Longinus with agonized, bloodshot eyes. A round of raucous laughter erupted from behind me. I turned to see several legionnaires kneeling on the ground, playing a game with dice. Their game table was a tattered and bloody cloak or robe spread on the ground. Looming over the soldiers, and standing between myself and them was a large wooden cross. And, hanging on this cross was a man. His body was badly beaten. His wrists and feet were the color of the dark iron nails that protruded from those areas, his blood having drained and stained his skin. On his head, he wore a hideous crown of thorns and blood. I knew who this man was. The world knew who this man was, or at least, it would know. He looked dead. But he wasn't.

I felt the indifference that I, and "my host" were feeling. He/I thought about joining the game going on under the cross. Can't do that, Longinus thought. I am their commander. What is Irena doing right now? he wondered. I sensed every one of his thoughts as if they were my own. They had been my own! Next, he thought about this man's death. The time had come. Enough of this, I heard him think. Longinus stepped up to the cross, and stood on the condemned one's right side. Longinus' left arm reached out and up. It was then that I saw it in his hand; the Spear, my spear! It looked new.

Slowly, as if in a bad dream, the spear's sharp tip inched toward the ribs of the man on the cross. "Jesu," my inner voice, Myrriddin's inner voice, whispered in recognition. The tip touched the skin in-between the condemned one's lower ribs. The skin beneath it stretched inward as the pressure was applied. Then the skin broke, tore, as the blade slid into the body. I heard a sickening sloshing and scraping sound as the blade rubbed against tissue and bone. For an instant, blood and body fluid spurted out of the wound, splattering a few drops on my face, Longinus' face. The initial spurt was quickly replaced by a slow flow of body fluid and blood which seeped out of the blade's entry point, oozing down the blade itself. Suddenly, the spear was yanked out of the body on the cross. The blood and body fluid then flowed freely from the wound.

I felt myself, both my Longinus self and my Myrriddin self—now virtually merged as one—recoil for an instant. What have I done? I thought. You've simply done your duty, came the next thought.

A rumbling sounded in the distance. It did not take long to realize that the rumbling emanated from both earth and sky. A storm approaches, came the thought. I felt the whole demeanor of my host, myself, harden. I looked at the one on the cross. Jesu, is that what you're called? Or are you called by a different name, Simon, perhaps? I knew not where that thought had come from. Surely this man was Jesu, and Longinus was simply in denial of what he/I had done in that moment.

The ground and sky rumbled again. The earth then shook, knocking three people, spectators, to the ground and nearly toppling one of the other crosses that were there, and its dangling occupant. It was then that I felt a small twinge of fear run through the body of Longinus.

Jesu made a sound, mumbling something seemingly to the sky. Then his head plopped on his chest. He was gone. Sheets of rain fell then—a torrent of tears from the heavens. The noise of it was deafening. "He's dead! Cut him down!" shouted Longinus. Two of the Legionnaires nearby, who were playing the game on the robe, seemed frozen with fear and awe.

A third Legionnaire yelled at them both: "Come on, you dogs. You heard the Centurion!" He slapped the soldier nearest him, knocking him out of his stupor. The other legionnaire followed suit, and they all ran to bring the Condemned One down.

I/Longinus began to back away. Suddenly, I looked down at the spear in my hand, at the blood on the blade's tip. I wanted to throw it to the ground, but could not. Then I heard it, The Voice: "What have you done, my son?"

Was it His voice, Jesus'?

I felt a yank on my mind, my soul, as if I were being violently pulled by a force beyond comprehension. Scene after scene began to rapidly play out before the eyes of my spirit; my life as Longinus after that fateful day. Irena. Friends Jacobi, Dosameenor and more. My sons. All were there. I lived that whole life over again in three heartbeats, up to and including my own upside-down crucifixion in Antioch. Then, it was done. In a flash of white light and a thud of hard landing, I was back in the bowels of the Crystal Cavern, lying on the still ocean slab, Myrriddin once again.

Slowly, I opened my eyes. The brightness was nearly unbearable. The light in the crystal room seemed even more intense than it had before.

"Ah, Master Myrriddin. You return," said Moscastan. I sat up on the slab, my heart still pounding from my experience; my journey of mind, of spirit. I looked at my hands —yes, solid flesh, my flesh. Next, I inspected the staff, the spear.

"You have complete understanding, complete knowledge, do you not." Moscastan said this as a fact, not as a question.

I looked at my mentor. He was once again standing just inside the room. Then, I looked back to the staff. Perhaps it was time for it to just be The Spear again. I began to remove the leather thong that held the piece of crystal at the top against the blade.

"I believe it would be best to leave the spear in its disguise. For now, at least. There are forces arrayed against us all, and part of what they seek is what you hold," said Moscastan.

After all that had happened that day, I knew that Moscastan was right. I retied the thong I had loosened and swung my legs off the slab to face the old man before me. I saw in his eyes the man I'd known in that life so long ago. "Jacobi...," I began.

"Moscastan, now, if you please," he replied.

"All right," I said, smiling with awe. "That was unbelievable! Have you..." I started, indicating the slab and the journey it seemed to induce. "...Of course, you have. Stupid question, that. Forgive me." My feeling of awe gave way to excitement. "I was there, really there! 'Twas no dream, Moscastan. I know it was real." I let this feeling of excitement wash through me for a moment. Soon, though, another feeling began to take hold: confusion. "But...why?" I asked. "You said a minute ago that now I 'completely understand.' I don't know if that's true. What am I supposed to do?"

"Do?"

"What am I supposed to do with this...knowledge or understanding?" I asked.

His brow crinkled in bewildered amusement. "Why, you are supposed to live your life," he said, laughing.

"You know what I mean," I countered. "Why show me all this without telling me what it means to my life now?"

"What you experienced was for you alone; to know your-Self completely, to know your greatness in the past, present and future," Moscastan replied.

Now it was my turn to laugh. "What I did in that life as Centurion Longinus, I don't think that everyone would call it greatness. They might call it evil..."

"The ignorant, perhaps. You simply played your part. Judgment is from fear and ignorance of The Workings, The Law."

"What does that mean...?" I had always loved Moscastan. In addition to being a mentor, he was like a father to me. But there were times when he was vague, to say the least.

Still, I remembered much of certain natural laws we had used in Druidic training to manipulate natural phenomena with and in the mind. But I sensed that was not what he was talking about here. I sensed that he was referring to something much bigger, and yet at the same time, something which all else was a part of and subject to. "...'The Workings, The Law'?" I asked more evenly, sincerely.

"Enough, for now. Let this day's events settle into your mind and soul," Moscastan said cryptically. "Come. Your friends await."

Yes, my friends. How long had I been in here? I wondered. And, my friends: were they still back where I'd left them? Or, had they found their way here, as I had? Something in Moscastan's tone just then made me believe that he knew they were near. But how?

"Come, and you'll find out," he said, as if reading my thoughts. With a snorting giggle, he ducked through the opening and back into the passageway.

I hopped off the slab and quickly followed.

~VII~

I followed Moscastan back out into the main chamber of the crystal cave.

"Myrriddin!" came the familiar voice of Igraines, un-stuttered.

She stood just inside the cavern near the main entryway.

"How did you find this place?" I asked, as I ran to greet her.

"I started looking for you," she said.

"You should've stayed put," I retorted, feeling a tad guilty, defensive.

"When y-you didn't c-ome right back, I thought to quickly g-get the poultice myself and maybe look for you, too. You'd b-been gone for hours. Th-thought to find you eaten by wolves, I-I did." Igraines managed to say.

"And Baldua?" I asked.

"I left h-him. Was c-coming right back. Got lost, though. Like you, I g-guess," she said, sardonically. "An odd mist d-down..."

"I know."

Igraines looked away then. I think she felt as stupid as I had initially for getting lost. She peered at the walls and the ceiling, a look of wonder spreading across her face. "What is this place?"

I looked to Moscastan, but spoke to Igraines. "Good question."

"'Tis a place of knowledge, a place of learning, a place of initiation—"

"A place for the soul to soar!" I added.

Now a look of confusion crossed Igraines' face.

"I'll explain later," I said, picking up the package of moss and mistletoe right from where I had left it. "Come. We need to get back to Baldua.

"But the m-mist is still strong," said Igraines.

"The way will not be barred," Moscastan declared, nodding toward the spear, the staff in my hand.

Igraines saw the nod. She looked at me with another look of confusion.

I walked out of the cavern, Igraines quickly following, Moscastan, with a knowing smile, trailing just behind her.

Indeed, the mist remained thick. But now I knew what to do. I breathed steadily, closed my eyes and went deep within. I held up the staff and saw in my mind's eye my deepest Self entering the spear and running through it, contacting the mist through the spear, contacting it at the smallest level of the mist itself; at the smallest and deepest level of being, where all things are made of the same substance, and are thus connected, and can therefore communicate. I knew to do this, at least in theory, through my Druidic training, but had never attempted to perform this type of feat with the depth of conviction I was feeling at that moment. Something in me had shifted back inside the cavern, on the slab. I now truly knew my Source, and I realized that by going within to my own deepest level of being, and aided by the spear, I could connect meaningfully with any and all things, for it is at this level, the level of Source, where all things are connected. I came to that level within the mist, merged with it (the mist) and asked it, urged it, to disperse, knowing that it would through the Law of Mind and Source. This Law, the workings of the One True Source, had been drilled into me on the Isle Of Mystery since I'd been a lad, but I was only now understanding it! Moscastan knew. He had said as much earlier.

"It leaves!" exclaimed Igraines in perfect un-stuttered astonishment.

Her exclamation broke my concentration and brought me back to myself. No matter. The work had been done. Within a heartbeat, the mist began to vanish, rolling back as if it had a mind of its own, revealing a green glen just outside the cavern's entrance and a breaking dawn. I dropped my hand, holding the staff to my side, pleasantly astonished in spite of myself.

Moscastan smiled proudly at me.

Igraines nodded toward the object in my hand. "A w-wizard's staff that i-is, truly."

"Not really," I said.

"We shall now go find your friend," proclaimed Moscastan, more I think to divert attention from the topic of the spear, than to prompt us to get back to Baldua.

I headed down the path, the same one I'd approached the night before. Igraines and Moscastan followed.

It was early morning. The sun's disc could not have been up more than an hour's time. Had I really been in the crystal cavern all night long? It did not seem possible. Though a thin, dewy morning fog a mere foot off the damp ground was present, the choking, cloaking mist was completely gone. It did not take long for us to find the spot where Igraines and I had left Baldua. He was gone. I expected Moscastan to question us as to whether this was the right spot. He did not, especially after we found indications that perhaps our friend had been taken away from the place. The ground had clearly been chewed up quite recently by horses and men—many men.

"By the C-Christ. He was layin' there," muttered Igraines, pointing to a spot on the ground. There were marks in the dirt trailing off from the exact place Baldua had last laid before she left—marks that looked like someone had been dragged.

Yet, for some reason, at that moment, Igraines' words bothered me more than the drag marks and what they implied. "Why do you say that, Igraines? You are not a follower of the Christ, this Jesu. You suckle the Mother-Goddess, Dana," I said more harshly than I knew why.

"Wh-why do you care what I say? It's just words! You don't follow the Ch-Christ either," she replied, obviously insulted.

She was right. I understood very little of the Christ's teachings. I had learned more during my spirit's travel, my vision on the ocean-slab in the crystal cavern, than I'd known before. Besides, what I knew of this Christ's followers, I did not like. I doubted that even they truly understood the teachings, for they spoke utterly against all things natural. From all that I'd seen of them thus far in my life, hearing their beliefs through a few of the wandering priests and preachers that had been around, they seemed to care more about controlling others than advancing their own souls. Still, inexplicably, Igraines' words bothered me. Perhaps I was just misplacing anger at my friend's disappearance.

Igraines followed the marks as much as possible. They went back into the main grouping of prints in the small clearing in the center of the area, joining with hoofprints and footprints. All the prints then seemed to double back the way they had come, which was the same direction Igraines, Baldua and I had come from the day before. "They took him. We must f-follow the t-tracks," she declared.

"I agree that it appears the vile enemy you encountered yesterday has taken your friend, but we would do better to go to our village. That is where they have gone," said Moscastan, anger seeping into his voice.

Igraines considered him doubtfully.

"We can follow those tracks, but I tell you they will lead to our village and beyond. That is where Creconius was headed," Moscastan continued, with more venom than I've ever heard from him. "We may already be too late."

"You d-don't know th-that!" Igraines headed off at a near run, following the tracks.

"Igraines!" I yelled.

"Stubborn girl," observed Moscastan.

"Yes. Well, I suppose we should follow the tracks," I said.

In fact, the tracks led back to a place some quarter-of-a-mile from the battlefield of the day before. Here, the tracks converged with a mass of other prints—human and animal—and headed off in the direction of our village. It was now clear that what or who had found Baldua had been an expeditionary force sent out to track down those who had escaped Lord Creconius' army. It was the mist that had saved Igraines and myself. There was naught to do but head to our village, quickly. But when we finally arrived there, we nearly wished we had not been saved by the mist.

~VIII~

Fortunately, Moscastan had a water skin and dried meat with him to sustain us, for it took up nearly the whole day to reach our destination. We arrived at the village near dark. We had seen the smoke on the horizon and smelled the burned carnage from a mile out. There was nothing left. Everything had been razed to the ground and smoldered still. This must have happened the prior afternoon or evening. Those left alive —which numbered more than I expected—wandered in a daze, collecting what belongings remained or piling bodies in the cooking pits for disposal; the same cooking pits which Leoni used to make the meals. Now, beneath the corpses was wood for a different sort of fire. 'Twas the Celtic way: burning of the body in a funerary pyre instantly released the soul to travel to the Otherworld.

Yet, there was another faction in those dark days that was beginning to exert much influence on this subject. They even believed that it was evil to burn the body, for then their God—who was supposedly the Infinite and Only God—could not raise them in resurrection upon a Day of Judgment. How absurd! If their God was infinite, then He would be able to resurrect one no matter what! This faction was the Christians, and their view on death and cremation offended my sensibilities as a Celt and further convinced me that they did not understand their Christ's teachings. There was a group of them here now also collecting corpses, but not for cremation in the noble, Celtic way. They were placing them on a mule-drawn, flat-bed cart for a Christian burial. Quite a few of our clan members, though still practicing the Old Ways, which included consulting with Druids on occasion, had, nonetheless, converted to Christianity, following the teachings of Jesu, or Jesus, as the present Christians called Him; the same man

347

Centurion Longinus had pierced—that I had pierced—so long ago.

"Bring them," called a man in a drab brown robe tied at the waist with a simple rope. Looped over the rope was a twine of wood-beads which ended with a small dangling Crucifix. The man's head was shaved in the style of one the Christian Ascetics from the new Monastery at Glastonbury. A Tonsure, it was called—the crown of the head was completely shaved with a circle of hair rounding the skull front, back and sides. I didn't know its exact meaning, but it made these men stand out as priests of their Order. I thought that it also made them look ridiculous. This priest was fairly young, perhaps twenty-nine summers, comely and appealing. He had a firm yet gentle way about his countenance. And his eyes: a deep brown, yet there seemed to be something more—a depth perhaps of things not of this world. He spoke to the two villagers who had piled corpses, some already burned from the raid, onto the cart.

"Yes, Father Pretorius," said one of the villagers.

That was another thing I did not understand about these Christians; why they called these priests Father. Did they adopt these priests as fathers? Perhaps I would learn the answers someday. Right now, I wanted to find Baldua. Then I saw Leoni, bent over a small fire off to the edge of the village. She was cooking something, lifting the wood spoon from the pot and tasting its contents' worthiness.

"Leoni!" I called as I ran to her. I embraced the plump woman, who, to my surprise, did not return the gesture. "You are unscathed?" I said, as I pulled back and looked into her eyes.

"Yes, yes. Important work now, though. I must feed all these people. They're working hard at cleaning up, you see," she replied, vacantly, falsely. She was clearly trying to act as if nothing had happened.

I looked her up and down. She was not unscathed. She was filthy from head to toe. Her hair was disheveled and her face lacerated. Her dress was torn in places and on the spot under which her legs met at her crotch, there was blood; a lot of it. She had been raped, brutally. Anger welled within me, intense hatred for the ones who did this. I would cut their hearts from their bodies while they lived and shove it in their screaming mouths.

"Myrriddin!" Igraines called from behind me.

I looked around and saw her standing next to the Cart. Then I turned back to Leoni and touched her gently on the side of the head, caressing her hair. She jumped with a start, but did not pull away altogether. She was not entirely gone. "I'll come back in a bit, all right?" I said.

She stared into the air for a moment, then turned back to the pot without answering. I left it there for the time being, and headed over to the cart.

Moscastan was not with Igraines. Scanning the immediate area, I saw him near a woman and two children, no doubt tending to their needs. I stopped in my tracks briefly when I noticed that he had once again assumed his younger persona. Interesting trick, that! I would have to ask him exactly how he achieved that glam. I wasn't sure whom I liked better— the young Persian/Britton Moscastan, or the old man I'd met in the cavern of crystal, the Crystal Sanctuary, as I was beginning to think of it; at least the longer this hideous day wore on. And which one was the real, present-day Moscastan—the younger or the older? I had thought the latter upon first seeing him, but now I was not sure. Why would he choose to glam himself as an old man? Perhaps because of what the Old Ones represent, or perhaps because it suited him best to be as he was when I knew him during the life of Longinus: old Jacobi. That, too, was something I would have to find out.

I continued on toward the cart. My heart began to thump as I saw what Igraines was pointing to in the pile on the cart. I arrived there just as they started to move it away, one man pulling it, another pushing, following the priest Pretorius across a field, presumably to bury the cart's contents. Rather than stop the laboring men, I simply walked alongside the cart, as did Igraines, and I looked at the man she had been pointing to. Though the man's face was burned, I could tell that it was not Baldua. Besides, this man was wearing a cross, denoting him as a follower of the Christ. Baldua was Celt, through and through. "It's not him," I declared.

"Y-you sure?" she asked.

I looked again. The man's face did resemble Baldua's, but it was not him. "Yes. I know it looks like him, but it's not. Besides, Baldua would not be seen dead with that Christian symbol around his neck," I said with a forced smile.

My attempt at humor in this horrific setting was lost on her. I was just pleased that it was not my friend.

"What about that?" she said, pointing to a small shoulder bag lying in the man's grasp. It was Baldua's. Yet, I didn't remember him having it with him the previous day.

"It's his. I-I've seen it b-before," she said.

"But did you see him with it yesterday?"

She thought for a moment, then shrugged her shoulders, not remembering.

"I don't think so," I said.

"That one was a raider," said the toothless, pudgy, middle-aged man pushing the cart; the same man who had addressed Pretorius a moment before. "Killed 'im myself, I did. Smacked 'im upside the head with a big torch and hit him a couple more times 'til he stopped floppin'. Stupid shit-holes. Who do ya think you are?!" he yelled at the corpse.

"He must have taken the bag from Baldua's hovel," I said.

We arrived at the burial site, a shallow pit had already been dug. Pretorius stood at the edge of the hole, eyes closed, apparently in meditation. I looked at Igraines who motioned with her head that we should get out of there. She obviously wanted nothing to do with this twisted practice.

"Stay, my children, please," said the priest. "No matter who these people were, what acts some of them may have committed in this life, they need to be sent to the Father properly. Your prayers and solemnity will aid in this."

I was loath to do so. Who was this person? Such presumption! I wanted to find my friend, to comfort Leoni and the others of our clan and destroy the demon that committed this atrocity. My anger, which to this point I did not even realize was there, suddenly burst forth. "Why? You are part of the cause of this, you and your kind," I exclaimed, pointing at the crucifix on his belt. "At least one of the dead men on that cart wears your symbol, and not one of our people!"

"Please," said the priest. "We are all of the One, regardless of what symbols we wear."

He didn't speak like most of the other priests of his religion that I had heard. He sounded more like Moscastan. There was something else, too: there was a familiarity about him; something about his countenance, his presence, that told me I knew this man. I sensed his spirit. I had known him previously to this life. I looked into his eyes and saw...a forest sanctuary in the mists from a long time ago.

"Paulonius?," I whispered.

"Pretorius," he replied, having heard my whispered recollection.

"No, I mean...never mind. You just remind me of someone from a long time ago," I said.

He looked at me quizzically for a moment before realization donned upon his face. "Ah, I see. You are a Celt and practice the Old Ways, then. Well, I understand your ways. Actually, my beliefs are not so far from yours. I am of a slightly different thought than most of my counterparts in the Church, more Gnostic, if you will. But I am Christian, and the need to tend to the Christian dead is great," he said, gesturing to the corpses in the cart.

"W-we need to find B-Baldua," Igraines said, grabbing my arm of the hand that held the spear.

The staff, the spear, had been silent; nothing from it. No vibration, glowing or anything since before we left the glen where Baldua had last been seen. With all that had happened to the village, I thought that the spear would have shaken in warning as we approached. It had not.

Father Pretorius was staring at the spear. "May I?" he asked, his voice nearly cracking, as he reached out tentatively to touch the object in my hand.

I could see in his eyes a recognition that he felt, but could not explain even to himself. I never let anyone touch this thing that I held. Yet, with this priest, it was different. I could tell that Pretorius knew what I possessed, but did not yet understand this knowledge. He did not yet fully understand his own soul's past enough to comprehend what it was that he was feeling. I held the staff, the spear, out to him. He touched it lightly and reverently, emotion welling up on his face in the process. Though still, I could see, he did not fully understand why he was feeling what he was feeling.

He touched the ancient wooden shaft lightly. Next, he caressed the crystal in its housing against the blade, touching the blade itself. Then it came: a tear of the soul long banished welled up in his left eye. "This is no Pagan Wizard's walking staff, is it, my friend? This is something from my Lord's realm. I feel it. It is old and not from here. Where did you come by it?"

"I...I cannot say," I replied.

"Cannot, or will not, Master...?"

"Myrriddin, just Myrriddin," I answered.

He dropped his hand from the spear.

"Will you stay for a few moments to see these people properly given over to God?" asked Pretorius.

"Yes," I found myself saying.

"M-Myrriddin," Igraines said in frustration, not wanting to waste any more time in finding Baldua.

"'Tis but a short time to see the dead off, lass," said Moscastan from behind. He had approached quite stealthily, apparently having left the village remains for the time being. "Father Pretorius, good to see you again," he said, addressing the priest.

"And you, Druid Master Moscastan," replied Pretorius. "Will you help me perform this rite for the passing of the dead?"

I was shocked by the invitation—a Christian priest wishing to join with a Druid Master in performing a rite of passing for the dead? Truly, this priest was not of the Christian thought that I was used to seeing. He seemed to allow for, even embrace, the differences of our cultural, spiritual ways. Perhaps it was not so much our differences he focused on, but our similarities, all being of the One, as he put it. I was then even more surprised by Moscastan's response.

"Yes, Priest Pretorius. I would be honored," Moscastan said.

"Moscastan?" I said.

"Why do you look at me so, Myrriddin? 'We are all of the One'. Have I not said that a-thousand times? The One has a myriad of appearances and faces and aspects, but it all boils down to the One. Young Priest Pretorius sees this, even if most of his power-hungry counterparts do not."

"Ah, now Moscastan, do not be too harsh," said Pretorius.

"You are right. I just fear that those of your faith with less understanding than you, which, unfortunately is most of them, are bringing an end to our ways, violently and permanently," said Moscastan.

"Understood. This is not my wish nor should it be the way of things. We all need to recognize that our true Source is One Source. I will do what I can, Moscastan. I will do what I can," Pretorius responded.

Moscastan stepped forward and placed a hand on the younger man's shoulder. "I know that you will, my friend," he said.

Pretorius gave another look to the spear in my hand. I could see in his eyes that he wanted to inquire of it further, but this was not the time. He nodded to the men who had pushed the cart and then turned toward the grave's hole before us. The cart-men began to gently drop the bodies into their final resting place.

Pretorius then began to speak a prayer for the dead. "Requiem aeternam dona eis, Domine; et lux perpetua luceat eis. Requiescant in pace. Amen".

It was in Latin, of course. Where was Baldua when I needed him?

"By the Holy of Holies, by Dana and Luna, I release the spirits to the Otherworld, the crossing be blessed and whole..." intoned Moscastan.

Back and forth went the prayers for the dead, in Latin by Pretorius, in ancient Gaelic by Moscastan. I anticipated feeling nothing but loathing for the whole ordeal and resentment for being made to stay on account of Moscastan's desire for us, Igraines and me, to do so. Instead, what I began to feel was tenderness toward the souls of the deceased in the grave before me. Caught up in the moment, it took me a few heartbeats to realize that the spear was vibrating in my hand. It was not a vibration of warning; it was a subtle vibration of sympathy. It was an aide to the comfort being created for the departed souls to ease their crossing.

After a while, the vibration stopped; the rite was over. I knew not how much time had passed, for I had gone into a deep meditation, harmonizing in thought, in spirit, in mind, with the moment. I felt a tug on my arm. Igraines was trying to pull me away.

"C-come on. E-enough of this," she said.

I came back to my senses and agreed. "We are going to find Baldua," I said.

"Wait," said Pretorius. "I wish to go with you." He had looked at the spear as he said this.

"Why?" I asked. "Are you not needed here?"

The villagers who had brought the corpses began pushing dirt on the bodies, filling the grave.

"I have done what is needed," he said, indicating the grave and the bodies therein. "I am no longer needed here. It is time for me to leave. Perhaps I can help you."

Igraines stepped forward angrily, clearly about to say something abrasive to the priest.

I grabbed her arm to stop her, looked into her eyes and shook my head. Turning back to the priest, I said, "If you wish, but I don't see how you can help."

"We shall see," was all Pretorius said.

"Moscastan, will you come, too?" I asked.

"I will follow. Those left here need the comfort of the Old Ways, at least for a time."

"As you wish," I said, then turned to Pretorius. "Which way did those raiders go?"

"South, I think. Their Lord, their General, seeks something," he said, and again looked at the spear. Igraines saw the look, too.

"Then let's go south. I'm sure Baldua is with him," I said.

"How could you know that? Perhaps he tried to get back here? Perhaps something else has happened, God forbid it," Pretorius said.

I met his eyes and knew that he had more knowledge of Baldua and of what this so-called General was seeking than he was conveying. But what could that knowledge be? And why would Baldua be of any interest to this General? The spear vibrated in my hand again, giving me an answer for the moment; now was not the time to press Pretorius. Fine. The spear stopped vibrating. "I believe that he is with them. Regardless, I will find him," I said.

"So be it," said Moscastan.

"Indeed," said Pretorius.

"Would all of y-you stop fl-flapping your lips and m-move it!" said Igraines, angrily.

"So be it!" said Moscastan again. "Go."

I looked back toward the village, to where Leoni had been. She was nowhere to be seen.

"She will heal, Myrriddin. I will see that she begins the process," said Moscastan, reading my searching eyes. "I saw you speaking with her a while ago."

I nodded.

After a few minutes spent gathering some meager provisions, Pretorius, Igraines and I headed south.

* * *

It was not difficult to follow the trail of the "raiders," as the villager had called them. It is nearly impossible to hide the tracks of a passing army. Equally, it was not difficult to find them. By the end of that same day, we had them in sight. We were careful not to stay out in the open too much, as I was sure Lord Creconius would have scouts fore and aft of their position at all times. I was also sure that it was indeed Creconius and his followers. We had not been invaded since the Romans first came. Fighting between tribes and clans, certainly; that had been going on since the beginning of time. But no organized body led by an outsider had threatened us for some time. Until now.

We stood in a small grove of trees on a ridge near an outcropping of rocks, with an opening in the trees to see the enemy encampment in the valley below. The outcroppings made the perfect shelter to sleep under and the trees blocked us from the army below. Staying there for the night was the best option. We needed to make some sort of plan to get Baldua and would do that over a small evening meal. We had gathered up supplies enough for a few days—if we were disciplined with rationing them to ourselves—which Igraines had insisted on carrying in a makeshift satchel.

I was a little surprised that Pretorius was still with us. He did not strike me as the type to quest about the countryside searching to liberate someone that he did not even know, let alone liberate this person from a blood-lusting rabble. Yet here he was.

I was leaning on the staff, the spear, and looking through the trees, Igraines and Pretorius next to me, when I felt a subtle vibration from it. "Myrriddin," whispered the voice of the spear.

I must have given a startled look, for Pretorius gazed at me quizzically. "What is it, my friend?" he asked.

"It's that th-thing," said Igraines, pointing to the spear. "It s-speaks to him." Then, she walked back toward the outcropping.

If daggers could fly from my eyes, they would have killed her instantly. I knew that she was aware of my communications with the thing, but it disturbed me that she would be so cavalier in conveying that to a stranger. Besides, how could she have known I had just heard the voice?

"Is this true?" Pretorius asked.

Again, I sensed the man's depth of character and sincerity. "It is," I said. "You were right when you said that this was no mere 'Pagan Wizard's walking staff,' as you put it."

An awkward silence ensued for a moment.

"Yes, well, that begs the question, doesn't it?" asked Pretorius.

I almost told him then that this was the spear of Longinus; the spear the Centurion had used to pierce the side of Christ while he hanged on the cross. But, I gave naught but silence.

"I see," he said.

"I don't mean to be rude," I countered, suddenly feeling guilty for being just that. "It's not easy..."

"You are afraid that I might not believe you," said Pretorius. It was a statement, not a question.

"Perhaps," I managed to say.

"L-lets eat," ordered Igraines, from under the outcropping. She had laid out a blanket and was divvying out food for the three of us. "They aren't going anywhere," she said, nodding in the general direction of the army encampment.

Pretorius and I looked at one another, suppressing laughter simmering beneath the surface. We joined Igraines for a humble meal of bread, dried meat, cheese and water.

After our meal, Pretorius went off to pray, leaving Igraines and me alone. It was dark and chilly. We lit no fire for obvious reasons, so we both huddled together for warmth. The spear was next to me, as always. We talked of things past and things perhaps to come, but mostly of the immediate threat posed by the invaders and what it might mean. Then, when the conversation seemed to lag, she touched the spear. To my surprise, I did nothing, somehow feeling that it was completely appropriate that she had done so; even that she had held it many a-time in another place, another time.

"Y-you know th-they seek this, too," she said in a whisper. "I don't kn-know how I kn-know. I just do."

I simply nodded, staring into her eyes. "Perhaps," was all I managed to say. I looked down at the spear, then gently placed it in a long nook in the rock next to me. I turned back to Igraines and stared into her eyes for a few a moments. We had known each other for a long time. In spite of her hard demeanor, she was becoming quite a woman through and through. And, yes. I admit that I was more than attracted to her; had been for a long time. I also believed that she felt the same toward me. The way she looked at me sometimes made me feel both excited and self-conscious.

She lay back, then, gently pulling me down with her and into an embrace. Slowly, tentatively at first, we kissed; a tender meeting of the lips. But soon the tentativeness abated, and our passion swelled. We became more excited and hungry by the moment, probing each other's mouths with eager lips and tongues. My heart was thudding. I could feel hers beneath her chest as well, as we pulled each other's body against one another. I do not remember exactly what happened next, save for the forceful caress of her hands, the heat of her body and the merging of our souls. If a paradise of heaven, as the Christians called it, existed, I entered it during that time with Igraines.

I felt her stir a little while later. I looked at her and a feeling of connectedness washed over me. Our passion for each other's body had been clear. But I realized that I felt more than mere lust for her, much more.

She insisted on taking a guard watch. Pretorius, back by that time and only half asleep nearby, did not see the need for any of us to stand guard. But then, he wouldn't. He was not a soldier. Not that I was, really, but I understood the need to keep a guard.

Still, she wanted to stand watch. "No," I had said to her. "Pretorius and I will stand watch through the night." That was a foolish thing for me to have said to her.

"Why? Am I n-not capable, that we three can't split the watch?" she asked, sitting up beside me, suddenly furious.

I always found it interesting that her stutter seemed much less pronounced when she was in a fit of anger. "Of course not," I said. "I just thought..." I began, looking at our bedding. To his credit, the priest said nothing about the coupling Igraines and I had obviously experienced earlier. Our clothes, though still on, were in quite the disarray, and our limbs, at least our legs, were still entwined. "Fine. Take the first watch, then," I said to her.

She got up and marched out to the small clearing not far away, near the tree where one could see the enemy's encampment.

We did not hear them come in the night. Nor, did we see them. I still, to this day, do not fully understand what happened. Thinking back, it seems clear that I should have taken the first watch. What I know for sure is that I awakened some time later with a broken body and another missing friend.

~IX~

Floating. Flying, actually. I could see the green hills and mountains below, bathed in a pale sunset. It was as if I were a bird flying above them. I came in closer, spying more details. The green hills gave way to a rocky, forested area. I recognized this place. But parts of it were different than I remembered. Some of the trees were larger; some of the foliage more lushly sprawled, and some of the rocky areas more eroded. It was as if some time had passed since last I'd seen this place. Coming in even closer to one area in particular confirmed my thoughts as to where I was. There, before me, was an opening in the side of a rock formation, a granite formation. It was a cave's opening embedded in the side of one of the mountains. But not just any cave's opening; it was the entry point to Moscastan's Crystal Cavern.

Two people approached it. One I thought to be Moscastan. The other person was a lad, a young man of no more than fifteen summers. I looked again at Moscastan and realized quite suddenly that it was not Moscastan at all. It was me, a future-self? The vision-Myrriddin was adorned in the regalia of a Master Druid, the highest of Merlins: a purple robe with crimson trim flowed over his body. His hair, my hair, what was left of it, was nearly all white. He still had a clean-shaved face in the Roman way, showing the face to have the lines and crags of the years and the wise. But he also looked pale and drawn, having seen much of life's offerings and disappointments. I did not sense that this version of myself was all that far in the future, if indeed these images were prescient. Though somewhat pale and careworn, he also looked solid in his Unification with the One; his bearing and countenance conveyed a surety of purpose, a confidence of self. Which made me think, perhaps the coloring and apparent ragged features were reflective of an inner power that my present-self simply did not yet understand. I could see this in his eyes, my eyes, still bright and full of youth, depth and knowledge and inner power.

There was a walking staff—clearly a true Druid's staff—walking with him. A new and very large Crystal Druid's Egg with a glowing green hue, adorned the top, concealing the spear's blade. There was something almost trance-inducing about the Egg, the Crystal. It was unlike any stone I'd ever seen. A greenish light seemed to come from within it. It pulsated a power that was beyond comprehension. Yet, I quickly realized what I was seeing: the stone was taking the power that coursed through the staff—the power of the Merlin, the power of the One—and amplifying it. Amazing! Where had this Druid's Egg come from? However, I could not tell if this staff was the spear I presently possessed. Why wouldn't it be? I wondered.

The lad and older Myrriddin were now very close to Moscastan's Crystal Sanctuary.

My vision-self, was in mid-sentence. He was speaking to the boy. "Arturius," Older Myrriddin said to the lad.

For amoment, I had the fleeting thought that I was simply dreaming, and that perhaps the boy was also a version of me some years earlier, speaking to his—my—future-self. But I had never been to the cave as a lad. No matter. Dreams are always strange that way, twisting our perceptions of time and memory and people. As I said, however, that was just a fleeting thought. This was no dream. I could feel its truth in the core of my being. This was a prophecy, a glimpse of some future event and time, a future in which I would tutor a boy named Arturius. The boy's name seemed familiar. But I knew no boy named Arturius in this life. At least not yet.

"Your father and Pretorius knew these things," Older Myrriddin continued, "but your father was wise in many other ways. He gathered many of the lands and clans together, did he not? You shall carry on that work, expand on it," continued my older persona. As they approached the cave's opening, the wonderful glow from within gently ebbed, flowed and spilled out of the entryway, onto the darkening ground. A look tantamount to pride played subtly across older Myrriddin's face. "I was a marvel at scrying and quite gifted with the sight, both past and future, you know. You may learn those things, too, during your stay here...if you wish it."

I felt my present-self grinning with heartfelt warmth at the older man's words.

"Yes. So you've said a-hundred times," the lad replied drolly.

They disappeared into the Sanctuary's opening.

"Merlin!" I heard from somewhere in the distance. "Myrriddin!"

The Crystal Sanctuary's entrance, the hills and mountains—the whole scene before me—evaporated.

My eyes snapped open. Slowly, they adjusted to the misty gloom. Cold. It was cold and damp. A hard surface was beneath me. Stone. A full moon was shrouded in misty clouds, peering out from its protective curtain on the mortals below. Light from torches flickered nearby. I should have been alarmed. Instead, I was disappointed. I was not quite sure why I felt that way. Perhaps it was because I half expected to wake up in the Sanctuary. Instead, I was outside on a cold, moonlit night, lying supine on a stone...altar?

Shapes took form nearby: upright, rectangular stone columns topped with stone lintels. I knew this place. Moscastan called it The Grand Henge, where the Ancients and ancestors plotted the course of the Universe; where the Otherworld met this one; where rituals of all sorts had been performed—from fertility rites to migrations of souls on All Hollows Eve; from sacrifices for various appeasements to the raising of the dead. This latter rite had only been a myth. But I got the feeling I wasn't lying on this Altar as some kind of living sacrifice.

It was then that I heard the chanting. Out of the corner of my eyes, I could see several white-robed, hooded figures, their faces obscured, but their voices clear. They stood six on each side of the stone altar, some ten feet away from me. They were chanting something in ancient Gaelic, only part of which I could understand. What I did understand, however, was unmistakable; it was a chant to bring the dead back to life, not the dead in the general sense, but one specifically: me. They were chanting to bring me back to life. Apparently, they had succeeded.

The chanting, the rhythmic voices, suddenly stopped. Sensing movement, I rolled my head to the right and looked at someone who approached the altar. Stepping forward, throwing off his dark hood and standing with his arms raised high to silence the twelve chanters, was Moscastan, somehow looking younger than I remembered him even as his younger self. Unlike the others, Moscastan was shrouded in a black robe adorned with gold stars and a prominent crescent moon on his chest. He stared at me. "You have returned. You have awakened," he said, stating the obvious, a hint of glee escaping from the upturned corners of his mouth.

But awakened from what? Ah, yes. We had been searching for Baldua and we had bedded down for the night; the priest Pretorius, Igraines and myself. "Igraines!" I opened my mouth to speak, but not a sound came out. Panic struck, I tried to grab my throat with my right hand, only to find that my hand would not move. Why? Trying my left hand proved slightly easier, but still challenging. I brought the heavily wrapped hand to my throat with difficulty and felt cloth around my entire neck—a wet, sticky substance seeping through the cloth.

I tried to sit up, but could not. The pain in my rib area and lower back sent searing bolts of agony coursing through my entire body. A slight, muffled animal noise emanated from my mouth in response to the pain. I remained lying down.

"Now, now Myrriddin," soothed Moscastan, "You've had quite an ordeal. We thought we had lost you. Your life's pulse faded and left not too long ago."

Forgetting the pain for the moment, I looked around as best I could, frantically looking for Igraines. Why I felt that she would be there at that moment, now seems ridiculous. I wasn't sure how or why I was there.

"It is here, Myrriddin. Fear naught," said Moscastan, pointing to a long, narrow object resting on a nearby portable wooden table, surrounded by ritual instruments. It was my staff, my spear. Not Igraines. That was something, anyway. Whatever had happened to us, my spear had escaped with me. But, how?

"It was...hidden, somehow, cloaked in a nook where the three of you had been sleeping. Did you place a glam on it when you retired that night?" ventured Moscastan excitedly. "So that no one else would see it?"

"I..." was all I managed to squeak out.

"My apologies a-thousand times, Master Myrriddin. I tax you needlessly. 'Tis good to have you back among us, truly, but you need to further heal," said Moscastan, turning to leave.

"Wh-where," I croaked, "is Geno..."

"Igraines?" Moscastan stopped and turned back to me. "You must complete the healing. We will continue to aid you."

The tone in his voice sounded grim. "What is it?" Speaking caused searing pain to shoot through my throat. But I had to know what happened to Igraines; indeed, what happened to all three of us that night.

Moscastan hesitated before proceeding. I could see in his eyes that he knew I would not be put off. "No one knows exactly what happened," he began, "other than the fact that you were attacked by the same brigands that sacked your village—the ones camped near where you bedded for the night. They apparently overpowered Igraines easily. There were drag marks on the ground from where she had been 'on watch,' as you might say. The priest Pretorius was beaten and left near a tree. He's the one who came and got me, and a few others. They let him live because he had buried their dead comrades 'honorably.' He was able to hear most of what happened to you. They had been watching you all along, trailing you nearly since your visit to the Crystal Sanctuary.

They want the spear and know you have it. But they couldn't find it. As I said, it's as if it cloaked itself, or you did, before you slipped into unconsciousness. I think 'twas the latter. I've seen you do something similar before, not even realizing you'd performed the feat of cloaking on the thing."

Yes, I remembered one occasion when I had willed the thing invisible during a bout with other boys. I was very young and the other lads wanted my "wizard's staff." They had pinned me down in an attempt to pry it out of my hands. At the very moment they were able to uncurl my fingers from around the shaft, the whole staff disappeared from sight. The boys jumped back at the display of apparent sorcery. I, however, could still feel the shaft in my hand even though I, too, could not see it for the moment. I remember laughing; laughing at my apparent power with the staff, or the staff's apparent power with me, and then laughing at the boys as they ran away. I almost laughed again now at the memory, but my face hurt too much.

Looking beyond Moscastan, I saw another figure lingering in the shadows just outside the sacred circle of stones. It was Pretorius. He, too, was in a white robe, but a large wooden crucifix dangled from around his neck. His hands were clasped in front of him and his head was bowed in prayer. I was surprised to see him in this Pagan place. I had a fleeting thought that his prayers were those of deliverance from this "evil place," as some of his contemporary Christians had called it. But I knew this man better than that. He had no fear of places like this. In fact, he would see it for what it had been: a place of focus for the One God to express in the only given way that our ancestors understood. In that sense, this place was sacred still. I had no doubt that his prayers were for me. I felt them; I felt their power. I felt the power of this priest and his understanding of the One's nature, which was the essence of everyone's nature. Pretorius stopped his mumbling of prayers and opened his eyes as if sensing my gaze. He smiled broadly and stepped forward into the henge's inner circle. He halted short of those who had been chanting, however, and looked at them tentatively, as they looked at him and seemed to convey that the priest should venture no closer.

Moscastan, turning serious, leaned into my face. "You are still in a broken state, but your body heals itself as I speak. You had left us for a time—you'd no life pulse, no breath. We brought you here, you and your spear."

He paused then, and turned to the table next to us. Tenderly and reverently, he picked up the staff, the spear of Longinus, with both hands. Holding it horizontally, he lifted it briefly above his head, acknowledging it and the powers that flowed through it to the gods, to the heavens, to the One. Its tip began to glow.

Soft chanting began again. Moscastan brought the spear back down and held it in front of his body. The small branches and foliage I had tied to the blade were disheveled. Some of the thongs were loose and the crystal was gone. The rest of the thongs still held fast, though, which in turn still held the branches onto the spear overall. With the missing crystal, the spear's tip looked more like a claw than the crowning top of a wizard's staff. Yet, still among the twigged branches, the blade glowed.

Moscastan laid the spear gently on my body lengthwise, the blade on my upper chest, the shaft running down the center of my body, with the lower part of the shaft resting on the touching heels of my splayed feet. I rested my right hand on the part of the shaft just below the blade. My mentor then stepped back silently, joining the nearest chanters in proximity and voice. Pretorius, too, had stepped back and resumed his chanting of prayers.

I held the spear tightly against my chest and closed my eyes. I felt energy coming from it. At first, it was in the form of a pulsating, soothing heat. But then the feeling changed to something akin to a charged, static or as if I were suddenly near a bolt of lightening: a powerfully charged bolt of lightening that was in the spear itself. From there, it went into my body, coursing through to the injured region. A binding and pinching sensation came from within, as my muscle and sinew that had been torn and shredded were now being fused and mended back together in an instant. The chanting intensified, adding and aiding powerful energy to the healing that was taking place. I surrendered, giving in to the moment utterly. Leaving physical consciousness and physical body behind, my spirit—body and mind drifted above the scene. I did this so that the healing could complete itself without hindrance of my conscious thought.

Floating. I was floating over the Henge. My body lay on the center stone, the spear atop my body. I could also see all present, as well as an Otherwordly light that surrounded the whole area. This light, which I could only see with disembodied spirit eyes, radiated from the spear to those present and back again. All were connected in the beautiful light of power; for that is what it was: a light of divine, healing power. I felt it, knew it to be thus. Though I hovered above this scene in spirit, the cord of my soul, which connected my spirit-self to my body below, was present. The light of power coursed through this cord as well, and into my disembodied being. I knew, then, that not only would I be whole again in body, but more than powerful in spirit, too. The ritual, those chanting, the power of this Henge—this spot on earth—and the spear itself, all contributed to the immense surge of power happening to me right then and there.

Time seemed to stand still as I hovered and joined in mind with what was happening below. Then, I thought of being inside my body once again, and it happened in an instant. With a violent jolt, the scene before me went dark and I heard the chanting voices no more.

And so it began. It was on that night that I was born once more.

~X~

"He awakens, Master Moscastan." It was Leoni's sweet voice.

The lids of my eyes were as stone. With great effort, they struggled to free my sight from darkness and open them to my new world. Finally, they succeeded. I was no longer at the Henge, but in Moscastan's small earthen dwelling in our village, resting on his sleeping pallet. Leoni was there, as was Pretorius.

Moscastan's smiling face peered down at me. "How do you feel?" he asked.

I thought for a moment, assessing my entire being.

"He's groggy, can't you see?" said Leoni, answering for me. "'Tis no wonder," she said to me. "You've slept for near three days."

Moscastan gave her a reprimanding look, to which she simply turned up her nose. "Hmph, I say. Time you awoke. Ye must eat or ye'll have no strength at all. I have some leftover oat cakes and porridge from the morning's breaking of the fast. I'll get them." With that, she left, squeezing her ample girth into the narrow dirt tunnel leading to the outside. "Don't suppose ye could make this into a normal portal?" she said to Moscastan as her form receded up the passageway.

Ignoring her comment, Moscastan looked at me. "She has recovered quite nicely, don't you think?" he commented flatly in an obvious referral to Leoni's traumatized state after the village was razed.

"Three days?" I asked, my voice a bit scratchy from lack of use, but normal. "I've been lying here for three days? I remember the night at the Henge. I was outside of my body..."

"It was a night to behold," said Pretorius. "God was truly present, as He always is, but that night, His power was undeniably there."

"Indeed," agreed Moscastan. "Again, lad, how do you feel?"

I tentatively moved my hands, my arms. They moved a little stiffly at first, but were perfectly normal. I felt my throat and found it to be healed. Then I sat up. Aside from a quick and fleeting sense of dizziness, I felt completely healed and normal. It surprised me, for I sensed that my injuries had been devastating. "I feel...well," was all I could manage. I swung my legs off Moscastan's sleeping pallet and touched the ground with my feet. Standing slowly, I found my legs to be somewhat wobbly, but nothing that a few hours of walking wouldn't cure.

Moscastan beamed. "Yes, yes! You are indeed."

"Truly, you have been resurrected, Myrriddin. That night, all of us, acting as one, within the One...truly amazing," said Pretorius, clearly pleased to see me.

"Master Moscastan," Leoni called from outside. "If ye don't mind, I think it better for Master Myrriddin to eat up here, outside. Fresh air'll do 'im wonders."

"Yes, Leoni," I called.

"Myrriddin? Ah good, then," she said.

Moscastan leaned in close to me. "Aye, air will do you good, but me thinks she'd rather not squish through to get into my den again!" He patted my shoulder and pointed to the corner where my spear stood waiting for me. It still had the small branches tied to it, but was also still missing the Druid's Egg, thus exposing the blade. No matter. I picked it up and crawled into the passageway that led out.

The day was bright, clear and crisp. A more beautiful day there had never been. Everything seemed more vibrant, alive. Such were my thoughts as I re-entered the world through Moscastan's passageway. I stood near the opening to his hovel, staring at the trees, the sky, the foliage, three animals—squirrels, I believed—scurrying into the underbrush.

Everything had a slight glow around it, the energy which held it all together, and I could see it. Things that were living, plants, animals and people—had an extra tinge of color to their fields of energy which were in constant flux and change. I was transfixed.

"You see the aura of things now, yes?" asked Moscastan, having climbed out of his home. He was followed by Pretorius, both of whom stood next to me. "The colors and light of the life-flow, the energy that holds creation together, that is Creation Itself. The—"

"Yes, Moscastan," I said.

"I see it on your face and in your eyes. You have been transformed, elevated in the eyes of the One, and are now able to see the things of worlds merged," Moscastan said.

"What?" I said, playing dumb. Though I knew full well what he was saying, and he was correct, I wasn't sure that I wanted to admit it. That would mean letting go of my humanness to a certain degree. On the other hand, it meant that I was merging with and into my True Self, blending the baser with the divine.

"Here, now. Wonderful to see you up and about, Myrriddin. Truly," said Leoni, waddling toward me with a wooden tray full of fowl, oatcakes and mead. "Come," she continued, indicating a short table to the right with a stool in front of it. "Sit. Eat." She placed the tray on the table as I sat on the stool.

I began to eat. Ravenously. The more I ate, the more hungry I became. Soon, I was practically shoveling food into my mouth and washing it down with weak mead. The others, now sitting near me on stumps of stools of their own, simply smiled as I gorged myself. I suddenly stopped as a thought occurred to me. "Igraines!" All sensation of having been brought back from the brink of the Otherworld, being given the gift of the gods, The God, The One in the form of the amalgamation of my spirit and body fell away. The horror, and the beauty, of the night I lost her came flooding back. We had one night together wherein our bodies had found ecstasy in and through each other. It had been one night together wherein our souls had found bliss as one. Only one night. I had known her most of my life. Yet, on that one occasion...what a difference one night could make. And then there was Baldua. "And Baldua," I asked—afraid to hear the answer.

Moscastan looked to Pretorius.

"Baldua will be thrilled you're back among us," said the priest.

"He's here?" I said, excitement swelling my throat so that, at least to me, I sounded like a squealing little child.

"He is that."

"What happened to him?" I asked, gaining my normal voice once more.

"Perhaps you can get him to tell you," Moscastan said grimly. "He walked back into the village, or what was left of it, on the fourth day of your...incapacitation, the day before you...died."

So it was true, then! I really had crossed to the Otherworld. I had been dead and then truly brought back to life. Why could I not remember my journey to the other side, then—my experiences there? But this line of questioning I would save for another time. I wanted to know about Baldua and Igraines. "He just walked in you say?"

"Yes. And, wouldn't talk about his experience. He just kept looking around and saying 'Mea maxima culpa, It's all my fault,'" Moscastan explained. "He'd just shake his head when pressed for what he meant."

Baldua. My dear friend. I was silent for a few moments, contemplating what might have happened to him. "And Igraines?" I finally asked.

"No sign of the girl," said Pretorius. "You are...close with her, aren't you?" he asked gently, clearly referring to our coupling that night.

I stared at the man, debating how to phrase my reply, or whether to even give one. "More than I realized, Father. Much more than I realized."

"We'll find her, Myrriddin," assured Moscastan.

I simply nodded my head, hoping he was right, knowing in my heart that it may not be that simple.

~XI~

I walked. I walked with the spear in hand, using it, as always, in the manner of a walking staff. The blade pulsated with a glow quite frequently now; softly, subtly, almost imperceptibly. Except to me. Its glowing was the pulsating of my heart, my life-blood. I was linked to the spear more profoundly now than ever before. I had been healed through the spear, but not by the spear. I understood that well. I had been connected with this instrument for much longer than just this time's healing.

I walked on. Most of my walks had turned into meditations. I contemplated all that had occurred over the recent past; the meaning of all of it; the knowledge both spiritual and practical to be gained. It had been three moons since the night at the Henge—since my resurrection. I had searched for Igraines in the interim; searched in vain. Pretorius and Moscastan came with me on my expeditions into the wilderness in search of her—her and the bastards that had so disrupted our lives. We followed the trail of the raiders, of Lord Creconius and his men. It led to the sea. That discovery left me bitter and disappointed beyond belief. I was so vexed, that I nearly lost all control; nearly hurled the spear into the ocean at the non-existent receding ship carrying Creconius and the raiders that had long since made its escape. Instead, I shouted at the sea in anger. I yelled at the top of my lungs, cursing Lord Creconius for this present life's transgressions against me, as well as his offenses in my former-life. He had also been known to my spirit as Draco. I knew that now for certain. I was consciously aware of all the connections with people in my current life—connections that spanned centuries on the plane of the Earth; eons on the plane of the spirit; eternity on the plane of the Universal. I didn't pretend to understand these connections or why they were there. But, that never stopped me from musing and speculating on them. For example, I would ponder that perhaps different souls are together through the same aspects of existence because they came from the same batch of ethereal properties, so to speak, much the same way several oatcakes come from the same batch of oat mix. Though there are many batches or bowlfuls from a single vat of mix, only a certain number of oatcakes can be made from a single bowlful, and those from a given bowlful or batch are forever linked together because of coming from that particular batch of mix. Trite, perhaps, but not an altogether inaccurate analogy, though Pretorius thought me daft when I tried to explain it to him. "By your reasoning, our souls aren't then eternal because they were created. After all, I do not believe that an eternal soul has a beginning or end. It simply is," he'd said.

The more I got to know this man, the more I realized how unlike his fellow Christians he was. "Maybe," I replied, "but even before becoming the mix for oatcakes, the individual parts within existed in a different form. They are thus eternal." He wasn't really convinced.

Lord Creconius, Draco, had been a thorn in my side for more than one of my incarnations. He had been instrumental in my demise as Longinus. And, he had now stolen that most precious to me. Well, near most precious, I thought, as I felt the spear's solidity in my hand.

Moscastan had helped to calm me that windy, cloudy day on the beach—the day we arrived at the end of the trail at the waters' shore. My anger at the raiders' escape, at Lord Creconius' escape, was equal to the anger I felt over wrongs Creconius had perpetrated on my being over the centuries, and equal to my anger over his abducting Igraines. "Be angry. You should be," Moscastan had said. "But see beyond the moment and do not become the anger. Otherwise, it will consume you. Seek not revenge. Revenge is for the impatient, the simple. Creconius will have visited upon him that which he perpetrates on others. Trust in the Balance of the One for that."

I stood there, arm raised with spear in hand, ready to fling it at the escaping ship that was not there. The ocean's spray was dampening my face and blanketing my spirit. I did not fling the weapon into the water. Instead, I brought my arm down and stared at the spear. Its blade was normal, not aglow. Though the blade still had the small branches around it that once cradled the Druids' Egg, one could easily see the blade itself. What parts of it remained unstained gleamed in the partial sunlight. The clouds seemed to accentuate the stains on the thing, making them deeper and more pronounced. His stains, they were: Master Jesus' from so long ago. And yet, it was just yesterday. A blink of the eye of God; a breath in the journey of my soul.

"I know, Myrriddin," said Moscastan. "I know your frustration. But look into your own scrying bowl to reveal information on your own life. You will see that he is a trivial aspect of it."

Trivial? I thought. What was he saying? And, besides that, I had never been able to look at my own future through the scrying bowl.

"Perhaps you've just not tried hard enough," said Moscastan, apparently reading my thoughts.

"I have tried hard," I retorted.

"Or, you've hardly tried!" he insisted.

"You know that's not so, Moscastan. I have seriously attempted it on several occasions. I am too close to the source of the information to be foretold: Me. You have said as much yourself in the past, so don't pretend otherwise," I said, anger from the day spilling into my voice.

I stewed for a couple more minutes, then began to calm down. Moscastan stood in silence, as did Pretorius, both men allowing me to process the day's events and regain my composure. Finally, I turned to Moscastan and held the spear out to him. "You said Lord Creconius wanted this. Why has he left without it?" I asked.

"He will be back, I am sure," replied Moscastan. "He has taken the other items he wanted from the same location in which you found the spear."

"He is satisfied for now," Pretorius chimed in, "but Moscastan is right. Lord Creconius will return to gain the rest of what he seeks," he said, glancing at the spear.

But it was what Moscastan had just said that stunned me. "What're you talking about, 'other items,' Moscastan?" I asked, looking from one man to the other.

"You found the spear in the Temple ruins on the Island Of Mystery when you were a wee lad," Moscastan began. "You found it along with a few other items which you considered at the time to be of...lesser value: a piece of wood—"

"A piece of the Rood—the Cross on which our Lord Jesus was hanged," Pretorius said for clarification.

"A bowl—"

"The bowl or cup is believed to be the one that He used during his final meal," Pretorius said, excitement creeping into his voice.

"And a book—"

"The original Testimonies of Thomas, Disciple of Jesus', and Mary of Magdalena, who was also a Disciple of Jesus. There have been ancient copies circulating for decades. These testimonies and others like them, which were also written by eye-witnesses to our Lord's life, are presently being condemned by my church as heretical," Pretorius spat, with obvious disdain and contempt for those doing the condemning.

A silence fell between us all. Of course, I remembered the items of which they spoke. And, Moscastan was right. To my child's mind at the time, the spear was the only real treasure there. Then again, perhaps there was more to it than that. The spear was not just a treasure—it spoke to me, even as a youth. I was particularly surprised just then, however, by something else that Pretorius had said about Mary. Had she really been one of the Disciples? Can anyone know for certain how many Disciples there had actually been? Truth be told, I knew little to nothing of the woman Mary. This church of

Pretorius', as far as I understood, shunned women, considered them to be inferior beings. But then again, the more I learned of Pretorius the man and his personal beliefs, the more I realized he was disenfranchised from his church, even at odds with it. "Why?" I finally asked, turning to Pretorius. "As you say, the accounts are from eyewitnesses. Why would the church condemn firsthand accounts?"

The priest regained his usual stoically reverent demeanor and stepped toward me. He placed a hand on my shoulder and said, "The Church has turned secular, my son."

It always made me laugh inside when he spoke to me as if he were my elder.

"The Church or many of those who run it," Pretorius continued, "are not as much interested in Truth and Enlightenment, as they are in power and control. Some in the hierarchy of the church have twisted the teachings of our Master Jesus so as to reflect an agenda of earthly ilk. A handful of us know this and will never adhere."

"At the risk of sounding naive, why do you stay a part of it, the church, I mean?" I asked.

"Because I love it so. God imparted His teachings through Jesus. Men made the church, or at least, made it what it is. It has simply lost its way. Perhaps I and others like me can bring it back to fold," answered Pretorius.

"Now who's being naïve?" Moscastan said sardonically.

"I believe that in their hearts, the Church fathers, from the Pontiff to the Cardinals, know the Church won't survive unless they hear and live the teachings of the Anointed One. They cannot twist and turn the teachings to suit their will. They will perish and the Church with them," insisted Pretorius.

"Please, Pretorius. They continue to destroy our way of life and subjugate our people in the name of your Jesus, and show no sign of letting up," Moscastan countered.

"Rome has done that."

"The Church is Rome now!" Moscastan said, displaying a rare moment of pure agitation.

"Now, now, Moscastan," I said, mocking his earlier tone with me. "Do not become the anger!"

My mentor smiled. "No, no. No anger. A bit of frustration is all. Come, Myrriddin. You, too, Pretorius, my friend. Let's go back and eat. We will consider more options in the finding of Creconius and Igraines. Perhaps Baldua will be receptive this night and he can aid us in this endeavor." Though Moscastan attempted to sound positive in his postulation, his eyes belied his true feelings. There was sadness there, a sadness that spoke to the truth of our mutual friend's condition.

Few words had passed between Baldua and me since my own recovery. He was tormented in the head. I was sure he'd break through whatever demons had hold of him; whatever demons Creconius had poisoned him with. But with each passing day, he seemed to sink deeper and deeper into the grasp of his demons. He had stopped saying that it was all his fault, which was something, I supposed. The problem now was that he was barely saying anything at all. He had withdrawn with his demons almost completely. I feared more for the loss of my friend's mind than ever.

It was near dark by the time we got back to the village. Our community had been rebuilt with astonishing speed and alacrity. A feasting hall had been built. We had a smaller one before the raiders came, but this one was grand; grand not because we needed a large hall—we didn't. It was grand as a symbol of defiance to those who thought they had destroyed us in flesh, as well as spirit.

Moscastan, Pretorius and I entered the hall. It was dimly lit, but lively. Many of the villagers were at several tables in the large room's center, feasting on the evening's meal. Leoni was in the middle of it all, serving food and drink, and scolding those who were grabbing at the fare for being impatient. Just near her was Baldua, sitting in the middle of a table, surrounded by many villagers clamoring for a meal, yet utterly alone. A vacant look filled his eyes. I turned to Moscastan. "I'll join you soon," I said.

Moscastan turned his gaze to where I had been looking. "Yes. See if you cannot bring him round. Be gentle and at ease, though."

I nodded and headed to my friend.

"Salve, Baldua! (Greetings, Baldua!)" I said in Latin, lightly, happily, as if nothing was wrong with the world.

Baldua had been absently pushing food around on the platter before him. He stopped, apparently recognizing my voice, and looked up at me. Though his gaze was upon me, my friend was not there. His eyes were empty. I sat next to him, facing out with my back to the table and hung my head for a brief instant, sadness nearly overwhelming me. I quickly shed the emotional weight and placed my hand on Baldua's shoulder. He didn't draw back from the touch, but he did turn back to the plate of food before him, and resumed playing with the food there. "What is it, Baldua?" I asked him. "Where've you gone, huh? You need to come back. I need you to come back. We've work to do, you and I. We need to find Igraines. We...we need to find the treasures that were stolen from the Temple ruins—you know about those, right? We need to find and destroy this Lord Creconius."

Baldua's head snapped up and his gaze bore into my eyes at the mention of Creconius' name. Hatred and fire spewed from those light colored orbs. He was present once again.

"Yes, Creconius," I said the name again, not sure how far to push my friend, but pleased that it was eliciting a response from him, any response.

He turned back to the table, fists balled up on either side of his plate. His body began rocking back and forth, anger spreading across the features of his face. He was fighting; fighting to get back. That is what I wanted to believe.

Moscastan appeared next to me. We exchanged a look. "I was wrong before. Press him. None too gently, I should think."

"My fault, my fault. It hurt, hurt badly..." Baldua said between clenched teeth. He was now rocking back and forth; a gesture both of comfort and of liberation, as if he were trying to shake off the demons.

"Why? Or, what? What is your fault? The village's destruction? Creconius knew where the village was without your help, so what could be your fault? And what hurt? What did that piece of shite, Creconius, do to you?" I pressed, emphasizing Creconius' name more and more with each saying of it. Baldua could be swallowed by the demons entirely, I knew that. But it was a risk I was willing to take to bring my friend back.

He suddenly stopped his rocking and began pounding his clenched fists on the table. His right hand landed on the side of his plate, catapulting the contents into the air and across the table. It landed on the arm or a large villager. Jostin was his name. He was of forty summers with many a swirled tattoo on either arm. He had the longest mustache I had ever seen, but kept the rest of his face and his head completely shaved for reasons none of us were ever able to figure out. We had not seen him for many a summer, for he'd relocated to his wife's clan four miles into the valley, and only came back when our village, his home village, had been razed. He stood now, ready to pounce on whoever had thrown the food at him. "Who dares?" he bellowed.

"Peace, Jostin," said Moscastan. "'Twas Baldua here, and he meant it not. You know that."

Jostin checked his anger and stared at poor Baldua, as many others in the hall were now doing. My friend continued to pound his fists on the table, bloodying his right, and breaking the other, as evidenced by the odd angle at which his pinky and ring finger were now bent.

"Baldua! What did Creconius do to you?" I yelled. Then, it hit me. Gently, I lifted the spear and placed the blade near my friend's head. The blade, indeed the whole spear, was glowing. I heard gasps from those nearby, as they pointed and wondered at the spear. "Breathe, Baldua." I reached up and broke one of the small branches of the wicker cage that still hugged the spear's top, so that I could touch its blade to Baldua's head.

At first contact, my friend ceased all activity. As if frozen in time, he sat there, stiff. Then, his breathing eased and he blinked three times and closed his eyes. Tears squeezed from his closed lids, dampening his cheeks. "Yes," he finally said to no one in particular

"What?" I asked.

"It is not you to whom he speaks, Myrriddin," said Moscastan.

Well, then who was he speaking to? And then it dawned on me. "Could it be?" I wondered aloud.

"Yes," answered Moscastan.

I looked at him with a mixture of confusion and I knew not what. I was the only one who had ever heard His voice through the spear.

"Oh come now, Myrriddin. Jealously does not suit you," said Moscastan.

"I'm not jealous," I said protesting a little too vigorously. Stop it, Myrriddin, I thought to myself. I realized that my friend was in need of the healing right then and there, and if part of that was to hear His voice through the spear as I had in the past, then so be it.

"Yes, I understand and know this to be so. So it is," said Baldua to the air. He fell silent then and breathed deeply, easily for some five minutes. The entire hall had fallen silent as well, as if in silent support, even prayer. I looked around and saw that many had their heads bowed, there lips moving in silent supplication. Pretorius, too, now standing near Moscastan, was uttering prayers under his breath much the way he had for me that night at the Henge. I, too, joined the silence, going within my being and seeing my friend as I knew him to Truly be: a whole and perfect being. Whatever was happening to him on the outside was of the human condition and not of his own True nature. With such a realization, anything could be overcome.

"You know this to be so," said the Voice of the spear in my mind, but not to me.

"Yes, I understand and know this to be so. So it is," Baldua said in reply.

Somehow, someway, I was hearing the communication between the Voice of the spear and Baldua. After a moment, I opened my eyes. The spear had ceased to glow and I withdrew it from my friend's head, realizing its work was done.

Slowly, Baldua's eyes opened. Silence still filled the halls. Baldua turned his head and stared straight into my eyes. I thought I saw my friend there, and not the vacant, demon-filled shell of a man he had been a moment ago. But, until he spoke...

"Well, how ye be, my boy?" came Leoni's voice from behind me.

Despite the situation, I smiled at hearing the matter-of-fact way in which she always expressed herself.

Baldua, still staring at me, then smiled, too. "She's always been rather gruff, Nonne consentis, Myrriddine, mihi frate? (Do you not agree, Myrriddin, my brother?)" he said, the first part in our native Celt, the second in his pretentious Latin.

"Indeed!" I agreed. I then flung my arms around his neck, embracing him as if he were in fact a long-lost brother.

"That...spear. It spoke to me, the way it speaks to you, Myrriddin," Baldua exclaimed.

"I know," I said.

"Ye still have not answered me question!" insisted Leoni.

Baldua took a moment, seemingly assessing his person. Finally, he nodded. "Fine. I am fine. But...I must admit to being the cause of horrible things." He said this last thing with a heavy heart and much remorse, but in a detached and accepting manner.

"You don't have to say it if you don't wish to," I said.

"A moment ago, you were prodding me for the information," replied Baldua.

"A moment ago, I would've done anything to bring you out of your...state of mind, to take off the weight of your burden."

"Still, I must say it to cleanse it from myself. "I..." my friend began tentatively. "...unspeakable things were done to me, to my body, to parts of me that only a lover should touch. I...the pain was unbearable. The fungus he forced down my throat, its poison drugged me, made the pain feel even worse and made me say things. He wanted to know where the ruined Temple was, and where the artifacts were that had been brought there three centuries past by a man called Joseph Of Arimathea. I broke down. I told him where they were, at least where I thought they were. All but the spear. I didn't break with that. Something stopped me," Baldua said, looking at the spear which was now at my side. "He still is unsure of where that is." More weight seemed to lift off Baldua in the telling of his torturous tale.

"'He' being Creconius?" I asked, even though it was the obvious.

Baldua cringed slightly at the name, but otherwise remained unaffected.

"But...how did you know where those things were?" I continued.

"Ach, Myrriddin," scolded Leoni. "Ye thinks ye be the only boy who's ever explored those ruins? Baldua was on the Island longer than you, lad."

A part of my childhood had just been shattered. I found that I was actually a bit hurt that my secret place on the Island had not even remotely been my secret place.

"What's more," continued Baldua, bursting my momentary bubble of self-pity, "I was the one that led a small group, including the pig Creconius, onto the Island and into the Temple ruins in the dark of a new moon."

A soft murmur arose in the hall. No doubt, most of our fellow villagers had no idea that there were treasures in the ruins of an ancient Temple on the Island Of Mystery. How could they, unless they had been chosen to serve or be educated there? So Baldua's revelation was just that to them: a revelation. The murmurs quickly started to become more ominous, though. "How could he have led them to that sacred place?" whispered someone behind me.

"Let alone robbed it," said another.

Moscastan whirled around and addressed those in the general direction from which the accusing words had come. "Enough of that talk!" his voice boomed, with an Otherworldly quality.

Everyone in the hall was silenced with awe, bordering on outright fear. "How dare you—you who would condemn without knowing the toll this lad has paid. Shame be upon ye! Show yourselves, those who speak so."

No one came forth.

"I thought as much. Those items which were in the Temple did not belong to us and most of you here knew naught of their presence to begin with. So, do not pretend to be sorely offended at their disappearance. Now, that being said, they were brought here for safe-keeping all those years past. They have been usurped by a force of evil and will be retrieved and kept safe once again, mark my words," Moscastan assured everyone. "In the meantime, help your fellow clansman back into your arms," he continued, extending a hand toward Baldua. "Keep him and understand what he's been through."

Those present looked to one another almost ashamedly. "Come," said Leoni as she picked up another full tray of food. "I did not slave over an open fire most of the day to see this venison and fowl wasted. These grilled roots are scrumptious, too, and you all will enjoy them!"

A festive rumble rose in the hall once again as those near Leoni began clamoring for food and drink once more. A tray that was precariously filled with mugs of mead rested on the table near Baldua. It, too, was descended upon by men nearby, as wolves to a kill. The evening's feasting continued.

~XII~

The day dawned bright, but damp. Our voices rose in chant when the sun's brilliant disk appeared as a sliver of reddish-orange light over the distant peaks. In a semi-circle, we stood in the middle of the Wood Henge: a smaller-scaled, wood version of the Grand Stone Henge where I had been healed and brought back from the Otherside. I had made it my morning ritual to join others here at the dawn of each day to give praise and thanks to Dana, the Goddess, for the light and Light of my blessings, and to welcome the rebirth of Creation in the form of a new day.

We were all in earthen-colored, hooded robes, faces obscured. We were spirits only, in harmony and synchronization in welcoming the new dawn. Spirits, perhaps, yet I knew full well that it was Moscastan leading the rite on this morning, and my friend Baldua, standing next to me. And, if I was not mistaken, it was Pretorius next to Moscastan.

Our voices soared at the rising of the sun's disk and the rapid spreading of its light. As the solar body quickly crested the peaks and became whole in its morning ascension, so, too, did my soul soar, ascending with the sun and the rise of our voices, declaring the new day, and with it, the rebirth of life; the rebirth of our souls.

All of us greeted the renewal of Creation as the renewal of our beings. And, we expressed this greeting with elation and a sense of oneness. It could be heard in our voices. We could feel it in our spirits through our connection with each other and the One. There was no separation.

As the sun continued its ascent, our voices became a crescendo, then faded. We ended the rite, filing out of the Henge in a single line, leaving the sun to continue its journey as we continued ours. None of us removed our hoods until we had all gone our separate ways.

Moscastan, Pretorius, Baldua and I met in the hall to break our fast. There were many others there, as well; no doubt some of whom had been our companions-in-ritual only a short time ago.

"Brother Pretorius," Baldua began in a jesting tone, as we all sat at the center table, food tray and mead cup in hand. "Was that you with us this morn, at the rite of dawn? Not too Falsorum deirum cultor (Pagan-worshiping of false gods), was it?"

"Don't be rude," I said to my friend.

"Back to old Baldua, as I understand, my lad?" smiled Pretorius. "Good to see. I don't consider the rite of dawn to be pagan. Are we not all of the One? Especially, when two or more are gathered, so is He. There ceases to be individuality for the moment. The robes accentuate that by hooding our features. So, you can't be sure it was me, can you? And if you are sure, why were you placing your attention on me and not giving your all to the moment, to the rite, to God?

"Indeed," Moscastan said, laughing.

"Pagan, so called, or not, Baldua, I know that we all adhere to the same Source, the same Laws, the same One, no matter what earthly form a given rite might seem to take," said Pretorius.

"All right, all right. Sorry I said anything!" Baldua conceded.

Yes, it appeared that my friend Baldua was back to his old self. A wave of sadness overtook me then. In that instant, I was reminded of the way things had been between me, Baldua and Igraines; between myself and Igraines, in particular.

"What is it, Myrriddin?" asked Baldua.

"She's around, lad," Moscastan assured me.

Baldua suddenly became sheepish, as if he realized that he should have understood what was the matter with me just then. "I'd not known your feelings for her, Myrriddin, truly. I'd have kept better watch on her, you know."

"None of us could do that. She's her own person. Besides, you weren't even there. 'Twas you we were searching for," I replied.

"Then perhaps I should've been more vigilant," Pretorius interjected.

"Thank you, but we've been through that. You know better," I said.

Moscastan looked thoughtful. "Try scrying again tonight, Myrriddin. Perhaps—"

"No," I said a bit too harshly. "No. It hasn't worked. Someone or something is guarding her closely with a glam I can tell. She is veiled."

"Or perhaps she's too far from here to see," Baldua offered lamely.

"Distance is irrelevant when using the Sight, Baldua. Have you learned nothing?" I snapped at him, instantly regretting it. "Sorry." We fell into an uneasy silence as we finished our meal.

"All right, then, my brethren," said Pretorius at last, breaking the gloomy mood that had descended upon our little group. "I've something to tell you." He said this last part with a heavy heart mixed with the subtle, adventurous glee of a child. "I must be off."

Baldua and I looked at one another somewhat confused. Moscastan smiled slyly. I could tell that he already knew what the priest was talking about. "Uh...all right. We will see you later, at the evening meal perhaps," said Baldua as a response, clearly fishing for more information.

Pretorius smiled indulgently. "No, lad. I must be away. I must leave. I've been recalled by the great Constantine himself. I go to Rome then to Constantinople."

"Ahh. Your heretical views have caught up with you," quipped Baldua.

Moscastan's sharp look to my friend showed that the latter's verbal arrow was closer to the mark than any of us knew.

"Is that true, Pretorius?" I asked.

"It will not be the first time, but I am not sure. The missive was vague," the priest replied.

"When do you leave?" asked Baldua.

"As soon as possible. I've delayed too long already."

"What? Why have you just now said this?" I asked, somewhat incredulously.

"You have had more important matters to occupy your time, Myrriddin," Pretorius said gently. "I will say this: it would please me greatly if you three would accompany me on my journey. You would be wonderful ambassadors. You could explain better than anyone what has befallen your people and all the people in this region. I'm talking of the Church's influence, for better or worse, yes, but also the lawlessness that has come here. Rome has abandoned you. Your testimony would be valuable," Pretorius finished.

"No," I blurted out.

Moscastan and Baldua looked at me surprised.

"My apologies, Father Pretorius. I thank you for your offer, but I intend to find Igraines," I said, softening my tone.

Pretorius and Moscastan exchanged a cryptic glance. Did they know something of her?

My heart began to race. "What? What is it?" I asked.

"Nothing, nothing, lad," soothed Moscastan. "As I said a moment ago, she is around. I feel it."

"Aye," I said, somewhat disappointed. "I know it, too, which is why I'll not leave now."

"But the question is where? Where is she? We all believe that she was taken by him, Lord Creconius, across the sea," Moscastan said. "What good then, to stay here?"

"What good then to leave?! What if she returns in my absence? What if I find out where they've gone, where they've taken her? I could then mount my own trip to retrieve her and the items that were stolen," I said, unintentionally directing

388

this last part at my friend Baldua. The color of shame splashed across his face for a brief moment.

"But we believe that he has headed back to the Holy land, to the origin of these things. 'Tis where they'd be most powerful and valuable," offered Pretorius, looking to Moscastan, apparently seeking the other man's agreement.

"Is this true, Moscastan?" I asked.

"You have been scrying for the incorrect query, Myrriddin. You need to be scrying for Creconius, himself. He's not very good at hiding himself in a glam of concealment. Never has been," Moscastan stated, absently. "You seek Igraines when you should be seeking Creconius. There you'll find your love."

I felt my own face blush at the mention of Igraines as my love. All at once, I questioned my motives for finding her. My love? Was she that? True; I had feelings for her that I'd not realized until that night. But perhaps I was making too much of them, making them something that they were not because of her absence and the guilt I felt over her disappearance.

"Nonsense, and you know it, Myrriddin," Moscastan said, apparently reading my thoughts. "You and Igraines have known one-another for many lifetimes, and have things to accomplish on the level of the soul together in this one. Do not dismiss that."

The intensity of his gaze gave me pause. The spear vibrated slightly in my hand; not in warning, but in a sympathetic echo of what Moscastan was saying. The spear knew Igraines' soul as it knew mine. I shook my head at the thought. How could it? But it was true. I felt it. The spear knew all of us at that table. Or at least, the power that coursed through it did.

"Scry for Creconius tonight," Moscastan continued. "Ask the spear to help you, too. You will see."

"Where we will end up will not be all that far from the Holy Land," added Pretorius.

I thought about what they were saying for a moment, not altogether convinced by it.

"I believe you'll come to join us. We're not leaving for three days' time," Moscastan said, interrupting my thoughts.

"You're going then? Just like that?" I said, surprised by the declaration. It didn't take much time for the entirety of what he was saying to sink in. It wasn't just that he was leaving for a day-expedition. He would be gone indefinitely. I suddenly felt like a child whose parent was leaving him in the care of another for the first time. It was true that we Celts reared each others' offspring, fostering them out to our neighbors and fellow clansmen. It usually didn't take place until one was six or seven years of age. Many times, that first moment of separation from one's actual parents was traumatic. But even so, that child would still see his parents from time to time around the village. Yet, actually, this was different; Moscastan was leaving and I did not know when, or if, I would ever see him again. There had simply never been a time that he was not there in my life. "That's not fair of you," was all I managed to say.

Moscastan leaned forward, placing a gentle hand on my shoulder and smiling. "'Fair' is nothing in this case. I need not a bye-your-leave, Myrriddin. We've been together for a good long time, now and in previous lifetimes, and our journey on that level will continue. But I must be off for my own growth. I trust that you understand. I also trust that you will come, too, so the point is moot."

"Heus! (Here, now). What about me?" Baldua said with mock offense.

"What about you?" retorted Moscastan, smiling broadly.

"As I said, Baldua, I would like all three of you to come," answered Pretorius.

Baldua's demeanor suddenly changed. I saw on his face high adventure and sights unseen in his life thus far. His excitement grew by the moment. "Yes!" he finally exclaimed. "Oh, but...I should stay, abide by you, Myrriddin, help you..." he trailed off as he looked at me.

"It's fine if you want to go," I assured him.

My friend thought for moment, clearly weighing the importance of staying versus going and clearly making a show of the decision-making process.

"Ahg, for Dana's sake! Just go, you know you want to," I said.

"I'll wait to see what you scry and what you decide," Baldua said, his tone turning serious. "'Tis the least I can do."

"So be it," Moscastan said.

~XIII~

The night was filled with darkness and foreboding. The mist swirled within the forest on the hillside and chilled my bones. A wolf howled in the distance, calling its mate or its maker, I knew not which. The moon was bright, made more so by the light's reflective quality from the mists. I looked up the hillside, to an opening in the side of the large earthen mound, a cave. The opening was manmade, its frame shored up by wooden beams. It was then that I saw her.

Igraines stood framed in the opening's threshold, silhouetted by light from within the cave itself, a fire for warmth, perhaps. Her face was lit by the moon's light. The light showed something else, too. Her form was different than I remembered: rounder. It took me a moment to realize what the roundness was. She was pregnant. Panic suddenly filled my being. Igraines was pregnant! It had been six months since last I had seen her. Could it be...mine? The other thought, what her captors might have done to her, was unthinkable. But where was she? I was scrying. Or was I?

I had entered my dwelling and begun scrying as Moscastan had suggested, looking for Creconius. Nothing had been revealed. I had stopped after an hour or so and decided to wander outside in the misty damp night for a while. I had only wandered a short distance when the spear began to vibrate violently in my hand. Its tip glowed, pulsating a blood-red. The energy I felt coming from it nearly knocked me to the ground.

"Heed the call," the spear's voice—Jesus' voice—said in my head. "Heed, Myrriddin, and learn."

I sat on the ground, my back against a mighty oak. Heat from the sacred tree emanated from within its core and engulfed my being. Perhaps the heat was from the day's sun, absorbed by the tree. Or perhaps the ancient sentinel was more alive than any of us really knew, generating its own source of heat from within. In that moment, it mattered not, for the tree's very being became a part of mine, as did the spear.

I looked out through my human eyes, but saw a land far away imposed upon the landscape before me. It was not all that different from the land I was now in, but it was more arid. It took me a moment to realize that most of the trees I saw on the hillside were from my own realm, but the hillside itself was from the...vision, for want of a better word. It was difficult to tell where the vision's world began and mine ended; the images were blending more and more. But it was clear that Igraines was in the vision's world. I tried to speak, to call out to her. "Igraines!" I yelled. She paused, tilting her head to one side as if hearing something well in the distance and attempting to identify it. In the end she gave up, turned back and went into the cave.

The scene changed. Soldiers I knew to be of a far away land, the land that now ruled the world—Roman, but not Old Roman, Old Roman being those who had occupied my land in centuries past—lined a road leading to palaces near a port. Creconius was there! He was speaking to three well-dressed men. Possibly, leaders of the community, by their dress and bearing. One was dressed in the black and collar of high Christian clergy. Next to Creconius was a wagon laden with wears under a canvas. He was gesturing to the wagon's contents for the men's perusal. All at once, Creconius stopped what he was doing and looked seemingly in my general direction, as if sensing my presence, my probing Sight. I immediately drew my attention away from him, and onto the palaces and nearby area. If my focus was taken off him he might no longer feel my presence. Near the palaces was a hillside. I could see a light coming from a small opening in the hillside. Though the opening was far away from this perspective, I had no doubt what it was. Igraines was there; I knew it! This place was either Rome or the other place which

Pretorius had spoken of, Constantinople. Either way, my decision as whether to accompany Pretorius or not had been made.

I was late. I knew it as I ran for the hillside, stumbling on my robe as I went. I heard their chants and saw the sun's light splash over the valley as the disc crested the peaks in the distance. The crescendo of voices told me at what point the rite was located, and there was no need for me to attempt to join in the circle. I would only disrupt the proceedings, which many would take as a bad omen for the day and the rest of the week's solar cycle. So, I halted. Catching my breath, I was moved to do something: to join in from right where I stood. I was perhaps fifty paces away from the circle of chanters. No matter. The robe's hood covered my face and my spear was hidden in the folds of the robe. I was simply a lone figure adding voice to the final phase of the morning's ritual. Perfectly acceptable. I was merely letting go of my haste, feeling the oneness with the moment, the sun—.

"Ah! Greetings, Myrriddin! I thought I was the only one too late to join in. Saw you coming up the hill back there. Well, you have it! Grand idea to stop here and give voice, since we can't make it to the circle!" declared Baldua, much too loudly for my ears.

The moment broken, I snapped at my friend. "What demon's in you, man? Have you no respect?"

"I'm just observing that you are brilliant to stop and join in. None'll be the wiser, eh, that we weren't here most of the rite, since we couldn't make it earlier?! Can't disturb it once it's begun."

Sometimes I just wanted to throttle my friend. "I stopped because I was compelled to, not for false praise while I hide under my robe?" I countered, between nearly clenched teeth.

"Who's hiding?" said Baldua, as he gave voice to the final chorus of the rite, hood off, face exposed.

I shook my head and attempted to refocus on the remaining moments of the rite, as the vocalizations nearby were fading.

"By and by," Baldua's voice said. Though, his voice was more of a whisper this time, it still crashed into my thoughts, disintegrating the moment for good. "Have you decided if you will go with Pretorius and Moscastan?"

I suddenly had the devilish thought of butting him with the end of the spear beneath my robe. The spear gave a short vibration as if laughing at me. "You'll find out soon enough," was all I trusted myself to say.

"Oh, come now," Baldua whined.

"No," I said, somewhat satisfied. Petty for me to hold out on him, but being an annoyance was something that my friend was adept at, and I felt that he must learn the consequences of that. Or so I kept telling myself. I knew he probably never would.

The circle of chanters broke and everyone began exiting the area single-file, hoods still on. Baldua apparently had a sudden change of heart. He hastily and clumsily reached over his shoulders and pulled on the hood of his robe, thus concealing his face. We both stood there, heads bowed, as the silent line of hooded participants began to pass by us on the nearby trail. Two of the hooded adherents stepped out of the line as they came close to us. They came to a stop and stood next to us, each flanking either side of Baldua and me as the others continued on. Though I still couldn't see their faces, I could guess who they were.

"Pleasant morn to you both and kind of you to make it," said the voice of Master Moscastan beneath the cloth cowl next to me.

"Aye, better to be late and seen than absent and not, right boys?" spoke the voice of Pretorius on the other side of Baldua.

"Thought we weren't supposed to know who each other is here!" Baldua said, whipping his head back to forcibly throw off his hood.

The other chanters had passed and were receding from us down the trail back toward the village. Moscastan and Pretorius pulled off their hoods, as did I.

"We'll speak with you now, lads, rather than at the morning meal," replied Pretorius somewhat gravely.

"'Tis something amiss?" I asked light-heartedly.

"We want to know if ye've decided to come with us," said Moscastan.

Baldua remained silent and looked at me, a smirk of victory tugging at one corner of his mouth. It seemed he would find out my decision sooner rather than later, after all. "I...was going to tell you at the evening meal and—"

"We'll be gone by then, Myrriddin," said Moscastan, now sounding as grave as Pretorius.

"What is it?" I asked.

"A vision," Moscastan replied cryptically.

"Well, what sort of vision?" said Baldua, sardonically.

"Hold your tongue, lad," Pretorius said gently. "You know Master Moscastan is quite the channel of the Otherworld, just as your friend, Myrriddin, here."

"I had a vision, too, Moscastan," I said. "I saw Igraines. She was, is, with child...I think."

"That would confirm what was shown to me," said Moscastan.

"I think it...well, I think it might be mine," I confessed, sheepishly.

Moscastan placed a tender hand on my shoulder. "There are larger things at stake here, my friend. She was betrothed by Creconius, Myrriddin, to a man named Lot of Orkney."

"What? What are you saying? That it's his child Igraines carries?" I asked, more harshly than I meant, feeling more hurt than I realized I would.

"I don't know, Myrriddin, but I don't think so. At least not yet. What I believe you saw was a future Igraines, not our girl of the present," mused Moscastan.

"But, she looked as she does now, or at least as she did when last I saw her. Besides, she looked right at me when I was scrying. Well, it seemed like it anyway. Just like that Roman officer did—as if she knew she was being watched," I insisted.

Pretorius looked at me. "I don't completely understand how these things work. Officially, the church's position on this is that scrying and any kind of magic are of the devil. Simpleton reasoning, me thinks. There's a lot more to God's Universe than the narrow view of one religion. But, why wouldn't the future Igraines feel she's being watched? She exists there as here in the Now. All are present-tense in the One."

I mulled over what the priest said.

"What the hell does that mean?" asked Baldua. "Never mind. Myrriddin also said she looks the same as she does now. Is that part of your present-tense-ness?"

"She's an eternal look of youth about her, I would presume," offered Pretorius.

"Enough," Moscastan interjected. "Myrriddin, do you come?"

The spear in my hand vibrated. I held it up for all to see. The blade was glowing a soft green.

"Myrriddin, what's it saying?!" asked a wide-eyed Baldua.

I stared at the blade, the glow, and was pulled in. It is your destiny, Myrriddin, came the voice in my head, the voice of the spear, His voice. It is the continuation of your work here, the work you started during your time as Longinus.

I looked at Moscastan, a vast smile suddenly spread across his face. "Ah. I see He speaks to you still. Just as before. Will you heed?"

I nodded. "To Rome first?" I asked, more to Pretorius than to Moscastan.

But it was Moscastan who answered. "Nay. We go to find Uther."

"What, pray you, is an Uther?" asked Baldua.

"Not what, but who," replied Moscastan. He then turned to me. "A distant cousin, for starters. All will be revealed. Come. Enough daylight has burned." With that, he walked briskly toward the village. There was naught to do but follow.

~XIV~

We were on the road within the hour. I hadn't the vaguest idea why it was so important to find this alleged cousin named Uther. Oh, Moscastan explained again to me the importance of what he, this Uther, was doing: driving out the likes of Creconius, uniting the various parts of the land under one banner—his banner; the Pendragon—but I could not get my mind off Igraines. Had she been given to this King Lot by Creconius as a slave? But why would a noble—a King, no less—marry a village girl? Unless, she really was much more. She had been on the Isle Of Mystery for a time. When she was still very, very young, no more than eight summers, the priests there decreed that she was destined for the life of a Royal, which was something that many scoffed at in private. She was sent back to the village elders for leadership training. She never quite took to it, which only served to prove the scoffers' point, at least to those who'd done the scoffing. Perhaps becoming the wife of this Lot was what the priests had seen. No matter. All I could think of was that she was now truly gone from me. Someone I felt as though I had known forever was now more out of reach than ever.

Moscastan gave her marriage even more weight than I did. He also clearly saw her pregnancy as even more significant, even momentous. I only saw it as annoying and hurtful, especially the fact that Moscastan insisted that the child she carried was not only not mine, but not Lot's either. Uther was the key to this mystery in more ways than one. Such was my dark mood as we plodded along the trail leading south.

"You'd understand a lot more if you'd get out of your own way," he said, seemingly able to read my thoughts yet again.

I snapped out of my melancholy state of mind to see that he was walking next to me. "I hate it when you read me so," I said.

"I'm not 'reading' you in the way you think. It's obvious, lad. I'd ask that you step outside your little self to see the bigger picture. Consult with the spear, that staff you walk with. You've barely used it 'til now. Allow it to help you see the truth of things to come. You'll be playing a pivotal role in the events of the near future."

"Well, I'm glad you think so." We walked on in silence for nearly a league.

"She will always be with you. She always has," he finally said, cryptically. "Your spear will tell you that as well."

"Moscastan," said Pretorius from a few yards ahead.

Moscastan hurried along to catch up to the priest, who had stopped at the mouth of the trail where it emptied onto a main road. He was not alone, but was speaking to a man dressed in very worn traveling togs. As Baldua, who had been trudging behind up to this point, caught up, the other man turned back to the main road, which I now saw held a large party of wagons and other travelers.

"We will go with these people for a time. They are from the Tremoriddin clan and are going to the Hallows Eve feast in the next Clan-dom," said Pretorius as I halted next to him.

I was surprised at the priest's carefree attitude regarding the matter. "All Hallows Eve festivities? That's about as pagan as it gets. Not too much for you?"

"Quite the contrary. I find the concept of allowing dead ancestors to inhabit the body for a night fascinating. Besides, I know the fellow to whom I spoke—stayed with his family last winter season. He's a Christian at heart," answered Pretorius.

"Ah, there's the rub of it," Baldua interjected. "A chance to convert him, aye?"

"Now, lad, you know me better than that by now," countered the priest. "Come."

We joined the Tremoriddin clan on the main road.

Darkness descended quickly. We had walked only another five miles or so when the whole company, the Tremoriddin clan and our little party, came off the main road and into a sparse grove of oaks to make camp. Cooking fires were started in the camp's center, and many of the women, and men, were preparing the evening meal. Venison was brought forth from some of the clansmen and we were invited to join them. Baldua, being Baldua, had already begun chatting to a comely lass with red-blonde hair. The odd thing was that she kept looking in my general direction even while engaged in conversation with Baldua. I turned more than once to look behind me in an attempt to assess if it was actually me she was looking at or someone, or something else. I could not figure it out, so I simply let the matter rest.

The meal was more than satisfying, and afterward, I sat near one of the fires for a time. Moscastan and some of the clansmen talked about the festivities to come the next evening. One clansman, in particular, was especially excited to allow his father to live again through his body for the night. Apparently, the debauchery of his dead father was insatiable— not unlike his son's it seemed, judging by the way he was speaking— and the son was more than willing to give up his physical form for the events this one night. I had never participated in the holiday in the purest sense of it. Our village and clan had ceased the practice of the tradition many generations before, though we certainly still honored our ancestors on the night.

"Will you join the rite?" asked a lilting female voice.

I didn't turn at the sound of her voice, not right away. I could smell her: light honey-suckle and lily. It was enchanting. Her voice only added to the odd sensation I suddenly felt wash over me. She sat down on the ground next to me, at which time I turned my head and looked at her. I hadn't even heard her approach, this young woman whom Baldua had been speaking with earlier. Her features were smooth and gentle in the firelight, and more beautiful than I saw earlier. Her hair

The Centurion's Spear/Maines

seemed more red then blonde in the light of the flames, as well. And her eyes were amber in color.

"Your friend—Baldua, is it?—said that you've never been a part of a true All Hallows Eve night," she said.

I looked around. Baldua was nowhere in sight.

"Oh, he's talking with my sister," she added.

"Who?" I asked lamely.

"Your friend," she replied, laughing. "He also said that your walking staff speaks to you from the Otherworld," she said, pointing to the spear at my side. "Is that true?"

"My friend says too much," was my curt reply.

"Please, don't be angry. I know his talk is just that. That is why I pointed him toward my sister. She likes to play those kind of games. But you—something tells me you've much too much of a deep spirit for such things," she said, smiling warmly, genuinely, her straight white teeth glowing in the light of the fire.

I was glad of the darkness and firelight just then, as I could feel my face flushing from her comment.

"Nimue," she said by way of introduction. "I am called Nimue, in case you were wondering."

"Ah. I am Myrriddin."

"I see. And are you one?"

"Am I one what?" I asked, confused.

"A Myrriddin?"

"Are you serious?" I asked, not sure if she was playing a game with me.

She nodded. "I ask sincerely. My grandfather was a great Merlin, and people used to call him Myrriddin as from the old tongue," she said. "You come from the land of the Mystery Isle, where you spent some time, or so I understand, so..."

"No doubt you understand that from my friend as well," I said, laughing.

"'Tis true."

A round of laughter burst forth from nearby as Moscastan, being a grand bard in addition to his other many talents, began a tale of love and woe and triumph over demons. The story began with a woman, the story's eventual heroine, singing a sardonic, stinging lament of love lost and revenge sought. Moscastan's falsetto and comedic rendition of a scorned woman singing was apparently what was garnering the laughter from those present, whose numbers seemed to have swelled in the past few minutes to include most of the clan. I had heard him perform this story before and always cringed when he began it, hoping that none of the women present would take offense and hurl hot coals at him. Offending anyone was always furthest from Moscastan's mind. Yet, he maintained that he must remain true to the story.

Nimue and I sat in silence for a long span of time, listening as Moscastan weaved magic with his story telling. It was the magic of transporting an audience to a different place, a different time, a different life. And, judging by the expressions on the faces of those present, all were entranced by the magic.

"Ye have not answered my question," Nimue finally said in a quiet voice.

"Oh?" I whispered back.

"All Hallow's Eve, the rite. Will you join in?"

"Well," I began, "Yes. Why not?" I found myself saying.

We sat in silence again, listening to my mentor, watching him animate the characters of the plot.

"But," said Nimue a while later, shortly after Moscastan passed the arc of his story. "You've not participated before, true?"

"Participated in the ritual?"

She nodded.

"I've honored my ancestors every Hollow's Eve since I was a lad," I said, a little too defensively. "But not in the way that you mean," I added, my tone softening.

"Then I shall be your guide, your partner," Nimue declared.

I felt my brow crinkle in confusion. "What do you mean? Will we contact our ancestors together?"

She laughed, giggled really. It was a sweet sound, but elicited a hushing scowl from two older women close by. "That's not exactly how it works," Nimue whispered to me. "Some drink the potion to help them go into a trance and...how would you say...to help them step aside so that an ancestor may come forth from the Otherworld. Something tells me, though, that you won't need any potion. Either way, 'tis best to have someone stay in their right spirit or right mind to serve as an aid to the one in trance. You understand?"

"I think so," I said, suddenly regretting having professed participation. I knew from personal experience that interesting things sometimes happened while in a trance state —things that a person might do without conscious recollection when finished. Though I had only just met the woman next to me, the thought of doing something potentially embarrassing before her while in a trance state, however unlikely that might be, was enough to make my face feel flushed once again. I could not back out now that I had declared my participation, though. That would mark me as dishonorable—to myself, at least. A man's honor is only as good as his actions are to his words, Moscastan once said. It had stuck with me. "I agree," I continued. "I don't think I'll need to take a potion."

Cheers and the slapping of hands on thighs suddenly burst forth from all those listening to Moscastan's tale as it reached its climax.

Suddenly and unexpectedly, Nimue quickly rose to her feet.

"Where are you going?" I asked, hearing too much disappointment in my own voice.

"Tremel said he'd take vespers with your companion, the priest," she answered.

"Tremel?"

"Yes, Tremel. My father," she said.

"Ah," I replied. I looked around at those present, but saw no sign of Pretorius.

"I don't see Tremel, either," Nimue said, apparently reading my look. "I'm sure they've begun the prayers and I know Tremel wanted me present."

I was unsure which I found more amusing: the fact that she called her father by his given name, or the fact that she and her father held with vespers and still practiced traditional so-called paganisms, such as the rite of All Hallow's Eve. "You would pray in the Christian way?" I asked.

She laughed liltingly. "Of course, the Christian God is simply an expression of the Mother Goddess."

"Aye, well, the good priest's church would see it much differently," I pointed out.

"Why?" she asked, genuinely perplexed. "There is only One Mother/Father Source for everything by any name," she said, sounding a bit like Moscastan. Before I could respond, she looked at my side. Her eyebrows suddenly lifted in surprise. "Your friend tells the truth, for the walking staff speaks to you now, me thinks."

I followed her gaze and saw that indeed, the spear's upper half glowed dimly, pulsating gently. After a moment, the pulsating glow ceased. The spear, my staff, looked normal again.

"What does it mean?" she asked sincerely, more with curiosity than awe.

"I'm not sure. I don't always understand it."

"Hm," she said. "Something tells me you will eventually."

Those around us who had been listening to Moscastan's story were beginning to leave the fires.

"Until the morrow, Myrriddin," Nimue said as she turned to go.

I hurried to get to my feet, but she had already walked away. "Indeed," I said, more to myself than to her receding back.

We heard the revelry from the main road, faint though it was. After a time, we left this roadway and traveled down a narrow path which wound through a dense forest. I could no longer hear the revelers very well and questioned Moscastan as to whether Tremel was leading us all in the right direction. Foolish, that, for I knew the answer before he spoke it. "come now," was his smiling response. "You know how a forest deadens sound."

"Yes, yes," I said curtly. Indeed, the forest we now found ourselves traveling through was thick with rowan, adler and oak.

The deeper we went, the deader the sound became – until a ringing silence filled the ear. Darker, too, it became. The forest's thick canopy thrust us into near blackness, though it was only late afternoon. Even though the actual path beneath our feet was packed – presumably from the trodding soles of many other travelers these past days who were also heading to the festivities – it was far from dry. There was a perpetual dampness to the forest floor which was due, like the darkness, to its thick canopy preventing Belenus' drying warmth from touching the earth's skin. This was also the reason for the pungent smells that bombarded our nostrils: sickly sweet mint, stale moist bark, foul rotting flesh and leaf, and everything in-between.

Nearly two hours we walked through the woods until finally, the path suddenly spilled out onto a large, beautifully flowered, thinly-grassed meadow, with mountains on one side and the forest on the other. Bright sunlight splashed on my face as we came out of the forest, warming my spirit though the day was chilly, and the cacophony of hundreds of voices hit my ears as if a door to a festival had been thrown open. Many, many people were already in full regalia and celebration of the sacred day – All Hallow's Eve. Traditionally, the actual rite did not fully get underway until late into the night: midnight to three by the Roman way of keeping time. That particular window of time was considered optimal for crossing between the world of the dead and the world of the living. "Worlds swirl near worlds and sometimes they are closer to each other than at others," a Druid priest on the Isle of

Mystery had once said. Yet, in spite of the time of day, the festivities here – if not the rite itself – had already begun in earnest.

Some of the celebrants were painted with blue or gold woad, a preliminary preparation for the main experiences of the evening. Others seemed to be slightly out of their heads, perhaps having already taken the potion Nimue had spoken of, or something entirely more potent. One man, for instance, stumbled toward us as we came into the meadow. "Welcommme to the realmmmm of the In betweennn, where all who live shall die, and all who've died shall liiive!" he said, speech slurring eerily in a high-pitched tone. The man was shirtless, and his skin unusually sweaty, which was odd because of the chilliness in the air – 'twas cold enough to see one's breath plume in misty vapor before the face. And his eyes had a far off, almost crazed look, pupils severely enlarged, as if he were possessed by demons or several creatures from a nether world. My guess was that he had ingested some of the small, leafy foscal plant that grew on the lower trunk of the sacred oak or the toxic mushroom that grew at its base. For some reason, both of these growths became a somewhat poisonous item when grown in direct contact with the oak. Mushroom and foscal that grow in contact with other trees do not develop this tinge to them. The poison is not enough to do any lasting harm, unless the mushroom or foscal is eaten in large quantities, of course. Yet, even then, the one ingesting the large amount would probably vomit most of it out before enough of the poison was assimilated in the body to kill. But, it is enough to alter the mind and "open the soul" as some claim. The fact that the mighty oak is where the "magical" foscal plant and mushroom were found exclusively only added to the mystique of sacredness to these wonderful trees.

Baldua had tried the foscal plant once in the hopes of crossing to the other side for a visit. "I'm simply curious," he had said. Truth is, I suspected that it was more because he had recently been informed that his birth mother had just passed to the Otherside during childbirth – the little one, the new life within her, having succumbed to death as well. We were isolated on the Mystery Isle at the time, having had no contact with our parents for some nine moons, having already been adept on the Isle for many solar cycles, many years. Baldua had been unusually close to his mother. Some even said – without judgment, mind you – that they were much more than naturally close; the child she had carried and died trying to give birth to was their proof. She had been seen with no man for many, many seasons. "Who else could be its father?" they had said. I'd made sure Baldua never heard these musings. If he had heard them, he paid no heed; gave no indication that he gave two shites what anyone else thought, what anyone else said. Such was his love for his mother. Whether the musings of others had been true or not, only Baldua knew. I cared not one way or another. He was my friend, had been for many lifetimes. His mother's death had been a hammer's blow to his soul. I had no doubt that his desire to visit the Otherside was perpetuated by his desire to see his mother.

In the throes of the plant's toxic effects, Baldua had appeared much as this man in the meadow – sweaty and crazed. Baldua must have had some kind of wonder-filled experience during his supposed sojourn in the Otherworld, for upon his return to his normal self, his normal state of being, he was more happy, more euphoric, more convinced of the reality of the Otherworld—the Otherside—than I had ever seen anyone be. He claimed that he had indeed seen his mother and spoken to her during the experience. What's more is that she had become the Goddess Dana during his time with her. Having left his body for travel to the Otherside, his mother, Dana, the mother of all, then took his spirit to yet another world altogether: a place in the future or distant past—he could not tell—but he knew by what the Goddess said that it was not of our time. All Baldua remembered of it was that this place was filled with tall glass or crystal buildings, and flying machines and carriages that moved rapidly on the ground without the aid of horses. Both the flying machines and the carriages transported people! He was utterly convinced that what he'd seen was real.

I, on the other hand, felt that the substance he'd ingested to aid him on to the Otherworld, the foscal plant, had simply twisted his mind. But then again, I had never swallowed the plant myself; never felt its effects, and thus was in no position to judge another's perception of the experience.

The man in the meadow before us began to spin, twirling on the balls of his feet with his arms flung out. "All manner of spirit awaits theee!" he sang. Like a dancer, he continued to spin, suddenly oblivious to all but the song in his head.

We moved past him, further into the meadow and across it toward the base of the mountains. There, people were not at a celebration point, but rather, were setting up tents of animal skins or make-shift shelters from bound, leafy branches. Trees of birch and small rowan were scattered about near the base of the mountains. Some of the people had draped canvases over the branches of a few of these trees, thus creating temporary shelters for themselves. This area had become a small village, complete with central cooking fires, set to one side, thereby leaving the center of the meadow for the celebrations to come.

Father Pretorius led us to a larger rowan whose low, over-hanging branches created a natural covering some eight feet off the ground, sheltering about twenty or so square feet of ground beneath it. The priest walked quickly to it, apparently surprised, as I was, that no one had claimed the spot yet, and stopped in the center of it. He turned to us as we caught up and raised his palms and face skyward—or toward the overhanging branches, now only a couple of feet above his head; I couldn't tell which. "Thank you," he muttered. He then looked at us and said, "'Twas meant for us, you know, this spot. We'll camp here."

"Indeed," agreed Moscastan, moving close to Pretorius. He turned toward Baldua and me. "You wish to partake in the festivities, lads, yes?"

"I don't...not especially," said my friend, his voice somewhat tinged with apprehension. He had been on edge since we had entered the forest from the main road.

I wasn't the only one who noticed. "What is wrong, my son?" Pretorius asked Baldua, gently.

"Nothing," replied Baldua a bit too quickly. He became thoughtful for a moment before continuing. "The forest, I suppose. Brought up...things."

"The past cannot harm you, lad, unless you allow it to," said Moscastan.

"Easy to say," remarked Baldua, with a bitter edge.

"Easy to do," countered Moscastan. "Just let it go. Let it flitter away. You are far more than any earthly experience you may have. Your spirit is eternal and therefore larger than anything that may befall you on this earth."

"Aye, 'tis true," put in Pretorius. "You are 'in this world' of experiences, but not 'of this world' of experiences. So it has been said. You understand?"

"I understand," said Baldua doubtfully, dismissively. "Why did we come here anyway? I thought this journey carried urgency. Why dally here in this place?"

"Do you tire of your new lady already?" Moscastan asked teasingly.

Baldua turned three shades of red, but held his head up high, defying embarrassment.

Moscastan smiled broadly and laughed. "Very well, lad. We do not dally here. These people are intrinsic to our goal. We began the inquiry for what we seek with Tremel, their leader, last night."

"At vespers," added Pretorius.

"But these things must be sought delicately, lest an affront to Tremel's hospitality be seen," continued Moscastan. "We should find out what we need to know this night." As Moscastan said this last part, his gaze drifted past Baldua and me to something beyond our shoulders. I heard soft footfalls approaching from behind, dead leaves on the ground crunching gently beneath them. They came to a stop.

"Forgive the intrusion," came the female voice from behind me. I recognized it at once. I turned and there she stood—lovely Nimue. I opened my mouth to speak, but then realized by her look that she was not here for me alone. She addressed us all. "Tremel asks that you join us for refreshments and libation presently, before the night's activities." She said this last bit to me, smiling as she ended the sentence, her secretive thoughts for me and the night to come left floating in the air for all to detect. With that, she turned and left.

I turned back to Moscastan and Pretorius to find both of them staring at me, each in turn with a gentle smirk on his face.

I felt my face flush and my brows crinkle.

"Me thinks that Master Baldua be not the only one smitten of late," Pretorius said to Moscastan.

"Indeed!" my mentor replied.

As Baldua defied embarrassment before our travel mates, so did I. Mustering my courage, I planted the butt of my staff onto the ground with authority. "Enough, gentlemen! You heard the lass," I said with more bravado than I felt. I spun on my heels and followed in Nimue's wake, leaving the others to secure our camping spot.

The fire was hot on my face, its flames intense, dispelling the chill in the night air around me. There were more than thirty of us huddled around the large fire. There were many such fires scattered about the meadow, lighting the area, each with as many or more people huddled around them as the one I was at. Around my fire some sat, some stood, but all – whether directly participating in the night's rites or simply being a guardian to another—felt the effects of this unique time. Those participating directly, each one, whether having taken a potion or not, had on his or her face an expression of...what? How can I describe another's journey to the Otherside, or his stepping aside to allow someone from the Otherworld to come through them? Judging by the expression on the faces of those participating, though, that is what they were experiencing. Some had another person near them – their partner, their guardian for the night's activities, as Nimue had described. These folks appeared watchful – not at all in the throws of the ecstatic passion of traveling to and from the Otherworld. They were watchful, but also solemn, some chanting as an aid to their charge.

Nimue and I had come to this particular fire two hours after dark-fall. It was now three hours past midnight. I had been in and out of trance since sitting down in front of the fire. But now...now I felt the inner pull on my spirit stronger than ever. There was something in the air, the energy and alignment of this particular time – this particular moment of the year, when worlds meet – and the alignment in mind and spirit of those present, made my head spin. Though I had been in and out of trance since we sat down, I had not as yet crossed to the Otherside, nor had I been contacted by any spirit from that world. In between my trance states, I simply observed those around the fire.

"You're very sensitive to this night, are you not? Nimue asked. "Your eyes..." she trailed off.

I said nothing, but pulled my gaze from observing those around the fire to the fire itself. I had laid the staff down on my right side. It rested between myself and Nimue, who was also on my right and sitting very close. She was so close, in fact, that I could smell her scent and feel her body heat in spite of the heat coming from the fire. Her left knee rested against my right thigh and over the shaft of the staff between us, on which my right hand rested. It was tempting to let my mind wander to Nimue, to her smell and closeness. Yet, there was another more powerful force drawing on me. A threshold of crossing was at hand.

I stared into the fire, concentrating on the primeval essence within. Gazing into the flame was much like staring into water – the water of a scrying bowl, for example. Yet, it could be even more powerful, for fire is more of a living thing —evolving, changing and expressing in every instant of its existence.

I continued to stare into the flames and felt the rest of the world recede. Forms began to take shape in the flames. Some were indiscernible spirits; some were clearly human. Some of the human forms looked at me as I looked at them – strangers from different worlds gazing upon one another through a seemingly impenetrable window. I heard things then: strange and ghostly whispers from the Otherside; from the forms within the flames. I heard something else, too—a sweet, lilting feminine voice singing a melody in an ancient tongue; a language so old, I had thought it lost to time. Though I did not understand the words, I recognized the tune. I knew it from somewhere in my past. Then I realized from whence I knew it. The image of my Na-na—my maternal grandmother—came to my mind as she looked down upon me in my cradle of rushes and fresh leaves. She had been beautiful with auburn hair and green eyes, and dots from the sun all over her face. I was no more than three summers as she sang the ancient song of protection in the archaic tongue to me. 'Twas a beautiful melody whose every note surrounded both singer and listener with an ever strengthening glam of protection. I suddenly felt that blanket of protection in the form of Love enfold me, both my toddler self and my adult self.

My mind came back to the present and once again concentrated on the flames. There within, among the forms from the Otherworld, was Na-na, just as I remembered her! I could still hear the melody of protection being sung, but I had the sudden realization that it was not coming from her. Her spirit's lips did not move, 'twas true, yet the song could have been coming from her mind to my mind, but it was not. It was coming from my world, from someone close to me – from Nimue. I knew that Nimue's people were of an ancient clan. Not surprising then, that she might know this tune. But to be singing it – something so obscure and from my childhood...Nimue was singing it for my protection, as my guardian and partner. The song also served another purpose. It helped propel me further into my trance. Deeper and deeper I went, until all the rest of my world vanished from my awareness, from my mind.

"Come, young Myrriddin," said the deep female voice from within the flames. My heart leapt at the hearing of her voice. "Come. I must show you something. Time on your side of the veil grows short. The portal will close sooner than anyone realizes," she finished, extending a hand to me.

Within an eye's blink, I was standing next to Na-na in the flames. Rather, my spirit was. In my hand, I held the spear, or a spirit form of it, an essential representation of it. The spear now looked as it must have soon after it was originally made. It did not have the additions I had put onto it. Its shaft was smooth and new. Its blade was polished and bright, except where crimson stains from Him remained. Though we stood in the flames of the fire, I could feel no heat. Indeed, though we were surrounded by an expanse of orange-yellow, I sensed that beyond it lay the infinite realm of the Otherworld. I could still hear Nimue's lovely voice singing the ancient song. When I looked in the direction of her sound, I saw her through the warbling effect of fire. More than that, it was also through the mysterious veil of looking from the Otherworld back into my own, where I saw Nimue sitting next to my in-tranced physical form that caused the warbling appearance. I, my spirit or soul, truly was now on the Otherside. I looked back into the expanse of flames, trying to see beyond.

"There are many levels to this side, this World, Myrriddin," my Na-na said.

I simply stared at her, realizing for certain that it was her, her spirit, and not some phantom from a dream.

"'Tis good to see you, my child. You've become quite the strapping lad. Although, I've watched you grow from this side, it's still pleasing to see you thus," Na-na said.

Even in my disembodied spirit form, I felt a slight self-consciousness at her words. "'Tis good to see you too, Na-na," I said, embracing her.

"I be surprised ye remember me. I passed through the veil when you were but five summers," she replied.

It was true. My Na-na had died when I was very young. Though it was tradition generally that we Celts fostered our children for the community to raise, such was generally not the case with our village and clan – except, of course, when a child was chosen by the Druids and Mystics for study on the Island of Mystery. In my very early years, I stayed with my mother, yes, but mainly my Na-na. I remembered her all my life and what came from her even more than what came from her own daughter, my mother. What came from my Na-na was always love, unconditional.

"Be not hard on her, lad," Na-na said, reading my thoughts again. "She always had one foot in the physical world and one foot in the Otherworld when she was alive, your mother did. She could never control it and it made her not well in the head, don't you know."

I looked past Na-na just then, half expecting to see my mum somewhere in the expanse.

"She's on one of those other levels I mentioned a moment ago," Na-na said.

"I see," I replied, somewhat at a loss for words. I suddenly had another thought. "Would you like to come into my world for a time, Na-na?" I asked, already expecting the answer. "'Tis what this night's truly for."

"It's easiest to journey between the two worlds this night, but I've no desire to inhabit another's body. Besides, I visit your world often in various forms and ways. I've been at your side many-a-time to nudge you to a decision and such. When you took that, for example," she said, gesturing to the spear. "Oh, 'twas yours many life-times ago, 'tis true—I was there, too—but you needed a nudging to truly recognize it, to reclaim it in this life, you see," she finished.

The spear began to glow softly, whether in warning, or why I could not tell.

Na-na saw it, too. "There's no time to explain. You must see something, something to come if you choose wisely," she said. With the wave of her hand, the flames around us faded, revealing another place, another time. Rolling green hills surrounded us and a sky as blue as the brightest day I could have imagined crowned our heads. Na-na stood next to me. She was looking off to her left, smiling. A sound came to me then; not Nimue's singing, but a sound equally as pleasant – children at play. I looked in the direction of Na-na's gaze—in the direction from which the sound of the children came. A group of children gleefully frolicked nearby. They were all dressed in rich and ornate gowns, not the offspring of peasant villagers were these. A short distance past the children, in the shade of a mighty oak, sat what looked to be a king and queen, judging by their attire and the craftsmanship of the chairs on which they sat. They were not exactly thrones, but nor were they field stools, either. Other people were around the king and queen—their court, I presumed. Standing off to one side of all of them was a very old man clad in the robes of a High Druid. It was me, a much older version of me—the same persona that had been at the cave with the boy, Arturius, in another vision. The old sage, my older self, next to the king and queen held onto a Druid's staff in one hand. But it was not the spear in guise that I now possessed.

The king was in a heated discussion with several men in front of him. He suddenly turned toward my older persona. "What say you, Merlin?" he asked.

"They possess the items, the Moors do, it is true. But, be sure that it's what you truly seek, Arturius," the older Myrriddin, or Merlin, said. Obviously, I would not be rid of the name Merlin in this life, if this future held true. But who was this Arturius, the boy who had now become king? And this land in which he was king, and I, his High Druid—was it still my homeland or was it elsewhere? And how was it that I could see future things or possible future things in the Otherworld?

I turned to ask Na-na the meaning of these things. She was gone! Panic briefly ran through my mind. The spear now glowed an intense red-blue, as if it were searing hot, even angry. Now, I had no doubt; it was a warning. All became silent. The sounds of the children ceased; the chatter of the king, queen, and the court went mute. I looked back at them. King, queen, court and children were still, frozen in time. And my older, Myrriddin self, Merlin, was no longer there.

Then came the rumbling. Steadily, it grew louder; so loud, in fact, that I should have been able to feel it as well as hear it. But this was the Otherworld, after all. Perhaps I wouldn't feel it since this was not my actual body in this world; not my physical body which I would need to feel such things. It then dawned on me what the rumbling might be. Next came the screams. They became louder and closer and left no doubt in my mind that they were coming from the Otherside, or rather, my side—the world of the physical. The veil was closed again.

"By the God," I whispered. The spear shook violently in my hand and I closed my eyes, commanding a return to myself. I felt a shuddering jolt, opened my eyes and found myself back in the world of men next to Nimue, and in the middle of utter, violent chaos.

~XV~

It took a moment to come full to myself upon arriving back in my body from the Otherworld. In fact, for a moment or two, I was paralyzed; my body would not respond to my will, nor could I hear anything. I felt my hand still resting on the staff, but that was all. I could see, however. I could see Nimue out of the corner of my eye. She was now standing next to my still seated form. Breathing. Breathing was difficult, not because I momentarily felt paralyzed, but because something was in the air, something I was breathing in. Was it smoke, smoke from the fires? I wondered. No. It was dust. It was then that my hearing came back and I heard the screams of terror, and felt the jostling of those nearby as they attempted to flee in panic. Some, still in their trance—induced stupor, stumbled and fell directly into the fire, adding to the terrible screams in the night. My body finally responded and I jumped to my feet, staff in hand, and spun to face the mêlée.

The attack had come at the height of the night's activities, when most of those who had gathered for the All Hallows Eve celebration were in the throws of ritual, including myself. I was fortunate in that I made it back from the Otherworld before anything befell Nimue or me. Na-na. For a brief instant, I let my mind wander to her. I felt the warmth of her love and presence.

"Pagans! All of you! Destroy them!" yelled a man wielding a battle-axe. He brought the weapon down on a defenseless naked man, cleaving off the man's right shoulder and arm. I recognized the victim. He was the one who had been boasting of allowing his debaucherous, deceased father to live again through him for this night. The man was obviously still in his trance, for his eyes were glazed and his face had on it a mindless smile. Perhaps his father's soul within was experiencing death again. The man crumpled to the ground in a fountain of blood. More and more of the attackers were appearing at the edge of the firelight, some on horseback—clearly the rumbling I heard from the Otherside—all brandishing weapons with crazed bloodlust in their eyes.

"We must fight or flee!" yelled Nimue over the din. There was no fear in her voice. She was simply stating fact.

I stayed rooted where I stood. I grabbed for the Roman short sword I kept at my side. It was not there. I had left it at our campsite. No need for weapons here, or so we had thought. I was sure, too, that no sentries had been placed at the meadow's perimeter. Why would there be? This had apparently been a gathering place for many, many generations. Someone crashed into me from my left, knocking me sideways into Nimue. We toppled to the ground in a tangle of limbs. I slammed to the ground partially on top of Nimue and heard a loud, horrible cracking sound as we landed. "Nimue?" I said, immediately believing that I had landed awkwardly on her and somehow broken a bone, or bones, within her petite body.

"It's all right. I'm not hurt," she assured me.

I quickly untangled myself from her and pulled us both to our feet. I then saw, to my dismay, what had caused the frightening sound: the housing of small branches I had attached to the blade of the spear to hold the Druid's Egg had broken and splintered into dozens of pieces when we hit the ground. Part of my body weight had landed on Nimue, but the other part had landed on the staff, crushing the branched housing. All that remained of the spear's disguise was the leather thong which now dangled loose on the shaft where it met the blade. It was no longer my walking staff, but a Roman spear again.

Nimue stared at it for a moment. "Interesting Druid's staff, Myrriddin," she said. "You know how to use it now?"

I was confused by what she said and must have looked it.

"As a spear, is what I mean!" she added. "Do you know how to use it as a weapon?"

Two more of the gatherers crashed into us, flailing in their panic to run away. We were not knocked over this time, though, but held our ground. The two who ran into us moved by us, and the assailant who was chasing them saw us and stopped short of Nimue and me, his quarry all but forgotten. He was a hairy brute with bare, muscular shoulders. He gripped a bloodied long sword in his right hand and was panting from his gruesome exertions. I brought the spear to bear its sharp tip pointing at the man's belly. I was not exactly sure how to use the spear as a weapon, but my anger at the turn of events of the night would guide me. Any advance toward us and I would skewer the brigand. But he made no move. He simply stared at us, then at the spear. Like its counterpart on the Otherside, its blade began to glow an angry red. The brigand's eyes grew huge at the sight, fear and awe shining forth from them. He took a step back and opened his mouth to speak, but nothing came out—at first.

"Here! It's here!" he said, facing me, guarding me, but yelling over his shoulder to the fellow raiders who had not caught up to him. "Holy Mother of Christ," he whispered to himself. "It's here!" he yelled again, this time turning his head to see if anyone had heard him.

In that instant, Nimue was shoved into me by others who were desperately trying to escape. Inadvertently, I lunged into the brigand, stabbing the spear into his abdomen. He howled with rage and pain. I froze for a moment, not believing what had just happened. I quickly recovered myself, though, and yanked the spear free. Though the blade had gone deeply into the man's belly, there was no blood on it, save for His blood from centuries past. Yet, even more odd was the smoke that trailed from both the blade's tip and the man's wound. He stood there for a moment staring at the wound which was now not just a slice into the skin, but strangely becoming an ever-widening, bloodless gaping hole. The brigand looked at the sky, with a faraway expression. He then looked at me with a

420

genuine smile of peace and happiness before he crumpled to the ground dead.

My astonishment at what had just taken place—the stabbing of another human being with the spear and the bloodless, gaping, smoking hole it left in the victim—was the only thing that was preventing me from vomiting over having just killed the man. Before I had any more time to think about it, Nimue was trying to pull me away.

"Come! There're too many of them. We must vanish into the night," she said, as she started to back away.

I turned to follow her. Corpses lay strewn about, making our escape slow and difficult. The more I saw of them and the violent hacking of these defenseless revelers, the more disgusted I became. My anger grew with each passing second. I had the only weapon on behalf of our side: the spear. I could not just run. I stopped in my tracks.

"What're you doing?" asked Nimue, stopping a few feet ahead of me.

"Defending these people," I replied, turning back to face the enemy.

"Just you and that spear against killers and Romans?" she asked sardonically.

Romans? I thought. I looked closer back in the direction from which we had come, toward the fires. There was a pocket of fighting, or rather massacre, taking place near the fire we had just left. Among those committing the atrocity, but with more practiced, disciplined efficiency, were Roman legionnaires, approximately two platoons worth. Nearby this pocket, just on the firelight's edge, were three men on horseback. They were still, observing the slaughter from their mounts. One of them was dressed as a Roman officer, a General. Another appeared to be wearing the cloak of a high-ranking official in the Christian church. A large, gold crucifix on his chest gleamed in the firelight—a Papal Legate, perhaps. But the third man...the third man on horseback was the one who had led the initial attack on my people, kidnapped Igraines and Baldua, and left me for dead: Lord Creconius.

He pointed directly at me and bellowed, "Seize him! Seize that spear! It is the spear of Longinus, the spear of Christ in Pagan hands!"

By the gods. My blood boiled at the words. The only Pagan on these grounds was the lower-than-shite thing from which the accusation came. And, how dare he attempt to usurp that which had been mine for Centuries. I am Longinus! I screamed in my head. As if to reflect my own outrage, the spear's tip pulsated a rage-filled red. I silently swore an oath to kill them all before allowing them to take it.

"That is not to be the way of it, Myrriddin. Have you learned nothing?" said the voice of the spear, His voice.

The voice conveyed power. I froze with indecision. I wondered where Moscastan was. He would know what to do. I attempted to calm myself; to call forth the power of the spear, my own power.

Guttural yells of bloodlust broke into the noise of the night from twenty yards away, as brigands and legionnaires converged against me, breaking my concentration.

"Myrriddin!" yelled Nimue, in a warning born of desperation.

That was it then; I would destroy them, regardless of what the voice had said. I ran toward them, planting myself some ten yards from my previous spot—more to give Nimue more room to escape than hasten the combat to come. In spite of my bravado, I did not know how to use the spear as the weapon for which it had been originally created. Impulsively, I began to swing the spear back and forth in wild arcs in front of me, daring anyone to cross the blade's threshold.

"Myrriddin!" It was Moscastan. I saw him off to my right. He looked dirty and bloody, as if he, too, had been in the fray. "Myrriddin, no!"

Too late. I was committed. "Leave here!" I called to him. "Take Nimue."

He moved toward Nimue, leaving my field of vision.

The first of the attackers arrived, followed quickly by the others, some ten in all. They stopped before the arcing spear, but none of them tried to come any closer to me. What they waited for, I had no idea. My feeble attempt at keeping them at bay could easily be thwarted with numbers. I never could have kept the spear arcing fast enough to keep them all away. Then I realized what had stopped them: fear. I could see it in their eyes. They believed that I held the spear of Christ and thus all the power it could yield. For whatever reason, that realization made me even more angry. I wanted nothing more than to make these men drop where they were; to have the power of the gods shoot forth from the spear and annihilate them. I brought the spear to a halt, bringing the blade's point to bear at the men before me. And then it happened: two of them attacked me at once. The electrical charge happened so fast that all froze in disbelief. A bolt of lightening shot from the blade of the spear and into one of the attackers, searing right through him and into the other in less time than it takes to blink. They contorted and screamed in utter agony. They were incinerated from the inside out and dropped dead as only the shells of men. Briefly, a silence filled the meadow. Only the crackling of the fires and the moans of those wounded or dying from the initial attack could be heard.

"Cowards!" Creconius yelled at his men, trotting his horse forward.

"Hold, Creconius," said the General, he and the Papal man keeping pace with Creconius. The three men halted their horses next to their men on the ground.

My arms felt weak, fatigued from arcing the spear and the slight electrical charge I had received when the bolt spewed forth from its blade. I held the blade toward the remaining brigands and Romans before me. It no longer glowed. I'm sure I appeared a pitiful threat. The General then raised a hand in the air and brought it down in a sharp chopping motion.

I never saw them coming, especially in the night. They hit me with such force that I was slammed to the ground on my back, dropping the spear in the process. The pain in both my shoulders began a few seconds later. In my fall, I had broken the front of both arrows, which had gone through my body and protruded out of my back. I now lay on my back staring at the night sky and seeing two feathered arrow shafts, one sticking out of the front of each of my shoulders. The pain was intense, like a poker in each shoulder. And, I could move neither arm.

"Myrriddin!" It was Nimue. Her voice came from far behind in the distance. I could not tell whether that was because she was escaping, hopefully with the aid of Moscastan, or whether it was because I was beginning to lose consciousness. I hoped the former.

My vision began to waver, but I could see two faces above me, looking at me with a mixture of fear, awe and curiosity. It was easier to focus on them than the pain. One was the young face of a legionnaire who couldn't be more than sixteen summers. Though his face was dirt-smudged, I could see that he was not from this land. My guess was that he was a conscript from the land where Moscastan hailed. The other face belonged to a toothless, filth—encrusted man, who prodded me none too gently with the butt of his weapon; a spear of some kind—a large stone, honed to resemble a sharp spear-head, tied in the fork of a split, hand-made shaft created from what appeared to be an oak branch. The spear was short, maybe four-feet long, but looked effective. The man, himself, was dressed in little more than rags and brandished a makeshift wooden crucifix on his chest. The thing dangled from a leather thong and looked to be little more than two twigs tied together cross-ways. He also stank of stale mead and human waste. I doubted whether the man had bathed in a fistful of seasons, and I guessed that he probably wiped his arse with his own cloak, if at all. His stench did more to prevent me from losing consciousness than any rough prodding with his weapon.

"He's alive!" declared the legionnaire in an accent that told me my guess about his origins was correct.

Other faces appeared over me.

Where is my spear? I suddenly wondered, panic gripping me. I could feel the dirt beneath my hands. My arms could move again. I moved one hand to feel the ground around me for the spear. "Agh!" I screamed. The movement sent a bolt of pain through my upper body. One of the men laughed.

"Looking for this, lad?" Creconius asked. I turned my head and the legs of those around me stepped aside. Standing some fifteen-feet away, holding the spear, was Creconius. The men around him were standing off by a few feet, giving him, or the spear, a wide berth. Fear drenched their features. It was as if they expected it to burst into flames. In spite of the situation, I almost laughed. These fools knew nothing of what they now possessed. Then again, for that matter, nor did I. All the time I had it, I never truly understood it or my relationship to it. Yes, I had the visions in the Crystal Sanctuary, and elsewhere, of my life as Longinus. But I no longer felt connected to that life, that person. If we have lived in human form previous to a given life, then why do the majority of us need to relearn the lessons there-from? Only a few Master Druids I have known were able to have that kind of recall.

I forcefully brought my attention back to the moment, my pain, the loss of the spear, all of it. I felt weak for having allowed the spear to leave my grasp. Then again, the arrows had clearly been targeted so that I would drop the weapon. I was alive. A part of me thought it better to have died if I was going to lose this sacred thing which had somehow been put in my trust...again.

"Kill him!" ordered Creconius.

"No," said a squeaky voice. This came from the mousy figure mounted next to the General. Compared to Creconius and The General, who, like Lord Creconius, was very tall even in the saddle and had the largest chest and arms I'd ever seen on a man, the Papal Legate was the size of a small girl with a voice to match. He was short and thin. His face was mostly obscured by the hood of his garment, but what I could see of it looked pale, even sickly. For an instant, I thought that perhaps this was a woman. Impossible, I thought. There was no doubt in my mind that he wore the Robes of the Church of Rome, complete, as I said, with the large gold crucifix. He trotted his mount forward to get a better look at me. When he stared down at me, something coursed through my body. I tried to discern what it was; fear? Awe? No. 'Twas power, but uncontrolled and unharnessed. There was no way of telling, therefore, if his power was used for good or evil. Power knows no person or intent. Only law; its own law of action. The intent, and thus the ultimate use, to which power is put, is up to the individual wielding it. In that sense, it is more frightening to face one who has the kind of power I was sensing now, but knows not how to use it, than it is to face one of evil and does know how.

The Papal Legate looked into my eyes. "Bring the Relic," he said to Creconius while staring into my face. The Legate held out his hand in apparent expectation of the spear being placed there.

"I am leading this party. You will not order me to do anything, Bishop," spouted Creconius calmly.

The Legate now whipped his head to face Creconius. Though I could not see the man's face, I heard the shift in power to his voice. It still squeaked, but there was now an undeniable force to it. "You dare defy the Church?"

I could see Creconius' face. It flinched, briefly. He, too, felt this power coming through the Bishop. He recovered quickly, though. "I care naught for your Church and..."

"You are here at the Church's pleasure, Lord Creconius. Do not forget your place. These soldiers are mine. Those," the Bishop continued, motioning to some of the rag-tag fighters nearby, "things are yours. If you insist, I can have the General demonstrate my point." With the nod of his head, the Legate signaled the General, who, in turn, inclined his head.

A yelp, and a sickening slicing sound came from nearby. Suddenly, the upper half of a body fell on top of my legs. His falling had moved the air around me such that I knew exactly who it was. I almost vomited from the fetid stench of the man

426

who had only a moment ago been staring toothlessly into my face. The legionnaire who had been next to him came back into my view, wiping the blood from his Roman sword. "I was tired of your shit-smell anyway ya scum," he said to the dead man, in his Persian accent.

The Legate moved a cloth to his nose beneath the hood, obviously having just received a pungent whiff of the man, now made worse by the loosing of his bowels upon death. "Och! Remove that putrid form," said the Legate, indicating the corpse on my legs. Two other legionnaires moved in and dragged the dead man away. The Legate again turned to Creconius. "I'll not ask again," he said.

Silently, arrogantly, Creconius walked over to the Legate and handed him the Spear of Longinus, the Spear Of Christ, my wizard's staff, defiance dripping from his face.

The Legate looked over the weapon with curious and loving eyes. He stroked it tenderly as he examined the shaft and made his way up to the blade. Upon arriving at the blade, he made a sharp gasp, seeing something there that delighted and astonished him. "His? Truly?" It took me a moment to realize that the question was directed at me.

I strained my neck to see to what he referred. But I need not have bothered. I knew what he had found on the blade: the dried Blood of Christ. I would give nothing away, however. "I know nothing of what you say," I replied.

"Come now!" said the Legate. Something in his voice caught me off guard. He said it like an excited little boy, not as the killer he had displayed himself to be a moment ago when he had ordered the General to make an example-kill. He slid off the horse and rushed to my side, kneeling next to me. He held the spear for me to see. "Here, the blood. It is My Lord Christ's, is it not? I have heard that it remained, that even the Centurion who possessed it, Longinus—the one who had pierced the Lord's side—could not remove it."

"It's just an old spear, man," I said. Stupid, that. Had I forgotten that bolts of lightening had just flown from the thing and killed two men?

"Yes. And the display you just created with it, what was that, dumb luck? Your...Druid's training?" asked the Legate. He said this last part also with boyish excitement, as if he were genuinely interested in the Druid's craft, not contemptuous of it. He was beginning to seem more like Pretorius than a true Papal Legate. "Besides," he continued, "I had seen it before you broke its disguise. Why disguise it if it weren't important?"

In spite of myself and the situation, or maybe because of it, I found myself warming to this man. "Perhaps you're right. But it is simply my...staff by any other name," I said.

He stood then, and pointed the spear at three of the men standing nearby: two more of the raiders and the legionnaire who had just carried out the murder of the foul-smelling man. All three of the men started. But the Legate made no threatening move toward them. Instead, he kept the spear's blade pointed at the men and threw off his hood. His face was indeed boyish. But in the light of the night's fire, he could have been fifteen summers or thirty-five; such were his features. His eyes seemed to be of a light color and sparkled in the sparse light with gleeful anticipation. He then closed his eyes and contorted his face with what appeared to be concentration. I knew exactly what he was trying to do. A part of me wanted to burst into laughter: he looked like a child trying to make an adult's toy work without knowing how. The other part of me, though, knew that even I didn't know how it worked. It just seemed to be a part of me, responding to my deepest, most intense intentions and emotions at any give moment. But then there was the voice: His voice that came unbidden from time to time through the spear. Could this boy-Legate hear it now? Would he make the spear do his bidding? If so, then I would surely die this night, for I now realized that this was why he had stopped Creconius from killing me.

The Legate shook with the effort of making the spear do his will. Nothing happened; no bolt of lightening shot forth, no glow emanated from its tip, and no vibration shook its shaft. He halted the effort, much to the relief of the three men at whom the Legate had pointed the spear. "Hmm," he voiced. "Yet we all saw the light that shot forth, killing the two unfortunates."

He approached me once again and resumed his kneeling position. "You are Merlin, are you not?" he asked sincerely.

"My name is Myrriddin," I replied.

"Ah, forgive me, Myrriddin," said the Legate. "But your name is simply the ancient form of Merlin, no? And, a Merlin is a high-ranking bard or magician within the ranks of Druids, no?"

I made no reply.

"And, you have studied for many years on the great Isle of Mystery, no?" he continued.

I was astonished that he knew so much about me, but tried to hide it. "Why would you care? And even if that's all true, why would someone like me have this sacred relic—if it's what you say it is, is what I mean?"

He laughed, giggled, really. "Oh, Merlin—Myrriddin—you know precisely why. Hundreds of years ago, several sacred relics of the Church, of the then fledgling new religion, were deposited on your Isle of Mystery for safe-keeping. They're all gone from there now." He leaned in closer to me, so that only I could hear his next words. "I've a good idea who has taken two of them," he whispered, inclining his head backwards slightly to indicate the now impatient Creconius. "In fact, I'm sure of it. My sources say so. Can't confront him on it, you see. Then we'd never get them back." He leaned back to his previous position. "They're probably long gone," he said loudly, so that Creconius could hear. "But the spear...my sources have kept me informed of you for some time. I feel as though I know you, Mer—Myrriddin," he said correcting himself again.

Why was he telling me all this? He wanted me to wield the spear's alleged power for him, no doubt, perhaps to train him in the use of it. But there was more, I sensed. Perhaps he wanted me, with the spear's help, to also help locate the other sacred items.

"I understand that you can view remotely even without the spear's help. That's a gift, you know. Oh, the Church frowns upon such things, but I think the Universe is a vast place and God is infinite in the way He uses it...and us," said the Legate.

I laughed out loud then, for he indeed sounded just like Father Pretorius. But, the mere act of laughing caused intense pain to shoot through my shoulders, and I grimaced at the agonizing sensation.

"I don't know what's so funny, my son, but we need to attend to you. General," he called, rising to his feet.

The General trotted his mount close to us.

"Let us be gone from here. See to my friend Myrriddin. Take him to my tent and summon my surgeon," ordered the Legate.

Creconius was incredulous. "You cannot be serious!"

"I can and I am," The Legate said to Creconius. Turning his attention back to the Roman, he said, "Carry on, General!"

The General saluted fist to chest, turned and barked orders into the night. Within a heartbeat, six men approached, one carrying a make shift field-stretcher. He laid it open on the ground next to me. None too gently, they jostled me onto the stretcher and lifted me up. I felt as though I would pass out from the pain. I looked over at the spear, still in the hand of the Legate. I then looked at Creconius, who was also eyeing the relic.

"I think not, Lord Creconius," said the Legate, reading Creconius' desire. "It'll be safer with me." He then approached my stretcher before the men started to walk away with me. He placed a hand gently on my left arm. "We'll have you fit in no time, my friend. And, trust me, Myrriddin. I will take great care of this," he said, holding the spear so that I could see it.

For whatever reason, I believed him. With his words, my world went black as I lost consciousness.

I did not know where I was when I awoke. The pillow beneath my skin was the softest thing I had ever felt, lulling

me into a sense of Otherworldly comfort and safety. I thought
I could lie there forever on this cloud of softness. Had I
crossed to the Otherside permanently? No. I could still feel the
pain in my shoulders, but it seemed lessened by ten-fold. I
opened my eyes and stared at the ceiling. Directly above me
was a cloth, a very rich-looking cloth for it shined and
shimmered as it moved slightly. I had never seen any cloth so
shimmery as this. I thought at first that it was the ceiling
itself, but quickly realized that it was a billowing drapery hung
from its edges just beneath the real ceiling. I could see
through the seam of the cloth to the actual ceiling: a canvas,
the top of a field tent. I was disappointed. I definitely was not
in the Otherworld, but some kind of lush commander's tent.
Then it all came back to me.

I noticed that the arrow shafts were gone. I then began
to look cautiously around at my surroundings. The interior of
this tent was huge. Ornate and expensive accoutrements for
living were everywhere: four wooden chairs, apparently
handmade—each appeared slightly different, but were clearly
from the same craftsman—polished and stained to perfection,
complete with golden inlays and gold lion's paws for feet stood
a short distance away. A very large matching table was nearby
the chairs. Thick and large carpets and rugs, rich in
appointment and artistry, covered every inch of the floor, and
many hung on the interior of the tent's walls as tapestries.
Each of those on the floor, at least the ones I could see,
depicted a battle being fought by Romans of old. But the
tapestries on the walls were different. Each of these had a
scene wherein a specific man was being hanged on a Roman
cross, or brought down from one, or showed a moment where
it was at some point in the middle of this event. My eyes
landed on one depicting the latter; one in which a particular
bearded soldier of Rome held his spear point to the ribs of the
man on the cross. My heart suddenly leapt. It was clear who
this Roman soldier was supposed to be. I studied the soldier
closer. The look is all wrong! I found myself thinking. I, he,
didn't look like that. To begin with, there was never any beard!

A sound came from nearby, from behind and to my left. It was a quiet, breathy, wheezing type of sound. It broke my concentration; my analysis of the tapestry.

"You recognize it, do you not?" said the squeaky voice of the Legate.

I strained my neck and head to see him. The pain shot through my shoulders again and my chest with the effort, too much so this time. I brought my attention back to my body. I raised one arm, then the other. The pain was there, but not as bad as when I tried to move my whole body.

"Three days," said the Legate.

I heard the creak of a wooden chair from behind as the Legate rose and stepped to the side of my...bed. I was on no mere pallet with rushes for a mattress, but a bed approximately four feet off the ground and covered with fluffed and sumptuous pillows; feather-stuffed by the feel of them. The Legate stood over me and I looked into his boyish face. He was no boy, however. The beginnings of wrinkles tickled the corners of his eyes. And, though he certainly looked youthful in features, he was sickly in color. He coughed then, spitting something into a sage-colored cloth, which he quickly brought to his mouth.

He quickly regained his composure. "Forgive me," he said. "A chill in the chest I cannot seem to be rid of. I no sooner think that it has run its course when it comes back again. I'm sure the activities of the other night helped it not," he said, pausing for a time. "Three days since that night—— that you've been here, in case you were wondering," the Legate offered.

I simply nodded. Three days. Better than the last time I was in a similar circumstance, I supposed. My gaze then drifted back to the tapestry.

The Legate turned his attention to it, as well. "You recognize it," he repeated while looking at the wall hanging. He said it as a matter of fact, not as a question.

I was not sure whether he referred to the whole scene in the tapestry, the soldier and the spear, or just the spear.

Given the events of the night two or three nights past, it had to be the spear. I wasn't about to tell him that I was the reincarnation of the soldier in the scene. Still..."The beard looks strange," I heard myself saying.

"Eh?" replied the Legate, obviously caught off guard by my comment.

"The beard on the soldier stabbing the prisoner on the cross," I clarified. "I thought soldiers of Rome were clean shaven."

"Ah, well you see, this tapestry is a product of its time. The artisan who created it lived during the time of Emperor Hadrian who lived not all that long ago. He always wore the facial hair. It became quite acceptable for a legionnaire to fashion one, as well, at least for a time," the Legate explained.

"So, this is a crucifixion at the time of Hadrian, then, not at the time of the Christ?" I asked almost dismissively, trying to deflect the direction of the conversation.

"Nay, Myrriddin. You know it's of Jesu. The artisan simply used the look of his time." The Legate paused again and studied me. "You'll notice, too, that the rank of the soldier is wrong as well. Is it not?"

It was true. The soldier depicted was a common foot soldier, a common legionnaire. Of course, he should have been depicted as a Centurion. But to the Legate, I feigned ignorance. "Is it?" I asked lamely.

The Legate simply smiled. He turned and walked across the tent's floor to a tall flap, an opening on the far wall of the tent. "I wish not to tax you too heavily. We'll talk again soon," he said over his shoulder. He stopped then, racked by another fit of coughing. He recovered quickly enough and looked at me from near the tent's entrance. "I'll see that a proper meal is brought to you," he said, and turned to leave.

"Wait," I called.

He stopped and looked at me, an indeterminable smile tugging at his lips.

"What of my staff, the spear?" I asked, a whiff of desperation filling my voice.

"As I said," he replied calmly, "we'll talk more later."

"And...my...did you take anyone else...prisoner?" My friends. Had Moscastan and Nimue escaped? What of Baldua and Pretorius?

"I would not call you a prisoner, Myrriddin," he answered.

"Oh?" I asked, incredulous. "Let me take stock," I began sarcastically. "You chased and killed many of the people I was with, you shot me and took my possession and brought me here against my will. Does that not make a prisoner?"

"As I said, I'd not say you were a prisoner."

"So I'm free to leave, then?" I said, becoming more angry by the moment.

The Legate stepped up to the tent's opening and pulled back the flap, silently inviting me to freedom. Daylight streamed in, as well as the sounds of activity in an encampment, surprisingly muted until just then.

I sat up and swung my legs off the bed all in one motion. And, I instantly regretted it. The pain shot through not only my whole body, but my whole being. I nearly passed out. I lay back down quickly. I panted heavily and was sweating from what ordinarily would have been a small exertion. One doesn't truly appreciate the body's abilities, no matter how minute or seemingly insignificant, until it is taken away. I then felt liquid on my shoulders. My wounds were seeping blood again.

"I'll have food brought to you, Myrriddin. And, my surgeon again," he said from the tent's flap.

"Thank you, Legate," I said, defeated.

"Rozinus," said the Legate. "My name is Bishop Rozinus," he said as he left me alone in the plush quarters.

~XVI~

"Fear not, Myrriddin," said Moscastan. He leaned over the pallet I lay on and looked into my face. I could move not a muscle. I tried to speak, but could not. I could not even move my lips. What had happened? I could not turn my head to see if I was in the same place, in the tent wherein Rozinus had left me. "You needn't have the spear. You have the Merlin within to do your bidding. You always have and always will," he continued.

"M-Myrrid-d-din, my l-love," stuttered Igraines. Her face appeared next to Moscastan, both stared at me with concern, yet joy in their eyes. What was happening? I screamed in my mind. I am here! Help me! I cannot move.

"You tried to safeguard the spear, but it matters not, lad. You did what you could," said Moscastan.

"Salve, mihi care amice (Hello, my dear friend). Are you coming back to us?" It was Baldua, speaking as his face joined the others above me. He turned to Moscastan and Igraines, "I think he's gone. His stare, it's blank," he said in perfect Gaelic.

'Twas true. I could not even move my eyes to focus on any one of them.

"No," said Igraines. "Th-they're still m-moist." Her face disappeared from my view for a moment as she turned away. I then heard an amazing sound: the wail of an infant. Igraines appeared back in my view, now holding a beautiful baby. "Look, Myrriddin, l-look. My son. I have named h-him Arturius. Y-You must teach h-him the w-w-wonders of the gods," she said, tears brimming her eyes.

Arturius! Yes! Yes! I know the lad. I've seen him, foretold of his coming, I yelled in my mind. But...I no longer have the spear to guide me, to guide us to...

"Look! His eyes water!" said Baldua. "He is with us still!"

Cold liquid dripped down my face, a small amount at first, then more, and more until I felt as though I would drown. I coughed, struggled for breath and sat up.

"I sorry," said the terrified girl sitting on my bed of fluffed, feathered pillows. "I bathe you, say Bishop. Too much water in cloth. I sorry," she rambled in broken Gaelic. She could not have been more than twelve summers. I knew little of the northern countries, but what I did know of them, this lass fit. She was yellow of hair and blue of eye. She spoke with the guttural accent of a Germanic tribe. She had, no doubt, been picked up as a slave during the Bishop's travels.

But what kind of slave she was, I did not want to think. I understood that most of these Christian priests now took vows of celibacy. I wondered if Bishop Rozinus did. I'd be not surprised by him either way. I did not understand their reasoning for such a vow. According to Pretorius, they thought by taking a vow of celibacy, it brought them closer to God and away from the so-called evil and baser aspects of being human. Yet, physical urges were not just natural to my people and the old ways, but brought us closer to creation by engaging in the act of creation itself; whether for the creation of new life, or the creation of something else, an outstanding harvest of a blessed crop, for example, by bringing together the opposite energies and spirits. There were those among the Druids who had reached a level of being beyond the physical; they were truly spirits living from their spirit only while housed in body. I saw that with them, the desire for the act of physical coupling was something that had simply fallen away; something that they had moved beyond, like a child that has outgrown a toy. To move beyond it for any other reason was to miss the whole point. One does not lead the ox with the wagon, as it is said.

"I sorry," the girl repeated. She looked as though I were about to strike her; not fearful, but simply resigned to it. Obviously, it was part of her master's routine.

436

"Do not worry," I said, realizing I could not only speak, not only move, but that I was also sitting naked on the bed. And, I realized, too, that my friends had been a dream. I remained a...guest of the Bishop's in his tent. "I was dreaming and you startled me, that is all," I said to the girl. "I can bathe myself."

"Nin," she insisted, shaking her head. "I water the hurts wid my mix," she said, pointing to a nearby bowl containing a dark, gelatinous liquid.

Though I was dubious, I looked at the wound in my left shoulder. It was nearly healed. If her mix had aided in that, then so be it. I then wiped off the remaining water from my face.

"I try to give you drink with cloth, but too much, me thinks," she said sheepishly.

I laughed, perhaps for the first time in days. "Me thinks too," I agreed. I then turned to her and motioned for her to apply her mix. As she worked, my mind drifted to the tent, to the fact that I'd lost track of my time here, to my friends and the dream I just had. To the spear! I resolved then and there to get it back. I needed it to fulfill the destiny that kept coming to me. Arturius, the boy who grew to be a king, at least if my visions were correct. Son of Igraines? But who was the father? I wanted to believe that I was, from that night Igraines and I lay together, which now seemed a lifetime ago. No matter. My destiny, or at least part of it, was apparently intricately interwoven with this child and with the land he would rule. And the spear; I must have the spear to guide me, to give me the power and ability to guide us all. I saw that now more than ever. It was truly my Druid's staff. "Quickly, now lass. I have things to do, you know," I said to the girl as she continued to slather her concoction on my wounds. The mix, or salve felt cool and soothing, and something else: it tingled. It felt as though tiny little creatures crawled over the skin. Not in a frightening or disturbing way, however. It was a special type of tingling and tickling sensation, like skin being rapidly mended back together. I had never felt anything like it.

"Yes, Master," she said shyly, but with a look that said, "You've been lying here for days and now you suddenly 'have things to do'?"

"Well, I do," I said defensively.

She continued about her work, saying no more.

The sun was bright and harsh as I stepped out of the tent. Or, perhaps it was more the fact that I been inside and bedridden that made it seem so. Two guards, helmeted, armed Roman legionnaires, flanked the sides of the tent opening as I stepped out. Neither moved, but stood stiffly, looking ahead and away from me. They made no move to stop me or question me. The girl who had been applying the salve to my wounds squeezed her way between me and one of the guards as she left. "Thank you," I called after her. She simply held up a hand in acknowledgement and walked on, never turning back to look at me. One of the guards snickered at this. I could guess what was going through his mind.

The activity outside the tent was sparse. I expected to see more people and soldiers. There were only a handful of legionnaires scattered about and a few of the raiders that had been with Creconius. It was then that I heard the voice of Creconius, heated, as though he would spew forth venom at any moment. "You said so," he claimed in a loud growl.

I took another step out from the tent and looked to my right, in the direction of his voice. There, near a corner of the tent, was Creconius, face-to-face with Legate Bishop Rozinus, who was flanked by two other Churchmen, judging by their brown robes and tonsured heads. "My good Creconius, I said no such thing," replied the Bishop calmly, even sweetly. "It is plain to see that you misunderstood."

I knew not of what they spoke. But something told me it was about me, and or the spear; more likely the spear. I took a step toward them. A strong hand grasped my arm and stopped me. "No, Myrriddin."

I almost spat at the man. How dare this rat of Rome be so presumptuous as to call me by my name. I looked into the

438

man's face and nearly passed out from the shock of what I saw. Beneath the brim of the helmet were the eyes of Baldua. "Salve, mihi amice (Hello, my friend)," he said in his pretentious Latin. 'Twas Baldua for certain.

"Enough with that talk!" said the other legionnaire guard; a female—Nimue.

I was stunned. With dirt smudged on her face and her hair obviously pulled back and up under her helmet, she looked more like an older boy than a woman to be sure. "What the..." I began.

"'Tis come in quite useful getting us this far, lass, don't ya think?" Baldua replied haughtily to Nimue's slight.

"What are you two doing here, and dressed like...like that?" I said too loudly, pointing to the Roman garb.

"Stop it, Myrriddin. You'll give us away now," said Nimue.

"Obviously, we came for you, ya ingrate," Baldua said to me. "You've been too ill 'til now. Thought we'd lost you."

"Yes," said Nimue, sternly but tenderly. "That we did."

"But...how did you..."

"Ah, by the gods, Myrriddin. Enough. We're here, are we not?" said Baldua, clearly thinking we were talking too much.

"Moscastan had us lead two soldiers into the woods," explained Nimue. "He glammed them——spelled them, I think. We took their uniforms and their place."

"And their compatriots didn't notice?" I asked.

"They were breaking camp when we arrived in the uniforms. Most of 'em were leaving with that general. Someone barked for us to stay. Didn't give us a second look," said Baldua.

"Lucky for you! Could you imagine if he had barked for you to go with those leaving?" I laughed at the thought of Nimue and Baldua serving in the Legions of Rome for the remainder of their days. Well, at least the thought of it happening to Baldua made me laugh for a moment.

Creconius yelled what sounded like a threat to the Bishop. He sounded as though he was losing control. His voice had shifted to a very high tone, almost to that of a woman's shriek. "I'll cut you through, I will!" he yelled again. Suddenly, a ringing sound was heard: the sound of a high-grade metal blade being unsheathed. In a whirl of his body, Creconius had brandished a hidden sword. The thing was nearly as long as a man and shined with the brightness of a full moon. Where he had pulled it from, I could not tell. He brought it down with the fury of a god, straight at Bishop Rozinus' head. But the bishop was fast, faster than anyone I had ever seen. In one move, he stepped slightly to one side and pulled one of the tonsured Churchmen toward him, effectively using the unwitting man as a shield against the sword blow. It worked. Creconius' blade missed the Bishop, but cleaved the other Churchman in one shoulder close to the neck, nearly cutting the man in two lengthwise. Everyone froze for an instant.

The man who was just hacked in two was fully awake and comprehending, at least for a moment. He looked at his mortal injury with stunned disbelief. "Oh, oh, oh," he said. He then turned his gaze to the sky, to the heavens. "I was not done here, my Lord. But if thine will is...is..." He dropped silently to the ground in a pool of blood. No one was watching the man die, though, for something more astonishing had happened.

Those who were within viewing of what had just taken place were watching Creconius; his face had changed, as if a glam had suddenly been lifted with the exertion of this shining sword. He had always had decidedly feminine features. But, now his face appeared even more soft. It was feminine, yes, but more that of a crone, a hag, a female Sorceress from the Old Ways——one who uses the knowledge and power and law of the Infinite, the One, to do Dark biddings.

"What treachery is this?" Bishop Rozinus asked, menace dripping from his words. "What demon are you, for you are not Creconius?"

"I am Creconius, you fool," Creconius said, regaining some of his normal voice. But his appearance remained that of the old crone. "I am Creconius-Mab, seeker and keeper of the Old Ways, and I'll have the spear or your head, Rozinus. Your church ways are an abomination and will be destroyed. I already have your other precious relics and the power they hold."

I felt Baldua tense up next to me. It was now I who reached out and placed a hand on my friend's arm to steady him.

"I knew it!" bellowed the Bishop. "Where've you taken them?"

"Far from here. Creconius-Mab laughed thunderously then. When he stopped laughing, his face became deadly serious. He brandished the point of the mighty sword at the throat of Rozinus. There was a crackling in the air, as if an electrical charge had pierced the area. The tip of the sword glowed a fierce red. Bishop Rozinus stared at it, transfixed. Not only did the blade shine immensely bright, but there was a glow to the hilt of the thing. It was not like the glow of the blade's tip, however. This one was soft and bluish-white and conveyed a feeling that was ... what? I could not understand it for a moment. And then it hit me. Creconius-Mab was having difficulty maintaining his glamour because of this sword—because of the power coursing through this sword. It was not meant for such a sorceress as Creconius-Mab. The blue light glowing from the hilt—it was the power of goodness; the positive attributes of the gods, The God. I could feel it; it was the same feeling I always felt from the spear. It took all of Creconius-Mab's power to stay in control over the magnificent sword.

"Impressive, is it not?" Creconius-Mab asked Rozinus as the Legate's stare remained transfixed on the sword. "Forged from a metal no man has seen before, honed to perfection and wielded by a so-called holy man of your ilk," continued Creconius-Mab. I looked at it closer. Indeed, the blade looked different than any I had ever seen; shining polish, yes, but it also appeared to be more solid, stronger than any blade I'd ever seen. It had sliced through the tonsured Churchman as if he were naught but air. There were symbols adorning each side of the blade, from hilt to tip. I recognized some of them as ancient Gaelic. The others looked even older, and more obscure. I believe Moscastan had drawn some like these once —said they were glamours of divine providence; invocations of ancient and sacred trusts. He had called them Runes. The hilt and grip were plain enough; a sturdy iron cross bar to protect the hand, both of its ends fanned out, and a smooth-handled grip with leather strips wrapped tightly around it. I could see part of the grip beneath his hand. It ended with a round crystal-like pummel. Nothing too special about the hilt, grip and pummel. It was the blade that set this weapon apart, and the power which coursed through it.

"You see the caliber of the blade, the weapon. You sense its power," he continued, taunting the Bishop.

"I..." Rozinus began, regaining his composure, no longer transfixed by the sword. He looked straight into the eyes of Creconius-Mab then, menace and contempt spewing forth. "I see one who is unworthy of such a weapon and sense that he is terribly weakened by the controlling of it. If you were worthy of such as this," he continued, as he casually brought a hand to the blade, "your wielding of it would be effortless." Rozinus then touched the flat of the blade with a finger and gently pushed it away from his throat.

Creconius-Mab began panting, his breathing labored as if from extreme exertion. For an instant, his glamour dropped completely. Before us stood a stooped, short, ugly hag leaning on the large sword whose point was now in the ground.

"Take him...her! Take the sword!" yelled Rozinus to no one in particular.

Before anyone could respond, or even know to respond —there were very few people left in the camp, very few soldiers—Creconius-Mab, the hag, gave a blood-spilling scream, threw her head back violently, and suddenly became Creconius-Mab, the murderous scum once more, fully glammed

442

with the large man's presence and being. Creconius-Mab then howled with rage and took three steps backward. Still howling his demented anger, he thrust the sword into the air and suddenly disappeared, vanishing completely from sight on a bright and clear day.

"By the gods!" exclaimed Baldua. The remaining tonsured Churchman standing next to Bishop Rozinus dropped to his knees and began to fervently pray through unbridled terror and tears. His words were in Latin, but his meaning was clear.

"He prays for deliverance from evil and ..."

"Yes, Baldua. I can guess what he's praying for!" I snapped at my friend as he began to play the role of interpreter.

He fell silent, as we all did for a moment, not quite believing what had just happened. The only sounds were a bird cawing in the distance, and the frantic mumblings of a terrified priest.

"Myrriddin," Nimue whispered from behind me.

I turned and looked into her eyes, beautiful even though her face was a dirty mess.

"You want your precious spear, follow me," she said. She seemed not at all affected by the Sorceress's disappearance. Slowly, she started to back into the tent I had just exited.

"You can't be serious," I said. "I'd know if it were in there."

"Obviously, you know not as much as you think," she countered as she went in.

"Go, Myrriddin. I'll watch here," said Baldua.

I said nothing, but followed Nimue into the tent.

It was stale. Though it was still the same large and luxurious space, the smell was sickly. My head hurt and my stomach lurched. I also felt weak. Perhaps I had made my exit from the tent too soon, I thought. The girl had been sent in to bathe me and continue treatment of my wounds. Maybe I was still injured and weak.

"Here," said Nimue from a large, freestanding wardrobe cabinet. It stood at least seven-feet tall. I recalled taking notice of it before at some point, but paid it no heed. Perhaps because of its location in the tent—several yards behind the head of the bed I had been in for ... two weeks maybe? Had I been here that long? Nimue stood holding the wardrobe's intricately-carved door open. A soft glow came from within. I approached slowly, cautiously, and peered inside.

It stood leaning against the back, right-hand corner inside the cabinet, the blade glowing softly with the same bluish hue as the sword hilt for a few moments. Was it in sympathetic connection with the sword? And how could I not sense the spear's presence in the very place I was convalescing, not think to look in the cabinet?

"You're scowling. I thought you'd be happy to see it," said Nimue.

"How'd I not feel its presence? And why did the Bishop not hide it away?" I asked, feeling a mixture of confusion and unworthiness.

"He probably kept it here to aid in your healing, don't you think?" she stated flatly as if it were the most obvious thing in the world.

"But I didn't feel it..." I started.

"I don't know," she said, exasperated. "Ah, Myrriddin, we haven't time for this. Take it." Nimue looked back to the tent's entrance flap and made a soft, bird-like cawing sound. A moment later, Baldua entered.

"We must leave. It's clear for now, but the shock of that Sorceress vanishing is wearing thin," he said as he stopped before us.

I took the spear in my hand. Its warmth was comforting. I took a deep breath and instantly felt my connection to it reassert itself. I was at home with this instrument, no matter where I was. Holding the spear, I suddenly realized that I also felt invigorated, healed, the sickly

444

feeling I had upon re-entering the tent all but gone. I looked at Nimue. "How'd you know it was here?" I asked.

Baldua answered. "The little lass that tended you a while ago – she's quite the chattering goose," he said, a smile pulling the corners of his mouth.

"What does that mean?" I asked incredulously.

"What do you mean, 'what does that mean,' Myrriddin?"

"Well, did you frighten her or did you ..."

"No! Of course not," he replied, genuinely hurt.

Nimue stepped in and said, "It means, Myrriddin, that your friend is a charmer of little girls as well as older ones. Well, some older ones," she said, clearly implying that she was above such things from him. "Enough. Let's leave."

I stepped toward the entrance when Baldua grabbed my arm, stopping me. "Not that way. There's a short flap at the back. The tree line is ten feet from it on the outside," he said.

Nimue led the way as we went to the very back of the tent. She pulled aside a lovely, expensive looking two-seat couch. There, near the base of the tent's wall, was a tied flap approximately three-feet-by-three-feet. "It's for ventilation, but makes a good escape hole," she said.

"You certainly reconnoitered the place," I observed.

She said no more, but dropped to her knees, untied the flap which hinged at its top, and crawled out. Dropping to my knees, I followed her out, Baldua behind me. Outside the back of the tent, the way was clear and we quickly made it to the tree-line. We entered the protective covering of the forest, escaping the Bishop and the remainder of his soldiers and Creconius-Mab's rabble. As I crossed the threshold of the tree-line, I looked back toward the tent. Not too far from the dwelling, in the midst of what had now become a bustle of activity—the group was apparently breaking camp—stood Bishop Rozinus. Standing before the Bishop and speaking to him, much to my surprise, was Pretorius. I looked at Baldua, who was looking in the same general direction as I was, but only briefly.

"Go, Myrriddin," Baldua said, as he pushed me into the forest.

~XVII~

We crept through the forest, quickly but quietly. We traveled for over a mile, weaving in between rowans and oaks and saplings as they became thicker in trunk, denser in population. At first I kept turning, expecting to see pursuers on foot. I stopped on two occasions simply to listen and nearly fell behind. No one was trailing us. The spear still glowed a soft blue; it had neither intensified nor diminished since leaving the tent. That was odd. Of course, it had glowed occasionally since the day I'd discovered it – in warning, in conveyance of some thought or message from the Otherworld; in empathic harmony with my own soul. Yet, it had never glowed this shade of color, nor with this consistency. I was still deeply connected to the spear; I felt it. But this glowing was in harmony with the sword Creconius-Mab had wielded, or had tried to wield. I did not understand it, but I felt it. Little did I know that the sword Creconius-Mab possessed then would one day aid in the making of a king. My immediate concern, however, was to proceed to safety.

We had traveled deep into the forest when we burst forth into a bright meadow near a large rock formation in the side of a green hill. Nimue, who had been leading us, stopped, Baldua and I alongside of her. The three of us stood in silence for a moment, the twill of birds and the soughing of tree branches in the late afternoon breeze the only sounds coming to our ears. Then Nimue added her own bird twill to the mix, calling forth a moment later a figure from between the craggy rocks. Moscastan. My heart leapt at the sight of him.

"Moscastan!" I yelled, nearly dropping the spear in my rush to embrace him.

"Ah, Master Myrriddin," he said. "We were a bit concerned there for a while." He turned to my two companions. "Well done." It was then that I noticed Moscastan appeared...different. He did not look as old as he had in the Crystal Sanctuary, but he certainly did not appear as young as the mentor I knew. The person before me was someone in between. There was something else, too: he was pale, as if something was draining his energy, his very blood. I was about to question him on this when Baldua interrupted my thoughts.

"Father Pratorius—he was there. We saw him when we made our escape!" my friend said, as he began to strip his body of the Roman uniform.

"Yes," added Nimue.

I had completely forgotten about seeing the priest. But in that moment, I knew not which caught me more off my guard; the fact that the priest had indeed been in the Bishop's camp, or the fact that my friends were surprised by it. I supposed that in the back of my mind, I had simply assumed the priest to be there as part of the ruse to free me.

"And the sword! Creconius-Mab was there and he had a sword the likes of which you've never seen, Moscastan!" Baldua was near babbling in his excitement.

"Calm yourself, lad. Come," Moscastan said as he turned and walked back the way he had come. The three of us followed, weaving our way into and through a craggy rock maze. We then ascended a steep, long set of natural rock steps and emerged onto a large plateau atop the hill, which was actually, as it turned out, not a hill but one gigantic rock formation the size of a small mountain that was covered with mossy grass, giving it the appearance of a smooth, green hill. The plateau was some seventy yards off the floor of the meadow and boasted naturally formed rock walls some four to six feet high around its circumference or perimeter. Thus, it was a perfect hiding place; a naturally formed and hidden refuge from prying eyes. The only way a potential intruder could spy on us here was if he climbed to the top of one of the tallest trees on the edge of the forest, which was not more than thirty yards away. But even so, the tallest of those trees could not reach the height of the plateau. I looked out over the nearby segment of four-foot wall toward the forest from which we'd emerged, and could only see the top of the forest's canopy. The sight of the canopy, the height and seclusion of the plateau——it was breath-taking.

"Wonderous," I said to no one in particular.

"Come, Myrriddin," Moscastan beckoned. I turned. He was standing near a cold fire-pit in the center of the plateau. Around the pit were many folks, celebrants from the evening of the All Hallow's Eve rite turned massacre. Some sat with arms and other appendages in wrappings still bloodied from wounds received that horrific night. Others stood nearby but with the vacant look of the undead in their eyes; that night's carnage leaving them so disturbed in mind that they had one foot in this world, one foot in the Other. The remainder looked fine in body and mind and were clearly giving comfort – or attempting to – to those in need. Anger rose within me. Rage again filled my being as it had the night of the raid, the murderous rampage. The spear in my hand finally ceased to glow blue. It vibrated in my hand and began to pulsate a vibrant red, reflecting the anger seething within me.

"Calm yourself, Myrriddin," said my mentor. "They need your help, not your anger," he said, noting the spear.

"My anger is for those that committed this," I said, waving my hand at the victims before me. And for Rozinus, I thought, feeling another surge of anger rise. I had allowed myself to feel complacency toward the Bishop for allowing me to heal. He'd have done better to finish what he started rather than allow me to live, I thought maliciously.

"Myrriddin," Moscastan said.

I walked toward him when he turned and entered a small nearby animal skin shelter approximately four-square-feet in size. It obviously had been hastily erected, using broken branches from the forest below. He pulled back a flap and disappeared inside the small shelter. He clearly wanted me to follow, but a part of me wanted to stop and immediately help the people here; I could feel it in my bones. I could feel it from the spear. It's what we were supposed to do—the spear and I.

"Go, Myrriddin," prodded Nimue. She had already shed her legionnaire's costume and stood before me as the daughter of Tremel. She was dressed now, however, in a green cloth tunic and animal skin riding breaches. She hastily wiped the dirt smudges from her face and revealed the beauty of it which I had nearly forgotten. Something stirred within me at a deeper level than what I thought I held for Igraines: a connection that was at least as old as the one I felt I shared with Igraines. I could not quite put my finger on it just then.

"Go," she said again, as she bent down to a man with an arm wound. She began to unwrap the bloody cloth. The unwrapping released a putrid odor of gangrenous flesh. I nearly gagged. Nimue paid no heed to the smell, or to my reaction. "He has something for you," she said, indicating the nearby shelter with a gesture of her head. "And in case you haven't taken note, he's not well, either." She stated this with a bitter edge. Why, I was not sure.

But at her words, my anger abated and genuine concern for Master Druid Moscastan took its place. I looked at the pitiful group around me. Yes, they needed my help and the spear's. But they could wait a few more moments, I supposed. I abruptly turned and entered Moscastan's shelter.

The space was tiny and dank and smelled faintly of Moscastan's underground hovel in our home village. A sense of comfort and security suddenly washed over me; a sense of freedom and learning and fondness of memory and peace. But it was false and fleeting.

A muffled scream came from outside. Clearly, it was from someone enduring pain; the kind of pain that comes from the tending of a wound that simply won't heal.

Moscastan already sat cross-legged on the hard ground and indicated that I should do the same. I did so, sitting opposite him, facing him, laying the spear next to me on the ground. It had ceased its red, angry glow and emanated the blue light once more. Moscastan stared at it for a moment. But I could see in his eyes that he wasn't just staring at the spear. His pained look also told me he was waiting for the muffled sound of the one in pain to subside. It almost seemed as if he himself was feeling the pain of this person, taking it on himself to lessen it for another. The sound finally stopped and my mentor brought his eyes to my eyes. What I saw there frightened me.

"I've done what I can for them, Myrriddin. You must heal them, break the glamour that binds them to the pain and suffering placed on them by Creconius-Mab that night as they fled," he said heavily. "I have fought it, but cannot break it. The wounds these people have do not heal. The spell must be broken for them to become whole. It is a travesty of the use of the One, the Law." He fell silent and became older in appearance before my eyes. I tried not to show surprise, but felt my eyes widen. "I have taken on their glamour as much as I can," he continued. "Attempted to show them that they have the power within them to deny the essence of pain thrust on them by another. But they're a simple lot. Some of them have even turned to the Christian's influence they've apparently experienced these seasons past, and now see their present condition as some form of twisted retribution for the sin of participating in the ritual that night. Absurd. 'Tis their own thinking that perpetuates the condition." He paused and drew a labored breath. "But I tell you nothing you don't know."

I stared at Moscastan, my heart suddenly feeling as though it were breaking. I had never seen him so. "Moscastan," I began, my voice cracking. "By the gods, what glamour could destroy you thus? You wield more understanding, more power of the Law than anyone I know."

"'Tis not the glamour, but the one who invokes it— uses the same laws of the Universe available to us all, but for the most sinister of purposes, the most reviled of reason, the most..."

"Moscastan." He had started to babble. "Save your strength, please," I said as I reached out and placed my hand on his shoulder. He was shaking ever so slightly. "What is happening? I've been in that Bishop's camp for over a fortnight. Meanwhile, the world I knew went from bad to worse still. Who could throw a glam of this power? One strong enough to keep those people out there in a bondage of evil and nearly destroy you? Is it Creconius-Mab? He is not what he seems. A sorceress! He changed before our eyes. Vanished too! He ..."

Moscastan shot a hand in the air to silence me. I was now the one who babbled.

"Yes, it is Creconius-Mab. But it is worse than that," my mentor said cryptically.

"I don't understand. Does he have a legion of demons at his bidding?" I asked sardonically, half joking.

Moscastan said nothing for a moment. I suddenly had the thought that perhaps my comment was closer to the mark than not.

"Baldua and Nimue said Father Pretorius was at the Churchman's camp. Was it so? Did you see him?" asked Moscastan.

"Yes. He was there at the Bishop's encampment," I replied.

"And Creconius-Mab, as well?"

"Yes," I replied, confused by the line of questioning. He seemed to be linking the priest and the sorceress together. Then my thoughts shifted to the amazing weapon that Creconius-Mab had brandished. "The sword! He or she; Creconius-Mab had a sword. It was nearly as long as he was and intricately designed. It was of a metal I'd never seen and infused with a power, too! Creconius-Mab had trouble with it, he did. Wasn't meant for him, I don't think. His glam dropped when he tried to use it and ..."

Moscastan's hand shot up again in the gesture to silence me. "So, it does exist," he said, his voice heavy with awe.

"Yes," I said confused. "How could you know about the sword?" I asked.

"Tell me this," he said, ignoring my question for the moment. "Were there...symbols on the blade near the edges?" he asked.

452

"Runes. Yes," I replied, surprised. "They ran the length of the blade."

Silence filled the space. Soft moaning could be heard from outside, but that was all.

"This sword," I finally said. "'Twas clearly endowed with great power. Creconius-Mab said that it had been used by a Holy man of the Church. He implied that its power was from this man.

"One named Constantinius, yes. But it was forged here, on one of the lesser islands in the lake, near the Isle of Mystery," Moscastan said. "It was indeed forged from a metal never seen before. But before Constantinius had it, the legend goes that it was used to kill one of the church's truly holy men. He was said to be much like the Christ, and as with your spear there, his Holiness, his power, was somehow transferred to the sword. After a time, the sword made its way back here, to the Lady on the island of its origins. A good woman and a high priestess of the Old Ways." Moscastan stopped his story. The look in his eyes became far and away as if he were reliving a memory. A smile of pleasure touched his lips. Obviously, the memory was a fond one.

It dawned on me what the memory might be of. "You knew this lady, this High Priestess?" I asked tentatively.

"Aye. She was my friend, my lover, my wife – for a time, at least."

"I never knew."

"No. You didn't. 'Twas before your time. She etched the runes to hold in the power of the divine that apparently coursed through the sword. It's much like your spear," said Moscastan.

"But the spear doesn't need runes to hold its power," I replied.

"Your spear actually pierced the Christ's side, did it not?" countered Moscastan. "The Christ's blood is the sealing stone for whatever power courses through it. But like your spear, the sword's supposed divine power can only be wielded by a righteous and just man."

His eyes bore into me then. I saw in those eyes the depths of his soul; many lifetimes of existence and trust in me, my soul. Am I worthy of such a title –righteous and just?

"Yes, Myrriddin," said my mentor, reading my face, my thoughts. "You're indeed such a man. You will help to found a kingdom based on truth and justice, and in the process, become the most famous of all Merlins."

Moscastan's eyes had glazed over. He was on the edge of trance, prophesizing. But something he said struck me. "I can't see that now. I always thought I would be father to a great Merlin to carry on what I've started," I said.

"No. The line of Merlins will end with you. You are already birthing yourself a-new. You are the son and the father," Moscastan said. "This supposed power in the sword will aid you in birthing the kingdom."

"And the spear?" I asked.

"A powerful Druid Staff indeed. But you will outgrow it," he replied.

"I don't understand," I said, confused and concerned.

"The power of the spear, the power of the sword, though clearly detectable, is naught but the power of the One focused. Nothing can harness this power more than the mind, the spirit. Nothing. You know this, but will soon fully embody it, thus outgrowing your need for the spear," he answered. He paused for a moment before continuing. "Yet, the spear and the sword are important symbols and instruments for now. The sword is in part what we sought."

"We?"

"Pretorius and I," Moscastan said nearly spitting the priest's name. He was also out of the semi-trance.

I wanted to know why he spoke Pretorius' name so, but a different question came to my lips. "How is it that Creconius-Mab has the sword?" I asked.

"She stole it from her sister."

"His...her sister?" I asked, completely confused. He said nothing for a moment. "You mean the Lady, the runes lady is the sister of Creconius-Mab?"

"Aye."

I was stunned. My face must have shown it.

"There's more," said Moscastan heavily. "I ask you this; When you saw Pretorius at the Bishop's encampment, was Creconius-Mab there?"

"No," I replied, struggling once again to discern this line of question.

"And when Creconius-Mab was present, was Pretorius?"

"Moscastan," I exclaimed, shocked, "what are you saying?!"

Moscastan sat staring at me for a long moment, thinking. "I'm not sure, Myrriddin. I'm not yet completely sure. So, I will hold my tongue. For now." He said this last bit with finality. Though a hundred questions leapt into my mind, the matter was obviously closed. He reached behind him to a bundle wrapped in dung-colored cloth. Gently, reverently, he lifted the bundle – which was nearly the size of a young man's head – and placed it in front of me. "As I said," Moscastan began, "the spear is presently an important symbol and instrument. "This," he said, indicating the bundle, "will go a long way to disguising the spear, and the Egg is exceptional. It will truly help to accentuate the spear's supposed – forgive me – the spear's power."

I unwrapped the bundle and found a beautifully woven oval-shaped wicker cage containing a flawless green crystal, a Druid's Egg, the size of a man's fist. I'd never seen anything like it. "Moscastan," I said, awed. "It's exquisite."

"Indeed. The cage is much sturdier than the last one you had. Place it on the spear's blade. It should fit well," he said.

I did as he bade, slipping the housing, the cage, over the blade's tip and onto the blade. The Druid Egg made a tap-sound as it came to rest against the metal. Instantly, a green hue lit the space around it. I could no longer see the blue glow that had been emanating from the spear.

"Secure it tightly," said Moscastan, pointing to the leather thongs on the top and bottom of the cage.

I did. When I was satisfied that the oval cage and crystal would not be going anywhere, I held it at arm's length, admiring it. "'Tis beautiful, Moscastan. Better than anything I have ever done. Thank you."

"Indeed. You're welcome, lad. Now, it's time—time to go out and help these people. Time to heal the land and found a kingdom, Master Merlin," he said smiling.

~XVIII~

As I emerged from Moscastan's shelter, the spear turned into a powerful Druid's staff once more in my hand. All those present around the cold fire pit stared at me, or rather, at my Druid's staff and its glowing green Druid egg, with awe and respect. All but Baldua and Nimue, that is. Baldua smiled, apparently glad to see the thing back to a familiar appearance. Nimue scowled. "If it and you are to aid these people," she said as she continued wrapping the wounded chest of a man, "then come."

I hesitated, but only briefly. I approached the man whose chest was being tended to by Nimue. "Remove the wrap," I said to her.

She looked at me with an expression of annoyance, having just wrapped the wound by running the bandage all the way around the man's torso. She quickly complied, however, and undid her work. When the last of the wrapping and the poultice pack was removed, the wound stood gaping before me. It was in-between his lower ribs on the right side of his chest and had the appearance of a stab wound. The wound was too large to have been caused by a knife or a sword, though. A spear must have caused this, I thought; a spear not unlike the one now disguised as my Druid staff—a soldier's spear. My heart raced as I stared at the wound. It was oddly familiar. The wound itself was festered, and the ridges of curled back skin around the opening were inflamed and pussey. I looked into the man's eyes. It was then that I realized who he was: Tremel, Nimue's father. I looked at Nimue kneeling next to him. "Help him, Myrriddin. Help them all," she said.

I simply nodded. There was nothing else to say. Looking at Tremel, I saw fatigue in his face and fear in his eyes. He stared at the staff, the glowing crystal. "Fear not," I said gently. "Lie back."

"Do as he says, Tremel, please," Nimue begged, the girl within the woman peeking out.

Tremel did as he was bade, relaxing on his back as best he could on the hard ground.

"Breathe deep and steady," I instructed.

He winced at first with the painful effort of simply breathing, but quickly settled into a steady, slow rhythm. Breath; life's essence. I too breathed deep and steady, but focused on the Druid Egg and the spear blade behind it, fusing with it in my mind. It started as a tingling in the hand that held the staff, but quickly became a constant charged vibration, as if a bolt of lightening were coming from the Universe, entering my body and the staff and collecting, converging in the blade, and especially the Druid Egg. It pulsated with a bright green-blue light. Several people nearby gasped at the sight. Slowly, reverently, I placed the cage of the staff directly on the wound. Then something amazing took place. The light that had been pulsating around the crystal and blade became more intense; then bent and streamed into the wound. I closed my eyes then and saw in my mind the wound being cleaned by the light, bathed in its healing power, and closing in an instant as if the wound had never happened. This final image had no sooner solidified itself in my mind than I felt the vibrating of the spear cease; the electrical charge disseminate. I opened my eyes and the light of the Druid Egg and blade were gone. But most importantly, the wound on Tremel's chest was completely sealed and healed. Only a pink line remained.

"By the God!" whispered someone nearby.

"How do you feel, Tremel?" I asked.

He thought for a moment, a look of astonishment and peace intermingling on the features of his face. "Hale and fit," he finally said. "As if something evil has been sucked from me."

A man hobbled toward me from behind Tremel. He hobbled because he was aiding a woman to walk. Blood seeped from a gash on her head and her eyes had the look of the walking dead. He stopped before me, holding his charge on her feet with great effort. He did not appear to be injured. But he did seem both fatigued beyond human limits and desperately sad. He looked at the woman he held, a comely lady of perhaps thirty odd summers – the same in years as he appeared to be – and then to me. Tears brimmed his eyes. "Some say ye be a Master Druid, a sorcerer of the Old Ways. Some say ye be a wizard that practices the arts of magic. Some even say ye be a priest of the new religion of the Christ," he said as he looked at my Druid staff, his eyes narrowing to see the spear blade within, I was sure. "But use the truth of Druids to wield great power. I care not what ye be. Do for my wife what ye did for Tremel. Please, my lord." His hold on his emotions broke. The man began sobbing as an infant. Two other men and Nimue jumped to their feet to steady the man, Nimue holding the woman, as the sobbing man nearly crumpled to his knees.

My heart and spirit went out to the couple and I motioned for Nimue to gently lay the woman down.

Darkness had long since descended by the time I finished treating those on the plateau. With each ailing survivor that I treated, the next healed even faster. It was a testament to the fact that their belief in the success of the treatment—whether they called it magic or not—was helping to dispel the glamour and heal them properly; as much, if not more than anything I was doing. Sprits had been raised; some even ventured forth to find kindling and wood to create a fire in the cold pit. Two of the men even brought back fresh water and venison—a feast compared to the paltry diet of roots and nuts they had been subsisting on for over half-a-moon's cycle. I was leery of starting a fire in the pit; didn't want to give away our position. But Baldua pointed out that there were only two ways to get to the top of this plateau: the way we had come and an even narrower passageway on the opposite end of the plateau.

"Two men could defend this place if need be," Baldua said. "Come, Myrriddin. We've all been through much and we've all been healed, including yourself. A decent meal and a warm fire is not too much for tonight."

I found myself reaching beneath my tunic to feel my own wounds. Each area where the arrows had penetrated was naught but a puckered scar; otherwise completely healed. They had not been so upon leaving the Bishop's camp. The only explanation that came to me was that the aid I had performed on the others had been instantly returned to me many fold.

"Praeterea, mihi amice(Besides, my friend), it's clear we've not been pursued," Baldua continued.

"Yes, but why not? is the question. And we still don't know why Father Pretorius was at the Bishop's camp," I said.

"You did not find out from Moscastan?"

"He alluded to something, but wouldn't complete the thought," I replied.

"Odd that. That Pretorius was there is what I mean."

"Odd too, that Bishop Rozinus did not pursue us once he saw I'd gone. He wants the spear, you know," I pointed out, needlessly.

Baldua smiled. "What spear? I see naught but a Druid's staff!"

"Yes, well, the Bishop will see through that," I said.

We stood in relative silence for a moment. Laughter came from nearby, near the fire pit which was joyously being prepared for night's fire.

"Your point is taken, Myrriddin. I'll post a man at both access points and a lookout on the walls," he stated matter-of-factly, authoritatively.

I looked at my friend quizzically. I had never seen him so serious, so commanding, so...grown up.

"Agh, now, Myrriddin! Why do you look at me so? These good folks have looked to me and Moscastan since that night. Moscastan began to take on their ailments of the

460

glamour and they looked to me for leadership. I can do it. I'm not just yer jester, don't ya know!" he finished, passionately.

"I know," I said after a moment. "I'd not be your friend if I saw naught more to you then a Latin-speaking jester," I replied sincerely.

I smelled smoke then and heard laughter from near the fire.

"Bring the meat!" said one of the men.

"Ney, let the fire burn hot first," replied another.

Both Baldua and I watched those near the fire pit ready for a meal. They appeared happy, celebratory. "I've not the heart to make three of them take watch. I'll take one," said Baldua.

"Show me the other path to this place and I'll take watch there," I said.

"No, Myrriddin. You've done enough for one day. Besides, they'll want you near. You're their...guide now, their spirit leader and healer, their shaman and, dare I say, their Merlin," my friend said.

"And what of Moscastan?" I asked. "And Pretorius?"

"Moscastan is your Mentor. He helped keep the glamour from destroying them. You took it away and healed them. Pretorius? He's become a mystery, has he not?"

Moscastan. I suddenly realized I'd not seen him since being in his shelter many hours earlier in the afternoon. "Excuse me, my friend," I said and headed for my mentor's shelter.

I crossed the short distance to the other side of the plateau, passing the fire pit on the way, which now contained a brilliant blaze.

"Hail to thee, Master Merlin! We be in yer debt forever!" called the man from earlier, whose comely wife now beamed with life and health by his side.

"Indeed!" she said in a sweet voice, tears of joy brimming her eyes. She let go of her husband as I neared and dropped to her knees before me, stopping me in my tracks.

She grabbed my free hand and kissed it. "Thank you, Lord Merlin, thank you," she said through her tears.

Of all the things I could say to her, I was about to correct her on my name; Myrridin, not Merlin, I wanted to say. But I did not. How trivial, it seemed. Myrriddin or Merlin. It, they, meant the same. "Rise," I said to her, pulling her to her feet. "You are welcome. But do not forget that you are whole again because you allowed yourself to believe you could be so," I said.

She looked confused. "I was aware of what you were doing," she said, "but...I..." she trailed off.

"Just trust that it is so," I replied.

She stood on her toes, kissed my cheek and ran back to her husband.

I smiled to myself and walked the rest of the way to see Moscastan. Three feet before his shelter, the staff in my hand began to vibrate softly, the spear's blade and Druid's Egg within, to glow softly in warning. I sensed that it was not a warning of impending hostility, though, but of something much more solemn. I didn't understand it just then. I approached the shelter's entrance and stopped before it. "Master Moscastan?" I said softly.

There was no reply.

Slowly, I poked my head in. He was lying down on a mat of straw, sleeping.

"I'll come back," I whispered, suddenly feeling foolish for saying something out loud to someone asleep. I was about to duck my head back out when the staff's subtle vibrations became more pronounced, more insistent. The Druid Egg and blade began to glow a soft, soothing white. It was then that I saw it: a misty, ethereal form floating just above Moscastan. I entered the dwelling and stood before my mentor, and the smoky substance began to take shape. Within a moment, it was in the form of a man, one that I knew—Moscastan. He, the ethereal Moscastan, floating above the physical one, appeared as aged as his counterpart on the mat. But the floating form began to change, becoming younger in appearance by the moment. Next, his face changed entirely. It changed to that of a stranger to me in this life, but one to whom I'd been close in another. This new/old face smiled at me and I recognized the toothless grin deep in my soul. "Jacobi," I said.

The form before me smiled even broader. The face then changed back to Moscastan—a young Moscastan. He looked at the aged form lying on the mat, then back to me and I understood; his mind speaking to my mind, not in words but in thought, understanding. It is simple to do, this conversing mind-to-mind, I now realized. "There is only the One Mind in which ours reside and are thus not separate, but connect points within the One Mind," Moscastan had once said. I now completely understood what he had meant. I also understood what was happening here in the dwelling. I looked down at his aged body on the mat, to his now craggy face. He had been much older than I'd ever known. Moscastan did not rest on the mat in sleep. He rested on the mat in death. And, his spirit was making the transition to the Otherworld. I suddenly found myself dropping to my knees, sad but honored to be witnessing this...event. I felt a tear roll down my cheek as I looked up at his still floating spirit. He smiled a sweet and loving smile and inclined his head toward me.

The white light from the staff suddenly brightened the entire inside of the dwelling. It became so bright that it was blinding and I had to cover my eyes. Immediately, I sensed that a doorway, a portal to the Otherworld was opening. My mind and spirit took over, aiding in thought and spirit to shoring up the portal. Connecting to the spear, my staff, I also asked for aid in this from those I sensed nearby on the Otherside. They abided and after a moment, I heard Moscastan's thoughts—in words this time—in my mind. "It is done, Myrriddin. Farewell," he said.

In an instant, I sensed the portal close and the white light dissipate. I opened my eyes. The ethereal spirit of Moscastan was gone. All was still in the dwelling, especially the now empty vassal of my mentor lying on the mat.

I sat in the shelter for quite some time, partly out of respect for my mentor; partly because of the sacredness of what I had witnessed. I felt no heaviness at Moscastan's transition to the Otherworld. A small bit of sadness, perhaps. I loved the presence of my mentor. More than his presence. The truth of it was that I loved him. Yet, he was not gone in the sense of a cessation of existence. I knew that for certain. Thus, I would be able to converse with him, feel his presence, his essence at any time. It would start in my imagination. Some may say it ends there, too. I pity those that do not know themselves and the nature of the Universe. Imagination is simply the mental imaging of Truth. I see Moscastan in my mind's eye and he is with me in truth, becomes himself to me again because it is him, his essence peeking back into this realm.

"Myrriddin? Moscastan? Is all well?" whispered Nimue from just out side the shelter.

"Aye. 'Tis well now," I replied. I leaned forward and kissed Moscastan's brow, stood and exited the shelter.

Nimue stood a few feet from the shelter silhouetted against the fire in the pit a few yards away and the light of a nearly full moon overhead. "We were beginning to wonder if something was amiss. You've been in there near four hours and..." She stopped speaking and stepped forward toward me. Though her face was still partly in shadow, I could see enough of its loveliness to tell that she was surprised by something; something she was seeing in me, for she stared directly into my eyes. She scanned my face and body. "Myrriddin," she said almost breathlessly. "There is a light that emanates from you."

I held up my free hand and saw a faint white glow surrounding it. In fact, the light was around my entire arm. It also surrounded my lower body and all parts I could see, including my staff. The blade and Druid Egg within also glowed with the white light. "So it seems," I finally said.

"What does it mean?" asked Nimue, with a touch of reverence, even awe.

"It means that Moscastan has begun his next life. It means that I aided in the opening of the portal and the perpetuation of his journey to the Otherworld. And, it means that I was truly blessed and honored to have witnessed his stepping through the veil," I said, as I felt a tear of joy mixed with sorrow slide down my cheek.

Nimue stood in front of me for a moment. Her eyes were narrowed in concentration, turning over what I had just said. Her eyes then widened in realization of what I was implying. "I thought," she began... "I thought that perhaps you and he were in meditation—that maybe you meant he was journeying out of his body to visit the Otherworld. But...you are saying that he's dead?"

"I am not saying that. But if that's how you wish to understand it, then you may speak of it so," I replied.

"Speak of what so, Myrriddin?" said my friend, Baldua. He approached from behind Nimue and came to a stop next to her. His eyes looked strangely at me. "Myrriddin, there's a light coming from you!"

"I know, Baldua."

"Your Master Moscastan has di—that is, he's left this world for the Other," she said to my friend.

It took a moment for what she was saying to come to my friend's mind. "Myrriddin. Is it true?"

"It is."

"Agh. I'm so sorry. I loved him, too, but I know how close you two had been over the years. Like father and son, yes? Though I'm not too surprised, you know. He had taken on so much since arriving here. He took on everyone's glamour, or at least as much as he could. No wonder it finally got the better of him. Still, when you got here, you and the spear, I mean your staff there," he said pointing to it in my hand, "I knew we'd all be fine and I really thought that Moscastan would be too, you know. No reason for him..."

"Would you clamp it shut, Baldua!" said Nimue. Turning to me she asked sweetly, "What can we do, Myrriddin?" I could have kissed her just then.

"What are you talking about, Nimue? He's dead, gone. What is there to be done?" Baldua asked contemptuously.

Nimue looked at my friend with daggers coming forth from her eyes. Upon seeing the look, Baldua's eyes grew wide with fear and he actually took a step back. It was all I could do not to laugh. "You cannot be that stupid, that lame, that numb in the brain. No, no! Perhaps you really can be. I was asking what we could do for Myrriddin, idiot!" Nimue spat.

"I am fine," I declared, taking the attention and wrath off of my friend. "I should like to cremate Master Druid Moscastan's remains in the way of our people, in the way of the Druids. However, I don't think we should do it here. I would like to say a few more incantations and prayers of blessing the spirit, though, before I wrap his body."

"Maybe the Priest can help. They were friends, were they not?" asked Baldua.

"What say you, Baldua?" I asked, the white light around my body suddenly dissipating. At the same instant, the staff began to vibrate in my hand and an uneasy feeling washed over me.

"Father Pretorius. He's at the fire pit. He just arrived."

"Just arrived? I thought you posted guards," I said more harshly than I intended.

"I did, Myrriddin. Why do you question me thus? The priest is known, was a friend to Moscastan. The guards let him through," Baldua answered, clearly offended at my tone.

I put up a hand, palm facing my friend in a gesture of apology. "Has he said why he was in the Bishop's camp?" I asked, calmly.

"Ney. As I said, he just arrived. He simply asked for you and Moscastan," Baldua replied.

I made to step around Nimue and Baldua; to immediately go to the fire pit.

"Wait!" cried Baldua.

I stopped and turned to my friend.

Baldua pointed to the shelter. "You can't leave the dead in there," he declared nervously.

"Why?" I asked. "Do you fear he'll walk away?" I turned again and resumed my short trek to the fire pit, stifling a small laugh at my friend's obvious discomfort over leaving Moscastan's remains for the moment.

I could smell the roasted meat as I approached the fire. The people had obviously cooked most of the venison hours earlier, but more was roasting on the spit. My mouth watered. I realized I could not remember when I'd eaten last. My stomach growled. I was famished. Yet my body's needs would have to wait. Everyone around the fire pit was standing, listening to Father Pretorius and another man. The other man was Tremel.

"Here, now. Myrriddin! See who's returned," said Tremel as I approached. He turned back to the priest. "Not seen him since that night," he said to Pretorius, clearly referring to the night of All Hallow's Eve.

"Come to think of it, I don't recall seeing you that night at all, Father," I said, as several folks stepped aside so that I could come to stand before the two men.

"Myrriddin, my son. 'Tis good to see you," Pretorius said with affection, ignoring my last comment. I searched his face, looking into his eyes for any sign of what Moscastan had alluded to. All I could see, at least for the moment, was a sincere man of the Church.

He stepped forward and embraced me as a long-lost family member. I returned his embrace as far as courtesy dictated, patting him on the back with my free hand. We parted from our embrace and stood at arm's length from one another, Father Pretorius eying my Druid's staff ever so subtly.

"You look and sound well, Myrriddin," he said.

"I am," I responded.

"The good folks have been telling me of your blessed work here. You're an Angel in Druid's garb, lad," Pretorius said.

I am a Druid, Father," I said, haughtily.

"Indeed, indeed. A true Merlin, I know. You may call it what you will, but it is God working through you and your instrument said Pretorius, pointing at my staff.

"And through Moscastan," Tremel added.

"Yes, yes!" said Pretorius. "Where is my friend?!" Pretorius said this last part with such genuine love, that, for the moment at least, I brushed aside any concerns Moscastan may have harbored about him.

"He...he..." I found myself stuttering as Igraines might do, all eyes present suddenly boring into me. Perhaps I was conveying the impending news with my tone of voice or a look in my eyes. But everyone present seemed to suddenly have the posture and bearing of one about to receive a blow. "He, Master Moscastan, is no longer here. He has left his body and crossed over to the Otherside," I said.

Several of those present gasped loudly in shock. Father Pretorius looked sadly at me for a moment. Then, to my surprise, he dropped to his knees. Many others followed his lead, going to their knees as well. "Come, Myrriddin. Please join me in prayer," the priest said.

I looked at all present. Roughly half had taken to one knee or both. Baldua and Nimue had rejoined the group, standing near and behind me.

"Come, Myrriddin," Pretorius said again. In the end, we will honor him in any way you see fit. But please allow me to, and join with me in, honoring him in my way for now. He would have liked this, I believe."

Would he? I wondered. In the end, he suspected you of something, he did. "Yes, Father," I found myself saying, "I believe you are right." I took a knee myself and looked back at Nimue and Baldua. They also dropped to a knee, as did the remainder of those who stood.

"Requiem aeternam donna ei, Domine; et..." Father Pretorius began his prayer in Latin. Baldua must be loving this, I thought.

We knelt in prayer for a few moments. Afterwards, several of the people came to me offering condolences, some even in tears. Tremel was one of them.

"Pretorius I've known for some time. Moscastan not as long at all," Tremel began through now controlled emotion. "But I knew his soul. I could tell, knew him for many lifetimes." He paused and turned to the priest. "Sorry, Father. Much of the old ways still live in me."

Pretorius simply smiled and waved a hand. No apology necessary, he seemed to be saying.

"Thank you, Tremel," I said.

"How did he pass, Myrriddin?" Pretorius asked.

"Peacefully," I replied. "He had assumed much of the evil that had been placed on these folks by Creconius," I stated flatly, looking directly into Pretorius' eyes for any sign of... For a brief instant, I could swear a veil behind those eyes dropped and went back up. In that same moment, the staff vibrated in my hand. Both things could have simply been tricks of my mind. But my intuition said otherwise.

"Yes. Taking the sins of another can be dangerous. It is a loving, Godly gesture, but fraught with danger," said Pretorius.

"What sins? I've not heard you talk of sins before. What so-called sins these people had were thrust upon them by another!" I was practically yelling at him.

"Myrriddin," Nimue said, as she touched my arm to calm me.

"That is all I meant, my son," said Pretorius.

An awkward silence filled the space for a moment.

"If you'll allow me, I would be honored if I could prepare his body with you," Pretorius continued. "I assume you wish him cremated in the way of your Druids."

"Yes," I said, "to both points. Come," I turned and headed to Moscastan's shelter.

~XIX~

We cremated Moscastan's remains at dawn. We did not use the fire pit, but instead built a pyre not far from it. The burning of his corpse took the better part of the day. What bones remained, I would take with me, I decided. I would inter them in the perfect place: the Crystal Sanctuary. Many prayers were said through the day. Many condolences offered. The people had come to know my mentor and to love him.

Pretorius had insisted that it would be safe to hold the cremation there on the plateau. He had been in Bishop Rozinus' camp to secure my freedom, or so he claimed. When the Bishop discovered I had escaped – with the spear – he had, of course, insisted on giving chase. Pretorius pointed the good Bishop and his men in the wrong direction. He had evidently witnessed our escape as we headed into the forest. He'd lied to protect us: myself and those on the plateau. "'Twas a lie for the greater good and God has already forgiven me," the priest had said. The Bishop broke camp and left. I had no doubt that once his scouts confirmed there was no trail of us in the direction they were told, they would double back to find our real trail.

Pretorius' story was quite plausible. Others who were within earshot of hearing it praised Pretorius as a brave hero. I, however, had my doubts. His story did not explain where he had been for the fortnight-plus since the night of the Rite. When I asked, he dismissively said, "Why, I was there in or near the Bishop's camp. You were too injured to recall, Myrriddin." I mulled over in my head what Moscastan had said, which, in the end, was not very substantial.

That night, after Moscastan's cremation, we all communed over an evening meal. It was decided that come the following morning's light, we would leave our plateau and each head for his or her respective home. I'd not had the chance to talk to Nimue alone. The thought of parting ways with her was weighing heavily on me. I wanted to go to the Crystal Sanctuary and lay to rest the bones of my mentor, but was unsure if Nimue would go with her father to their home or come with me, were I to dare ask.

Tremel, Pretorius and several others had retired to a far end of the plateau for the night, away from the fire pit which still contained a small blaze within. Baldua, Nimue and I sat alone near the pit. I was about to ask Nimue to walk with me so that I might discern her plans when Baldua spoke with whispered urgency. "The priest Pretorius wishes to come with us, Myrriddin. He wants to see your cave of crystals." There was an edge to my friend's voice that disturbed me.

"Why?" I asked. "Why would he?" I thought for a moment.

"Obviously, he and Moscastan were close. I could see that when they both held vespers with Tremel," Nimue put in, as if it were plain to see.

"Perhaps, but I think there's more to it," I said.

"What?" asked Baldua.

"I know you don't like these men of Christ, Baldua," interjected Nimue, "but this one is open to our Old ways unlike most of the others I've met."

"Is he? Is he really? Or is it all an act, a ruse? Is he even of the followers of Christ?" I said.

"Yes, he's a man of the Christ and yes, he's open to our ways," Nimue said defensively. "He was at the rite of All Hallow's Eve, was he not?"

"I never saw him," I countered. "Did you?"

She thought for a moment. "No, but he had to have been. He came with you, after all."

I turned to Baldua. "Did you?"

My friend shook his head indicating that he had not. "What are you saying, Myrriddin?" Baldua whispered conspiratorially.

It all struck me then exactly what Moscastan had been implying. I supposed I'd realized it when Moscastan said the words, but somewhere in my mind, deemed it impossible. Not anymore. I told them what my mentor had said in the shelter after telling him of the glam we'd witnessed at Rozinus' camp: how Creconius' glamour dropped and the sorceress Mab stood before us, attempting to wield the sacred sword forged at the lake whose powers had been sealed into the weapon by her own sister. I then told them of the line of questioning Moscastan had convened upon me and its implication.

Baldua and Nimue sat in stunned silence for a moment.

"Impossible, Myrriddin!" Baldua finally blurted out. "Impossible!"

"And why?" asked Nimue.

"Yes, why? Why would he or she appear as an enemy's leader on a battle filed, then capture me, have his men do unspeakable things to me, then appear to you as a priest, even helping to bury the dead in the Christian way? Not to mention visiting Nimue's people here on numerous occasions as that same priest. It makes no sense! Don't you think I'd be able to look into those eyes of the priest and see the evil one behind them; the one who did those things to me?" Baldua's passion was laced with intense anger. He obviously had not completely released the tragic events that had befallen him, nor forgiven the one responsible.

"No," I said simply, gently. "That is the whole purpose of a glamour—to deceive the perceiver of a reality by creating a false one. A master at it will leave no doubt in your mind as to the truth of what you're seeing, even though it's not the truth at all. You saw Moscastan's dead face. He was in truth decades older at his death than he ever appeared to us in life every day. Death dropped his glamour of youth for good," I said.

"Yes, but we always knew it was Moscastan," he retorted. "This, what you're saying about Creconius and Pretorius, it's not possible."

472

"Nothing is impossible within the One. No application of Its Laws is out of bounds for someone who knows how to use them. No matter how twisted and disturbing you may think the application is, there is no judgment within the One. Its laws know only to respond," I concluded.

After a moment, Baldua rose. "No. It's not possible. I concede that you know more of these matters than ever I'll understand, Myrriddin. But this is too much," he said, leaving Nimue and me alone by the fire.

And you, Nimue?" I asked.

"My head holds with Baldua's argument. But my heart holds with what you say, Myrriddin. I've always thought Pretorius was a good man. He visited us often, never really pressuring Tremel or our people to follow his Christ," she said. "But I always sensed something else there, some other reason for him to take interest in us."

"What will you do tomorrow, Nimue?" I asked, completely changing the subject.

"Do?" she asked, confused.

"I...will you go with Tremel?" I asked, feeling sheepish.

She laughed. A sweet laugh, but indiscernible. "Why, Myrriddin?"

I felt myself squirm with discomfort on the inside. On the outside, though, I remained rigid, giving nothing away; nothing of my inner discomfort.

"Well, Master Myrriddin," she began, "I'm not sure I want to be married to a powerful Merlin."

Married! I thought. I'd said nothing of marriage.

"Although I would like to see your home, this Crystal Sanctuary," she said, straight of face so that I could not tell how serious she was.

"It's Moscastan's Crystal Sancturary, not mine," I said lamely.

"It is yours now, Myrriddin, and you know it," she stated flatly.

"Marriage," I said under my breath.

"Please, Myrriddin. I'm teasing you," she said. She then placed a hand on my hand, the one that was resting on my staff. "I go with Tremel. He will want to be with our people at least for a time. Then, perhaps in the spring, if you wish it still, I will come to you."

"And how will you know if I wish it still?" I asked.

She smiled seductively and leaned in toward my face. "You are the Great Merlin. Come to me in my dreams and tell me." She kissed me then, passionately. I returned her kiss equally. We embraced as our mouths continued to explore one another's, promising a future—a tender, yet solid time of oneness. I lost track of time as we slipped into the shadow of the plateau and quietly, feverently made love.

At our parting the next morning, Tremel's people treated me with the deference and respect of a High Druid and Priest, bowing low before me. Two women even tried to kiss my feet, groveling on the ground in front of me. I would have none of it. "Please," I said as I bent down to them, helping each in turn to her feet. "I can't abide being worshipped," I said.

"You are a great Merlin and are due the respect of one so connected with the gods," said one of them: a thin, wide-eyed, toothless lady of perhaps forty summers.

"Aye, or God himself," said the other woman, a doe-eyed, younger version of the first. "My mother sees through the eyes of the Old Ways, I through those of the New, True Path," she added. "You are God's servant."

"Indeed," I replied.

"We are all servants of the One," Pretorius said. He stood behind me, along with Baldua. The two women bowed their heads and retreated back to Tremel, who stood a few feet away with some others, including Nimue. I caught Nimue's eye. She smiled radiantly. We had said our farewells the previous night, but it was not goodbye. I knew in my heart, my soul, that we would not only see each other again, but be together in a more profound and permanent sense.

Baldua, Pretorius and I had hastily made—one for each of us and with the help of Nimue and a few others—a small pack from skins and woven plants in which to carry cooked venison for our journey. I had made mine slightly larger to also carry Moscastan's wrapped bones, which included his charred skull. I considered the carrying of his bones to rest in the Crystal Sanctuary a pilgrimage.

Just before we set out, I felt the staff vibrate in my hand. I realized instantly what it meant; the way we were to go. It began to pull, more of its own accord, pointing toward a specific region of the forest nearby. I asked Tremel and he confirmed what the staff was conveying. "Yes, yes!" he declared excitedly, as he watched the staff point the way. "It speaks true! You will recognize the way once you're on the other side of the forest. I know Pretorius will."

And so we parted, leaving the safety of the plateau, Tremel, Nimue and the remainder of their people going off in one direction; Baldua, Pretorius, I and the remainder of my mentor's bones going off in another.

We had been traveling down a path, walking a slow pace through the dark forest for some eight hours. The staff had been silent and still since we had entered the forest, which I interpreted as a sign that we were at least going in the right direction. But I had yet to recognize any part of the forest as being from our initial journey to the place of the All Hallow's Eve rite or my flight from Bishop Rozinus' camp. Pretorius had been leading the way when the path we were on came to a fork. He went down the left fork without even breaking stride. Though Pretorius could not see it, the staff began to vibrate the moment I set foot on the path that went left. I stopped immediately. "Wait," I said. Baldua stopped alongside me. Pretorius stopped as well, though he was some fifteen feet ahead of us on this new path. "I don't think this is the way," I declared.

"Come, Myrriddin," exclaimed Pretorius. "Do you not see the burned out crooked oak there?" he said, pointing to a huge oak up and off the path. The large tree's trunk was bent at about four feet off the ground and much of the remainder of it had grown parallel to the ground for some twenty-five yards before bending skyward again. It obviously had been there for decades if not centuries, such was its girth, length and proliferation of branches. Yet, its branches were now barren, its core-body split and blackened and charred from an ancient lightening strike by the look of it. Though its surroundings were plush with life, the tree was dead. Long dead. The sight of it made me sad, for it clearly had been something majestic to behold when alive. This feeling also made me realize that I certainly would have remembered seeing this tree previously, which was obviously what Pretorius was implying by pointing it out. Baldua and I exchanged a look. I cocked an eyebrow, silently questioning him. He shook his head and turned back to Pretorius.

"I have never seen that, beate pater (my good Father)," said Baldua, the latter part in Latin.

"Nor have I," I said. "I would have remembered it."

"Agh. No matter. I do. Follow me, lads," the priest said, as he started down the path once more.

It began as a warmth, as if I held a pole that had been placed in proximity to a blazing hearth, but not in the fire itself. It rapidly changed, though, becoming so hot that I nearly let go of it—my staff.

"Wait!" I called to Pretorius. He was already some ten feet farther down the path. He halted and walked slowly back toward us, stopping directly in front of me. For a brief instant, an uncharacteristic gleam of anger flashed in his eyes.

Before I could respond to Pretorius, however, my staff's Druid Egg began to glow, pulsating on one side only. Intuitively, I knew what it meant, for the side it glowed on was nearest the other path, the other fork in the trail we had been on. The heat of the staff became more intense and the staff began to pull me toward the other path. As I walked in that direction, the heat and the glow lessened the closer I got to the other path. Upon setting my foot on that path, the glow and heat ceased altogether.

Baldua came up behind me, Pretorius behind him. "This is the correct path," I declared.

Baldua turned to Pretorius. "So much for your crooked tree, Priest," he said.

Pretorius said nothing, but looked from my staff, the spear, to me.

"You can go where you will, Father," Baldua continued. "Myrriddin and I go down this path." He pushed past me and walked down the new path.

I stared at Pretorius for a moment. There had been a shift in his persona these past days. But I still could not fully tell what it was, which either meant that I was wrong or that he was hiding it well. I would stay vigilant and observe. For the moment, however, I followed my friend down this new path. An instant later, I heard Pretorius' footfalls behind me. He had decided to stay with us, after all.

Darkness came early. We did not make it through the forest that day as I had hoped we would. I even began to doubt the path we were on. But the spear had pulsated often, and in a beautiful green hue, conveying the fact that we were indeed on the right path, or so my intuition told me. So, I put my momentary doubts aside. What did it matter if we were not through the forest in one day?

"We need to make camp. It's too dark for trudging any farther," said Pretorius. "We might have been through by now, but such is not the way of it."

I could not tell if his comment was a slight on me or if he actually believed the other path was the one we should have taken and was simply voicing a perceived fact. I chose, for the moment, the latter, but made remembrance of the former. It would be yet another indication of his shift in persona if true. Pretorius was not one to reprimand – at least not the Pretorius I thought I knew. Perhaps I was looking for signs from the priest of what Moscastan had suspected. The problem with looking for signs is that we often end up seeing what we wish, regardless of what's actually there. "Pretorius is right, Myrriddin," put in Baldua.

"Yes," I agreed. A thin group of trees was off the path to our right. Odd that, for the forest to this point had been immensely thick with all kinds of oak, saplings and rowans in extreme proximity. Each tree in this thin group of trees had many feet between them, and, in fact, were spaced in apparent perfect symmetry from each other, in a circle shape. The trees in this group, some twenty odd, seemed to have grown stunted—most only fifteen feet or so high—and with branches stripped of most of their leafy foliage. Looking up, I could see that the higher branches of the taller trees which surrounded this smaller group had grown over the tops of the small group, creating a canopy, a roof over the grouping of trees. We stopped on the path, Pretorius and Baldua halting next to me on either side. I stared at the small, thin group of trees, debating with myself as to whether we should make camp in their presence. And then it came to me as to what I was looking at. At the same moment of my realization, the staff vibrated in my hand and the Druid Egg glowed bright green. And then an amazing thing happened: the ring of small trees—for that is what it was, a ring of trees, I saw that now—began to glow the same hue of green as the Druid egg, as if in empathetic harmony with my staff, my spear and the attached Druid Egg.

"Diis!(By the gods)!" exclaimed Baldua. It was a beautiful sight; the ring of trees glowed as if...as if...Of course! I thought. I had realized a moment before that this was a naturally formed – more or less – temple ring of standing monoliths, like the standing stones built across the land and the one that Moscastan had brought me back to life in. This one, this Henge, however, was made of wood, of living trees. But more than that, I suddenly realized the singular power in this place: it was a portal, perhaps a focal point, for the divine energy of the Universe. I was enthralled with the prospect of spending the night in this place.

"We can't stay here, Myrriddin," said Pretorius, contemptuously. "Surely, we cannot, if you were thinking of it, that is."

Pretorius was standing on my left. When I turned to look at him, I was facing away from the forest henge. But in the darkening forest, the glow was visible in the eyes of the priest, reflecting therein. The reflected glow in his eyes helped to reveal something. There, behind Pretorius' eyes, hiding, was an Otherworldy malevolent rage. Pretorius was indeed the priest I had known for a time, but he was apparently more than that now. I cold see it, sense it. It was not that Pretorius was someone other than whom I knew, or Moscastan had known; it was that someone or something else was in his being, as well. This other thing looked out at me and suddenly, the staff in my hand grew hot as if also sensing the malevolence within the priest. As if knowing I could see it, the thing within Pretorius suddenly retreated. I could see it, sense it no more. The staff in my hand stilled and cooled, and the glow thereon dimmed. So, too, did the glow of the Henge.

"We will stay here tonight, Father Pretorius," I said gently. "There is nothing harmful here, save for a few creatures of the forest."

Pretorius inclined his head in acquiescence, all of his contemptuousness gone. "As you wish," he said.

"Here, now," said Baldua, "Have I no say?"

"You just said that we should stop and make camp, did you not?" I pointed out.

"Yes, yes I did," he said. Baldua looked at the henge off the path. "Bonum est('Tis good). This spot will do nicely," he declared with dramatic flair.

"Thank you. I'm glad you approve," I said, patting my friend on the shoulder as I moved past him toward the Henge.

It took us a few moments to find a suitable spot on which to settle; far enough off the path for us to be away from possible prying eyes, yet not so far away that we couldn't see the path. Though the Henge we all saw was directly off the trail, there were actually two more of the same dimensions farther in off the path just beyond the first one. It was in the center of the third one that we chose to stay the night.

"I see need of a fire. 'Tis a bit brisk tonight," said Pretorius. His demeanor was odd; nervousness seeped through his words.

"If Bishop Rozinus' men are about..." I started.

"I doubt that very much, Myrriddin," he said with a little more authority; even too much.

Still, there was indeed a chill in the air. "Of course," I said.

"I'll get some kindling," offered Baldua.

"Ney, lad. I will." With that, Pretorius left hastily.

"He's become a strange one at times," observed Baldua.

"You don't know the half of it," I said.

Baldua looked at me intently. "You're not on with that again, Myrriddin?"

"Aye. Only it's not what I thought."

"Good."

"It's worse," I said.

My friend sat on the ground heavily and drew a skin from his pack. He uncorked one end and drank a strong draught, satiating the days' travel with the water in the skin. I followed his lead, sitting next to him and withdrawing my own water skin. After a long pull of drink, we sat in silence for a moment, the sounds of small, nocturnal forest creatures coming to life around us.

"So tell me, Myrriddin, what is the priest about?" asked Baldua, smugly. "I don't hold with his condescending Christian ways, but he is not so bad. He's become a little strange at times, yes, but..." he trailed off.

"You're right," I began. "Pretorius the man is not a bad seed. I believe that. And, I also believe that he exemplifies his Christian beliefs truly and honorably, not like some of the other rules-ridden, power-devouring priests and leaders of his faith I've come across. But there is something else there, something else within him, using him."

"Ach," my friend said, disbelieving. "To what end?"

"To get the spear, most likely," I answered.

"I could think of a bushel of other ways to get the thing," he said.

The sounds of the night forest coming to life abruptly stopped. The ringing in my ears told of the utter silence that now engulfed us. Usually oblivious to such things, even Baldua noticed the change. He looked at me, questioning me with his eyes, thus echoing the preternatural quietude we were now in. The staff's Druid Egg and blade suddenly came to life, pulsating a vibrant red-green light.

"Prepare yourself," whispered a man's voice urgently. It came from the staff, the spear. "Prepare yourself."

Looking at Baldua, it was clear he had not heard the voice. It was meant for me.

The first scream came from the edge of the Henge we were in: the edge farthest from the path. It was an agonized, terror-filled female wail to freeze the blood. No sooner had that one died out, then another took its place. This one, however, seemed to come from even deeper in the forest and was clearly male, although it had the same desperate, horrified quality as the first. It subsided and the first voice screamed again, this time from a different location, some twenty feet closer to our position, though still in the tree line outside the Henge and thus its source remained unseen.

"Forest demons!" Baldua cried, jumping to his feet, brandishing from beneath his tunic a new-looking Roman gladius. It was obviously a souvenir he had kept from his borrowed legionnaires uniform.

I too, rose, to my feet, the staff in my hand, its Egg and spear's blade glowing more intensely by the moment. "Doubtful your short sword will do much good then," I said. "Against humans, maybe, but..."

My words were cut short by yet another scream coming from still another part of the forest. They seemed to be coming from everywhere, the screams. They were agitating Baldua, who spun toward the sound of each scream in turn apparently expecting to see some horrific sight, which was not to be seen.

I, on the other hand, became calmer with each scream. I felt myself ease into a confident centeredness wherein I could and would deal with anything that might come, and deal with it triumphantly.

"Show yourselves!" my friend yelled into the darkness.

"Peace, Baldua," I said calmly.

A red flash came from where the first scream had seemed to emanate. The flash came hurling toward us in the form of a ball of light, screaming a feral, Otherworldly sound of terror. Baldua and I both ducked as the thing swooshed violently through where we had both been standing, arching away and back into the forest. An instant later, another screaming, angry ball of red-light came flying at us. Each time, we ducked or rolled out of the way. Baldua, caught standing at the last assault, deflected the ball with the flat of his sword, sending it spinning violently out of control through nearby trees. It smashed into the trunk of a mighty oak, exploding on impact. I expected small fires to break out from all the sparks that the explosion had produced, but the sparks and remnants of the ball dissolved on the ground and in the trunk – where some had become embedded – and disappeared entirely. With that, the assault halted, at least for the moment.

"Forest demons, I say again. They don't want us here. Maybe the priest was right," my friend said, more with anger than fear.

"I've never known you to believe in the likes of 'forest demons,'" I pointed out, "let alone anything Pretorius had to say."

"Yes. Well, we all change, do we not?"

"You speak as if you're surrendering to that which you despise," I said.

"Sometimes surrender is the best option," countered Baldua.

"Surrendering your stubbornness, yes. But surrender at the sacrifice of your spirit is foolish. The latter is what I am hearing from you, my friend," I pointed.

Baldua stared at me for a moment. "I hardly think this is the moment for a Moscastan-like discourse on the advancement of one's spirit," he said.

"Moscastan-like or no, shouldn't every moment be an opportunity for learning?" I countered.

"Agh! By the gods, Merlin!"

I opened my mouth to speak, but Baldua was not through.

"I know, I know. Myrriddin. Not Merlin!"

"It matters not, Baldua," I said.

I then turned my attention back toward the origins of our attack. "'Tis not demons coming against us, trying to drive us out."

"Are you mad? They've thrown those...things at us from all over!" said Baldua, getting agitated once again and flailing his hand in the direction from whence the objects came.

"Trust me, my friend. It is not a handful of demons. It is but one individual and it is not just trying to drive us away, but to kill us," I said. I knew this to be so—in my very soul. The words from the spear came to me once again: "Prepare yourself." Indeed, I had never felt so prepared for anything as I did that moment, though I knew not exactly what was to come. All my training in the Druidic Arts; all my mentor's years of patient tutoring, and above all, the molding and connecting I now solidly felt to the spear of Longinus, my Druid staff. All these things suddenly culminated in that moment within me. In that instant, my understanding and awareness of the All and my Self, my Spirit, transcended everything of this world. I truly knew what the Christ meant when he had said, "I am in this world, but not of this world," as I had been told by various followers of this Christ I'd met through the years. I also realized now that most of them did not fully understand the words; did not completely embody them.

"You see?" Baldua proclaimed nearly shouting and snapping me out of my moment of profundity. "You said 'it.' Is that not a demon, then?"

"Fine," I said. "She and he, if you prefer. Creconius Mab."

Then came a rumble. It started low. We could barely hear it. But we felt it beneath our feet; the earth shook. The shaking grew strong, knocking us both to the ground. The Druid Egg and spear blade grew fiery red. So bright did they become that I momentarily thought they would burst. They did not. But the mighty oak that the last ball of light had smashed into did burst. It rent asunder with such violence, such force, that its great trunk split in two, smoke and fire spewing forth. The crack and groan of timber splitting was deafening, and the booming crash of the two halves of the trunk hitting the ground shook the earth with one giant jolt. Then, all was still, save the tall figure standing in the middle of the split and now dead mighty oak.

~XX~

"Who dares summon me?" demanded the loud, thunderous voice from the figure in the split tree: Creconius Mab in his imposing warrior form. He appeared much as he did the day I first saw him on the battle filed, save now, he was cloaked in an Otherwordly glow of red-menace.

"Shite. Him again," sighed Baldua.

"Merlin," said the figure, all but ignoring Baldua. "Your legend grows. As does the fable of your...wizard's staff."

"Druid's staff, is more the like," I said.

"The spear of Longinus is more the like," he countered. "That which pierced His side. Carries His power, much like this!" From the folds of his cloak, he withdrew the long sword he possessed that day in Bishop Rozinus' camp. It was magnificent, even more so this time than when first I saw it; the runes along the blade, the quality of the blade itself, the glow. It glowed green. As it did, the Druid Egg and blade of my staff, the spear of Longinus, began to glow green as well, changing from the angry red in a heartbeat. It, they, were glowing in harmony – the spear and extraordinary sword. For a moment, it had me in a trance state. The staff in my hand vibrated softly, bringing me back to the present. After a moment, the vibration ceased, but its green glow continued in harmony with the sword's. "You see? They belong together— the sword, the spear. Together, their owner would be invincible!" Creconius said, an evil glint in his eyes.

My mind began to see the truth of this moment, of what the figure before me was saying. "No one can own these instruments, Creconius Mab. They hold no power in themselves other than what we endow them with. One need only be in harmony with them, in mental equivalence of the desired effect. You do not have the proper mind to ever attune with the sword or the spear," I said, not quite knowing from whence the words came.

Something in what I said, however, hit this sorcerer, (or sorceress) hard. Anger seethed from his being, contorting his face in rigid rage.

"No one summoned you, Creconius Mab. No one cares that much," I said. "You came of your own accord. Now, be gone!" I yelled, glamming my voice with power beyond this world. I intoned the last word with a deep note, sustaining it with this power and thus releasing the power through it. The sound reverberated off all the trees that surrounded us, shaking their limbs. Even some of the clothes on our intruder's body jumped suddenly as if struck by a gale force. And, I saw, out of the corner of my eye, Baldua throw his hands up to his ears, so power-filled was the sound of my voice.

At the apex of the sustained sound, I raised the staff over my head. In my mind's eye, I saw a bolt of light shoot forth from the spear's blade and the Druid Egg. It was so intensely real that I felt its reality course through my entire being. Then it happened: it happened in actuality. A crisp and powerful bolt of the green light shot forth from the spear's blade and Druid Egg. The force of it nearly knocked me down. The bolt shot out and violently connected with the sword's blade, creating an arc of immense force and power.

It held fast, this arc. I held it with great intent in my mind at the exclusion of all else, and it was so in the real world. The sound of my voice faded to be replaced by the crackling and humming sound of an electrical charge in the air.

"Aghh!" yelled Creconius Mab, thus adding his voice to the sound of the charge. He agonized to break the arc, to break the hold. The effort was draining his being of vital energy, his very life spirit. Or, perhaps I should say her; for the glamour of Creconius, the warrior, began to drop. In a pulsating torrent of light and darkness, the true person was revealed beneath the façade: Mab. Finally, the glamour of the warrior faded completely; the arc too, the latter ceasing completely. A preternatural silence filled the forest. Next to me, Baldua rose to his feet.

The figure in the tree before us was a pitiful sight: a small, aged, haggard female figure who dropped the great sword's point into the ground and leaned on its still glowing hilt—which nearly came up to the top of her head—panting like a fatigued animal.

"Well done, Myrriddin!" exclaimed Baldua in a hushed voice.

"'Tis not over yet," I said, giving voice to the feeling of unease that had begun to crawl into my being.

Ignoring what I had just said, Baldua took a step toward the figure in the split tree. "We must take the sword!" he said, with childlike glee.

"No, Baldua!" But my warning was too late. With the speed of a coiled serpent, the crone Mab struck. The great sword came up in a burst of blinding red light, striking my friend broadside in the side of his chest – at least from what I could see. So bright was the moment of impact that for an instant, I covered my eyes. When I uncovered them, the bright light was gone. And, so was my friend. Baldua had disappeared.

A strange sound: a low-level cackle, a malevolent laugh, came from the ugly figure who now stood outside the split oak, near the spot where Baldua had been a moment earlier. Once again, she leaned on the still-glowing hilt of the great sword, whose tip was presently in the ground by some six inches. Except for the glow of the sword hilt, darkness surrounded me, and in more ways than one. The cackle sent chills through my body, but I quickly quashed the feeling, consciously replacing it with the intent of ending this absurd being's menace. I'd had enough. Baldua, my dearest friend was gone, presumably obliterated from the earth. Rage, mixed with the worst sorrow, began to rise within me.

"Be still, Myrriddin," said the voice of the spear. "Be still and know the Oneness of All. You can no more destroy the one before you than you can destroy yourself," It said.

"Sooo..." hissed Mab. "It speaks to you. Yes? I knew it. Your eyes betrayed you just now. It speaks to you, but you don't know its full potential or how to use it completely. Is that not so?"

"This...staff is a part of me, always has been. That's all you need to know," I said, flatly.

"Indeed, indeed. Which tells me volumes. The Spear of Longinus is meant for me! As was the rood, and that precious book and bowl that were so clumsily placed in that ancient Temple, which your friend so willingly led me to. These things hold power beyond mortal imaginings and I am the one to use them.

"You are mad, Creconius Mab. I say again: There is no power in these things but that which we endow them with."

"You lie! You hear the voice of the spear, the voice of Chr...of Chri..."

"You can't even speak it, can you?" I stated, nearly laughing. "I hear many things, Creconius Mab. Or should I call you...Draco?"

"Agh!" she screamed, as if the very name of Draco inflicted physical pain.

"I know it's you, Draco. Though it's been three centuries, Draco, it is you. I remember!" I said. Each time I spoke the name, Draco, Mab reacted as if being stabbed with a hot blade. I knew not why this was. Perhaps the name Draco conjured the true evil that was within Creconius Mab, reflecting it for her to see, to feel, without preamble. Whatever the reason, I cared not.

"Draco, Draco, Draco!" I chanted.

She mumbled something. It sounded like it was in Latin. For a moment, she repeated the same phrasing over and over, building in volume with each reciting.

I raised the staff, the spear, in anticipation. I was about to speak my own incantation, my own glamour, rather than wait in a defensive posture for what Mab was calling forth. But I wasn't quite fast enough.

Creconius Mab pulled the sword from the ground, pointed its sharp tip at my chest and yelled, "Id jubeo! (I command it!)"

The flutter of thousands upon thousands of wings came from within the forest, growing louder and louder by the moment. The winged creatures – whatever they were – were getting closer and closer. The trees surrounding the Henge began to shake. So, too, did the staff in my hand, the blade and crystal egg now emanating a pulsating green-red light. As one, they washed over us and the Henge like a large ocean wave, engulfing the entire area, crashing into trees and my body, knocking me to the ground in the process. Ravens. Tens of thousands of them, their cawing vocalizations all but drowned out by the deafening collective sound of their wings. I looked up from my position on the ground. Darkness pervaded now; such were their numbers. But I could see a few inches in front of my face. The ravens that now came close to me, to my face, did not crash into me, but pulled up briefly, flapping their wings and hovering in front of my face. A glazed sheen covered their eyes. They had been glammed, spelled no doubt by Creconius Mab. But after only an instant of hovering before me, these particular birds were then smashed into by their fellow ravens flying up behind them. They were thus absorbed back into the flocking hoard.

Even above the din of flapping wings and frantic cawing, I could hear Creconius Mab's cackle nearby, now madly hysterical. The initial wave of ravens had turned into a cloud, obscuring all. Though they fluttered and flapped in a frenetic cacophony so close to me that I huddled on the ground in a ball for protection, now none of them actually touched or attacked me. The initial battering I took was more likely a result of undirected headlong flight than a purposeful intent to knock me down.

"Id jubeo!" came Creconius Mab's now high-pitched command. It was laced with panic. Obviously, the birds were not performing as the crone wished. "Id jubeo!" she yelled again. This time, her voice was a shrill, out-of-control shriek.

Still huddled in a ball on the ground, I realized for the first time that my staff was no longer in my grasp. I groped around in the dirt surrounding me. Nothing. Now I began to panic. Had the ravens lifted my staff, the spear? Are they even now taking it to the crone?! I wondered. Anger quickly replaced the panic. "Draco!!" I yelled.

Then, in my mind, the din of the ravens, the cackle of Mab, receded in the distance. It was replaced by the voice, the voice of the spear; Jesus' voice. I knew it was His voice as surely as I knew I was present in my body. "Stand, Myrriddin. You need not rely on it, the spear. Just as I've told you in a past age, I am within you, because I am you. You know this, but are finally feeling it. That is the essence of True knowledge; the feeling of a Truth. Stand now, and cast out this evil in your midst," said the voice.

"I will destroy the evil Creconius Mab!" I replied in my mind.

"Ney, Myrriddin. That whom you call Creconius Mab is a fallen one, turned to the evil use of the One Law. You cannot destroy evil, only cast it from here. Balance is the nature of All," the voice of Jesus said. "Now, stand in the nakedness of your soul and cast the beast out."

The din around me came back to the fore. Still on the ground, I looked before me. It was not as dark as a moment ago. Light, a now very bright glow from the sword's hilt was illuminating the area. I stood and raised my hands. The ravens continued to swirl and dive and dart all around me, at an even more frenzied, chaotic pace than before. And, as with a moment before, none of them touched me; none swooped to attack me with their sharp talons and beaks. Another raven— or perhaps the same one as before; they all looked alike— suddenly stopped in mid-air in front of me, flapping its wings madly to keep aloft. In that instant, I knew what to do. Reaching out with my mind, my awareness, I entered the mind of the raven.

Its mind was simple. I could sense it, feel what it felt. It did not comprehend my presence in its mind. But what I found astonishing was the fact that this particular raven was but a pin-point, an individualized aspect of the collective mind of the frenzied horde of birds. There was something else there, too. I knew that this collective mind was being held together by this something else, this other presence, as surely as I could sense the evil of it. Creconius Mab. She was controlling the flock by controlling the individual minds as one.

From within this one individual raven's mind, I expanded my awareness farther and farther into the collective mind of the flock of birds by bird. I felt Mab's aggravation as my consciousness seeped in farther and farther until I broke the hold she had on them. I saw in my mind's eye what Creconius Mab had tried to get the ravens to do to me. Without thinking, I reversed the image in my mind and made her the object of the ravens' madness. Instantly in the Henge, and almost as one, the thousands of ravens around me turned and attacked the figure near the split oak.

"Agh!! Ney, Merlin! Demons be upon thee! Agh!" she screamed as beaks and talons ripped through her flesh and bone. In addition to the fluttering chaos around her, many had landed on her person, gorging themselves on her living flesh, tearing bloody chunks from her body and carrying them off in flight. Another raven would land where one had just left to take its turn at the gruesome meal. Two birds suddenly went aloft from her face, each carrying one small white orb in their sharp beak. Mab would see no more.

Still screaming, she crumpled to the ground in a bloody heap, pieces of muscle and tissue missing. Finally, her screaming ceased as one of the ravens viciously ripped her tongue from her mouth with its beak. Then more of the flock descended upon her, covering her, obscuring her from sight.

Then, I released them from my mind. The birds left, scattering away through the trees. Most flew erratically as if they had been released from a cage and knew not which way to fly. Some did not leave, however; some stayed behind, and took their turn feasting on the corpse. I stepped toward them and flapped my hands, scattering them as well. "Thank you, my friends," I said to them as I watched them fly off.

"Humph," came the sound from the corpse, as air and body gases made a final escape. I looked down at the bloodied, pecked and gouged body. The great sword lay next to it, the hilt still aglow with a green-red hue. I could see by the glow of the sword's hilt, a mist, an ethereal mist, forming just above what remained of the face of Creconius Mab. The mist began to take form; a form which I remembered from a past age: pasty-white, nearly translucent skin, black hair and ice-blue eyes—Draco! The face then changed, becoming more familiar to me in the present—Creconius Mab, the warrior. It changed once more, this time becoming the face of Creconius Mab, the hag, the crone, the dark Sorceress. The words of the spear's voice, the voice of Jesus, echoed in my head. He was right. Evil is not destroyed. It but changes form and anger, rage, hatred and fear are its tools. For all those things I felt from this misty form too.

"Enough," I said. "Be gone from this place. I command it."

Nothing. It, the misty form did not move.

"I said, be gone!" I commanded again with a violent, dismissive wave of my hand, at the same time banishing the thing in my mind's eye. Slowly, the misty face, the ethereal form, dissipated and was gone.

The corpse on the ground was now truly empty. And, the sword next to it, its hilt now only glowed a soft green, a beautiful hue. I was utterly drawn to the weapon. As if in a glamour, I approached the sword and tenderly lifted it by the handle. I held the blade before my face and closely took in the details of the runes, the quality of the craftsmanship and the powers I knew they held. I also observed the metal of the blade. I had never seen anything like it; no metal could compare—its shine, its density and quality. I could tell that one would not be able to even lay a scratch on the blade; flatten or chip its sharp edge. It must have been forged of something from the Otherworld. Or, so I wanted to believe. It shined brighter than any blade I've beheld, but it also had a reflective quality beyond mere polish and buffing. In fact, no amount of polishing and buffing could be attributed to the high reflective aspect of the metal. It was mirror-like. I could see myself, my dirt-splotched face—unshaven for a moon or so by the look of it—staring back at me. So clear was my reflection, that it seemed I was looking into the highest quality glass mirror, not the blade of a sword.

"Magnificent," I said to it. "You are truly of the highest caliber, are you not? Highest ever."

The sword responded. Its green glow began to pulsate. From pommel to blade tip, it pulsated with light. And it sang. A medium pitched tone emanated from the blade as it vibrated. It sang and its light expanded. And it pulled me. Like my Druid staff, the spear of Longinus would do, the sword began to pull me in a particular direction, away from the Henge and deeper into the forest. I went, knowing there was a greater purpose at work here.

I walked, with the sword's guidance, perhaps twenty-five yards into the forest when I saw and heard where it was leading me. There, leaning against a whole and hail mighty oak, as if someone had gently placed it there, was my Druid's staff! Its Druid Egg and spear's blade on top were alight with the same pulsating glow as the sword. What's more, it sang too! The spear's blade vibrated, singing a tone which was two-steps higher in pitch than the sword. Thus, each instrument was in harmony with the other. My heart leapt with joy at the sight and sound. I stepped over to the tree and grasped my staff, feeling my face stretch into a broad smile.

"Heus (Here, now)," said a voice from above. "the way yer carrin' on, you'd think that hunk of wood and metal and such was your best friend!"

I looked up to the branches of the Oak and was astonished to see a battered but living Baldua sitting sprawl-legged over a large branch some twenty-feet off the ground.

"Baldua!" I yelled, my heart now completely bursting with euphoria. "I thought...I thought..." I stammered, unable to verbalize what I was thinking.

"That I was killed?" Baldua said, verbalizing it for me. "That sword there sent me sailing through the air with a bang when the hag hit me with it," my friend said, dubiously eying the weapon in my hand for a moment. "I lost consciousness on the way. Awoke on my perch here, I did," he continued, patting the branch on which he sat. "A few bruises and cuts. Coulda been a lot worse, I suppose,"

"Well, come down from there," I said.

"Don't you think I would have by now? Woke up just as you were scattering those black birds from the corpse. Did you do that, get the birds to attack, I mean? Of course you did. But how did you get all those black birds to attack Creconius Mab? That's who it is, right? Or, was. I..."

"Stop, Baldua. They were ravens and, and..." I began.

"I know!" he declared, as if he had just uncovered a great secret. "You used both the sword and the spear to weave the magic to control the birds!" Before I could respond, he started in again, this time more in a counter argument with himself than addressing me. "No, you couldn't have because the spear, I mean, your staff, was here against the tree. All right then, just the sword, eh?" he said, once again focusing on me.

"If you saw me scatter the birds from the corpse, then you saw me pick up the sword from the ground," I pointed out.

I could see by the look on his face that he was thinking about what I said. His eyes grew large, then. "What say you, Myrriddin?"

"I am not 'saying' anything, Baldua," I replied.

A sound wafted to us through the trees. It was faint, from off in the distance, perhaps, but definitely not a sound of the forest. Clanging metal was the sound. Another sound began to seep in just underneath the clanging: yelling voices – many of them.

"Do you hear that, Myrriddin?!" exclaimed Baldua.

"I do." We both listened intently, discerning what the sounds meant.

"A battle," my friend concluded.

He was right.

~XXI~

I leaned my Druid staff against my chest to free the hand holding it. Still grasping the sword with the other, I now used both hands to guide the sword over my shoulder and through the straps of my satchel. I brought the sword point down, sliding it between my back and where the straps joined together between my shoulder blades. The place where the straps joined was, I hoped, small enough to catch the crossbar of the hilt, thus preventing the sword from sliding all the way through to the ground. It was. A crude scabbard for such a wonderful sword, but one of function.

"We must..." A loud scraping sound cut me short of what I was about to say. Suddenly, Baldua dropped at my feet, his back to me, arms and legs wrapped around the oak's large trunk – at least, they were wrapped around as far as he could reach, so large was the trunk. He then flopped on his back, his face contorting with pain. The underside of both his arms were bloodied with fresh scrapes and cuts from his descent down the tree trunk.

"You just said you couldn't get down from there," I said in mock reprehension.

"No, I didn't. I said that I would have. That's to say...well, I was asleep. Couldn't do it before waking up."

"That's not what you implied," I teased.

"That's not the same as saying I can't!" he said defensively.

"All right," I said, letting the matter rest. "'Twas painful, it appears, sliding down the tree that way."

His hands went to his groin. "You don't know the all of it."

The sounds of the battle became a little louder.

"Are they coming this way?" Baldua asked.

"I'm not sure," I said. I held the staff at arm's length, looking to it for guidance. The green pulsating light was even brighter. "Let us find out."

My friend's eyes went wide. "You mean join the battle? Why would we do that?"

"Not join it, necessarily. But we must go to it," I said.

"Ah, for shite's sake, Myrriddin. I say we go the other way and get away from here altogether," he said.

There was someone I needed to find and he was nearby, at this battlefield, I felt it. "You may do as you wish," I said. "I must go." I started to walk back through the henge toward the main trail that we'd come from, toward the clashing sounds of fighting in the distance.

Baldua scrambled to his feet. "What of the priest?" Baldua asked.

"Pretorius may be there, at the fighting," I found myself saying. Baldua caught up to me, walking along my right side. "So that's why we go?"

"I'm unsure." I said.

"Then why go?"

I simply shook my head. "As I said, you needn't come." But he did.

We made it to the trail and headed off in the direction we were originally headed in, which was the same direction from which the sounds of battle were coming. I set a brisk pace, even with the sword flopping on my back. It seemed to get heavier with each step, yet at the same time, it was no burden. If anything, its weight gave me strength and determination. It would be an intrical part of the future; I sensed it.

We marched on in silence for a while, the sounds of battle nearer, but not as strong, exemplifying the ebb and flow of such things. I could see out of the corner of my eye that Baldua kept glancing at me, my Druid staff – which I was presently using as a walking staff – and the sword on my back, especially the sword. "I...could carry that if you'd like," he said sheepishly.

"Thank you, but no," I said.

He made no reply, but I could see disappointment in his face when I looked sidelong at him. We trudged on for another half mile or so. I must have been lost in my own thoughts for a while, for it suddenly dawned on me that silence now prevailed. I stopped, Baldua halting a step farther. "What is it?" he asked, turning to face me.

"Listen," I said.

Baldua did. "It has ceased."

Up to this point, the smells of the forest had been our constant companion: the musty dampness of the forest floor, the pungent sweet smell of the lush varieties of plant, and the putrid smells of dung and dead plant life dominated. I had become so accustomed to the odor of the moist, plush environment, that I ho longer noticed them. That is why the new smell, which began to assault our nostrils, was so obvious.

"Smoke! I smell smoke," said Baldua.

"So do I." I broke into a trot, Baldua once again by my side.

The mad battle cries rose so suddenly and from so close that it startled us both into dropping to the ground. What sounded like dozens and dozens of voices rose in a frenzied cry of bloodlust. They were answered by what seemed like another large number of voices equally mad in their desire for blood. An instant later, the clanging clash of weapons colliding rolled over us again, this time closer than ever.

"It seems it was but a lull," I said loudly, over the din of battle.

I rose but remained hunched as I made my way off the trail to our left. Light was filtering through the trees. It was not daylight. Too soon for that. Much too soon. It was firelight. I approached a large rowan and using it for cover, peered out into the area beyond the tree line. I recognized it at once; it was the meadow where the All Hollows Eve rite had been held.

"Diis! (By the gods!) It's..." cried Baldua over the noise.

"Yes, it is," I replied.

My attention then turned to the source of the smoke. There, in the same spot as the large fire I had been near the night of All Hallows Eve, was a huge fire casting light across the entire meadow. Light to fight by. Men engaged in violent and brutal acts on one another, hacking at each others' person and limbs. The noise was deafening, the sights were horrific. But the more and closer I watched, the more I noticed the odd behavior of those of the one faction. On the one hand, there were those who were dressed more or less as soldiers; they wore what looked like the remnants of Roman military uniforms. On the other hand, were those whom the soldiers fought. These wore little more than rags. They were undoubtedly the remainder of Creconius Mab's rabble. Brigands to a man. But in that moment, they were something else, too. The more I watched them, the more I realized that their behavior was beyond odd. It was disturbing to my very soul.

There were about one hundred men fighting hand to hand. There seemed to be one soldier for every two brigands. The brigands not only fought with Otherwordly strength, but some wielded a sword in each hand, parrying one soldier's attack while thrusting a blade into another, yet they would not die when struck by what should have been a fatal blow. They would not die! Twenty feet from me, a brigand's arm was lopped off by a soldier. This same soldier then ran the brigand in the chest with his sword. He then kicked the enemy in the stomach to remove his weapon. The one-armed brigand crumpled to the ground in a spout of blood from his arm stump and chest wound. The soldier screamed in bloodlust and obvious frustration, lunged on the body and stabbed it viciously, morbidly, repeatedly. Over and over he stabbed at the body's chest, stomach and face. So violent was his ongoing attack that chunks of bloody flesh flew, silhouetted against the fire's light. Bone fragments, too, flew from the body, scraping and chipping sounds preceding the fragments of bone. The soldier finally collapsed from exhaustion, rolling onto the ground next to the still body. After a moment, the soldier got up and looked at his work, staring at the mutilated corpse.

Then, astonishingly, it moved. Not just the twitch of the dead, sinew and tendons snapping, but purposeful movement. The corpse was trying to rise.

"Impossible!" said Baldua, watching the same drama play out as I.

"Nothing is impossible," I said.

The soldier screamed. His tone indicated naught but utter frustration. "By the Christ, why won't you die?!" he yelled at his quarry.

Now standing, holding a sword in his mangled one-armed hand, the corpse, the now faceless brigand, made no sound but lunged at the soldier with cat-like speed, stabbing the man in the center of the chest. The soldier fell in an instant and was dead. The corpse/brigand moved off, apparently to find others of the enemy.

Looking across the meadow, I saw at least thirty similar engagements as the one I'd just witnessed. One of them even resulted in the head of a brigand being lopped off, yet still the headless thing fought on until all the body's blood had spurted out. Then, and only then, did the body fall and lay still.

"'Tis madness," said Baldua. "An army of the undead. Perhaps we opened a portal at this place on All Hallows Eve. Maybe the dead are crossing back over to seek revenge through this rabble. What've we done?"

"Quiet, Baldua. We have done nothing," I reprimanded. I searched my spirit; reached out with my mind to find the meaning of what I was seeing on this field. And there it was: the essence of evil that was Creconius Mab. I felt it, sensed it, and it was strong. But it was residual remnants of the thing itself. "It's not this place, Baldua. Come." I left the hiding place of our tree and headed to our left.

"Wait!" I heard his call from behind me. I kept moving in the shadows and quickly felt his presence next to me. "Where're you going?" he asked.

I scanned the darkness and found what I thought I might see: two men on horseback—one in a Roman officer's uniform, the other in the robes of a high churchman. "There," I said, pointing to the two figures.

They were approximately one hundred yards away near the tree line. We, Baldua and I, followed the tree line darting and ducking in the shadows so as not to be seen until we were near the two men on horseback.

"Wait, Merlin, Myrriddin," said Baldua. I did not wait, but kept moving, as did Baldua. "Is that who I think it is? We helped you escape his capture not long ago. You miss him that much?"

I searched my mind. Baldua had a point, but I knew I could help this situation. I searched my spirit and another answer came. "He's not what we thought he was. I'm not what he thought I was. He knows that now. I'm sure of it."

"I hope you're right," my friend said.

I hoped I was, too.

~XXII~

The men on horseback faced the large fire and the carnage taking place around it. Three foot soldiers—legionnaires—were not far away, staying close to the churchman as guards, no doubt. All of them, the men on horseback and the legionnaires, had their backs to the tree line. Thus, they had not seen Baldua and me as we made our way along the edge of the trees. Finally, we came out of the shadows and approached them.

"Darkness prevails this night," I said, startling all of them. The three legionnaires immediately ran at us, gladiues' at the ready.

"Hold," Bishop Rozinus commanded of the men from atop his horse. The soldiers stopped a few feet in front of my friend and me, but kept their swords pointed at our chests. Bishop Rozinus and his companion on the other horse – the same Roman officer that was with him on the night of All Hallows Eve, I noticed – studied us, me in particular. Realization dawned on his face.

"Bishop," he said, his gaze falling to the staff in my hand.

Bishop Rozinus looked as though he was about to speak, but when he opened his mouth, what came out was a rasping cough. So violent it was that for a moment his whole body shook. He put a hand to his mouth, a dark cloth within its palm and continued to cough into the cloth, his chest rattling with each violent spasm. The coughing fit finally subsided and he pulled his hand away from his mouth. It was then I saw in the fire's light that the cloth he held was not of a dark color from a dye. It was dark from the staining of blood.

"I see you still have a chill," I said.

"Aye," the Bishop replied. "'Tis good to see you, Myrriddin."

"Bishop, shall I"..." the officer began.

"No, General Trystor, you shall not. You will leave Myrriddin and his companion be," Rozinus stated flatly. He addressed me directly. "We have much to discuss, you and I Myrriddin, should we survive this night." He said this last part in aggravation, staring back out to the insane battle taking place before us.

"This place is cursed," said the General, a scar-faced, leather-skinned man of middle years.

"'Tis not the place," I said, "but the glamour remaining from Creconius Mab that infects the souls and bodies of this rabble."

"I agree," said the Bishop. "We, too, were somewhat under Mab's spells when we fought alongside this...rabble as you put it, the night we captured you. We have since shaken off the effects. But Creconius Mab's men, they have not shaken the effects. What's more, they became...I don't know how to say it, but... He stopped in mid-thought, racked by another fit of coughing. It was a short one however, and he quickly regained his composure.

"They became nearly impossible to kill?" I offered.

"Yes," he replied.

A thought suddenly occurred to me. "When did they become...like this?" I asked.

"A very short time ago. They attacked us when we were passing here. No provocation. But they became demons only a short time ago," the General explained, clearly open to offers of any help.

"Why were you passing here?" asked Baldua.

"Later. That's not important now," said Rozinus.

"I think I can help," I said. I had been using my right hand to hold and use my Druid staff on the trail as a walking staff. I now transferred it to my left hand. With my right hand, I reached over my head and shoulder and grasped the handle of the sword still secured on my back. I pulled the thing up and free of its housing, brandishing it with dramatic flare before me. The three legionnaires holding us at gladius point took a step back almost as one, unsure of my intent. One of them even gasped audibly.

"The great sword," observed Bishop Rozinus, his tone noncommittal. His eyes, however, betrayed him. He was impressed that I had it in my possession.

"A short while ago, I killed Creconius Mab," I began.

"With a flock of savage black birds, no less!" exclaimed Baldua, proudly.

"Ravens. And that's not exactly the whole of it," I corrected. "But regardless, he or she is dead. The evil left the body..."

"And came here," Rozinus said.

"Perhaps. It may have followed its own essence, which had already been spent in this rabble, these men, and was still here," I concluded.

"Finding its own kind, its own likeness, you mean, instead of leaving," said the General who I now realized was in fear and awe of what he was seeing this night. His comment was not exactly what I meant. But it was as close to the mark as the General would understand.

"In a manner of speaking," I said.

The great sword, as General Trystor had called it, glowed red, pulsating from tip to pommel. So, too, did the spear's blade and Druid Egg of my staff. They pulsated in conjunction as before, then ceased, the glowing becoming normal once more.

"By Mithras!" exclaimed one of the legionnaires fearfully. His eyes grew large as he watched the two instruments glow. "You are a sorcerer?" he asked me.

"Calm yourself, man," Rozinus interjected, addressing the now terrified legionnaire. The Bishop dismounted and approached me.

I had almost forgotten the appearance of this sickly boy-man. He looked even more ill than the last time I had seen him, even more pale and thin.

He stopped before me and remained facing me while speaking to the rest.

"This is Merlin," he began, "formerly know as Myrriddin. He is a great Druid who understands the workings of all things. He is no evil sorcerer, but uses the same principles as the likes of a Creconius Mab. The difference is that Merlin here uses them to minister for the good on behalf of the most High." He paused for a moment, then spoke to me directly. "You are already becoming the thing of legends, you know. 'The great Merlin' is what some are hailing you as——simple folk, who've heard of your feats on the plateau. My own scouts told me you healed many up there, chased out the demons or the glamour placed upon them."

"I'm sure it's been exaggerated, the reports of my so-called feats, I mean," I said.

"And yet, you possess the great sword. The only way that happened is if you killed Mab, which you said you did. The only way that happened is if you were more powerful in the use of God's Law. You Druids may call It by another name, but make no mistake," Bishop Rozinus continued, becoming intensely serious, "there is One God operating through His One Law. The Law itself knows no person. It only responds. You, therefore, invoked His Law powerfully, yes, but for good, and thus also with divine grace," he concluded.

"Divine grace?" I asked, losing patience with what was beginning to sound like a sermon from this follower of Christ.

"Yes. Any use of the Law for good is by its very nature of and by God's grace," he said as if I were daft.

"That does not make a lot of sense to me. A Law responds equally to all, good or evil," I replied.

"Yes, but God is all good, you see," he said, "so any invocation for good is inherently of God."

"By good, then..."

A horrendous crash and a scream to boil the blood came from close by. I looked in that direction and saw that the crash was from burning timber collapsing in the fire. It was suddenly clear, however, that the timber did not collapse by the flames devouring it. Something was flopping in the flames on the timber. Or, rather, someone, which is where the horrible screams were coming from. In the next instant, it became apparent what had happened. In the middle of a cluster of fighting men, one of the rabble picked up a wounded soldier from the ground. The soldier, whose left arm dangled from the elbow down like rocks in a sock, was hitting his assailant with his right hand in a vain attempt to get free. With seemingly Otherworldly strength, the man lifted the soldier over his head like a doll of straw and threw him into the fire.

"No!" shouted the soldier as he crashed into the flaming timbers. His screams of pain and terror pierced the ears and made the soul cringe.

"Enough! I've had enough of this night!" the general yelled.

"Agreed," I said. Holding the sword and staff high in either hand, I walked toward the large fire.

"What's he doing?" I heard General Trystor ask from behind me to no one in particular.

"Just you watch," answered Baldua as he caught up to me. Side by side, we walked to meet the threat.

We stopped some twenty feet before the large fire, its heat intense upon my face. The possessed man—for that is what he was—that is what all the rabble had become: men whose minds and bodies had been taken into possession by Creconius Mab—turned to face my friend and me. His eyes had the same vacant sheen to them as did the raven's earlier. But unlike the ravens, this man, indeed all of the rabble, were under a residual glamour, not directly controlled by another, I felt it. Creconius Mab's evil spirit had been dispelled back to its source. For now. Three more of the possessed rabbles closed in on us.

"Whatever you're about to do, Merlin, now would be a good time," my friend said.

I closed my eyes and entered the state of solace within my head. Once there, I reached out in my mind to touch the mind of the men before me. As with the ravens, these men were under the glamour of a collective mind essence. But, as I suspected, this was a residual glammer. Thus, there was nothing or no one to turn it back on, as it was with the birds, and it was easy to dispel. With my mind, I touched each of the men around the fire, pulling forth their individual minds, their individual spirits to reassert themselves once more. As dirt washes from the body in water, so, too, did the evil fall away, dispelling out of their beings. I opened my eyes. The men—the rabble before me—blinked in confusion as if waking from a sleep. More and more of them gathered before me and Baldua. I could tell by the look on most of their faces that they did not comprehended what had just happened. But one of them, the man who'd been throwing soldiers into the fire, apparently did. He fell to his knees and began to weep.

I dropped my arms, resting the staff against my chest and placing the great sword back in its place on my back. General Trystor, now on foot, too, and Bishop Rozinus approached Baldua and me. They stopped alongside us, surveying the men. More of the men, the rabble, now being of right mind, began to drop to their knees as well upon seeing the Bishop. Others, I suspected, were dropping more in fear of repercussions for their barbaric actions than out of deference or respect for anyone else.

Indeed, some of the remaining soldiers, approximately thirty, began to vent their anger at the night's events. "That's right—on yer knees! Every damned one of you!" barked a legionnaire. He hit a nearby man, one of the rabble, in the back of the head. The blow sent the man sprawling on his face into the dirt.

"Cease!" bellowed Rozinus to the legionnaire. "You will control your men, General," he said to Trystor.

"This filth has committed an atrocity this night," General Trystor protested between clenched teeth. "I have lost good men, some in such a manner that even I will have nightmares about it."

"They were in the grips of an evil beyond your understanding, General," the Bishop replied.

"Then why weren't we?"

"We were for a time."

"But we shook it off, Bishop," Trystor pointed out.

"God was on our side, my good general," replied Rozinus.

I rolled my eyes. Would that it be so simple, I thought.

Bishop Rozinus must have caught my skeptical look. "Merlin? Do you not agree?"

"I do not know much of your God, I confess," I began, my use of the word 'confess' eliciting a small smile from the Bishop. "What I do know of Him is from various of His earthly representatives who seem more intent on subjugating people than freeing them with Truth. And as to God being on 'our' side, if He is truly God, then He or She or It, would be everywhere, in all places and thus on everyone's side," I said.

"Very well said! A bit trite, but well said," replied Rozinus.

"No one, no thing, can truly take command of you, your mind," I continued. "But the simpler one's mind, the easier it is for him to believe the opposite, and thus the easier it is for a glamour to take hold," I finished.

"Then it takes a powerful mind to free the enslaved mind, does it not? Such is how you healed those on the plateau, killed Creconius Mab and dismissed the evil here tonight," said the Bishop. That and with the help of your...instruments," he added eying the staff and sword on my back. "But I submit to you that it was God working through you that enabled you to do these things."

"As you wish," I said dismissively, tiring of this debate.

"Enough talk," said the General, apparently also tired of the line of dialogue. "I want justice for my men," he said, turning to Bishop Rozinus, controlled anger seeping from his very being.

Bishop Rozinus turned to face his military officer. "I will decide what justice is served here," he said. Though his tone was firmly kind, it was laced with deadly measure, an illicit threat contained therein. "As Master Merlin pointed out, these men," he continued, indicating the dozens of men now on their knees in front of and around us, "are of a simple mind. Their acts were not their own."

"That's not exactly what I said," I interjected.

Ignoring my remark, the Bishop pushed on. "I believe forgiveness is in order here, don't you, General?" Again, the Bishop spoke with kindness, mixed with a deadly air.

The General was silent for a moment, a long moment. Why is he not insisting on punitive justice, but instead, standing in silence? I wondered. The answer came to me like a bolt of lightening. Bishop Rozinus was clearly General Trystors' superior and General Trystor was obviously a Christian. A wooden crucifix dangled from the front of his armor, which I noticed for the first time. Perhaps he was even a priest as well as a soldier. Regardless, implied in the Bishop's tone was the threat of being thrown from the Church's bosom – excommunication, I believe it was called. Eternal damnation would follow if you accept that sort of thing. Obviously, the General did. His silence grew longer, his face became a mask to hide what I could see in his eyes; fear – the fear of this excommunication.

"Forgiveness is a hard thing, Father," General Trystor hissed.

Father? I supposed any higher churchman was called Father.

"It can be," Rozinus replied, "or it can be the simplest thing in the world." He turned back to those kneeling, and paused in dramatic silence, the crackling of the fire the only sound filling the air. Finally, he said, "Your sins of this night are forgiven, for you knew not what you were doing. In the name of Christ almighty, I absolve you and forgive you. Amen." He turned back to the General. "You see, Trystor. It is done. 'Tis that simple."

"As you say, Father," said the General. "I'm trying, I am. But there're times that God asks too much."

"Nothing that cannot be met, my son," replied the Bishop. He then faced the still kneeling sixty or so men. "You have been forgiven this night, given a new chance, a new life. But it comes with a price. Every one of you to a man will now swear fealty to General Trystor. You will serve in his army as he sees fit. No harm will come to you by his hand. Is that not correct, General?" he said, looking to General Trystor once more.

The General's expression softened a little, placated somewhat by the Bishop's effect on these men. "Aye," he said. "I give my word, but I tolerate no slotheness!"

"So be it!" said the Bishop. "Rise, then," he commanded those kneeling.

They did as he bade, rising slowly, but surely, to a man. Most looked relieved at the turn of events. But more than a few stared at me with fear and awe in their eyes. The man that had thrown the soldiers into the flames, and who had dropped to his knees weeping, looked at me with wide eyes, his dirty face streaked with the tears he had shed. "He called you Merlin," said the man, clearly referring to the Bishop's addressing of me.

"My name is Myrriddin, but yes, I am called more by Merlin now it seems," I said, looking sidelong at my friend who still stood next to me. Baldua merely shrugged his shoulders.

"You rid us of the demons which held us," the man continued. "You are truly a powerful Druid," he said, bowing his head in respect.

"He is indeed," Bishop Rozinus added.

"Decurion," barked the General to one of the legionnaires who only a moment before had held Baldua and me at blade point. The man trotted up to the General, and stood stiff as a tree trunk upon arrival. "Take our new...conscripts. Have them first tend to any wounded, then have them gather the dead and bury the bodies. I don't care if it takes the rest of the night. In the morning's first light, line them up for inspection. We'll proceed from there," General Trystor finished.

The legionnaire gave a crisp salute, closed fist to chest and turned to the rabble. "All of you, follow me," he said.

Almost as one, the men who only moments before had been an army of the undead, followed the Decurion as he began to walk to the other side of the fire, presumably to now organize the rabble into part of an army of men.

The rest of us stared after them in silence. "Merlin," began Bishop Rozinus, "I thank you for your service and aid. In spite of what you think, I know God worked through you this night, as He does always," he said, staring at my Druid staff, the spear. "Curious though," he continued, "that when you arrived, or shortly thereafter, the spear, for I know that's what it is – the spear of Longinus – was glowing, as was the great sword. But when you approached the men to cast out the evil, there was no glow. Oh, you held each above your head with grand flourish, but neither one was aglow."

"I had not noticed," I said, for truly I had not.

"I did. I remember, too, how the spear glowed in response to you, and the intent you held for us that night almost in this very spot," said the Bishop, holding out his hands to indicate where we were. "And in the next instant, it shot forth a charge that killed. Yet, just now, it did not glow. It did not seem to respond to you at all."

I said nothing.

"Perhaps you have grown beyond it, assumed your own God-given power, eh?" Rozinus said, eying the staff even more reverently.

On the night of All Hallows Eve, I had assumed that the Bishop wanted the spear for the same reasons as everyone else who sought it: for its alleged powers, to wield it for their own gain. But I saw something else in the eyes of Bishop Rozinus right now—reverent awe, bordering on worship. I realized that to him, the spear of Longinus was a Truly Holy relic. It was to be revered, respected and protected. My feelings about the man before me went from indifference to great respect.

"Do you know what has happened to the other items that were with the Spear of Longinus, the ones that were hidden with it?" I asked.

"You speak of the holiest of holies: a book of testimony in the first hand, a piece of the cross on which our Lord was hanged, and the sacred cup from which our Lord drank at his final meal, and from which he performed the first sacrament," said the Bishop. "Alas, Creconius Mab has stolen them and whisked them far, far away." He looked at my friend then.

Baldua looked away, a mixture of shame and anger washing over his features.

"I do not blame you, lad. Not at all," said Rozinus. He stepped forward and placed his hand on Baldua's shoulder. "Your name?"

"Baldua," my friend replied, looking the Bishop in the eyes.

"I know the story of what happened to you. Unspeakable things to get the sacred items. No man could have denied your tortures," Rozinus said soothingly. "And, of course, now that Mab's dead, we'll not know for sure where they have gone," he said, turning to me.

"She never would have told you anyway," I pointed out.

"I know. We have a good idea where they went, though," he said.

"Bishop Rozinus," Baldua began tentatively, "how is it that you know what happened to me?"

Rozinus paused, looking at us both, clearly considering how to answer. "I'm sure you wish to be on your way, both of you. But I think you should come to my tent for a brief respite," he said. He then turned back to Baldua. "Therein you'll find the answer to your question, Baldua."

~XXIII~

Bishop Rozinus led Baldua and me away from the fire toward the foot of the hills and a stand of trees. Within the stand of trees was a spot underneath some overhanging branches. It was perfect for a small encampment. I recognized it at once. It was the same spot where we had set up camp the night of All Hallow's Eve. In the spot now, however, was one large tent surrounded by several smaller ones. A half-dozen legionnaires were about, with more trickling in from the battle field, dirty and wounded. Two guards flanked the large tent, which I suddenly realized was the same tent I had been held in to recuperate, or held in as prisoner, depending on the way I chose to look at it. I felt myself stiffen, but held my stride behind Rozinus.

Bishop Rozinus stopped before the entrance to the large tent, Baldua and I halting, as well. The Bishop turned and faced Baldua and me. He leaned toward us, and speaking in a soft tone, he said, "Please wait here for a moment. I need to make sure my guests feel presentable." He then turned and entered the tent.

Presentable? I thought, suddenly becoming self-conscious, remembering the reflection of my unkempt face in the flat of the great sword's blade.

"Presentable?" said Baldua, in an echo of my thoughts. "Why would Pretorius need to feel presentable?"

"You think it's Father Pretorius in there?" I asked.

"Who else could it be?" he countered. "The priest certainly knew what happened to me."

"He said guests, Baldua."

"What?"

"Bishop Rozinus said he needed to make sure his guests... plural, more than one," I said.

Baldua's brow crinkled. "What of it?" he asked, perplexed. "It doesn't mean that Pretorius is not in there."

"True enough," I admitted.

The tent flap opened and Rozinus motioned for us to enter. One of the sentries held open the tent's cloth flap, and Baldua and I followed the Bishop into the shelter.

It was dimly lit, a handful of candles scattered about, providing but a scant amount of light. The area was decorated somewhat as I remembered. The large wardrobe in which the spear had been stored was still in the same place. The bed I had recuperated on, however, was not. It was pushed up against a far wall. In its place was a large round table, parchments scattered on its top. On my left, standing at the end of the table, holding a large bowl of fruit was the young lass who had salved my wounds on my last day in Rozinus' previous camp.

"Hello again," I said, truly pleased to see her.

She silently inclined her head in greeting.

I then caught sight of two other figures standing on the opposite side of the table from where I was approaching. Baldua and I stopped at the table. Bishop Rozinus, to my right, stopped at the other end of the table from where the young lass with the bowl of fruit stood. My eyes, however, were stuck on the two figures opposite Baldua and me. In the sparse light, it was difficult to discern their faces. It was clear by their figures that one was male and the other female. I noticed movement behind, and it became apparent that at least two others were in the shadows behind them. I could see the glint of metal and sameness of clothes: soldiers or guards of some kind. They came closer to the figures at the table across from my friend and me. Now I could see them better and they were indeed dressed in a uniform of some sort, though not of Rozinus' or General Trystor's ranks. They presently flanked the two figures across from me as if protecting them. My eyes focused on them. The man was clearly not Pretorius. He was not as tall, nor as broad. His face seemed rugged, but regal; his full, dark beard neatly trimmed. His hair was shoulder-length and thick. He wore a finely made leather riding tunic with gold and sliver lace. And, his bearing was that of one who gave orders, not of one who received them.

The female next to him was partly in shadow, but her scent drifted to me and I recognized it.

"Igraines?" I asked, feeling my heart thump in my chest.

For a brief moment, a silence hung in the air like a mist over a bog. It seemed to linger for an eternity. Perhaps I was mistaken, I thought. But that thought was suddenly dispelled when she spoke.

"Yes, M-Myrriddin. 'Tis I," she said with her lovely stammer. She moved forward an ever so small amount so that her beautiful face came into the light. "I've m-missed you."

I felt my face flush and was grateful for the dim light in the tent. "And I you," I responded, nearly stammering myself. Though it had been barely two moons and a little more, perhaps a fortnight or so more, it seemed much longer—so much had happened in that time. I suddenly had an unexpected feeling: I wanted to touch her, to hold her. However, that would have been unseemly. That and the large table between us made it all but impossible anyway.

"Igraines!" Baldua blurted out, looking as though he was about to jump out of his skin.

"Aye, Baldua," she said, without stammering. There was something in her voice. I noticed it now, but realized that it had been there when she had greeted me, as well. It was a demurity that was not of her character.

The well-dressed man next to her came forward into the light. Seeing him more clearly confirmed my initial assessment of the man's appearance and stature. The only thing that I saw now, which I did not see while he was in shadow, was that his face was lined with the crags of age, not scars. Standing next to Igraines, he could have been her father twice over. His voice also conveyed one of many years and much experience. "I am Gorlis Lot, King of Cornwalls, Merlin. It is a great pleasure to meet you," he said, his voice deep and resonate with authority.

"The pleasure is mine, King Lot," I said with a slight bow of my head. "I have heard of you through my friend and mentor, Moscastan," I added.

"Alas, M-Merlin, we have heard. I am deeply s...sorry for your loss," said Igraines.

"Indeed, man. My condolences," added Lot.

"You knew Moscastan?" I asked.

"A great man's passing is mourned by all, just as a great man's feats are admired by all." He spoke this last part directly to me.

I was not sure how to respond to the remark, so, I simply said, "Thank you."

"How come you by King Lot, Igraines?" asked Baldua in his usual tactless way.

Though it may have been tactless, it was precisely the question burning in my mind. I, however, was too concerned with decorum to ask it; or, too cowardly, might be more accurate. Lot bristled at the question, his face contorting angrily as if insulted. The two guards in the background stepped forward in a near-threatening gesture, clearly taking a stance to protect their king.

I held up my free hand, palm facing them in a gesture of peace. "Please. This is my friend Baldua. Our friend," I said, indicating Igraines and me. "His name is Baldua and he means no offense."

"I don't need you to defend me or explain me, Merlin," Baldua said angrily. He then turned to Lot. "Merlin is right when he says I mean no offense. You say you are a king and I accept that. But I do not know you, and the question has naught to do with you. It was put to my dear friend Igraines, who was taken against her will in the same attack that my friend Merlin here was left for dead! He was brought back from the Otherworld in the Henge, the Temple ring of stones near our village."

"Yes," said Lot. "We heard that too." I saw the beginnings of a smile tug at the corners of the king's mouth. It appeared he was no longer angry, but was enjoying Baldua's diatribe.

"So I ask again," Baldua rolled on, ignoring the king's remark and turning once again to Igraines: "How came you by King Lot, Igraines?"

She did not answer right away. It was apparent that she was deciding what to say. I could see it in her eyes. But I saw something else there as well, fear. Twice she looked sidelong at Lot, as if silently asking permission to tell the tale. It accentuated and confirmed the demureness in her voice I had heard a moment ago. Something was wrong. What had happened to the strong, even fierce, Igraines that I knew and loved—yes, loved? Anger began to rise in my heart. Baldua was asking himself the same question as I, for his body went rigid next to mine. But then the real blow came.

"Igraines is my wife," declared King Lot.

Stunned. I was stunned into utter silence. I kept my faced rigid, but my insides began to roil. I suddenly felt as though I would be violently ill.

"Wife?" Baldua declared, nearly shouting.

"You will keep your tone, my young friend," said Lot, a deadly edge to his voice.

"I'll speak as I wish, and again, I do not address you," spat Baldua.

The two guards flanking Igraines and Lot tensed and began to draw their swords.

Blinding light filled the space. In my mind's eye, I saw it so and at the same instant in the tent, it was so. Light, white and bright, exploded from the Druid Egg and spear blade and from the great sword on my back. I could feel a tingling sensation running near the length of my spine and knew it was energy coursing through the sword.

The girl to my left squealed in fear and dropped the bowl she had carried, the sound of it crashing to the floor, filling the tent.

"Call off your dogs, King Lot, or this will be the last moment they draw breath," I said with Otherworldly depth and authority.

"Down, boys," said the King.

I heard the distinctive sound of metal blades sliding back into their sheath and the nervous murmurs of the men. An instant later, I released the light in my mind and it was gone from the tent.

Silence and dim candle light once again were our companions. It took a moment, but our eyes finally readjusted to the sparse light.

"By the Christ," exclaimed one of Lot's men.

"What the devil was that?" the other asked nervously.

"That was impressive," said Lot.

Rozinus seemed almost giddy. "You see?" he said to Lot. "The tales are not exaggerated."

"Indeed," replied Lot. "With you on our side, Merlin, no one will oppose us."

"What are you speaking of?" I asked suspiciously.

"We, the lesser kingdoms, unite under one banner, that of the Pendragon—Uther Pendragon," said Lot proudly. "One nation, one country united to drive out foreign invaders."

"'Lesser kingdoms'? What is that? Various of our tribes and clans have occupied many regions for centuries before even the Romans came," said Baldua. "But what kingdoms?"

"The very tribes and clans and regions you speak of have been uniting under one leader as individual city-states, to use the Greek," said Lot impatiently. "You do know what I speak of, yes?"

"We were subjected to a broad education on the Isle of Mystery," I interjected. "Mathematics and philosophy and hence, a partial history of the Greeks was a part of that education. "We know of what you speak."

Baldua glanced sideways at me, his look saying, I must have slept through that part.

"Yes, well," Lot continued, "we also unite under one central leader, Uther Pendragon."

"Unite?" cried Baldua. "Most of the clans that I know of are only good at fighting each other. How are they to unite as one?"

"Takes a powerful leader, it does. Uther Pendragon is that man," Lot replied. "Besides, you speak of your smaller, localized clans. I speak of the larger tribes across the land." He paused for a moment before pulling his attention back to me. "What say you, Merlin? Will you join us?"

I did not answer straight away, but thought for a moment, remembering that Moscastan had mentioned this Uther Pendragon. And, I knew in my soul that part of my destiny was to help in the creation of this country under one leader. I had seen it in my visions. But in my visions, there had been a different leader; a different High King than Uther. Yet, I had been an old man in those visions. A distant future, then. Perhaps the King in my visions—Arturius was his name—was the future son of Uther Pendragon. Yes, that was it, I thought, and knew it to be so. I looked at Igraines then, and knew another truth; felt it in my soul: she is, or will be, the mother of this future King Arturius. The fact that she was now married to the present King of Cornwalls was irrelevant. The future of my visions would be fulfilled. I would make sure of it.

"Myrriddin. Are y-you not w-well?" asked Igraines.

It was only then that I realized my eyes had been closed and that I had been in a light trance, feeling the future and my part in it. I opened my eyes and looked into her lovely face. "Yes, Igraines. I am quite well. And yes, King Lot," I said, looking the man squarely in the eye, "I do join you. My destiny and the movement you speak of are intertwined on levels even you are unaware of."

"Indeed. Splendid," he said.

"But presently, I wish to speak with Lady Igraines in private," I said.

"Yes, we..." began Baldua.

"In private." I repeated, turning to Baldua. I wanted to speak to her in private, 'twas true. But denying Baldua's presence would also be a concession to Lot. My man would not be there, either.

There was hurt in Baldua's eyes, but he acquiesced. "Very well," he said.

"Yes. M-Myrriddin. We must talk,"

She then turned to Lot, placing her hand gently, but firmly, on his arm. "It will not take long, husband, and this is my long-time friend."

Lot's eyes narrowed, accusingly. And lover, they seemed to say in reply.

"And, he was with me the night I disappeared. I owe him the story up to now. Trust me, husband," she finished.

He considered for a moment, then smiled. "Of course, I trust you," he said. "Come, all of you. Let's give the friends some time," he said to the others. Lot walked to the tent's entrance, his guards, Rozinus and the girl following in his wake. Begrudgingly, Baldua followed a moment later.

~XXIV~

In the dimness of the tent we sat in silence. I had placed the great sword and spear on the table and pulled up two chairs for us. We sat next to each other, neither wishing to be the first to speak. But Igraines finally did.

"You are becoming quite f-famous, you know," she said, by way of small speak.

"I don't know how," I replied lamely. "I've done what anyone would have done in my place. Besides, my...experiences have been fairly recent. Word can't have traveled that fast."

"Words do travel fast and you kn-know they do," she said.

Again, we sat in silence. Until I realized something. "Your stammering—it's not as pronounced as it was," I observed.

She smiled sweetly. "I am comfortable with m-my station in life, Myrriddin. Perhaps for the first time, I know I'm where I belong."

I felt my brow rise. "Comfortable, but not complacent, I hope," I offered.

She simply smiled once again.

"What happened?" I asked, turning serious. "From that night, what happened?" I could not help but hear the desperate disappointment in my voice. It was caused by realizing my feeling for her on that night and sensing a possible future with her, only to have it all yanked away with her disappearance. The emptiness was then solidified permanently with the knowledge of her marriage to Lot and my own visions of a truer future. Upon reflection, however, this last point brought some comfort and perspective. I am, after all, to be an integral part of a future much larger than just myself.

"My real father, of noble birth, had come for me," she said, breaking my thoughts with the astounding statement.

"What?" was all I could manage to say.

"It was not the raiders of Creconius that attacked us, carrying me off and leaving you for dead. It was my father's men."

I was speechless.

She touched my arm with her hand, compassion flowing forth. Her eyes brimmed with tears. "I am so s-sorry for what they did to you, Myrriddin. I pray your forgiveness. Those men didn't know what you are to me. To them, you were simply in the way," she said.

I stared into her eyes, feeling the sting of bitter tears brimming my own. A question burned in my mind. But I did not speak it; dared not speak it for fear of a flood of emotions washing me away.

Yet, she must have seen the question for she answered it, nonetheless. "You are my first love, since I was a little lass. You are my dearest friend and my first lover. My first. You will always be those things to m-me, Myrriddin. I love you still," she said, her hand leaving my arm and going to her abdomen.

"Are you ill?" I asked

"Not any longer," she replied.

I remembered the visions of her being pregnant, and suddenly had to know. "Are you with child?" I asked.

"Yes," she said flatly.

"Is it Lot's?" I asked, rather indelicately.

Anger flashed in her eyes, but quickly abated. She made no reply.

"Is it mine, then?" I asked, as if grasping at air.

Igraines sat thoughtfully for a moment before answering. "Lot will be father to the child I carry, M-Myrriddin. She will be his daughter and will know n-no other," she proclaimed with the fire and conviction I had always known her by. "It is the way of it. It is the way it must be. You know of what I speak. I know you have seen a true future for us all."

"I know nothing!" I said angrily, lying. "The very least of all, you. You spent many years with us on the Isle of Mystery, then many more in our village, with our people, a stuttering peasant girl." I saw anger flash once again in her eyes, but I pressed on. "Then, one day out of nowhere, your father of nobility appears and whisks you away, nearly killing me, ney, really killing me, as Baldua said, at the time. Why? Why did this father of yours leave you with us there, and pluck you at his convenience? Why did you not tell us of your nobility?" I had become agitated. The great sword's hilt and the spear's blade and Druid Egg pulsated an angry red for a moment. Igraines looked at them with reverent awe, but no fear. I took several deep breaths to calm myself. The sword and spear's pulsating, an echo of my state of mind, ceased. "My apologies. I simply wish to know," I said.

"And deserve to know," she said, in an effort to ease my mind. "I did not tell you of my nobility because I did not know. I did not know until I met my father the day after I was taken f-from you. I suspected something am-miss, for I expected to be raped when my captors ar-rived at their camp. The opposite happened—they treated m-me like royalty. One of them was even be-be-headed by his captain for leaving a bruise on my arm during the c-c-capture. The next day, my father explained it all to me: how he had left me on the Isle for training and rearing. Paid handsomely, too. For my own safety, my lineage was kept secret, even from m-m-me." She paused for a moment. "I was n-n-never supposed to have left the Isle," she continued. "But as the years went and my father being far and away w-with no word..." she let the words trail off.

"After you were captured, how did you know he was really your father?" I asked.

"I was very little when he l-left me on the Isle, 'tis true. But I remember him, never forgot his face as he was ferried away, s-starring at me," she said.

523

There was a distance to her now, to her face. I could see it. Clearly, she was reliving the memory. I wanted to reach out, to embrace the little girl in the woman before me. But I did not. "I see," I said instead.

Another silence fell between us for a time. This silence was different, not awkward. It connoted comfort; the comfort two friends share in one-another's company when a truth has been revealed and accepted.

"A woman child," I said, looking at her abdomen. No sign of a growing life within could yet be seen beneath her traveling togs. Of course, it would only be a matter of time.

"Aye," she smiled happily. "A girl child."

"How are you so certain?" I asked. The moment the words were out of my mouth, however, I felt foolish for having asked; a woman knows.

She looked at me a bit incredulously. "How is it you are certain of something unseen?" she asked.

"I feel it deep in my soul and know it to be so," I replied sheepishly.

Igraines simply cocked an eyebrow as if to say, "There you have it."

"So be it," I said. I looked at her for a moment deciding how best to ask the next question. Finally, it was obvious that the best way was to simply ask it. "One last thing and then I will leave you to your life. "Marriage. Why?"

"The marriage was the reason my father came to find me. I had been betrothed to King Lot many years prior. 'Twas time."

I was surprised. "You say that with such ease, such acceptance. The girl I knew never would have put up with such an arrangement made by another."

"The girl you knew is but half the woman I am," she said. "To be sure, I did fight my father in the beginning, even had a kn-knife to him at one point, threatened to k-kill him or anyone who thought they could force this upon m-me. But I came to understand the higher purpose, the reason for the unification of people and kingdoms through marriage and fealty, and my place in this higher purpose, just as, Myrriddin, Merlin, you know yours. You've seen yours."

I could not argue the point, for I had indeed seen glimpses of things to come and my place in them. "Yes," I said.

"Come." She took my hand and stood, pulling me to stand too. "Let us leave the gloom of this tent and begin our futures."

Before I could stop myself, I felt my hand leave hers and go toward her abdomen, its palm landing ever so gently on her stomach area. I closed my eyes and could sense the new life beneath.

A soft hand lay itself gently on top of mine. "Fear not, Myrriddin. She shall be treated as the princess she will be."

"I know," I said, my voice cracking. Her hand remained on mine. I could feel her warmth, her spirit, through her hand. I closed my eyes and immersed myself in her spirit, allowing myself to be carried away to another time, another place. It was the time of the Christ in a region called Gaul. I, my spirit, was in the form of Longinus, former Centurion of Rome. And Igraines, her spirit was there; her then female form resting next to me on a sleeping pallet in a shelter. Our bodies were naked and sweating. We had just made passionate love. She raised herself on one elbow and looked into my eyes, smiling radiantly. But the face that looked at me, Longinus, was not that of Igraines. It was "Irena," I heard my Myrriddin self whisper aloud. The sound of my voice made the vision vanish and snapped me back to the present, to Rozinus' tent, to Igraines.

Igraines smiled. Her smile was not unlike that of her former self. "Irena," she repeated thoughtfully. "We have known one-another before, Myrriddin, have been together intimately and beyond. I know that. I do not know what my name has been, but Irena certainly...feels right," she said. After a moment, she withdrew her hand.

I dropped my hand from her abdomen and picked up the great sword, returning it to its makeshift scabbard on my back. I then picked up my Druid staff, the Spear of Longinus, my Spear. The feel of it in my hand briefly sent me back to that life as Longinus again. In a flash, images raced before my mind's eye from that time; images of myself and lessons learned and not learned. In the next instant, I was Myrriddin once more with this life's purpose – my life's purpose as Myrriddin – affirmed in my mind and heart. I looked into Igraine's eyes. "We have different roles this time," I stated.

With a tear in one of her eyes, Igraines simply nodded, turned and headed toward the tent's entrance. With a mixture of nostalgic sadness and excitement for what lay ahead, I followed Queen Igraines out of the shelter.

~XXV~

The next morning, I helped with the wounded as much as possible, healing those I could, praying with Rozinus for those I could not. I spoke with some of the rabble, the men that had fought for Creconius Mab. None of the men that I spoke with had any recollection of what had taken place. Some were aghast at their atrocities when it was brought to their attention. It was obvious that at least a few of them were not the mindless rabble and common thieves one might take them for, but were simply a product of their circumstances in life; circumstances that they were powerless to change. Or so that is what they truly felt and believed. I saw nothing of Igraines or her husband. No matter. I knew that it was only a matter of time before our paths would cross again in this life. Indeed, I had thought much about my visions and experiences as Myrriddin and as the eternal soul that I am. I knew with more certainty than the day before what lay ahead for me, for Britain, for all of us in the coming years. We were all connected on the level of the profound for certain, but also on the level of the mundane.

By the time the sun had reached its zenith, I was ready to leave. I still had another task before starting the rest of my life: to lay Moscastan to rest within his Crystal Sanctuary. I gathered provisions and sought Baldua, assuming he would still wish to accompany me back to our village and the not-too-distant Crystal Sanctuary. I didn't have far to look. As I approached Bishop Rozinus' tent, I could see that the Bishop and my friend were in the middle of a discussion, Baldua looking quite perplexed. I walked to the two, clapping my friend on the shoulder with my free hand upon arrival. "Pray tell me what the matter is, Baldua? Is the good Bishop confusing you with his Church's rhetoric?" I teased.

"Worse," my friend replied.

"Baldua here was asking after your Priest friend, Pretorius," replied Rozinus.

"Ah," I said, noncommittally. I still had my doubts as to who, or what, Pretorius was.

"As I tried to explain to Baldua here, Pretorius was in our camp last evening," he said.

I was surprised, but dared not show it. "When?" I asked.

"Just prior to your arrival. Well, two hours prior, is more likely, to be sure," said the Bishop. "He warned us of the glamoured men who were about to attack."

"What happened? Where is he?" I asked.

"That's the rub," put in Baldua. "He seems to have disappeared.

"Once the attack began, we paid no more heed to the Priest, as our attention was elsewhere. I'm sure you understand. I only now recalled Pretorius' presence when Baldua inquired of him," explained Rozinus.

I thought for a moment. "And...you are sure that it was the man, Pretorius?" I asked.

Now it was the Bishop's turn to look perplexed. "What is your meaning?"

"You sure he was flesh and blood and not spirit?" I clarified.

"Has something happened to him?" asked Rozinus.

"Merlin thinks..." Baldua began.

"It matters not what I think. What matters is what the Bishop saw," I said sternly. "I ask again—was he of the flesh or of the spirit?"

Rozinus thought for a moment. "I would wager of the flesh."

"Ha!" exclaimed Baldua, victoriously.

"If of the flesh, then why did he leave?" I asked my friend.

"I don't know," Baldua said in a way indicating that was precisely why he was confused – though, he, of course, refused to take my version of the priest into consideration.

"I, for one," Rozinus said, "am no longer surprised by anything that men do. Your friend, Pretorius, was a bit of a renegade as far as the church was concerned on any account."

"I don't accept that," said Baldua. He would have stayed with us.

"Obviously, lad, you were mistaken," said the Bishop.

"But..."

"I beg of you, Baldua, enough," I said. "I came to see if you still wish to come with me. I have another task, if you'll remember."

"Aye. Of course, of course I'm with ye," he said, almost apologetically.

"You leave us then," said the Bishop, his eyes drifting to the staff in my hand. "I thought that you'd be a part of us now. What you said in the tent last evening..."

"I stand by what I said. I will meet you within two moons time. I must lay my mentor to rest, you understand, and see to my village."

"Ah, yes. I am sorry for your loss, truly and for my forgetfulness. I pray your forgiveness," he said sincerely.

"Naught to forgive," I replied.

"Give me but a moment to gather my things," said Baldua as he dashed off. I watched him as he ran. My eyes then drifted to something beyond my friend some distance away. Standing alone in the middle of the meadow was a figure, whose back was to me. Around the figure, in a perimeter of about ten feet, were beautiful meadow flowers. Odd, that, for it was past the winter solstice. Though it was unseasonably warm for the time of year, it was still too cold for flowers to be growing there. Then, a possible explanation became apparent. The figure turned and faced me. It was Igraines.

The afternoon was bright and brisk. Baldua and I trekked through the woods in silence for the most part. My friend was brooding. I suspected that it had something to do with the fact that Pretorius had become an enigma, one that I was apparently able to dismiss a little easier than Baldua. Ironic that, for I had assumed that my friend had never particularly cared for the priest. I no longer believed the priest to have been Creconius Mab. But there had been an evil, malevolent force within the man's being when last I looked into his eyes. I was not sure whether the dead sorceress had been responsible for that or not, but perhaps whatever it was had finally driven the priest away from us for good. Some mysteries are better left alone.

We made camp at dark-fall near a crag of rocks at the edge of the forest. The next morning, we gathered what food the forest offered up in the way of nuts and roots and continued on our journey. The second day's travel found both Baldua and me in a lighter mood than on the previous day, and I thoroughly enjoyed my friend's company in the manner I did when we had been boys. On the third day, we began to see familiar sights, the ridge of hills and trees that surrounded our area, familiar game. The final indication that we were home came when we stepped onto the field where we had drilled with our pretend army. Then it hit us: the smells of cooking fires and food being roasted thereon. I looked at the sky, the fading light and the setting sun.

"'Tis time for the evening meal, yes?" asked Baldua, echoing my thoughts as we both stopped to savor the aroma.

"Aye," I replied. We began walking again, toward the smell. I looked up and saw the smoke from the fires billowing lazily above the trees and found my steps becoming quicker and quicker, as were Baldua's, until my friend and I were at a near run, the great sword flopping on my back. We were giddy in our excitement to have a decent meal for sure, but moreover, to be home. We found the main path leading into the center of our village and flew down it as if our lives depended on it. The closer we got, the more we could hear voices, many voices, more than would normally be at an evening's communal meal. They sounded joyful, celebratory. Before long, we were in the village and we stopped dead in our tracks, astounded at the sight before us. The whole village had been rebuilt. Not just rebuilt, but made better than ever. It was as if the murderous raid had never taken place. What's more was that there were many more buildings than had previously been in our village, large ones made of wood and stone. A throng of people hovered around the cooking fires

"How can this be?" whispered Baldua with awe. "Perhaps this isn't our home."

"Of course, it is," I insisted. "We were just on our drill field. That was our village's path we just took."

"No, I mean maybe someone else, others, have taken over and..."

"AGH!!" came the woman's scream. All activity ceased, all eyes turned to us.

"Merlin?" someone whispered.

"Couldn't be," said another.

"And Baldua," said a third.

Then a woman came forward, the same woman who had screamed. She came slowly toward us as if approaching two spirits. She was plump and her face smudged with soot from the cooking fires, but there was no mistaking who she was. I felt my face break into a huge grin. "Hello, Leoni," I said.

She stood blinking away disbelief.

"Hello," said Baldua.

She took us both in. Others began to gather around us.

"Well, Master Merlin, Master Baldua. Ye've come in time for the meal, haven't ya?" she said.

"We've come home," I replied.

"So ye have, so ye have."

We stood in silence for a moment, the other villagers murmuring.

"Now," Leoni began with mock perturbation, "I know ye to be a powerful Merlin and all, but does that mean yer too good to hug yer Leoni?"

"Never," I said stepping forward to embrace the woman; the only mother I had ever really known. She wrapped her arms around me with such force that I thought I would be crushed. While still hugging me, she reached out with one hand and grabbed Baldua and pulled him into the reunion embrace as well, both of us nearly suffocating in her ample bosom. A wild cheer went up from those nearby and others began clapping us on the shoulder in welcome. We were home.

~XXVI~

It turns out we did indeed arrive back in our village at a time of celebration. The final structures of the village had just been completed and the neighboring village had moved in with our people to our village. They were our clansmen, after all, and for safety's sake, everyone seemed to agree that it was better for all to live together. We sat around the fire for most of the evening, gorging ourselves on the food and regaling our fellow villagers with the story of our journey. Most already knew of Moscastan's passing, but were saddened to the point of tears upon hearing my first-hand account of it. Finally, the moon's trek across the night's sky was descending, the hour was late and many began to drift to their homes. Leoni sat near me resting her head on my shoulders, Baldua on the other side of her.

     "How did you get all these things built so fast, Leoni? All these new buildings, too? Did you have a master mason or the like?" asked Baldua playfully.

     "Ye might say that. He's an odd sort, to be sure," she replied.

     "Who," I asked, my interest peaked.

     "Don't know his name. He won't give it. He helped us tremendously, you know, with the design, the building, the organizing, he was quite a carpenter, too." She said.

     "Why did he do all this?" Baldua asked.

     "Don't know other than he said it's his purpose. He'd talk like one of those Christian priests, but..." she trailed off.

     Baldua and I exchanged a glance across Leoni. "What did this man look like?" I asked.

     "Couldn't tell ye, nobody could. He'd show up in the mornings lookin' like he's been livin' in the forest all his life—long, matted beard and hair that covered his face. And he always looked down, not wanting to meet yer gaze like," she said, as if realizing it for the first time. "Then he'd up and disappear near night fall. Never even took a meal with us."

"Will he be back tomorrow?" asked Baldua.

"Doubtful," Leoni said sleepily, "Two days ago, he said his work here be finished. He was moving onward."

"And he never gave his name?" I asked.

"Ney. Just called 'imself, 'The Messenger'"

Save for a few of the villagers still about, we sat in solitude.

"I'd like to retire, Leoni. I have something to do in the morning," I declared.

"I know," she said. "Will ye be takin' his hovel or the Crystal Sanctuary?"

My face must've shown surprise.

"Well come, lad. Don't act so taken back. Ye've taken his place now, in more ways than one," she said. "The villagers all embrace it. And, they be proud of the fact that ye've come back to lay 'im to rest here. They're also proud of the fact that perhaps you'll be stayin'," she added.

I thought about her words for a moment. "The Crystal Sanctuary," I said.

"So be it," she replied.

By the time I arrived at the Crystal Sanctuary the night was nearly gone. I could not remember the way at first, which cost me a little time. But ultimately trusting my sense of direction and intuition, I soon found myself on the correct path through the woods. The way was much longer than I recalled, but with a near full moon's light still casting to help me and a steady gait, I came to the place near dawn. Unlike the last time I had been to this place, there was no mist near the ground outside of the opening or entrance to the cave or Sanctuary. There was a solid stone wheel in front of the hole in the side of the granite rock formation that was the cave's entrance, effectively sealing the opening. At first, I questioned whether I was in the right location, for I had never before seen or noticed a round stone door anywhere near the entrance. But I recognized the granite rock formation and surrounding area as being correct. This was Moscastan's Crystal Sanctuary, no doubt. I stepped up to the stone wheel, which was at half a man's height and approximately eight-inches thick, and shoved with one hand—my other hand held my Staff. Nothing. It would not move. I then made the attempt again, this time using my entire body weight, leaning my shoulder into the thing. Again, nothing. A momentary panic seized me. How am I to move this thing from the entrance? I wondered. It would take three men.

"You think as a man, not as the infinite spirit you are, aligned with the Unlimited Source of all," said the Voice of the Spear, His voice. "Do you have such little faith?"

I looked at the Druid staff in my hand, at the spear's blade and the Druid Egg thereon. I expected to see them aglow with some kind of light or to feel the staff itself vibrating slightly in my hand to correspond with the voice. Such had been the case in the past. This time, however, such was not the case. Perhaps there's no correlation this time. Perhaps I'm just hearing it in my mind, I thought.

"Perhaps you are," The Voice answered. "It does not matter. The thing you look to is just wood and metal. You have said so yourself. The question remains: do you have such little faith? You have fought and destroyed one who possessed a great evil, using the Infinite Power of the One, allowing it to course through your being with your understanding of the Natural Laws that govern the Power. Yet, you doubt yourself now? The thing before you is but a stone. You know how to use the Laws of the Universe. Command it to be flung into the sea and it shall be so."

I smiled. Yes. The Voice was right. I could move a mountain if I chose, or rather, the Power that coursed through me could. I closed my eyes and concentrated on the stone, on the air around it. I saw in my mind's eye the air becoming dense near the stone door, so dense that it, too, was becoming solid. I then blended with it in mind, becoming it and pushing the stone door, the wheel and rolling it to the left as I faced it. I saw this happening in my mind, saw the stone wheel, envisioned it rolling away from the Sanctuary's opening. I heard the sound of heavy stone grating on dirt and gravel; heard it with my ears in the actual world. I opened my eyes and the stone was indeed rolling gently, effortlessly to the left along the side of the granite wall. It disappeared behind a thick growth of vines and vegetation growing from the ground and cracks in the granite rock formation. Light from within the Crystal Sanctuary spilled out from the opening and onto the surrounding area. I stooped and entered the brightness.

The smell of the sanctuary's interior hit me. I had forgotten about the wonderfully clean aroma of the place. It took a few moments for my eyes to adjust. When they did, I marveled again at the beauty of this sacred place. Twilight of the gods, Moscastan had called it. It was even more dazzling than when I'd been there last. After drinking in the sight and absorbing the peaceful divinity of the place, I turned my mind back to the task at hand. I had been thinking of the best place to lay the remains of my beloved mentor in this Sanctuary and the answer had come to me during my night's trek. I made my way through the Sanctuary, down a passageway that Moscastan had led me, and entered the small hole in the side of a wall. I stood before the Crystal Alter, as Moscastan had called it. It was an even deeper blue in color than I recalled. It still looked like a solid piece of the ocean set in the room, but there was something more; I could see movement within the block itself, not any one thing moving, but the whole of it. There was an internal undulation to the thing, as if it were liquid inside, moving and sloshing to its own tidal forces. I blinked in disbelief as I realized I was indeed looking at a piece of an ocean set in a rectangle before me; a piece of the Otherworld's ocean or the sea between worlds. There was no leakage of any of it, it was not liquid being contained in a glass box of some sort. It was liquid being held in its shape from the Otherworld, I could sense the presence of spirits and guardians from beyond this realm. They were waiting. And I knew what they were waiting for.

I leaned my Druid Staff against the wall near the entrance. I then removed my satchel and the Great Sword from it, leaning the latter against the wall with my Staff. Finally, I gently withdrew the wrapped remains of Moscastan from the pack. I had thought to create a niche in one of the walls of this room in which to place the wrapped remains, then close it up, sealing them into this place forever. But something now compelled me to place the remains on the solid, but undulating, liquid Altar. I did so, gently, reverently, silently saying an incantation; a prayer for peace of spirit for Moscastan. Though the inside of the Altar continued to undulate, the top of the Altar felt hard. I loosened the wrapping and opened it, allowing the ashes and bones of my mentor to be exposed. I stepped back from the Altar, head bowed, maintaining my silent vigil. And then it happened. The remains, cloth wrapping and all, began sinking into the Altar, being absorbed into the mass in front of me. For an instant, I could see the bones floating in the liquid. In the next moment, Moscastan's smiling face appeared in the middle of the Altar. It mouthed the words, "thank you," and then dissipated, as did the bones, vanishing from sight. Next, the undulation of the Altar stopped. It was once again solid: a beautiful, solid blue block. The feeling of those from the Otherworld being present left as well. Though somewhat surprised by the remains assimilating into the Altar, I smiled to myself. It had been a perfect close to Moscastan's life.

I turned, intending to retrieve the Great sword and staff. There was something else now leaning against the wall next to them. It was long and thin, approximately the height of a man and wrapped in cloth. It reminded me of what the wrapped spear had looked like when first I found it all these years past. The object had not been there when I had placed the sword and staff against the wall. Somehow, I knew Moscastan had placed it there and that it had belonged to him in this life. He was now passing it on to me. "What have you left me, Master Moscastan?" I said out loud.

I crossed to the object, picked it up and knew instantly what it was. Unwrapping it confirmed my belief. It was Moscastan's own Druid staff. But it was different than I remembered. In fact, it now looked more like my Druid staff, my disguised spear than Moscastan's Druid staff, complete with a small wicker cage atop and a Druid Egg within. Running my hand the length of the shaft, however, reconfirmed that this was indeed Moscastan's Druid staff. He had made carvings, incantations, in the wood of the shaft when first he had earned this Druid Staff. I looked from Moscastan's Druid Staff, to my Druid Staff. What he was suggesting by this gesture was clear. And, he was right. "You continue to dispense lessons even from the Otherside. "Thank you," I said out loud. Leaning my gifted Druid Staff back against the wall, I picked up mine. It took but a moment to untie the leather thongs that held the wicker cage in place. I removed the cage and crystal Druid Egg, placing both in my satchel. The thing was no longer my Druid staff. Its blade shined as if it had recently been polished, all of it save for the area where His stains remained. It was the spear of Longinus once more. I wrapped the spear in the cloth that Moscastan's staff had been in, placed the sword back in its place on my back with the satchel and left the small chamber. As I walked back toward the main chamber, I could not help but sense that I was home. Perhaps Leoni had been right. This was my Crystal Sanctuary now, my home.

Voices—the sound of voices in rhythmic unison could be heard. I entered the main chamber and realized that the chanting, for that is what it was, was coming from just outside the Sanctuary. Must be dawn, I thought. But the sounds were close. The Sanctuary was nowhere near the place where Druids and others gathered to sing in the new day. Besides, the chant was uplifting, yet somber. Not one of the usual songs of greeting and welcome normally reserved for the rebirth of the solar disk. I stooped to exit the opening to the sanctuary and was touched by what I saw.

In the burgeoning light of the new day, standing in a semi-circle in the clearing in front of the Sanctuary's entrance, were more than two dozen sage-colored, robe-and-hood-clad Druids and worshipers; those who would normally be bringing in the new day in the traditional place near the village, were doing so here. But this gathering was more than that. Recognizing the chant they were singing, it became clear to me that this was a gathering of respect and help for Moscastan: Respect for the powerful Druid that he had been and help for his crossing over to the Otherside, something I did not doubt he had done with ease. It was in no way mournful, the chant. It was a celebratory song of life and the fact that Moscastan has indeed been reborn in the Otherworld, which is a joyous thing to Celts. It means that we will all see him again. I found myself bowing my head and joining the chorus of song. It wound its way to its height and then dropped off to a single sustained note, fading in volume as the breath did of those singing, symbolizing the last exhale of the departed in this life. Then, silence. The birds of the dawn twilled and the sound of forest animals waking to break their fast were the only noises we heard for a few moments.

In utter silence, the robed figures before me began to file out of the clearing in a single row down the narrow path that leads here. One figure remained. He pulled back his hood. Baldua. I was not surprised that the others had found their way here. Druids knew of other Druids Sanctuaries, if they had one. And this place was probably the most profound of them all. But I was surprised to see Baldua. I knew he had never been here. Obviously, he had followed the others. Regardless, I was pleased to see my friend. I smiled broadly and embraced him, albeit, a bit awkwardly as I was carrying the wrapped spear and my new Druid Staff.

"I hope you don't mind that I'm here," he began, apologetically. "After you left last night, I overheard some of them," he said, indicating with his hand those who had just left, "saying that they would make the trek here for the dawn's rite and to send Moscastan to the Otherside. I simply showed up at their meeting point and joined their ranks to come here."

"Gods no, Baldua. I am glad of it. Moscastan is too, I'm sure," I assured him.

He looked over my shoulder at the cave's entrance, his eyes growing large at the light shining forth from it. "I heard tell that there's an unearthly beauty to the place," he said with a childlike tone that revealed his true meaning; he wanted to see the inside, but knew he must be invited to do so.

"I would be delighted to show it to you, but I was about to undertake another task," I replied.

"Alas, another time, then, for I am here in part on a task myself. Rozinus is here, at the village, I mean. He says he's leaving for the east. Constantinople, I think is the name of the place."

"The East?"

"Aye. Lot is here, too, with Igraines," he said.

"Do they follow Bishop Rozinus?" I asked, confused.

"No, no. But the people of the village were astonished to see her with Lot, and married no less. It was fun to watch Leoni, especially. She..."

"To the point, my friend," I said, before Baldua could get much further into his irrelevant tangent. "I didn't expect to see them for a time. In fact, I was going to seek Rozinus. It's time his people—his church—have something," I declared, holding up the wrapped Spear.

Baldua looked from the wrapped item to the Druid Staff in my hand. His brow crinkled with concern. I could tell by the look in his eyes that he was not fooled by the Staff I now held. "What are you doing, Merlin?" he asked.

"What is right to be done," I said, but explained no further.

To his credit, Baldua said nothing more on the subject.

"Rozinus, Lot and Igraines...who else is in the village?

"Uther Pendragon," Baldua replied.

"Just the three of them?"

"Hardly. Between Lot and Uther, there looks to be a legion of their soldiers camping outside the village," said Baldua. "They wait for your council, respectfully. They know that you are here, laying your mentor to rest. But there is urgency in them. Apparently, a ruthless king to the north is refusing to join Lot and Uther Pendragon and the other kings, and is, instead, threatening to have us all under his yoke."

"I see," I said. Images began to float before my mind's eye: images of impending battles between two Dragon emblems, images of illicit encounters, one of which would be between Igraines and Pendragon, producing a King that I would rear. My mind began to drift in trance.

"Merlin. Myrriddin!" Baldua called to me, bringing me back to the present. "Stay with me. We all need your council," he said.

"Indeed," I said. "Let us go meet them." I walked past my friend and proceeded down the path away from the Crystal Sanctuary, my Crystal Sanctuary.

"By the by," Baldua said tentatively as he followed me into the forest. "What did you see just now? It was obvious that you were seeing something. You always get a faraway type of look in your eyes when you go into trance and I bet it was something to do with the future this time. So, what was it? I can ask you that, yes?"

"I saw the future, yes. But, nothing is written in the sky save for what we put there," I replied.

"You're not going to tell me. Is what you're saying?" Baldua said glumly.

"Trust me, my friend. You don't need everything revealed to you. You are to make your own discoveries. And, you are going to have more excitement in the coming seasons than you'll know what to do with," I said.

"I see," said Baldua. "I forgot to mention that someone else is waiting for you at the village, as well," he said, cryptically.

"Oh?"

"Yes. She arrived late last night," Baldua said slyly, as if holding a secret.

"Well, who is it?"

"That, I'm afraid you are going to have to discover for yourself!" he said laughing.

In my heart, I knew who it was: Nimue. I would not have to wait 'til the spring solstice to call to her in my dreams, after all. "So be it!" I replied.

We walked through the forest on our way to the village, to meet our future.

VOLUME III

MASOUD

MASOUD

"In the name of Christ, the Lord!" yelled the commander. Others around him, clad in similar armor and helmet, but with white tunic emblazoned with a red cross on its front, Templar knights, repeated the call as one. I was among them as a common crusader and soldier. We brandished our swords as we invoked the Lord to the side of the righteous: our side. It was our battle cry, or at least one of them, as we prepared to engage the infidels' army.

They stood before us no more than fifty paces away from our front line. Arrayed before us dressed in black from head to toe, save for the brown leather chest plates of much of their infantry. They appeared a formidable foe. They, too, had a battle-cry. "Solom Allah!" they yelled, or something like it. The infidels' army would scream their battle-cry on the heels of ours, thus invoking their Lord's name to the side of...what? Heathens, they were. Or, so I believed.

"Did you hear?!" exclaimed Henry as he turned to me. My friend, Henry Tobiason Andrews, and I had come on this crusade together, enamored with thoughts of glory and a place in history as being among those who helped rid the Holy Land of the Muslim invader. We would also, Henry and I thought, be fulfilling a sacred duty to the Church. The crusader army was made up of volunteers, volunteers of a sort, truth be told. Many crusaders were the cut-throats and thieves of society, but all of us were promised eternal salvation by the Pope for coming here and freeing the Holy Land. "Did you hear?" my friend said again, his long, flaming red hair spilling out from beneath his too-small helmet. Henry was in the line of soldiers in front of me, both of us in the fifth and sixth lines respectively behind our front line. The two armies, ours

Christian, theirs Muslim, faced each other, only yelling battle-cries for the moment.

"Hear what?" I asked.

"They have it," he said, pointing in the direction of the opposing army, eyes dancing nervously. "It's been seen!"

"Have what, damn it? I don't know what you're on about," I retorted.

"It just came down the line and..." Henry began.

"'Tis true!" said the man next to me, a boy really. His tunic and helmet were much too large for his small stature. His wide, boyish eyes peered at me from beneath his helm's brim. He could not have been more than thirteen years of age. "My mate saw it this morn, he did!" the boy proclaimed.

"The Rood, Liam," Henry said to me. "The wood from the actual cross our Lord perished on. And the Great Spear of Longinus too, the very weapon that pierced our Lord's chest! Think of it!"

"Yes, yes," I said doubtfully, nearly shouting to be heard over the chorus of yelling voices, invoking Christ and Allah in turn.

"The infidels paraded it before some of our men this morning to taunt us," Henry insisted.

"They did, they did," added the boy-soldier.

"They know it to hold the power of our Lord, but the fools know not how to use it. They can't, the devil spawns!" Henry said, laughing. "They have the Grail and the Spear of Longinus too, just as King Richard said. I truly believe it now."

"I'm sure you're correct, Henry," I replied sardonically. Ridiculous, I thought to myself. There was a time I believed these things existed. In point of fact, I had sold all of my possessions, even indentured myself for a time to a local blacksmith in order to supply myself with weapons, armor and the tunic I now wore in service to the Crown—which most crusaders had to supply for themselves. I did it to join this idealistic quest for the Holy relics of Christendom and the liberation of the Holy Land. When first I became part of King Richard's army bound for Jerusalem, I was indeed an idealistic crusader with noble intent. No more. The blood of others I had shed, the innocent lives I had taken, the fact that Christians and Muslims know the same God but by different names—for want of a better word—had shown me disillusionment as to the purpose of this farcical quest. The madness of this venture had even led me to the point of heresy; the so-called Holy relics are naught but wood and or metal and nothing more, if they existed at all. Such was my heretical line of thinking. A part of me envied my friend's continued passionate belief. "I'm sure you are correct, Henry," I repeated, with less sarcasm in my voice.

The poor boy-soldier never saw it coming. None of us did. We heard a soft thud which seemed to come from the boy. Henry and I turned our eyes upon the lad. The arrow had entered his left shoulder on the top, having descended from a high, arcing line of flight. It penetrated down into his body with only the guide feathers and notched end protruding out just behind his collar bone. The boy said nothing. He simply stared dumbly at the thing in his shoulder.

"By the Christ!" Henry exclaimed. The boy looked at us then, realization dawning on his face, tears of sadness—not of pain—filling his eyes: a young life denied. He crumpled and died at our feet.

Suddenly, the yells of our battle-cry became screams of agony and chaos. Arrows rained down on us all, hundreds of them, finding their marks in crusader flesh, spreading fear, confusion and death. Some in our ranks tried to lift their shield for protection. My friend and I had no shield. Many of our fellow crusaders had them—either because they could afford to purchase one or were issued one because they were part of the King's regular army—but some of us did not. Regardless, our close proximity to one another proved, at least for the moment, to render any shield all but useless. Bedlam ensued as the arrows came down in wave after wave, forcing all the lines of our men to collapse in a mass of crowded bodies, each man hunching and huddling against those next to him in an attempt to protect himself. The closely packed bodies thus made it all but impossible to draw one's shield as a protective umbrella.

"Hold the lines, damn you!" bellowed our commander of the moment from atop his white steed. Sir Jonathan James was his name. He was a handsome, gruff man with short cropped grey hair and a cropped grey beard (unusual for a Templar Knight, which he also was, for the Templar knight was never supposed to shave) who never wore a helmet in battle. Approximately forty-five years of age and a veteran of many bloody campaigns, rumors told that he was not only a warrior but a priest in the Church as well. Intriguing. At the moment, however, Sir Jonathan James was our commander and none-too-happy with his troops' performance. "Stand up and re-form the lines, now! Those with shields get them up high. Make the shell! Those without, get beneath the shell. Move, move, move!" Commander James yelled, his horse prancing anxiously beneath him.

The men, all of us, obeyed, such was Commander James' sway. He was a strong man and a charismatic leader. He was the type of leader that all men would follow, the type of man that every man wanted to be. Almost as one, every crusader in our ranks—nearly four centuries by the old Roman way of counting and categorizing troops—stood and formed disciplined, tight lines despite the fact the there were dead and wounded lying at our feet. At the same moment, shields came up and over most of our heads, held flat above by their owners, thus creating a protective barrier between many of us and the deadly flock of arrows still coming down. Ideally, all of the shields would overlap, creating a solid ceiling above us, with those in the front lines holding their shields in front of them, thus utilizing an age old defensive technique: a Tortoise Shell, as the Greeks once called it. Unfortunately, there were many gaps in our shell. Many of the feathered missiles still got through. Crusaders were still hit by the arrows and dropped dead or severely wounded. Still maintaining our line, Henry and I moved to two nearby fellow crusaders holding shields above their heads. In the process, I tripped over the body of our boy-soldier, slamming hard on my knees. I winced as the pain shot through my leg and body. I glanced at the boy's face. It now looked more blissful, more peaceful than sad, and I had the fleeting thought that boy was better off this way; he had avoided the carnage that was sure to come. I quickly got to my feet and joined Henry under the shields. We crouched there, swords drawn, waiting for the attack from the sky to end. But a moment later, the worst began.

A thousand and more voices in front of our ranks rose in the fevered pitch of battle frenzy. The Muslim army surged forward and slammed into our front lines. The first few lines of crusaders were utterly crushed and killed in an instant. As a common foot soldier, I was not usually in a vantage point to know exactly how many of the enemy we faced on a given battle field. Of course, we would hear rumors of what the scouts had seen, but would not truly know how many we faced until engagement. Such was the case here. But the force of the enemy's initial charge left no doubt that they had overwhelming numbers. I was knocked down, the weight of many bodies nearly crushing the life out of me. The fetid stench of these dirty, sweating bodies, loosed bowels and fear permeated my nostrils. Add to that the coppery smell of spilt blood mingled with dust kicked up in this barren place by so many feet and so much violence, and it was enough to nearly make me vomit. Most of those who had fallen into me were alive and trying to get up and out of the crush themselves. Some were not alive. Indeed, as I got to my feet I found that my sword was caught in something. I looked closer. It was hilt-deep in the back of a crusader. I was horrified. I pulled the sword free and rolled the man over as best I could in the crush of everyone. His dead eyes stared back at me from a face I did not recognize. He had obviously fallen into my weapon or had been pushed into it during the attack. Guilt seeped into my mind. If I had only held my sword higher, I thought. Nay. It was a part of war. I thanked God then, as horrible as it may seem, that it had not been my friend Henry. I looked for my friend then. He was nowhere that I could see. "Henry!" I called, trying desperately to be heard over the din of battle. I could not see him.

Man-to-man combat was breaking out all around me. The whoosh of a sword's blade came deadly close to my face. From the corner of my left eye I saw several thick strands of my own light brown hair fall away. It was then I realized that my helmet was gone, fallen or knocked off in the melee, no doubt, and that the sword which had just swung dangerously close to my head had lopped off some of my own shoulder-length hair. I turned but saw no specific assailant. He had either moved passed me or had been cut down in the crowd. Suddenly, the press of fighting bodies to my left separated. An also helmet-less Henry, long flaming red, tousled hair whipping about with his movements, was defending himself against two Muslims who were hacking at him with their scimitars—large, curved bladed and wide-ended swords. Our swords were straight and approximately four feet long and double-edged. They were not as formidable as those the Muslim army used, but our fighters were inherently more skilled in swordsmanship. It was something one started at an early age. I was proud of my friend. He was the best of the best, an expert swordsman. He was dancing around his opponents, confusing them and easily parrying their attacks. But I could see two more of the enemy coming up from behind Henry, about to join the fray against him.

"Henry! Behind you!" I called as I began to run toward him. The blow came so suddenly that I had no time to react. Pain exploded on and through the right side of my head about three inches above my ear. Intense bright light flashed before my eyes as I felt myself crumple to the ground. Then, all went black.

~||~

I dreamt. I dreamt of being in a cavernous space where the tall walls and high ceiling were made of crystal stones and gems, millions of them. The place was bright, as though the crystals expanded a small amount of natural light into the brightness of a mid-day sun. The place was also sacred; a sanctuary for the spirit, for my spirit. This place was my home, had been my home at some point in time. I felt it. But I had never been there. Or, rather Liam Arthur Mason had never been to this crystal sanctuary. No matter. I took comfort in being there now in my dream. I knew I was dreaming, felt it in my soul, knew it in my mind. But this place had been real, was still. I felt that too.

Someone else was with me in my dream, in the crystal cavern. The person was an old man dressed in a flowing blue robe. He had long white hair, a white beard, and the oak staff he leaned on had intricately carved symbols on it; symbols of an ancient religion. The old man looked like a powerful wizard from legend, perhaps even the great Merlin himself. And, his staff was clearly a wizard's staff. Or, as my mother would call it: a Druid's Staff. My mother, though a pious and devout Christian woman, still, on occasion, made reference to the "Old Ways"—the the Old Ways being the ancient religion, for want of a better word, of our peoples headed by the Druids. Depending on the company she happened to be with at a given moment, the reference was either in praise of the Old Ways and its Druids combined with sadness that the Christians had all but destroyed them, or condemnation of them as evil. But one thing she often said to me when I was a lad was, "Be upright and true as a Druid's Staff."

The man, the wizard, the Druid standing before me in my dream looked to be wise—it was in his eyes. I wanted to ask him about this place, this crystal sanctuary, and why it felt like home. And then the answer came. I looked deeper into his hazel colored eyes, into his very soul and saw...myself.

♯ ♯ ♯

I awoke, my eyes opening onto the actual world. My head throbbed horribly. I lay flat on my back and had no idea where I was. The guttural sound of the Arabic language, a language I had come to understand a little and despise a lot over the past year that I had spent in this region near Jerusalem, was all around me. It came back to me then: the battle, Henry fighting two—or had it been four—Muslims, and the blow to my head. I stared at the thick cloth or canvas ceiling some ten feet above my face. I was clearly in some kind of field tent. I listened more closely for a moment to those nearby. I heard no English, only Arabic. Not a good sign, for it meant that I had been captured.

I reached out and touched the right side of my head. Wet warmth greeted my fingers. Blood, no doubt. But I also felt something beneath that: cloth wrapping. Someone had bandaged my head. That surprised me. Most of us in the Christian army had been under the impression that the Muslims took no prisoners, let alone bound the wounds of the enemy. Perhaps I had not been captured after all, for, would they not have left me for dead if they saw I was unconscious, and killed me if they saw I was alive? I wondered.

"Do not touch!" came a scratchy male voice next to me, as the stranger slapped my hand away from the head-wound. His words had been in English, but heavily accented with Arabic. "La, la. No, no. You must let it heal, you see," he said.

I turned my head to the right until it hurt too much to do so. But it was enough to see the man who spoke to me. He was dressed in black from head to toe—from his wrapped headdress on down. His face was exposed and was very dark, even for an Arab, with the start of wrinkles around his eyes. I

551

guessed him to be near thirty-five years of age. His slightly hooked nose and furrowed brow gave him the look of a vigilant hawk. His eyes were too close together, thus he seemed perpetually cross-eyed. Despite that, his dark eyes twinkled with the delight of one who was in a constant state of happiness. Interestingly, his dark beard had streaks of red in it and was parted oddly down the middle, from his chin to his collar bone—such was its length—ending in two points.

"I thought..." I began, finding it painful to speak. "I thought you killed any who lived...any of the enemy, is what I speak of."

"La. No," he said in Arabic. "We are not the...how you say...barbarians in this, you see."

"Your king executed a-thousand captured crusaders I heard."

"Our Sultan," he began, emphasizing my incorrect use of the word king for their leader, "did so in retaliation for your generals' and king's slaughter of our people," he said patiently, as if speaking to an ignorant child. "But such is not always the case, you see. You live, as do some others of your kind."

I looked at my surroundings. I was indeed in some kind of field tent. Its sides were open. Sleeping pallets, approximately two feet high, with wounded crusaders on them, filled the nine-hundred-some-odd square foot insides of the tent. I saw Commander James on one pallet, but saw no sign of Henry. The commander's chest rose and fell with breath, but he was unconscious. I was surprised that he had been allowed to live given that he was a high ranking officer. But, perhaps the Muslims were unaware that he was a commander. His outer tunic with colors denoting his rank was missing; it was not on his person. Commander Sir James lay on his back in his grey under-tunic and leather breeches. The under tunic was stained red on the side facing me, his right side, where it covered his lower ribs. And his head was bandaged, another red stain decorating the right side.

There were eleven of us wounded crusaders on pallets that I could see. "Is this all?" I asked.

"I do not understand," said the Arab.

"Is this all that you took prisoner?" I asked with a motion of my hand, indicating the others lying about.

"Oh, la, no, no. Many have already been sent to God, or your devil, you see," he replied.

"You make my point," I said, anger seeping into my voice.

"But...you live," the Arab said, apparently perplexed by my attitude.

"For now," I said.

He was silent for a moment.

I suddenly became aware of the sounds of moaning from inside the tent and bustling activity outside the tent.

"I am called Alhasan," said the Arab.

I said nothing, did not offer him my name.

"And you?" he finally asked. "What are you called?"

Still, I said nothing. There is no harm in it, I thought after a moment of silence between my captor and myself. "Liam Arthur Mason," I said.

His brow crinkled as he attempted to say it. "Lum Arter Masoud?"

"No. Lee-um Ar-ther May-sun," I repeated slowly, phonetically.

"We have several names as well. Perhaps just one is best, you see," said Alhasan.

"Mason," I said.

"Hmm. Masoud is close, no?"

"Not really. But close enough, I suppose," I replied, too tired to argue.

"Most excellent! You rest now, Masoud." With that, he turned and left the tent.

⸎ ⸎ ⸎

I slept. I dreamt. I dreamt again of the Crystal Sanctuary—though I could not say exactly what about it I had dreamt this time around. I dreamt of other things too: of ancient places and ancient times, of ancient people and their lives. All were strange to me, Liam Arthur Mason. Yet, at the same time, they were all oddly familiar to me on a deeper level than I knew how to explain. For example, a mentor from a by-gone era whose name was Jacobi or Moscastan or something in between, I could not recall. A Christian priest from many centuries past came into my dream too; Pretorius was his name.

I also had dreams of questing for Holy things, relics of our church. At least, in my dreams I knew them to be holy relics. However, I could not remember what the relics were, save one. It was an ancient weapon; a spear. This relic, this spear was a part of me, I could feel it, at least in my dreams. Yet, at that time, most of my dreams made no sense. But dreams often make no sense.

I awoke slowly, my eyes adjusting gradually to the dimness of my surroundings. Oil lamps and candles now lit the interior of the tent, whose fabric walls had been unrolled to seal the tent from the outside world. These curtain-walls had ornate designs; scenes of things and battles, of people and their lives and what I took to be their spiritual leaders, which were all completely foreign to me.

Across from the pallet on which I lay was an opening through which one could enter or leave. It was the height of a man. Beyond the entryway, the dark of night speckled with the flicker of nearby torches. Though I could not be sure, I sensed that the hour was late. I must have been asleep for quite some time. I also saw that the entryway on the outside was partially flanked by two very large guards, each dressed in the black and brown of the Muslim army. I could not see their faces, of course, because their backs were to me and the interior of the tent. I did notice something else about them, however; they each wore a black, silk sash around their waist, the end of which dangled equal length off of their right hip. I had never seen such before.

Soft moans came from a nearby pallet, one to my left. A crusader moaned softly, but fitfully, in his sleep. His torso was wrapped in cloth even over his outer crusader tunic. Whoever wrapped this man did so hastily, not even bothering to remove the man's battle tunic. The upper portion of the red emblazoned cross on the tunic he still wore stuck out of the top of the blood-soaked cloth bandage he was wrapped in. The sight gave the illusion that the cross was drowning in blood. How appropriate, I thought. I shook off the thought and turned my attention back to the wounded man. It was obviously a stab wound he was suffering from, a large one judging from the amount of blood, perhaps even from a spear. The man's moaning subsided only to be replaced by whimpering from elsewhere in the tent. It came from the other side of him, from the pallet next to him and further from me.

I lifted my head to see over the stab-wounded crusader to the one who made the whimpering sounds. This one did not wear the red cross emblazoned tunic of a crusader, but a plain grey tunic with a brown cross on it. His garb denoted that he was a servant to one of our officers, perhaps even to Sir Jonathan James himself. He was young, sixteen years at most. I saw no indication of injury to his body, but he was whimpering and looking around with wide frightened eyes, lifting his head off his pallet and swiveling it side to side as if he was expecting something or someone to be there next to him. There was no one near him. It looked odd, only his head lifting and swiveling. Why is he not sitting up? I wondered. But then I saw why. He was strapped to his pallet. Grey leather straps ran over his chest and through the pallet. His wrists and ankles were bound to the pallet as well.

"Mon Dieu! Mon Dieu!" he whimpered in the Franc tongue. He suddenly looked at me, or rather, through me. His eyes were unnaturally dilated. "Ils viennent pour moi!" he said in French.

"What? Who is coming for you?" I asked. "En English, s'il vous plait. My Franc is not so good."

"Les Démons viennent pour mon âme!" he cried.

"Demons? Is that demons you say? Demons are coming for your soul?" I ventured, confused. The boy put his head back down and continued his whimpering. I began to think that the lad was not right in the head. But there had to be more to it; his pupils were too large to be that way for no reason. Then it dawned on me. We had heard stories of the Muslim army drugging captives with the "Satan's Brew", as crusaders called it, and thus driving the prisoner mad, forcing them to confess even beyond their knowledge, then killing them. That was enough proof for many of us that these Muslims were indeed spawns and pawns of Satan. I admit that I too had let that notion slip into my belief about these people. But I had begun to doubt all the tales regarding the enemy of late.

I looked closer at the area around the lad's pallet, which also happened to be in the center of the tent. Near the head of his pallet was a waist-high, wooden table. On this table were a few items—rolls of white cloth, for wrapping wounds I presumed, metal instruments for cutting and clamping by the looks of the blades and pincers, and several small bowls with some kind of liquid within. Each bowl had a small cloth soaking in it, part of which draped over the edge of the bowl. What's in those bowls, I wondered. Just water, or something a little more intoxicating? Curiosity got the better of me. I looked around the tent. There were fewer wounded crusaders lying about than earlier. There were now several vacant pallets. That was disturbing. What happened to them? I would find out later, I decided. But, I was not looking around the tent to see how many men were left. I was looking around for any of our Muslim captors. None were present. That too was odd, but with the two guards just outside the entrance, well, none of us who remained were going anywhere, especially in our condition. No matter. For the moment, I simply wanted to know what was in the bowls.

Slowly, quietly, I got up from my pallet and stood. Pain shot through the right side of my head. But to my surprise, it was a tolerable, dull pain, not an intensely sharp one as I expected. I felt dizzy, but able. Cautiously, I walked to the table near the whimpering lad. The table was much longer than it had appeared to be from the low angle perspective on my pallet. On the other side of the instruments and small bowls were five larger bowls, all containing liquid as well. In two of them the liquid was clear. In the other three the liquid was tinged red. These five larger bowls were wash basins, I assumed. I dipped a finger into one of the large bowls with clear liquid and tasted it. Indeed, water. It was obvious, then, what the red tinge was in the other three bowls. That left the initial mystery of what was in the smaller bowls.

I picked one up. The liquid within was not clear. It was cloudy and had a thickness to it that was beyond mere water. It was almost creamy in its consistency. I held it to my nose. A sickly-sweet odor wafted to my nostrils. As with the larger bowls, I dipped a finger into the substance and brought it to my mouth to taste it.

"Don't, my son," whispered the voice of Sir James. He stared at me from his pallet with pain-filled, yet vigilant eyes. "If you wish to keep your wits about you, do not so much as taste it."

"Is it...the 'Satan's Brew'?" I asked.

He started to laugh, but stopped from the pain of it. "Fools and the ignorant call it that," said Sir James. "Opium is what it is. Or, some opium concoction."

"Are the stories true then? They use it for torture and to get information?" I asked.

"Don't know what stories you speak of. It's medicinal. They," said the commander, lethargically waving his hand toward the outside, indicating the Muslims, "use it in here to dull our pain. But, if one is not careful, one begins to have a need for it at all times. I've seen it, lad. Our own surgeons use it to help our wounded. Comes from a plant. Chew it, smoke it, stew it. Satan's got naught to do with it."

I said nothing, trying simply to take in all that the commander just told me. I looked in to the small bowl again and the cloth therein, and began to understand. The cloth was soaked in the opium concoction then probably placed between the lips of the patient to drip into the mouth. What Commander Sir James just told me also explained other things

I had observed during my time as a soldier. For example, I had noticed more than one previously wounded veteran crusader gnawing on a specific kind of plant stalk, or smoking from a hose pipe. Perhaps it even explains why my dreams have been so vivid and varied while being in this tent.

"Come, lad," said Sir James. "Dawn approaches. Rest some more."

The moaning crusader and whimpering servant had ceased their laments and were both sleeping soundly. My head was beginning to throb with intense pain. More rest was good advice. I walked back to my pallet and lay down. I stared at the tent's ceiling for a moment in contemplation. "Why do they keep us alive, sir," I finally asked, not really expecting a reply.

"I'm not sure, but I believe it must have something with what you did," answered Sir James.

I was utterly confused. "What I did, sir?"

"You don't remember," he said, more by way of a statement, than a question, but clearly surprised.

I thought for a moment, but drew nothing from my memory of what Sir James could be speaking of. "I...I was hit in the head in the battle, lost my senses and woke up here, is all I remember, sir."

"Hmm. Well, you shall find out soon enough," he said.

Fear and confusion shot through my being. I desperately wanted to ask him what I had done, but decorum and fatigue won out. I remained silent.

"Rest now, soldier," commanded Sir James.

"Mason, sir. My name is Liam Arthur Mason," I offered.

"So be it. Rest, Liam Arthur Mason."

~III~

I slept through part of the next morning and awoke to the sounds of bustling activity outside the tent; the sounds of a military camp in full active detail. But there was more. As I lay on my back listening, it became clear that there was more going on in the camp than just the normal routines of an army preparing for the day. There was none of the organized, chaotic urgency to the sounds that would indicate preparation for an impending battle, yet there was something. Perhaps, then, the Muslims were preparing to break camp and move on. Muslim army camp or Christian army camp; the sounds of the specifics were not that dissimilar. Were we, Christians and Muslims, that dissimilar as a people, then?

My trite musings were abruptly interrupted by the crashing and shattering of what sounded like a large, ceramic bowl. The shattering sound was immediately followed by an angry voice shouting in Arabic. I glanced to my left and saw a very young, eleven years old at most, Arab boy being chastised by an older Arab man for dropping what I now realized by the smell of it was, or had been, a ceramic pot full of urine. Though I could not completely understand what the Arab man was saying, his tone of voice, hand gestures and angry facial contortions made his meaning clear. Finally, he pointed to the shards of the pot on the ground and slapped the young attendant on the side of the head. The wounded side of my own head throbbed in sympathetic harmony with the boy's.

I brought my attention back to my immediate surroundings and noticed that the pallet next to me was now empty. The moaning crusader who had been on the pallet the previous night was no longer there. In fact, several more of the pallets that on the previous night had still held wounded crusaders now lay unoccupied. A sense of sadness mingled with foreboding washed over me. Henry. I thought once again of my friend. Still, he was not in the tent and I had not seen him since the battle. Perhaps he had been killed in the fighting after all, or worse; killed after being captured. Or, perhaps he had escaped the battle's obvious outcome and was even now on his way home to Britain. Not likely, that, but the thought lifted my sadness a bit. The tent's walls had been rolled back up and the outside air, as dry and hot as it was, flowed freely through the interior of the tent.

The reprimanding Arab ceased his berating of the lad, which allowed me to now hear another voice. This one was also a male, but it was speaking in Latin and at the level of a murmur. "The Divine Essence of All permeates my soul..." the voice said.

I looked to its source. Sir James. He lay on the same pallet as last night. His eyes were closed, but he shook and sweated as one in the throws of fever. His voice went down to a whisper, then only his lips moved, mouthing the words over and over.

After a moment his voice rose again, but to no more than the level of the previous murmur. "The Divine Essence of All permeates my soul...and brings forth...and brings forth..."

"He's been muttering that for two hours now," said yet another voice; Alhasan's. He stood next to my pallet. "Do you know Latin?" he asked me. "I do not know Latin but for a small amount. It resembles a prayer or chant to me; an incantation, perhaps."

I had not seen Alhasan enter the tent nor sensed his presence. But I listened again as Sir Jonathan James continued his unconscious repetition. I did know the Latin language, and indeed, what the commander was uttering sounded like a prayer or chant or fragment thereof. Oddly, though I had never heard this particular prayer before, it felt familiar to me. The commander's words fell to a mumble again, then to an inaudible nothing. Only the lips moved mouthing the words as before.

"You see?" said Alhasan. "Repetition is one part of an incantation."

"I would not know," I professed.

"Oh come now, Masoud. I am sure you know the nature of spells and magic," he insisted, "you demonstrated as much before us all."

I had no idea of what he spoke. I thought back to what the commander, Sir James, had said the previous night; that I had done...something. Was Alhasan speaking of the same thing? I wondered.

"Masoud? You look as though you are in confusion. You must remember, no?" He paused, but I made no reply. "Ah, you clearly don't. Well, such is the way of these things at times."

"What things?" I demanded. "Comman—that is, my friend there," I began, nearly revealing that Sir James was a senior officer, "mentioned something of my actions upon capture. I remember nothing."

"As I say, such is the way of the Mystery at times," replied Alhasan. "I am not surprised by it. You were with Allah at the time," he explained.

"What say you?!" I exclaimed indignantly.

"Forgiveness, Masoud," he began.

"Mason," I corrected.

"Maasoon," he attempted, feigning difficulty with the pronunciation of it, I was sure. "Masoud is, close enough, as you said, no? Do you not wish it? It is an honorable name. It means, happy, lucky, you see."

I sighed and gave in. "As you wish, Alhasan. You were saying...?"

"Ah, yes. You were deep within God, if you prefer," he said.

"That is no help at all," I replied.

"One may say, then, that you were deep in...trance, I believe is your word for it. When in trance you, your everyday mind, slips aside and your soul connects to the loving bosom of the One God, you see," he finished, obviously proud of himself for having explained it so perfectly. Or, so he thought.

"Your interpretation of what a trance is...is interesting. But it doesn't explain anything about what I'm supposedly not remembering," I countered.

"I understand," said Alhasan. "But, forgiveness, please. It is not for me to inform you, but for one far greater than I to do so."

"Oh, come, Alhasan. You can tell me. I won't reveal any knowledge obtained through you," I said, somewhat pleadingly.

"Ah, Masoud. There would be no honor in that, you see," he said nicely, but firmly. "You will be given council with His Greatness in short time. That is, if you feel well enough."

"And who is His Greatness?" I asked, annoyed.

"Why, Sultan Salah al-Din, of course," Alhasan said as if there could be no other.

"Salad...what?" I asked, cross sarcasm seeping into my voice.

"Have respect, Masoud," Alhasan said with a harsh tone. "Salah al-Din, or Saladin, as your people are coming to call him. Salah al-Din means Righteousness of Faith," Alhasan stated dreamily, "and he is a great Sultan and General and leader of our army, you see."

"And my captor," I said.

"Your host," Alhasan corrected.

"As a guest, then, I can go if I please," I stated flatly.

Alhasan smiled almost wryly. "Yes, yes you could, but it would greatly displease Salah al-Din," he said, his words dripping with implied consequence. "He has been most generous to you."

"How so?" I asked.

"You live, do you not?" Alhasan replied, pausing briefly. "Salah al-Din will meet with you later if you feel able. You and your muttering commander," he said indicating Sir James.

So, they know his rank after all, I thought. "I feel well enough," I said.

"Excellent!" exclaimed Alhasan. "I will come for you both shortly, when the sun reaches his zenith." With that, he turned to leave.

"The...commander may not feel well enough," I pointed out.

Alhasan stopped and looked at Sir James. The latter had not muttered for a few moments, but his lips continued to move in silent recitation. Alhasan then faced me once again. "Your commander will attend if Salah al-Din bids it, you see," he declared with finality. "Until the zenith, then..." Alhasan bowed his head slightly in my direction then strode from the tent.

ﺕ ﺕ ﺕ

The sun's zenith came quicker than I wished. "Rise, Masoud," said a deep male voice contemptuously. Still lying on my pallet, I rolled my head to my right, toward the sound of the voice. Four large, darkly clad Arab soldiers flanked a short, stocky dark man robed in grey. His head wrap was burgundy and his black beard was cropped short. His brown eyes were intense as he jutted out his chin, causing him to look down his stubbed nose at me in a manner that spat pretentious importance and condescension. "The Sultan will hold audience with you now. He commands it," the stocky Arab said arrogantly in perfect English.

"Where is Alhasan?" I asked.

"Silence and on your feet!" he bellowed.

"I don't feel well enough to-"

"Do as he says, Liam," said Sir James. I immediately sat upright and looked at my commander. He slowly sat up as well, looking weary and pale, but alert. "We may yet live. Do as he says, I order it."

"Yes. And you, commander. You are to come as well," added the stocky Arab. "Bring them," he ordered to the soldiers with him. The darkly clad men—curved scimitars at the ready—stepped forward; two toward me, two toward Sir James. Without further preamble, my commander and I rose from our pallets. The Muslim soldiers tied our hands in front of us with leather thongs, leaving one long strand of the chord tied to each of our individual bindings, thus tying us to each other, as well. We then gingerly walked with our escort out of the tent.

~IV~

The sun was indeed at its—or his, as Alhasan had said—zenith. It beat down with the intensity of fire, but I was not uncomfortable. It was simply good to be out of the hospital tent. My head still throbbed, but not nearly as much as on the previous day. I inhaled deeply. The hot and dry air burned my lungs as it entered. No matter. I was glad to be walking. The four Muslim soldiers surrounded Sir James and I with the stocky Arab leading the way. I glanced at Sir James. He was clutching his side and doing his best to keep the pace of our cross-camp march, which was brisk and set by our handlers. The camp was large. I didn't see tents as such for the common Muslim soldier. Instead, I noted many large, cloth canopies held aloft by poles. There were no sides to these shelters. Many men could fit beneath the protective canopy. Sir James quietly grunted in pain. I touched his arm and made a slight motion with my head when he looked at me, silently asking him if he needed to stop and rest, not that our captors would have allowed that, but I would plead his case if I had to. But that would not be necessary, for, courage and defiance filled his eyes. Sir James shook his head and we carried on.

The camp was full of Muslim, Arab soldiers going about their duties. Some stopped and stared, even pointing at us as we walked by. I saw no other crusaders, prisoners or otherwise. Again, the question as to the fate of my friend Henry briefly entered my mind.

"Move aside!" our stocky Arab leader shouted in Arabic. There were several platoons of soldiers in our path. They parted and I was able to see our apparent destination; the largest and most ornate free-standing field tent I had ever seen. It was dark in color and its front sprawled before us and it seemed to be the size of a castle. There were no turrets, of course, as on an actual castle, but the top of the tent went up into several high peaks. "Holy Christ!" I mumbled in awe.

Sir James let out a small laugh at my surprised uttering. "No doubt the size of this thing is a match to Salah al-Din's high opinion of himself, eh lad?" he quipped in a whisper.

"Quiet!" said the guard on Sir James' right, hitting my commander in the back with his sword's pommel, causing Sir James to stumble forward. He did not fall, though, and he did not let out a cry of pain. He recovered his step quickly and we walked on.

The closer we came to the tent the more dwarfed I felt by it. And, the more detail I could make out on its tall sides, sides that seemed to reach for the sky by some thirty feet. Large mural-type scenes adorned the sides of the tent. They almost looked embroidered, such was their quality, and depicted conquest and battle, Sultan-ness and Muslim piety. The whole of the tent's exterior was dark in color. The scenes, though clear as to what they were when up close, had been created with muted tones of the earth, thus blending in with the tent's overall color from a distance.

We halted before a long tunnel entryway flanked by two guards. The tunnel was made of the same material as the tent. It was approximately six feet wide and ten feet tall with a covered roof, and arched the whole way leading into the tent proper which was some twenty feet in length. The tunnel's sides were dark as well as straight and vertical, and extended from the roof down to approximately one foot off of the ground, thus leaving an open space near the ground, presumably for ventilation. In fact, as I looked once again at the whole of the large tent itself I noticed that its sides' bottom was the same as the tunnel's; extending from the top down to about a foot off the ground. I suddenly noticed something else too; there were Muslim soldiers, guards, positioned about every twenty feet all along the tent's outer wall, guarding the ventilation space so that no one could slip under it and into the tent, no doubt. I hadn't seen the guards until now because their uniforms were the exact same coloring as the tent itself, thus causing them to blend in to the tent's wall. Interesting, that. Someone nudged me in the back and we moved forward into the tunnel.

It took a moment for my eyes to adjust to the darkened interior. We were still being led by the stocky Arab and flanked by the guards, but we were now cramped shoulder to shoulder in the relatively narrow tunnel. The body stench of our captors nearly overwhelmed my sensibilities. But, then again, it was probably at least in part my own foul un-cleanliness that I smelled.

"Be respectful and stay alert, lad. God willing, we may yet get through this. 'Tis up to you, Liam," whispered Commander James.

Up to Me? What in hell does that mean?! I thought, wanting to scream.

The tunnel opened into a small room; an annex of sorts, or a waiting vestibule. Indeed, one of our guards grunted and shoved my commander and I hard in the back, shoving us to the ground. We both landed on our knees. I immediately attempted to stand.

"No, Liam," whispered Sir James urgently, as he reached out a hand to keep me down.

But it was too late. I was already nearly back on my feet when I saw bright white light splashed before my eyes from the stinging blow I received in the back of my head. I crumpled back to the ground, landing in the arms of Commander James. "They want us to stay on our knees, lad." he said.

"How was I to know? You've had more experience at being captured, commander, no doubt," I replied, slurring my words from the pain. I did not lapse into unconsciousness, but nearly so. I swooned for a moment then heard the sound of voices frantically speaking in Arabic around me and about me. The one speaking the most frantic was directing his words at the guards and stocky Arab, reprimanding them, it seemed. He then turned to me. It was Alhasan.

"Achh! Masoud," he began in English, apologetically as he helped me to my feet. "A thousand pardons, please. They are oafs, these guards, hemorrhoids on the asshole of a cow. That is why they are usually given mindless duties. They were not to harm a hair on your crusader head, you see. But, one cannot give gold to a mindless pig, you see?"

"I think you mean pearls to swine," I said, attempting to correct his reference.

"Eh?" he replied, confused.

"Nothing," I said.

"You treat these things as equals? These are the pigs!" said the stocky Arab defiantly and again in perfect English, pointing to Sir James and myself.

Alhasan whirled on the short man, jutting his hooked nose into one of the man's eyes. "You dare defy His Greatness, the Sultan?! For this is from where the orders come, my small one!" shouted Alhasan. The stocky Arab said nothing. "I thought as much, you see. Your job here is done." Alhasan stepped back and pointed back down the tunnel. "You and your...men are now to leave."

Hatred bore into Alhasan from the eyes of the stocky Arab. Clearly, this was not the first confrontation these two have had. Indeed, something told me that this was an ongoing discord and that the only thing keeping Alhasan from the grave by this one's hands was his proximity to His Greatness, Sultan Salah al-Din. The stocky Arab and his guards suddenly turned on their heels and marched back down the tunnel to the outside.

Alhasan turned to me once again. "Come, Masoud. And you, as well, Masoud's commander," he said to Sir James. "The Sultan awaits you both."

⌣ ⌣ ⌣

We entered what appeared to be the main area of the tent. The space was huge, large enough to hold seventy or so people. It was richly appointed with fine rugs on the floor and tapestries on the inside walls of the tent. There were a dozen or so people, some richly dressed in dark robes and turbans, some soldiers, officers in the Muslim army judging by their attire and bearing. They were engaged in intense conversation with a black robed figure sitting in a high backed, hand carved, wooden chair. This person also had plain brown, military breastplates on his upper torso. Though he wore a black turban, tuffs of grey hair spilled from beneath, dropping in ringlets about his neck. His black and grey beard was neatly coiffed. He appeared to be approximately forty years of age. His demeanor at present seemed to be one of annoyance, impatience, toward the men chattering before him. Then, he looked at me.

His gaze was intense, so much so that I briefly averted my own gaze partly out of fear and partly out of a sudden sense of awe I felt toward the man before me. When I looked back at him, his gaze still held fast upon me, but I mustered the courage to return his look. His eyes were dark and conveyed a depth of spirit, an infinite intelligence and strength of character that belied ruthlessness when pushed. I sensed that he was a man that could be trusted, but should also be feared. Salah al-Din. The man before me in the high backed chair had to be the Sultan himself.

He suddenly shot up a hand and all before him fell silent. They then followed their Sultan's gaze to me. One of the military men who had been speaking to Salah al-Din became angry, stepping toward me and raising hand to strike. "Eyes to the ground, you heathen!" he yelled at Sir James and I in English as he approached.

"Stay your hand, Commander Hakim, and command what you have captured. He is Crusader Mason, or Masoud, as our beloved Alhasan has named him," said Sultan Salah al-Din. His voice carried a smooth, authoritative power to it. It was more than just the power of authority, however. It was the power of inner stillness, the power of inner righteousness. Not arrogance, but Righteousness: the kind that comes from a profound, singular and personal inner connectedness to the

One Most High, and the knowledge or perception that what you do in the outer world of men with this Righteousness is naught but Good, regardless of the fact that it might be in the form of war and destruction.

"You honor this crusader dog with a Muslim name?" Commander Hakim spat at Alhasan. The Muslim commander Hakim was a slight man of perhaps thirty summers. An angry scowl crossed his features. It was one that I guessed had been there for a long time, judging by the permanent creases they had already created in spite of his apparent young age. His head was bare, turban-less, and I was surprised to see short-cropped red hair adorning the top of his head, and a closely trimmed red beard clinging to his face. Save for his dark features and eyes, he almost appeared to be of Anglo decent. "Has he renounced Christianity then, and embraced Islam?"

"Hakim," Salah al-Din said calmly, but sternly. "You will stand aside."

Hakim's eyes narrowed threateningly, contemptuously at first to Alhasan, then to me. But he did as he was ordered and took a step back and aside, becoming an observer to what was about to play out.

Salah al-Din then spoke directly to me. "Come here," he said with softness.

I glanced at Sir James out of the corner of my eye, a part of me seeking my commander's permission to obey the foreigner. I realized the absurdity of my glance immediately. Sir James' brow crinkled, silently saying, don't be an idiot, lad! Go!

Alhasan quickly came to me and pulling out a small knife, cut the bindings around my wrist and the long thong that connected Sir James to me. I stepped forward to the man in the high-backed chair. A feeling of utter respect for the Sultan suddenly washed over me, compelling me to avert my eyes to the ground out of respect as I approached, no doubt to the satisfaction of Commander Hakim. I stopped three feet before the chair, eyes still to the ground. An awkward moment of silence passed. I suddenly felt all eyes in the tent roving over me, assessing me, weighing and measuring me, quartering me through and through.

"Alhasan," Salah al-Din finally said. "Bring the instrument."

I felt Alhasan's presence depart. My heart began to race and my mind to reel. What instrument? I wondered. Something of torture? Worse? I managed to sneak another questioning glance at Sir James. To my amazement, he was smiling.

~V~

I stood before the Sultan and his court for what seemed an eternity, though I'm sure now that it had been no more than a moment or two. I felt a bead of sweat trickle down the left side of my face. I dared to look in the face of Salah al-Din then. What I saw astonished me. He too, like Sir James, was smiling. It was not a malicious smile, quite the contrary. It was one of kindness, mercy and curiosity. "We shall see if the other night was the trickery of your devil or if Allah truly works through you and the spear that pierced the Prophet Jesu's side," he said.

Before my further confusion could be given voice, Alhasan came back into the room carrying a thin item that appeared to be over six feet in length. The thing was wrapped in what appeared to be some kind of shining white cloth—silk, I was told later. It could have been a thin pole, such were its length and shape. Or...a spear. My head, where the injury was, began to throb with pain. Images suddenly impinged themselves before my eyes. I swooned briefly. The images seemed in part to be from the other night. But other images were from an age in the long distant past, images or visions which contained people that I knew not, and scenes and things that were alien to me; crucifixions of persons unknown, a spear with a unique pattern of reddish stains on its blade, a battle between ancient armies. Yet, I sensed that I was connected to all of them. The distant past images suddenly rolled rapidly by my eyes to be replaced by images still in a distant past, but not as far back. In these images I saw a group of Druids and a Merlin, a Master Druid of old, in and around the Great Henge of Stone in my homeland. Specifically, they encircled the great center stone altar in the middle of the Henge and the figure, a man, lying on this center stone altar. The same spear from the previous images lay upon his body—I recognized the stains on its blade. This vision rolled by and was replaced by a recent scene, one from a previous night in the present time. In this vision I held the same spear before the Sultan and Alhasan. I was awash in a white glow.

The images abruptly disappeared and I came to myself once more, standing before the Sultan and his court, Alhasan now next to me, still holding the wrapped item and looking at me with awe. I was panting heavily and sweating as if I had just made the run of my life. Perhaps I had.

"You see, great Sultan? Masoud becomes as one with the spear and he has not yet touched it again!" exclaimed Alhasan.

"Hmm," was the Sultan's response. Then, "Unwrap the spear," he ordered.

Alhasan did so hastily, but reverently, as if the thing were a firebrand and a sacred artifact all at once. Perhaps it was. Alhasan finished the unwrapping and held it out to me, cradling it with both hands, the wrapping now draped over his palms, the thing, an ancient spear, resting on top of the wrapping so as not to actually touch his palms. He then bowed his head slightly toward me, indicating, I presumed, that I should take the spear.

Two things ran quickly and immediately through my mind: one; take the spear, which, though old, appeared to be intact and able, from its stained blade to its somewhat chipped and dented shaft, and level it at the Sultan's chest and demand our freedom. Or, two; do nothing—refuse to take the thing. The first thought would have been foolish at best, for when the others saw Alhasan offering up the weapon to me, the military personnel present stepped forward, unsheathing their scimitars and holding them at the ready in the process. The others, the robed figures, merely stood by, passively watching the proceedings but with obvious interest.

"Take care, Alhasan," hissed Hakim.

"You take care, Hakim!" Salah al-Din barked, sending the soldier a withering look. "Alhasan does my bidding. Do you?"

Hakim's features became soft for the briefest of instances; a humiliated child in the presence of an angry parent. "Great Sultan! How can you question me thusly? My loyalty knows no bounds!" he said, with bravado. But it rang as insincere, an act.

"Ah, but that requisitions the question, does it not, Hakim? Is your boundless loyalty to me? Or to yourself?" asked Sultan Salah al-Din. I was not the only one to have seen through Hakim's pretentious bravado. "Put your weapons away," he said to his men, "and step back, Hakim," the Sultan continued, forgiving Hakim a bit too easily, which seemed odd. He then turned his attention back to me. "Take the spear, Masoud."

It was a soft, but stern command, not a gentle request. Forgetting all about the two thoughts that had raced through my mind a moment ago, I turned to Alhasan, still holding out the ancient weapon for me to grasp. "What am I supposed to do with it?" I asked to no one in particular.

"Listen to it, you see, let it speak to you" Alhasan said softly.

I reached out a hand and let my fingers wrap gently around the old wood. I then lifted it and held it before my eyes, examining the Blade. The stains were there, stains from antiquity, by the look of them. The shaft was chipped here and there, as I said, but overall was whole and hale. I then listened, as Alhasan had instructed. I listened for what seemed like quite a few minutes. Nothing. I heard nothing. I shook my head.

"Do you feel It?" Alhasan asked. "Do you feel a presence from it? His presence, the Power's presence?"

I felt nothing and shook my head once more. A piece of wood and metal, this was. Yes, it was very old, perhaps, but still just wood and metal.

"Well?" asked Salah al-Din of Alhasan, his tone now laced with impatience.

"Sire, your Greatness, we all saw what took place that night, the glowing presence, the Power that came from the spear, through Masoud and into his crusader friend, healing him!" Alhasan's voice was becoming high-pitched, excited.

"A magicians trick, I say," said a voice from beside Hakim. The figure was in black from head to toe; black robe and turban whose tail wrapped around his head and covered the lower half of his face. I did not know why I hadn't noticed this one until now. There were other figures behind him whom I now saw as well, all cloaked as he was but in the shadows of the tent. I could not make out any of the features of the men behind the one who had spoken, except one; one of them had a pair of yellow-gold eyes that peered out intently from an otherwise cloth-wrapped face. "A magician's trick," the first man said again. He was an imposing figure, the one who had spoken; at least a head-and-a-half taller than I—some six-feet, five-inches in height by my reckoning. One of his eyes was black as coal, the other as white as snow, its pupil opaque. I could not tell if the opaque eye was blind or not. But one thing I could tell was what I was sensing when this one spoke; a darkness to his countenance to match the darkness of his robe. I shivered in spite of myself.

"No, I don't agree," dared Alhasan. He then turned back to Salah al-Din. "We all saw what happened that night. The prisoners were seated on the ground, lined up on the dirt, hands and feet bound. Masoud was as if in a waking sleep from his head wound, but still held the hand of his friend, his fellow-invader, who leaned against him and who we all saw was dead. Then, Great Sultan, it happened. The cart carrying the rood and the Spear of Longinus, the same spear that pierced the Prophet's side and contains the Power of Allah, came careening out of control, its horse gone mad with fright, and crashed, you see, the long rosewood box splintering into a-thousand pieces and laying the Spear of Longinus out for all to see. Then, slowly, Masoud gets to his feet and with the strength of ten men breaks the thongs that bind his feet and hands. He walks to the spear and picks it up. It glows at his touch, giving us all pause," Alhasan said, now telling the story with theatrical intensity, clearly living it in his mind as any good bard will in the regaling of a dramatic yarn.

"Yes, yes. Again, I say a magician's trick," said the dark-robed, opaque-eyed man.

"Except for the next part of the story, my good Master Rashin. The raising of the dead is no magician's trick. Only Allah the Merciful can do that, and that he did through the Great Spear of Longinus and Masoud!"

I was stunned by what Alhasan was saying. I remembered nothing of it. I tried. I stood there shaking my head, willing myself to remember. Nothing. I remembered nothing of that night. But something else impinged itself on my mind; not a memory, but a reasoning. "Alhasan. You said, that...that I...I can scarcely say it...that I, with the aid of this spear," I said, indicating the thing in my hand, "brought someone back from the dead?"

"It was Allah, God working through the spear and you, you see," he replied.

"Was it the friend on the ground next to me?" I asked, my words brimming with hope.

"The same. Your friend..."

"Henry?!"

"I've heard enough of this," said the opaque-eyed Rashin. "Sultan, Salah al-Din, by your leave, I will tend to other matters."

The Sultan, clearly disappointed and none-too-pleased with my performance, or lack thereof, simply nodded his ascent to Rashin. The dark one shot a contemptuously daggered look at Alhasan and I, then let out a low, menacing cackle and left the room. Again, I shivered at the man's countenance.

Hakim stepped forward then. "Shall I dispose of the prisoners, Sultan?" he said in a strange, offhanded manner.

"No," Salah al-Din stated flatly.

"But..." Hakim began, foolishly.

"I said, no!" Salah al-Din said as he grabbed a thin short object next to his chair, a riding crop by the look of it, and suddenly lashed out with it, striking Hakim on the face which left a welting red line in its wake. "Your insolence will be your undoing. You may go and attend to your business as well."

To his credit, Hakim showed no emotion and looked at neither Alhasan nor I. He simply left.

"Leave. All of you may go. Alhasan, you and Masoud and his commander will stay," the Sultan said. Perhaps I should have been afraid, but he had not said it unkindly, but rather in such a manner that indicated he simply wanted to speak with us alone.

The others all filed out, save for two very large men. They went to the entrance of the room and turned back, standing at attention, on guard.

Sultan Salah al-Din turned his attention back to the three of us, then specifically to me. "Yes, Masoud. We all saw what happened that night, your interaction with the Great Spear of Longinus, if that be what it truly is. Our...mystics...sought to use it against your crusaders. I never believed it to have any powers whatsoever. It was simply a useful tool to play against the minds of your kind." He paused briefly before continuing. "Still. That night when you raised your friend-in-arms from the dead, I too thought this was truly a power-laced weapon. Briefly. But the power came not from the Spear, but from you, Masoud and..."

"And, from Allah Himself through the spear!" interjected Alhasan.

"Indeed, from Allah, Alhasan. Which perplexes me, Masoud. Why would Allah, praise be His name," Salah al Din said, looking up as he uttered the praise, then looking back to me, boring his intense gaze into my tired eyes, into my very soul, "why would He choose to wield His power through a Christian crusader, a butcher of my people?"

Despite my fear over the situation, angered welled within me. "I am no butcher, Sultan," I said.

The Sultan's eyes narrowed. He was clearly insulted by the way I addressed him. To him, I was not just the enemy and a butcher of his people, but the very definition of an infidel to a Muslim. "You will take care, Masoud."

"I mean no offense, Great One," I began again, forcing myself to civility and respectfulness. "But the more I see of your people, the less I see a difference between us." Something happened then. I still held the Spear of Longinus in my hand. To my amazement, I began to feel warmth coming from the thing, from where I held it. I almost dropped it, but something forced me to hang on. "You call God, Allah, Praise be His name," I was shocked by what I heard myself saying, but could not help but let the words come out. "But there is only One God by any name. You know this to be so or you'd not've allowed me to live to this point."

A dead silence filled the air around us. It did not feel ominous, this silence—as if the Sultan were about to burst with outrage—but I did not expect Sultan Salah al-Din to hold with what I had just proclaimed. The warmth from the Spear vanished. I looked sidelong for an instant at my commander, Sir Jonathan James. Again, he was smiling, and this time even broader than the last time I had glanced at him. I did not understand why he was smiling.

The Sultan looked at Sir James, as well. "Commander, you are of the...Templars are you not?"

"Aye," said Sir James, meeting Salah al-Din's gaze with equality.

"Your...student, a neophyte in your order, perhaps?" he said nodding at me.

I shook my head, both in silent answer to the question and disbelief at the question itself.

"Soon to be, me thinks," my commander answered, whose smile became even larger.

"Presuming you both live to see that day," the Sultan pointed out.

The shouts from outside the tent came suddenly; voices in chaos, frantic with the fear and panic. The Sultan stood at once, and addressed the guards that remained. "Find out what is happening," he ordered.

One of them turned to leave, to carry out the order, but was knocked down by Hakim as the latter ran back into the main area of the tent. "They attack! The crusaders come again with smoking weapons!" he declared angrily.

"With what?" I asked lamely.

The explosion that immediately followed my words knocked us all to the ground. My ears rang for an instant as I was showered with dirt and debris. I lay motionless for a time, unsure of whether I lived or not.

~VI~

Day light streamed in through the torn ceiling of the tent. Dust and smoke choked my lungs, loud voices and the din of nearby battle filled my ears. I lived still. Orders were being shouted from all around. I looked up and saw not only the gaping hole in the ceiling but one whole side of tent gone, blown out no doubt by the explosion. It was the side of the tent that had been behind the Sultan's chair. Indeed, not just a wall, but the rooms which had been on the other side of it had been leveled. I could see several bodies among the expanse of the tent's cloth, the ruins of the tent's rooms.

An explosion? I wondered. I had heard that our army was able to create a fireball made of wood, dung, oil and other elements that contained the magic of a lightning strike when fire was held to it. But I had never seen it used. I could smell burning cloth, wood and skin. Putrid was this last unmistakable smell. I coughed and rose to my feet to see Salah al-Din running toward the outer reaches of what had been the tent's parameter, shouting orders as he went. A rough hand grabbed my arm, pulling me to one side.

"This way, Masoud, quickly," said Alhasan as he pulled my arm and lead me—still holding the spear—away. I looked to Sir James who was just rising to his feet, coughing and sputtering from the debris filled air. His hands were still tied. I reached out with the blade of the spear and cut through the leather thongs that bound his wrists. To my surprise, the blade still held a sharp edge and sliced through the leather with the ease of a knife through lard.

"Masoud, no!" exclaimed Alhasan.

"Masoud, yes!" I retorted.

"Let us be gone from here," said Sir James, by way of an order more than a suggestion.

580

"You cannot escape, you see?!" said Alhasan, panic lacing his voice. I interpreted his tone to reflect what will happen to him if he let us flee more than an attempt to imply the impossibility of us being able to flee.

Muslim soldiers began gathering at the opened side of the tent. "Back the way we came in, lad," said Sir James. We did just that, heading back through the long entry tunnel which had come through the explosion unscathed, and out in to a smoke-filled, chaotic morning. To my surprise, Alhasan was right behind us. "Wait! Masoud, please!" he cried.

The smoke was thinning and what I saw was not what I expected to see. No crusaders. Only Muslims. Hakim had said the crusaders were attacking. I saw none. What I had taken to be the sound of nearby battle from within the tent was actually naught but the Muslims converging on the scene of the explosion, yelling all the while, their scimitars at the ready.

We heard it then; a screeching sound to still the blood. From across the sky it came, shrieking as if it were a demon just released from the shit-stenched bowels of hell itself. "Cover! Now!" ordered Sir James, looking to the sky.

Following his gaze my eyes beheld a frightening sight; an arrow the length of a man, its shaft nearly as thick as one, was descending right toward us, trailing a smoke tail and screeching its death yell. "Bleeding Christ," I muttered at the sight.

"Aye. Its shaft is mostly hollow, filled with the fire-stuff, launched from a big crossbow," remarked Sir James. "Not very reliable, tend to explode at the bow, they do. Used for long range assaults on occasion." He grabbed my arm and pulled me away. "Run!"

Fire-stuff? came the absurd and inappropriate-for-the-moment question in my head as my legs began to carry me away. There was nowhere to hide, no shelter to seek. Why the Sultan had placed his tent so out in the open now baffled me. No matter. We simply ran.

The impact of this apparent second arrow or missile knocked us through the air. I landed atop my commander, bounced off his body and crashed hard to the ground, then tumbled some fifteen feet before coming to a stop. A split second later something or someone slammed into me, Alhasan. We had not been struck by the missile itself, but rather, we had felt the sweeping effect of its initial impact some twenty yards away from our present position. All was black with smoke and unearthed dirt from the point of impact. My ears rang with near deafness from the sound of the massive explosion. I coughed and sputtered from smoke and debris in my mouth. I pushed an unconscious Alhasan off of me. "Alhasan?" I said, shaking him slightly by the shoulders.

He groaned and opened his eyes, coughed. "Powerful weapons. We have the 'fire-stuff' too, you see," he said smiling, "though, we've not used it in such as a large arrow."

The surroundings began to clear. More voices in chaos could be heard gathering at the point of impact. It became clear that not all the voices were expressing chaos. Some were voicing anger and outrage. I looked around the immediate area, searching for my commander. I spotted Sir James some fifteen feet away. He was clutching his injured side again and being helped to his feet by someone dressed in the under tunic of a crusader. I recognized the man aiding Sir James at once. It was Henry! "Bleedin' Christ!" I said again.

My friend heard me and nearly dropped our commander in his rush to greet me. We embraced as long-lost brothers. He looked at me and then at the spear I held in my hand. "That...thing. And, you. You healed me, brought me back to life!"

"So I've heard," I said in exasperation. "But I don't remember a damned thing of it! Where were you? Why did they not keep you with us?"

"I don't know," he replied.

"Time enough for that later, lads. We need to move, now! Take advantage of the attack and get out of here," said Sir James, already moving off in the direction from which the last missile had come, its entrails of smoke still visible in the air, though rapidly dissipating.

"No, Masoud!" pleaded Alhasan, now on his feet and joining us. "You must stay!"

We ran for our lives. The entrails of the large missile arrow were all but gone, yet it had pointed us in the right direction, away from the Sultan's tent and the encampment proper, and toward our own people and our freedom from captivity. We ran and ran and saw no sign of pursuers. Hope crested in my chest as we ran up a rise in the desert. I knew what we would see on the other side, even though they may still be a ways off: we would see our army and the lovers of the Christ, the noble crusaders of God. In that moment I had all but forgotten my change of heart toward the Muslims; that they were in reality no different than us, that they were not the evil infidel they had been portrayed to be by the stagy and corrupted Church. All that had been set aside for the moment as I raced up the rise. But what greeted us was not our Holy army.

Commander James, though clearly in pain as he ran up the rise, was the first to make its crest. He froze in his tracks. Henry and I nearly crashed into him as we made it to the crest as well. Alhasan, still with us, stopped along side of me. We all panted with fatigue. "You see?" said Alhasan, pointing to the other side of the rise. There before us, sitting on horseback were Hakim and the dark-robed, opaque-eyed man, Rashin. They were flanked by a century of Muslim soldiers. The soldiers stood calmly, quietly, all facing us. Their demeanor reflected that of Hakim and Rashin. They were completely ignoring the din of noise going on behind us at the points of impact. It was as if they were there waiting solely for us. My heart sank. But I was also shocked to see Hakim. He was just in the tent! How could he have beaten us here? I wondered. I then noticed Rashin looking intently at the spear in my hand, his opaque eye moistening and squinting lustfully at the thing. It was then that I was struck with a most extraordinary sensation; I knew this man. Impossible! I berated myself. I could not possibly know this man. Perhaps he was a Muslim or a Sufi Mystic and Magician I've heard our priests rail against, and thus he has me in some kind of spell to make me think I know him so that he could get to the spear and...my mind was rambling. I caught it and stopped it, but still the feeling persisted, I knew this Rashin.

"I think not. You dogs will not escape this day," bellowed Hakim, from atop a black steed.

Rashin sat tall on his brilliantly white and tremendously large stallion. He said nothing, but continued to eye the spear and me.

Still the feeling of familiarity persisted. For the moment, I pushed it aside, being pressed by the more urgent matter and threat of reentering the state of captivity.

"The spear," called Rashin, "I want the spear."

"But, my lord, it does nothing, as was just demonstrated, you see," answered Alhasan.

"Then Masoud will have no opposition in giving it to me," Rashin countered.

The spear grew warm in my hand, vibrating as well. I looked at the thing and I was suddenly thrust back a thousand years in my mind's eye. I saw a darkly cloaked figure with paste-white skin. I was in another body, looking upon this individual and a company of ancient pagan, Druid priests of the Old Ways, as my mother would say, flanking him. A fire, the fires of the Wickerman, burned near them. Wickermen: the ancient Celtic method of dispensing with an enemy via placing him in a giant wooden cage in the shape of a man and setting it alight with fire. The flames purged the enemy of evil and released his soul to cross over to the Otherworld. At least, such was the belief. But the practice had been outlawed. Yet, here I was, watching the ritual burning of a Wickerman through the eyes of...of...Longinus. I looked at my hand, Longinus' hand. The spear, the same spear I now held in my hand as Masoud, was there and vibrated. I felt Longinus concentrating, placing his attention on the elements. The rains fell then, smothering the fires of the Wickermen, putting them out. The dark cloaked one was infuriated. "Draco," my Masoud-self whispered. The vision vanished and I was on the rise again, staring at Rashin, comprehending to a degree, but nothing more. I felt one other thing from this Rashin; though he was obviously strong of will, he did not seem as powerful as he had in that ancient lifetime as Draco.

"What did you call him, Masoud?" asked Alhasan.

"Draco," Sir James answered for me. "It means 'dragon' in the Old Tongue. Apt name for him lad."

Sir James clearly misunderstood my reference. But I said nothing to correct him, to make him understand. How could I when I did not understand it myself?

"Allah help us!" exclaimed Alhasan, eyes growing wide as he looked at the spear in my hand. "It speaks to you again."

The spear pulsated a bright red. I almost dropped it, believing that it was about to be too hot to hold. But it became no hotter than the warmth I had felt from it earlier.

A murmur arose from those in Hakim's ranks. It was the murmur of fear, bordering on outright terror. They were all, to a man, staring at the spear, watching its seemingly supernatural display. I held it aloft, not quite sure why I was doing it, nor knowing what I was going to do. But my display and apparent command of the spear of Longinus was enough to cause the soldiers who were with Hakim and Rashin to cower, sending most of them to their knees in a posture of supplication.

"On your feet, all of you, or I will have you flogged right here!" Rashin bellowed.

The moment dragged on. I had no idea what to do. "Go on, lad," urged Sir James.

"I hate to say this, commander," I began in a whisper through tight lips, "but I don't know what I'm doing, it's just for show, my raising the spear,"

"No, no! You know what to do, you did it to bring back your friend, you see," said Alhasan. "Think, concentrate."

"On what?!" I asked nervously.

The men in the opposing battle group before us began to murmur again, but this time it was the murmur of confusion tempered with anger; they were beginning to realize they had been duped, that my gesture was empty, that I was a fake. Though the spear still pulsated, the other men rose to their feet, a cry of anger and vengeance escaping their mouths.

The intuitive realization of the spear's glowing pulsation, its meaning, then came to me like a fresh breeze, quickly but gently enfolding my being and washing me in the truth of its caress: it was a warning. I started to back away.

"Liam, what are you doing?" asked Sir James.

"Yes, Masoud, do not flee, especially in the direction we have just come," echoed Alhasan.

"It's a warning, the spear's glowing, it's a warning that we must leave here, now!" I turned and ran back in the direction we had come.

I felt the others follow more than saw them. There was no time to turn and see, to make sure. A split second later, we heard a howl in the air and a third missile hit not more than a few feet in front of where we had previously stood. It had apparently landed right in front of Hakim and Rashin's men. We were all knocked down by the blast. The smoke cleared after a moment and I could see Hakim and Rashin lying on the ground not far behind us. They had obviously spurred their horses into following us and thus missed the brunt of the explosion. Their men had not been so fortunate; bodies and body-parts lay everywhere. Moaning and crying of the wounded and near dead filled the air. Rashin, as if possessed by a demon, suddenly sprang to his feet as if he had only been taking a nap. He roused Hakim who was much slower to stand, but stood nonetheless.

I felt the spear—which no longer glowed—in my hand. It was tugging, almost pulling me to the left, away from the large tent we had been in just a short time ago, and back toward the hospital tent we had initially come from. "This way," I stated flatly, no longer feeling the doubt that plagued me a moment before.

"That way leads..." Alhasan began.

"I know where it leads. The spear, it's pulling me that way. That's all I know," I replied.

"So be it," said Sir James.

I ran, the others followed. We were completely ignored by the dying, the injured and the chaotic as we made our way to...I knew not, but my intuitive sense to follow this spear's lead had taken over my being. I, we, had little other option at the moment.

We made it to the hospital tent, which was still standing, and went beyond it. We all stopped in our tracks, confronted again by a platoon of Muslim soldiers, scimitars at the ready. They seemed to be as surprised at the sight of prisoners on the loose as they were by the aerial attack.

"Stop them!" Hakim yelled from behind us. He and Rashin were on foot with naught but a small contingent of soldiers. "Do not let them escape!"

The lead Muslim soldier in front of us stepped forward to carry out the order. He was dropped to the ground, dead before he could complete the first step; an arrow sticking out the side of his head. I looked in the direction from whence the arrow came and was greeting by a blessed sight: a host of crusaders swarming on the Muslim encampment. I looked back at Hakim and Rashin. They were gone.

"Praise be, eh, lad?" smiled Commander, Sir James.

"I must...I must..." cried Alhasan backing away.

"Stay with me, Alhasan. I will see to it that no one harms you! If you leave they will kill you to be certain!" I said to him. "There's no choice in it, 'you see'," I said to him, using his own favorite phrase, hoping he would not see it as a mocking of his English, but as a sincere form of adulation. "Please, my friend, allow me to help you as you have helped me."

Fear was on his face, but trust filled his eyes. "As you wish, Masoud. As you wish," he said.

~VII~

The soldiers of Christ overran Salah al-Din's camp, but had no follow-through. Their arrogance was such that the initial success of the catapulted exploding arrows lulled them into a false sense of superiority; that they would simply be able to walk into the Muslim camp and be in command. As such, the ignorant fools, much to the consternation of their commanders, lost discipline and began looting and pilfering what they could.

"Agh! La! La!" screamed a woman nearby, a harem bride by the look of her richly appointed attire. No mere camp whore was this. Three men, crusaders, had her pinned to the ground. A forth, a sergeant no less as indicated by his particular tunic, was ripping her gown and undoing his belt and tunic all at once.

"You there! Sergeant! Cease! Secure the edges of..." barked a nearby commander. He was cut off in mid sentence, however, by an arrow through the neck. The sergeant and his fellow soldiers, having given the commander barely a glance to begin with, now proceeded unabated with the rape.

Someone had a hold of my arm and was pulling me in the opposite direction. "Come, you, away from here!" said a voice with the accent of a Franc.

I turned expecting to see my commander, Sir James, holding my arm and perhaps Henry nearby. Instead I was staring into the face of another man who wore commander's insignia, but who had the toothless grin of a commoner, not a noble; obviously, a commander by circumstance, not by birth. It was he who held me by the arm. "Where is Sir James and Henry?" I demanded.

"Who?" asked the toothless commander in his Franc accent.

"My commander and my friend," I said. "The men who were just with me."

"Most likely on their way to the general's tent for debriefing, as should be you. Come, S'il vous plait," said the toothless commander. It was then he saw Alhasan. "Take that one prisoner!" he yelled, addressing any crusader within earshot to capture Alhasan. Most were in the process of looting, raping or killing the remaining remnants of Muslim soldiers, but two heeded the order and stepped toward my friend.

"No! He's...with me," I said, stepping in front of Alhasan. The crusaders stopped in front of me.

The toothless commander looked me over and his mouth broke into a lecherous grin. "Aye. Not enough of the lovelies in this hostile land, mon ami? Keep your...servant then. Does not matter."

"Agh! La! Laaaaa!" the woman screamed now between sobs. She was putting up an intense struggle, frustrating the sergeant's efforts at making penetration. He raised a bare hand across his shoulder and backhanded the woman's face. Blood began to seep from the woman's mouth.

I stepped toward them, the toothless commander grabbing my arm tighter. "Plan to join 'em?"

The spear began to vibrate in my hand, then to glow as before. The toothless commander's eyes grew wide with fear as he saw it and he let my arm go. The two other crusaders in front of me stepped back with awe in their eyes. I then turned and ran toward the four men attempting to rape the woman. "Release her! Release her now!" I yelled at the men. They ignored me. Though I had never before used the spear, or any spear, as a weapon, I suddenly found myself wielding the one in my hand as if I had been born with it attached to my limbs. It was an extension of me. The butt of it found its mark in the temple of the raping sergeant. It sent him sprawling to the ground unconscious, his small, exposed, erect penis flopping and deflating as he landed. The other soldiers who had been holding the woman down now became enraged. They stood as one, releasing the woman, who scurried off like a cat which had just escaped a pack of dogs.

"You are dead," stated one of the men flatly, staring straight at me.

"I doubt that," I replied defiantly, arrogantly. What happened next was a blur, both to the eye and to my mind. Alhasan later told me that I had closed my eyes in that moment, Attuning with the divine spear! as he put it, and used it to thwart the men, whirring and whirling the thing as a windmill, striking each man precisely on the side of the head above the ear with the butt end of the spear, never the blade, thus mercifully incapacitating the men, but doing them no lasting damage. All I remember is that a moment later, I came back to myself, holding the spear at rest while four men lay at my feet. Feeling eyes upon me, I looked to my left and saw the woman I had rescued. Her eyes were incredible; beautiful lavender colored eyes stared at me from behind a pile of baskets and large broken ceramic. Terror was still in those eyes, but she managed a nod of her head toward me which I interpreted as a thank you. It was then I noticed a cloaked and turbaned figure near her, crouching behind a partially destroyed supply wagon. His eyes—which was about all I could see of the man's face—were a stark gold in color and focused intently on me, as if watching, observing my every move. I recognized the man as one of the men who had been in the Sultan's tent; one of those who had stood silently behind Rashin in the shadows then, watching my every move just as he was now. A shiver ran up my spine as I returned the man's stare. And, another feeling of familiarity washed over me. I had known this man before as well, but could not presently place his past identity in the forefront of my mind. The only thing that did come to mind about him was that he had been some kind of Christian priest in that past existence.

"Ah, Masoud! You show again your connection to the spear and the power therein, you see?" said Alhasan gleefully.

I looked from the gold-eyed man to Alhasan, then to the toothless commander, who stared at me dumbfounded. He looked at the men I had just dispensed with. "That will not sit well with the general," he said.

"If he's any kind of general, if he's got any kind of honor, he will not condone such behavior from the crusaders of Christ," I replied.

"'Honor'? 'crusaders of Christ'? You speak as one of them." he stated.

"One of them?" I replied, annoyed at this wretch's insolents and confused by his words.

"Knights of the Temple. You talk like them. If you are, I meant no offense, I just..."

Sir James suddenly appeared from behind the man, placing a hand on the toothless Franc commander's shoulder. Henry appeared just behind Sir James. "He is not. Yet. But take care, my friend, how you would address him. You don't know to whom you speak."

"Yes, sir," said the toothless commander. "But you should be at the general's tent by now. All of you," he said looking to me.

"I simply came back when I saw the commotion," replied Sir James.

I looked back to where the woman was. She was still there, staring at me. I then looked to where the cloaked man with the gold eyes had been a moment before. He was gone.

Shouts came from the other end of the camp, from the direction we had come.

"Your men, commander..." began Sir James

"Commander Laffite," said the toothless Franc commander with a false mantle of authority.

"Your men lack discipline. They care more about looting and causing mayhem than they do about gaining and securing this camp," said Sir James. "I suggest you tell your men to fall back before it's too late."

"You are not in command here. I will..."

Three Muslim soldiers descended on a pair of crusaders some forty feet from our position, cleaving the arms off both men with their scimitars. Both crusaders stood in stunned silence as their life's blood spouted from their shoulder stumps.

"Salah al-Din will retake his camp, by leave of your incompetence," said Sir James.

Laffite hesitated for but an instant more before taking Sir James' advice. "Replier! En arriére!" yelled Laffite. "Fall back!"

The crusaders had indeed become enamored and thus distracted with the lust of a would-be conqueror. Salah al-Din and his army raided their own camp with merciless brutality, taking back what was theirs and disemboweling any crusader who was stupid enough not to immediately follow Laffite's orders. Lafitte, Sir James, Henry, Alhasan and I were fortunate enough to make it out. Alive.

‡ ‡ ‡

Night comes slowly to the desert, especially when a near full moon rises at the same time the day's sun relinquishes its command of the sky. Such was the way of it this evening. The crusaders, including Sir James, Alhasan, Henry and myself, made it back to an English encampment in tattered rags and fatigued bodies, fortunate not to have been pursued by Salah al-Din and his men. For now. At the crusader encampment we had been given quarters, a change of tunic and wash basins with which to cleanse the past days from our being. We were summoned to the general in short order. A golden hue washed the land as we walked with our escort across the camp to the general's tent. The sky looked as though God himself had sprayed it with his breath of the most high, so golden it was. But there was something ominous, foreboding about it too; as if a portent were being conveyed of sorrows yet to come. I could not put my finger on it, but I felt it at the core of my soul. The spear too, which I had not let out of my sight since arriving in the camp, seemed to sense something, for it was in a constant state of mild vibration in my hand.

We were ushered into the general's tent, which was large on the outside, but not nearly so as the Sultan's. The inside was also large, but filled with all things practical for the work of a commander who sent men at arms to death or glory. I laughed to myself at the thought of our generals having such an ornate, even audacious, of a dwelling on the field of battle as the Sultan's was. But, then again, Salah al-Din was a king. Perhaps our own king—generals, King Richard's for example, had similar richly appointed dwellings in the field as the Sultan's. I had never been in a king's tent, let alone a general's. This general, General Blackthorn, was no king. He was a large man in his sixty-fifth year by all accounts and was also known as a Templar Knight. He stood before us now in the middle of his simple general's field command tent, large though it was. His eyes were dark and intense; full of authority and questions. His beard was grey as was his shoulder-length, grease-filled hair. The smell of lilac flowers filled the air and I realized it was coming from the general himself. The man seemed attached to cleanliness. Most men I knew, myself included, washed periodically, yet bathed only once in a moon's cycle, if then. I came to find later that General Blackthorn, a haughty member of the English nobility, bathed twice daily if at all possible before becoming a Templar Knight. But once a Templar he had to adhere to their code; not to bath and always remain dressed for combat. Apparently, he insisted on using oils from the lilac flower, thereby giving him a fresh aroma at least, if not a truly clean one. The scent was quite contradictory to his appearance; that of a hardened soldier and leader of men. Just above his grey beard, on the cheek below his left eye ran a scar. It traveled down from his lower left eyelid and curved around the cheek to his left ear which was missing its lobe, no doubt from the same event that caused the scar itself. He looked to me to be in the bloom of late forties rather than mid-sixties. But then again, I had always been a poor judge of another's age.

Several crusader commanders were in the tent with us, including the Franc commander, Laffite, who stood off to one side.

"You there," Blackthorn said in a deep voice by way of addressing me, "you are the one who brings the Spear back to us, back to its rightful home, yes? It is an honor, my son, to meet you. I am Sir Horatio Blackthorn, commander of the host of crusaders and liberators of Jerusalem."

"But I thought King Richard leads us," I said lamely.

"Aye, 'tis true. But the king sees fit to consort with our Franc friends," replied the general, looking at Laffite, "than to actually be here with us. I lead in his stead and by His Majesty's grace, along with a couple of other generals who are en route to us," He looked directly at the spear. "Bring it to me," he ordered.

I was taken aback by the command. I suddenly never wanted to let anyone else touch the instrument I held. Still... "I...by your leave, sir, I must warn you that it may not...that is, it may become..."

"Oh, come lad. Do you disobey a direct order?"

I looked to Sir James and Henry, neither of whom looked to offer me any help.

"My son," Sir Blackthorn began in a gentler tone, "I have heard of all the feats you have performed with it; the restoring of your friend here to life, how it glowed in warning to you, leading you away from certain death; how it became an instrument of defense and magic in your hands, thwarting evil from our midst."

I could only guess that his last reference was to the combat I had entered into, which resulted in the saving of the Arab woman who was being raped. "There was no magic to it, Sire," I said.

"Oh? Its glowing is not magic? Would you say it's not of God, our father then?" asked Sir Blackthorn.

"I do not know of such things, Sire."

"But it does communicate with you, does it not? What does it say, lad? What does it say?! Does it tell you when our

Lord Christ will come again? Soon, I hope!" The general was becoming excited, like a schoolboy wanting a secret to be revealed. He waited a moment for my response. But when I offered none his smile grew large, stretching the scar on his face such that it appeared he had two smiles. He threw back his head and laughed a belly laugh as I have never heard. I was confused by it and that confusion must have shown on my face. The general stepped forward and clasped his large, strong hand on my shoulder, sending a shooting pain throughout my upper body. "I jest with you, lad." He leaned in close, his lilac scent nearly overwhelming my senses as he whispered into my ear. "We all know the Good Christ's second coming will be in the mind and hearts of all men, that we will come to see the Christ beholden in each other as ourselves. We all know that's the Lord's true Second Coming, do we not, soldier?" He stepped back then and stared into my eyes, looking questioningly as to how I would respond to his query. I had never heard anyone say such of the Christ's next coming; that it would be in our minds, our hearts, through us, as us. This man spoke like no Christian I had ever known.

Yet, what he said sparked a realization within my own mind and heart. "I know naught of these things, Sire," I said again. "I am but a humble man from poor origins. But, what I have seen in this land has led me to question everything I was ever taught on the side of our Lord Christ. These people in this land worship God as we worship Him."

A snicker came from the direction of Laffite or someone standing near him.

"Silence!" the general bellowed. "Go on, my son," he said to me.

"I don't know, Sire. As I said, I know naught of these things," I replied.

"You know more than you think. Much more. Does he not, Sir James?" Blackthorn said, turning to my commander.

"I would say so, your Grace," replied Sir James.

"You are right. He will make a splendid candidate," said General Blackthorn.

"Candidate?" I asked.

"We will speak of it later, my son. For now..." said the general, holding out his hand for the spear.

I slowly stretched out my hand and reluctantly released the spear into the general's palm.

"Aagh!!" the general screamed in agonized pain at the spear's touch. I was horrified. He abruptly stopped the scream and stared at me. In the next instant he burst into another belly laugh, the rest of the company in the tent joining him this time. "Again, I chide you, my son. Oh, you are too easy. Come. Let us dine whilst I examine the instrument that pierced our Lord's side. It is amazing that it's still in such good condition..." the general babbled as he looked at the spear oddly, I thought, almost lustfully. Food was brought in. We reclined on pillows and I had the most sumptuous food I had eaten in quite some time.

~VIII~

We finished our meal and retired to our quarters. I looked forward to a wonderful night's sleep; one that filled the mind and soul with heavenly peace, restored the heart to truth and faith, and replenished the body to full strength and vigor. But it was not to be. Every sound in the night, no matter how small, impinged itself upon my senses, keeping true rest and peaceful sleep at bay. It did not seem to be affecting my quarter-mates that way. Henry slept on a nearby pallet like the dead, snoring rhythmically, and Alhasan snuffled quietly next to me on his own sleeping pallet, oblivious to the nocturnal noises keeping me from slumber. I noticed at one point that Sir James was not in the tent with us. I was not surprised, however. He was a senior officer and an English noble, after all. He would have option to be housed elsewhere. Still, when I looked to the empty pallet that was near our quarter's entrance—our quarters being a simple four-man field tent—the commander's belongings, his dirty tunic and side-arm, were there.

"The soul floats nightly," whispered a heavily accented voice from just outside the tent. The accent was Arabic. I immediately grabbed the spear, which Sir Horatio Blackthorn had reluctantly, begrudgingly, I thought, given back to me at our meal's end, and brandished it at the ready. "The soul floats nightly," said the voice again.

I threw open the tent's flap which revealed a man dressed in black and brown. I had seen the attire before, but could not immediately place where, though I knew it to be Arabic. The man, whose face was obscured save for the slit in his headdress that allowed his eyes to peer out, jumped with a start. "Do not move," I commanded. I was about to sound an alarm, to yell at the top of my lungs that we had an Arab intruder in the camp, for that is surely what he was.

He then stopped me with a familiar voice, no longer a whisper. "Wait. Do not call out. I was informed that this was the quarters of the Temple Master," Hakim said. I was stunned to silence. "Give him this." He handed me a folded paper. I examined it. It had a strange seal on it: a pouncing lion made of Arabic letters. In addition to the lion, there were symbols on it which I had never seen before. It seemed to be an alphabet comprised of triangles and dots.

"I don't..." I began. But, when I looked back to Hakim, he was gone. I could only assume the folded parchment was meant for Sir James. Why was Hakim, who had seemed so ruthlessly antagonistic toward us, delivering a message for Sir James?! And, how did he get past our sentries?

"What troubles do you have?" Alhasan asked from inside our tent. I turned and saw my Arab friend sitting up on his pallet, groggily rubbing his eyes and yawning. "Is it urgent? I hope not, for I would greatly like to sleep a fortnight, you see."

"I do see, for I'd like to sleep a long sleep as well. There's no trouble...least I think not. This is most odd, though," I said, once again examining the strange markings on the sealed parchment in my hands.

"What is it?" Alhasan said, suddenly becoming excited. He leapt off his sleeping pallet and bounded up beside me to see what I held.

"Ahh, your Knights Templar. It is their code, the writing there," he stated.

"You mean these strange open triangles and dots?" I asked.

"Yes, yes! It is their language, their secret alphabet. It must be the name of whomever the missive is for, you see." he said.

"This reads, 'Sir James'?" I asked, doubtfully.

"No. They would not use the actual name, but the title or rank within the Order," Alhasan pointed out.

"The messenger said it was for the 'Temple Master'." I said.

"You see? And the messenger delivered it here. Your commander, Sir James is a worthy guess." Alhasan looked out the tent. "The Templar messenger has vanished into the night."

"But that's just it; I don't think it was a Templar messenger. It couldn't have been," I said. I turned over the missive and showed Alhasan the Lion emblem in Arabic letters.

His astonishment was palpable. "Masoud, who delivered this?"

"You won't believe it. It was Hakim." I said.

"Truly?"

"Truly."

"That explains much," said Alhasan cryptically.

"Do you know what the lion script says?"

"It is the emblem of the Ismaelian Knights, Masoud," said Alhasan gravely.

I thought for a moment. I had heard of that Order before, but always in the context of it being called by another name; one of an Order of unholy and near satanic men. "You mean, The Order of Assassins? They are cut-throats and degenerates, smokers of the hashish and opium, are they not?!" I asked, now completely dumbfounded.

"No, they are not, Masoud," Alhasan said defensively. "You have been listening to too much of your crusader ignorance. They are a noble Order of Knights which is akin to your Knights Templar Order. The Order of Ismaelian Knights or Assassins, as you call them, even work with your Knights Templar for the betterment of all and the perpetuation of the concept of the One God."

"I don't know anything about the Knights Templar, save that they protect Christians on pilgrimage. But you seem to know a lot about the Order of Assassins," I said haughtily.

"You will soon come to know much about them too, and your Templar Order. Look..." he said pointing to the spear in my hand. Its blade glowed a beautiful, soft green.

I held it up, looked at it closely. Somehow, its glow was soothing.

"What does it mean, Masoud?"

"I don't know, Alhasan." The soothing feeling I received from it quickly abated and was replaced by a feeling of frustration. Contrary to what I had just said to Alhasan, I suddenly felt as though I did in fact know all the answers regarding the spear and my connection to it, already knew in my soul all about the Knights Templar and everything to do with all things relating to the One that Alhasan had just spoken of...but I could not fully remember. I closed my eyes and willed the frustration to leave, willed the deep seated knowledge that I possessed to come forth. I laughed oddly at the thought of being in possession of such knowledge.

"Masoud?" asked Alhasan. "Are you not well?"

I did not answer him, but kept my eyes closed to let the soothing quality of the spear's glow wash over me again.

"Yes, Masoud, turn to it and to Allah, for the answer. All the answers you seek are there," Alhasan said, apparently understanding what it was that I was doing. His voice altered in its timbre to an audible gentleness which matched the visual softness coming from the spear.

"I...must lie down," I heard myself say. My eyes still closed, I next felt myself being gently guided toward my sleeping pallet. I lay down on the soft rushes, the spear by my side, and let the feeling of softness wash completely over me.

And then they began again; visions of things from many centuries past. But they were different from previous visions of the past: a forest; a sorceress; a Merlin by the name of Myrriddin——me. I saw a battle between good and evil, wherein the evil was thwarted but not destroyed, never destroyed. Balance to all, in all of ALL. Leaping ahead in the vision, in this same time frame, this same life, the visions showed our Britain's true founding king, Arturius himself; King Arthur, as he is known to us now, at least by legend. Many doubted a man, a king the likes of him ever actually existed. But I saw him now through my vision, through the eyes of my former self; Myrriddin. He, Arthur, was tall with green eyes and fair-skin like his mother, Igraines. Yes, Igraines had been her name; mother to this great king. His face was handsome like that of someone from the High country and his hair was light brown and shoulder length. Uther Pendragon had been his father. The thoughts, images and memories came flooding into my mind as if I were reliving the events in the present. Arthur turned to me, said something to me, "Bring it back, Merlin," he said, "'Tis up to you. You, who are the legacy, the bloodline, of him to whom it belonged, of the one who pierced our Lord's side. You gave it to the good bishop Rozinus all these years past, in good faith, I know. But it now resides with the Grail in the hands of blasphemers and infidels. Wrest it from them. Bring it back whether it takes this life or more."

"'This life or more,'" my Liam Arthur Mason self, my Masoud self said aloud. The vision faded.

"Masoud? Masoud?" Alhasan said.

I opened my eyes and looked at Alhasan. "I am well, my friend. I am well," I replied. I looked at the spear. It had ceased its glowing.

"What did it show you?"

"It?"

"The spear, Masoud. Surely it was showing you something. Your eyes moved beneath their lids as if you were watching something. Your lips moved as if speaking in a dream or being spoken to in a dream, you see," Alhasan said excitedly.

"You're quite observant," I said. "I don't know that the spear showed me anything. But I did have a vision; a vision of the past or a past."

A loud snort came from the other side of the tent. Henry stirred on his pallet. He rolled away from us, coughed violently, then rolled on his back, eyes still closed. I noticed, perhaps for the first time, that my friend looked thin, too thin, as if he had not eaten in days. I then noticed something else; a stick protruding from his clenched teeth. His jaw moved as Henry lightly chewed on the object even in his sleep.

"What is that?" I asked quietly. "He may choke." I sat up on the pallet intending to go to my friend Henry and take the stick from his mouth.

But Alhasan's hand stopped me. "No, Masoud. It is the only thing that enables him to sleep fully now, you see."

I was confused. How could chewing on a stick enable him to sleep? But then I remembered something that Sir James had said in the healing tent. "Is it...?"

"It is the opium, yes. It has become his best friend, I fear," said Alhasan.

"I had no idea," I replied sadly.

"He hides it well, or so he thinks."

Before I could think on how to help my friend, the tent flap opened and Sir James entered. He stopped and looked oddly at me, as if he suddenly felt that he had interrupted something. He then looked at Henry and back to me, a look of understanding spread across his face. "You did not know," he stated, referring to my friend's addiction.

I shook my head.

"It eases his pain. When the time is right, we'll help wean him from the opiate's teat."

Though I nodded my understanding, disappointment and renewed concern for Henry's well being coursed through my being.

"What do you hold there?" asked Sir James regarding the folded parchment I held in my hand.

"It was delivered for you by...Hakim, of all people," I replied, handing him the sealed item.

Sir James examined it.

"From the Order of Assassins!" I volunteered.

"They are actually called the Order of the Ismaelian Knights," he gently corrected.

I glanced briefly at Alhasan, who looked just a little smug.

"The Order of Hashishim, too," I said. "They suck the hash pipes and kill. I heard that they murdered the Christian

King of Jerusalem; Conrad of Montferrat? It is their method, murdering for their benefit."

"They do not murder," Alhasan said. "They also see what they do as intrinsic to preserving our way, the way of Islam, and our land and people, you see."

"Sometimes, Master Liam Mason—Masoud—one man's murderer is another man's savior," said Sir James.

I was stunned again. Not only had Sir James received a missive from the Order of Assassins or Hashishim or Ismaelian Knights or whatever they were called, but he was standing before me defending them. It was then that I noticed he was wearing a crisp, white outer tunic with a red cross upon it. I had seen him in something similar many times before and I knew it to be the attire of a commander within the crusader ranks. But this one was different, longer, down to his shins and the cross on it seemed to be sewn on from silk or satin. I now understood this tunic's underlying symbol; it was the tunic of a knight or commander within the Knights Templar. He was also wearing a brown garment underneath the white outer tunic; I remembered that the brown under tunic symbolized the simple priest that Sir James apparently was in addition to being a knight.

I looked at Alhasan. He was in black as he always was. For a fleeting moment, I considered the possibility that Alhasan was a servant in the Order of the Knights Templar—servants in the Order of Templar Knights always wore black. I immediately dismissed the thought as absurd. He was a servant, true, but a servant to Sultan Salah al-Din. But, then again, perhaps he was also a servant in the Order of Hashishim Knights that served his people.

I must have appeared confused, even fearful, for Alhasan softly touched my sleeve. "Masoud, our Order of Hashishim Knights was begun by Hasan-i-Sabah. Our faction of Muslims has always been persecuted by the Sunni faction, you see. The Order began to assert our rights to exist, to thrive and worship, by wiping out those who would seek to destroy us. The Sunnis now fear us!" concluded Alhasan.

"By 'us' do you mean the Order of Hashishim Knights, are you a part of them? Or, do you mean your faction, the..." I asked, concerned.

"Shiite," Alhasan replied.

"What is the difference?" I asked.

"Oh, Masoud, you do not know? Why, our Shiite Caliphs, which are the only true leaders of Islam, are direct descendants of the Great Prophet himself. The Sunnis' Caliphs are not. They are elected," Alhasan spat.

"There is much more to that and the establishment of your Order of Knights, Alhasan," said Sir James. "Perhaps another time would be more appropriate to..."

"Of course there is, but you are correct, commander. Masoud is not yet a Templar so one must curtail the specifics of the details until he is avowed, you see," answered Alhasan. "Another time, indeed."

"I only meant that right now we must tend to other matters," said Sir James as he opened the missive.

A thousand questions came into my mind. The questions ran from why people kept saying or implying that I am to be a Templar when it was not something that I had sought out at least yet, to questions that revealed my desire to have a deeper understanding of Alhasan's faith. I suddenly had immense guilt over being in this land and trying to kill his people when I had not the vaguest notion of their beliefs beyond that which our own religious leaders wanted us to believe.

"Well," stated Sir James as he looked up from the missive and directly to me. Do you wish to become a Templar Liam Arthur Mason, also known by the Muslim name of Masoud?"

I was taken aback at the question and my commander's grave tone in asking it. "I thought it was something that one was not asked, but sought out."

"And there was also a time when it was only for the nobles of our lands, which I believe you are, but that is beside the point. Time is of the essence now, lad, because of your apparent connection with the spear of Longinus which you hold there. We are asked to attend a joint session of the Knights Templar and your Order, Alhasan, to discuss the matter," he said, looking to my Arab friend. So, then Alhasan was a Hashishim, I thought. Sir James then addressed me once more. "Should you decide to seek the Templar entry, lad, I would be honored to sponsor you and to speak for you. And, tonight would be a good time to declare your wish to be a part of the Knights Templar, lad."

This was almost too much to take in; the Order of the Knights Hashishim and the Order of the Knights Templar holding a joint meeting?! I should make my voice heard tonight to become a Templar?! This was nearly too much. Nearly so.

Sir James seemed to read my mind. "I know. 'Tis a great deal to think about in quick manner. But search your heart, Liam, your soul," said Sir James in a calming voice. "I think you will come to realize it's where you belong in this life. Come. Come. We should just make it," he said as he headed out through the tent's flap. I looked lamely at Alhasan.

"After you, Master Masoud," he said. Spear still in my hand, I left the tent, Alhasan following me.

~IX~

We strode a short distance across the camp toward a nearby church, Sir James leading the way, myself following and Alhasan behind me. Very few other soldiers and crusaders were about. The camp was quiet. I was still unsure of exactly where we were. Near Jerusalem, that much I knew. But I had not realized there was any church close by. Yet, when I looked closer at the imposing structure we were approaching, I questioned whether it was a church. Its dome was huge and high and contained on the top of it the crescent moon and star; the symbol of Islam.

"We go to a mosque?" I asked.

"A church, a temple, a mosque," replied Sir James quietly. "It has been all of those things. They all serve God, do they not?"

"But, the crescent and star atop the dome," I pointed out.

"It has served the Muslims of late, the Christians before that and the Jews before that. We, the Christians have reclaimed it. We have simply not yet put our Lord's cross back on top," Sir James said.

We crossed through its courtyard, went through the large portico and entered the massive main entrance. The ornately carved wooden doors had already been propped open, beckoning us in. The large entry area was dim, lit by a nine-candle chandelier hanging five feet above our heads. The entry area was rectangular, spreading out to our left and right. It was empty; not just devoid of people, but also empty of anything save a small bowl of water atop a chest-high pedestal before the sanctuary's entrance, some fourteen feet before us, across from the church's main entrance which we had just come through. I crossed the entry area and stood in the threshold of the sanctuary. I could see into the huge area of the main sanctuary. There was sparse candlelight and sconce-light within, so it was difficult to see very far. But what I could see took my breath way. It was immense. The interior height of the dome was astonishing. It was inlaid with gold and ornate carvings; Muslim over Christian and in some cases utilizing the Christian art that had been there for many a century. I stepped through the threshold and began to wander further into the sanctuary.

"No, lad. This way," said Sir James.

He and Alhasan were standing near a narrow door off of the entry area. I had not noticed the door before, apparently because its design and appearance was that of the wall of the entry area, thus blending in to the wall itself. It was now open, having been opened by Sir James, no doubt, and opened to a staircase that descended into the bowels of the place. I approached my companions as they turned and descended the stone steps, Sir James again leading the way.

The passage downward seemed to become narrower the further down we went. A dry, musty smell filled my nostrils. It was not unpleasant, however. The deeper we went the cooler it became. Finally, we came to the bottom of the steps. We stepped into a large, square room with several doors on the walls. Torches burned in sconces on the walls, illuminating the space and revealing a shadowy group of men near a pair of large wooden doors on a far wall. There were ten men that I could see. The dry musty odor suddenly mixed with the slight smell of smoke from the wall sconces. Another scent then joined the mix as well; the scent of lilac. At least one of the men present must be General Blackthorn. I looked closer at the men; they all had their faces obscured by cloth and they all seemed to be in ritual garb—six of them in white tunics with red crosses emblazoned on the chest. But four of them wore black robes, each with a red-crescent moon and star on the chest. The Knights of Hashishim were indeed with the Knights of Templar. One more man came out of the shadows; another Hashishim. I turned and looked at my friend Alhasan and was astonished to see that he had donned a black outer tunic which also displayed the crescent moon and star symbol.

"Wait here, both of you," Sir James ordered. He left us and approached the group of men. After a few moments of private consultation with one of them, Blackthorn, I presumed by his stature, Sir James returned to us. The wooden doors near the men slowly opened and the eleven men filed in to the room beyond. The doors slowly closed, leaving the three of us alone in what I was beginning to feel was some kind of ante-chamber. Sir James turned to me. "Well, lad. The time has come. Do you wish to become a part of the Order?"

I thought for a moment before answering, the weight of the question bearing down upon me. "It is now or not?" I asked, not quite knowing why.

"No. There may come another time, but not one such as this. We are at war and I do not know how much longer the alliance between our two Orders," he said nodding to Alhasan, indicating the symbol on his chest, "will be able to meet like this. For you, because of your connection with the Great Spear, it is important that both Orders are represented at your initiation."

Initiation? I thought this was strictly a petitioning? I wondered. I closed my eyes for a moment and sought clarity. Two things welled up inside of me. One was a feeling of fearfulness; that things seemed to be happening too fast. But the other was a feeling of...You are coming home, whispered a voice. The voice startled me, but it had echoed the other feeling I had. I looked at both of my companions and could tell by the expressions that neither one had heard the voice. I looked at the spear in my hand and realized that the voice seemed to have come from it. I suddenly felt as though I was indeed coming home. That sensation completely subdued the feeling of fearfulness. I felt a deep, inner connection to what was apparently about to happen this night. Though I no longer felt any weight associated with the question Sir James had just asked me, there was one other question that came to the forefront of my mind. "Why?" I asked.

"Why what?" he asked.

"I am connected with the 'Great Spear', as you called it," I began, "that I know. But why must I join the Knights Templar? And why should the Knights of Hashishim be present?"

"Both of our Orders of Knights go farther back in time than just their recent history would reveal, lad. Both Orders are offshoots of ancient organizations and schools of the Mysteries that predate Christendom or even the Druids of old. We are descendants of the groups that were thriving during the time of the Pharaohs of Egypt. We were also at the time of Christ. Search your soul. You will come to know that you yourself have been a large part of all these, as well as a great adept on your own. I sense it in you, even though I do not know the specifics of your soul's journey, save for your connection with the spear you hold. The initiation here this night is the linchpin that binds you to your past and your future. It is a necessary step on your path of reconnection. You have sensed it up to this point and have had fleeting manifestations of it, but have not yet lived by it. You will, by your actions in becoming a part of the Order or Orders here tonight, be unleashing the power within to live again through you and the spear," Sir James finished.

What he said washed over me, bathing me with a confirmation of what I had been feeling and seeing in my mind's eye: the visions I had earlier in the evening, for example —my ancient self as Myrriddin in counsel with King Arthur. It made sense to me at the level of my soul, if not at the level of my thinking mind.

"Here, tonight, we are all of the same Order of Knights, we all stand for the One Truth," Sir James said.

"It is so, Masoud," added Alhasan.

"And tomorrow?" I asked.

"We live in the present, Masoud," answered Alhasan.

"Well said, my friend," said Sir James.

I wanted to think for another moment before giving an answer. But my soul answered for me. "So be it," I heard myself say. "In all haste, let us be on with it."

"So be it," said Sir James. We turned and faced the large wooden doors shoulder to shoulder, Alhasan on my left, Sir James on my right. We then approached the doors, step by step, as one. "Hold," said Sir James when we were two feet from the doors. The three of us stopped in unison. Sir James then stepped forward, raised a clenched fist and in dramatic and purposeful fashion struck one of the wooden doors once, twice, thrice. The sound reverberated off of the walls of the ante-chamber. An eternity seemed to pass as the three of us stood before the doors. In truth, I am sure that no more than a few seconds had passed. And, then it happened.

I held the spear in my right hand, its butt resting on the ground next to my right foot. The blade's tip was higher than my head by some four or five inches. A vibration began; it started at the blade, specifically at the place of the ancient stains that still resided thereon. I looked at the stains on the blade. A soft, green glow then appeared on the spot of the discolorations.

The vibration and the glow descended the blade, then the shaft and went into my hand. My hand tingled slightly from the vibration, as if a small charge had come into my palm. Then, my hand also began to glow the soft green. Yet, while the soft glow stopped at my hand, the tingling sensation continued through my arm and into my body, coursing through my entire being. My breathing became deep. Something profound had entered my being, my very soul. I searched it for meaning and found it to be a sensation, an awareness of my connectedness with and to the past, present and future; to everything and every person that has ever existed or ever will exist and that our connectedness is due to the fact that we are all made of the same thing—the same soul substance—the same Mind that is God's Mind, whether one calls himself a Christian, a Muslim, a Jew, a Druid of old or an adherent to any other religion.

Religions are of men, said a voice in my head. We are all simply individualized expressions of this God-Mind, the One Mind, the voice continued.

The emotion that accompanied this sudden insight, this gift of an ultimate understanding nearly overwhelmed me. My breathing began to quicken.

All knowledge, all answers are within. The voice seemed to come from the spear and deep within the core of my soul at once. It has always been in your soul, but is re-learned or revealed to your small, human mind over and over in part through several life-times, the voice continued.

Why? I asked in my mind. If this is so, why must it be that way? Why can I not simply and easily remember my past experiences, my past lifetimes? Why can't any of us? The concept of reincarnation was not at all foreign to me. As I have alluded to, my mother was a good Christian woman, but still held with some of the Old Ways of our Celtic ancestors. The notion that our souls lived many lifetimes in different human bodies was one of them. But the question remained: if we revisited this earth in different human forms, why do we not immediately remember our previous lessons learned? Why must they remain there, in our being, but hidden from our mind?

A gentle hand touched my shoulder and I became aware of the fact that my eyes had been closed and my breathing had become shallow and rapid. I opened my eyes and forced myself to breathe deeply and normally, my inner dialogue suddenly silent. Sir James stood before me, his arm extended, hand on my shoulder. "That's the way, lad. Breathe steady and true. You left us for a moment. A deep trance is what you entered. The spear glowed and you were gone—in spirit, at least," he said. I glanced at the spear. It appeared normal, the glow was gone. "I know you are ready for this night," added Sir James.

"Yes! Truly," said Alhasan with awe.

At eye level, a small panel on the wooden door slid open, prompting Sir James to turn back around to face it. The opening was in the shape of a small triangle; about six inches from bottom corners to apex and six inches across the base. All we could see through the opening was darkness. Suddenly, a pair of eyes, a piercing ice-blue in color, appeared in the triangular opening. The eyes peered at all three of us in turn, remaining on Sir James. "Who seeks entry into the inner sanctum?" asked the shrill, squeaky voice in perfect English behind the eyes. Who was this person? I wondered briefly. But I quickly released the thought, dismissing it as irrelevant. I was still in the fog of the trance, as Sir James had called it, and I wanted to linger there. Indeed, something told me that I needed to remain in that profound state of mind for what was to come.

"The noble Keeper and Guardian of the Great Spear; one who has guarded said Spear through the centuries," intoned Sir James, assuming his role as the Temple Master. "One who has guarded it even back to his original ownership of it, back to the time of the second-to-last Great Prophet, my Lord Jesus the Christ. And one who has served our Orders in its various incarnations over the past thousand-plus years. He has always served with honor and humility through every one of his lives."

The eyes in the triangle shifted to me. "Is this true? Are you and have you always been the Guardian of the Great Spear?"

I hesitated. My little, all too human self wanted to say, I am not at all sure! But fortunately, still being in the mists of a trance, I spoke from the depths of my spirit, my soul. "I am the Guardian of the Great Spear," I heard myself say.

"And having been among our ranks, one of the Brethren in lives past, do you now wish to renew your vows in this life, thus reaffirming your devotion to the Order of Knights of the Great Brotherhood; Keepers of the Great Mystery of Mysteries, and protectors of the faiths and faithful?" the voice behind the eyes asked.

I was surprised by the words, but felt in my soul they rang true, even as the Temple Master had said; I had been in the Brotherhood for many a life, of course! "I do!" I intoned with all sincerity.

"And who will vouch for and speak on behalf of the candidate?"

"I, the Temple Master and High Knight of the Order," answered Sir James, the Temple Master. "The office of Knighthood is also to be bestowed upon the candidate—the Guardian of the Great Spear—at my behest."

I saw the eyes in the triangle widen at this. Indeed, I felt my own eyes grow wide with surprise at the behest. A knighthood? I had not dared to even think of it.

"His Guardian's status and soul's journey through the centuries speaks to this, as does his deeds in this life," added the Temple Master, Sir James. "They exemplify the pinnacle of all that is True and Good and Honorable about our Order, so say I!"

There was a brief pause. The eyes in the triangle looked askance for an instant, as if the person behind the eyes was listening to someone else near him. The piercing blue eyes then came back to me. "So be it! Enter the inner sanctum and prepare for initiation once again into the Mystery Mysteries, into the Order of Knights of the Great Brotherhood," proclaimed the voice behind the eyes. The panel slid shut, closing the triangular opening. With the creaking of ancient hinges, the two large doors before us began to open inward, inviting us to enter the dim interior of the sacred, inner sanctum. The Temple Master led the way, followed by myself; the Guardian of the Great Spear, and then Alhasan; the devout Servant of the Brotherhood.

~X~

We took three steps into the room and halted; the Temple Master on my right, Alhasan the Hashishim servant, on my left, the Great Spear in my right hand, the shaft's butt resting on the ground. A haze filled the room, this sanctum. It was a long, rectangular room. The interior was dim with candle-light and the scant light from three torches in the wall. But it was enough light to see all. On the far wall from where I stood at the sanctum's threshold there was a wall mural made to resemble an open-air end of a temple—ancient Egyptian, by the look of it—thus giving the painted impression that this far wall was open to the outside. A rising sun was cresting the painted horizon: the east. The far wall was made to represent the east, I was sure of it. I had entered the sanctum from the west end. A cowl-hooded, looming figure in a Templar robe stood before the eastern wall. Again, judging by the man's stature, I recognized the figure to be General Sir Horatio Blackthorn. Between Blackthorn and I, which was some thirty-five feet I estimated, were two objects resting in the center of the sanctum. The one closest to Blackthorn was a chest high pedestal, an altar, with three lit candles thereon. Direct and centered between the altar and I, was a wooden rectangular box on the floor. It was approximately three feet wide, six-and-a-half feet long and two-and-a-half feet deep. It was positioned lengthwise to the shape of the sanctum itself. The thought struck me that this box very much resembled a coffin. I nearly laughed at the thought. But the laugh never came forth because the realization hit me that it resembled a coffin because it was a coffin; a simple wooden sarcophagus. I felt panic well-up in my being, but squelched it before it could take hold.

I noticed then that flanking the walls on my left and right—the northern and southern walls respectively—were pews running lengthwise along the walls. In these pews, four to a side, were the other men I had seen a few moments ago outside in the ante-chamber. Interestingly, every other man was a Templar or a Hashishim Knight. It was not the case that one side contained Templar Knights and the other Hashishim Knights, as for whatever reason I expected. All were of One Order of Knights in this place, on this night.

"I am the Master Knight of Initiation," intoned the figure of Blackthorn. "In this life, you have been among your brethren but ignorant of our great work, blind to the Great Mystery of Mysteries to which we adhere and practice. You have lived the life of our brethren in other of your soul's existences, but seek now to shed the veil of ignorance in this life, to die to an old, outworn small self, and awaken to the Grand real Self of your being, to connect to and with your True nature and learn the Mysteries of our Order once again. Candidate, is this not so?" asked the Master Knight of Initiation.

It was then I noticed that there was an edge to his voice which I found disturbing, almost a resentfulness, I thought, trying to place it. But that would be absurd, I told myself, dismissing the perceived edge in his voice as theatrics for the initiation. "It is so," I replied, bringing my focus back to the moment.

"Your deeds in this life and your exemplary behavior as the Guardian of the Great Spear in your previous lives is known to us," continued the Master Knight of Initiation. Because of this and your desire to enter into our midst once again, we gladly confer upon you this night the office to which you aspire. You will now repeat the oath of our Order. Obedience, Trust and Honor, Chasteness and Secrecy will be tantamount to the oath. Repeat after me: It is not for my will, but for the will of God and the betterment of all that I serve the Order—"

"'It is not for my will, but for will of God and the betterment...'" I heard myself saying, as I began to fade into the depths of my soul. The trance had come upon me again. I heard the Master Knight of Initiation continue to administer the sacred oath and my voice repeat what was said. Deeper and deeper into the trance I went.

Several minutes went by. I heard myself repeat the phrase; "I Am in God, And in God I Am. So it is. Amen."

"It is time for you to die to this world of darkness if you are to be born into the world of Light," intoned the Master Knight of Initiation. I felt hands lightly grasp my upper left arm and my upper right arms simultaneously. My eyes opened as slits and I saw that I was being gently guided, spear still in hand, to the coffin. We circled it several times as the Master Knight of Initiation continued the incantation, "Die to this world that ye may be reborn into the world of Light. Die to this world that ye may be reborn into the world of Light. Die to this world that ye may be reborn into the world of Light! So be it!"

As if floating, I was then guided to a lying down position in the wooden sarcophagus. I kept the spear with me, lying it on top of me, resting it lengthwise along the right side of my body from just below my right foot to the top of my right shoulder and beyond; the shaft's bottom at my foot, the blade near my right ear. Through my trance-haze, I could see the silhouettes of the men standing above the coffin; they were those who had just guided me in. They then placed a sheer, white cloth—a shroud—over the top of my sarcophagus. Once their duty was complete, the figures disappeared from my sight, presumably to retake their seats in the pews.

"Your body," intoned the Master Knight of Initiation, "is of the earth and to the earth it will return. Contemplate your True nature, the nature of your Soul and be reborn to it."

My mind went deeper into my soul. And all went black. I died to this world then, at least for a time.

My mind, my spirit drifted. I could smell the smoke from candles in the sanctum. The smell of incense also drifted to my nostrils, something I had not noticed before. And, the faint sent of lilac wafted to my nose as well. But then another smell abruptly took their place; the foul smell of rotting earth and mud mingled with the fetid stench of loosed bowels and spilled blood. My mind reeled at the odoriferous reek. All thought of being in a coffin in a secluded underground sanctum left me. A scene came bright before my eyes; a Roman crucifixion played out in front of me. Three men on crosses before me hung in utter agony, their blood draining from wounds—wounds, by the look of them, inflicted by sinister implements of torture— and spilling on the ground at the base of their crosses, mixing with their own loose excrement which had dripped down the perpendicular post of the wooden cross and to the ground below.

One of the crucified men, the most brutalized and battered of the three looked directly at me, though I didn't seem to have any form in this...vision. But his eyes chilled me to the bone. He looked nothing like the depictions I had seen in the artwork of the twelfth century and before. He was much darker of skin and His eyes, though blood-red in the whites, were dark brown in the iris. Yet my soul recognized Him instantly. My Lord! my mind whispered.

A centurion approached my Lord Jesus then. I willed my perspective within the vision to move so that I may look at the Roman, as I could not see his face from the angle I was viewing from. With the speed of thought I was in front of him, the cross with Jesus upon it now between the Centurion and myself. I looked into the Roman's face and saw one very much resembling my own—Liam Arthur Mason. With no hesitation, the centurion reached out with his spear and stabbed the crucified Christ. No!! my spirit yelled. But even as it did, the scene abruptly changed.

I was now an ethereal observer in a King's court; the court of King Arthur or King Arturius, as he would have been known then. I knew it was the King Arturius by the attire he wore—a deep burgundy felt tunic emblazoned on the chest with his family's emblem; the Pendragon. He stood near a large, but plain chair, a throne that befits a king for and by the people. Nearby was a huge table, oblong, yet near round.

There were four people in this room; a young, Franc and Nordic-looking, blonde-haired man, a knight of the realm no doubt, judging by his silver tunic—also emblazoned with the Pendragon—and his stature; an old woman dressed in fine silk and bright yellow cloth who was undoubtedly a beautiful lass in her day; and a white-bearded, cowl-hooded old man robed in the way of the ancient High Druids—a purple robe with ancient symbols on it, symbols that if memory served me were called runes. He leaned on a large, ornately carved walking staff. But my memory again told me that it was no walking staff he leaned on but a Druid's staff or a Wizard's staff. My memory suddenly also served me for another purpose; the recognition of the old woman and old man.

Her face was known to me, to my soul, my spirit. Igraines, my mind said. And, the old man too; I knew him, felt it. Again, as with the centurion, I willed my perspective to a different position within the vision so that I may see closely the face of this old one. The vision quickly shifted and I was now in front of the man as he spoke. I looked into his wrinkled face and knew him instantly—Merlin, Myrriddin, was the thought in my mind. He stopped in mid sentence and seemed to look right at me much as the Christ had done on the cross in the previous vision. It was then that I looked into his eyes and saw my own soul. His face did not resemble mine as Liam Arthur Mason, but I knew him to be me in this former life; it was in his eyes—his soul, my soul, looked at me through those eyes.

"Well, Merlin," said the King. "What say you? 'Tis time we retrieve what is rightfully ours, I say. Do you not agree?"

The aged wizard looked on his King, the ethereal presence of his future self, me, all but forgotten for the moment. Anger flashed in his voice and his eyes. "Do you seek a war, Arturius? For that is what you will have. These items are naught but material things."

"Powerful material things," answered King Arturius.

"False power, I assure you," answered Merlin.

"You wielded the spear's power yourself all those years ago, or have you become so long in tooth that ye forget, my friend?" quipped Arthur. "I have asked you before to retrieve the spear and the other things. Yet you've ignored my bidding."

"Have you learned nothing I taught you? The spear, the grail—if it is even a thing at all—the rood; none of them hold any real power save what we give them," the aged wizard replied.

"If they hold power which is bestowed upon them, then that is power truly, is it not? 'Tis the power of faith, of politic. Either or, it is still power." Arturius went silent as Myrriddin stewed, clearly not happy about what the king was leading up to. Arturius stepped up to Merlin and lay a hand gently on the wizard's shoulder. "If one withholds something I desire, and I am angered by it, then the thing itself contains power over me, for it is of my desire to possess it."

"Only in your mind does it hold power," said Merlin. "But these...artifacts of the Christians—of which I alone possessed the spear of Longinus for many a year—contain naught but the power of death and destruction if you pursue the course of action you are proposing."

"You said yourself that your visions revealed wars over these things."

"Many, many years hence, Arturius. But your actions here may be the catalyst that sets all that in motion," Merlin replied gravely.

The king returned to his chair, plopping in it with what seemed to be exaggerated exasperation. "The Holy Region is being overtaken by certain nomadic...infidels," he said. "It is said that they have obtained our most sacred relics, and..."

"'Our most sacred relics'? Have you completely abandoned your Old Ways, Arturius?" Merlin asked.

"No, Merlin, I have not,"

"Then you know," began Merlin as he approached the king's throne, "that one teaching of our Old Ways beseeches us to be unattached to things and the conditions we find, for all is transitory; of the One, and thus not ours to begin with. Why do you think we Druids keep our temples in the open, in the forests of our Mother, Dana? Why do you think we keep no written records?"

"I always thought you kept no written records because you guarded your secrets with all jealousy!" joked Arturius, clearly attempting to lighten the mood.

"Pray you be not serious, Arturius. You know us too well for that notion."

"And as to your temples being only the forests? What are the Henges that we see dotting our land?! Wood or stone, are they not temples; permanent structures built by the hands of your kind!?!" said Arturius, voice now raised, humor abated.

"No. Those are demarcations of power centers; places where the Mother's power, the power of the One is focused and harnessed or used for good. You know that, Arturius," said Myrriddin.

"Ah. So things can hold otherworldly power, eh, Merlin?" countered the King.

"The power in this case is not of the Otherworld, Arturius."

"But, all power is, 'the Power of the One', right, Merlin? That's what you always tell me."

"And that is true, but you play with my words," said Merlin.

"Will you both cease this?!" said Igraines. I had forgotten that she was present. Apparently, so had Arturius and Merlin, for they both jumped with a start.

"Forgive us, my lady. You must be tired from your journey," said Arturius, leaving his chair and going to his mother. He gently took her hand and then turned to the other man in the room, whom I also had lost mind of. "Lancelott, please see to my mother's comfort,"

"Certainly, my Lord," answered Lancelott, who had the brow of an eagle; furrowed and eternally serious. His grey eyes pierced one to the soul. A striking fellow he was indeed. He took the lady Igraines' hand from Arturius' and began to lead her away.

"My sister?" inquired Arturius, causing the queen to stop and look at him quizzically. "Morgaines; is she to join us too?" asked the King with an odd, lecherous excitement that I found unsettling.

Igraines' expression was masked, but I could tell that beneath it there was sadness. It was no doubt a reaction to Arturius' question. "Yes, Arturius. She will be joining us tonight."

"Good. That is good," said Arturius.

Igraines and Lancelott left us then, Merlin, my former self, thoughtfully watching her leave. For a brief instant I felt his/my feelings for her well-up in my being; loving emotions that had truly spanned centuries. They were there for only an instant, though, before being suppressed back to the netherworld of my soul's experiential library.

"Come, Merlin. Let us retire to my chamber to discuss this further. We have already established an Order of Knights to grapple with this. Let us not waste the Knights of Jesu. Let us instead make all haste in deploying them for their divine purpose." said Arturius contritely.

Merlin did not immediately respond, only stared after Igraines.

"Merlin, Myrriddin, I beg thee, come."
Finally, the wizard turned to his king. "All military endeavors profess to be of divine purpose. Ridiculous. How human, solely human."

"I beg thee, Merlin; come," Arturius stated again. He turned to leave and Merlin followed. I willed myself to follow too, but a mist enshrouded me, preventing me. Then, all went white.

~XI~

A moment later, the mist cleared. I looked up and saw a thin white cloth draped over something that I was otherwise enclosed in. There was semi-darkness beyond the cloth. I was back in the coffin at my initiation. I could not tell how long I had been in the coffin, or on the sojourn of my soul. All was quiet in the chamber, the sanctuary, as a meditative silence hung in the air. I closed my eyes again, concentrating on the visions of Myrriddin, or Merlin once again in the hopes of being able to resume my observations there. Nothing. Then, suddenly...

"Myrriddin! You're here! I thought not to see you again," said the sweet voice of Igraines. I opened my eyes to see a lovely face; a much younger Igraines. Obviously, my soul had journeyed further back in its history than it had the last time. She was beautiful. We stood in a large chamber room, in front of a large, fireless hearth. She stared right at me. I, Masoud, was not only an observer in this vision, but was in fact looking out through the eyes of my former self, Myrriddin or Merlin. She stood before me, Igraines did, with a small female-child of about four years clinging to her leg. And, in spite of the long flowing light blue gown Igraines wore, it was evident she was very pregnant. She looked down at the little girl clinging to her. "Well don't be rude, child. Say hello to Master Myrriddin, Morgaines," Igraines said.

The child Morgaines looked as if she were angry with me for some inexplicable transgression. But I quickly realized her apparent grave expression was actually one of seriousness whilst performing a mental exercise. She was assessing me. At last, her small mouth curved up slightly at the ends, no doubt the result of her conclusion that I posed no imminent threat.

"Are you the great warlock I've heard tell of?" she asked none too timidly.

I smiled. She had the brashness of her mother, to be certain. "Some call me wizard, child. None call me warlock. That title bespeaks of ill intent, does it not? I seek only the good in and for all," I replied.

"I've told you, Morgaines," Igraines interjected, "Myrriddin is a High Druid."

"But King Uther says the Druids don't live anymore, that those like Master Myrriddin are but wizards and warlocks using magic," Morgaines said as a matter of fact.

"Aye and Uther Pendragon forgets much, not the least of which has been the service which Master Myrriddin has given to him and this land, 'magic' or no," replied Igraines, a bitter tone seeping into her voice.

I kept my eyes on the child Morgaines. "'Magic,'" I began with mock seriousness, "is but a term the ignorant use to describe what is simply the use of natural laws or The Law. And I serve Uther and the land by extension. In truth, I serve only the One."

"He has been saying that for as long as I've known him," said Igraines to Morgaines a little too sardonically.

We stood in silence for a moment, a sudden awkwardness weighing down upon us. "Morgaines, go play while I visit with Myrriddin for a spell," Igraines finally said.

"Yes, mother." Morgaines left her mother's side, skipping to the other side of the chamber.

"Well, Myrriddin. It has been four years at least, since our eyes last met. Since just prior to Morgaines entered into the world," Igraines said.

"'Tis true."

"You helped Uther and the Bishop Rozinus rid us of the Saxons and then you disappeared to that cave of yours, or so I was told," she said, with a poorly concealed sour edge. "Though I know Uther has seen you since. Tell me, Myrriddin; did he ask something of you? Did he ask you to give him a...what did you used to call it...a glamour, a spell of some kind?"

I sensed that my Myrriddin self knew exactly what she was talking about, but I, Masoud was at a loss. She pressed on.

"I carry his child, Uther's. I think you know that," she blurted out. She paused for a moment, clearly trying to decide whether to go on. By the look of her, she had a story that needed to be told and I was the pertinent audience for whom it was meant. "My husband Lot came home from battle one night, a new fresh scar on his left cheek. His handsome face had always been flawless so I noticed the scar instantly, even though he seemed to be hiding it. I should have seen something amiss immediately: he was trying to hide his face that night, I know that now. He kept in shadow and used a cowl covering. I assumed it was because he was embarrassed by the new scar or because he didn't want to be seen by servants as having come home from war even for the night." Igraines fell silent for a moment, obviously reliving the events of the night in question, smiling in spite of herself. "Lot was more amorous that night than I've ever seen him. He insisted we couple right then and there, couldn't even wait for the bed chamber. He threw me down with the passion of a demon in lust and impaled me right there in the entry hall. He eventually near dragged me to the bed chamber where he thrust into me again, over and over and over, dumping his seed in me at least five times that night. I awoke near dawn, my weeping servant shaking my shoulder. 'What is it?' I asked her. 'Oh, terrible, terrible news!' she said. 'Your husband is dead, Master Lot is dead! Killed in battle yesterday!' she screamed. 'No,' I said, 'he's right here.' I turned to the other side of the bed. The bed was empty. 'His corpse is at the gate, my lady. They travelled through the night to bring his body home, they did,' said my servant," Igraines recounted.

Though Igraines did not weep openly, tears came to her eyes at the telling of her tale. She turned from me then and went to a chair near an open window. She sat heavily in the seat and stared out at the pasture below and the horses passively grazing there. The peaceful sounds of birds' songs wafted to our ears from the trees beyond. I crossed to her and simply stood patiently near the chair, waiting for her in her own time to continue.

"There was a cart at the gate," she went on, "and several men on horseback surrounding it. I paid no heed to them but went straight to the cart. Something was in the cart, under a blanket of animal skin. I threw back the skin and there he was; Lot of Orkney, my husband. Shock and numbness filled me." Igraines hand went to her swollen belly, caressing the life beneath. "Had I slept with his ghost? I wondered. But that was ridiculous and I knew it. Then I looked at his body, his face. He was dirty and bloody from head to toe and his tunic and mantle torn and rent. But his face was still unblemished; there was not a scar on his face, no fresh scar on the left side of his face! As if to seek an answer, I looked at the men on horseback. One of them was Uther," she said looking up at me accusingly. "And he had the scar on his face! The same scar I'd seen the previous night! He had appeared to me as Lot, even wearing his clothes! I felt completely betrayed and despoiled. Why would he do that?! I thought. And then it struck me; he had made many advances toward me which I had spurned. He had glammed himself as Lot that night to rape me," she said.

"No," I heard my Myrriddin self say. "Lust, yes, but not the other."

Igraines laughed. "Do you say that to appease your guilt, Myrriddin?"

I made no reply. Her words hit close. A long silence ensued. I nearly turned to leave, knowing not what further to say. But then Igraines spoke again.

"Uther said that you are to take the child when he's born, to rear him," she said through a veil of soft tears. "It is a boy, I know it. He is a bastard, but is the taking of him necessary?"

"Yes. It was my doing. All of it," I, Myrriddin confessed, turning back to Igraines. "You now carry the future hope of the land and people. I saw it, saw you carrying this male-child, our hope, long before this pregnancy. When Uther was insistent on having you I knew the fulfillment of my vision was at hand. I'm sorry, Igraines, but the needs of the people, the future...they are more important than the needs..."

"...Of one woman? How convenient, Myrriddin. Uther is king and will reign for a long time. His other son, Ramey, is heir and will follow his father to the throne."

"Uther will die in battle and so will Ramey," I said in an urgent whisper, leaning in to Igraines. "I have seen it in the scrying bowl as well, just as I saw his seed, his future son, whom you now carry, as king of this realm," I said, falling silent for a moment, allowing my words to wash through Igraines. "Uther does not know that I have seen his death and that of Ramey's, and he must never be told. I say it again; the son you carry is the future king."

She sat in shocked silence for a time. "The future is up to us, I've heard you say such," said Igraines after a time. "So why not tell Uther of what you've seen that he may avoid it, chart a different future?"

"Because for him or Ramey to live will mean the destruction of all of Britain," I replied.

"Which you have seen as well, I suppose," offered Igraines without sarcasm.

I simply nodded.

She fell contemplative for a time, looking at her swollen belly, at the unborn child, the uncrowned future within. "The people, the council, will not accept him as Uther's heir to the throne," she finally said.

"That is why I must rear him; to prepare him for his rightful place; that he may prove to the others his worth," I explained. "Uther thinks I take him to cleanse his conscience of that night and the bastard he left behind. Let him think what he will."

"So that is why you have come back; to take my child?"

"You are not yet due. And I will not receive him until he is well weaned from the teat. I am presently here to reclaim two items of great import which I foolishly entrusted to Uther and Bishop Rozinus respectively.

"The sword and that spear? Why? You've always tried to convince others that they are naught but metal and wood," Igraines said. "You gave the spear to Rozinus and the sword to Uther."

"Because I believed they knew their worth. They have chosen to revere the items as holding powers beyond this realm. This has corrupted them and their followers. Bishop Rozinus pledged to give the spear to his Church. He broke that pledge, instead keeping it for himself in a vain attempt to wield power over others," I said more contemptuously than intended.

"So only the righteous may possess them; namely, you?" she said sarcastically. "And besides, they do hold power, I've seen you use them, especially that spear."

"The power to which you refer is in each and every one of us. It is from the One, from the Source of all. I am able to use the spear in particular as an extension of myself to channel this power, that is all," I explained.

"Me thinks there's more to it, but I'll leave it there." She still had a hand on her belly. Suddenly, her other hand flew to her side. "Ah! He kicks. Feel, Myrriddin!" she said with gleeful surprise.

She removed her hand from her side so that I could place mine there. I did. The future king kicked my palm forcefully. "He is strong. Like his mother," I said.

I pulled my hand away from her side but she grabbed it, clutching it between both of hers. Igraines looked at me, tears once again brimming her eyes. But this time, I could see they were tears of joy mixed with the fear of the unknown. "I have always loved you Myrriddin, always. In our previous lives to now. I have always trusted you. I trust you now in all that you say. You will rear my son, our future king and I am glad of it."

"Fear not, woman." I said.

"Forgive my emotion, it's all just..."

"Overwhelming?" I offered.

"Yes. Well perhaps. Everything affects me now. I am quite pregnant, you know," she said smiling.

I laughed. But my laughter was cut short by a loud explosion. The whole building shook. "By the One, what was that?" I said.

"What was what?" asked Igraines calmly. She still sat in the chair as if nothing had happened. Indeed, nothing was amiss in the chamber; we were where we had been for the past few moments and Morgaine still played at the other end of the room, the beautiful birds' songs still wafted to our senses from outside. Then I realized what was happening.

Igraines began to fade from sight. "Igraines!" I yelled. The whole room went dark.

"Igraines!" I cried again. I had the sudden realization that I was being dragged upright down a corridor, my feet, barely touching the dirt ground, yet bumping objects as we went. I came back to the present and opened my eyes.

"Quiet now, Sir Masoud!" said Alhasan. He was under one of my armpits, Commander James under my other, my dangling arms around both men's necks as we moved rapidly along, both men trying their best not to drag my feet as we went.

~XII~

We were traveling down a dimly lit, tall but narrow, musty, dirt corridor, the walls little more than shored up earth, with a few small, lit torches in them. The explosion hit again, sending a fair amount of dirt and dust tumbling from the walls, but not collapsing them.

"What is happening?" I asked, coming fully back to my present self; Liam Arthur Mason.

"We're under attack," Alhasan answered. "We finished the initiation, at least. Then, it hit; the first explosion."

"We finished the initiation?" I asked.

"Do you not remember?" began Alhasan. "We lifted you from the coffin, you recited after the Master of Initiation and accepted the sword as a Knight Templar, though I am not surprised if you do not remember. You were in trance the whole time, even though you spoke the recitations!"

I suddenly panicked. "The Spear of Longinus! Where is my Spear?!"

"It's here, on my back, Sir Mason," replied Sir James with mirth in his voice.

I looked back over my shoulder to his back and saw the great spear sticking blade up, rising well above his head. There was something else there too; a sword hilt. "Is that...?"

"Your knight's sword, yes," he said. "We should halt."

We stopped and the men put me down. We listened for a moment. Silence. It was then that I noticed I was in the tunic or mantel of a Templar Knight. The pristine white tunic with Red Cross emblazoned on front and back had obviously been place over my head and tied at my waist at some point during the initiation, though I did not remember it happening.

"It seems to have stopped for now," said Sir James. "You passed out at the end of your initiation, as soon as you held the King's Sword that was bestowed upon you. You said, 'at last' as you caressed it, and dropped."

"I don't remember. May I see it?"

Sir James reached behind him and loosened the straps that held the things on his back. First he handed me the Spear. It felt good to feel its weight in my hand. Then he handed me a sword; the most beautiful thing I had ever seen. I took it by the hilt and became light-headed at the feel and sight of it. I knew this instrument, had held it before in the distant past I was sure. I was sure in the same manner I had been with the spear. The thing was nearly the length of a small man. Forged from a metal I had never seen—at least in this life—and engraved with ancient runes up and down its magnificent blade. I was awestruck.

"Much debate went into bestowing this upon you," said Sir James. "But in the end, it was determined that he who was the keeper of the Great Spear was to be the keeper of the King's Sword as well. It is said that this sword was the one given to the legendary King Arthur by his wizard, Merlin the Magician. "Some call it Excalibur."

I looked directly into Sir James' eyes, my attention to the sword broken by something my commander had said. "Merlin's name was Myrriddin and he was a High Master Druid, not a mere magician," I said rather too defensively.

"What?" asked Sir James, his brow crinkling with confusion.

I almost laughed. "Nothing. 'Tis not important," I said. "If it had belonged to the past great King of Britain, should it not now belong to our present king, King Richard?"

Sir James' face contorted in obvious disapproval of the thought. "That pig is a pawn of the Franc. He deserves naught," Sir James stated. "The King's Sword has been in our Order's possession since one of our incarnations as the Knights of Jesu, founded by our King Arthur...and Merlin. Today, some call that Order the Knights of the Round Table, although I don't think there was really a round table. Just a story, that."

"No, there was one. But it was more...oval, almost round, shall we say," I said, recalling my vision from earlier and thus correcting Sir James. He looked at me quizzically. "Perhaps you're right; just a story."

"In any event," continued Sir James, "it is more appropriate that the sword stay within the most inner circle our Order of Templar Knights today, of which King Richard is not a part. He is not even aware of its existence, this inner circle. It was furthermore deemed appropriate, as I said, that the keeper of the Spear be also the First Knight of Excalibur. Do you not agree? It feels right in your hands, does it not?"

"It does indeed," I said. Suddenly, the building shook with yet another explosion. "Where are we?"

"We went down, deeper into the church's bowels, when the first explosion hit," said Alhasan.

"And the others?"

"Scattered," replied Sir James. "As I said, you passed out at the conclusion of the initiation. We had picked you up and were starting to file out when it hit. The others scattered to the outside, I think. I thought that too vulnerable, so I took us down here."

I looked around at our bleak surroundings and saw things on the ground in the dim light, the things that my feet had been bumping into: skulls and bones—human skulls and human skeletons. Some of the latter still had rotted clothing clinging to their morbid frames. "What in God's name is this place!?" I said.

"The Pit is what it's called," answered Sir James. "Certain prisoners were cast down here...forever."

"And this is where you thought to have us escape?" I said more forcefully than I had intended.

"Take care with your tone, Sir Mason. Your status has been exceptionally elevated, but I am still your commanding officer," said Commander Sir James authoritatively.

"Yes, sir. But can we please leave now, before we become the new residents?" I asked.

"Aye, you're right. I did not intend for us to come down this far to begin with; simply wanted to keep you safe until you came back to your senses. Can ye walk on your own now?" he asked me.

"Yes," I replied. "Lead the way, sir."

With that, Sir James headed back the way we had come, followed by Alhasan. With the Spear of Longinus in one hand and the great sword of Arthur in the other, I headed out with them.

⚜ ⚜ ⚜

A chaotic din of voices in panic assaulted our ears, becoming louder and louder the farther up the steps we went. The way up and out of the bowels of the church where Sir James had thought to take us—me—for protection seemed to go on forever. As we approached the main level of the church from within, the chaotic din of voices from without became more pronounced as screams to curdle the blood; human screams of agony.

We poured out of the church, Sir James in the lead. He suddenly stopped on the church's large portico, causing Alhasan and I to nearly slam into him. We peered out into the church's courtyard. Many soldiers and crusaders were running about, apparently trying to avoid the explosions and subsequent flying debris, or racing for their arms, as some of them came running back to the courtyard, side arms of swords in hand. Others lay on the ground, bodies or limbs torn asunder by the hurled exploding instruments of destruction. It was these poor, retched souls from which the agonized screams emanated. The area was no longer dark with night, but dim with a cloud of choking smoke from the explosions. A breeze parted the vile cloud for an instant and I could see the orange of a birthing new day peek through.

"They timed their attack precisely," noted Sir James. "Dawn: assembling of the troops here in front of the church."

"Dawn? It seemed only moments ago we entered into the sanctum of initiation," said Alhasan with genuine surprise.

"Alhasan! I thought you said your people don't have exploding missiles!" I said.

"We do not. We use the fireballs, you see!" he replied.

"But..." I began. Before I could finish my sentence we were violently knocked from our feet as one of the hurled balls of fire hit the church's dome, exploding and sending hot particles raining down upon us. It was all we could do to scramble out of the way and under a sturdier portion of the portico's roof. Where we had stood only an instant before was suddenly crushed by a huge, fiery section of flaming church dome. It was the size of a large pig and smashed the entire portico where we had been standing. Something else too; a black, slick liquid accompanied the fire and explosion, falling on part of the portico. Debris and oil came down in the courtyard, the oil splashing on the hapless victims writhing on the ground, inflicting further agony, but withholding the mercy of death.

"Oil. They're using hot oil in their fireballs as well," yelled Sir James over the ever increasing loudness of the din.

A feeling suddenly arose within me that was completely unexpected, one that only days before would not have entered my mind. But something had shifted at the core of my being these past days, culminating in the initiation and the visions, the realizations, of the profound past of my soul. Passionate anger rose within me at the absurdity of our plight in the moment and at our overall plight in this part of the world, and by extension the sheer stupidity of war in general. It was made all the more poignant by the fact that only hours ago, there had been many of us from so-called opposite sides of this conflict working in harmony and like-thought to install someone, me, into an Order of like-minded, gallant purveyors of Truth. And now this?! But stupidly, I directed my anger at Alhasan. "Where are your people from earlier tonight, your Hashishim Knights?! I don't see them," I said. Indeed, none of them were around; only Christian soldiers and crusaders, running to arms, to put out fires, to help the wounded. "Had they run off to give the order to attack?!"

"That's enough, Liam!" ordered Sir James.

"And where is Commander Blackthorn?!" I yelled. "Why did he not see this coming?"

"My good Knight Mason! That is enough, I say!" barked Sir James. "I tell you, you will not insubordinate yourself. You will..."

He stopped in mid sentence, staring at me with a mixture of awe, respect and even a little fear. Or rather, he stared at the weapons I held—one in each hand: the Great Spear of Longinus and the King's Sword of Arthur. They both now glowed with an angry red, and the glow began to pulsate in a steady rhythmic manner after my own seething emotion and my accompanying pattern of breath of the same. Gaining the rein of my anger, I stepped off of the portico, or what was left of it, and out into the middle of courtyard, gently stepping over the wounded and dying.

Stopping in the center of it all, I looked toward the heavens and raised the weapons over my head, the Great Spear in my right, the King's Sword in my left. I had no idea what I was going to do, but let my controlled anger, and more importantly my soul—my Merlin self, so to speak—be my guide. My eyes closed. "By the One Source of all there is and all that is...by the One Source which courses through me and all; I bid you come through me now! End this night of destruction and death, and sow the seeds of peace and life here and now. So Be It!!" I intoned. "By the One Source..." I began again, repeating the incantation, for that is what it was, over and over and over again. With each saying of it, I felt my mind fusing more and more with the words, and more importantly, with the thoughts and passion behind the words. Thus, in that instance, I truly came to know the reality of the power of the One Source. This Power began to course through my being. I, Liam Arthur Mason—Masoud knew not from where these words and thoughts, passion and Power came from. But my soul knew. I simply got out of the way and let it be so. And what happened was astonishing.

I felt the power well up through the earth, up through the ground beneath my feet, enter into the lower portion of my body and vibrate its way up my legs and through my chest as if a fiery, shaking snake was rapidly winding its way up and through my whole body. It suddenly went into my limbs, raging through my arms and bursting forth from the spear and sword. Light, as if from a lightning charge, bolted from the weapons in my hands and into the air, disappearing into the smoke and dawn beyond. Then the winds came; howling winds that carried with them a strong, lovely, sweet smell; it smelled like candy. I felt the effects of this scent instantly. It soothed the mind, the senses, and thus the body. The winds raged, instantly overwhelming the fires as the breath blows out a candle flame. The smoke in the area swirled rapidly on the wind and dispersed, leaving the area altogether. We then saw two more fireballs hurling through the sky in the distance, heading directly toward us. Two more bolts shot from the instruments I held, one from each. The explosion was bright even in the dawn sky as each fireball was destroyed in mid-flight by the bolts from the Spear and Sword, thus preventing both fireballs from ever reaching their targets.

The bolts from the Spear of Longinus and the Sword of Arthur suddenly ceased. A moment later the winds suddenly abated. And then the truly marvelous occurred. We watched as one by one, the injured stopped their cries and began to rise. Some, whose limbs had been torn from the explosions showed visible signs of weakness in the previously injured limbs, but were nonetheless healed; limbs had been put back together and in some, even reattached or re-grown in an instant. It seemed impossible, but the evidence was before us. Unfortunately, the dead did not rise, which I thought strange. Supposedly, I had brought Henry back from the dead. Why not these men?

I lowered my arms, putting the weapons, the instruments, to rest at my side. I sensed Alhasan and Sir

James rush to my side. The three of us stood in observation of the miracle unfolding in the courtyard.

"Allah be praised!" exclaimed Alhasan. "I told you Masoud. I told you that Allah works through you and the spear! Just as that night with your friend. It was the same, you see! Or nearly so."

"Aye, Sir 'Masoud'," said Sir James mockingly, but kindly. "Dear Jesus. Unbelievable. Truly. But why did the dead not rise as your friend had? You brought Henry back that night," asked Sir James.

Alhasan turned to Sir James. "Why, these souls have already willingly departed. 'Enry's had not on the night in question or at least not completely, you see," he answered, as if it were the most obvious thing in the world. "Is that not so Master Masoud?"

"Indeed," was all I said. It sounded perfectly reasonable.

"Still, your power with the spear and sword is amazing," said Sir James.

"'Not I, but the Father within doeth the work.' Wouldn't that be more accurate, Sir James?" I asked.

"Or the magician in you," he replied.

"The Father, the Magician, the Merlin; by any name it's the same thing: the great Source of All working through me as me, or you."

~XIII~

It took nearly the whole day, but we gathered the dead and created a mass burial site for our dead brother-soldiers and crusaders. Interestingly, it was those who had felt the direct effects of the healing at dawn that insisted, almost as one, on gathering our dead comrades from the church's square and from elsewhere where they had fallen, and bringing them to the burial site. The Christian rites were said by priests and the dirt shoveled into the great hole in the earth. Finally, by late afternoon, with The King's Sword in a make-shift scabbard on my back and the Spear in my right hand, I made my way back to our dwelling amid the stares and murmurs of those of my fellow crusaders and soldiers I passed along the way. Word had spread quickly about my use of the Spear of Longinus and the Sword of Arthur. Most who looked upon me as I walked to my tent did so with awe or fear etched upon their face. Some, however, looked at me with a mixture of contempt and disbelief. It was as if they were saying, I believe not the story being told of this one! Or, who is this would-be knight? One thing was certain: my life had just been irrevocable changed within a handful of hours.

As I approached the tent's opening I became excited to share all that had happened with Henry. I darted into the dwelling only to find it empty. Henry was nowhere to be seen. Although, why should I think he was still in here after all these hours. It was late afternoon, after all. A horrific thought suddenly occurred to me: Perhaps he had been injured in the attack! I turned to run out of the tent and back to the church's square, but I was stopped, jarred as I ran into someone just outside of the tent's threshold, knocking him flat on the ground. The collision knocked the breath out of my own body for a brief instant. Alhasan lay sprawled at my feet.

"What the devil, man? Are you my shadow? Am I not to have a moment's peace?!" I said much too harshly. My harshness was a vain attempt at covering my own startled embarrassment at having been so easily snuck up on. Besides, this was after all Alhasan's tent too.

"Ah, Masoud. Shadow, no. But I must be your aid, your servant always now. There are those who would seek to exploit you and I must remain at your side to help fend them away," he explained. "It is my...how you say; calling, you see. It is my place in the Order of the Hashishim Knights."

"Ah. And how do you know this is your calling?" I asked, mirth and suspicion warring within me.

"As you know your place as the Keeper of the Spear of Longinus and the Sword of your Great King, so too do I know my place is by your side, my Lord Masoud," he said, picking himself up off of the ground, the floor of our tent and bowing deeply before me and holding his bow.

He held the position, clearly waiting for me to release him from his bow and thus acknowledging his official position as my servant. "Or, perhaps it was ordered as your calling by your Order of Knights, or better yet, by Salah al-Din himself, as more a mission of espionage than servitude, eh?" I said.

Alhasan slowly unbowed himself, standing upright and staring straight into my eyes with genuine hurt and insult. "You aggrieve me, sire, truly. What have I done to earn your wrath so?" he asked.

I smiled and put my hands up, palms outward toward him in a gesture of surrender and apology. "Alhasan, I pray you forgive me. The events of these past many hours have been enlightening and tumultuous, inspiring and confusing all at once. I simply have trouble understanding why you choose to stay with me when your people and my people war so. It's simply confusing. Your people attack us when we had just held vigil together in a joint initiation. Why would they do that?"

"Those that attacked are not those who were with us in the sanctuary. Remember; they too were caught in the attack. They are working within a system that has taken on a life of its own; that has become a beast in its own right. It is the same with every war, is it not? There comes a time when the enemies cannot stop the beast they created because the beast has come into a life of its own, you see. Such is the way of this war too," Alhasan pontificated. "Yet, as in past conflicts between our peoples, there are those bodies in the beast who will aid in its ultimate destruction to preserve the overall Truth of being. The beast is thus slain from within. You are now important to that process, Masoud, you see. And I serve to slay the beast with you."

"What you say is more riddle than anything else, my friend. But my heart feels the truth of what you say," I said. "So be it, then. But just give me a little solitude now and again, will you?"

"As you wish."

"Right now," I said, looking around at the empty tent, "I would very much like to find Henry. You have not seen him, have you?" I asked. Alhasan's expression suddenly changed to a somberness that distressed me. "You have seen him. What is it? Is he...is he dead?" I asked, bracing myself for the answer.

Alhasan shook his head. "His body lives, barely. But his soul is slowly being pushed out, I fear."

"I don't understand," I said.

"It would be most simpler to show you," said Alhasan. "I would venture that he is where he is most days at this time; where he's gone daily since...since the night you brought him back from the side of the dead. But, be warned: you will not like what you see."

"Lead on," I said. Alhasan nodded turned and walked away from the tent. I followed him.

⊥ ⊥ ⊥

We walked for nearly half-an-hour. The sun was now beginning to set and I had the latent thought that this day had been the oddest of my life. Yet, it was not over. We left the outskirts of the encampment, traversing the rugged area on the western-most side and leaving the perimeter guards there, soldiers from the ordinary rank and file—that which I had been a part of on just the previous day—agape at the sight of the Sword and Spear I carried, as well as the tunic that I wore.

"See to it that you say nothing of my whereabouts," I said.

"Aye," one of them managed to say. "What of him?" he asked, eyeing Alhasan suspiciously.

"He is with me. That's all you need know," I replied.

"Yes, sir. There's naught out there but the latrines and the den, sir, you know," said the guard.

I ignored the comment. The latrines I knew of. But the den I knew not of. We moved on, Alhasan and I.

The stench of the latrines was soon upon us and we moved down an embankment and into the bed of a stream which had a good and steady flow of ankle deep water running through it. To our left some thirty feet away and up on the other side of the embankment were the mounds of a freshly dug area: the trench for the latrines no doubt. "Are they daft?" I asked rhetorically. "Who gave orders to dig the latrines so close to a water source?"

"I doubt those who dug it were properly supervised, My Lord Masoud," answered Alhasan.

"Would you stop that, Alhasan!" I said. "Stop calling me Sir, Master, Lord. Just Mason, or Masoud! Much has happened this past day, but not that much! And where in hell are you taking us, anyway?"

"'Where in hell,' indeed!" he said cryptically. There were rocks whose tops protruded through the surface of the water, giving stepping stones of a sort to the other side of the stream. The embankment of the other side was approximately ten feet away. Alhasan easily hopped from rock to rock across the stream and up the five-foot embankment of the opposite side. He stopped at the top of the other side of the embankment and pointed to something off in the distance. "There is our destination," he said.

I reached the top of the embankment and stood next to him. Before us was an olive grove whose trees reached some twenty feet in the air with branches full of their offering. At the other end of the grove was a hillside. In fact, the grove actually butted up against this hillside. In the hillside was an opening, a dim light emanating from within. It was the opening in the hillside to which Alhasan pointed. A steady stream of smoke also came out of the opening. "A cave?" I asked. "Henry is in there?"

"Come," Alhasan said gravely, walking through the olive grove. I followed.

It was dim in the grove because of its canopy of branches, and it was still warm from the day. But the air within carried a staleness to it that seemed foreign to the immediate area. I then realized it was the staleness of a smoky residue. I stopped briefly at one of the trees. Its trunk appeared a little darker than would a normal olive tree trunk. I ran a finger down part of the trunk and came away with a black residue of smoke on my finger tip for the effort. Yet, in spite of this same dark coating on many of the trees, they still bore the harvest of their olives. However, the fullness of the branches I thought I saw a moment ago was not because of the healthy fullness of the offering of these trees, but because of a droopiness of the branches' leaves. I looked ahead at the cave's opening and the smoke coming out, which did not seem to be a terrible amount at the moment. But I realized that this was the source of the trees' smoky layer and the reason why the branches were drooping. There must always be a steady stream of smoke coming from this cave, I thought. But it just did not seem possible that enough smoke could come from the cave to coat the trees even over an extended time. Then I noticed the ground at my feet. I was standing in the remnants of a now dead and cold campfire. Surveying the area I saw dozens and dozens of old, ashen camp fire spots dotting the area within the grove. It was as if at any given time, this grove was used for a camp. No wonder the trees had this residue on them. The trees' leaves were choking from the smoke being layered on them from all the fires that had been here. They could not breathe. The notion suddenly struck me as ridiculous; trees don't breathe! But the spear's voice suddenly and unexpectedly asserted itself. They are living beings made from the same substance as you. Never forget that, it said. I looked at the spear. It was normal; neither glowing nor shaking.

"Masoud. Come," said Alhasan. He was standing at the opening, the entrance to the cave. I made my way through the rest of the grove and joined him. He ducked through the five-foot by five-foot opening and disappeared into the dimness beyond. I ducked and entered as well.

My eyes stung from the haze that hung in the dank air. It took a moment for my vision to adjust. The cave was big on the inside. It extended far back, some sixty feet. Its ceiling seemed to rise to a peek at about thirty feet. The cave itself splayed out in a fan shape from the entrance to be approximately eighty feet wide at its widest point deep within. About twenty-five feet in was a central fire. Several sleeping pallets lined the walls and piles of rushes were strewn about the dirt floor near the central fire. Men lay on most of the piles of rushes, reclined in sleep or apparent stupor or both. Three of the forms on the pallets near one wall appeared to be wrapped from head to toe in rags. The stench of sickness hung in the air and seemed to be coming from the direction of these wrapped men. I dared not think what illness had them.

Also near the fire were what appeared to be clay jars, the kind the locals used for carting water and grain; each stood two-feet tall. There were five or six of them. But these jars had been altered for a use other than the carrying of liquid or grains. Several hoses, each made from what appeared to be tightly woven straw, protruded from each jar near the bottom, spaced equally apart around the base of the jar. The top of the jar housed a metal bowl. Smoke trailed up from most of these bowls. There were about thirty people lying or sitting about. In addition to those on the rushes, there were those on the pallets along the other wall. Some, with eyes closed, were ranting mindlessly in sleep, or in some fixated dream-state, in a place in mind or spirit that seemed more a place of torment than pleasure, judging by the tone some had; it was fearful, as if they were small children living out some demon infested tale of woe. Still others who were on the rushes near the fire and the jars, were sucking on the end of a hose extending from a given jar, drawing in the smoke of the opium—for that was obviously what they were doing—draining their soul with every inhalation. I looked closer at the men before me. To my utter surprise, not all were soldiers of Christ as I had presumed. Several of them, judging by the appearance and clothing were actually members of the Islamic army under Salah al-Din!

All are One. In richness, in poverty, all are One, said the voice of the Spear. You <u>are</u> the richness. You <u>are</u> the poverty. "I understand. 'I am that, I am'," I heard myself say aloud.

"Liammm?" said the slurring, but familiar voice of my friend, Henry. "Is that truly you?"

I moved toward the sound of his voice. There, on one of the piles of rushes near the fire was my dear friend. I removed the heavy sword from my back and placed it on the ground along with the spear. I sat next to my friend; Henry on my right, the weapons on my left. I was silent for a moment, looking at the others who sat near us on the rushes. They were oblivious to my presence. I looked then to Alhasan. He remained respectfully away, staying near the entrance. I turned my full attention back to my friend. Henry looked even worse than on the previous night, or perhaps I was truly just noticing his appearance in its entirety. Even in the dim firelight of this smoky place I could see that his skin had a yellowish tint to it. His thinness was sickly. "You look horrible, Henry," I said.

He laughed a drunken laugh as he placed the hose end he was holding into his mouth. He inhaled deeply, drawing the opium smoke into his lungs. He rolled his eyes and tilted his head to one side with the pleasure of it just the way an infant does when drawing the life-nurturing flow from his mother's teat.

"Why?" I asked, stupidly.

He did not answer right away. But instead, held his breath, and hence the opiate smoke, inside his lungs. Finally, he released the smoke from its prison. Little of the stuff escaped from his mouth, giving me pause that much stayed in his body. He closed his eyes and smiled the grin of one who was not entirely in this world...and loved that he was not. "'Why?' you ask?" he finally said, keeping his eyes shut. I...went home when I died," he said, with surprising lucidity.

"Home? I don't understand," I said.

He laughed for a long time. Finally, he drew another inhalation on the hose, holding this one in only half as long as the previous one. He opened his eyes and looked at me. Though his eye lids drooped like the branches of the olive trees outside, it was Henry who stared at me and not some half-witted, drug-controlled person I did not recognize. He was somewhat detached, but it was him. Yet, it was clear by his next bit of rambling that he was connected to a deeper part of himself because of his state of mind. He regarded my Templar tunic. "I see you be one of them now, eh? Matter 'o time, was all, is that not right, Myrriddin my friend," he said to me. "Or Longi...Long-i-nus, or whatever name you be using this time. You remember me? I was hanged with you, right next to you, on the cross over all those centuries ago, I was," he stated. He then began to laugh as another thought, another memory apparently entered his now inebriated mind. "They hanged you on the cross upside down, do ye remember? Pissed 'em off you did!" Henry laughed uncontrollably, until a coughing fit nearly had him vomiting.

Though I was surprised at his memory, I did not show it. "You're a Christian. Since when did you start believing that you've been here before?" I said.

He made no reply.

"Come," I said as I took hold of his arm.

"No!" he said vehemently as he jerked his arm from my grasp. "I am fine here. More than fine here. I remember things with this," he said, holding up the hose.

"You don't need that to remember things," I said. But my words felt empty, and thus sounded empty even to my own ears.

644

"What do you know of it?" Henry replied. He then looked at the weapons at my side, the Spear in particular. "They hanged us for that thing, all those centuries past. And, here it is againnn. And againnn and againnn and againnnn will it keep showing up in our lives," he said as a statement of fact. "But you...you think it's destiny, I suppose. Well, I want off," Henry said raising his voice to a near yell, "ye 'ear me?! I want off this ship!"

"Shut yer yap, ye shit-hole!" said a voice from a pallet deeper within the cave.

Henry laughed again. He leaned in to my ear then, as one about to reveal a great secret to me alone. "I haven't shit in near a week!" he whispered. He sat upright with a laugh. "'ave ya heard of such?!" he said in a normal, matter of fact tone. "I feel like I gotta, but..."

"Let me take you back to the tent," I offered.

He did not answer me, but became silent for a time, staring into the fire in front of us. A tear brimmed one of his eyes. "I was home for a time, Liam. I was," he said in a lament-filled voice. "It was so beautiful. Then I was yanked back to here. By you and that...spear of yours. Why? Why? Didn't you let me go?" He began to weep, sobbing as a babe in the arms. I tried to think of something to say. But there was nothing to say. I put my hand on the spear thinking perhaps it could help. It had helped work wonders earlier. But I knew that was futile. Henry's condition was of the mind; one that was a conscious choice on his part, and as such only he could change it. At last I did what he probably needed most from me in that moment. I simply put my arms around him and held him as the friend I loved.

We stayed in the embrace for a few moments, tenderness and bitterness warring within me; tenderness for my friend, bitterness at my inability to help him. I looked over towards the entrance. Alhasan stood just inside the entrance. But there was someone else now there as well. The other man was silhouetted in the entrance itself by the light spilling in from outside. But I could see his gold eyes staring at me from beneath his turban. I turned my attention away from the gold-eyed man and back to my friend, and gently laid him down on the ground. He was already asleep. I then jumped to my feet, determined to speak with this gold-eyed man. I took one step toward the entrance and froze. He was gone. The gold-eyed man had vanished. Again. I ran up to Alhasan. "Where'd he go?!" I asked. I poked my head out of the cave for a brief moment. There was no one about.

"Who?" asked Alhasan.

"The man, the Arab with the gold eyes. He was standing just there," I said indicating the cave's entrance.

"There has been no one here but me. No one else has come in. I would have known it, you see," he replied vainly.

"I know what I saw, Alhasan," I said. "This man was also in Salah al-Din's tent. He stood behind Rashin, dressed as him but had stark gold-eyes. You must know of whom I speak, as you know the men who attend the Sultan and his hangers-on."

"I do, I do, Masoud. But...Masoud, there is no one in attendance of the Sultan or Rashin who appears as you say, no one with eyes of gold, you see," replied Alhasan.

I was dumbfounded.

"Come, Master Masoud. You are tried and tired from the day's event," he said nodding back toward my now sleeping friend Henry. He then turned and left the cave.

There was naught to do but follow him.

~XIV~

I left Henry at the den that day concerned about my friend and mystified by the stranger with the gold-eyes. I could no more force Henry to come back with me than I could force him to let go of the opium. It was his friend, or at least that was his perception for the time being. I cursed myself for not having seen his plight before. He had not been in the healing tent while I had been there. And, I did not see him until that day in Salah al-Din's tent. It was with heavy heart that I entered our tent, Alhasan at my side, and spent the rest of that evening and night in a state of self-loathing, guilt and moodiness over my friend. I finally fell into a restless sleep. But it was sleep nonetheless and I remained in it for a time. Until the visitor came, that is.

It was near dawn when I heard the scratching at the tent's flap. My first thought was that an animal was digging for something just near the tent. Alhasan and I exchanged a glance. He had clearly heard it too. But it became obvious that the scratching sound was in a purposeful, rhythmic manner; three scratches and moment of silence, followed by three more scratches. Over and over, the sound came. It was no animal making this noise.

Finally, I got off my sleeping pallet. I glanced over at what had been Henry's sleeping pallet. It was still empty, which disappointed me. So, too, was Sir James', though that did not surprise me at all. I grabbed the Spear of Longinus and slunk stealthily to the tent's flap. "Identify yourself," I said in a harsh whisper without opening the flap, spear at the ready.

"'Sultan Salah al-Din wishes a word, Sir Masoud," said the squeaky voice in a hushed whisper. I recognized the voice at once: it was the same voice that had greeted us at the sanctuary's door through the small, triangular shaped window or opening on the door just before entry for my initiation ritual.

Slowly, I pushed aside the tent's flap just enough to peer out at the visitor. He was alone and covered from head to toe in the black of the Knights Hashishim. As at the sanctuary's threshold, only his stark blue eyes were presently visible, this time through a slit in the cloth around his head and face. "You. I thought you to be one of us," I said, genuinely surprised.

"Ah. My English is quite good, is it not?" he replied, with pride.

"Yes. That and you're bright colored eyes led me to an incorrect conclusion," I said.

"Yes. The eyes. Franc mother, truth be told," our visitor stated flatly. "I say again; the Sultan wishes a word," he insisted.

"The last time I was in the presence of your Sultan I was a prisoner. And you expect me to now just walk into his camp and his tent to bid a fond and warm salutation?" I asked, sarcasm dripping from my words.

"Your life's position has been quite lifted, he is aware. He is also aware of the fact that you performed a great feat with the aid of the spear and the sword," my uninvited caller said.

"That does not answer my query," I replied.

"He wishes to ask you something, something of great import, something that could bend the way of this conflict," he said. There was an unspoken meaning to his words which I saw reflected in his eyes, I could see it, sense it. I sensed too that this meaning was of a profundity that needed to be heeded. My skin tingled at the realization and the spear gave a subtle vibration in my hand. My guest seemed not to notice, or pretended not to. "Your passage and safety is guaranteed, you have Salah al-Din's solemn oath on the matter."

I thought for a moment. It could be utter suicide, walking into the camp of the enemy. But then again, was I forgetting all I had experienced the past couple of days since the initiation?

"The Sultan's word is gold, Masoud," said Alhasan from behind me.

"Is that so?" I asked rhetorically, not looking back at him but instead keeping my eyes on our visitor.

"It is," replied Alhasan. "We must go to him if he wills it."

I now allowed the tent's flap to fall back into place, rudely falling in the face of our visitor, the messenger, and turned to Alhasan. "'We?' And what of you? You served the Sultan. Will he not want you back if you accompany me?"

"If it be the will of Allah."

"Or Salah al-Din's,"

He considered for a moment before answering. "I serve you. If Sultan Salah al-Din has invited you with guarantees of safety then that extends to your property as well... which includes the Spear, the Sword and me," concluded Alhasan. "But, as I say..."

"I know, I know; 'if it be Allah's will,'" I said. I turned back to the tent's flap and opened it. My caller, Salah al-Din's messenger waited patiently. "Very well, but give me a minute."

"As you wish," he said with a bow. He then stepped backward some ten feet and waited in the shadows.

I closed the flap again and began to gather my tunic. Alhasan just stood there watching me. "Well, come on," I said.

"I am presently ready, Masoud," he said.

Indeed, he was already dressed in his black servant garb of the Knights of Hashishim, something I had not noticed until that moment. "I see. One might think you half expected the messenger, Alhasan," I pointed out.

"I did, by 'half', as you say," he replied.

I stopped putting on my tunic, my head barely through the neck hole of the thing. "Then do you know what this meeting is really about?" I asked.

"No."

"Do you know this messenger outside? An acquaintance? A friend, perhaps?" I asked.

"Yes," was all he said.

I was unsure whether to be annoyed or amused at Alhasan's quick and crisp responses to my questions. I choose the latter and resumed dressing. "Just thought I would ask," I said. I placed the sword on my back and picked up the spear once again, then exited the tent into the waning night.

The messenger guided us stealthily through our camp, moving tent to tent, shadow to shadow, avoiding any of my people who were still about, which were very few. I thought it unnecessary. "We needn't move so through my own camp," I pointed out.

"And where would you say that you are going with myself and Alhasan here, especially dressed as we are?" he was quick to point out.

"Then you should've dressed differently. Besides, where I may go does not concern them," I said, knowing full well that it was a false statement.

"I had no time to 'dress differently'. And, your officers would state otherwise," he said.

Regardless, we were outside of the camp in quick order. The moon was half full and waxing, providing enough light in this desert land for us to see where we were going. We journeyed for not more than half-a-mile, before coming to a rise, a small hill, which we surmounted with ease. Before us was the encampment in which I had been imprisoned only a short time ago, now rebuilt from the attack perpetrated by the crusader army. My heart began to race. The dawn was still an hour or so away. I felt a sudden desire to be back in my own camp by then. Despite the messenger's assurances, I did not want to be seen in Salah al-Din's camp in daylight. We paused briefly at the crest of the hill and looked upon the Muslim camp. Some cooking fires were scattered about. As there had been in my camp at the present hour, there was a quiet lull to this camp as well; the quiet before the dawn.

"Come, Sir Masoud," said the messenger. "This shant take long."

We descended the other side of the hill and entered the camp of my former imprisonment.

Indeed, there were very few Muslim soldiers up and about. But there were a handful. Those who saw the three of us looked away, paying no heed, at least, at first. No doubt they simply thought that two of their comrades were bringing in a crusader prisoner. The attire of Alhasan and the messenger of Salah al-Din, and my crusader/Templar tunic spoke to that. But then, upon seeing that I held weapons, they stopped whatever they were doing and stared, some even stepping toward us. Those who did this were assertively waved off by the messenger. We moved through the camp, across it and to the other side. On the outskirts of the camp stood the grand tent of the Sultan, Salah al-Din.

The guards at the entry tunnel to Salah al-Din's tent eyed me as I approached with my two companions but showed no surprise at my appearance. No doubt they were expecting me. They simply stepped aside, allowing the messenger, Alhasan and me to pass. We walked into the tent's stuffy entry tunnel and came out the other side on the interior of the tent and into the main chamber where Salah al-Din held council.

The space looked the same as the first time I had been there, the tent's walls and ceiling having since been impeccably and imperceptibly sewn back together after the violent explosions that had torn them apart. Salah al-Din was in the same high-backed chair. Some of the same soldiers and court appendages that were in attendance the last time were there again. Among them: Hakim, the commander that Salah al-Din had slapped with a riding crop, who then turned up at our tent dressed as a Hashishim Knight, and the dark-robed, opaque-eyed man, Rashin too. He stared at me, Rashin did. I felt that his discolored eye saw me better than his normal eye; it felt as if he were probing my very soul with it. The sensation of knowing this man returned to me. Only now it was more

651

pronounced and more definite than it had been the day on the hillcrest. A name came to me unbidden, then another, and I spoke them both aloud without thinking; "Draco. Creconius Mab," I heard myself saying aloud to Rashin, yet not to him. A wide grin appeared on the man's face as if he knew exactly what, or who, I was talking about. And indeed, perhaps he was completely aware of the names I had just spoken as being those he had been identified with in two previous existences.

"Rashin," said Salah al-Din.

I looked at the Sultan with what must have appeared to him as an expression of confusion.

"His name is Rashin and he is, how shall I say," Salah al-Din began, looking at the opaque-eyed man with humorous contempt, "my court soothsayer..."

"I beg the Sultan's indulgence at my interruption, but I do not use that archaic term, great Sultan. I am of the extreme Sufi..."

"Yes, yes," said Salah al-Din irritably. "You are a great mystic and are able to see the future. That is one of the definitions of a soothsayer, but I use the term more in jest than anything else, you should know that," he said with finality. He then turned his attention back to me. "I thank you for coming, Masoud. It shows courage on your part. Congratulations are appropriate as well. You have risen yourself to a grand height and proven beyond doubt that you are the Keeper of the Spear of Longinus," he stated flatly. I could not tell if he was being sincere or sarcastic. He paused, then. The silence in the tent dragged on for more than a few moments. In fact, it hung in the air for so long that I began to become aware of sounds outside the tent; the sounds of a military camp beginning to come to life in anticipation of the campaign's new day. "We will speak in private, you and I," Salah al-Din said at last as he stood and stepped toward me.

"Great Sultan!" Hakim said. "I must insist that we be present at this...undertaking."

"No," was the Sultan's terse response.

"Salah al-Din," began Rashin as he stepped forward, brazenly stopping between myself and the Sultan, effectively blocking Salah al-Din's path in getting to me.

The Sultan's face flooded with controlled rage.

But Rashin did not back down. In fact, though his back was to me, I could hear that his voice was filled with authority; the kind of frightening authority that comes from the depths of the soul or from the depths of a soulless beast, depending on one's perspective. "I am the one who controls the item we have and the power that it contains. Do not forget, my Sultan," Rashin said.

I peered around the form of Rashin to look at Salah al-Din, to gauge his reaction. The Sultan's eyes appeared as though they were going to pop from his head, so anger-filled he was. He took a deep, visible breath before he spoke. "You have yet to prove that to my complete satisfaction, Rashin. You will wait here in this chamber while I speak to Masoud. Alone. Move aside."

A tense moment ensued as Rashin appeared determined to defy his Master's orders. But, after a moment, the opaque-eyed man deferred to his superior and stepped aside. Rashin then turned his gaze upon me, or rather, on the spear in my hand and then the sword on my back. His gaze at the sword was particularly intense and the look on his face was strange, even lustful; as if he were staring at the object of his most base, carnal desire, not unlike, oddly enough, Sir Blackthorn's gaze at the spear when first he beheld it.

"Come, Masoud," said Salah al-Din as he brushed past me. I turned and followed him out of the tent's main chamber, but I could not remove Rashin's licentious expression from my mind. I glanced back at Alhasan who had been standing this whole time near the entrance through which we had come. He simply inclined his head toward me. It was a gesture I interpreted to mean that I should obey the Sultan as he, Alhasan, is by staying put. Thus, I followed Salah al-Din.

~XV~

The two of us walked out of the main room and through three other adjoining rooms or chambers which were nearly as large as the main receiving room we had just been in. We then proceeded down a hallway of sorts. The chambers and hallway served as reminders of just how large this tent structure truly was. Finally, the Sultan led me into a chamber that was small by comparison to the others. It was brightly lit by several hanging oil lamps and tall floor candles. Laughter seeped into this chamber through the tent wall and venting space at the bottom of the wall. The sound appeared to come from the room immediately next to the one we were in. The laughter was lilting, pleasant and feminine. Women. The next room contained women. A harem? I wondered, a room to house the Sultan's wives and concubines? Some tales I had heard in my travels claimed that Salah al-Din was married to over one-hundred women. Of course, they were just that: tales; tales that were meant to further paint the people of this land as infidels and fornicators in need of annihilation. Perhaps he was not married to one-hundred women, but a handful. By the sound of it, five or six women occupied the next room. Every tale has an element of truth, or so it is said. What of it if these women are his wives in the pluralistic sense? How is that different then our forefathers of the Old Text taking more than one woman as wife, or even any 'Christian' married man taking a mistress? I thought to myself.

There is none, said a voice from deep within my being. The spear vibrated in conjunction with the words, shaking slightly in my hand and emitting a low, subtle humming or rattling in harmony with its movement and the thoughts in my mind. There is no judgment save by man, by woman. Rules are made by men, not God, not the One, the voice continued. The standard by which one conducts oneself is set by the consciousness within his own mind—which is part of the overall Mind of God—for his soul's learning, not by anything without. The voice went silent, the spear became still.

"It speaks to you indeed," said Salah al-Din, eyeing the spear in my hand. Obviously, he had seen or heard the thing vibrating.

The laughter from the room next door died down and the sound was replaced by the soft, muffled voices of the women conversing among themselves in their native Arabic in what seemed to be casual conversation. I smiled at the sound. It was sweet and natural, even though I could not hear precisely what was being said, let alone understand too much of it even if I could.

"I bring you to this room because none of my men would dare follow me us here," Salah al-Din said, in a hushed whisper, obviously having taken note of my awareness of the women in the next room.

I looked into the Sultan's eyes. Rashin would, I thought, but did not speak it.

He then looked again at the Spear of Longinus in my hand, then to the King's Sword hilt rising above and behind my right shoulder. His hand then moved to his side, pushed the folds of his dark robe back and came to rest on the jewel encrusted hilt of his own weapon; a bare-bladed, gleaming scimitar fit for a king or a Sultan as the case may be. "I am a much more skilled fighter than you, Masoud," he began, "but no doubt you could kill me where I stand with those weapons of yours and the power that you wield through them," he said softly, the corners of his mouth tugging up into a grin.

"You know that is not why I am here," I replied. I am here at your request, though I cannot fathom what your desire to see me is regarding."

His grin faded and his features softened into a look of contemplation and thoughtfulness. He stroked his beard for a moment. "We are not that different, you and I. Our beliefs are not that far apart, that is to say," he declared. "Allah and

Jesus' God is One God, the only God. They are the same. We Muslims have the same forefathers as you Christians and the Jews."

"But Jesus is not your Savior," I stated observationally.

"Is He truly yours?" he asked rhetorically. "Or do you see more, understand more now, Masoud? Muslims do not believe one is born in 'original sin', as Christians call it. So, there's no need for us to have the type of Savior you hold in Jesus. Besides, no one person—claimed to be a Son of God or not—can take away another's sins. Still, as I say, we are not that dissimilar, you and I." He turned then and stepped to a nearby table with two chairs near it. On the table sat a bronze, lit oil lamp and an ornately decorated, gold tea set. He lifted the pot by its single, angled, extended handle and poured the dark contents into two small gold sipping cups. "You English like tea, yes?" he asked as he turned back with the two cups holding out one of them for me. I had no time to respond, let alone tell him I take mine with cream. Hesitantly, I took the small cup he offered. I allowed Salah al-Din to sip from his cup first. I did this out of a sense of decorum, although the thought flashed into my mind that the Sultan might be insulted by this, thinking I was fearful of being poisoned.

But he said nothing. He held his cup to his lips and sipped the tea therein with a slurping noise that indicated his pleasure with the act and ritual of partaking in tea. I followed suit.

The liquid was dark and bitter. It was all I could do to keep my face impassive. I certainly did not wish to offend the Sultan, but his tea was horrid. The taste in my mouth was so foul that it was all I could do to swallow. A stinging tear watered my eye with swallowing the rank substance, giving away my distaste for the stuff.

Salah al-Din laughed heartily. "It does not quite meet with your English sensibilities?" he observed.

"I...uh, no, sire," I stammered, trying to speak through the fetid taste still in my mouth. No one makes tea with the art of an Englishman, I thought.

Salah al-Din fell silent for a time, savoring the tea from his cup and once again became contemplative. "As I was saying, we have many similarities," he said after a time, resuming his former line of conversation. "There is much within our Five Pillars that is quite similar to your Christian code."

"Five Pillars?" I asked, unsure of what he was talking about.

"To be truthful and to be sure, they are an oversimplification of a Muslim's practice of Islam, but they do serve to aid one in his practice and for the outsider to understand," he stated as a matter of fact as he moved back to the table and poured himself more tea. "They are the five basic tenets of practice that a Muslim must adhere to and live by: Declaring our faith or bearing witness daily, Salaat or daily prayer, fasting, charitable giving and service to others even if it is just in the form and of a simple smile," he said turning back to me and grinning, his eyes twinkling in friendship. "And of course, pilgrimage—in our case to Mecca," he continued. "As I said, these things oversimplify our belief or practice, but they are a good start and essential. And, surely you see by these that we have similarities, yes?"

"Yet, we war," I replied.

"Indeed we do, though it is not by our will," said Salah al-Din. "It is in our defense that we war."

"I could beg to differ. But, I've come to know that the whole of this war is pointless; the death, the destruction," I said. "It's foolish at best, especially knowing we serve the same God, the One God, call him what you will."

"Wise words, Masoud," replied Salah al-Din.

"Indeed," I said. A silence then fell between us for a time. I began to waver in my decision to be there. In fact, it seemed that we were skirting the issue of why I was there. "With respect, you did not summon me here to teach me the tenets of Islam or debate the merits of the war," I finally said, the slight edge of impatience slipping into my voice. "If you please."

"As you wish," he replied graciously. He drank from his cup of tea, throwing back the remainder of the second cup with vigor. He placed the cup back on the table and stepped up to me, his face turning gravely serious. He stopped so close to my face that I could feel his breath on my cheek and smell the bitter herbs from the tea thereon. "You have heard tell of the Rood, yes?" he asked in a hushed whisper that connoted a secretive agenda.

"The Rood. Do you speak of the wood from the very cross that the Christ was hanged on?" I asked.

"The very same," he answered, as he took a step back to a more respectable distance. Still keeping his voice in a hushed tone, he continued. "It is said that this Rood contains power much as your spear and sword."

I wanted to point out to him that I was coming to fully understand that these items contained no power in and of themselves. I refrained from doing so, however. "So it is said," I replied, wondering where this line of discussion was headed.

"We are in possession of the Rood," Salah al-Din declared.

I was not completely surprised by the Sultan's claim. They had initially possessed the Spear of Longinus before I came to have it. Rumor had also stated that they possessed the Rood. But questions did begin to enter my mind as to how they could have come by the Rood, and the Great Spear for that matter.

"We do not possess the entire cross, mind you. But we do have the cross section. It was apparently cut into pieces at one point..." Salah al-Din said.

At his last words, a sudden flash of heat wafted over my entire body. My head and face felt flush and I felt as if I would faint. An image impinged itself on my mind. I was looking out through the eyes of Centurion Longinus again, many centuries past. There were others with me/Longinus, a woman, an old man and a large red-haired Celt. I knew them all. Or, I had known them in that life: Irena, my love. Her name came to my mind. So, too, did the old man's and the Celt's;

Jacobi and Dosameenor, respectively. But it was where we were and what we were doing that was the most interesting in this...vision. We were in the back of a covered wagon on top of the wagon's load; wood—the rood. We had a saw in hand and were cutting the Rood into sections, thirteen, to be exact...

"Masoud?" came the Sultan's voice, yanking me back to the present. The vision faded and I was once again before Salah al-Din in mind and body. "Masoud, are you ill?"

"No, no. It's just that...nothing. I am fine. Pray continue," I said.

"Yes, as you wish. We managed to fasten the pieces we have back together and it is definitely the cross section of the Rood. His blood, your Christ's blood stains the end pieces near where the nail holes remain even now. It is where His hands were...secured," the Sultan said, clearly trying to be respectfully delicate in his description.

"How do you know it is the Rood?" I asked. "How do you know that it is His blood? Perhaps it is a cross piece used in a crucifixion. But it could be anyone's blood, if that is indeed what it is."

"The same way we knew the spear you now carry was the one that pierced the Prophet Jesus' side; its powers were unleashed by one of our own," he continued. "No ordinary cross or spear would have performed thusly. Though, in the case of the Spear of Longinus, no one demonstrated its powers like you."

I pondered, mulled over, really, what the Sultan was saying and implying. "You say one of your own unleashed power from this Rood?"

"Indeed."

"Was it Rashin, by chance?" I asked, already knowing the answer.

"The very one. It was also he who was able to draw some of the spear's power out, though that display was not very impressive. However, what he did with the Rood was most fortuitous as to its potential use for us," Salah al-Din explained.

"Perhaps it's more that Rashin is a powerful individual. Or, perhaps he simply knows how to wield the Power of the One regardless of the instrument," I replied. I cringed from the very core of my being at the thought of Rashin wielding this power. I withdrew deep into my own thoughts. "The power of the One acts only by its own Law and may be executed for evil purposes. The power knows only to respond by the individual's intention," I said under my breath, deep in thought. But, apparently I did not say it far enough under my breath.

"One man's evil is another man's deliverance," replied Salah al-Din. "Or so I have observed. Given that, is there any true evil outside of what we rain down upon each other, what we ourselves create? And, if there is only the One Power, as you say, then there is no good or evil to It. It simply Is, is it not?"

"Yes, but do you really believe that?"

"Allah is all there is, and there is none greater. That is what I believe," he answered cryptically, smiling, smirking, as the words came out of his mouth.

"But your very words clarify my point: Rashin will use the Rood for the purpose of destroying us..."

"As you would use the power of the Spear and Sword to destroy us!" he retorted in a sudden burst of anger and impatience. "So you see, Masoud, in that sense, at least, we have a stalemate." His words hung in the air a time. "Masoud," he continued after a moment more calmly, "I believe we will eventually win this conflict and drive you all back to your homes, Allah willing. And I will accomplish this by intelligent use of my army and by superior battle strategies. I am merciful. I will hold none. Those who wish to stay may do so and even continue to worship as they see fit," the Sultan stated calmly, superciliously.

"How generous of you. But, you're a bit premature, are you not?" I asked, angered by his arrogance.

"I think not."

"Still, you would not be telling me about the Rood unless you feared the Spear and Sword and the Power..."

"The Power you wield through those instruments and the Power we wield through the Rood will destroy each side proportionally. And, then I would still win. Why succumb to all the unnecessary death only to have the same result in the end?"

"You don't know how it will end," I replied, lamely.

"Have it your way, Masoud. But do you not see my point; regardless of the final outcome, there will be mutual loss, and hence unnecessary destruction in the meantime, do you not agree?!" he said, his voice rising again with anger.

"I see your point," I finally conceded. The silence that followed lingered for a few moments. "I agree not to use the Power for such ends."

"As do I," he said, calmness once again pervading his voice.

A silence lingered in the air again. Silence all around, for it was then that I noticed the women's voices had gone silent in the next room. Disappointment seeped into my being. "May I return now to my encampment?" I asked after a time.

He walked over to me. "Yes, Masoud," he said and then placed his right hand on my shoulder. "I thank you for your wisdom in this. Your wisdom is rising. For that and other reasons you are showing the signs of becoming a great leader."

I stood in silence, not sure whether I should make a response to the compliment, but realizing it would be bad form not to. I inclined my head in a gesture of acknowledgement. He released my shoulder and stepped toward the doorway that we had come through. "If you will wait here, I will send Alhasan back for you. Please help yourself to some more tea," he said looking back at me with a wry smile.

I felt myself smiling as well. Salah al-Din turned and was nearly out the entrance of the small chamber. "You said, Sultan, that Rashin had not proven to you adequately that he could use the power of the Rood," I heard myself blurting out as the thought came in my head. "That is, you didn't actually mention the Rood back in your main receiving chamber, but it is what you were referring to when you spoke to him earlier was it not?"

Salah al-Din stopped in the entryway and turned back to face me. "Sometimes, Masoud, one must tell a subordinate that he is not meeting expectations in order to have him exceed them."

"That can work both ways, sire. Rashin is one to keep his own secrets. Me thinks that he could yield more power than he's showing you. He is probably keeping it hidden for his own nefarious purposes. I would bet on it," I said.

The Sultan smiled. "As a Muslim, I do not gamble. But if I did, I would bet so as well. You speak with such surety, as if you know him, Masoud."

I thought for moment as to how to answer. "I know the spirit of the man," I said vaguely. "He would love to possess this spear and sword I carry as well, I know that to be the truth."

"No doubt," he replied.

"Beware of him, sire, is all that I am conveying to you," I said.

"Thank you, Masoud. Alhasan will be with you shortly," he said. He then turned and left the chamber. I was left suddenly feeling quite alone; just myself, two weapons and bitter tea.

~XVI~

I remained in the small room or chamber for what seemed like an hour. I even tried some more of the tea which did not taste any better than it had the first time. Twice I went to the entry doorway of the chamber and looked out and down in both directions of the tent's hallway. There was no sign of anyone. The thought crossed my mind that perhaps I should just leave, not wait for Alhasan or anyone else. But then again, that would probably be among the more unintelligent things I could have done. A lone crusader with spear and sword would not exactly be tolerated walking through a Muslim military camp. Finally, I went over to one of the chairs near the tea table and sat, determined to simply wait for Alhasan. The room was quiet and the women's voices from the adjacent room were still silent. I wondered if they were there, perhaps sleeping, or if they had moved to another room altogether.

The silence dragged on. "I beg pardon," said a whispered voice, a whispered female voice, in English but with a heavy Arabic accent. The voice came from the other side of the tent wall, from within the room where the women had been. She was close to the wall, close to me by the sound of it, as the wall that the tea table rested near was the joining wall of the women's room.

Though it was but a whisper it startled me, so unexpected it was. Is she speaking to me? I wondered.

"Master Masoud?" she asked as if in answer my thought.

I leaned toward the tent wall, toward the sound of her voice. "I am Masoud, yes. Or, rather that is what your people have chosen to call me," I said in a conspiratorial whisper. My words were met with silence. The quietude dragged to a point where I thought perhaps she had gone. "Are your still there?" I asked.

"Yes," she replied timidly. "I heard you speaking with the Sultan and recognized your voice."

Confusion crept into my mind. "You recognized my voice?" I asked.

"You...you came to my aid," she replied.

I was stunned by her answer. I could not fathom when I might have come to the aid of a woman in this campaign, much less to the aid of a Muslim woman. I was speechless.

"You do not remember," she stated with a tinge of disappointment.

"You must be mistaking me for another," I said.

"No," she insisted, her voice now becoming more assertive in tone. "I inquired as to your name after the...incident. And, as I said, I recognized your voice a few moments ago." She paused briefly before continuing. "Several of your own men were...how do you say in English...raping me, I believe is how it is said. You stopped them, killed one, maybe."

Of course. It came flooding back to my memory then. She was not mistaking me for another. We, Sir James and Henry and I, had still been in the Muslim camp, prisoners, when our soldiers and crusaders had attacked. During the course of that battle, a woman had been attacked by my own fellow crusaders. I had been appalled and intervened on the woman's behalf, fighting my own men. In the present moment, the woman's lavender eyes were all I remembered of her. "I remember what you speak of," I said.

"I am pleased that you remember and I thank you most sincerely for your bravery. You risked much in doing what you did," she said.

"The acts of those men were not befitting the honor and principles of our beliefs," I replied. "I could not let them get away with what they were doing to you."

"Much of your own behavior seems to be setting the example for all to see. And follow," she said. "Even my Uncle respects you enough to speak to you privately, negotiate with you, that much is clear."

"Your Uncle?" I asked, surmising the answer, but surprised nonetheless.

"Sultan Salah al-Din, of course," she said nearly laughing. "Who did you think I was speaking of?"

"I thought...that is, I mean...I thought..."

"...That I was one of his wives?" She now laughed genuinely. It was a lilting, intoxicating sound. "You must have heard us, the women, in here when first you came in, yes?"

"Yes. That is true."

"I understand, then, how you might have thought what you thought," she replied.

A long pause of silence engulfed us then, as if we had run out of things to say. It had been a long time since I had been in the presence of a woman, any woman, let alone spoken to one. I wanted to see her face, look into those lavender eyes. I wanted to rent asunder the cloth and canvas wall of the tent that separated us. It was such a flimsy barrier really, but it might as well have been a wall of brick and iron, so separated were we by culture, by creed. I then noticed something on the wall, in the lamp's shadow. It was a closed flap near the edge of the table. The flap was square—approximately a foot-and-a-half square—and was held closed by a tie at its top. A window of sorts is what it appeared to be; a window to look into the adjacent room. Slowly, I reached out and pulled the tie loose. The flap, held secure at its bottom, flopped open, revealing the next room. A woman's face slowly appeared in the window's opening. I could see her clearly even in the lamp and candle light of the room. Though I had laid eyes on this woman once before, this was the first time I was actually seeing her, taking in her appearance. Her cheek bones were lovely and high and tapered down to her mouth—the corners of which rose slightly in a perpetual, warming smile—in perfect symmetry with the rest of her face. Although she wore a light-blue head wrap, black ringlets of her hair fell from beneath, resting on the medium-dark brown skin of her forehead. The eyes had an ever-so-slight almond shape to them and flowed gently to her slender, delicate nose, simply adding to the perfect proportion of her face. And, the shining lavender color of those eyes was stunning, as if the light of a-thousand light-purple stars twinkled therein; the priceless capstone on what was, in my opinion, the most perfect female face. She was beyond beautiful. I was instantly enamored. "What is your name?" I asked, near breathlessness.

"Najeeba. My name is Najeeba," she said shyly.

"Najeeba," I repeated, savoring the sound of it and the way it rolled off my tongue. "And what does it mean?"

"It means, 'Of Noble Birth,'" she declared.

"Apropos, given that you are the Sultan's niece," I said, suddenly becoming aware of the fact that I was grinning from ear to ear. I became self-conscious, even embarrassed by my own boyish giddiness. Yes, she was immensely beautiful, but how could I be so taken by this creature in such short order? I wondered. I stared deeper into her eyes, searching for...what, I was not sure.

"Many pardons, Sir Masoud! A thousand pardons for my delay!" Alhasan yelled as he came bounding into the room.

I jumped to my feet, toppling the chair I was sitting in. My thighs bumped the table violently as I stood, toppling the carafe of tea as well, spilling the dark contents onto the table, and nearly knocking over the lamp that was there too. I had been so startled that I found the King's Sword in my hand—I had obviously instinctively pulled it out with the sudden appearance of Alhasan, perceiving a possible threat in the moment—as well as the Great Spear in the other. "Damn you, Alhasan! Have you no manners?!"

"A thousand pardons, Sir Masoud! I was only just informed to retrieve you, you see! Please forgive me," he pleaded.

I looked over to the window. Najeeba's lovely face was gone. I leaned over the table and poked my head through the square opening in the tent wall. Peering into the next room I saw nothing but richly appointed throw cushions and lit candles. The room was devoid of anyone.

"Come, Sir Masoud. We must be off and away," said Alhasan.

"Very well," I said with unbridled disappointment.

~XVII~

The day's sun was near gone as the mists enshrouded the land and the stones: the great monoliths of my people's bygone time. My soul knew these rock beasts as if they were of my own flesh, my life's blood, my very spirit, for they were. Many generations had passed since the carving and placing of these magnificent entities of the ages. They were alive, centerpieces in the vortex of natural and Infinite powers. I often came here when I was vexed or perplexed, when I was grappling with an issue of great import or of grand significance to the schemes and dreams of men. But I had come here many a time simply for the sake of my own spirit as well. Indeed, I had even been brought back from the dead once here during my life as a Roman Centurion, and had helped to shape and build the place many lifetimes before that. Now, I was in the light of a full moon, leaning with my backside against what remained of the center altar piece, the same place upon which I, the centurion, with the aid of the sacred spear, had been recalled from the Otherside.

A cowl covered the top my head and my eyes were cast down in contemplation. A gentle hand touched my face, stroking my left cheek lovingly. "Myrriddin," said Igraines.

I warmed instantly to her touch and her sweet voice. I brought my gaze upon her lovely face and looked into Igraines eyes, now turned the color of brilliant lavender.

"Myrriddin, my dearest," she said staring back at me.

I saw in those eyes Irena too, the persona of Igraines' soul I had known as Longinus. And the lavender color of her eyes now reflected yet another guise of Igraines soul; Najeeba. Such were the thoughts of my spirit in the present vision, dream, soul experience, whatever one wishes to call it.

"What vexes thee?" she asked soothingly.

"You have always known the ways of my spirit, have you not, my love," I stated.

"Always," she replied. "But it's not difficult to know something troubles you when you left the dinner so abruptly, almost angrily. Please, Myrriddin, what is it? Is it Arturius? His men?"

"Aye. 'Tis both, Igraines. They know not what they are about to spark. They follow an irrational order from the Church, to which they usually give only half attention, and are bent on beginning a legacy of death and persecution," I said.

"They are good and true men, Myrriddin. You judge them too harshly," reprimanded Igraines. "Besides, you have said that what they begin here will not come to fruition for many years."

"For many centuries will the pain of what they seek to do inflict itself upon the people of that which they call the Holy Land," I stated, rising in frustration and walking a few feet away before turning back to face her. "It will end with bitter divisions between people and their faiths for millennia to come. I have seen it."

"The men wish only to wrest the Holy relics from the Moors and make passage for Christian pilgrims to the region safe," she said.

"And would that be all it remained," I replied. But it will not. Their desire for the Holy relics will turn into lust for power and the absurd assertion that the church's way is the only way to God and they will end in attempting to destroy the others' faith just as they've attempted to destroy our Old Ways."

"Arturius and his men will not do that! They have sworn an oath by your command and initiation to uphold all that is true and decent and honorable," she said defensively. "What you suggest is..."

"It is not Arturius' men that will perform what I speak of," I said. "But it will be part of the legacy they help to create. Many of those who come long after them will pervert the original purpose of the undertaking to come. Especially when the Last Prophet is come to earth near three centuries from now by the Christian calendar, I have seen this as well. He will inspire thousands to attempt the destruction of Christendom in part because of what is about to begin here."

"It cannot be so, Myrriddin. What kind of man, prophet or no, would do such a thing?!" she said.

I, Myrriddin, did not answer her, but instead walked to one of the nearby standing stones touching my palm to it. The warmth of the day's sun was still emanating from the thing. Images entered my mind, images of holy wars and crusaders and men that I, Masoud knew. And, I saw myself, my Masoud self holding the spear in the court of Salah al-Din. The image suddenly vanished and I was Myrriddin once again, yanking my hand away from the standing stone as if were hot coal.

"What is it Myrriddin?" asked Igraines suddenly at my side. "I know you see things when you touch these stones. What was it?"

"It was a future self. In many centuries to come, I will be in the midst of all of which I speak," I, Myrriddin replied.

ل ل ل

I awoke to find a half-naked, dirt-streaked, very lucid Henry sitting on his sleeping pallet staring oddly at me. "You were speaking in your sleep. Kept me awake, ya bloody bastard. And, who on God's earth is Igraines?" he asked, a look of confusion creasing his brow. "I feel as though I know the name, but can't place it."

"It is a lengthy story, my friend. But, you're looking well, if not a bit dirty," I said, genuinely surprised to see him here in our tent shelter. It was then that I heard the noises of the camp outside. "What is the time?" I asked, noticing daylight coming in through the tent's seams.

"Late afternoon. You've been asleep all day," he said.

"All day?" I asked in wonderment, rhetorically. My thoughts turned to Najeeba and then to the dream or vision I had just awakened from. It was clear that my mind was seeing Najeeba and Igraines and Irena as one in the same. Or, perhaps my mind was correlating the women as a representation of my desire for a female companion. Yet, I knew better. It was much deeper than that. I felt it in my soul.

"Well I'm off," declared Henry as he stood and began dressing, throwing his filth encrusted outer tunic over his bare torso. The stench of his soiled clothing moving through the air of the cramped tent's interior wafted toward me. I nearly gagged from it.

"To where?" I asked, trying to avoid the urge to directly point out his lack of personal hygiene. "You haven't told me where you've been, how you've been. That is, the last time I saw you..."

"You should not have gone there, to the den, I mean," he interrupted.

"I was concerned, Henry. I wanted to help you."

"Hmph," was his cryptic reply.

"But you look well! Rested," I offered, trying to change the subject of the den, trying to stay focused on the positive.

"I occasionally get a good night's rest. Or day's rest, as it is sometimes," he replied. "Except when my bunkmate talks in his sleep."

He began to leave. "Where are you going?" I asked.

"Where do you suppose I'm going?!"

Disappointment crept into my being. "Back to the den," I stated, hoping he would deny it, even if the denial was false.

"Aye. My home away from home," he laughed sardonically.

"But what about your duties here? Surely, you've not leave to..."

"I do not need a 'by-your-leave' from you, Sir Liam Mason, or Sir Masoud, or whatever in the Devil's hell they're callin' you these days!" Henry said tersely, venomously. His sudden burst of anger was palpable and unexpected. "But, yes, I have been given leave by higher-ups to tend to my...ailments." He began to limp toward the tent's entrance. "You, on the other hand, are a grand knight now. I suggest you get off your arse and answer to the day before the day is done." With that he left, leaving me in contemplation as to how a bright glimmer of hope for my friend could so instantly turn into the anguished heaviness of defeat.

Henry was gone no more than five minutes when I decided to put him out of my mind for the present and move through the rest of the day. His banishment from my thoughts was not to be, however. My dear friend was stricken with the opiate crave and I, for all the Power of the One, was powerless to do anything to help him directly. But that was just the point; we all have this Power coursing through us, because It is us. And as such, we all have the choice, the free will to do with It as we will, for better or worse. This realization was sinking in more and more, day by day, as I continued on this strange odyssey which began with Henry's apparent trip back from the dead, the first time I came into contact with the Spear of Longinus. At least, it had been the first time coming into contact with it in this life. But then it struck me; what I could do for my friend in the present moment was to give him my thoughts and prayers of healing; to hold him in my mind as the perfect, whole being I knew him to be, regardless of the temporary, outward appearance. I had never thought along these lines before. Oh, I had prayed a beseeching prayer to God for whatever reason on many an occasion. I had always prayed the type of prayer that I was taught by the Church; a manner of prayer in which one speaks to God in a pleading fashion, hoping beyond hope that He may see fit to answer. Of course, He may not see fit to answer. Yet, I was coming to an inner realization that the power of a prayer is not exterior to the one praying, but in the intent and thought on the interior of his mind, and also manifested by the degree of feeling and conviction at the level of his heart, his soul. In other words, the Power of a prayer is to Know, unwaveringly, that the one who is ill is actually in a condition of appearances and not in a natural state of being. To Know this is to deny the condition its hold on any kind of reality. Thus, I decided to pray from right where I sat, to treat Henry in mind, to treat my friend and the condition he was presently caught up in, and have the Knowingness that the condition was not Henry, that Henry was but the jovial, healthy person I had known these many years. Taking a deep breath I simply let the words come of their own accord. "I know there is but One Power," I began, "One Source for all things, for any and all healing, and that this Source is All there is. Since this Source is all there is, I am an aspect of It, and the Power thereof flows effortlessly through me now and always, and through every other person on this earth because it is us, It is what we are. The Power of this Source is here now and always in the form of abundance and perfect health, and flows through me now and through Henry Tobiason Andrews. He is perfect in health and perfect in mind. He has released the crutch of the opiate and is hale and whole. I see this now and know it to be so! I am grateful for this sight, for the knowledge and I let go of it knowing that it is done! So be it! In the name of the Christ, Amen!" I drifted in thought for a time, having induced through the prayer, a kind of trance state in myself. I then felt myself float out of my body, out of the tent and to a location not all that far away. I did not travel through time as with my other visions, but stayed present in time and found myself at the side of my friend, Henry as he continued his walk toward the den. He was alone, utterly alone, walking with his head cast down as if traversing the terrain in shame.

He stopped briefly and looked directly at me, or rather, where my form might be if my body had actually been there. He looked quizzically at me. "Liam?" he said, sensing my presence and suddenly spinning around, looking for me but not seeing me. He stopped then and simply looked straight forward in the direction he had been walking in. "You're quite the magician now are ye not?" he said to the air. "Either that or I'm goin' mad," he said under his breath.

"Know yourself, Henry. You are whole and hale," I said. Though he did not actually hear me, Henry closed his eyes and took a deep breath. He opened his eyes as he let the breath out and looked at the sky. A small flock of doves flew overhead. He watched the birds' flight and smiled, apparently savoring the moment and perchance life itself. Perhaps he had heard me after all. But the moment quickly passed and without saying another word, he walked on. It was a start, anyway.

I opened my eyes and found myself back in the tent. That was interesting, I thought to myself. I had been next to Henry in spirit just a moment ago. It had certainly been a present time journey of my spirit and not simply a traveling vision pulled up from the memory of my soul. I thought of the prayer I had spoken and laughed at myself for delivering the last part about the Christ. It had been a different kind of prayer than I'd ever spoken, but some habits fail to fall away. The thought then struck that I should save this prayer in my mind and recite it often for my friend, as often as needed.

The spear caught my eye and I looked at the thing standing upright—blade up and butt on the ground—against the tent's wall next to my sleeping pallet, the Great Sword of Arthur in its makeshift scabbard standing hilt-up next to it. Something grabbed my sense of intuition: a message was being conveyed to me. Now it was my turn to feel as though an unseen presence was with me attempting to tell me...what? But the presence was not in the form of a human spirit. The intuitive tingle, if you will, I was receiving was coming through the spear and sword. To my surprise, however, neither spear nor sword was aglow with warning or message as in the past. Yet, I suddenly and inexplicably knew I was needed elsewhere immediately. I threw on my tunic, grabbed the Great Spear and the King's Sword and left the tent.

~XVIII~

I followed my footsteps, not knowing exactly where I was going, only knowing that I must get there as soon as possible.

"Now! Get your asses into place!" yelled a commander with a Franc accent.

I looked in the direction of the voice and saw Christian soldiers scrambling to form up into ranks of ten, weapons at the ready, their commander, Laffite, barking orders and threats to make the soldiers fall into their proper lines of presentation. I made my way to them and stopped near Laffite and the men. Laffite looked at me and smiled, his gapped tooth grin exhibiting a strange mixture of contempt and respect.

"Ah...Sir Mason...forgive me, Sir Masoud," he said. "Come to join us, or are we now beneath your dignity?" he said.

I could not tell whether he was serious or being a jester. His tone was intense but not sarcastic and that grin stayed cemented on his face. I looked at the lines of men forming and knew the urgency I was feeling a moment ago had something to do with this. "What is happening, Lafitte?" I asked, choosing to ignore his taunt.

"We storm the citadel!" he proclaimed with a dramatic flair, slurring his words in the process.

"What citadel?" I asked.

"Jerusalem herself, sire!" he replied. It was then I noticed his bloodshot eyes and smelled the reek of inferior, self-made liquor on his breath. He was drunk.

"By whose order do you call the formations?" I demanded.

"Mine, Liam," said General Blackthorn from behind us. I turned and saw the general on a grand white horse trotting up to the formations. "Well, truth be told, King Richard himself has given it. Glad to see you here, lad. And your weapons," he added indicating the spear and sword I held.

Four other officers on horses of their own—one was Sir James, another was a lower ranking captain whom I had seen only in passing, and two others; lieutenants whom I had never seen before—accompanied the general, reined in their mounts next to Sir Blackthorn. The captain had an extra horse in tow. This mount was saddled, but rider-less. Presumably, it was for Lafitte. The captain and lieutenants stared at me and my weapons or instruments, as I preferred to call the Great Spear and the King's Sword.

Sir James grinned, apparently amused at the men's fascination with me. "Yes, gentlemen. It is he, Sir Liam Arthur Mason, also dubbed Sir Masoud, keeper of the Spear of Longinus and guardian of the King's Sword, the sword of King Arthur himself," exclaimed Sir James. "He has performed great feats of healing and miracles with these items, and will surely lead us to victory in our endeavor!"
I made to speak, to tell these officers that the commander exaggerates and that I am no leader of men; keeper and guardian of the Spear and Sword, perhaps, but not the leader that the commander professes me to be. I also wanted to tell them of my pact with Salah al-Din to not use the instruments in such manner. But I would not betray that agreement.

"Sire," began the captain holding the reins of the riderless horse. He was a fair-skinned, red-haired and red-bearded man who reminded me greatly of Henry. "Sire," he said again in a deep voice by way of addressing me, "your mount." He held out the reins of the horse, a magnificent beast of a deep brown and black, toward me. Apparently, the beast was not for Lafitte after all.

"Magnificent, is she not?!" exclaimed General Blackthorn with boyish excitement, nodding toward the horse. "I obtained her in Spain, I did. Please accept her as my gift to you. Her name is Macha."

My heart raced. I knew the name. Somehow, I knew the name. I approached the animal and looked into her eyes. Within those dark windows I saw and sensed an old friend and familiarity. It seemed as though her spirit was smiling at me. I was at a loss to explain it, but had learned not to question these things. Just accept it as so, I thought. And so I did, both the gift of an old friend and the gift from my superior officer. "Thank you, General, for such a lavish gift. I hardly feel worthy," I said.

"Nonsense! Can't have our Great Guardian and Knight without a mount," Blackthorn said.

"Come, Liam," said Sir James, "Mount. We must be off."

"We proceed to Jerusalem?" I asked.

"We do," he replied.

"But I thought our people were gaining much ground in her retaking?" I asked, confused. Part of the reason our particular regiment was stuck out in the open regions of this land was to keep Salah al-Din's men harassed, thus allowing the bulk of our crusader army to concentrate on obtaining the Holy City once again. Even Salah al-Din himself had come out from the City and camped to aide in fending us off.

"They, we, are, lad. But the campaign falters, they need our reinforcements," replied the general.

"Where is your Arab friend?" asked Sir James.

"Alhasan?"

"Aye."

I looked around as if I half expected Alhasan to appear on cue. Of course, he did not. "I know not," I said, "I have not seen him since early this morning."

"We need him as an interpreter. He is your servant now, is he not? I heard him speak as much," said Sir James.

"Yes, that is, he has said as much as you say."

"Take your leave and find him then rejoin us here. We march within the hour," ordered the general. "God willing, we join our men near the Holy City tonight under cover of darkness. We attack the enemy within by dawn. Go, lad."

With that, the red-haired captain tossed the reins of Macha to me. I mounted the fine horse and nodded my thanks to the captain. "Sir Blackthorn," I began, turning my attention back to the senior-most officer present. "Might I retrieve my friend Henry as well, sir? Will we not be needing all able-bodied men?"

But it was Sir James who answered in the general's stead. "Do not worry about Henry, Liam. The men at the den, at least ours, are being rounded up now, even as we speak."

That sounded more ominous than I wanted to admit. "You will do them no harm?" I asked.

"They will be fine, just find Alhasan," said Sir James, as he directed his horse toward the men still stumbling to assembly.

"'Tis more than I can say for the men of the enemy who also occupy that den of iniquity," said the general somewhat maliciously. "Mustn't let our plans be made known, eh, lad?"

These men, Sir James and Sir Blackthorn, seemed to be a contradiction. On the one hand they were Templar Knights who work with our Islamic brethren of the Hashishim Order for the betterment of all, or so they say. Yet, on the other hand, they were fierce warriors willing to spill that same blood in the name of Christianity. And, on the other side were the likes of Hakim who displayed this same apparent duality. All in the proper context, came the thought in my head, jarring me from my judgmental musings of the men. The thought seemed to come from deep within my own being, from the part of me I now knew to be eternal, where ultimate Truth and Knowledge are one and the same and completely accessible. Although I had only recently begun to truly pay attention to this aspect of myself, I was quickly coming to know and accept that it was just that; My Self—my True Self. The rapidity with which this understanding was impinging itself upon my mind I attributed to the various experiences, knowledge and information from my soul's past which had been coming to the forefront of my awareness these past few days with ever increasing speed.

"Off with ya, lad," said the general with urgency.

I said nothing more, but turned my attention to the horse beneath me. Macha felt sturdy and energetic as she pranced about for a moment. And, she felt perfectly natural beneath me. I spurred her gently forward and back to the tent in search of Alhasan.

The trip back was quick and revealed a camp in mid-disassembly; tents and shelters were coming down and being made ready for transport. Men were rapidly running here and there attending to the duties one has when breaking camp. It was interesting how rapidly I had become accustomed to our community of tents. I nearly lost my way because so many of the temporary dwellings were already gone and thus my points of reference as to the exact location of my own dwelling were gone with them. That, and the fact that the tent I had been sleeping in only a short time ago was already collapsed. Alhasan stood from his labors in folding our shelter at my approach.

His eyes grew wide at the sight of Macha and I. "Ah, Master Masoud!" he exclaimed. "Truly befitting of one such as yourself! You appear as royalty, a Sultan in your own right!"

"Thank you, Alhasan. I had wondered where you had gotten to. Woke up not long ago and you were gone," I said as I dismounted and began helping my friend to finish with the folding of our tent.

At that moment two soldiers approached us with a supply wagon. "We'll take that for you, sir," said one of them, a child-faced lad.

I looked from the first to the second and saw the mirror image of the first: identical twins. They were tall, nearly six foot each. But their pink, hairless, child-like faces belied a youth of not more than twelve I surmised. "What in God's name are two doing here?!" I asked. "You can't be more than twelve the both of you. You should be home taking care of a farm or your parents, not out here in this..."

"Sir, our mother's dead by birthing a stilled baby sister and our father ran off," said the first in the cracking voice of a boy turning man, which merely served to confirm my guess at their age.

"Went mad, he did. Blamed us for mum's death and the baby's too for that," added the second, in the near same crackling voice, almost speaking over the first.

"Yes, called us 'devil's spawn,'" said the first on the heels of his brother's words, "said we were not his, never believed we were his."

"Yes, and hated our mother for a long time, claimed she had fornicated with half the village and we were the curse for it," said the second.

"But then when she became with child again he said he knew it was his, and he was happy for a time," the first continued.

"Until the birthing time when she didn't live nor the little one," the second lad said.

My head started to spin trying to keep up with the two.

The second suddenly turned to his brother. "I would have liked a sister," he said.

"I as well," replied the first.

"All right, boys. Enough. I'm truly sorry for your losses on all fronts. But to come here?" I asked. "What are your names?"

"My given name is Cain," replied the first.

"And mine is Lucifer," replied the second.

"Of course," I offered, sardonically, looking to Alhasan. My friend seemed more amused than anything else.

"But I prefer Canter," said the first.

"And I prefer Luscious," said the second.

"So be it, Canter and Luscious. Here's our tent for the wagon. I helped the boys load the now folded shelter onto their wagon. "Thank you," I said.

"Our pleasure, sir," replied Canter.

"Yes, our pleasure," echoed Luscious. "'Tis an honor to serve the likes of you!"

With one in the front of the wagon and the other in the back, they pulled and pushed the thing to the next grouping of dismantled tents.

"Come," I said to Alhasan after a moment. I mounted Macha again and held my hand out to Alhasan for him to grasp so that he could jump up behind me.

"I could not possibly, Masoud!" he said.

I could not tell if he was afraid or did not want to seem disrespectful by riding with me.

"We do not have time for this," I stated flatly. "The general wants your services as an interpreter for our new venture, so jump up here or have us both at the whip's end."

"Your general would not dare to treat you so!" he said, appalled.

"It's a jest, Alhasan! Now get your ass up here, that's an order!" I barked.

He did as I bade, taking my extended hand and leaping onto Macha's back with surprising agility. We trotted off to join the others.

~XIX~

The organized chaos of a moving army is tempered only by its slowness. On the other hand, perhaps it only seemed chaotic to the individual soldier making his way as a pinpoint in a sea of men. Sitting on horseback as I was, however, gave me a completely new perspective. I could see over the heads of the sea of men and thus the entire army arrayed before me—or behind me, depending on which way I looked. I was traveling in the middle of the marching crusader army. Dust choked our nostrils and stung the eyes. Darkness was falling, but we were determined to travel on into the night in order to make our destination. Alhasan still rode behind on me on Macha which garnered stares of disapproval from some of the men. A few of the stares turned to whisperings, a handful of which I happened to overhear during the course of our journey; idle rumors and gossip mainly. One had Alhasan and I as lovers, claiming that was where my true power came from; an unholy coupling, as they said it. Still another said that I was a spy for Salah al-Din and Alhasan was actually my contact posing as my servant. Ignorant fools. None of these men would dare say these things to my face, of course. No matter. They would all have the challenge of their lives before long, so let them have their entertainment even if it was at my expense.

"Agh!!" Alhasan suddenly exclaimed from behind me.

"What is it?" I asked, alarmed.

"A pox upon me, Masoud! I have forgotten to give you something," he said.

A moment later his hand reached around me and held a folded parchment in front of my face. "What is this?" I asked, taking the item from his hand.

"A message."

I recognized the seal on it as being from the Sultan. "From Salah al-Din?" I asked, suddenly feeling a sense of foreboding.

"Nay. From another in his midst, you see," he said with a curious blend of mirth and disapproval.

I broke the seal, unfolded the parchment and began to read the delicate lines of broken English. My sense of foreboding was quickly replaced by joy as I read.

Sir Masoud, I beg forgiveness at the boldness of my person in putting words forth to you, and for my poor use of your written English language. Writing to a man of your faith or any man is not something I have dared do in past. I beg forgiveness also for taking leave of your person so swiftly this past time of our meeting. Alhasan has known me many years, since I was but child, and has great affection and respect for my person. I had no cause to vanish in his presence. I thank you again for rescuing of my person from direness and for opportunity of meeting with you. I wish only that our meeting had been extended. Perhaps in future it will, though I know not how that be possible. I saw in your face a fondness and recognition of my soul. I too felt this for your person and know it is truth. I again beg forgiveness for my boldness, but could not let these words go unspoken to your person. If you choose, Alhasan will carry any reply to me. I bid you a fond farewell until we stand before one another once more.

Najeeba al-Din

My whole body trembled with delight. I read the words again. Afterward, a feeling I had only felt once before in my life suddenly washed over my entire being. Love. Oh, I had experienced many forms of love before, but only once before like this. I could have stepped off Macha and walked on the air. But, the thought interrupted from the so-called thinking part of my mind, you don't even know this woman! "Bullocks!" I heard myself say out loud. You have known this woman before and many a time, said the voice of my spirit, my soul. That was the truth of it! As she said herself, I indeed had a fondness and recognition of her soul! "Najeeba," I said softly.

"Speak not her name, Masoud!" Alhasan whispered from behind me. "Grave danger if she is found out. You should destroy her words now that you have seen them, for her sake and for yours, you see."

"You...care for her, yes?" I asked over my shoulder.

"She is as a sister to me. I wish her happiness," he replied.

"But you don't approve of her writing this to me," I said.

"As I said, it is dangerous," he replied. "But I would do anything she asked of me."

"Anything? Are you sure?"

No reply was forthcoming from my riding partner. We rode on in silence, the darkness of night folding in around us. No moonlight was there to guide us. The lunar disc had not yet risen. There was scant light for our march but we trudged on. Then we saw it; a line of light off in the distance. We were traversing the crest of a hillside when the line of light on the horizon came into view. "Jerusalem," someone whispered in awe.

"The Holy City," said another.

"God's City!" said still another.

A murmur of excitement flowed through the men. Ironically, though we had all been in this region for some time, most of us in the company had never laid eyes on the city herself. She was, after all, the whole reason we had come on the crusade in the first place. I felt caught up in the men's excitement. Briefly. Over these past months I had undergone a drastic change in my reason for being here, culminating in the events of the past few days and weeks. There were other lights as well, small groupings of lights dotted the landscape before us just in front of the line of light. We proceeded on, cautiously marching down the hill's embankment in the near darkness and onward toward the Holy City. The line of light we were seeing in the distance now rose before us, growing clearer and more distinct. It was a line of torches and firelight atop the city's walls and battlements, daring anyone to challenge her sanctity and protected perimeter. The small dotted groupings of light on the land were campfires. They were campfires from the crusader army that had been here for weeks already, no doubt. Darkness had completely descended when we reached the land not far from the wall of the City.

"Sir Masoud," said Sir James trotting up alongside of Macha, myself and Alhasan. I suddenly found it curious as to why he was calling me by my Muslim name and not my Christian one of Mason. "We're going to set a camp here and blend in with the army that's already here. I'm assigning you a century of men. Do not light anymore campfires. We don't want Salah al-Din to know how many more men are here," he finished.

"I, you're raising me in rank?" I asked.

"Aye," he replied. "Actually, Blackthorn suggested it, with my whole-hearted agreement, lad. Ye've proved your mettle," he said with a large grin on his face.

"What I've proved doesn't amount to the leadership of men," I said, a little too forcefully.

His grin turned to the smile of an understanding father as he nudged his mount even closer. "Be not afraid, Liam. You can do anything you choose. Anything that you put your mind to," Sir James said with all sincerity. "All of the One Mind, right? Whatever you put it to, It will respond in like form. Besides, I've more men than I have leaders for. Yours is the Crescent Century and will flock under the banner of the green Crescent moon three-hundred yards to the north of us," he said, pointing off to his right.

I sat in rather stunned silence for a moment.

"Well commander?" said Sir James by way of addressing me. I stared at him, a-thousand responses rolling through my head. "But, the men I am to command; they are to flock to a crescent banner—a crescent being a Muslim symbol

—and follow a commander that is now commonly known by the name of Masoud—also Muslim. Do you not see a conflict there?"

"No," Sir James stated flatly.

"I..."

"Just make it work, sir Masoud. I know you can and will." With that he yanked his mount's reins, turning the beast's neck around, and galloped away.

"Your commander has strange humor," Alhasan observed. "Or, perhaps he has a grand plan in his mind."

"Strange humor, is more the like," I replied.

"Still, you possess the Great Spear and the King's Sword! All will bow down to you," he said.

"I don't want anyone to bow down to me. But we shall see how this plays out." I trotted Macha gently in the direction that Sir James had indicated, scratching my growing beard in thought. Of course, as a Templar I no longer shaved, as per one of the rules. Some of these rules, however, I would not adhere to in private; not bathing and remaining dressed at all times, for instance. Absurd. We trotted for a few moments, avoiding others in the somewhat crowded immediate area. In the dim light of the few surrounding campfires I could see a white flag fluttering in the night breeze. It was now but a few yards away from us. In the center of this white flag was a dark green crescent shape.

"I see the flag there, Masoud," Alhasan said, echoing my thoughts.

"Yes, Alhasan. I see it too."

"Your men await!" Alhasan said with excitement.

My men, I thought. My stomach suddenly lurched. I did not want to lead anyone. And what if they don't wish to be lead by me? I looked at the spear in my right hand, standing upright, its heel in the stirrup of my right foot and my nervous fear began to flow from me. It was slowly replaced by an inner confidence. I am them, they are me. I lead myself by leading them. We are one body, one mind. One.

"Sir Masoud!" Alhasan said loudly in my ear, breaking my transcendent musings and forcing me to rein Macha to a halt before I ran over some of the very men I was to command. The white flag with the green crescent presently waved not six feet before my face. A group of drop-jawed men stared at me, apparently shocked that I almost walked my mount right over them.

"Are ye daft?!" exclaimed one of them, an older, grey-haired, filth encrusted soldier whose regular army tunic, though carrying the markings of a sergeant, was soiled nearly beyond recognition. "Ye nearly ran us down," he continued in a Gaelic accented English, denoting his origin in the peasant-filled hills of my homeland.

"Whhhat matterrrr, Taliesin," said another soldier in slurred English, thick also with a Franc accent and flailing an arm with dramatic flamboyance. He held a large flask in the hand of the flailing arm and was a much younger man than the first one who had spoken. He was also obviously drunk. "Whattt matter, for we all die on the morrow in any event!" he continued in a louder voice, drawing many of the other soldiers in the immediate area to us. "Bet...better to die here and now than bleeeeeed to death in this place on the morrow," he stopped in mid sentence staring straight at me, squinting his eyes in the darkness to get a better look. "Bleeding Christ. You be him," he said in astonishment.

The first man, the one called Taliesin, walked forward, stopping within arm's reach of the spear shaft. He reached out to touch it, but thought better of it and pulled his hand back. He then looked behind me at Alhasan then at the King's Sword on my back. "You're right, lad," he said addressing his younger counterpart but not taking his eyes off of me.

I looked deeper into those eyes and yet another of my soul's images burst forth into my mind; two Roman legionnaires suddenly stood before me in my mind's eye; one older, one younger. They were from my life as the Centurion over a thousand years ago and I knew in that moment that I was familiar with this Taliesin's spirit as being the older of the

Roman legionnaires. He had always been a loyal soul friend, as had the younger Roman soldier from that life, perhaps now in the body of the drunk young soldier before me. I smiled. "Taliesin, is it?"

"Aye, sir. That's what I be called," answered the man.

"You look in need of a bath and tunic change, Taliesin," I said.

"Ha! Aren't you Masoud, the Great Keeper of the Lance of Longinus and King Arthur's very sword!" exclaimed the younger man. "And that's your profound greeting to mon amie, Taliesin?!"

Taliesin turned suddenly and slapped his younger counterpart hard with the back of his hand, knocking the latter to the ground. "Had enough 'o you, I have! Shut yer yap, ya whiny shit or I'll dig yer grave here and now and fill it with ye! Show respect to your betters or by the Christ I'll do it!"

Bursts of laughter erupted from the men nearby. "Aye, and I'll help 'im!" said someone.

"I'm with you, Taliesin!" said another, eliciting even more laughter.

Taliesin turned back to me. "I apologize for his arrogance, my lord. He's been a pain in our arses for weeks, he 'as, whinin' and carryin' on about the end of our lives."

I did not address him right away but instead, looked to all the men who had gathered near the flag; nearly one-hundred by my reckoning. A century of men, is what Commander James had said was to be mine. I turned my head slightly and addressed Alhasan over my shoulder. "Slide off of Macha," I ordered quietly. He complied and was on the ground in an instant, standing near Taliesin. I then turned my attention to the gathered men, looking at many of them in turn as I spoke. "My name is Sir Liam Arthur Mason. And yes, I am also known by the Muslim name of Masoud. Whichever you choose to call me is your concern. I have come to be equally proud of both." I looked briefly at Alhasan as I said this last part, and he smiled with both surprise and pleasure. Turning my gaze back to the men, I continued. "I am indeed the guardian of the

Great Spear of Longinus and the King's Sword. I am here as your commander by order of General and Templar Horatio Blackthorn and Commander Sir Jonathan James. We..." I froze in mid sentence. Some of the men gathered were men from my own company mixing in with the men like Taliesin who had been on this desert field waiting for weeks if not months. My eyes landed on one of them in particular from my company; Henry, looking weary but alive and awake. Relief washed over me at the sight of him. He was not only alive but with me. I could not have asked for anything more. "We will blend in together here and await orders," I continued after recovering from the surprise of seeing my friend. "The morning will be telling, but it will not be the doom of our forces as some have called for," I said, indicating the slapped soldier who was only now regaining his feet. "That I can assure you!" I said, thrusting the spear's blade tip into the air in a show of bravado.

"We are with you!" someone said.

"Aye!" said another. All of the men were now staring at the spear and murmuring softly in agreement and good cheer.

I brought the spear back to rest in the stirrup. The gesture had not been meant to imply I would use the now presumed magic weapon as the instrument of our salvation. But, that is clearly how the men perceived it. No matter. If it garnered their acceptance of me as their commander for now then so be it.

I swung my left leg over the top of Macha's neck in front of me, lifted the spear at the same time from the stirrup and dropped to the ground on Macha's right side, landing in front of Taliesin. Though I dismounted her on the wrong side, to her credit, Macha did not flinch. I smile at her and patted her neck, and then turned my attention to Taliesin. Our eyes met on level ground, our height being the same. "Thank you Taliesin for your aid in quelling an awkward situation," I said referring to the young drunk Franc crusader. "The men seem to look to you. I have need of you and them in the hours and days ahead. May I rely on you and your influence with them?"

"Your character comes before ye. They already know of you and respect you,"

"They may know of me and the things I have done but that's not the same as knowing the man," I said. I looked at the Crescent on the flag. "And, gathering under this symbol—that may garner resentment."

"Nay. I see it as mocking the heathens, sire! That symbol is a part of our Old Ways back home, if ye be knowin' what I mean, which is a great bit older than these upstarts' religion," Taliesin said with a wry grin.

"Master Taliesin," I said with amusement, "you sound like a Druid of the Ancient Ways."

"Aye. Been accused of worse, I 'ave," he replied.

The young man Taliesin had slapped now appeared standing behind him. It took a moment of looking at the lad's face in the semi-darkness, but his face took on a familiarity that I finally placed. "You!" I said, realization dawning on my mind. "You were in the field tent, the Muslim hospital tent with me and Commander James!"

"Oui, I was," he said.

"You were mad with fever, I believe, ranting about the devil coming for you," I said.

"I was mad with the opiate crave, being brought off of it, is what I mean," he replied.

My thoughts began reeling. Perhaps he could help Henry off of the smoke. The lad took another swill from his flask. Then again, this young Franc crusader appears to have replaced one craving for another. Yet, I could not accept his behavior now. I needed every man to have his wits about him. "I'll want you sobered by morning," I said.

Taliesin turned to the lad. "Ye've a count 'o ten with that thing," he said, indicating the flask. "If I see it after that, I break it."

The Franc youth turned to walk away. Taliesin grabbed him by the scruff of his neck. "Ye've not been given leave by your commanding officer, crusader François Drusee," he said.

The lad looked directly at me with defiant, bloodshot eyes. I waited for an instant for him to ask for leave. He did not.

But this was a tiny battle of wills not worth inflaming. "You may go, Francois," I said.

Taliesin released the lad who then scurried off in obvious embarrassment. After a moment, Taliesin looked to my Arab friend as if noticing him for the first time.

"This is Alhasan," I said. "He is my servant and assistant. He is to be completely trusted, do you understand, Taliesin?"

"Yes, sir. If ye be a trustin' 'im then that'd be good enough for me and the men."

"Good," I replied, relieved. Perhaps this command would not be as difficult as I'd feared. I looked at the night sky, now completely dark. "Beg yer pardon, sire, but don't ye Templars hold with Vespers at darkfall?"

"Most still do. But times have changed and I suppose I am not the typical Templar Knight Taliesin," I answered truthfully. "My prayers seem to come at various times, especially when I sleep, and are more trance-like meditations where I see...visions," I explained, not quite sure why I was telling this man these things. But then again, if the intuitive revelation from my soul regarding this Taliesin was correct, then I had trusted this man's spirit for over a millennium. No surprise then that I would share with him the fact that I had visions nearly daily of late.

"And these...visions; be they of this time or a past? Perhaps of Roman times?" he asked tentatively, expressing an obvious awareness of his own soul's journey through time.

"You, my dear Taliesin, are more than an ancient Druid of our Old Ways. You are a Seer, are you not?" I asked dryly.

"Humph," he voiced with disgust. He then leaned in closer to me and said in a whisper, "I been accused of such by the Church's men at the local parish. They think all us of the Hills be witches and wizards, warlocks and devils, beholdin' only to the Old Ways. I be Christian but I practice the Old Ways too. The Christ," he said, unconsciously crossing himself in the Church's prescribed manner, "performed miracles. But I say them that's witnessed it got it wrong. It weren't nothin' but the natural powers of Dana bein' wielded anew in front of ignorant folk. Our Druids and wizards been doing the same thing for thousands of years, don't ye know."

"You speak as a heretic, Taliesin," I said.

He looked at me oddly for a moment, clearly wondering if he had misjudged me.

I smiled. "Fear not. I understand what you say. And, yes; some of my visions had been of a Roman life, with you in it."

"Aye. I knew it. Good to know ye again, sir," he said.

"And you, Taliesin. But tell me; if you practice the Old Way ways of the Druids, how can you be a Christian at the same time?"

"The Christ's teachin's are for everyone, ain't they?" he replied as if I were daft. "And, as I see it, Jesus 'imself was the greatest of Druids; performin' the likes of raising the dead and what have ye. Much like ye, now. Ain't no miracle ye bringin' yer close friend back from the Otherside." Even in the darkness he must have seen the surprised look on my face. "Aye, we all heard of that one. My point bein' that you, that spear and that sword just be pullin' on the same power that the Christ used."

"But, it's said that Jesus is, the only begotten son of the Father, implying that the Father's power only comes through Him," I countered, more as point of argument than anything else, for truth was that I agreed with what he was saying.

"Nay, sir. 'Tis originally this: Jesus is a begotten son of the only Father, or of the One, we might say in the Old Tongue!" exclaimed Taliesin. "Been told so by a village elder and that's how I see it. He also be one of the parish Fathers, this Elder. Studied here in the Holy land, he did, when a lad. That's the proper way of readin' the Holy words, he says. It also means that all of us can do what the Christ did. We're all Druids."

I was not sure whether Taliesin was a foolish man or a man of superior faculty. But was there really a difference? I have found that one man's fool is often another man's sage. I looked at Alhasan who was simply grinning ear to ear in apparent agreement with Taliesin's point of view.

"Well, Taliesin, I should like to continue this discussion with you. But for now, let's bed these men down for the night," I said.

"Aye, sir," he replied. He then turned and began barking soft orders for the men to settle in for the night.

"He is an old soul, you see," said Alhasan said, referring to Taliesin.

"Aye. He is that," I replied.

~XX~

Darkness swirled about me. A mist enshrouded my surroundings. Voices. Voices in argument came to my ears. They sounded far off, as if in a distant land. I could discern that they were male, but could not decipher what it was they argued about. Willing myself closer to them, I found myself being catapulted through the mists at an alarming rate of speed; as if I were being shot from a giant crossbow.

The mists cleared. I looked out through the eyes of Myrriddin once again. Men surrounded me and shouted at one another and me in turn. We were in the castle room that had the huge, oblong table. The men were Arturius' men, regaled now in their ornate armor of King Arthur's Knights Of The Round Table lore, complete with the Pendragon emblem, Arturius' family crest, emblazoned on the front, and a Christian Red Crucifix on the back. Lancelott was chief among the ones arguing. His face contorted with rage, and his thick Franc accent made him difficult to understand. He seemed to be directing his anger at another knight in particular. "Mon Dieu, Sir Perceval! You dare question your king? You are a coward, I say! And unchristian!"

This garnered another round of even louder protest from the rest. Arturius stood next to Lancelott, silent, head hung as if in shame.

"You condemn me as unchristian when you fornicate with your king's wife?!" countered Perceval, a young, exceedingly handsome and stoic knight. His mane of dark hair and obvious muscular frame gave him the air of one from Greek legend.

The entire room fell silent at Perceval's outburst. Arturius bristled at the accusation from Sir Perceval and stepped toward the tall knight. "You will hold thy tongue, good knight."

Perceval was silent for a moment, as was Arturius again. "'Tis true then, my king?" he finally ventured, obviously disappointed that his king was not denying it.

"I will put this to rest now," Arturius began with an edge in tone that demanded attention, respect and a finality on the subject. "God has chosen that my seed be devoid of life," he began, addressing the men. "My First Knight came to my wife's chamber at my behest to aid his king in giving this realm an heir," he said, glancing at me while saying this last part, thus clearly conveying that the idea was not solely his after all.

"'Tis sacrilege!" someone said.

"Silence!" my Myrriddin self bellowed. The man who spoke the last words withered under my gaze. "What your king has done was done to aid the kingdom and should be considered an act of ultimate honor and sacrifice."

"No, Myrriddin. I have sinned grievously against God and man," confessed Arturius, hanging his head once again in shame.

"No, you have not," I said angrily. "The only sin you have committed is listening to the pompous asses of the Church, who shower you with praise and then threaten your immortal soul if you do not comply with their arbitrary rules and whims. Once was the time when you heeded them not. Once was the time when you saw fit to adhere to our Old Ways. Once was the time when you would have seen that what you requested of your First Knight was for the betterment of an entire race and perfectly righteous for the assurance of the longevity of us all, not to say that it followed the natural and perfect law of Dana and the Universe. But now you have been poisoned by these alleged men of God, these pretentious Holy Men. The shit that comes out of my ass is holier than these men."

Arturius suddenly looked up at me. "Myrriddin, do not speak so. You damn yourself by your words," he said. "It is not too late for your soul's salvation."

"Do you not see, Arturius! My soul, your soul is in no need of being saved, except from these so-called men of God! The Christ's very nature is within your very being because it IS your very being!" I was yelling.

"We are all born tainted by original sin, Myrriddin," continued Arturius as if speaking to an ignorant child. "The Book says so."

"A misreading of a book that was written by other pompous men of God!" I said, nearly screaming in frustration.

"Arturius, my king, I believe your wizard is going mad," offered Perceval, who looked at me with a mixture of extreme caution and fear; as if I were suddenly a dangerous rodent that needed to be killed.

I drew a deep breath to relax my tension. "Typical. 'Tis not I who is mad. Where madness reigns, sanity is deemed madness," I countered calmly. "I speak naught but the Truth. You would do well to remember that, my good knight."

The men murmured amongst themselves for a moment.

"The more pressing issue at hand is the road to the Holy Land. We embark on the sunrise again to make the way safe and to retrieve our rightful artifacts," said Arturius, clearly, desperately attempting to change the subject of his condoning, even sponsoring, his wife's infidelity.

"Aye," said someone.

"Yes," said another. Others nodded their head in agreement. Most of the men seemed willing to let the king's transgression fall by the wayside for the time being.

But Perceval was not so easily quelled. "This is not finished, my king. I will not be part of this venture if there be one rule for the common man and another for the king. The highest among us must be held equally accountable for his folly and sins," he proclaimed self-righteously. "And you, wizard," he said turning his wrath upon me, "you are an abomination to the Christ and all he stands for. I say your days at court are few in number."

"You overstep yourself, Perceval!" said Arturius, rising and stepping toward the knight, drawing the magnificent

King's Sword, the very one I presently possessed in my life as Masoud. The blade rang a high, pure note as it was drawn from its leather and iron scabbard. To the fearful protests of the men, the king leveled the point directly at Perceval's chest, which was but a mere four inches from the sword's sharp point. Perceval, a hardened, battle tested warrior, nonetheless stepped back in fear and shock at the audacity of his king. "Draw one more breath against Myrriddin and it will be your last," Arturius stated through clenched teeth.

Sir Perceval seemed to waiver for a moment, unsure of what to do. Finally, he gathered his pride, turned and stormed from the room. Several of the other knights followed in his wake.

The mists enshrouded me again and hid the room from my view. The remaining men's voices continued in debate, but became distant once more.

☘ ☘ ☘

The pallet was comfortable as I lay on my back. A thick layer of soft rushes were beneath me upon the top of the pallet, creating a softness that rivaled the supple skin of Najeeba. Her naked form lay atop of mine and I kissed her neck tenderly, allowing my tongue to linger there. Her skin had the sweet taste of the gods' nectar in the morning. Our body's fit flawlessly together, our parts made for each other. To slide into her was to slide into the perfection of being. Our nude bodies entwined now, her dark breasts squished against my chest as our gentle thrusts of passion, lust and love echoed the formation of the universe itself. Looking at her face I saw the continuation of our souls' respective journeys. But she was Najeeba in this life, my Najeeba, at least for this moment of ecstasy. Our passion, our thrusts became quicker, more urgent, until our bodies reached the threshold of their ultimate release. The seed of my body welled up from deep within my loins and I exploded into her with the force of creation itself, she at the same moment bursting as the receptive form of the

Great Mother Earth. Panting with exhaustion, our bodies collapsed together, as we breathlessly professed our feelings.

"I love you, Najeeba," I said.

"And I you, Masoud. I have loved you forever," she replied. I smiled and closed my eyes to rest, satiated on every level of my person.

After a moment, I felt a nibbling on my ear. "Najeeba," I whispered. I opened my eyes in the light of a predawn and turned my eyes toward the source of the nibbling. A scorpion crawled near my face, near where my ear had been but a second before, its wicked claws open and no doubt feeling for its breaking-of-fast on my ear but a moment before. It was not a soft pallet filled to overflowing with plush rushes on which I lay, but a cloth on the cold desert floor. Disappointment flooded my mind. It was then I noticed the dampness of my trousers near my groin. A nocturnal release spoke to the seeming reality of my time with Najeeba on the other side of night's veil. Dreams are but the realm of the soul, I thought. I wondered if she had dreamt of me on the previous night too. Our souls were obviously connected. I was sure she had held me in her dreams last night as I had held her. If we could not be together in the outer realm, then we would be together on the inner realm. The mind and body knows no difference.

My mind then drifted to the meaning of the vision of Myrriddin and Arturius or Arthur. There was a link between Arthur's knights and The Knights Templar, or so my vision had implied. The Templar Order was initially created to protect pilgrims on their trek to the Holy Land. At least, that was what the commoner thought. It seems as though Arthur's knights had taken on that duty first. But, why was I reliving some of my soul's past? Perhaps there was information I needed to learn again from that time for use in the present, but it eluded my mind for the moment. No matter. I would trust that all would be revealed at the proper time.

"Sir," Taliesin whispered nearby. I looked to my left and saw the man squatting next to me, his filthy tunic now brushed as clean as he could get it. He obviously did not have another. "The men begin to stir. What orders have ye?"

Orders? I thought. I had no specific orders, but could not let the men know that. I looked over Taliesin's shoulder and saw the sun cresting the hills to the east which rose above and behind the city from our position. The light began to bathe Jerusalem and gently cascade down onto the desert floor where we were. From what I could tell, we were quartered outside the northwestern wall of the city. A hill loomed before my eyes. It lay between our present position and the outside of the city's northwestern wall, which itself was elevated to a slight degree above the desert floor. Both of these features had been imperceptible in the darkness of the night before. The hill itself had apparently been walled in at some point, judging by the multitude of broken stone blocks around its base. But no more. I looked closer at the hill, which seemed to rise only some fifteen feet off the desert floor. Though I had never been to this spot, something about this hill was beyond familiar. My heart began to pound inexplicably, my palms to sweat. What was happening? I wondered. Then I understood what it was. "This is where He was crucified," I heard myself say out loud.

"Sorry, sir?" asked Taliesin, obviously confused by my statement.

"The hill there; it's Golgotha, the Hill of Skulls. It's where the Christ was crucified," I said in wonder.

Taliesin rose to his feet and looked behind himself at the hill, then back to me. I rose to my feet, bed cloth wrapped around my waist, lest the night's emission be seen by any, and stood next to the sergeant.

"I don't know 'bout such things, sir, nor much care," Taliesin stated flatly. "Mean no offence, mind ye. Ye bein' a Templar and all, I suppose it means something to you. But I'm sick of this place and all its religious shite from both sides. Just wanna get home, sir."

"I understand completely and no offence taken. I admire your honesty and agree with you on all counts," I replied. I said nothing for a moment, assessing what exactly it was that I was feeling about the hill. Realization donned slowly upon my mind. "My interest in this hill is deeper than I can explain, Sergeant."

He smiled knowingly. "Aye. Been here previous 'ave ye?"

"No, I haven't," I replied. Just..."

"Just not in this body, eh, sir?"

I smiled at the man's accurate assumption. "Tell the men quietly to awaken, break their fast, and gather here before the hour is out. Orders are forthcoming," I said, making it up as I went along.

"Aye, sir," he said, spinning on his heels and walking quietly away to carry out his orders. I quickly changed my under tunic and breeches, preparing to meet the day and my past.

~XXI~

A light fog enshrouded the crest of the Hill of Skulls. I trudged up to where the top of it met the sky. Was this really the right place, the place the Christ was crucified all these centuries past? It was. I could feel it as if I had been there, for I had been there. As far as hills are, this place, Golgotha, was quite unimpressive. Puny in height by the standards of other hills— perhaps fifty feet at its crest—and not all that large in circumference, its one side butting up against the northwestern wall of the city. Still, it did not matter how large this place was. What mattered were the events that happened there. And, in my soul I knew those events all too well. The spear in my hand vibrated as if to confirm my insight. It too had been here with me as Longinus nearly twelve centuries before. My heart still pounding, I closed my eyes, fully expecting to see in my mind's eye the events of that day, a day that changed not only the path of a lowly centurion of Rome, but one that changed the course of the world as well. Yet, nothing came; no vision of Christ on his cross, no reliving of my stabbing his chest with the spear I now held. The feeling of the experience lingered in my spirit and mind, but I would not see the event played out again. Why? I wondered, somewhat disappointed. But then again, what did I expect to achieve by reliving the event, some sort of profound revelation or experience, maybe even redemption?

"Strange, is it not?" said the voice behind me.

I turned to see the figure of a man standing not more than six feet from where I stood. We were alone at the top of this Hill of Skulls. He stood with his back to the east, the rising sun, just above and behind him, silhouetting his body, his face, making it impossible to see his features, though I could discern that he was dressed as an Arab in a dark cloak and headdress.

701

"Who are you?" I asked, annoyed at having my solitude invaded.

"Forgive me," he said, stepping to one side, allowing the light of the sun to play on his face. His gold eyes seemed to light up at the touch of the morning's rays.

"You!" I exclaimed. "You have been...I don't know, watching me?"

"In a manner of speaking, my son," he said, cryptically. "There are many who would be grateful for what I do."

"That presumes they know what you do. I do not," I replied.

Silently, he gazed skyward for a moment, apparently lost in his own thoughts. "It is strange, the perception of passing time. When one truly understands it, he comes to realize that there is really no passing of anything. It all exists here and now," he began, his handsome face contemplative. "Some of us remain here to aid others we have known for...well what you would call a very long time. Is that not so, Masoud? Or would you prefer to be called Longinus or Myrriddin?"

My head began to spin and I closed my eyes. Images flashed before my mind's eye. Not images and scenes of the crucifixion of so long ago in this place, but images of a different place and time; images, visions of Myrriddin flooded my mind in rapid succession. I was not in his body in these as I had been in other visions, but instead, I was looking from the outside in as an observer. Most of these images contained other people, but one person in particular; a Christian Priest who did not adhere to all the ways of his Christian brethren, but rather accepted the ways of the Old Religions as all being part of and expressions of the One God. The images stopped and before my mind's eye was the face of this priest from the past. I knew him well. Or had.

"Master Masoud!" yelled Alhasan.

"Sir!" yelled another.

The image of the priest and past snapped into oblivion. My eyes shot open and before me stood not the gold-eyed man, but Alhasan, the twin lads Canter and Luscious. They stood now where the Gold-Eyed one had stood moments before. My eyes darted all around the hill. There was no sign of the gold-eyed, Ancient Priest. None.

"Whom do you seek, sire?" Canter asked.

"Am I mad?" I asked rhetorically to myself.

Canter and Luscious exchanged a look of concern.

"Fear not, my boys. Your commander is quite well," Alhasan said confidently. "He now experiences things from the Otherside of the Veil; things that most of us cannot fathom, things that would drive most men mad, but not your commander, you see!"

The boys stared at me. "What are you all doing here?" I asked, gathering my wits.

"We came for you, sir," replied Alhasan, "before the others do. Commander James has come for you at the camp. The boys here have been given to you as servants."

"We asked for the duty sir," said Canter eagerly.

"Yes, yes, as soon as we heard of your promotion. Wanted to be a part of your crew," declared Luscious on the heels of his brother's words.

"'We must!' we said! 'He'll have us, he will!'" said Canter.

"Yes, yes! You will, sire, will you not? Please, sire?" asked Canter.

"Yes, please?!" echoed Luscious.

I laughed in spite of myself. These two were entertaining if nothing else. "Aye, lads. I'll have ye as my help as long as you stop chattering when I ask it!"

"Done!"

"Done!"

"Let's be off then." I said.

They turned and headed back down the hill toward the camp. I lingered just long enough to view the spot once again where the crucifixion had taken place. I then looked to where the gold eyed man had stood moments before. I was not mad. I knew that. And perhaps Alhasan had hit the mark; I was now in harmony with something much greater than myself, something that traversed time and caused me now to live from the place of my spirit more than I realized. More than I even cared to admit to myself. I headed back down the hill.

꜔ ꜔ ꜔

The commotion in the camp was frantic, yet quiet. The men gathered their meager belongings together with silent urgency. Each man knew that he must work in silence so as not to give too much away to the enemy regarding our numbers and intention, the latter still being somewhat of a mystery to more than one of us. Each man's face showed a tenseness that belied an uncertainty of the day's coming events. I still knew not what I would tell these men, my men, as to what the day's orders would be. But, fortunately, it became quite apparent that I would not have to. Commander Sir James and General Blackthorn, sitting high on their large mounts, were now in the middle of my men. The general and commander appeared to be waiting for someone, as they simply sat there, observing but not interacting with the men. It suddenly dawned on me that it was I for whom they waited.

"General. Commander," I said to one then the other in turn by way of greeting, shouldering my way through the busy men. Alhasan and the two lads were nearby, gathering my own belongings and placing them on Macha.

"Liam," began Sir James. "We assault the north-western wall within the hour. You will lead your men to the fissures in the cornerstones there," he said, pointing back up the hill to the somewhat crumbling corner of the distant wall. My heart jolted and a feeling that approached the sensation of what I took to be blasphemy—having never experienced a sense of blasphemy before, it was the only thing I could equate it to in the moment. The thought of marching my men up this sacred hill and over the actual site where He was killed, where my former self had stabbed Him, was near too much to bear. But I ignored the feeling, knowing full well the more pressing issue would be the sure loss of many numbers of my century.

"But...commander!" I stammered.

"I know. It will be difficult. Your men will take the brunt of an aerial assault from the tops of the walls, no doubt," he replied, "but it is necessary. And you are to remain at the back on your mount. Let the enemy see your weapons; the Sacred Spear and the King's Sword! Let it strike fear to their very core!"

"We cannot trudge over this holy ground! Do you not know where you are?!" said the none-too-quiet voice with a slight Franc accent from behind me. It was the companion of Taliesin from the previous evening, Francois Drusee, apparently sobered but heated, echoing my initial thoughts.

"Shut yer yap, Francois!" said Taliesin in more than a whispered hush, both men now appearing at my side.

"It is for this exact reason that we want you, Masoud," stated General Blackthorn, "to do this. The spear and its eternal owner have returned to claim the city, the hill, all of it! Roo-hah!"

I was dumbfounded on more than one level. Outwardly, it was a twisted, but good strategy; having me and the spear surge up the hill. But his reference to me being the eternal owner of it; was he seriously invoking my spirit as Longinus the Centurion? Or, was he being cruelly sardonic? I could not tell. His face was impassive. The scent of lilac wafted to my nostrils. It was mixed with the foul stench of body odor. It was obvious from whom both smells were emanating and in my mind accentuated the notion that Blackthorn was indeed being maliciously sarcastic. It was then too that I saw the glint in his eye; something I had not seen before, something he apparently kept well hidden from sight: a wickedness that lurked beneath the surface and seemed poised to burst forth at what I took to be the thought of the blood and death that was about to come. Bloodlust in the heat of skirmish was not a new concept to me. In battle, I had seen the glee play upon the faces of those in its grip as they slaughtered their fellow man in a moment of animalistic rage and frenzied, bloody destruction. I had heard that for some so-called seasoned warriors the mere smell of blood was enough to send them over the edge and into the gruesome bosom of the frenzy even years after their days of battle had ended. But what I saw now in the general's eye gave me more pause than witnessing a soldier momentarily caught up in the passion of blood-letting on a battlefield. What I saw in Blackthorn's eye was the darkness of an anticipatory joy in it, the near sexual gratification of potentially seeing another's grisly, bloody death. Yes, I received all that in the glint of the eye and knew it to be true. General Blackthorn, with his lilac smell poorly masking his real stench, suddenly took on a completely new persona to me.

"My good Masoud," he said to me smiling slightly, "are you in agreement with your man here?"

My face was obviously telling him of my dissent, but he was not clear on its meaning. My dissent was suddenly about his apparent dark character trait. I had never actually been with the general before or during a battle. My immediate commander, Sir James, could not have been more different in this context: calm, decisive, efficient in duty and the ways of battle and war. A born leader. Blackthorn, however, now seemed more to me the arrogant, aristocrat who simply had the title of general laid at his feet because of his station in life.

It matters not, Liam, Masoud, said the voice in my mind. None have another's soul and path. Each chooses his own.

I was confused by the voice's assertion. Was it talking about Blackthorn and his apparent penchant for a wickedness that I simply did not comprehend?

There is no wickedness in the eyes of the One. Law only and how it is applied. You have forgotten, remember...remember the Law of the One and that it is up to each as individual expressions as to how it is used, the voice said.

"The victims of wickedness may feel differently," I said.

There are no victims. Only participants.

"What are you mumbling there, Sir Masoud?!" demanded the general.

"Nothing, general," I replied.

"You will carry out your orders post-haste. Gather your men, inform them and execute your duty." He spun his mount and trotted away, nearly knocking over some of my soldiers as he left.

Anger splashed across Sir James' face as he watched the general leave us. My commander then dismounted and came up to me, looking back at the general then to me. "He gets this way before a battle," he said. "Like a different person. Dangerous to cross him when he's like this, Liam."

"Understood," I said.

~XXII~

An equine snort from behind me drew my attention around and away from Sir James. Macha stood behind me with Luscious holding her bridal and Alhasan standing on her other side. A firm hand clasped my shoulder and I turned my attention back to Sir James.

"Do as the general bade, Liam, but stay farther back," began my commander, "even farther back than Blackthorn says, so as not to be in harm's way of any arrows, yet still within the enemy's sight from the wall. They may see you and know who you are as well."

I bristled again on the inside at the thought of what that meant for the men now under my command. "And let my men perform the fatal charge on their own, while I rest comfortably out of range?! You would not do that and nor will I!" I replied, anger at the stupidity and pointlessness of this whole conflict rising within my mind once again.

"Liam. Masoud, take care. You border on insubordination," Sir James said with a wry smile of pride. I took that smile to mean he was hoping for that reply, but had to officially reiterate the general's commands. He mounted his horse and rode off in General Blackthorn's wake.

I spun on my heels and mounted Macha. I then turned her and trotted a few yards away, stopping in the middle of a large group of men gathering their meager belongings and weapons. "Those of the Green Crescent Banner gather to me now!" I called in a loud voice, no longer caring to hide us or our intent from the enemy. The men gathered quickly, Taliesin and Francois at their lead. Every one of the men had trepidation etched upon his face to one degree or another, caused by the anticipation of the impending orders, no doubt. They all stared at me now, waiting. I hesitated in conveying the orders. Guilt seeped into my being over the fact that I was about to send most of these men to their death. As if to seek help—or some kind of absolution—I looked at the spear in my hand. I then brought my attention to the weight of the King's Sword, still sheathed on my back, and then back again to the spear.

The help—or absolution; I knew not which to call it—came in the form of an epiphany, a sudden comprehension of a profound truth. The comprehension washed over me like a cascading waterfall. It was not something I had never heard before, but this was the time I understood it, felt it to my very soul's awareness. There is nowhere that He is not—no place not contained in Him: God, The One, Allah, He is the same by whatever name one chooses to use. Further comprehension flooded my soul. All are <u>always</u> in and of The One and thus there is and can be no death, only Life; eternal existence in a myriad of forms and levels of being!

"Masoud, sir?" said Taliesin, obviously concerned at my hesitation.

"He visions, you see," replied Alhasan now standing next to Macha.

"Ney. Not a vision, Alhasan," I said. "'Tis a voice I hear that speaks the truth of Truths to my mind." I then looked at the men, the soldiers before me. "Men!" I said in a loud voice for all to hear. "We make history this day! Here, on the very hill where the Lord was crucified," I continued, watching the men, some of whose faces showed astonishment at my confirmation of the significance, the sacredness of this particular hill, "yes, where He died to this world but did not perish; where He stepped willingly into His destiny with honor, demonstrating to us all on the third day that there is no thing as death, only life everlasting! We storm the wall at the top of this sacred hill to take back what is rightfully ours..."

"And kill the Muslim infidels!" someone shouted, garnering to my surprise—and pleasure—only a few, half-hearted cheers of approval from the men.

"They are not infidels!" I countered. "Invaders, perhaps, but not infidels. We all, Christian, Jew, Muslim, worship the One

God by whatever name," I said, voice raised with authority, Macha dancing gently beneath me. "We take back the city that had been ours for a-thousand years and the Jews' for longer than time itself. We take it back now for our own, yes, but to also share it; that all may worship here as they wish and be part of Her sacredness." Yes, Salah al-Din said as much; that in his great mercifulness it is what he would do when he drove us away once and for all; that those who would stay may worship as they see fit. He was right. It was the way it must be. I felt sure the Sultan would not mind that I borrowed his merciful notion. Though I doubt my commanders would feel the same way. But none were within earshot of hearing me just then. Some of the men reacted with murmurs of confusion.

"Yes!" exclaimed Taliesin to the men, the crusaders and soldiers. "Our commander speaks the truth! We are merciful and tolerant, for all be one in the eyes of God!"

I cocked an eyebrow in surprise at my new friend. His use of the word we implied all of us present to be Christians which included himself. His statement seemed contrary to the attitude toward any of the Christian faith he had voiced on the previous night. But then, what I had just spoken of was not regarding any single human contrived religion, something Taliesin obviously understood.

"We are with you, Sir Masoud! Are we not, lads?!" Taliesin yelled to the men in a tone that dared any of them to defy him or me. It also revealed, at least to me, that whatever he was saying in the moment was being said to solidify the men's support.

"Aye," said some of the men, less than convincingly.

Taliesin jumped upon a nearby, small boulder, elevating himself some three feet off of the ground. He was now in clear sight of all of the men. "I say again," he began with intense fervor, "we are with you, Sir Masoud, are we not, Lads?!"

"Aye!!" rose the cry this time to an earsplitting battle-cry. "Aye!!"

"Lead us, Sir Masoud!" cried one crusader.

"Send the blessed Spear of Longinus before us! May its Christ powers protect us!" yelled another.

"And the King's Sword too!" said still another.

I let their excitement swell, their yells churning into the bloodlust of the righteous. When I judged the yells to be at its peak I gave the order. "Turn about and form ranks!" I commanded sternly. So new to my leadership role was I that I had a momentary doubt as to whether or not that was the right command. Yet, I had been a crusader long enough to know that the command was not that far off the mark. The men's response, however, alleviated any fear on my part. Almost as one they turned to face the Hill of Skulls, and the walls of Jerusalem beyond. They crisply formed up ten rows of ten, weapons—spears and swords mainly, some with bow and arrows—at the ready. It was then I noticed thousands of the other crusaders and soldiers across the increasingly sunlit field beginning to fall into formations of their own as if following our lead. "Forward!" I called to my century of men.

"Roo-hah! Roo-hah! Roo-hah!" Taliesin began chanting in a loud cadence, others picking up his call and cadence as we marched forward and up the hill.

I trotted Macha around the formation to take the lead in our march. Regardless of what Sir Blackthorn had said, I would not stop at a safe distance in leading my men to the wall. I will trust in my protection, I thought, grasping the spear tighter. A warmth suddenly seeped into the palm of my hand. It felt as if it were saying, Indeed, do not fear. A voice then spoke in my mind, the same voice as a moment ago. Fear not, it began in an echo of the message contained in the spear's warmth, trust in Truth. Trust in the eternalness of yourself! A shudder of new understanding went through my being. I felt my spirit relax and give in to these words, as well as to the words I had spoken only moments before.

The cheers and vocal cadence of the men continued to grow in intensity. I looked back at the men I was leading, into their faces. I now saw no trepidation, no fear there. Only the lines of hard determination were etched upon the features;

determination to accomplish the mission of scaling these walls. It was then that I remembered something. I had forgotten to give a crucial order; the order calling for the assault ladders and bowmen. Obviously, we would need the ladders for the walls and bowmen to lay a cover barrage! Fool! I berated myself. Panic ran through my veins at the inept, incompleteness of my orders. But then I caught sight of Taliesin. He was trotting in front of twenty to twenty-five men, who were carrying the assault ladders, approximately twelve of them, two to three men to a ladder! I had not noticed the men missing from the formation, but apparently Taliesin had broken them away shortly after we began the march up the hill in order to carry the ladders. The men were now making their way up alongside of the main formation, looking to take the front where I was now. "Blessings upon you, Taliesin," I whispered to myself. "You know how to cover your commander's ass." I tugged on Macha's reins, turning her to meet the ladder-men and stop all my men at the hill's crest, which we were upon. "Halt!" I shouted, raising my free hand. Almost as one the men, the formation stopped. Though we were at the crest of the hill, the wall of Jerusalem was still a-hundred yards before us. "Those of you with bow, to me! Form a line here before me, shoulder to shoulder, facing the wall!" I ordered. The bowmen in my troop were not necessarily their own distinctive unit. Each of them was dressed in similar tunics and breeches and breastplates of leather as any of the other men in this group of soldiers. They also usually fought sword in hand alongside any of their comrades. Yet, as I learned in that moment, they could indeed become an elite unit unto themselves when called upon. Surprisingly, nearly a third of the men stepped forward in answer to my call, bows in hand, filled quivers on the back. I had not realized my century contained so many so many bowmen. They did as I bade, appearing before me in a crisp line of shoulder to shoulder men. I trotted Macha sideways, back and forth, inspecting the line. "As soon as the rest of us draw fire, you will shoot to cover our assault," I commanded. I had the feeling that I should say something more, but could not pinpoint what that something should be.

"May I, sir?" offered Taliesin who was now standing beside me and Macha.

I inclined my head in acquiescence, unsure of what he was going to say but intuitively trusting it to be the addendum needed to what I had just stated.

"Ready position!" Taliesin yelled to the bowmen in a tone that clearly conveyed his familiarity with this particular leadership role. All at once and in unison, the bowmen dropped to one knee, pulled an arrow from the quiver on their back and notched it to the bowstring. They then rested the armed but relaxed bow across the upright knee and awaited further instructions.

"Superb," I said in masked awe.

"Impressive!" exclaimed Alhasan, who suddenly appeared next to me panting breathlessly. He had no doubt endeavored to keep up with Macha and I as we ascended the hill.

"Impressive, indeed," I reiterated. "Thank you, Taliesin."

"You are most welcome, sir," he replied. "Hamish here is your man," he continued, indicating the bowman on the end closest to us, a large, cropped-haired, facially tattooed man. His tattoos were a mixture of ancient Celtic symbols; swirls and circles within circles denoting the eternality of existence, and those of Christianity; a small Celtic cross adorned his left cheek and a fish, the latter being in the middle of a Celtic swirl adorning his right cheek. "He has led this troop of arrow-men for some time, he has. "Trust 'im to give the order as to when and where to fire."

"After the leadership skills you just displayed, one would think..." I began.

"I go with you, sir," Taliesin proclaimed in no uncertain terms.

I stared at the man for a moment, admiring his character and forthrightness. "Indeed," I agreed. I then turned to Hamish. "The duty's yours, Hamish," I said to him.

"Thank you, commander," he said in a mousey, squeaky voice, which did not at all match the image of the man before me. I was stunned by it for a moment, but quickly recovered and looked to the ladder bearers.

"Ladders to the..." I started. But the words froze as my gaze fell upon the front man who had his left arm through the end rungs of what was obviously a heavy burden. Henry. I nearly leapt off of Macha, such was my desire to embrace my friend. But the decorum of my new found position of authority would not permit such a publicly blatant display of favoritism, nor would the urgency of our overall current situation. Henry looked pale and gaunt. Beads of sweat trickled down his trembling brow. His mouth moved as if involuntarily chewing on something that was clearly not there. Anger coursed through my whole body at what the worship of the opium had done to him. One might argue that the symptoms he displayed were due to the exertion of the march up the hill under the burden of a heavy assault ladder. Yet, none of the other men who had carried the ladders exhibited such symptoms or appearances. They were a bit winded, perhaps, but that was all. I knew better. There was no doubt in my mind that Henry's condition was the result of not having suckled on the opiate's teat this day or for perhaps many a day. I forced a smile to stretch my face and nodded in greeting to my friend. He managed an unreadable, feeble smile in return, but that was all. I would look after him later, presuming of course we made it through the next few hours alive. But it was my full intention on surviving the next few hours and well beyond. I turned my attention away from Henry and back to the matter at hand. "Those with shields to the ladder bearers!" I commanded. Most of the formation broke, shields in hand, and huddled close to those carrying ladders. The remainder scurried to be near those with the shields, not wanting to be left out of the semi-protective umbrella when the time came. I looked to the leader of the bowmen. "At your discretion, Hamish," I said.

"Aye, sir," he replied.

"To the walls of Jerusalem!" I ordered to the rest of the men. The company lurched forward as one entity, Taliesin leading the way.

~XXIII~

No war cry rang out in this leg of the march. We marched on in determined silence. Within moments the first enemy arrow struck the forward most ladder, its flame-lit head sticking mere inches from Henry's hand. "Shields up!" I yelled. Those with shields complied, raising them up flat to the sky over their heads in protection of the nearest ladder bearer, themselves and whoever else may fit underneath. No two shields were alike, as none were of regular military issue. They were all the personal armament of the individual soldier. Some were long and rectangular and three quarters of a man's width and height, others were small and round or square, but effective nonetheless in offering at least some protection from the rain of arrows that was sure to come. With our shields in place I looked back to Hamish and our bowmen. Even as I was turning my head to see them, Hamish was giving the order to his fully loaded, bow-stretched archers, hand raised in the air.

"Loose!" he commanded with a swift downward stroke of his raised hand. The unison thudding sound of many bowstrings being released at once rushed to my ears as a barrage of small missiles flew from our bows. No sooner had the arrows been loosed then Hamish gave the next order. "Bowmen up! Advance the line!"

As the line of bowmen quickly got to their feet and advanced closer to our position, now only some thirty yards from the wall, the arrows they had released were finding their marks on the enemy. More than one agonized scream was heard from the top of the wall nearest our position. One Muslim soldier suddenly toppled from the wall, landing in a bone-crunching pile in front of us, two arrows protruding from his upper body.

I turned and looked at Henry who yanked the burning arrow from the ladder with his free hand and tossed it to the ground. Several more enemy missiles hit the ground in front of us, falling just short of the men. Odd, that, I thought. Surely their bows had the range to strike us where we now stood.

"Final position!" Hamish barked. I watched as within only an instant of time our line of bowmen dropped to one knee, notched an arrow to their bowstrings, took aim at the wall's top and pulled the sinew string taught, ready to shoot. "Loose!" commanded Hamish with the same chopping motion of his hand as before.

At that same instance I gave the final order. "Advance! Double it!" I yelled. The company ran forward as one, doubling their pace as I trotted alongside atop Macha.

"Agh!" cried one of the shield men near Henry. The man fell to the ground clutching his right knee, an arrow shaft sticking out from the joint. The man's large, oblong shield dropped to the ground as well, exposing two other men; Henry and a fellow soldier. The fallen shield bearer had been between Henry and the other soldier who had been on the outside of the group as a whole. The exposed soldier now darted toward Henry in an effort to gain protection near the larger group.

But he then stepped in front of Henry. That step proved to be fortunate for my friend Henry, but fatal for the other soldier. The distinctive and gruesome thump-sound of an arrow biting deeply into a man's upper torso told the soldier what had happened even before he looked at his chest. The man, and indeed the whole company, continued to move forward as his eyes grew wide with the shock and realization that he was about to leave this world. With a terror-filled gaze he then looked at his chest and the arrow shaft protruding from it. Helplessness crossed his face as blood began to trickle from a corner of his mouth. I looked at Henry, who starred at the man with a surprised, yet knowing look on his face; that arrow would have struck him had the soldier not stepped directly in front of him. What happened next took place so rapidly that it was completely unavoidable. The arrow-struck man's now limp body stumbled forward and collapsed to the ground, but in doing so it caused a chain reaction. Henry tripped over the man's body, dropping his end of the long and heavy ladder, thus causing the others carrying his ladder to topple in turn. The soldiers in the closest proximity now fell over them, most of them ending up on the ground, but some falling on top of the ladder itself.

Yells and screams of confusion filled the air, as did another sound for a brief instant; a snapping sound akin to a dry wood branch breaking, intruded upon the ears. "Aghhhh!!" cried someone who was obviously in stomach-churning pain. I looked to the fallen men and saw one in particular whose legs had been caught under Henry's ladder. "The devil be damned!!" the man screamed in a fierce but pain-filled, cracking voice. It was then I realized that the snapping sound had been one of the caught man's legs being broken underneath the ladder. Chaos reigned for a time.

Yet, even amidst the chaos my men kept their heads. The ladder was quickly picked up, the man with the broken leg was dragged to safety by a friend, and the rest of the company made it to the wall in short order in complete control of mind and body as evidenced by the determination on their faces and purposeful execution of their body movements. Ladders began slamming upright against the aged stone barrier. My men immediately jumped onto them and ascended. I pulled on Macha's reins, halting and spinning her to face the rest of the men, nearly knocking down Alhasan in the process. My Arab friend stood before me, mouth agape. Next to him stood the toothless Franc sergeant, Lafeit—whom I was unaware of as being company until that moment—also with a mouth wide open in surprise, even shock. "Mon Dieu!" Lafeit exclaimed.

"What, by the God, is the matter with the two of you?!" I said, suddenly infuriated at this distraction and perhaps feeling just a little naked by the way these two stared.

"Sir Masoud has Allah's favor!" said Alhasan.

It was then I realized that it was not me they were gawking at. It was the spear I held. I noticed something different about it even before looking at it; the weight of it. It suddenly felt much heavier than it should have. Slowly, I raised the spear and looked at it. To my astonishment, the spear's shaft was riddled with enemy arrows. On one side and all up and down its length arrow shafts stuck out of it like the quills of a porcupine. I had not felt nor seen any one of these arrows come so close.

"'Tis true, just as they say!" said LaFeit. "The power of Christ All Mighty is within the great Spear of Longinus. It has drawn certain death away from you!"

Before I could respond, howls of pain and outrage came from one of the ladders. Five ladders had been placed against the wall, several men now scrambling up each one, a couple of them nearing the top which landed only a foot or so from the top of the wall, some thirty-five feet off of the ground. One of the ladders with a man nearing the top was being dowsed with a dark liquid from the wall's summit. It was black and had the consistency of thin mud. It also steamed, indicating that its temperature was hot, very hot. Pitch. The liquid was a vile substance known as pitch; sticky, boiling oil mixed with water, dirt and excrement. The Devil's Diarrhea some called it. The substance was poured from caldrons atop the walls. The liquid was not completely unexpected, as pitch was often used by defenders of a walled city under siege. But, one could never be fully prepared for it or for its nauseating stench. Some with shields had ascended the ladders first, shields raised—as much as possible while climbing the rungs of a ladder—to help protect other climbers below from raining arrows and whatever else may be hurled down at those assaulting the walls. The shields did little now, however, to protect against the disgusting liquid. Horror filled my being as I watched the men on the one ladder inundated with pitch. Immediately, they fell, plunging backwards to the ground in the throes of searing pain. More than one man's face and hands broke into dark blisters when the foul, hot liquid came into contact with their body. Those that survived the fall to the ground wailed and writhed in ungodly torment as the pitch stuck to the skin.

Anger coursed through my being. I shook the spear violently, loosening all of the stuck arrows and sending them to the ground. A trail of pitch ran down the wall from the caldron above. The large, round iron caldron—which was big enough to hold three men—was still tipped on its front, its lip barely hanging over the wall's top edge, the dark liquid still spilling out from it, but now barely a trickle. The momentum of all the liquid that had been inside was now gone with only a few drops creating a trail down the wall's outer side directly in front of the ladder which had been its target. My anger crested. In my mind's eye I imagined a bolt of lightning come forth from the sky and setting alight this dribble of Devil's Diarrhea. It would burn well. So great was my focus and intent with this image in my mind that my body began to shake with the real feeling of it happening.

Then, it did. It came not from the sky, but from the spear in my hand, from the Spear of Longinus. A bolt of blinding white lightning shot forth from the spear's blade, striking the dribble of liquid Devil's Shit. I suddenly realized I had just broken the pact with Salah al-Din. But it was too late for regret. A flame burst out and trailed up the pitch staining the wall. The enemy at the top saw what was happening. From what I could see, there were seven of them. Five of them disappeared from sight, apparently cowardliness getting the better of them, judging by the tone with which their comrades yelled at them. One of the two remaining Muslim defenders motioned for the other one to man a side of the heavy caldron. Together, they attempted to shove the huge iron pot over the wall. But even if they could have pushed it over they were not fast enough. The flame ran quickly up the trail of pitch, onto the caldron's lip and into its interior. The large pot ignited and exploded, spewing out a flaming fireball. The caldron itself shot backwards from the exploding pressure within it, knocking the two defenders down, one falling out of sight, the other falling off the wall to the outside. He landed near Macha's feet, his dead eyes staring emptily up at me. For a brief instant, our section of the wall was clear at the top, no enemy fighters or defenders could be seen and for that brief moment I thought we might be able to rapidly breach the wall. But at least ten more Muslim defenders suddenly appeared at the top of the wall, most of whom had bow and arrows.

"Roo-hah!" came the battle cry to my left and above. Henry. It was Henry and he was yelling at the top of his lungs wielding his sword while standing on the top of the wall. Three enemy fighters were locked in combat with him, trying to cut Henry down with their scimitars. But it was Henry who had the upper hand. He spun and ducked and weaved with his sword in a deadly dance with the enemy, cutting each of the them down in turn, chopping the sword hand from one, spinning and nearly cleaving a second in two. Henry appeared his former, fearsome self, for the moment at least. He had managed to scale his ladder and breach his part of the wall, thereby creating a hole in the enemy's defenses. I was proud of him. But, as with the nearby section of wall from where the pitch had been dumped, the breach was quickly sealed as Muslim fighters swarmed to fill the gap.

I looked along the rest of the wall as far as I could see. The whole of our crusader army had begun the assault and was meeting a similar difficulty as my men and I were here. They were being repelled on ground and wall. I looked back up to where Henry was. He was there no more. In fact, he was nowhere in sight; not on the wall, nor on a ladder, nor on the ground. One of the ladders was being pushed over by Muslim defenders using the butt of two spears. They succeeded. The ladder fell backwards with at least seven of my men still on it.

"Commander, use the power of the Great Spear of Longinus again!" someone shouted.

I held the spear aloft and impulsively grabbed the King's Sword from its sheath on my back. The blades of both spear and sword glowed with a green hue, a soothing sight quite opposite to the tension of our present situation. I held both weapons aloft for all to see.

"Yes!" shouted someone else.

"Praise the All Mighty!" yelled another.

Cheers began to ring throughout the entire army as one by one they all saw the glowing weapons.

"Destroy the walls, Sir Masoud!" yelled still another soldier.

I attempted to focus my mind on just that; the walls crumbling before us. But doubt was in my heart. I felt it. And nothing happened. I shifted my focus and sought to destroy those on the walls, rather than the walls themselves. More doubt crept into my being and with it, anger at my inept use of this power. Or perhaps it was guilt over breaking my word with Salah al-Din that I would not use the spear and sword so. Regardless, nothing happened.

Arrows, rocks and more pitch began to assail us from the wall's top.

"Now, sir, or we're doomed!" said the same soldier who had last spoken.

But no bolt of lightning or other display of power came forth from either weapon. In fact, the glowing on the blades was beginning to fade.

"Look!" said Taliesin, who now stood at Macha's side. He pointed to a spot on the wall's top to our left and some fifty yards away. A blue flame shot forth from an object held by someone standing atop a turret on the wall. The object seemed to merely be a piece of wood as tall as a man. But then I saw who held the object and knew the object for what it was. The one who held the object was Rashin and the object was a piece of the rood. The blue flame, or rather, a blue flaming ball, shot forth from the rood and sailed into the midst of two centuries of Christian soldiers and crusaders near where Rashin stood above them. It exploded violently. Most of the two-hundred men were killed instantly. Incinerated. But the rest, or at least most of the rest, were set ablaze.

"No!" I shouted impotently. I spurred Macha hard and galloped off in the direction of Rashin at a break-neck speed. My outrage grew as I approached the carnage. I looked up at the turret from where Rashin had hurled the destructive power through the rood. Rashin was gone. "Rashin!" I yelled angrily. I pulled Macha to a halt in front of the base of the wall below the turret, craning my neck to see the turret and the now empty spot where Rashin had been a moment before. He seemed to have simply vanished into the air. I looked to the field around me. Moans and cries filled my ears. A sea of death and suffering lay before me. Grief, confusion and emptiness washed over me. Though these men lying before me had not been in my company I felt that I, he who wielded the Spear of Longinus and King's Sword, should have been able to thwart this. I suddenly felt less than inadequate as a leader. I was a pretender, not at all qualified to have men under my command. Holding both the spear and sword before my face I silently cursed the situation I was in. "Show me the way," I pleaded to the objects in my hands. They said nothing. And, they no longer glowed at all.

A loud hissing sound flew past my right ear, then another. The palm of my right hand suddenly stung as something collided with the spear's shaft directly opposite of my right palm. Another enemy arrow had struck the spear. I then felt something hit the King's sword in my left hand, a metal clanging sound rang in my ears as an arrow bounced off of its blade. Another one hit the sword's hilt, nicking my thumb in the process. I instinctively let go of the sword and instantly regretted it. The Kings swords hit the ground with a metallic ringing.

Before I had time to react and retrieve the weapon a flash of pain coursed through my head, then another. I felt warm liquid ooze down my face. But it was not pitch from above. I touched the side of my face with my left hand and discovered the liquid to be blood; my own. I looked up toward the top of the wall just in time to expose my face to the next stone that was being hurled at me from the top of the wall. The large-fist-sized rock smashed into the top of my forehead at the hairline. The last thing I remember as I fell from Macha's back was the erroneous inner thought of, why? Why has the spear's power abandoned me?

Its power is your power, came the response in my mind. You have simply begun to lose faith, to forget, to doubt.

My body hit the ground in a painful heap. Then, all went black.

~XXIV~

"Remember, Myrriddin," said Moscastan, my mentor, "you are always connected to the Source, always. It is your awareness of It, and especially your feeling of It, that creates a condition desired. Doubt, lack of Faith, destroys the condition sought and renders the circumstances you are feeling; in this instance, states of doubt and lack of faith and their corresponding conditions, however that may appear to you. What you are Truly feeling is always what will appear before you as your circumstances."

"I understand," I heard myself, my Myrriddin self, say.

"You must awaken now," Moscastan said in an odd voice and in a strangely accented tongue. Yet, I knew these qualities of voice. Not as Moscastan's, but...but...

"You must! You must to awaken now, Masoud!" said the voice urgently.

My eyelids felt heavy. It seemed to take all of my effort to open them. When I did I found I was Masoud once again, lying on the ground on my stomach, my right cheek in a small puddle of my own blood. The smell of smoke filled my nostrils along with the stench of death. Slowly, I rolled over and sat up, my forehead throbbing, and stared into the face of Alhasan. Taliesin was next to him as was Sir James, grave concern plastered across their respective faces. Beyond them I could see that the bulk of our army had pulled back, retreated, leaving the dead, their corpses littering the field and Hill of Skulls. The sun appeared at its zenith. Midday. "We've retreated?" I asked to no one in particular.

"Yes, lad," replied Sir James. "You've been out most of the morning."

I noticed then that I was nowhere near the wall were I had been struck down, some three-hundred yards away from my estimate.

"We pulled you away as soon as we could," explained Alhasan.

I nodded in understanding. My head suddenly throbbed worse than it had a moment before and for a time I gave into the pain, hanging my head in silence and willing the pain to vacate my skull. I touched the area of the injury with my right hand and felt the wet bandage which someone had dressed onto the wound. My attention shifted to the rest of my body in an attempt to assess whether or not I had any other injured regions. I did not. The King's Sword, I thought suddenly, for its weight was no longer on my back. I remembered. It had been knocked out of my hand by an arrow! And the spear; I must have dropped it when I was struck in the head. Certainly, someone retrieved them! I thought. I forgot about the pain in my head for the moment and looked around the ground near where I sat, expecting to see them resting nearby. They were not there. A panic began to run through my body as I turned my head to view my immediate surroundings in a frantic attempt to look for the sacred weapons. "Where are they?!" I asked, hearing the cracking of fear in my own voice.

The three men before me exchanged a look, a look that told me they had certain knowledge but were loath to share it for how I may react. "They've gone, lad," said Sir James at last, "taken by the enemy."

"I don't understand," I replied, dumbfounded.

"They came through the wall when you fell, Masoud. They took your King's Sword and Great Spear, but not you," offered Alhasan.

"But," I said as I tried to recall in my mind's eye the exact location I was in when struck down, "what do mean they came through the wall? Do you mean a gate? I was not near a gate when I fell," I heard myself babble.

"There are passages, you see, blocks in the wall that open," said Alhasan.

I sat in silence for a moment, feeling shame for the fact that I had lost the sacred instruments. "Your Sultan has them both now, does he not, Alhasan," I stated as a foregone conclusion. "Punishment for a broken promise," I whispered under my breath.

"He does not!" exclaimed Alhasan, clearly insulted that I would even think such a thing. "He knows they are connected to you. He could have taken them already and long ago had he wished, but he is not dishonorable! It was not by his order your spear and sword were taken, but by Rashin's, I am sure of it."

I thought for a moment. What Alhasan said made sense. "You are probably correct, my friend. And your Salah al-Din is honorable. Still, we, I must get them back."

"How, commander?" asked Taliesin with the gleam of adventure-to-come in his eyes.

I looked to Alhasan. "You said there are passages in the wall, blocks that open."

"Yes. That is how Rashin's men snuck out and stole your weapons," answered Alhasan.

"And you saw them?" I asked.

"No," he admitted. "But it is the only explanation."

"Do you know where these passages are?"

"Not the certain one that was used to take your weapons," Alhasan said. "But I do know of one. I can take you correctly to it."

"Why did you not tell us of these passages before?" asked Sir James in an accusatory tone.

"As I said, I only know of the one. Useless to know of only one. Can an entire river rush quickly through a tiny hole without detection? I think not," said Alhasan. "And, I had forgotten about them until this time, you see."

"Umph," was Sir James' cryptic response. "I say we find the one that they came through to steal the sword and spear."

"Commander, you or I could search for days for that one particular movable block and never find it, so well are they concealed," said Alhasan.

"Then we will go through the block, the passage that you know of, Alhasan," I said. "Will you lead me?"

"Of course, Master Masoud," he replied.

"I do not think..." began Sir James.

"I am going, Jonathan, Sir James," I said forcefully, hearing the desire for redemption echoing in my voice. "Strip me of my new command and title for abandoning duties if you wish, but I am going to take these holy instruments back."

Sir James smiled. "I was simply going to say that I do not think you should go alone, is all."

"Perhaps," said Taliesin, "we could sneak in many men after all and..."

"No. That will not do. Alhasan was right; one small passage would not be enough to stage an invasion," said Sir James.

"Aye, But be just one of us to get to the gate from within..." replied Taliesin.

"They are not the gates of your experience," said Alhasan. "They are on machine lift-cranks and hinges. If you do not know how to work them, they will not open. In addition, they are too fortified, you see."

"There it is, then," I said. "Alhasan, you will lead us in. Sir James, will you accompany us in?"

"Honored to, lad."

"And I be at your side, Sir Masoud," Taliesin declared proudly.

"I would prefer that you stay here with the men, Taliesin." I hated to thwart the man's desire, but he was too valuable an asset between me and the soldiers. "They respect you and listen to you," I said.

He hesitated, disappointment playing across his face. "If it be your wish."

"Aye, it is. And this undertaking must be kept between the four of us," I insisted.

"Agreed," said Sir James.

"Yes," said Taliesin.

Alhasan simply nodded.

"So be it. We will go in tonight," I said hoping my redemption would be waiting for me.

⌁ ⌁ ⌁

The air was cool, the moon one-quarter and just rising, cresting the walls of Jerusalem and silhouetting the city, bathing it in a heavenly glow. Night had fallen some five hours past. Silently, we made our way along the wall's base near where Rashin had stood on the turret earlier in the day. Alhasan led the way followed by myself and Sir James. Sir James and I had discarded our crusader tunics for plain brown travelling togs that denoted us from no particular country, no particular political and religious persuasion. We could be slaves. As much as I had wanted Commander Sir James with me, I thought initially that he would be ordered to stay with his men. He would then have to decide whether it was worth the risk of accompanying me in the hopes of getting back before anyone was to notice that he had gone missing. Yet, my commander only answered to General Horatio Blackthorn. And, as it turned out, the lilac scented general had not been heard from nor seen since the day's main battle. Presently, our dead and injured had been cleared from the field of battle. Blackthorn had not been accounted for. Some speculated that he had been captured, taken prisoner. But according to eye witnesses, only those who had made it to the top of the walls, as Henry had, were taken prisoner. Blackthorn had certainly not been one of those. Regardless, Blackthorn's absence left Sir James in his place. With only two other generals to command the army presently in the immediate region, Commander Sir James' sense of duty nearly precluded him from joining me. But in the end, he delegated his duties temporarily to a subordinate under the admonitions of silence and it being a mission of biblical importance.

My thoughts drifted to Henry. So much had happened to us since arriving in this land. Neither one of us were the same people. I could only hope that he had indeed been captured. At least then he would be alive and I might even be able to help him once inside.

We traveled quietly in the darkness along the wall for some time. Finally, Alhasan slowed our pace and felt along a given section of the wall with his hands. "Here," he whispered as he placed his fingers into a crack in the stone wall. The crack was about two feet in length, at chest height and ran perpendicular to the ground. At first glance, it did not look like anything but a line, a cosmetic blemish on the aged stone wall. He dug the fingers of both hands into the crack and gave a tentative pull.

"Wait," Sir James whispered. "We can't just stroll through the door there."

"There is, how you say, an antechamber on the other side of this stone door. Then, another door leading out into the city, or still another one leading to a nearby building, I forget which, you see," explained Alhasan.

"And no one on guard in this antechamber?" Sir James asked.

"These passageways and moving blocks are a secret and only used by the Hashishim Knights," answered Alhasan.

"You mean they were a secret. I doubt those were Hashishim Knights that snuck out of the passage and stole the spear and sword," I said. "The knights of the Hashishim Order I have encountered would not have performed such thievery, knowing my connection with the weapons as they did," I concluded, trying to convince myself.

"As I have stated, Rashin gave the order to take the Great Spear and King's Sword, I am sure. I am also sure they were Hashishim Knights," said Alhasan with confidence.

"How can you know that?" I asked indignantly.

"You are alive. Out of respect for you, your Templar stature and your brotherhood with the sacred weapons, they did not kill you, you see," he replied matter-of-factly.

A slight chill ran up my spine. "Yes. I do see."

"Come," said Alhasan, indicating the crack. "I am in need of your help." Sir James and I wedged our fingers in the

730

crack and pulled. Slowly and with a slight scraping sound, the stone block hinged open toward us. We opened it just enough to squeeze through one by one.

The antechamber, as Alhasan had called it, was small and dark. There was a damp and musty smell to it that suggested the tiny room never saw the light of day. Alhasan pulled the stone block-door closed behind us by what looked to be a leather strap attached to the door's inside. The stone door closed with the slight scraping sound again, as well as a gentle and quiet thud, plunging us into a near complete darkness. "Now what?" I asked.

"To prayer!" said a muffled voice speaking in the Arabic tongue. Though I could not yet speak the language myself, I found that I was understanding more and more of it. It took but a moment to realize that the voice was coming from the other side of the antechamber's wall, the city's side. The voice was joined by another, also speaking in Arabic, but inaudible. By the fading sound of the voices, they appeared to be moving off.

"Come," whispered our guide, Alhasan. As my eyes adjusted to the room's dark interior, I could see Alhasan standing in front of a short, wooden door. It had a small window in the middle of it which was in the shape of a crescent moon, a sliver of light leaked through it and spilled onto the room's dirt floor. The door itself stood only four feet high and was curved at the top. Alhasan pushed the door's splintered handle down and slowly opened it inward, toward himself. Cautiously, he peered out. Apparently satisfied that the way was clear, he slipped out of the room, motioning for us to follow.

Our small group emerged onto a darkened street, its clearly Roman built stone slates long since cracked and crumbled. We had come through what was called the Second wall of Jerusalem and emerged near what had been known as the old Gennath Gate, now, judging by its appearance, dilapidated and sealed with stone and mortar. Torches cast poor shadows onto the street from their sconces along the city's wall, but there was enough light from them and the ascending moon to show that the street and immediate area were all but deserted.

"Where is everyone?" I asked.

"Prayer?" offered Sir James.

"Yes, but no. I believe the defenders of Jerusalem think they have won," Alhasan replied, "that they have defeated you. But not all of Allah's soldiers rest and pray," he said, pointing up to the top of the wall.

I looked to the top of the wall and saw figures patrolling there and watching the outside of the city. Alhasan moved forward and we followed, pacing ourselves cautiously along the wall we had come through which was on our right. We had walked quietly for only a few moments when we came to a bend in the road and yet another stone wall. This new wall met the wall of our emergence at a forty-five degree angle and went off to our left for as far as I could see in the dimness of the night. What I could see of this new wall—new to us, that is —was that it had many sections in need of repair; holes and gaps abounded. I touched this wall and a curious sensation began to radiate from within my spirit. It was an inner warmth. Just as a warm drink on a cold day warms and soothes the body from within, so too did this sensation warm my spirit. The spear was calling to me. I felt the connection swell in my heart, in the seat of my soul. This wall was an important link in retrieving the Spear of Longinus and the Kings Sword. I felt it. "We go through this wall?" I asked, eager to move on. But something in my heart immediately told me that going through this new wall at this juncture would be premature.

"No," said Alhasan, confirming my feeling. "Do not lose the prize for haste in obtaining it. This wall was the First wall of the city and we will follow along it. It will lead us to what was called the Antonia Fortress. It is where Salah al-Din is as well as Rashin. I believe there is where you will find your sacred weapons."

My heart began to race and my soul to smile. Alhasan spoke the truth, I felt it. I also knew that the ancient fortress hugged the First wall, as Alhasan had called it, in the northeastern quarter of the city. According to Sir James, General Blackthorn had commanded the host of crusaders and Christian soldiers which was to breach the section of wall nearest the Antonia Fortress, between the Golden Gate entrance to the city and the Mount of Olives. His troops had been annihilated and the lilac general had disappeared. From what Alhasan had just said, we would be approaching the fortress from the opposite side and from within the city herself. "How far is the fortress?" I asked.

"Approximately under one mile along this wall," replied Alhasan.

"Lead us," I ordered.

"As you wish, Master Masoud." The three of us crept on, with Alhasan and the First wall as our guide. We had travelled nearly a quarter of a mile without incident, looking through the various gaps in the wall along the way. At one point there were several Muslim soldiers on the other side of the wall, roaming or patrolling what had been known in the time of Christ as the Upper City area.

Something entered my mind, then, something that was in opposition to what my heart had indicated only a short time ago. "Alhasan, the turret upon which Rashin had wielded the power through the Rood," I began, "that was near where we first entered the outer wall or the Second wall as you called it..."

"It was the Tower of Hippicus upon which he stood, lad," answered Sir James in Alhasan's stead. "That was its name at the time of our Lord."

"Interesting, commander, but..."

"It was close to Herod's Palace," he continued, apparently intent on giving the unsolicited history lesson, "and on opposite sides of the city from the fortress. Herod's Palace; now that's a place that has more than a few secret passages!"

I knew Sir James had been to Jerusalem on campaign before, but I was surprised by his apparent intimate knowledge of parts of the city. However, I set that aside as being fodder for conversation at another time. "Then why would Rashin leave the tower or Herod's Palace for the fortress?" I asked.

"Sultan Salah al-Din wishes his close advisors to be close at hand," answered Alhasan.

"Especially the ones he trusts the least, eh?" Sir James commented wryly.

"This is perhaps the truth of it," replied Alhasan.

We moved silently onward toward the fortress, ducking in the shadows of the wall when patrols came to near.

Curiosity got the better of me and I decided not to wait for some other time in conversing with Sir James regarding his knowledge of Jerusalem. "You've been stationed to this region before, Sir James, I know," I whispered, "but you seem to know quite a lot about various regions of the city, especially, given that we've not occupied it of late."

"Herod's Palace and her secret passages, you mean?" he replied. "Anyone could find out these things. The historian Josephus wrote about them."

"You are not just anyone, and you implied a much deeper knowledge, based on experience I'd say, than your words indicated or some historian might write about," I said.

"Did I now!"

"Aye. Well, at the very least, I sense that you know a lot more," I replied.

"Indeed."

We continued on in silence for a few more moments and I was beginning to think that he would say no more. I was wrong. "I know the intricacies of Herod's Palace and a few other important spots, yes," Sir James continued. "I know them as a Templar, just as Alhasan knows them as a servant of the Hashishim Order, is that not so Alhasan?"

"Yes, yes. Many rituals and ceremonies together here, you see," replied my Arab friend, albeit somewhat cryptically. "No doubt you too will participate in them quite soon, Sir Masoud."

I still did not understand how our two factions—the Order of Templar Knights and The Order of Hashishim Knights

—worked together on certain, deeper fronts, yet warred with each other on the outer fronts. Regardless, that was not my concern at the present. "Right now all I care about is getting back the spear and the sword," I replied.

"And so you shall," assured Alhasan. He suddenly stopped and crouched, startling Sir James and I and causing us to instinctively do the same.

"What is it?" I asked. My head wound throbbed from the quick drop and my hands flew to my head in a vane attempt at keeping the pain at bay.

"Masoud, Liam are you well, lad?" Sir James asked.

"Yes. It will pass," I replied. The pain throbbed for a moment more and subsided. "Why did you stop, Alhasan?"

"We are here," he said, peering around the corner of the wall we had crouched near. I peered around Alhasan and the wall's corner. It turned out not to be a corner at all, but a large chunk of the wall jutting out and over the section of wall we had been moving along. Upon further inspection, it was clear that the portion jutting out was actually a patchwork of wall laid or built over the main wall, as if it were a large patch covering a hole in the this particular section of the wall. Following Alhasan's lead, we moved out and around the patched portion and could see that the main wall stretched on for at least another one-hundred-and-fifty yards, and to my surprise, immediately in front of our position began a steady and gradual increase in height, ending at a near seventy feet in the air by my estimation. It also culminated in at least one huge turret or tower. We had arrived at the fortress. But my heart sank. From our position the wall and tower looked formidable, impenetrable even from this side which was technically inside the city proper. Yet, I refused to give in to despair. "There has to be a way in," I declared, "a gate perhaps."

"This was the gate for this section of the wall," said Alhasan, indicating the jutting patchwork of wall which we had just come around. "It was sealed some century ago, you see."

"Why?" I asked.

"I do not know," he replied matter-of-factly.

"Even if the gate were still here, lad, would you have us simply walk right through unnoticed by any of the enemy?" asked Sir James sardonically.

"Your point is taken, commander, but the underlying question remains; how do we get in?" I said. In near unison, Sir James and I looked to Alhasan for the answer.

"My good Sirs, would I have led you to this point without a way of entering the desired place?" Alhasan said with mock insult. Yet, the tone of his voice gave me pause; I sensed that his reaction of a mock insult was more of a cover for an inexplicable nervousness than anything else. Sir James and I exchanged a glance. He had clearly heard the uncertainty in Alhasan's voice as well. I looked back to my friend, my servant. "Alhasan..." I said, letting the sound of his name and my voice trail off as if calling out the deceit of a small child.

"La, la! No! Sir Masoud. I have plan! Truly," he said defensively.

"Well then, what is it?" I asked. "Surely you..." my head began to throb again with intense, searing pain. But the origin of the pain this time was not my head wound. It was something else entirely. The spear, something was happening with the spear! I felt it. I closed my eyes. In my mind I saw a darkened stone room. Inside this room stood several hooded figures standing in a loose circle. In the circle's center stood Rashin, hooded as well, but face exposed. Upon his face danced an unearthly red glowing light. The source of this light came from three objects in front of him, each on its own makeshift stone altar. The objects were the Rood of Christ, The King's Sword and The Spear of Longinus. Power was arcing through these sacred objects in the form akin to lightning in the sky. The power was clearly being directed by Rashin, each object magnifying the power through the other. I then noticed yet another hooded figure step from the shadows near Rashin and come to stand next to him. The arcing power also coursed through this individual, through Rashin and subsequently through the objects. Though I could not see the new figures face I instantly knew who he was, for the scent of lilacs suddenly filled my ethereal nostrils. "How can this be?!"

"As to your general, I cannot say. Each makes his own choices," said a nearby voice. But the voice did not come from Sir James or Alhasan. I turned my head and looked directly in to a pair of gold-colored eyes. I was stunned into silence. "But the objects have become a conduit," he continued, "a conduit for the Power of the One that flows through each of us equally yet is only expressed to the degree of the individual's understanding of it."

"How did you..." I stammered, finding my tongue at last.

"The law of the One knows only to respond to the belief of the individual," the ancient, golden-eyed priest continued, oblivious to my partially posed question. "According to the individual's belief, the objects will act as a multiplier, again, if that is what he believes. You knew all this at one time, but are in need of reminding."

"But they have to be stopped!" I said, ignoring his last apparent jab at the accumulative knowledge of my soul.

"Masoud!" said Alhasan in a reprimanding tone.

"Go to the last gate," said the ancient priest in my mind as he faded from my mind's eye.

"Who were you talking to," asked Sir James.

"Where is the last gate?" I asked Alhasan, ignoring the commander's query.

"The last gate?" replied Alhasan, confused. "That would depend upon which gate you're start from counting."

"Sir Masoud..." began Sir James,

"I saw Rashin in my mind's eye using the spear, the sword and the rood as a conduit for bringing Power here I believe for purely destructive purposes," I explained. "And that is not all; Blackthorn was with him."

"You saw this in your mind, Liam. It doesn't mean it was actually so," replied Sir James none-too-convincingly.

"Then the gold-eyed...the voice I heard said, 'go to the last gate,'" I continued, ignoring Sir James' reply.

"There is not a last gate in distinction, no first gate and subsequent last gate, you see," said Alhasan.

"Not in distinction, but in passing," noted Sir James.

Yes. I understood. We all three understood. The three of us looked to the last gate we had passed, sealed now. Or, so it appeared.

"It has to be this gate," I said, but not knowing where to begin looking for an opening or way through the patchwork.

"Begin at the bottom," said the priest's voice in my mind.

The priest's name came to me then. A name from my spirit's distant past. "Thank you, Father Pretorius," I whispered knowing that to be the golden-eyed, disembodied priest's former name. I stepped to the patchwork segment of the wall and began looking around its base.

"What do you look for, Master Masoud?" asked Alhasan.

"I'm not sure. I just know to start here and it will be revealed," I replied. I began to run my hand along the base of the wall where it met the earth, digging my fingers into the dirt. Nothing but sand and dirt and hard stone met my efforts. Until, that is, one of the base blocks moved ever so slightly, as if it were balanced on the point of a deeper stone below it. The patched section of the wall had been constructed with what appeared to be rough blocks of stone approximately three feet tall by two feet wide and laid unevenly atop one-another and overlapping each other. Little mortar appeared to have been used to seal the blocks together, thus creating more of a balanced wall of stacked blocks than a solid, cohesive one. Consequently, at least one block was bound to be loose and of no particular anchoring quality. Once I was confident that the moving of this loose block would pose no threat of the entire patchwork wall section tumbling down upon us I began to dig dirt from its base, and continued to do so, Sir James and Alhasan joining my efforts when they perceived the stone block was indeed loose. As dirt and debris loosened around the block, a two inch gap appeared at the top of it. Putting my hands beneath the block as if I were cradling a babe, I pushed up once, twice, thrice. The stone lifted slightly, loosening the rest of the dirt and sand that had lodged itself between the block and those next to it. "Help me pull it free," I said to my companions.

"Perhaps the whole section of wall will fall should we free this stone," said Alhasan.

"Not likely," replied Sir James as he examined the wall section. "I'm no engineer, but judging by the way they all overlap, this one stone, if removed would present no threat," he said, echoing my earlier assessment.

"Come then. Help me," I repeated. The two men knelt beside me, wedging their fingers in the now visible gaps around the loose stone block. "Pull." We pulled and wriggled the stone block toward us. The block, though heavy, turned out to be atop other smaller, round stones which effectively acted as ancient rollers. Slowly, it became looser and looser, sliding out of resting place ever so begrudgingly. "One more effort, now," I said. Our obvious success thus far inspired us to heave our backs and legs into it with even more vigor. Soon we could nearly wrap our arms around the block to gain more of a grip and were surprised to find that the block just seemed to keep coming out of its slot, so long it was—long in the sense that it extended through the wall from our side to the other some five or more feet. The stone block was heavy, but with a gallant effort and the aid of the ancient roller-stones beneath it, we three were able to finally pull it out completely.

As soon as the block was free I got on my hands and knees and peered through the opening now at the base of the patched section of wall. A small and short tunnel greeted my eyes. The moon was higher in the sky and looking through the tunnel I could see that the ground on the other side of the wall was bathed in soft moonlight. Without preamble, I lay flat on my stomach and pulled myself through the tunnel.

~XXV~

Upon closer inspection of the fortress and its walls and towers, it was quite obvious that my initial awestruck assessment of the fortress as being impenetrable and formidable had been severely misplaced. Though two of its towers and most of its walls still stood, the fortress itself was very unimpressive. I could imagine that during the time it was built it had been a most functional and, perhaps, formidable structure; part fortified city, part palace. Presently, however, it was a partially destroyed, crumbling shadow of its former self. I came to find later that it was named Antonia Fortress after the famous Roman Triumvir Marcus Antonius, or Mark Antony as he was also known, and was partially torn asunder by Rome herself a few centuries earlier. No wonder it was currently so un-noteworthy. It was also the place, according to some, wherein Jesus had been put on trial.

Unlike most of our journey this night, many Muslim soldiers were now about. The moon had risen and though it was a quarter waning, it still gave off enough light to find one's way to the fortress proper, as well as view the quantity of Arab troops we came upon. Sir James and I had wrapped our heads in the Arab manner. Alhasan led us and we followed in a way that denoted us as his servants; walking slightly behind him with our heads bowed respectfully and eyes averted so as not to look directly at our betters, as it were. We moved rapidly through the court and the ancient temple, or what was left of these structures, and arrived promptly at the remains of the fortress itself. Alhasan led us through one of the walkways and to a rampart leading up into the center part of the main structure. The rampart took us into a very large, high ceilinged room with four passages leading off in different directions. Though the room was partially lit by many torches in wall sconces, it was still dark and foreboding, foreboding because the large space now more resembled a huge cave than the large, well-built room of a fortress. I looked to the passages before us as we walked on. They appeared to be dark openings to dark tunnels beyond. Until, that is, one of them on our right caught my attention. It looked no different than the others, but something about it spoke to me on the deepest of levels as being the passage through which my task would be accomplished. "Stop!" I barked, my two companions halting cold in their steps and both staring at me in a reprimanding way, keep your English speaking voice down, you fool! spoke their look.

A troop of Arabic guards was walking nearby, heading out in the direction through which we had come. I looked out of the corner of my eye at them and saw that two of the men had clearly heard the non-Arabic words I had uttered. I ignored them, drawing my attention back to the passage on our right which had called to me. The calling was a feeling in the center of my heart; a feeling that told me, compelled me, to take the passageway. My heart pounding, I took a step toward it.

But as I did, a hand grasped my arm, stopping me. "La, Masoud. I believe Rashin to be in another part, not that way," said Alhasan gently, quietly.

"I do not know why, but my sense is to follow this passageway," I replied, "and I trust my inner sense more than ever."

"I understand, but..."

"Who are you?!" demanded a strong voice in the Arabic tongue. The two Arab soldiers that had looked at me a moment ago now stood before us. Though I did not raise my eyes to look at them directly, I did, nonetheless, peer at them from beneath my brow. They looked at me in an accusatory manner, and the hands of both men rested on the pommel of their as of yet still sheathed scimitar. "Who are you?! Answer!" demanded the one man again.

"I am," began Alhasan, drawing at least one of the men to look at him rather than me, "servant to Salah al-Din and these two are my servants."

The Arab soldier who had spoken and who also still stared at me now turned to Alhasan. "This one," he said, pointing at me, but speaking to Alhasan, "spoke in the crusader tongue and you answered him in it. I will ask but once more, both of you; who are you?"

"And I will answer you but once more," Alhasan blustered in an arrogant tone. "I am personal servant to Sultan Salah al-Din and these two men serve me," he stated indicating Sir James and me. Do you not think that a great leader such as our Sultan would have those near him who speak the enemy's tongue? Salah al-Din himself speaks the crusader tongue or are you too dim to understand the intricacies of leadership or even what I have just said?"

Rather than back down, the Arab soldier became angry and took a threatening step toward Alhasan. Though Sir James and I both carried standard issue, sidearm crusader swords— beautiful weapons that were part long dagger, part sword— beneath our tunics we dared not draw them lest we give ourselves away and bring reinforcements for the Arab soldiers and certain death for us. Fortunately, that point was rendered moot as the Arab soldier's comrade proved to be of a more amenable disposition and thought. "Come, Abbas," he said, gently taking the arm of his hot-headed partner. "Leave them. They are unworthy and I for one do not wish the wrath of the Sultan on my head should we bring harm to his property."

Screams and yells of confusion suddenly assaulted our ears from within the city near the fortress and diverted all of our attention from the immediate situation. A fraction of a second later the fortress rocked with an explosion, causing dust and dirt from the ancient stones above us to sprinkle down upon our heads. More yells found their way to us. All at once, four more Arab soldiers ran by us heading out of the fortress. "Come! We are assaulted!" one them commanded to Abbas and his comrade as he ran past with the others. The two before us did as they were bade, the belligerent Abbas giving me a look of utter contempt and spitting at my feet before joining his fellow soldiers.

"What is happening?" I asked, addressing no one in particular when the others were gone.

It was Sir James who answered. "Catapults, I should imagine. They and the siege engines finally arrived just before you woke up. I suspect fireballs of pitch and wood are being launched over the walls and at the gates."

This news was completely unexpected as was the realization that came next into my mind. "Why did we not wait until they were in place before attempting the assault yesterday?!" I asked, appalled. "Countless lives might have been saved!"

"Blackthorn did not want to wait, said he didn't trust the runners' reports that they were on the way," replied Sir James in a tone of disgust. "Blackthorn's a fool. I doubt very much if the catapults and siege engines are going to help now. We've not enough men left."

"Blackthorn is appearing more and more a wretch," I said.

"Aye," was all Sir James could muster as a reply.

I then looked at the passage still to our right, the one I was about to head into a moment before. I took a deep breath and silently asked my inner sense. The feeling was stronger than before; this was the passage to follow. My feet were moving of their own accord, carrying me in the direction of the passageway's mouth, some forty feet away.

"Masoud!" said Alhasan. But he was not going to stop me this time. I entered the passageway just as another explosion shook the fortress, striking even closer than before and nearly knocking me off of my feet. I looked back briefly and saw, with relief and satisfaction, that Alhasan and Sir James were now following me.

The passageway or corridor was dark, barely lit by a scant three sconce torches which were spaced very far apart, approximately every twenty yards or so. The corridor was wide, by some ten yards across, but low in height, a mere six feet high at most. Another surprising thing; the remnants of the fortress appeared tall from the outside, with the tower appearing to be at least seventy-five feet or more tall. Since we had entered at the ground level I had expected these inner passageways and corridors to incline upwards. The one we were in, however, inclined downward and became steeper with every step.

We rushed on for a moment in silence until we came to the last of the lit torch sconces, at which point I stopped us for a moment. "I still protest, Master Masoud," whispered Alhasan urgently. "I believe we should be going to another part of the..." he was cut off by yet another explosion, jolting all of us. This one obviously had been a direct hit onto fortress.

"No. I'm sorry, Alhasan, but I still believe I need to go in this direction and down this passageway," I replied. Yet, a moment of doubt splashed into my mind as I looked ahead and saw nothing but darkness. Regardless, I ran on. A moment later, however, my feet suddenly went out from under me and I was falling. But before I could voice my surprise and fear, I hit solid ground again in the form of a profoundly steep incline. Landing on my rear with a thud, I then began to slide and roll downward in the darkness.

I heard my companions land behind me with an equally hard thud and begin their own slide and roll into God only knew what. Finally, I went airborne again. A few seconds later I landed in a soft pile of what I took to be straw or hay by the feel of it. The smell of stale urine filled my nostrils. "Allah!" Alhasan exclaimed as he apparently went into the final free-fall. It suddenly dawned on me that I was going to be his landing cushion if I did not move quickly. I did, scrambling out of the way just in time to feel Alhasan land in the straw beside me. Unfortunately, Alhasan was not so lucky. Before he could react at all, Sir James plummeted in, landing directly on top of him, at least by the sound of it in the complete darkness.

"Agh! Commander!" cried Alhasan.

"My apologies, Alhasan," said Sir James as he rolled off of Alhasan. "Liam, are you here?"

"Yes, sir."

"What the devil have you gotten us into?!"

"I'm sorry, I don't know why I was led to this point," I said lamely.

"And just where is here?" asked my commander.

"I was hoping one of you could answer that," I said.

"La. I know some of this fortress, but little," said Alhasan.

"That's just..." began Sir James. But he inexplicably stopped in mid sentence. I was about to ask him why, when I heard the reason; voices, faint voices were wafting to our ears. But from where?

"You hear that," he asked in the darkness.

"Yes," I replied. But there was something odd about the voices. They seemed distraught, but there was something else, a quality that seemed out of place in the middle of this place of battle. "Children?" I asked, horrified at the prospect of any child being in this place.

"La. Not children," answered Alhasan. We sat in silence for time, listening. We could not discern what was being said or who the voices belonged to, though I still felt that it could be children. "Look!"

"What?" I replied, confused. "Look at what? It's black as pitch in here." But then I saw it; a sliver of light on the ground nearby, some ten feet away by the look of it. Slowly, I crawled toward it, bumping into two objects along the way which impeded my progress. I decided that I did not care to know what the objects were. Thus, I made my way around them and kept on moving toward the sliver of light. I reached out and touched the line of light and it became quite apparent what it was. "There's a door here," I said. "The light is coming from underneath the door at the bottom."

My friends crawled over to my position and for the first time in a few harrowing minutes I was able to see their faces from the soft bounce of light beneath the door. "You are correct it appears, Masoud. It is a door." Alhasan felt up the door's center-left side until he located what turned out to be a leather strap or handle. Giving a tentative tug the door easily opened inward.

~XXVI~

We all three stood and looked out into a gloomy but lit hallway. This hallway was nothing like the dilapidated one we had initially come through, however. This one was pristine, complete with dark marble-tiled floors and tapestries on the walls.

The voices still came to us in a muffled and distant manner, but were a little more audible. The hall extended some forty feet and cornered left. "We've come this far. Let's push on," commanded Sir James, drawing his sword. Following his lead I did so as well, though I did not feel the need. Besides, it now felt odd to be holding any other sword or weapon than the King's Sword or the Spear of Longinus.

"Is that necessary?" asked Alhasan.

"I doubt that the ploy of being your servants will work down here," answered Sir James. "Something tells me we've truly entered the monster's bowels."

"You are probably most correct commander, though I'd not classify it as the monster's anything. There are two monsters at least in any conflict, you see." said Alhasan. We stepped out of the room and began our trek down the hall.

As we reached the corner, the voices suddenly went silent. After a moment, we tentatively peered around the corner. There was no one there, no one to impede our progress. We rounded the corner and continued on. Three things became apparent. The first was that this part of the hallway was extremely long. It seemed to go on as far as the eyes could see. The second was that there were many rooms off of this section. Beginning some thirty yards ahead of our present position there was light spilling out of doorways. The third thing was something completely and utterly unexpected; the stale urine stench of a few moments ago, which seemed to follow us as we went down the hall, was suddenly replaced by the sweet but faint scent of perfume. I thought instantly of Blackthorn and his perpetual lilac scent. But that was not it. This smell was not of lilacs per se. It was distinctly perfume, decidedly feminine and intoxicating. "Ah, laddie," said Sir James as he sniffed the air. "Have you led us to a harem now?" he asked rhetorically in a tone that denoted trouble was at hand.

In my mind's eye a pair of beautiful lavender eyes stared at me. "Najeeba," I whispered.

I felt real eyes upon me and turned to see Alhasan's stern look of disproval. "I doubt very much that she is here, Masoud. Do not be distracted from the duty at hand."

"She is not a distraction," I said defensively.

"Najeeba? Who is that?" asked Sir James.

"She is niece to the Sultan. Sir Masoud was of assistance to her some time back," explained Alhasan, "and is presently, how you say, enamored with her. Quite inappropriate, you see."

"You cannot place a judgment on such things. I can't explain what I feel other than to say she and I have known one-another for centuries, daft as that may sound," I said.

Sir James stared at me for a moment. He seemed to understand. "You have become more attuned with your soul, Liam, to be sure. And I believe what you say. However, we are not here to rescue a maiden, soul partner or no. We are here to retrieve the sword and spear."

"We create what we are here to do and perhaps we will do both," I retorted, brushing past both men and slowly making my way down the hall.

"Liam. Masoud," Sir James whispered loudly from behind me.

"There is no point in attempting to dissuade him, commander. You will not succeed," said Alhasan.

"Aye. I'm more his follower now than his commander as I see it."

Ignoring my companions, I made my way to the first
door and looked in. Nothing. The room was empty except for a
few throw pillows and carpets. The next room proved to be
the same, as did the one after that. But the fourth, the fourth
was the source of the smell of perfume, for it lingered in the
air as I entered the room. Throw rugs and rich accoutrements
dotted the space; a gold-leafed table here, silken shawls and
thick silken pillows there. "Well, they are gone now," said
Alhasan from behind me, clearly relieved.

"Don't be so pleased, my friend. The night is new. We
may come across her yet," I said. I turned and left the room,
my companions following.

Still, the hall seemed to go on and on, bending and
curving one way then the other.

"What the devil," exclaimed Sir James. "It's like a maze.
We'll not get anywhere like this. Think, lad. Do you feel the
spear or the sword, here a-bouts?"

I closed my eyes briefly, searching my mind, my soul
and saw the Spear of Longinus and the King's Sword. In my
mind's eye, I saw them in the same room as before. But this
time, a light from the spear reached out to me, making its way
through to where I presently stood in the hall. My eyes popped
open, obliterating the vision in my mind's eye. There was no
light extending from anywhere and making contact with me.
But what I felt next was the unseen connection with the Great
Spear asserting itself on my being. The hair on my neck stood
on end. A tingling sensation began at the base of my spine
and ended at the area of my heart. It then gave me a tugging
sensation, pulling me forward. My steps began slowly, moving
me forward further down the hall.

"Masoud, it speaks to you, yes?" Alhasan said.

I did not respond for fear of breaking the connection
with the spear, thus losing direction once again. I moved some
thirty feet more and came to an open doorway on the left. But
it was not a doorway as such. It was the entryway to an
extensive, left-spiraling staircase leading down, lit only by faint
light coming up from below. "Agh!" cried a woman from deep

down the staircase, breaking the connection with the spear. No matter. It was clear that descending the ancient stone stairs was in order. I looked back at my friends for the briefest of instances. A momentary crease of disapproval furrowed their brows in near unison. But for Sir James' part, it was quickly replaced by a smile of support.

"Ah, the devil be damned. If we're going to jump in, may as well go all the way, eh lad," Sir James pointed out. "Let's go then!"

Like three bolts of lightning, we descended the stairs, going round and round and down and down, nearly stumbling more than once in darkened space and on the crumbling stone steps. Finally I did stumble, catching my foot on the sharp, jagged edge of one the final steps. I completely lost my footing and flew headlong into a flimsy door at the base of the staircase, crashing loudly through it and sprawling on the floor. The crusader sword which I had been holding flipped out of my hand as the latter hit the ground hard. It clanged and slid across the floor, coming to rest under a black boot as the boot stepped upon it. I looked up and into the face of the boot's owner; the opaque-eyed soothsayer, Rashin. "I am quite impressed. Your connection to the ancient weapons is indeed strong for you to have made it this far."

Alhasan and Sir James came rushing through the door and froze at my side. I made it to my feet without pretense, forcing my embarrassment over the entry I made to the basement of my mind. The hooded figures I had seen in this room within my mind's eye were all present, all but Blackthorn, that is. But his smell was there; the faint but unmistakable scent of lilac hovered in the air.

It was then I noticed out of the corner of my eye that Sir James' sword was raised in a ready-defensive position.

"It is unwise to brandish your sword just now," said Rashin to my commander. "Do you not agree, Sir Blackthorn?" he said over his shoulder.

From the shadows behind Rashin a figure emerged. The figure threw off his cowl and revealed his face; General Sir

Horatio Blackthorn, Commander of the crusader army and in that moment, traitor to his race and religion and soul. Anger welled within my being. I had not wanted to believe the vision I had earlier of this man being in the midst of those who stole the Great Spear and King's Sword. Indeed, until that very moment I had not truly believed the vision. Yet, he was here.

"You are a disgrace, Horatio," declared Sir James.

"My good fellow," replied Blackthorn condescendingly, "quite the contrary, we are merging our powers, the Order of Templar Knights and the Knights of the Hashishim Order. These weapons are our legacy, they are our birthright!" he said.

"You are mad. And, you do not speak for the Templar Order," I said.

"Am I mad? Quite the contrary, I am one of the very few who is in his complete right mind," laughed Blackthorn. "You cannot remember, though your soul knows. Your soul knows everything of your journey, Masoud. But instead of using this knowledge for your soul's advancement and incarnating as an advanced divine being on this earth, instead of incarnating as a man knowingly connected to his advanced soul as you did with your last life as a Master Merlin, you chose to reincarnate in this life as an ignorant foot soldier barely connected with his spirit's knowledge," Blackthorn said, pausing for what I interpreted as being nothing more than the drama of it.

Some of what he said made sense. Yet, my feet were firmly on the path they had always been on. Even in this life as Liam Mason-Masoud, I had been experiencing much of those lives of Longinus and Myrriddin, or rather, re-experiencing some of the moments of great learning and importance, and with each re-experiencing, solidifying the lessons and seeing them with a new layer that was not apparent before. The fact that someone else could not see this was of no concern to me. We are each of us on our chosen journey, this and every life, the purposes of which, the objectives of which, remain hidden to all but the individualized soul. To say that one soul is more advanced this time around or that time around is to miss the point of the subjective journey within the One Mind, which is this: that Mind may experience Itself, as Itself, through our individualized experiences within Itself.

"We have all been with you on your soul's journey, Master Masoud," Blackthorn continued. "All for our own purposes, of course, but there nonetheless. Yet, you were oblivious to one of the greatest Orders of Knights even as the Roman centurion who set all this in motion. The Militia Crucifera Evangelica, protector of the newly birthed Christian sect, deflector of Rome by way of deception and magic, it was they who ensured that the roots of the new religion could take hold. Do you think as Longinus you languished in the Mists with the likes of the Celts for those years all on your own? Our Orders," he ranted on, now indicating Rashin and his men, "have been in existence since the dawn of knowledge in one form or another, ensuring that only the select and worthy know the Eternal Light and Infinite Knowledge, the Great Secrets, the True Workings of the One and The Law that governs our very nature."

"It is not for you to withhold anything," I said, angrily. "All are equal by the One and under the Law of the One, and by the Law enact experiences to the degree of their understanding," I countered, not exactly sure of where my words were coming from, but not questioning them either. "Who are you to deny them the knowledge of their very being, their very essence?!"

"You should be bowing before him, Blackthorn," snarled Sir James, indicating that the general should be on his knees before me.

"You have been keeper of the Great Spear and King's Sword until now, this is true," said Blackthorn, ignoring Sir James' taunt and my question. "And for that, we are truly grateful," he said, sounding falsely contrite. "But you have not always had it, and while some still see you as the weapons' keeper, the time has come for all of the relics to come back into the fold of the Order, the true guardians of the Eternal

Light and Infinite Knowledge. We had been waiting to see if this was indeed the Great Spear of Longinus and the King's Sword and for you, your soul, to appear and demonstrate the fact. Together with the Rood, The Grail, the Shroud and the bone of the Apostle, the Power of the One can be infinitely multiplied and directed."

"If not mad, then you truly are a fool," I said, "for if you were the true guardian of the Eternal Light and Infinite Knowledge, you would know that you do not need these things to multiply and direct the Power. You need only your unwavering confidence in belief and knowingness in the very nature of your being."

"Enough of this," declared Rashin as he stepped away from us and deeper into the room.

~XXVII~

As Rashin walked deeper into the room, I realized for the first time that the space was a large, cavernous, high ceilinged, cathedral type structure. Stained glass windows banked the walls, eerily lit from behind by torches and candles. Though we were obviously deep underground, the windows were meant to mimic the outside night's light of an above ground cathedral. Instead, in this vast underground place it appeared as more the devil's church then a Christian cathedral. It was then I noticed that the high ceiling was designed to resemble the inside of a Mosque. This place did no service to either of these great religious sanctuaries. It was a poor representation of their blending, almost a mocking.

There were no pews as in a real cathedral. In the center were the pedestals that I had seen in my vision. One contained a piece of wood—a part of the Rood—another The Spear of Longinus and still another The King's Sword. Yet, there were three other pedestals as well. One contained the Shroud of the Christ—that which my spirit recognized as the burial cloth of Jesus—folded so that His emblazoned image faced all. Another pedestal had upon it a plain wooden bowl. The Holy Grail? I wondered. It must be. Yet, I sensed nothing special about this bowl. And finally, one more pedestal held a small, pointed object which stood upright. It took me a moment to realize what it was; a human finger bone. I tried to approach the pedestals but was prevented by four very large, dark robed, hooded figures. They unceremoniously took me by both of my arms and led me to a spot just outside of the six-pointed configuration of pedestals. Sir James and Alhasan joined me, escorted by other hooded figures. Two other hooded figures appeared, having come from the cathedral's far end, near what would have been the area of the altar in a real church. "You did not succeed," stated Rashin to the newcomers.

"We did not, sire. She is gone," said one of them.

"No matter," said Rashin.

For the briefest of instances, my eyes darted around the whole room, trying to discern the room's overall layout, yes, but also, I suddenly realized, looking for the female whose voice we had heard from atop the spiral staircase and obviously who the men had been looking for.

The woman all but forgotten by our robed and hooded hosts, we were flanked by several of these men. My companions and I faced the pedestals while Rashin, Blackthorn and eleven other dark-robed ones encircled the sacred relics. "You see before you the power of God conveyed in these objects," stated Rashin to us. "The Rood by which your Jesus was hanged, the cloth in which he was buried, the cup with which he drank the first Holy Communion," continued Rashin, pointing to each object in turn, "the finger of Paul, one of your Prophet's great Apostles, Excalibur—The King's Sword—and finally, the Great Spear, that which you Masoud, as Longinus, used to stab your Prophet, your Anointed One while he was on the cross, killing him. Behold now the power!" he finished, taking his place near Blackthorn. Nodding to the lilac general, the...ceremony, for want of a better word, began.

In high theatrical pose, Blackthorn raised his face and arms toward the ceiling, the heavens, and closed his eyes. "Abwûn d'bwaschmâja Nethkâdasch schmach Têtê malkuthach," he intoned in a tongue that was so ancient it had not been heard in a thousand years. Yet, it was not so far removed from my mind, my soul, as to be unrecognizable; Aramaic, the language of Christ's time. "Nehwê tzevjânach aikâna d'bwaschmâja af b'arha. Hawylân lachma d'sûkanân jaomâna..."

"'Oh thou, Oh Birther! Father-Mother of the Cosmos from whom the breath of life comes...,'" Sir James whispered next to me, interpreting the ancient Aramaic chant as Blackthorn droned on in the background. In that moment I was not sure which surprised me more; the fact that Sir James understood Aramaic or the fact that I had the sudden realization that this was no ordinary chant. It was the Lord's Prayer, in its original form and meaning, in its original language of Aramaic. "'...who fills all realms of sound, light and vibration. May your Light be experienced in my utmost holiest. Your Heavenly domain approaches. Let your will come true—in the Universe just as on earth. Give us wisdom for our daily needs, detach the fetters of fault that bind us like we let go the guilt of others. Let us not be lost in superficial things, but let us be freed from that what keeps us off from our true purpose. From you comes the all-working will, the lively strength to act, the song that beautifies all and renews itself from age to age.'"

"Amên," finished Blackthorn.

"'Sealed in trust, faith and truth,'" Sir James said, thus concluding his interpreter's performance of the Aramaic words.

Silence filled the room. All the robed figures seemed to be in a deep state of meditation. An odd way to tempt the power of God, the power of the One through these artifacts and the ancient Lord's Prayer, yet...

A tingling sensation filled the room, making the hairs on my body stand on end. An energy entered that seemed to fill the space with a strange buoyancy. I had the sensation that I could float off of the ground if I set my mind to it. "Abwûn d'bwaschmâja Nethkâdasch schmach Têtê malkuthach," came the words again, but this time in unison by all the hooded figures present, chanting the prayer and focusing their individual minds to be of one collective mind and hence joining directly with the One Mind. The energy that had entered the room now centered itself on the sacred objects. From all but one of them came a light with an odd, unearthly blue glow, radiating the light from an unseen source. The one object that remained darkened and plain was the so-called grail. As I had sensed previously, it appeared to be a plain bowl or cup. I saw Rashin's eyes then also looking at the wooded bowl. His eyes narrowed with anger at the bowl's apparent falseness, his discolored eye watering with the emotion. By the look of his face it was all he could do to not let the anger consume him, thereby breaking the spell being cast, the power being summoned. The other five objects held the Otherworldly glow, however. I could feel the power coming through the objects, particularly the Spear and the Sword. The power grew, building and building in intensity as evidenced by the pressure being pressed upon my body from without. It was as if a giant hand was squeezing me. I looked to Sir James whose expression told me he felt it as well. As if to further confirm the sensation, the power and the glow began to expand from the objects, taking the form of a vaporous cloud, engulfing the room, seemingly becoming too large and potent to contain, yet singular in its concentration, its locality.

"Strengthen the bonds of power!" said Blackthorn loudly to the air, to the power coursing through the objects and the room, speaking to it as though it had a conscious mind, for indeed it appeared to, directing its attention first to those near the objects and then the individuals nearby. The power, the energy, while engulfing the room we were in also localized itself into a stretched, oblong vaporous sphere with one round end that seemed the head of the thing. It was as if the power, the energy, was looking at all with unseen eyes, assessing, even asking, who dares call me forth?! It was directly in front of Blackthorn when the general had said the words. It now moved around the circle of hooded and robed figures, and came to Sir James, Alhasan and myself, stopping in front of me.

It hovered before me and my first instinct was to fear it. But I did not. There was nothing to fear from a power that is from the One Source, for it was my power, everyone's power. Nothing but peace and devotion, happiness and abundance is what I held in my mind. And, within a heart's beat that is what I felt from it, this mass of power-filled energy. Overwhelming feelings of warmth and comfort, prosperity and peace and yes, love is what radiated back to me. I was receiving what I was giving and to a tenth degree more. It was the most wonderful sensation, as if I was in the lap of God and, of course, I was. Right there and right then, I was. I also knew truly that we are always in this presence because it is us. It only appears missing, absent, when we turn our intention and realization away from It.

"Death! Destruction! Oblivion to the enemies of the Eternal Light!" Blackthorn yelled at the powerful sphere of energy in an enraged tone.

In that moment I pitied the lilac scented general for he had absolutely lost his way. He was no knight of the Templar Order. He was displaying everything the Templar Order was not. As with the knights of Arthur's legendary round table, those who were among our predecessors, the Templar Order stood for truth, justice, service and protection of those less fortunate. We were the keepers of the Light and Sacred Knowledge, yes, but not to the exclusion of others. In fact, it was for the preservation of these things that they may be taught to all and held by all to be the right of all that we kept them safe and out of the hands of those who would seek to control the populace by keeping the knowledge for themselves. Blackthorn had truly lost sight of that.

"Oblivion to the enemies of the keepers of Infinite Knowledge!" yelled Blackthorn.

It is done unto you as you believe, said the voice in my mind, the voice of the golden-eyed priest, reciting the great Truth.

The sphere of power turned and floated back to Blackthorn. "Direct your power to them and destroy the enemy!" he commanded of the sphere. The sphere of power complied, giving Blackthorn what he was giving it. The sphere stretched itself and embraced Blackthorn, wrapping itself completely around his body in a slow, near sensual manner. He was lifted off of the ground to the astonishment of all present. Instinctively, everyone took a step back and away from the oblong sphere. "Aaaggghhh!!!" screamed the general in utter agony. A rumbling sound began to fill the room, growing in volume as if thunder were approaching. The next sound was that of a horrific crunching sound, bones being crunched within the body of the floating Blackthorn. The rumbling grew louder, the large room began to shake, sending chunks of the stone and tiled ceiling plummeting to the floor, striking three of the robed figures in the head—two of whom were the men who had searched for the female—and killing them instantly. The remaining figures panicked, including those guarding Sir James, Alhasan and myself, dropping the ceremonial pretense and bolting for the door I had come through. Another rumble and shaking of the room brought down more of the ceiling and some of the wall, blocking that door. Hoods now flew off of our former guards and their eyes darted back and forth seeking another way out but clearly not knowing of one.

Now was my chance. I lunged forward toward the pedestals, intent on removing the relics from their resting place. I tossed the Rood to Sir James who enfolded it in the extra cloth of his tunic and slung it on his back. I then gently wrapped the Finger Bone, Bowl and Shroud in the spare cloth of my own tunic for safekeeping. Finally, I took the Spear of Longinus and the King's Sword from their pedestals. The sphere of power dropped the limp body of General Blackthorn on top of Rashin, who appeared to be stunned, in a complete state of shock by the events. The building shook again, more crumbling ceiling fell but struck no one this time. The sphere of power then turned toward me. I held the Spear of Longinus and the King's Sword aloft to it, not in a threatening manner, but in a manner of victory. You will be led to freedom, said the golden-eyed Priest's voice in my mind again. But this time, I knew the voice to be coming from the sphere of power. But how? Was it truly the priest I had known as Pretorius in my previous existence? Or was it the One appearing in a given form? Or Both?

"Where to go, Masoud?" asked Alhasan standing next to me. "Our previous way is now blocked."

"You will die before I let you take these things!" yelled Rashin as he tried to push the dead Blackthorn off of him. "Do not let them escape!" he yelled to the remaining robed figures.

"This way!" I said, not knowing exactly where to go, but realizing we could not stay here. I ran to the far end of the large room, the large pretend cathedral, toward where an altar would be if this were an actual church, the direction from which the two men had returned from while apparently searching for the escaped female. Unless she was hiding in the cathedral, she must have escaped out of some opening on the altar side of the room. Two heavy wooden doors were there on either side. I crashed hard into the one on our right, presuming it would give way and I would fall into another room or hallway. It did not. I might as well have flung myself into a solid stone wall. It would not budge. The next door proved to be the same. It became clear that like the stained glass windows, the doors were there for appearance and not function. I began to lose patience, and allow fear to creep in. Another thunderous rumble jolted the room. A large wall near where we had been standing with the pedestals broke free, crushing three more of the robed figures and the pedestals and nearly crushing Rashin. Rashin was free, standing near the remaining robed figures and pointing at us.

"La, here!" said a female voice from our left. I looked in the direction of the tender but urgent voice and saw a darkened archway. In the archway was silhouetted a petite and slender figure. Her face was in shadow but an arm extended from the figure and into the light, beckoning us into the archway. "Quickly," she said in Arabic accented English. "There's no too much time."

In spite of myself and our situation my whole being smiled. I could not help but look at Alhasan, who, also recognizing the voice, could only give a look of resignation.

~XXVIII~

Immediately, I began to walk toward the shadowed figure.

"Wait," insisted Sir James.

I halted briefly and looked at my commander.

"This is Najeeba, I presume? What's she doing here? This could be a trap," he observed.

I looked back at Rashin and his remaining robed men, now gathered in a group and heading toward us. "I'd say we're already trapped, commander."

"Aye," Sir James admitted, seeing Rashin and his men as well. "On with ya, then, but be on guard!"

"Always," I said as I turned and dashed toward the darkened archway.

Najeeba stepped into the light just as we arrived, her lavender eyes bright in spite of the gloom of this place. I froze at the sight of her beauty, nearly losing sight of our need to escape. "Follow," she said in hushed but urgent tone. She turned and ran back through the archway. We did as she bade and followed. She was fast, running down a darkened corridor as if she knew every step. It was all we could do to keep up. Though my spirit soared at the sight of her, I could not help but expect others, perhaps her keepers, to jump out at any given moment and apprehend us. I chastised myself for such thinking. Trust. Trust, I kept telling myself. We had no choice, as it was anyway. We could hear Rashin and his men entering the corridor behind us from the pretend cathedral. They were not far behind.

"Here," she said, ducking into a room. We followed, ending up in some kind of small storage closet, Alhasan closing the door behind us. We were as cramped together as wrapped fish. Yet, for a moment I was glad of it. I was pressed up against Najeeba, could smell the lovely scent of her hair, so close was I. I could barely see any of her features, so dark was the closet. What scant light was there came through cracks in the closed wooden door. But it was enough to reveal half of Najeeba's face. She turned that lovely face to mine and our eyes met in the semi-darkness. There was a kindness and depth in those eyes. I also felt a connection with her that truly spanned time itself. Sir James had referred to her as my soul partner. Indeed, I sensed the truth of it in that moment. But there was no time to revel it. We heard Rashin and his men run past the closet, could see their shadows pass us through the cracks in the closet's door. We remained in the cramped silence until the footfalls receded.

Slowly, quietly, Alhasan opened the closet door and stepped back out into the corridor, the rest of us followed. "They will come back, I believe," observed Alhasan.

"Yes. And they will bring Sultan's men." said Najeeba.

"Where are your women," asked Alhasan sternly, suddenly switching to Arabic.

"Are you so ungrateful as to insult me?" asked Najeeba, replying in Arabic. It was all I could do to follow their conversation, and it became obvious that Najeeba did not yet realize that I could understand her language.

"You take great risk," Alhasan continued in his native tongue. "Your women and watchers have been negligent."

"All other women have been sent East. I am here at my request, as are two other of my woman friends. My uncle can never say no to me, danger or no." Najeeba said, displaying none of the demureness I noticed at our first, actually our second, meeting. "I have no watchers as you call them. I am here now to aid Sir Masoud," she said turning her eyes to me, but continuing to speak to Alhasan. "He saved my life, my very soul, as you know, Alhasan. I do this now because of that and because of...because of..."

"Say it," urged Alhasan with quiet irritation.

"Because of love," she admitted as she still stared at me.

My heart swelled at the hearing of it, yet I gave no hint that I was following their conversation in Arabic, let alone understood what she had just specifically said. Though I wanted to embrace her passionately I simply held her gaze instead. After a moment, I looked to Alhasan who had the look of a crestfallen school boy.

"Love?" he finally said.

"Yes," she stated, now looking back at him. She saw his look and knew it for what it was. She stepped to Alhasan and stood before him. "You have served my uncle and me well, Alhasan. You are as a brother to me, but you know I've never had feelings for you beyond that, nor would it have ever been appropriate for me to."

"These revelations are all quite interesting," Sir James said in clear Arabic, quite irritated at the distraction. He had been pacing the immediate area, patrolling and guarding, making sure no one was yet coming back after us. "But we need to leave before none of us get the chance to discuss it further. Now?!"

Najeeba was obviously surprised by the commander's use of the Arabic language. She suddenly looked at me with an expression that was a mixture of questioning realization and embarrassment. I read her look instantly. Do you understand my language too? she seemed to ask silently.

"I understand enough," I said in English.

She held my look for a moment longer before getting back to the matter at hand. "This way," she said as she turned and headed back toward the cathedral.

"But, we just came from that way!" I said.

"Follow!" she said as more of a command than a request.

I looked to Sir James who simply shrugged and began to follow Najeeba. A moment later, we found ourselves back in the pretend cathedral.

The thunderous rumbling had ceased, the sphere of power was gone. Yet, there was still an unmistakable energy to the air, a tangible sensation of infinite possibility. Najeeba led us past the bodies of the robed figures and Blackthorn. Sir James paused and stared at the general's body.

"We should keep on move," said Najeeba in broken English.

"Would that we could take him back for a proper rite," said Sir James, ignoring Najeeba for the moment.

"I understand," I replied. "He lost his way, but was still a servant of the Light."

"A great one for a time. What led him astray?" wondered Sir James aloud. "Ah, impossible though, to take him back, I mean."

I looked at the face of General Horatio Blackthorn and did something impulsive. I reached out the spear and touched its blade gently to the general's bruised and battered forehead. All went dark around me as I turned my sight inward intending on blessing the general and his service up to his wayward turn, but even still blessing that too, for it was all of The One. However, my intention notwithstanding, what happened next shocked me to the core of my being. In my mind's eye, I saw General Horatio Blackthorn in all his fine Templar regalia on a younger day, the day of his installation as a Grand Master of The Knights Templar many years earlier. His face conveyed an idealistic vigor that shined with divine purpose. The general seemed to look directly at me and I saw into his soul, saw all his former selves. I had known the general in previous lifetimes but had not recognized him, his spirit until that moment. His face changed, shaped into a familiar from my time as Myrriddin. He was, had been, my mentor, Moscastan. The shock of seeing his face now brought emotion and memory to the surface I had not anticipated; nights and years of tutelage under my beloved Master Moscastan, observing the wizard becoming the age and persona of his desire at will in any given moment, for example. Or, the carrying of his bones to be placed within his crystal sanctuary, which had become my place of solace as Myrriddin the elder. His appearance shifted again and he became his soul's expression before Moscastan; my beloved mentor and friend Jacobi during my life as Longinus! How had he come back to this earth as a wayward general and knight from such two previously lofty, advanced soul's incarnations?!

The words then echoed in my mind; to say that one soul is more advanced...is to miss the point of the soul's subjective journey within the One Mind, which is this: that Mind may experience Itself, as Itself, through our individualized experiences within Itself. It seemed some lessons must be repeated. "Blessings to you, my old friend," I heard myself saying to the image in my mind's eye. "And may your soul's journey be swift and effortless." The image of Jacobi/Moscastan/Blackthorn faded from my mind. I opened my eyes and was fully and completely present in the Devil's church, the pretend cathedral once more. I removed the spear's blade flat from the general's forehead and stared at the body before me.

~XXIX~

"Come," said Najeeba, "No more time!" She took three steps toward the entrance Sir James, Alhasan and I had originally come, only to see it was blocked by rubble. Undeterred, she then darted to the left, and came to a crumbled section of the room's wall with ceiling debris and rubble piled at its base. She began to remove some of the rubble, clearly looking for something. Rather than waste time in questioning her, Sir James and I left the dead general's side and began to help her, pushing aside debris near the base of the wall. "There!" Najeeba said as Sir James uncovered what was a four foot in diameter dark hole near the base of the wall.

"A ventilation duct," Sir James stated.

"La, no." replied Najeeba. "I believe it to be an escape tunnel. This place was once used as prison."

"How do you know of these things?" asked Alhasan with a mixture of awe and dismay, as if to say, a woman should not know of these things!

"I venture to explore," she said with pride.

Sir James took one of the nearby torches out of its sconce on the wall and entered the small tunnel on his hands and knees. Najeeba went next, followed by Alhasan and myself, tucking the sword in the cloth belt of my under-tunic thus leaving one hand free as I hung onto the spear with the other. I pulled some of the debris back over the opening as I went in concealing the whole from Rashin or anyone coming after us.

Once again, darkness engulfed us, save for the torch that Sir James held at the lead. The tunnel we now found ourselves in was cramped, barely enough room to crawl forward on hands and knees in a single-file line. On and on we went, the tunnel bending to the right and then the left and then returning to a straight course, all the while making a steady, gradual incline toward the surface. After a time, the air became stale and thin, making it difficult to breathe, as it became apparent that there was not much air ventilating through this tunnel. I began to think that rather than escaping we may have entombed ourselves, never to see the outside world again or breathe fresh air. Each of us began to cough as smoke from the dying torch flame swirled back on us with nowhere to escape, and I put part of my tunic cloth over my mouth and nose in an effort to help my breathing and filter out the smoke. The others were doing the same. Sir James extinguished the torch in the dirt of our tunnel floor. We would continue on in utter darkness. But a better idea impinged itself upon my mind. No sooner had the torch gone out when I began to fully concentrate on the spear and sword, holding the image in my mind that they both were leading us in light, their blades glowing to show the way. So fully was the conviction of my desire and intent that almost instantly the spear's blade began to glow a soft green. I removed The King's Sword from my tunic's belt. It too glowed a soft green and in the same hue, in harmony with the Spear of Longinus. And, to my astonishment, after a few seconds I was able to breathe with less difficulty. It was as if the spear and sword were providing enhancement of our air, producing the necessary qualities in it for our sustentation. "Sir James, take the King's Sword as it will illuminate the way," I said in a raspy whisper, passing the instrument forward. As I did, each of my companions audibly breathed easier.

"Allah be praised," sighed Alhasan.

"Amazing," said Sir James.

We continued on, our hands and knees becoming raw with the effort of the crawl. The hours passed by as if time itself crawled. We travelled for what felt like several hours, though in my mind I could not believe that it was so long. Suddenly, our journey began to become more difficult, not because of a thinning in the air around us again, but because the tunnel had begun a steeper incline, much steeper than any before this point. Also, the tunnel passageway had become narrower. We were all on our stomachs pulling ourselves forward. "Here's something!" Sir James finally declared.

Each of us suddenly emerged into the ruins of a large, high domed ceilinged room not too dissimilar in configuration than the pretend cathedral we had left below. Blessedly, though, this one was obviously above ground. Bright light, sunlight streamed in through the upper window openings on the dome. I breathed deeply and nearly started to laugh, so pleased I was to be in a large space and above ground.

"The day has dawned," exclaimed Sir James, noting the wonderful light entering the room from windows. We apparently had indeed been in the tunnel for several hours.

"The tunnel. We were in the tunnel for very, very long," observed Najeeba. "It took longer than last attempt."

"'longer than last attempt?'" Alhasan asked horrified that she had made the journey through the tunnel before.

"Yes."

"But, how? Why?! I, la, la. I do not wish to know," concluded Alhasan.

"Listen," ordered Sir James, as he held his head high to hear the sounds of our surroundings. But there were none, no sounds. All was silent; no sounds of soldiers urgently running to their task or even simply going about their duties, no sounds of nearby battles, no sounds of catapulted fireballs exploding and the chaos they bring.

"What has happened?" I asked.

"The battle is won by the Sultan?" Alhasan asked Najeeba.

"Yes," she replied, firm with the knowledge of it. "Not many are presently present."

Were it not for my sudden sense of isolation I may have smiled at Najeeba's use of English, so endearing it was at times. But the matter was grave if she was correct. At least, it was grave for Sir James and I. "How can you be sure the battle's won?" I asked.

"It was so before coming to you," explained Najeeba. "I wanted you not prisoner. I desired to escape you out. The Sultan and his men are now talking with prisoners at your army's camp. He is most merciful. But others will demand your head, for you control those," she said pointing to the spear in my hand and the sword in Sir James' hand, "and that you lead Templar Knights."

"But..." I began in protest.

"You said, 'I escape you out,'" Sir James said to Najeeba. "Escape him or take him out to where, to here, to the Sultan?"

"Commander, I should as well to leave him down below as to that," she replied. She then turned to me. "I take you to freedom, both of you," she said, addressing Sir James for the last portion.

I looked to Sir James and saw a personal battle waging across his face. His sense of duty was no doubt at war with his desire for freedom from this place. My own sense of duty and honor reared up from within. Am I to leave this place and return home, or should I rejoin my men and fellow soldiers and crusaders? I wondered. At the thought of joining my men, Henry came into my mind. What had become of him? "Where would prisoners be in this place?" I blurted out.

"No, Masoud. You must not. You must not search for your friend!" said Alhasan, understanding my meaning.

"But I told you where prisoners were," said Najeeba, ignoring Alhasan's outburst, "where I led you from was prisoners' place. They are gone now." she said, obviously confused by my question.

"But I thought you meant it was originally a prison, not that it had been made into a type of holding room," I said.

"I aided to some of men there, cleaned wounds. It is why it looks like your churches and our mosques," she said. "Sultan, my uncle, is most merciful, allowing all to worship as they wish, even as prisoner. I believe some made and escaped through tunnel we came through. The rest taken to your camp."

"Perhaps your Henry is still alive then, Liam, Sir Masoud," said Sir James. "But now you are charged with a higher duty," he said, handing me the King's Sword and the Rood. "It is your duty as Templar Knight and Guardian of the sacred relics to take these items, all of them, to safety, to the safety and protection of our Order in our homeland. I order you to do that. Go with Najeeba," he said looking at Najeeba, but speaking to me. "Something tells me her uncle, the great Salah al-Din had a hand in planning this, your escape." He smiled, then. To Najeeba's credit she kept her face impassive, giving nothing away.

"And you, Sir James, Jonathan?" I asked, not wanting this to be our parting, but knowing it to be so.

"I will remain here in hiding for at least a few hours so as not to draw attention to you," he explained. "I'll then make my way back to our men, come what may. Go now and discharge your duty, lad."

"I...I...yes, Sir. Thank you for everything," I stammered.

"Come, this way," said Najeeba, as she moved off. I followed tentatively, Alhasan behind me all but prodding my back to go. I looked back one last time at my Commander Sir Jonathan James. He was already gone.

Epilogue

"I have not been unwise in the discharge of my duty, have I, my love?" the old man asked.

"La, you have not, Masoud," replied the aged woman with lavender eyes. Though many years had passed since their first meeting on a crusader battlefield, beauty still lived in those eyes and in that soul. Indeed in the soul of Liam Arthur Mason, renamed Masoud all those years passed, resided the very soul of Longinus the Centurion and first keeper of the spear, and Myrriddin, Guardian and keeper of the Spear of Longinus and the King's Sword. The soul of Masoud, Myrriddin and Longinus were one soul and had never strayed too far from this Earth, this plane of existence.

But the time had come for this soul to sojourn on another plane. "It is time, father," said the voice of Aiden Alhasan Mason.

Masoud and Najeeba turned to see their firstborn, handsome son standing before them in the full regalia of the Grand Master he was. His hair was as dark as his mother's and his eyes were hers too; lavender. His skin tone was a mixture of the people of the Isles of Britain and the Arab nations. Standing near Aiden were five Master Templar Knights, also in the ceremonial robes of the high Templar. They filed past Masoud, each bowing in respect to the aged Master, then slipping through the portal into the secret, darkened Temple beyond. Two servants came to stand next to Aiden, one on each side, each holding the sacred relics of Christ wrapped in silk cloth.

"Unwrap them," said Masoud. It was not a request. He would not see the new dawn. His soul's journey was to continue elsewhere, at least for a time. "I will behold them one last time, before charging you for their safe-keeping, Aiden."

"As you wish, father," Aiden replied, nodding to the servants next to him to do as his father bade. One by one, the relics were unveiled. Masoud stood on hobbled legs and gingerly shuffled across the antechamber to the servants. He touched each relic in turn, pausing long enough to feel their energy. At last he came to the Spear of Longinus. "Wood and metal you be, old friend, but keeper of the Divine too, yes?" he whispered to the thing. He reverently kissed the spear's blade. He then turned to face the Temple doors which opened for him. The small procession then entered the Temple for the rite of passage, including Najeeba. Unprecedented, this was, for a woman to be allowed into the inner sanctuary of the Templar Knights. But this was to be no ordinary rite, but a rite of the transference of Templar Power and Guardianship of the Sacred Objects. It was also to be the rite of Transition of The Soul or in this case, of two souls; Masoud's and Najeeba's. It was their choice to leave this plane, together and on this night.

All took their places within the Temple's darkened interior. The servants, lead by Aiden, walked Masoud and Najeeba to their place of honor in the middle of the Temple. They sat, side by side, in the west-facing high-backed plush reclining chairs. The drink was given to them and the ceremony begun. They sat hand in hand, did Masoud and Najeeba, as they began to drift in mind and spirit to the threshold of the Otherworld, to the chorus of chants and rites being read. Drifting, floating, was Masoud. He began to see things of his soul's journey, from its past, though time in this state was rendered nonexistent. They flashed by his mind's eye, and he relived each in an instant. Finally, a place, a time, a persona came into view. He settled there for a span and enjoyed the cool mists.

The mists rolled across the headlands as waves across a shoreline. Masoud walked down to the edge of the lake on this moonlit night and stared across the water at the Isle of Mystery and the ancient temple ruins thereon; the very place where he, as Myrriddin, had found the Spear of Longinus all those many years past. A part of him remained at One with the mists now, calling them and keeping them here as a comfort the way one clings to a blanket in childhood.

"Masoud, Myrriddin?" Igraines said as she approached him from behind. Her voice was still as sweet as a summer robin's song. Though they were both well aged and long in the experiences of living even in this place, his passion for her had never waned no matter in what form. Indeed, the more experience his soul received the more he lived in that passion and the more he allowed it to carry over from life to life. He turned and looked into Igraines' eyes—and hence the soul of Irena, his love during his embodiment as Longinus—now turned a brilliant lavender. But...how could that be? he wondered. They had never been lavender before. And then it hit him. Myrriddin/Masoud, was not just dreaming the dream of his soul, reeling from the continuous thread of his existence from one life to the next to the next, and the overlapping of his partner souls, the good ones and the challenging ones, that he moved with through eternal existence and growth and expression. He was crossing to the next expression of his journey, leaving the persona of Longinus, Myrriddin and Masoud behind and parting, for now, from his partner soul of Irena, Igraines and Najeeba. His soul had chosen this place and his Myrriddin self through which to exit.

"Myrriddin, my dearest," she said staring back at him.

"Yes, my love, my queen," Myrriddin said. She stood next to him. He looked deeper into those lavender eyes and took comfort in them as he took comfort in the mists. Her face was still lovely. "'Tis near time for me, Igraines, near time to travel on."

"Do not speak so, Myrriddin," she said sadly.

"You have never been afraid of the truth before, my love. Do not fear it now," I replied. "Besides, I have done all I can here."

"You have been of great service, 'tis true. But, what of us? We missed so much of each other because of our duties.

We've only just begun spending more time in each other's company," she lamented. "One lifetime is not enough."

"We each answered a greater call. Yet I have no doubt that we will have the opportunity to be with each other again and again and again if we so choose," I said.

"I do so choose, Myrriddin." She stood on tip-toe then and kissed his lips. He returned her kiss with the lost ardor of youth, their youth.

Their lips parted and something shifted within his being. He knew the time had come. She must have seen it in his eyes, for she simply nodded in understanding, in acceptance, a tear of sadness rolling down her cheek. Attachment is the root of our sadness at loss. He suddenly thought. With no attachment there is no loss. That is not to be understood as indifferent detachment, however. Compassionate non-attachment is an aspect of unconditional love. Such were his thoughts in that moment. He looked once again to the Isle of Mystery across the Lake and stepped onto the lake's surface. With one foot after the other, he walked on the surface of the water all the way to the Isle's shore. Looking back in the direction he'd come, he gave one last wave of his hand to the lone figure of Igraines still standing on the opposite shore. She waved back and turned, walking away and fading from sight, continuing on the journey of her soul. He then turned and walked toward the ancient temple ruins to say farewell to his lives as Longinus, Myrriddin and Masoud, knowing that though these figures are gone they may be forever revisited at any time and in the blink of an eye. He knew too that his soul's journey was just beginning. A soul's journey is always just beginning, for it is never ending, always present in the eternal moment.

Made in the USA
Columbia, SC
30 November 2021

50094328R00462